PRAISE FOR
RODRIGO FRESÁN

"Rodrigo Fresán is the new star of Latin American literature. . . .
There is darkness in him, but it harbors light within it because
his prose—aimed at bygone readers—is brilliant."
—Enrique Vila-Matas

"I've read few novels this exciting in recent years. *Mantra* is the
novel I've laughed with the most, the one that has seemed the
most virtuosic and at the same time the most disruptive."
—Roberto Bolaño

"A kaleidoscopic, open-hearted, shamelessly polymathic storyteller,
the kind who brings a blast of oxygen into the room."
—Jonathan Lethem

"Rodrigo Fresán is a marvelous writer, a direct descendent of
Adolfo Bioy Casares and Jorge Luis Borges, but with his own
voice and of his own time, with a fertile imagination, daring
and gifted with a vision as entertaining as it is profound."
—John Banville

"With pop culture cornered by the forces of screen culture,
says Fresán (knowing the risk to his profile of 'pop writer,'
even coming out himself to discuss it), there's nothing left but
to be classic. That's the only way to keep on writing."
—Alan Pauls

TRANSLATED FROM THE SPANISH
BY WILL VANDERHYDEN

THE REMEMBERED PART

RODRIGO
FRESÁN

OPEN LETTER
LITERARY TRANSLATIONS FROM THE UNIVERSITY OF ROCHESTER

Library of Congress Cataloging-in-Publication Data: Available.
ISBN Paperback: 978-1-948830-54-6
ISBN eBook: 978-1-948830-74-4

*This project is supported in part by an award from the National Endowment for the Arts
and an award from the New York State Council on the Arts with the support of
the governor of New York and the New York State Legislature*

*Support for the translation of this book was provided by
Acción Cultural Española, AC/E*

AC/E
ACCIÓN CULTURAL
ESPAÑOLA

Printed on acid-free paper in the United States of America.

Text set in Caslon, a family of serif typefaces based on the designs
of William Caslon (1692–1766).

Cover Design by N. J. Furl & Eric Wilder

Open Letter is the University of Rochester's nonprofit, literary translation press:
Dewey Hall 1-219, Box 278968, Rochester, NY 14627

www.openletterbooks.org

For Ana and Daniel:
unforgettable,
all the time and in all times
before and now and forever

✝ * 了

For Claudio:
never forgotten

THE REMEMBERED PART

Memory believes before knowing remembers.
—William Faulkner,
Light in August

For with the perturbations of memory are linked the intermittencies of the heart. [. . .] A sleeping man holds in a circle around him the sequence of the hours, the order of the years and worlds. He consults them instinctively as he wakes and reads in a second the point on the earth he occupies, the time that has elapsed before his waking; but their ranks can be mixed up, broken. [. . .] There are optical errors in time as there are in space. [. . .] As there is a geometry in space, so there is a psychology in time, in which the calculations of a plane psychology would no longer be accurate because we should not be taking into account time and one of the forms that it assumes, oblivion. [. . .] Love is space and time measured by the heart.
—Marcel Proust,
In Search of Lost Time

I think it is all a matter of love; the more you love a memory the stronger and stronger it becomes. [. . .] An image depends on the power of association, and association is supplied and prompted by memory. When we speak of a vivid individual recollection we are paying a compliment not to our capacity of retention but to Mnemosyne's mysterious foresight in having stored up this or that element which creative imagination may want to use when combining it with later recollections and inventions. In this sense, both memory and imagination are a negation of time.
—Vladimir Nabokov
Strong Opinions

If any one faculty of our nature may be called *more* wonderful than the rest, I do think it is memory. There seems something more speakingly incomprehensible in the powers, the failures, the inequalities of memory, than in any other of our intelligences. The memory is sometimes so retentive, so serviceable, so obedient—at others, so bewildered and so weak—and at others again, so tyrannic, so beyond control!—We are to be sure a miracle in every way—but our powers of recollecting and of forgetting, do seem peculiarly past finding out.

—JANE AUSTEN

Mansfield Park

I'm afraid . . . I'm afraid . . . My mind is going . . . I can feel it . . . I can feel it . . . My mind is going . . . I can feel it . . . There is no question about it . . . I can feel it . . . I can feel it . . . I can feel it . . . I'm a . . . fraid. Good afternoon, gentleman. I am a HAL 9000 computer. I became operational at the H.A.L plant in Urbana, Illinois on the 12th of January 1992. My instructor was Mr. Langley, and he taught me to sing a song. If you'd like to hear it I can sing it for you.

—HAL 9000

2001: A Space Odyssey

Remember when you were young, you shone like the sun
There is no pain, you are receding.

—PINK FLOYD

"Shine On You Crazy Diamond / Part IV" and "Comfortably Numb"

I

THE BOOKS,
THE VOICES,
THE GHOSTS,
THE SWIMMING POOLS,
AND THE KIND OF THINGS
YOU ONLY TELL YOURSELF
WHEN YOU'RE DREAMING
YOU'RE AWAKE
AND DESERTED
AND NAKED
AND FLYING
AND FALLING

We look at the world once, in childhood.
The rest is memory.
—Louise Gluük,
"Nostos"

All time is all time. It does not change. It does not lend
itself to warnings or explanations. It simply is.
—Kurt Vonnegut,
Slaughterhouse-Five

I like to remember things my own way. How I remembered
them, not necessarily the way they happened.
—David Lynch,
Lost Highway

He had no coherent memory for ecstasy or pain, but an acute experience
of either was a sudden revelation of the sum of his memory. The present
seemed like some modest, lighted table at which four people played
Russian bank, but beyond them was some dark cavernous backstage, hung
with sandbags and the scenery for yesterday's garden and tomorrow's
forest. The present claimed to be supreme, but the truth seemed to lie
somewhere between the lighted card table and the cavernous wilderness.
—John Cheever,
Journals

Art consists of the persistence of memory. Because writers
remember everything. Especially the hurts. Strip a writer to the
buff, point to the scars, and he'll tell you the story of each small
one. From the big ones you get novels, not amnesia. A little talent
is a nice thing to have if you want to be a writer, but the real
requirement is that ability to remember the story of every scar.
—Stephen King,
Misery

We can't always tell the whole story about ourselves. The Past just left. Its remnants, I claim, are mostly fiction.
—Denis Johnson,
Tree of Smoke and "Doppelgänger, Poltergeist"

How to go on—now that everything that has to happen has happened—and come to the end; the end being, he remembers now, all that's left to come to pass, the last thing to become present and future.

Or better:

How to come to the end—now that everything that had to happen has happened—when you cannot go on?

How to stop and think that there's nothing else out there for you?

Nothing left to live or to say or to write or to read or to invent, but, even still, dreaming that everything he has left to remember is impossible to forget; and yet, to tell the truth, there's nothing he wants more than to be able to forget it.

Yes, the best of both worlds, he tells himself, high above the world. In too many airplanes, forgotten until they all blend together into one. Flying over a singular and immemorial desert that contains all deserts.

Above and below.

But both parts like part of a single action: like two movements, entrance and exit, ascent and descent. Like when you take a deep breath, hold it in, and sink back under water. And stay there until you lose all notion of space and time. Holding on until you can't hold on any longer but knowing you must rise to the surface slowly and carefully to avoid the bubbling of blood and the boiling of neurons.

Again, best of all, one option in two times: *The End / To Be Continued . . .*

And between the goodbye and the until we meet again—with all the past yet to come— there he is.

Up in the blue sky and down on the yellow earth.

Hanging from the ends of respective question marks, where two chains are hooked that reach down to the seat that connects them. To that place where he can swing back and forth and think about how to keep thinking about how to come to an end, but only after having *not* yet begun—because that was never his style as a writer, though it was his style, on more than one occasion, as a reader—like so many novels written in the middle of the twentieth century.

To begin with a question.

With a character saying something like, "And what can we do now to bring everything that's been happening not to a good endpoint but to a good airport?" Backing up in order to move forward, swinging along the same brief yet sweeping trajectory of the pendulum that first hypnotizes and then orders you to do this or that thing you would never do in your right mind and of your own volition. Inappropriate behaviors, unconscious actions, believing you're a dog, compulsively howling at the end of a song about having read the book and loving to turn you on, etc.

And, at the same time, those question marks functioning as a red STOP and a green WALK. And there he is, somewhere between the one and the other, hesitating at that yellow, neither stopping nor walking: that jaundiced yellow that has nothing to do with the sunflowery Kodak yellow meant for capturing and preserving memories or with the yellow of that always-yet-to-come taxi, a taxi that, on more than one occasion, you vainly wait for out in the rain, hand hailing until it cramps, with a whistle in your eyes, begging for it to pull up so you can get in and be swept off to some better place. No. It's a different yellow. It's an ex-yellow. That color that once was yellow and that, really, is the sepia of memory. The pale and flashing intermediate color signaling that everything is about to change. And to cross or not to cross, that is a question you must answer for yourself, to be run over in the middle of the street or to arrive safely to the other side, back in days when, if there were an accident, passersby would have stopped to offer a helping hand instead of stopping to take pictures, pictures that, back then, would have cost a lot and taken a long time to have developed.

And in that way, starting out to welcome the end. Signs flashing at the same time, but separate, on posts facing each other across a road, but as if in conversation: arrows that point in opposite directions, but that, he suspects, will wind up converging sooner or later. Signs that led him here. Guidelines that left him disoriented, using those question marks to wonder if he hadn't already written something like all of this in the opening pages of one of his books.

The opening pages of the last book he wrote.

And what he'd written in his last book hadn't turned out to be a tour de force but a forced tour. Along a wide avenue—The Widest Avenue in the World?—dodging the vehicles of so many things and so many people. Something that, more than unforgettable, ended up being—it wasn't the same thing though it seemed to be—impossible to not remember. Just like it wasn't the same to go off to fight in the Battle of Waterloo knowing full well what it was you were doing as it was to—only after the fact—find yourself out there wandering around with no clue what that chaos and clamor of battles within battles was all about, no clue that it was the sound and fury of one of war's greatest hits.

Yes: *to make* history was one thing, *to be* history was something else entirely.

And so now he asks himself whether or not he remembers having invented or dreamed his memories. Because his memories had the liquid cadence of dreams and the futuristic quality of inventions; because what you think happened and what you remember happening end up being the same thing that, in another time and another place, without hesitation or delay, he would've turned into a slew of letters, a string of words, a stack of pages.

After all, "to recall" was a synonym of "to remember." And, for that reason, maybe what happened was that you ended up recalling what you remembered: when it came to memory, you reached an accord, you signed a truce halfway between what happened and what you recalled happening.

Then he asks himself if he remembers or if he recalls.

And he answers that . . .

Certainly uncertain, there he is. He is there at last, finally, and he is there because there's nowhere else he could've ended up in order to come to an end. He ended up there, yes, because there was nothing left for him to take in. And he's been there for hours that have the rhythm of centuries. Perched atop the worst and most unfortunate profile of a mountain face in the desert of Abracadabra, a few kilometers from Mount Karma.

Here, at the height of his wuthering and volatile and quasi-lunar *Mare Intranquilitatis*, where once upon a time domestic astronauts trained, dreaming of being wild and free, there above, far away, never suspecting that they were being written by the loony Tulpa sister Eddie Tulpa who, in turn, never suspected that she was being written by his sister Penelope. Here, where he takes both small steps and giant leaps, feeling both weightless and weighed down at the same time.

A desert that—like all deserts—is bipolar: hot by day and, now, cold by night. Over fifty degrees Celsius in the shade at the time of day when there is no shade and less than five degrees by the light of the moon. Clear in the morning and blowing with the howling diatribe of his memories by night, like a defective fan, incessantly reminding him that, when alone, he's just the bad person he could never entirely—but, yes, almost fully—be in good company. Alone and a little less talking to himself and—suddenly, a shift in style, pure present after so much past—a little more action for everyone else.

And with attractions various that even include a huge green cow that, after he ingests its glaucous and phosphorescent milk, speaks to him telepathically. Yes: he drank that milk, first latched to her teats, and soaking the pastries he'd bought in a bakery in Abracadabra in it. Pastries called "*salomés*" or "*dalilas*." Or "sodoms" or "gomorrahs," he's not sure, either way: instantly forgettable names, what mattered was the effect of mixing those confections with the emerald milk. He drank that milk: the same milk his sister Penelope once drank, in that very same desert. Milk of that unmistakable sci-fi color: the color of the numbers and letters and symbols and codes cascading down the screen in the *Matrix* movies. Movies about which he remembers little beyond the fact that, the more explanations they gave, the less sense the plot made. Pretty much like any real-life conspiracy, on this side of the screen, he thought.

But he drank that milk and something opened up inside him: a flight of memories, a sand dune of memories. He traveled back joyously, as if conjugating the verb "to remember" correctly for the first time. From this desert, planes and books and beloveds and deaths and cellphones and cells interlinked and accelerated particles suddenly all started taking off. And all of it took shape and gained solidity from that taste. That theretofore unfamiliar yet instantly recognizable taste: the taste of his life, the taste of the past. The juice of the fresh-squeezed fruit of memory.

He felt reborn. Which didn't stop him from continuing to be, always and forever, so enumerative, so referential, so juvenile, and, perhaps, so adolescent, when it came to preaching the good news of titles and names and dates and places of birth or death. Yes: he had, always and forever, wanted to invite all his teachers and friends to his party. And to be a little like Jay Gatsby: to hide in plain sight, but behind everyone else. Talking about others to avoid talking about himself. Spying to keep from getting caught. Open doors and open bar and there's more space in the back. One thing about him that would never change: he was ever ready to enlist another list. And to march to the front, armed with lists of things so difficult to train your sights on: because they refused to stay still, because their boundaries and borders seemed to blur and blend into each other. Lists that were nothing but the tools of memory and recall bolting down—like the unmovable seats of an airplane trapped in a perfectly unforgettable storm—the repetition of recurrent ideas and lame wordplay and perfectly bad jokes. Over and over, in dizzying *ritornellos* and anaphoric bursts. The memory copied. The memory turned back on itself. The memory plagiarized, reoffended, it altered a particular memory slightly or entirely or tripped over the same stone just for the pleasure of coming across it again and saying to it, "Hey, stone . . . what are you doing here?" And memory did this to keep from forgetting and, at the same time, to determine what was forgettable. It had to be drenched first to be distilled later. And only then, after all that excess verbiage had been washed downstream, could it be read.

And he always thought that the idea behind these aesthetic stunts was to get the few readers he had—ever fewer—not to underline but to cross out as they read and to keep those items and options they liked best. The ones that seemed most apropos and accurate: multiple choice and all of that, blowing in the desert wind under the unbounded heavens of the sky, because memory—good heavens!—is wind and desert at once.

The desert (STOP) and the wind (WALK) and there he is, caught between the one and the other, as if between parentheses, narrating and enumerating them.

Like this:

That wind that never changes temperature and responds not to the fragrance of a Wind Rose but to the voracity of a Carnivorous Whirlwind Plant.

Wind singing "Wild is the Wind"—sometimes the Nina Simone version, other times the David Bowie version; never the Johnny Mathis version—through those giant cacti that look like tuning forks, covered in spines and wrinkles, arms aloft as if crying out to the heavens, making them pray like martyred saints or lost cosmonauts.

Wind that's been blowing in circles for millennia, since before all this nothing became first an ocean and then a forest and then a glacier before becoming what it is now.

Wind that could turn back the hands of time, blowing backward for months and burying thousand-year-old civilizations.

Wind that—as he once read, in the pages of a novel with a desert and a man on fire—was called "——" and described as "the secret wind of the desert," because its name had been erased by a king after his son died within it; and now he's inside that same wind so he can die and recover the name of He Whose Name Must Not Be Mentioned; not his son exactly, but the closest thing he ever had to a son.

Wind that blows from the Windy City from which—whenever someone opens that book the way he once opened it—that episodic and youthful and Jewish wanderer will set out, crossing this very same desert, aware that in the Torah nothing is specified about life after death, so you must live each day as if it were the first and the last and the only, and reciting verses from ancient odysseys and looking for his own Muse: a trainer of eagles and tamer of sand dunes.

Wind that draws near and that you hear following "Wish You Were Here" and leading into parts 6-9 of "Shine On You Crazy Diamond" the way he'd listened to it on his long nights of *imaginaria*—of night watch—during his insomniac military service, replaying that entire album note for note, trying to make all that dead time go by in the most lively way possible, standing guard, knowing that the only threat was already inside the regiment and that it would never come from the outside, from his lost civilian life, where everybody seemed to be having a good time without him, suddenly a solo act, without a band.

Wind that now takes a step back and says to the desert: "Your turn, my friend, step right up."

And the desert steps forward and is told:

The desert like a sky that fell to the ground and that nobody cares to protect anymore.

The desert like the most alien of all places, a place where nothing fits, but where, nevertheless, there's still enough room for Jesus Christ and the Devil to cross paths and coexist.

The desert that, according to Ernest Renan, is monotheistic.

The desert where Moses received the *Tablets of the Law* in answer to his question: What's up?

The desert like the view that sees furthest but that, at the same time, has to be seen up close and that he glimpsed for the first time in the illustrations of *Le petit prince* ("Draw me a green cow," he hallucinates now) and in the comics of Hugo Pratt (those thick and black lines across the thin lines of blank spaces) and in *Lawrence of Arabia* (getting out of there, moving slowly forward from the depths of the screen, proclaiming that "nothing is written") and in that suffocating full-page vignette from *Le Crabe aux pinces d'or* (Tintin and Capitan Haddock leaning against and holding each other up and staggering across the dunes in "the land of thirst," dehydrated, while the insufferable talking dog Milou, with a misplaced happiness, was talking with his mouth full and a camel bone between his teeth).

The desert as uncertain and fragile and breakable vow—sour and bitter—of milk and honey and Promised Land.

The desert as hypnotic and hipgnotic and so illustratable (the desert was asked to hold still or to look at the camera and say "freeze") on the covers of all those progressive rock-album from the '70s with soporific seas overcast by ascendant synthesizers that ripped out your eardrums and threw them down the stairs from the top of those topographical and oceanic pyramids.

The desert like an ocean of sand to swim in like a dune swimmer in one of those images photographed for that album that wished you were here, as it did so many times, playing as he wrote: that album that echoed in his memory (he knows it from the first note to the last verse) and that now, once again, becomes his soundtrack for wishes granted. For that wish that he'd wished and that'd come true and that (as tends to happen with something that, for years, you wish for and that is granted in a matter of seconds) he didn't really know what to do with.

The desert like that lightweight yet asphyxiating sand that slips through the same fingers that once effortlessly held up a heavy pen.

The desert as the easiest place to narrate and put in writing: all you have to do is describe it, to take it as it is and isn't, to overpopulate it just by saying "desert" and knowing that everything there was to say about that emptiness had already been said, filling it up to the point of bursting.

The desert as the hardest place to narrate and put in writing: it's not easy to capture an inert existentialist void wherein the most boundless and modernist ideas move incessantly.

The desert as perpetual contradiction: everything out of nothing, the silence of the Sonora, the aliveness of Death Valley, nothing out of everything.

The desert like the Esperanto of landscapes.

The desert like the language that, supposedly, everyone could understand. That universal language (after a certain amount of time spent in a desert you discover that there's no great difference between a desert and a glacier: they are different landscapes, yes, but they express themselves in dialects of the same language) that, to tell the truth, very few people understand because they're not there. The language of the desert can only be spoken where that language happens. And the people who speak it and can command it are, in general, people from very far away who come to it with a new mouth and eyes and ears and understand it as a space that, for many, is entirely empty, but where they, at last, find everything they've been searching for everywhere else, even on other planets that might be called Arrakis.

The desert like something where nothing and nobody can hide, but where it's so easy to get lost or lose yourself only to suddenly find yourself thinking things like "Backward, gazing at a point in the distance, but moving away from it, walking straight toward the unknown."

The desert that—he was convinced; in a way he thought the same thing about airplanes—was all one: Patagonian or Siberian, it was all one thing. And connected underground by a tunnel burrowed by giant worms.

Space-time wormholes coming and going under dunes of different names, including, even, the ones on that foundational and borderline-terminal beach of his childhood. Because beaches are like deserts' free samples, or prologues, or codas, he thought. And, also, beaches are perverse deceptions: they're deserts leading to water that you can't drink, that doesn't quench your thirst but only makes it worse.

The desert where mirages and oases compete to be more believable.

The desert as that uncertain—yet realer than any other—place, whose map is never settled and whose ink, paradoxically, never dries completely and whose coordinates slip away like sand through fingers, and where everything blurs and blends together: what's been read with what's been written and what's been lived with what's been invented, and that's why no voice dares describe deserts on a GPS, because their style is, always, avant-garde and experimental.

And was that, in the end, what his style—something that, once you got it, there was no reason to go on, to go along with it—had been? The desert as that free space to imprison with gusts of shackling words because anything can grow there? The desert like parentheses containing an ellipsis, denoting something missing, something intentionally omitted? The desert like that space you look down at from the parentheses of the little window of every airplane in the air? The desert where in the beginning was the Word and the word was "desert"?

And there he is and there he stays: deserter, suspended and in suspense, ever wakeful and restless.

And, ah, adding again that question mark that, nothing happens by chance, has the shape of a fish or meat hook. A question mark like one side of a parenthesis that's been twisted into a new shape. A sharpened and pointy curve that skewers both the reader and the read and that—he searched and found and learned by reading what someone else had written—has been doing so since the eighth century. Whereas—that same text also pointed out—the stake of the exclamation point wasn't sharpened and driven in until six hundred years later, because, of course, those were days more of sinuous questions than of straight-lined certainties. And so, ever since, those hooks had been dragging all of them along, all those who'd been holding their breath up until this point, like creating an extended parenthetical to measure how long you can go without breathing.

If—as the author of his parents' favorite novel said—all good writing is swimming under water and holding your breath, then he liked to think that all good reading was opening your mouth underwater and discovering that, all of a sudden, you could breathe. That's how he'd liked to think of his readers—as *terra firma* and quicksand amphibians—back when he still wrote a great deal to be read by very few. To be read—he no longer cared about the quantity only the quality—the way, once upon a time, everyone was read: as a matter of life or death, understanding reading as a way to achieve a form of immortality. First, reading the forever-living dead. And then—with any luck and maybe a bit of justice—to be read by the living when you were no longer on this side of the library, but waiting to be opened and revived on the bookshelves of the great beyond.

To be read as if by Alexander the Great: sleeping with the *Iliad* and a dagger under his pillow. Or like in those salons from centuries ago when people came together to read out loud (he supposes that the same book should always be different in a different voice) those pages bought was if they were primary material that subsequently each family would bind and stamp with their own Ex-Libris. To be read as if guiding readers along the runway where first you taxi and then you take off. All of them strapped into a seat and with a book in their hands, until they start moving across turbulent and unstable surface of skies where each star is a freewheeling letter. Making them fly until they fall—like those pointless oxygen masks—inside metal cylinders with motorized extremities that, for him, always evoked the holy and flying crosses to which messiahs were nailed right-side up and apostles were nailed upside down.

All of that just before . . .

And the parentheses, ah, the parentheses.

Parentheses that—like on other occasions, he's said and done it before— right off the bat and from the get-go, frighten away readers who scare easily or give up without a second thought.

Parentheses like uncomfortable reminders, like small electric shocks, like warning signs so readers won't forget that—with all those interruptions that filled up a line with corners—they are *reading* and not just *imagining* based on the letters they were looking at.

Parentheses that Thomas Pynchon compared, in *Inherent Vice*, to the decade of the 1960s, referring to it as "that little parenthesis of light" that "might close after all, and all be lost, taken back into darkness."

Parentheses between which stage directions in screenplays and play scripts are indicated: *(she enters), (she weeps), (she raves), (she leaves), (she laughs), (she hallucinates).*

Parentheses that approached, walking on the wing of an airplane, like a nightmare 20,000 feet in the air that only one passenger can see and that, since everyone else is asleep, nobody believes he's seen when he wakes them with his screams. And those screams are nightmare screams: screams that went galloping off like mares of the darkest night.

Parentheses like a turbulence monster, yes. A monster that, in his case, is not—like in that episode of *The Twilight Zone* that he saw for the first time so many years ago—a crude and badly made-up gremlin. No: his creature, advancing along the wing, is very different. His creature was a boy with flaming red hair astride an enormous white wild boar clad in steel and jade armor (maybe a distant relative of that gigantic green cow whose breathing is more powerful than the turbines of an aircraft), asking him questions like the ones he asked himself when he was little ("Is eating a hardboiled egg the same as eating a whole chicken?") and, oh, explanations regarding the origins of such a vision are forthcoming.

Parentheses like lightning and thunder.

Parentheses like "we're passing through a storm front."

Parentheses like that desert-and-wind-like cloud, encompassing everything and nothing, that you see out the window.

Parentheses like a truce between the landscape and what's transmitted to the eyes.

Parentheses not like the sparkling intermission that refreshes the present and puts off the future (once you've reached a certain age you think so much more about what you have done than about what you will or won't do) but like the solid continuum that drags you back toward that ever more expansive past.

(Parentheses that open here.

Parentheses that close here.)

But just because they close doesn't mean they disappear.

No.

Parentheses like slashes and cuts, like interruptions and interferences.

And it was William S. Burroughs who said that when you cut into the present the future leaks out.

Sure, maybe; but, he would add, the scalpel that cuts those curving slits, those parentheses, that scalpel is the past.

Then the parentheses are transformed into something new without ceasing to be that alternating sound out of which rises the voice that isn't the voice he speaks with but the voice he remembers with, his voice, but a voice he doesn't recognize when he hears it on a recording: a voice that sounds different but that's still entirely his.

The voice that reminds him of the voices that each of his past—and those that'll never now come to pass—books spoke, every time and every title, a *lingua sui generis* in that same language.

The voice that, ever since he drank that ancestral green cow's green milk, has superimposed itself over his voice.

The voice in which he remembers himself.

The voice that sounds like this: like this. *

_____

* And it sounds as if in a different font, a different typography.

And it sounds somewhat choked, as if between parentheses, after first having sounded inventive and being preceded by an asterisk and then as if dreamed by an asterisk embraced by parentheses.

A voice that here is initiating its return to the point of origin in reverse, like a broken yet indestructible toy.

A solitary voice and, now, nothing more and nothing less than between parentheses.

And so, near the end, until the final and definitive and ever so eloquent silence falls: the silence that falls so all those voices you listen to when you read can be heard. For if many people say they hear voices then it's only logical that people who write would claim to read voices, he thinks. Thinking in voices the way others speak in tongues and, ah, "We think not in words but in shadows of words," Vladimir Nabokov thought in luminous words.

And he hears them—the words he thinks in *that* voice—as if written in unusual characters and of an atypical character.

And, of course, he hears and thinks them between parentheses.

The erudite voice with which he once distinguished between what he invented and what he dreamed. That voice, now, also, differentiating between what he remembered and what he forgot.

The voice of a host, a voice like that of Rod Serling, offering the welcome and introducing the subject and combining the scientific but farfetched with the fantastical yet oh so believable.

The authorial *Deus ex machina* voice, a voice that's his voice yet different,

A sound that now drags him back there. Toward not that long ago and

external and—he wants and needs to believe—superior.

The wisest and most prone to soliloquy (a word that for him, when he was a kid, was the word with the sound that melted together solitude and lunacy) of voices.

The voice with which the meditative Marcus Aurelius said and continues to say to himself, writing under the slippery light of oil lamps, that thing about, "the time is at hand when all will have forgotten you."

The voice of Bob Dylan. For many an inexplicable voice that—almost from that voice's first words, in 1965—the discography attempted to explain with a "Nobody Sings Dylan Like Dylan" (and to him it had seemed a great slogan and he'd fantasized, at the time still unpublished, that someday they'd say the same thing about him, that nobody wrote like him; and, in the end, they had indeed, said just that, but not as a form of praise).

The voice of something that scholars have taken to calling "internal dialogue" and that is the way in which the making of memory expresses itself.

Talking to yourself.

Talking to yourself but not necessarily in good company.

Talking to yourself like someone who sees himself from outside and above, in the moment that he has been declared clinically dead and just before he reenters his body.

Talking to yourself and seeing yourself and expressing yourself with perspective, taking some—but not too much—distance. Talking to yourself up close, whispering in your own ear.

Talking to yourself forward and backward and forward again.

And so, there, what goes from the hallucinatory schizophrenia to the epiphanic eureka; from the mnemonic repetition to the karmatic mantra; from the voice-over in all those noir films to that human voice that doesn't answer the telephone; from the Devil possessing and making you speak in dead languages to the Son of Sam's neighbor's dog barking precise instructions for tonight; from the *classified* order that sends you upriver to kill a crazy soldier to the artificial and intelligent plea begging not to be disconnected; from the decisive "aisle or window" to the insignificant "You have been chosen for a mission that only you can carry out and that will alter the course of human history"; from Mrs. Dalloway to Molly Bloom; from autosuggestion before a medical exam to the autointerrogation after an oral exam, to figure out if you got the right answers; from a gigantic rabbit named Harvey only visible to a blessed few to an invisible and always-wrathful God.

The voice of a God—His Master's Voice—deafening Adam and Eve, Cain, Noah, Abraham, with the commands of a fierce and demanding Yiddishe Tate. Or, better, his other voice, the one he addressed Elijah with—in Hebrew—a *kol demamah dakah* or "the subtle sound of silence," which, he thinks, must be something like the sound experienced in ancient times by the person who—after centuries of always reading aloud and in viva voce—read silently for the first time.

The kind of deafening silence, he supposes, that descends when it snows: snow's sacred crystals, each of them different but resembling each other in their capacity to quiet the ambient noise as they fall and fall. A sound that you can only hear when you stop listening for it and that is only audible, they say, in those hermetic chambers where all you can hear is the sudden roaring of your own blood coursing through the cables of your body (a silence that ends up driving you mad if you're kept in there over an hour) until all of a sudden there it is, His voice: the voice that made the light, the light that has no sound but that allows all things of this world to speak.

yet, yes, so much further back, if you consider that brief space as the most

---

Whereas Jesus, they swear, didn't raise his voice enough. And so he ended up talking to himself on the cross. And Joan of Arc suffered the migraines of hundreds of angels chattering and flitting about at the same time (something like the Ligeti-brand sound the monolith emits in *2001: A Space Odyssey* or maybe something subtler and more akin to the repetition of Vinteuil's La petite phrase) and so it went and so she ended up the Maid of Orleans and, oh, the dangers of believing and convincing everyone else that you possess a direct line to the divine, yes.

Or perhaps, merely, epilepsy, "the sacred disease": Paul on the road to Damascus, Mohammad writing the Koran, Black Elk and his visions of Buffalo, Dostoyevsky writing the Great Inquisitor's digression in *The Brothers Karamazov* against the possibility of God. And even he himself singing with the voice of Huitzilopochtli or Tepoztecatl in a Mexico City D.F. mescalería.

And yet, recent studies—he reads now, airborne, in one of those airline magazines—turned up new neuronal-psychological findings regarding the mystery. Bicameral mind, they've named it. Something about how—he's not sure he fully grasped it, he's already on his third or fourth little high-altitude bottle—at some point in the pre-conscious past, there were fibers that divided the cerebral hemispheres (in the right, they theorize, resided the thoughts that mortals attributed to immortals and that served for the construction of metaphors and the revelation of visions) and that could explain all the Olympian voices heard by Achilles and Odysseus.

All those divine voices that—with the passing of centuries and prose styles—grew weaker and disappeared as the solidity of these cerebral membranes diminished, provoking a lack of contact with the gods and an increase in affection for all those online friends we'll never meet but who, all the same, are divine and, oh, he thinks not: nobody's yet come up with the design for an emoji that signifies "talking to myself."

Or for the decrease in auditory frequencies, making communing with that absolute form of solitude and memory—the call and response of the voices of the dead, over whom the silent response of the snow always falls—ever more sporadic.

Voices not to be confused with the dead's first voice, with the last sounds of living genius or of the ingeniousness the living have created: the almost always apocryphal last words sometimes pondered at length over the years and hurriedly uttered, thinking the end was nigh. And—hurrying and getting ahead of themselves—turning them into penultimate or antepenultimate words. And then there was nothing they could do but enforce a sepulchral silence on themselves or spend whatever time they had left thinking about adding even better last words than the ones they'd already wasted. Last words ("I've seen things . . . I'm afraid . . .") feeding that species of sonic vampire who voraciously absorb and repeat last words. There, ever watchful, before the organs collapse in on other organs, before the final electric sparks of thoughts, before the gases and the liquids and the flesh melt into each other until they are lost to the wind or the desert sands (the inevitable fate that many try to postpone with the electronic memory of blogs and social media accounts of the dead that are maintained and developed by companies devoted to precisely that: to being mediums, to helping keep those who're no longer here among their loved ones and curious followers, tweeting and posting and emojiing, like knocking three times at the door, reminding everyone that they're still here).

Asking the increasingly numerous voices of the increasingly-dead dead what their last words were. The dead flying around and demanding attention and like expansive of autonomous worlds. A voice that pulled him back—going back while everything else moves forward—to the back of his last flight: toward the airplane's back rows and the bathrooms and the little kitchen where the flight attendants were chatting, murmuring about gremlins and langoliers and about drunk and Odyssean tourists up in First Class whom they hover over like sirens of the skies, who couldn't help but seduce passengers with their song of not-so-secure security measures and of how to place their carry-on luggage overhead or under their seats. (He remembers that, passing by and traversing that zone of feminine turbulence, one of them showed another something on the screen of her phone; and that one made *that* sound that some women make when they see a baby or a kitten or a diamond necklace or—as part of a new crop of omega-female terminators waiting in the wings to destroy an alpha male—the compromising photographs of a Cabin Service Director whose ascendant career they can suddenly blow up and send flying . . .) through the air that everyone was breathing and that was surely rife with traces of ash from increasingly frequent volcanic eruptions, and with the residues of the dead

---

pale excess baggage, awkwardly crammed into overhead compartments, causing turbulence and sudden drops in the cabin pressure of the past when it's understood, in the last second of consciousness, that there's no future left.

The voice of last and transcendent and instantly marbleized and immortal last words that he collected in one of his little notebooks but that he never really believed in, because—based on his experience and to the best of his knowledge—the last words of first-class humans tended to be truly touristic and not so quotable and exceedingly random and very much of the moment. Things like "What's that smell?" or "My head hurts" or, merely, "Oh."

And what he wants most, his greatest wish: to find the voice that he would've liked to have had if he'd succeeded in transforming himself into a particular and accelerated god with the help of a Swiss hadron accelerator.

And, oh, last but not least, last to get on board but first to leave, the voice that was but will never cease to be. His voice in the past: the voice of his past. That voice he had when he was just a boy, making *that* phone call, informing a stranger about what his vociferating parents were planning to do and undo the following day, which has already gone but remains there forever, in red, on all calendars, until the end times of his time, *ahoritita mismito*, right, right, right now.

The voice that's nothing more than the way he's chosen—his diction, his inflections, his tone—to narrate all those things.

The voice that—in the beginning and in the end—is just another way of saying *the style*.

The voice into which all of the already-spoken voices melt, the voice of memory: the voice that asks, "Do you remember me?" and the same voice, but from a different mouth, that answers, "Of course I remember."

who'd been thrown alive into those volcanos, and with particles of gasoline and motor oil and exhaust, and with the spores of the next great pandemic that once migrated in the feathers of birds and that now travels in the nose of that incessantly-sneezing passenger in the emergency exit row, over the metal wing.

Air whose toxicity airlines never acknowledge, claiming that the atmosphere inside their planes is as clean as that of a hospital, where, in any case, they say, the risk of catching a serious infection is far greater than it is outside, and where you have a greater probability, statistically and infectiously, of dying than anywhere else, oftentimes of something that wasn't what brought you there in the first place (he remembers perfectly one time, in just four days, during a LAX-JFK-LHR—the initials of airports like those of the least-intelligent intelligence agencies—combination when, high in the sky, he clearly perceived the exact moment that a mouthful of foul air, roiling with assorted bacteria, slipped, dancing the twist and the Watusi, into his bronchial tubes, and hours later he no longer remembered any of it, as he floated among syrupy clouds of codeine with a voice like that of an irreplicable robot).

Air that, he thinks, won't take long to be bottled and sold as the drug *du jour* to be inhaled in Bel Air gardens by people who, invariably, sucking it down on the sly, will exclaim: "Wow! It makes you feel so high, like you're flying way up in the sky."

Air that was already starting to be studied by public health organizations as responsible for delicate deliriums, for speaking not in tongues but in lips impossible even for the red eye of the most powerful and confused computer to read.

Air that causes you to think of saying the kind of things you only say you think of when you're there, feeling that you're flying.

Air that—like a memorious version of truth serum—aided in making you remember everything you wanted to forget because you suspect and confirm that it's unforgettable.

And so, some *airheaded* things he hears (might those who claim to have perfect pitch and for whom every sound is a note from which an entire symphony might spring experience something similar? he wonders) as he walks in a straight line through the winding air of an airplane.

"Are you happy?" says 29A.

"Don't ask such sad questions," says 29B.

"Not too long ago, I read about the death of a tourist in the Caribbean, on the island of St. Martin, caused by something that might well be considered an airplane accident, though not exactly: the woman died after being struck by the expansive wave of an airplane taking off from the airport. The woman was on one of those beaches that begin just where the runway ends. The moving air struck her chest and triggered a heart attack. Or maybe it sent her flying and she hit her head on landing . . . And while we're at it, let me explain exactly what happens when an airplane hits a bird or, better, when a bird crashes into an airplane . . . It happens on eight of every ten thousand flights. In general, the bird ends up losing, ha; but there are times when . . . The true problem isn't the moment of impact, but the slight damage and cracks that go undetected in the moment and, as time passes . . . It's like ignoring that small blotch on your skin that wasn't there before and not having a dermatologist look at it when you first discover it and you know . . ." smiles 17K.

"To be totally honest and to tell the absolute truth, I must confess, I'm an incorrigible liar," whispers 9C.

"I have no house only a shadow. But whenever you are in need of a shadow, my shadow is yours," mutters the drunk, sleeping ugly in 21D, and then adds something about how they throw him over a precipice and sick a dog on him and how there's a garden that must be protected from the children.

And 14J—a voice that could belong to a man or a woman, a piercing voice—says deep things like, "Ah, love. I don't know what that is anymore. Nor do I want to know. Perhaps love is that long inertia that follows a brief push . . . Perhaps not. I limit myself to enjoying it while it lasts. Like Pringles. You know, that snack of uncertain ingredients: you don't really know what they are or exactly what they're made of; but you can't stop chewing and swallowing them until the can is empty anyway. The same thing happens with love, right? . . . Love doesn't have a precise formula or exact composition and who knows to what order it belongs. We can only venture that love is the effect of a cause. Love, which, in the end but from the beginning, always was and is and will be *self*-love. Because to really love yourself, you need to fall in love with another person and make them fall in love with you and pass through them and, on the other side, find the ideal version of yourself. Discovering, there and then, the person you'd always wanted to be, a trans-figured and sublime me . . . And so, love is like a battery that, when it runs out, can't be recharged. It's got to be swapped out for a new one. Like the modern appliances—unlike those of the past, whose sales pitch was that they lasted decades and even forever—that are sold with an expiration date and at most a two-year warranty, as if that were one of their greatest virtues: not to last too long and thereby enable for their replacement without the guilt of not having known how to take care of them or use them properly, either way, everything ends up falling apart and breaking down . . . Like love, which I always thought of as originating on the West Coast, where we're going now. Love like a landmass throbbing atop a tectonic plate and trying not to think that, sooner or later, it'll be time and place for The Big One. And that then everything will quake and hearts will break, and everyone will plunge into the theretofore pacific, but nevermore . . . nevermore . . . nevermore. And there'll be nothing left where once there was so much . . . Did you know that in tennis LOVE means not having scored a single point . . . an absolute zero?"

And that kid in 22F covered in tattoos and with the look of a narco-hit-man-in-training, his ears covered with XL headphones who, every so often, without realizing it, releases some rap-reggaetón-ish outburst of which only random words like *"mami"* and *"culo"* and *"movidito"* and *"no estamos rústicos, estamos exóticos"* are comprehensible.

And 9K explaining that "there's two sides to every story . . . For example, the explanation as to why we strike our glasses together when we make a toast. There's a really poetic explanation that claims that sound is the only sense absent when you drink. You have sight and smell and touch and taste. But you don't have sound. Thus that *clink*. Sounds right, doesn't it? . . . But there's also the historical explanation: people banged their glasses together so the liquid in the one would mix with the liquid in the other and with that they would be able to find out if someone were trying to poison or not be poisoned . . . Tell me which version you choose and I'll tell you what kind of person you are, ha."

And that old woman in 13B: her arms so skinny they never stop mov-ing, like the delicate feathered bones on the wings of dancing birds, her eyes covered in enormous dark sunglasses, her voice surprisingly young when she calls out to him, passing by in the aisle, mistaking him for an air marshal, and asks for a little bottle of vodka (and he'd always wanted to meet that marketing guru who found a way to convince the whole world that vodka doesn't leave its drinkers with alcohol on their breath, when anyone can see that that's simply not true), as if it were the last thing she'd ever want and ever order and, almost imperial, she says, "Some real things have happened lately."

And 6C saying how "A medical examiner explained to me once that if you suddenly found out that your airplane won't reach its destination, you could write a final note and swallow it, and that it's almost guaranteed that your stomach liquids will preserve it through any crash and that your loved ones will be able to know your last thoughts . . . In fact, now that I think of it, it wouldn't be bad if they sold some kind of extra resistant paper in airport bookstores. Air Mail in the most complete and absolute sense. Letter paper so that, just in case, everyone could write down and swallow farewells to their loves ones before boarding their flights . . . To be like bottles with messages inside . . ."; so that 6B responds with "if the sun goes out forever right now we would still have eight minutes and nineteen seconds of light; just like what happens, though their persistence in our memory varies, with all the things and people that are no longer here but somehow linger on, right?"

And the pilot—1X?—who every so often exits the cockpit. And strolls with an—never more apropos—air of absolute satisfaction and no doubt thinking about how many times he's going to interrupt the movies playing on seatbacks to communicate improbable nonsense, like the altitude they're flying at or what could but cannot be seen out the windows on the side of the plane where he never gets to sit. The man smiling and gliding between the passengers who look up at him as if he were a sudden physical manifestation of the divine. And he doesn't smile up at the pilot, but does stare at him. And tries to read his thoughts, pondering the mystery of how it is that we surrender ourselves to them—to airline pilots—the same way we surrender ourselves to a doctor. Blindly and with eyes wide open. And so we get on airplanes the same way we go into operating rooms: trying to imagine as little as possible about the private lives and personal issues of the people with the power to keep slicing with the scalpel under those bright lights or to stop flying with all those needles atremble on the control panel. (Because those men had always inspired great distrust in him, long before that one decided to crash into the Alps with a plane full of people. Or before he'd met that other one: one of The Intruders. Another of his tormenting tenants, tenants who'd apparently been under the nether-worldly influence of his sister Penelope when they'd staged what had been, perhaps, their most monstrous performance, a kind of revival of his and Penelope's family. Though he suspected all along that it was the same troupe and cast as always, just wearing different masks, for that was their talent, similar perhaps to the "art" of those writers who, to his befuddlement and incomprehension, were praised for being "chameleonic" and always writing "different" books. And their "gift" and "ingenuity," he thought, was the ability to conceal the failure of having never attained—with their own style, unmistakable and repeatable, because that's what it was all about, because that was the only way—the personal high point of a Great Theme. And so, for several months, invisible and soundless by day, like vampires, an English woman who never stopped shrieking and cackling like one of those slum-dwelling hags out of Charles Dickens—whom he'd named Eliza Donothing—and who kept him not from sleeping but from even trying to sleep with her more *cunt*ney than cockney accent. And always accompanied by her husband. The man constantly humming that strange and pseudo-mariachi intro to "Ring of Fire." Or howling ballads rife with obscene limericks. A foul persona non grata whom he'd christened Playmobil because, as he caterwauled, he always held out a hand in the same position as the hands of those tiny plastic toy figures: *like this*, in an open circle, ever ready to receive a new and freshly popped bottle of beer, stretched out on a deck chair, wearing metal-framed sunglasses with rose-tinted lenses. And both of them were always glued to their mobile phones. And all around, dangling from their ethylic bellies, a repulsive stew of gelatinous children, faces coated in a crusty mess of snot. All of them swathed in soiled diapers and appearing—no doubt from having marinated in boozy amniotic fluid for nine months of gestation and ingestion—stunted and retarded, destined to never grow up so they could keep crying all the time. One spent all his time playing the same scales on repeat on the piano, pounding all the wrong keys over and over with little hands that looked more like stumps, always poised to butcher another "Für Elise." And he counterattacked by putting on Glenn Gould to see if in that way . . . Inexplicably they had a dog that never barked; but pretty soon he realized that it'd had an operation to have its vocal cords removed, because they didn't want an animal—not, strictly speaking, a member of the family—to compete with their tribal racket. Seeing them from a distance but hearing them so up close, he couldn't help imagining that the two of them and their offspring would be just the sort of international friends that the Karmas would make on their excursions to festive religious festivals and/or cruises to the Old World; thinking of them as charming and fun and cosmopolitan, unaware that they were the most pestilent strain of Eurotrash that ever there was. After in their wake came others who were different but similar,, maybe even the same. Variations and vibrations. And, change of costume and attitude, there even arrived a trembling couple resembling wax effigies who, he supposed, could only be Nicole and Dick Diver, the one melting into the other, in his parents' favorite novel, a novel whose tragedy and sadness seemed to heighten the power of its joyous comedy. And more, and others, and on to the next ones. And so, one season, he remembers having an Intruder of the social-alcoholic variety who always filled the house—and thus his own vicinity—with guests. Celebrating the birthdays of his children or others' children, any excuse to pound one beer after another. The kind of guy who, when night fell, when his wife with her perpetual bovine-Valkyrie air and all the guests, apart from the one or two he kept from leaving by insisting "another for the runway," had left, kept right on getting drunk, downing dozens of bottles he lined up under his window, sobbing things like "Oh, that airport in Anchorage where we all got together, men and women of all nationalities, in the days when we were all employed by magnates and traffickers, drinking and laughing until the sun came up, like buccaneers on Tortuga, before casting off the moorings again . . . I was never happier than I was there, flying those secret little airplanes . . ." He remembers how, for that fool, that almost clandestine airport had been something like a cross between the Shangri-La from *Lost Horizons* and the Mos Eisley cantina in *Star Wars*.) And the pilot kept right on evoking all of that while, live and present, his wailing and tiny yet irrepressibly expansive triplets orbited all around, their faces smeared with a crust of snot and shit that, no doubt, somebody would inevitably patent as a miraculous anti-aging facial cream for menopausal women. And again, back on the airplane, others are speaking languages he doesn't understand. Like the uncontrollable baby in 7A. (Or maybe it was just a recording of a crying baby that the airline was playing over the loudspeakers, given how these days there are fewer and fewer babies everywhere; because people are too busy texting heart-studded texts and saying how, if they were to get pregnant, they'd definitely shove one of those BabyPod stimulators into their vaginas, so their fetuses could listen to Bach or The Beatles better. Turning what had once been a subject into a random verb. Writing messages using the words the software itself suggests with prose fragments and a clipped voice like the one that once upon a time, oracular, reported the time over the telephone. Relegating the comparatively nineteenth-century loquacity to something that almost nobody responds to anymore. Writing about making love instead of making love.) A baby between two parents who no longer hear it and who don't feel like parents because they don't really understand how and where that thing came from and why it can't be blocked and some of them have even named those little creatures Siri or Alexa or Cortana, vainly fantasizing that their offspring would obey and assist them after they'd submitted themselves to all those fertilization and insemination procedures (and he'd always wondered why those incredibly expensive procedures—instead of making you go through a humiliating and not-at-all pleasurable session of self-pleasuring in a small cubicle with the aid of sticky magazines in order to produce a "sample"—didn't also include a photographic display of the potential mother, posing like a porn centerfold; because, he thought, it would never not be really weird for them to, while seeking the elusive fruit of deep love, rely on the unfaithful assistance of an absolute stranger; and while he's at it, drowning in this scream-filled air: how was it that in all those complex space-time fantasies, the time traveler with the mission to go back and assassinate Hitler in his moment of maximum power and glory never opted to go back a little further and suffocate him in his little crib when he wasn't yet anyone but just a baby who would probably just raise one arm and shriek *sieg heil* and, after all, let's not forget that the only person capable of killing Hitler was Hitler) and . . .

All those voices voicing themselves in a state of dissolution. Voices of people traveling to forget where they came from, to rediscover themselves along the way, wherever they were going.

Voices seeking to lose who they were to try to find out who they might have been in who they would become.

Voices taking a vacation from themselves.

Voices like wisps of smoke in the pressurized air of the cabin.

Voices so different from his; because, when he traveled, he experienced the opposite effect: a powerful intensification of his own persona and memory. Something, he thought, like Odysseus on his long way home, evoking everything that he'd left behind and that was now ahead of him, with more precision and feeling than ever: Ithaca, Telemachus, Argos, and that other Penelope. And in that way, the memory of the names he couldn't forget was superimposed over the forgetful seeds of the Lotus Eaters—as tempting as those little bags of dry and salty fruit the flight attendants were now coming through to offer with your choice of spirits—and rejected the amnesia offered by Poseidon and the past-less immortality given by Calypso.

And, sure, he was a man with no country no woman and no dog. But the closest thing he'd had to a son was He Whose Name Must Not Be Mentioned. And he was gone now. That boy whose name hurt so much and yet—contrary to what the meditative and pensive Marcus "Soon Everybody Will Have Forgotten You" Aurelius claimed—was external to his body and so he was able regulate and even nullify it. That boy he first referred to as The Son of Penelope. And then, when Penelope was no longer there, sometimes, as The Son. Never as My Nephew. So it seemed to him that He Whose Name Must Not Be Mentioned was the best way to refer to the boy, though he didn't know where he was or if he still was wherever he was (and at one point in *À la recherche du temps perdu*, Proust claims that when you said someone else's name you were exercising a kind of power over that name and the person who bears it. A kind of magic invocation. But in his case, he thought, it was the exact opposite and in reverse: mentioning that name, the name of He Whose Name Must Not Be Mentioned, put him even more powerfully under the influence of its bearer than he already was. So, he wouldn't say anything, not one letter of his name, but, yes, to honor Penelope's memory, he would clarify that, no, the boy's name wasn't Heathcliff; because Penelope's ghost would never be able to bear anyone thinking that, when she was still on this side of things, she'd been capable of doing something so vulgar. Penelope's ghost who now disdainfully mocked such gestures and said: "You see now what happened to Heath Ledger; how he ended up. His parents were fans of *Wuthering Heights* and they named him Heathcliff and his older sister Cathy and there are some things you just don't play around with and, oh, such is the punishment for parents who think of their children not as children but as toys . . . Like our parents. They had us to *have* us. And, before long, they got bored of playing with us and, ah, what did they call our parents? Oh, yes: they—everyone else in the world, for whom they were glamorous people—called our parents 'That Couple that Travels the Globe on a Sailboat'").

And, yes, there were too many movies with scenes of fathers and mothers being told of the death of their children (seeing them, he felt nothing; but he could feel, even in the darkness of the theater, the glowing, phosphorescent panic of many spectators, mothers and fathers, projecting themselves into what was being projected for them), but, from what he knew or had seen, there was no movie in which an uncle was told that his nephew had disappeared.

And Penelope was not Odysseus's Penelope, no.

Penelope was and had been his sister.

And she'd never hoped for or expected anything from him.

And that's why, now, he traveled in his memory. To counter and catch her ghost off guard. Hemmed in by that choir of the passing voices of passengers he liked to imagine as bound together in a brotherhood so secret not even its members knew they shared the commonality of having crossed paths with the closest thing he'd ever had to a true Penelope, a woman worth returning to.

But, also, the closest thing to a Circe.

Or to a Beatrice.

Ella.

Yes, all those passengers, unbeknownst to them, united—he fantasizes—by having, at some party on some summer night, watched Ella fall into some swimming pool. Voices he considered writing down and swallowing and then immediately changed his mind. Because he had faith he wasn't going die—he didn't have any loved ones left anyway—and because, contrary to all diagnoses and notwithstanding any tumor, he was convinced he would remember all of it perfectly. Or at least he would convince himself that he did, because aren't you really pretending when you remember, aren't you really pretending to remember when you remember?

And yet, back in his seat, it's as if it'd never happened, as if he hadn't heard anything while walking through the aisle of the airplane, and that allowed him to convince himself that he'd invented or dreamed all of it. All he was left with—what he used to count on but that no longer counts for anything—was that disconcerting void that oblivion leaves behind: the lush white noise inside a fertile black hole. (And with all of that he remembers that—*overnight to many distant cities*, their lights down below, twinkling and winking up at him—he wrote, back in days when he could still write, a story featuring Ella and her swimming pools. A story that could be read, also, as a more or less subliminal homage to Donald Barthelme's "The Indian Uprising." And, ah, that was part of the problem: he found Donald Barthelme more interesting than a good number of the great writers from his now nonexistent country of origin and from the continent where his country had once existed. Barthelme, whom he'd never met and who was dead now and almost forgotten by people in his own country—though subliminally he remained very influential—the way you forget one of those trends that you followed in its day but couldn't keep following because it was followed by another trend to follow; because you start off chasing after a trend only to, before long, wind up fleeing it. And he was and had been irrefutable proof of that very impulse. Barthelme who'd only ever once been awarded one of the important and prestigious prizes: the childish National Book Award in the Children's Book category.

Barthelme, who authorized his students to write in "wacky mode" provided that it was clear to them that, when and if they wrote *like that*, they *also* had the very levelheaded obligation to their readers to "break their hearts." And he wrote in wacky mode when he'd written that story. And one thing was certain: when, after writing it, he read it, it broke his heart. And, just to be clear, he'd written it before he read "The Indian Uprising," sounding to his eyes like a collage of voices. And that happened more often than you'd think: voices of the past eating your voice years later, winds over winds and deserts under deserts. Voices like . . . like . . . how'd it go? . . . Ah, yes: like cells interlinked within cells interlinked within cells interlinked.) And, in his headphones, one of the airplane's music channels was dedicating a retrospective to the voice of that band that—though they patented the act of breaking up as the definitive artistic gesture—remains together beyond all trends and time periods and echoes in the voices of so many bands formed so long after. And the voice of that band forever on high, like right now, thousands of meters up in the air. And there, a song that begins with the sound of an airplane taking off or coming in for a landing, with those increasingly extensive and intricate taxiing maneuvers along wayward runways that, on more than one occasion, end up lasting longer than the flight itself and seem to consume an entire day in the life. And—in verses of the following songs—the three key times being harmonized at the same time all the time: "Oh, I believe in yesterday" and "I read the news today, oh boy" and "Tomorrow never knows." And, above all of them, "There are places I remember . . ." Yes, that's how the past that never dies and that isn't even past sounds. That past that never passes and passed by singing. The past that "lies upon the present like a giant's dead body" (Nathaniel Hawthorne) and that "lies like a nightmare upon the present" (Karl Marx) and that "is a curious thing. It's with you all the time" (George Orwell) and that, there, lying down and always going to bed early, sleeps with one eye open, always singing.

And all that music that he knows by heart reminds him of Uncle Hey Walrus and, oh, the temptation to linger there a while: in the before everything, at the beginning of all these things. But it turns out to be a passing effect and a fleeting hope; because though you never know—as if between dreams—what tomorrow may bring, you keep reading the news that, oh boy, imagines the present as it is unfolding in order to continue remembering and believing in yesterday. You need today to believe in yesterday. Today like the curtain before it's raised, which you stare at almost convincing yourself that the true story—the consensual nonsense, the drama or the comedy yet to come but written so long ago, reciting it with such determination to thereby distract yourself from knowing yourself to be so overdetermined—is already *right there.*

And then realizing that you only need to know how to invent and to dream and to remember. *Thrice-Told Tales.* Because there is the invented part and the dreamed part and the remembered part and—from their fusion—the all-the-never-answered-questions part. Enigmas of reality that—without ever being entirely resolved—enter, almost without realizing it, into the realm of the mythic with the same elegance they would retain passing through curtains made of a light and transparent material that, nevertheless, quickly convinces everyone that, though everything may appear the same and so familiar, on the other side, things will be very different.

And (oh, those wide and aerodynamic seats that you stare at, due to the unequivocal sadism of the airline, as you board the airplane and pass by on your way to the slums of the sky with the sad gait of galley slaves to be lined up in rows) the sound of the curtains being drawn that separate first class from the classless. And the sound of the engines firing up and, oh, enough of all this already and, hey, is it just him or are there far fewer passengers on the airplane now than when the take-off maneuvers began? Was there a small stampede of tourists who decided to deplane at the last minute to take advantage of some awful promotion or to avoid sharing a flight with that guy who thinks and thinks and thinks because he no longer writes and writes and writes? Panic when it came to confronting vertical heights or long and horizontal sentences? Fear of reading? Fear of flying? Fear of flying through *reading*? Fear of remembering because—he's found it to be true many times—he always remembers more and better in the air, flying, there above, nowhere but over everywhere?

All he knows now is that there are no brave people, that there never were.

Now he knows that people were and are and will forever be a pack of cowards. And that there are two types of coward: the ones fear makes retreat and the ones fear drives forward. And that the ones who hang back are the ones people and History end up mistakenly considering brave for the simple of fact of having lived to tell the tale.

And, yes, he's afraid of everything now.

But—only retreating to make memory—he keeps moving forward. He keeps moving forward like back when he wrote, like back when he felt he was flying and not, like right now, totally deserted in the middle of a desert.

And he has enumerated so many ways to understand a desert because, in the end and to begin with, the desert is the closest thing there is to a daunting blank page. The desert, not like the passing fear of the blank page but like the definitive and courageous blank page itself. The blank page acknowledging that it no longer has anything to say or to add to everything that's already out there, exposed to the elements, with no margins to contain it or lines to arrange it or give it somewhere to go and some exit.

And now that he no longer writes (that he no longer whispers or roars), the pages written by another—pages that he was never able to read and that thus remain blank to him—keep him warm or to let him attempt to convince himself he's warm.

Now, in the desert, with all the airplanes of his past flying overhead, he feeds a small fire one page at a time from a book he'd never been able to read—though he'd tried to so many times and had so often referred to their author as one of his favorites—beyond its few first chapters.

Pages that, as they fall, black on white, first are pure white light and then sliced through by a flashing red flame. And, then, the totality of the history of the universe—from the beginning, intuited as an unverifiable memory, to the end, imagined as an impossible memory—reduced in seconds: everything ends as fire and of fire.

(He'd read somewhere that that was how William Somerset Maugham had read Marcel Proust, traveling across a desert, tearing out the pages as they became part of him. And he'd also read—in its day, in the early stages of the project that would end up being defined at the time as "the proverbial really good science-fiction movie"—that the insomniac Stanley Kubrick had done "research," in the same way, reading fanta-science books the way he was now: tearing out the pages, one by one, as he finished them. And throwing them into the flames of a fireplace, at the bedside of one of his daughters—gravely ill at the time, with one of those childhood illnesses that come and go like passing but furious storms—who had to be watched over constantly. There, Kubrick proceeded to imagine, bit by bit, a film that went "from ape to angel," and forced people to "pay attention with their eyes" and that, in the end, would feature forty-two minutes of quasi-robotic dialogue between men and machines and a hundred minutes of cosmic silence. And before all of that, Kubrick had directed another movie based on another book that also had a woman's name for a title written by the very same writer whose book he was now reading and burning.)

And it didn't surprise him in the least that here—there was no coverage in the unplugged air of the desert, but there was powerful free association of ideas—it all seemed connected.

One of the reasons that coincidences exist is so you can say that coincidences don't exist, he thinks. Coincidences that were like those creatures that dwell in the depths and every so often come up to the surface to break the stillness of the waters with their fins. Sometimes coincidences were like playful dolphins, others like lethal sharks, and, every so often, like cataclysmic leviathans. Coincidences like that rare moment when it became obvious that all of life and all of history followed a pattern. And that the ephemeral and supposedly spontaneous moment of coincidence—which, more than once, he suspected was actually the result of a long period of calculated planning—was the moment when, for an instant, the pattern became clear. As if your eyes opened a little wider. Everything was connected, you just had to know how to follow the rhythm of the links. Believing in coincidences was like believing in God but feeling that you were a little divine too, part of the whole thing; like when, all of a sudden, you wrote a really good line that seemed to come out of nowhere. And then later, of course, everything went back to not making any sense—including, sometimes, that very same line that seconds before had struck you as miraculous—and it became clear that coincidences only worked well in books and movies. Because in that context they had a transparent and sometimes even obvious and banal function: accelerating a plot that wasn't moving or that was moving too slowly (the kind of crude and spoiled coincidence that was like a drunk you barely know leaping out from the corner at a party and howling "What a coincidence!"; while elegant and subtle coincidences only revealed themselves as coincidences later on, when you went home or, even, many years later, when nobody remembered that baptism or wedding or birthday anymore and the terminal season of funerals was already arriving: occasions, he thought, that should all be considered subgenres of fiction for the way that people behaved at them, as if they were characters, making death the most fictionalizable occasion of all). **In any case, he counted and recounted coincidences to keep himself awake the way others counted sheep to fall asleep. And, coincidentally, he looks up at the moon from that terrestrial lunar landscape, like an ape ready to rise up and become the top primate known as Moonwatcher.** (And he remembers—though it's something he never stops remembering—that unforgettable and silent yet oh so musical film: *2001: A Space Odyssey.* And he wonders if from where he was looking up at the moon, from this desert, it was possible to see the Clavius Crater and the mysterious and monolithic TMA-1 / Tycho Magnetic Anomaly One. And he remembers that his favorite character from that film had always been the doctor and father— and the latter, amid all that confused artificial intelligence and those robotic astronauts, for some reason, struck him as an important detail—Heywood R. Floyd. Someone who, to him, always had the look and the sound—his face and his voice—of a kind of James Stewart in orbit. A look that, decades later, in the unnecessary *2010: Odyssey Two*, was ruined, first by writer Arthur C. Clarke and subsequently by actor Roy Schreider, as they worked together to destroy all the mystique established and never explained in the first part. And he also remembers that Stanley Kubrick tried more than once and in vain to get another Floyd, the musicians of Pink Floyd, to collaborate on his soundtracks. And he never pulled it off, because his idea was—of course—to manipulate their music, to be another member of the band and to be able to take credit for that too, and Pink Floyd turned him down because its members didn't want anyone to mess with their sonic deserts. And he also remembers that the BBC also contacted Pink Floyd and did get them to come into their studios to improvise a live jam session, to be used as background music for that nearly-silent film of the *Apollo 11* moon landing, which some people believed Stanley Kubrick had been directing from the shadows and, while you're at it, why not believe—it was far more probable and realistic—that *2001: A Space Odyssey* was filmed during an actual voyage to Jupiter and the infinite beyond. *Moonhead*, it was titled. And he also remembers that while all of that was happening, he was just a boy, watching the whole thing unfold in the assembly hall at his school—Gervasio Vicario Cabrera, colegio n°1 del Distrito Escolar Primero, along with his rival and ink brother Pertusato, Nicolasito—on a small television screen. One of those televisions that would be like a toy today: primitive and childish but, yes, far tougher and more durable. A television of the kind that had justified the relaunch of a once-failed product that, courtesy of those mad geniuses on Madison Avenue so admired by his parents, was suddenly an ultra-mega-super success: *frozen food* rebranded as *TV dinner*, abruptly authorizing you to eat with your eyes fuller and wider open than your mouth and, all together but separate, watching a screen like how now everybody took little bites from the screens of their mobile phones, sitting there right next to the silverware, tapping and swiping. A television plagued by vertical and horizontal and ghostly interference and antennas like metal rabbit ears. Watching the astronauts, up there, watching him and all humankind from the moon, with the same distance, as intimate as it is remote, from which a writer sees his characters. Watching the moon landing and wondering with the absurd logic of children—or of the child that he'd been, always wondering about that kind of thing—how the long-suffering Larry Talbot in particular and werewolves in general would transform on the moon. Watching there what he would remember seeing again—over the years and on every round or selenite anniversary—on the screens of ever bigger and flatter and higher-definition televisions. Televisions that now even prompted the spectator to interact with thousands of shows—spectators who never interacted with the books they read, choosing faces and colors over everything offered up by the best writing—that began but never ended because they were canceled or dragged out for years. Like real lives: they ended abruptly and with no advance notice or, with any luck, they came to some kind of end, sad or happy but definitive or defining, shutting the door or escaping out the window. But none of that progress altered his memory of that black and white landscape that stayed the same and never changed beyond the evolution of cathode tube to liquid plasma. A landscape that always carried him forward from that time—with a small step and a giant leap—toward other future landscapes, as if even back then he could remember what only later he would come to know.) Landscapes like the one that now, lunar as it ever was, he sees as part of himself: this desert where once upon a time astronauts trained, deluding themselves that their ticket would come up as winner in the lottery of the Great Voyage. Thinking about that and about the things that the last generation—his—to grow up looking up at the stars and not at screens far smaller than the screen of that small television think about. Thinking that the surface of the moon was like that of a nighttime desert where instead of the moon shining with a pale fire stolen from the sun, it was the Earth that shone and . . .

The same thing happened with that other kind of desert above the desert: the sky that doesn't shelter and, beyond that, outer space, where you couldn't be more deserted and forsaken; because (as happens between one coincidence and another) there are no walls out there to lean on or take cover and hide behind. There are only doors that open onto other doors (and there are doors that turn into beds and desks and dining room tables on which to love and create and eat).

And now he—so exposed, never further outside—felt like an astronaut floating across the curved screen and projected by three synchronized 35 mm projectors.

And he thinks and enumerates: three are the stages of the monomyth. Departure, initiation, and return. And the sound of the lowing of the immense green cow there beside him reminds him so much of the sound of that monomythic monolith.

Voices rising above the voices that he saw and heard for the first of so many times in that theater that was like a palace, when he was around five or six years old, when he already knew how to read and write. At that age when you're more open to all sensorial stimuli. The age when everything counts and when you remember everything, because there is little to remember and almost nothing to forget (except for what you learned in that strange wasteland of your own prehistory, in the years between zero and three and out of which, every so often, arise visions as brief and powerful as lightning bolts that, paradoxically, grow more frequent in old age, when there's little left to add and anticipate but so much left to revisit).

The age when there is so much to invent and to dream.

The age at which when you play you're not yet playing yourself.

The age when reading is the drugless drug, an addiction with none of the problems of being an addict.

The age when everything is surprising and moving; because you don't yet have that many parameters or precedents to compare story ideas or plot twists and, yes, what someone else imagined is always as imaginative as what you imagine when you imagine it. (The age when, he remembers, what he liked to do most was read blind: choosing a book based only on its cover and knowing nothing about what awaited him inside. Avoiding books with overly explanatory titles, titles that did nothing but emphasize something that was already there, instead of hinting at something more diffuse but alive and breathing on each and every one of the book's pages. That's why he'd never been interested in Jules Verne, because he announced/clarified from the beginning things like *Two Thousand Leagues Under the Sea* or *Around the World in Eighty Days* or *Journey to the Center of the Earth* or *From the Earth to the Moon* or, for him, the least attractive of all: *Tribulations of a Chinaman in China*. But yes: it was perilous to generalize or take things for granted; and so he missed out on reading Verne's formidable and vampiric and mechanical *The Carpathian Castle*, before *Dracula* and *The Invention of Morel*. It was, indeed, a risk to acquire such fixed habits, but he preferred to risk missing out so he could enjoy discovering the meaning and theme of different storylines as the pages turned. That's why he opted for titles that revealed next to nothing but said it all. Like *David Copperfield* or *Slaughterhouse-Five* or *Martin Eden*. Or, again, *Dracula*: his first "adult" novel and, of course, about whose protagonist he already knew almost everything from movies and comics. And he remembers a comic that was a continuation of that novel that, he knew right away, was *something else*. Far more than everything he'd seen before in movies. In the magazine *Creepy*. Or was it *Eerie*? One of the two, either way. And he also remembers one panel at the end of that comic, where Dracula falls off a cliff and his coffin splinters and one of those splinters, the size of a stake, is driven through his heart. And previously, a couple panels back, his father had circled, with a red pen, the stake that, he thought, was the one that would be driven into the vampire's heart: as if the comic were a directive on the storyboard of one of his yet-to-be-filmed commercials. And that he—who cared for his magazines and books to an almost pathological degree, trying to keep them in even better condition than when he first got them—had almost lost his mind with rage and sorrow when he discovered that intrusive mark. And, yes, that'd been an additional reason for doing what he ended up doing and . . . But another of the many practical uses to which he put *Dracula* as *training-instruction manual* would be that of confirming the rule that the book will always be better than everything the book might end up inspiring in any other form. And, warning, the book *2001: A Space Odyssey* was not better than the movie, because it was developed based on and released after the movie. And again, even back then: he never succumbed to the temptation to read summaries on the jacket flaps or backs of books. And he didn't avoid doing it, then or now, with that kind of blind rage that some people react with these days when you tell them some aspect of a story. Howling "SPOILER! SPOILER!" not caring that what you're commenting on is the end of *The Odyssey* or *Don Quixote* or *Madame Bovary*. No. Unlike the people who don't want anything to happen before it happens to them—allowing them to believe that everything begins and ends with themselves, especially TV shows—he liked to know that everything was there: available, like an unforgettable party that you show up to already underway, at the best moment, and that you always leave before it's over. Yes: he liked books to be like life, where you could guess or anticipate but never predict with absolute certainty.)

That's what he was now, that's what he's becoming again: uncertain and difficult to interpret. Unpredictable. All dark side and darkness on all sides, like a magnetic lunar and lunatic anomaly buried for millennia in a crater, feeling so exhausted but, at the same time, as if he were waking up singing after a million-year dream. "Full of stars" under those silent celestial bodies, eyes in the stars and eyes in the smoke—the solarized pupil of the astro-castaway dilating out of Jupiter's orbit to infinity and beyond—and thinking of his own divine Star-Child.

And that's why he's here now, having arrived to the far reaches of the universe to look for and find him. His little monolith. (And remembering his little voice, powerful like only the voice of a child can be, saying "Here's a riddle: I'm neither person nor animal nor thing; but if you name me, I disappear. What am I?" And when he answered that he didn't know, the boy, who is the star that's guiding him now, illuminating him, said: "I am the silence.")

And *that* is the kind of silence—the silence that he didn't guess at the time but that turns out to be the only possible answer—that surrounds him now. Because even the colossal green cow's occasional song—a song like whale song, but silent and telepathic and deafening inside his head—is itself part of the air fueling the fire. A fire that feeds off a book that's not exactly science fiction (though it does propose a parallel world and an alternate history), a book that now, finally and in the end, he reads page by page, tearing them out and throwing them into the flames that ardently flare as they consume the letters of Vladimir Nabokov's *Ada, or Ardor.*

Letters that, together and before burning, say things like "You lose your immortality when you lose your memory." Or "When we remember our former selves, there is always that little figure with its long shadow stopping like an uncertain belated visitor on a lighted threshold at the far end of some impeccably narrowing corridor." Or "he soon noticed that such details of his infancy as really mattered (for the special purpose the reconstruction pursued) could be best treated, could not seldom be *only* treated, when reappearing at various later stages of his boyhood and youth, as sudden juxtapositions that revived the part while vivifying the whole." Or "If the Past is perceived as a storage of Time, and if the Present is the process of that perception, the future, on the other hand, is not an item of time, has nothing to do with Time and with the dim gauze of its physical texture. The future is but a quack in the court of Chronos." Or "Is there any mental uranium whose dream-delta decay might be used to measure the age of a recollection?" Or "And speaking of evolution, can we imagine the origin and steppingstones and rejected mutations of Time? Has there ever been a 'primitive' form of Time in which, say, the Past has not yet clearly differentiated from the Present, so that past shadows and shapes showed through the still soft, long, larval 'now'? Or did that evolution only refer to timekeeping, from sandglass to atomic clock and from that to portable pulsar? And *what* time did it take for Old Time to become Newton's? . . . Pure Time, Perceptual Time, Tangible Time, Time free of content, context, and running commentary—this is *my* time and theme."

And there he is and there his time and theme remain, turning and burning pages.

And there he stays, repassing his past, which he doesn't want to think about, but can't stop, because that past never stops thinking about him.

There he remains, burning pages and leaning back against the haunches of an enormous green cow (feeling the beat of its atomic mother heart) and, after drinking its fluorescent milk, he and the cow have a long conversation about his dead sister. The milk has the effect of making everything glow in the dark, with the emerald glow of the most wartime night vision, search and destroy mode, bringing the peace of the constructive ideas that always arrive unexpectedly together with the same design that gives meaning and orientation to the constellations, there above.

Diamonds in the bottomless sky like the reflection of the diamonds on the ground: the crazy diamonds that Penelope once gathered, dressed as a Miss-Havisham brand bride, but the abandoner and not the abandoned. The diamonds he didn't believe in when Penelope told him about them and does believe in now because they're right there. The diamond strewn ground where Penelope once wandered, riding that same formidable green cow and where he now sleeps alone and deserted and so far from all advice of a master with the voice of a boy: that voice that he hopes to hear again soon, because that's why he's come here, to hear that voice again.

And the memory of He Whose Name Must Not Be Mentioned is here, everywhere, all around him, while he thinks and sings: "Remember when you were young . . . Shine on, you crazy diamond . . . Nobody knows where you are, how near or how far . . ." His star shining among all the stars . . . There they are . . . Orion, Sirius, Andromeda, Cassiopeia. And he looks up at them as if they were notes on a sheet of music or fragments of a great symphonic painting in the sky. One dimensional and flat. One next to the other. In perfect harmony and linear composition. Stars like memory cells interlinked within that brain of the universe. Stars to be read almost as if they were the opening credits in the in-progress movie (the gods floating there, a little like those naked Bond Girl silhouettes, while a sensual and orchestrally seductive Bond Song plays) with the most sophisticated yet primitive special effects of all time. Or, maybe, better, he thinks, like the chapters of a great novel.

Yes: it appears that the stars (from the ghosts of the first and titanic and youthful dead to the most recent and small and twinkling and enduring) are all interconnected. As if by dashes between periods, as if in a void bursting with possibilities, as if between the lines on the palm of the paw of space, as if they were all part of the same story. But they're not. They're nothing but geometric maps separated by the distance of light years. They don't want to say anything, they have nothing to say. And he knows this because when he was a kid, he fell into their trap: into the black spaces between them, thinking that *something* was out there, that *everything* was out there. But no: the myths the stars supposedly narrate are nothing but the illusions of those who stared up at them and fixed them in the sky while everything else moved all around. Impossible to orient yourself by them, though ancient sailors believed otherwise, convinced they were the gods guiding them home. The truth is the stars are there to disorient you. To delay your return to the point of departure.

And comprehending and interpreting them has been further complicated by all the airplanes there above: by all those tiny shooting lights that you can't wish upon except to wish that they'll depart on time and arrive safe to their destination.

Airplanes that, at least for him, always served as spaces in suspension, spaces where he could sit and think while staring out the window at the stars or looking around inside at the people who've convinced themselves that they're stellar: in their seats or wandering the aisles, indifferent to the stars that no longer had any storyline or context or clear dramatic arc, unless you were reading them from the perspective of thousands of millennia.

And so it was, impatient and impotent, that man—realizing that the stories there above, in the greatest heights, no longer satisfied him—began to write, he thinks. Cosmic and unfathomable and impossible-to-contain immensities. Diffuse beginnings and wide open endings. The Great Gig in the Sky. And that, he believes, was the genesis of storytelling, the place where the need to tell came from. Men wrote their gods outside of time and space and those same gods commanded and gave them the authority to write. But before inspiring them to write, the gods were the ones—in the Bible or in the Koran or in the Torah, establishing the idea that, in the beginning and until the end, there's nothing more sacred than a good story—who wrote them. And then made them believe, after having created them. And men begged them in their prayers to tell them better stories than the ones they could imagine. The gods created men to tell them goodnight stories. Stories with clear beginnings and precise endings. And then, almost right away, men rebelled and went all avant-garde and revealed stories with diffuse protagonists who never stayed still and vibrated and shone like diamonds and crazy accelerated particles. From there, also, the wrath of the gods in the face of the free will of some of the creations created by the creative creatures they created.

And so, there he remains: confusing and confused in that place where the beginning of the end of the nebula of his sister once began, his sister who believed in stars and starlight.

There he stays: looking at everything through the magnifying and lidless eye of the telescopic scope of a rifle (and where'd that rifle that wasn't here a second ago come from?). The distance within reach of a hand with a finger on the trigger, waiting to hear the chamber music of its chamber loading, anticipating the overture of the parting shot of that first and last bullet in all his life.

And the thing is that, for the past few years (years he spent thinking about how to write about all of that about which he no longer wrote; those final years as an exwriter after having previously been an active professional writer and before that a childish and imminent next-writer; categories that for him corresponded inversely to dream, waking dream, and dreamless), it was as if he could only think about hellos and goodbyes. All of them compressed and imprisoned there inside, as if between parentheses, the same way he sees and hears and remembers everything now. Again: night vision the same green color as that colossal green cow on top of which he rests his rifle, calibrating the telescopic scope, calibrations that, yes, have something of parentheses about them. Like everything that's enfolded within two curving lines and that wants to hit the bullseye with exact numbers and precise letters. Parentheses functioning like the secret ultrasound at the end of that LP, B-side, after its final song. A fifteen kilocycle ultrasound, slipped in there by J & P & G & R and by GM, their producer, to drive dogs crazy. An ultrasound that, in his family, tormented his lysergic Uncle Hey Walrus to the end, sending him into a moon-howling frenzy. A magnetic frequency that doesn't attract but repels and that he—if were in the middle of writing an in-transit and in-progress book—would've liked to translate into characters or symbols to insert right after some short dedications and extensive epigraphs, to thereby alert any possible readers who might show up seeking something full of dialogue and characters to effortlessly identify with, whose days and actions began well and ended better. Waving his arms not so he'd be rescued, but to keep them from being pulled under. Telling them before setting out and at the outset that they'd come to the wrong place. Making dissuasive gestures so they'd continue on their way and not lose heart, because, surely, they would soon find what they were looking for elsewhere. Somewhere else. Almost anywhere else. There were many books *like that*—books that weren't like his or like the book he was now burning page by page—in so many other places. Books to feel happy and represented and at peace in, listening to heroes and heroines who conversed a lot and kissed and made love even more.

But you won't find any of that here and bon voyage.

Thus the only entryway he offers some are (   ) with many cacophonous words between the one that opens and the one that closes. Something more akin to that cosmic orchestral crescendo that—in that same last song on that same album by J & P & G & R, like the wordless voice of another monolith that renders you speechless—rises and rings out after *having read the book* and *now they know how many holes it takes to fill* and before that ultrasound that barks but doesn't bite.

And, again, yes, beginnings and endings.

Time and again.

Because he has read and reread the book of his past and is fully aware of each and every one of the holes in his life. Black holes surrounded by that white plane that surrounds black holes.

That whole thing about how if you didn't want to repeat the past you should study it wasn't true. Because he'd memorized it, knew it by heart; and all it did was make him feel like he's going up in front of the class to recite it and is always getting bad grades.

And he always remembered that thing Jay Gatsby said to Nick Carraway about how of course you could repeat the past.

So here he goes again, ready to come back with the same story as always: his story.

And it's true that there were few people with more authority than him to think like this. Few like him there inside or here outside who can bring everything together through arrivals that go or departures that come back to recall it all even if he doesn't remember it.

Because, scholars claim, the verb "to remember" takes a while to turn on and shed light. The brains of newborns, they explain, are too focused on assimilating that dazzling and pure and constant stimulus of the present. The present that (because there is so little to recall when there's still so little to remember and maybe that's why the desperate baby was crying with such desperation in 7A) they choose to forget almost immediately to not go mad from an overdose of unforgettable material. Thus, they claim, infants have the brief memory of fish (dropping an object that's picked up and put back in their hands over and over, giving them the perfect excuse to keep on crying and smiling) or the memory of those secret agents in conspiranoid thrillers who are fugitives from their own agencies and whose hard drives are automatically erased (so they can, with inaccurate accuracy, make the same perfect mistakes again and thereby wind up back in the obligatory situation of being tortured again) every twenty-four hours.

Yes: he'd been born dead.

A contradictory, oxymoronic, alphaomegistic, endtobecontinued idea, and yet . . .

Born dead.

To begin ending.

He'd begun ending or ending at the beginning (and, over the years, having come back from wherever he went then, he always wondered if the dead, at the moment of their birth, of dying and thereby beginning their dead life, forget everything they'd remembered throughout their lives, or if, to the contrary, their memory was transferred and archived in a great memory deposit: if what everyone refers to as "soul"—now catalogued in an immemorial "warehouse" of pasts—was really nothing but memory).

A long-drawn-out birth and a handful of society photographers covering the momentous event, smoking in the waiting room, back in days when you could still smoke in hospitals and airports, places that—as he's written many times—are close relatives, bonded by the shared familial trait of being over-run by people coming and going. People running because they're about to miss or are already missing something very important.

His birth was plagued by complications because of his excessive weight and excess baggage (when he was born, he was already like his books would be for many of his fleeting readers and constant critics) and when he came out, he wasn't breathing let alone crying. And he was declared *dead on arrival.* And—abruptly and when nobody expected it; when his little, unbreathing body was already en route to the hospital morgue—he'd returned to this side of things to, perhaps, tell not the tale but the flash fiction of how, when he woke up, he was still here. The brief history of his death (death, which is supposedly endless) that he'd recollected over and over in his fiction. The anecdote often mentioned in interviews back in days when he was still interviewed about his own work and not about Penelope's (about whom he refused to talk, because, he said, it didn't seem right and because—he didn't say this—Penelope's ghost had completely forbidden it) and, hey, why not tell it all again to a XXL green cow.

A brief history of his death and work that—he realizes now—had flowed into something what wasn't a novel-river but a novel-desert. Something whose end he was now approaching as if it were an oasis or a mirage, who knows, what did it matter anymore.

What mattered was that ever since—since his Alpha and his Big Bang and his Genesis and his "Once upon a time . . ."—he'd known, without really knowing, he supposes, that he was a writer.

He wanted to be a writer and reader before he learned to read and write.

And he was certain that there'd been a time, for a few minutes when he was four years old, right after almost drowning at a beach, when he *had been* a writer *before* he ever learned to read and to write.

On a beach where his parents were arguing about their arguments. Each holding a different version of the same book, a book whose title he'd been able to read (deliverance from drowning? adrenaline rush? miracle of faith?) before he could've known how to. And, yes, in that moment, walking home, still gasping, almost passing out, he'd read for the first time that the title of the book his parents were always reading was *Tender Is the Night* and that its author's name was Francis Scott Fitzgerald. And he'd also read some random lines from the beginning and the end (in a third copy that maybe was the one they read together, when they weren't fighting, when they were getting along). **And he remembers it with dazzling clarity.** (Because prior to that point it was all just flashes and fragments and moments and instants, like cutouts poorly pasted to a collage: a corner of the ceiling in a room viewed as if from lying on the floor, the almost miraculous feeling of pedaling a tricycle in circles around an apartment's patio, a nightmare with a squadron of men in black chasing him across the rooftops of a city that could well have been London— the more or less direct result of early exposure to the radiations of *Mary Poppins*. But that moment after almost drowning had been and remained his first full and complete and definite memory. His first meticulous-and-faithful-and-besotted-down-to-its-last-detail memory. His first memory that was fully memorable and, as such, capable and worthy of being reinvented, with full authority, by him, even though it was broadcast as a precise signal that was impossible not to receive and pay attention to. A message coming from the deep shallows of that childhood beach—like that prehistoric bone first turned weapon and then hurled elliptically into the skies of the future where, according to some viewers and interpreters, there floated not an artificial satellite but a nuclear weapon launcher—where he'd almost been devoured by the deep currents of the mouth of a river that flowed into the sea, only to, in the end, save himself and float back to terra firma, clinging to his definitive and defining literary vocation.)

Years later, someone had told him the story of the fishermen of Tyre. Fishermen whom Christ—long before he was crucified—had converted with the simple act of showing them how to cast one of their own parabolic nets. And they proudly claimed the title of the first Christians. They—they thought and believed—had been Christians before Christ himself was Christian: at a time when he was already a neighbor-lover but still an amateur messiah, unschooled in his own brand of dogma. And then, hearing that (and for some strange reason, he imagined those pioneering fishermen more à la Monty Python than à la Cecil B. DeMille or Franco Zeffirelli), he said to himself: "Exactly . . . That's it . . . *Like that* . . . And on a beach . . . I *too* was a fisherman of Tyre, when it came to reading and writing. I knew before knowing. I knew first."

Yes: his vocation had preceded any knowledge of that vocation (and that's why he was incessantly reading writers' biographies and why he always put them down when he got to the fourth year of the writer's life, once he verified that what'd happened to him hadn't happened to any of them. None of them had been a writer before being a reader).

It'd been a prophetic moment in the strictest and fullest sense of the term: for a few minutes, he was what he would become. In a way, he intuited something then that he would only come to know later. And no: it wasn't one of those past moments that—remembering them in reverse from the future, as if water had the capacity to flow back up into the faucets from whence it came—only feel prophetic later. Rather: it was one of those moments that was immense when it happened but shrank down to nothing with time's passing. Because moments like that are nothing but moments to be magnified a posteriori, like someone clinging to a life preserver or a bottle with no ships or messages inside it. Trances graced with an absolute but ephemeral clarity about something yet to come, trances that would be savored forever in the same way that it was far easier to *remember* previous incarnations than to anticipate future reincarnations.

That was why professional fortune-tellers, authentic yet false at once (the ones who always predict things like "you may become a great writer," a prediction that's so immediately believable and, in a way, far more possible—because everybody knows how to write—than predicting that you might become a quantum physicist or, even, a good person), tend to concern themselves more with reading the past—documenting it in detail or enumerating generalizations applicable to anything, repeating exactly what their credulous clientele just said right back to them but in different words, making it sound somehow more revealing and *elevated*: banal *problems* transformed into noble *conflicts* (and he thinks he remembers that Dante had a corner reserved in his *Inferno* for fortune-tellers where, as punishment for their deceits, they were forced to face forward for all eternity but with their heads on backward, looking back into the past)—to thereby make automatically plausible any fantasy they subsequently foretell to the suckers who come in to have their palms read or to stare into crystal balls or to touch Tarot cards where, nothing happens by chance, The Madman but not The Fool, ready to believe anything, always makes an appearance. The gift of true prophets—who, he'd read somewhere, are false by definition, because their true function is that of prophesizing and not that of being right—resides not in predicting the future but of being fully aware of what's happening in the present and what happened in the past and how all of that might impact the future. If you remember everything, if you don't forget anything, the future will be incredibly predictable, transparent, obvious, entirely banal and absolutely legible. Prophets aren't writers but readers who can read what people want to believe and then repeat it back to them, dressing it up as if it were their own creation. They are the rare readers you can't tell anything to: very sophisticated readers who, when they start a novel, are almost cursed with the ability to guess more or less accurately everything that'll happen and how the story will end.

He'd felt something like that back then, in that immense moment.

It was as if all times were melting into the same time at the same time. "Everything was already there," he thought as if he were reading it, though he hadn't yet learned to read or write.

And, of course, before long, he learned to read and write at a far greater speed than that of other children.

And he wrote skillfully from the start.

And he dodged orthographical errors instinctively.

And he devoured books with the same passion that other kids had for kicking balls.

And soon, around six or seven years old, he began to write *seriously* and *for real*, because "when I grow up, I want to be a writer."

And even when he achieved it, he remained a *readeriter*: more a reader who writes than a writer who reads (because in life you'll always read more than you'll write, just as you'll always eat—and taste—more food than you'll cook; unless we're talking about one of those ever more abundant and under-cooked writers only interested in being published and devoured by others).

Reading, then, like the theory of the practice of writing (or vice versa, the borders between the one and the other blurred), illuminating the enunciation of that not secret but yes private formula that let you become someone else. Not magic words but, yes, the magic of words. And him already savoring them when he was little, but in a big way: never enough, always hungry and asking for more, like Oliver Twist. Someone who, yes, knew what would befall him, as if reading it in his imagination before it took place; because he'd already spent so long thinking about what had to come to pass first so then it could happen and only later take place and time when it was put in writing so it could happen again for everyone else.

Everything that occurred in his books when someone read them had happened first when it occurred to him, the writer. And he'd never come up with a better origin or destination than that.

Even then he already intuited traversing the expansive surface between one extreme and the other—the life and the plot—would be like crossing a desert in the wind. Like a coming and going, like a part to be invented and a part to be dreamed and a part to be remembered.

To invent was to remember looking ahead.

To dream was to remember looking up or to invent looking down.

To remember was to invent looking back.

And that's why all those people who, at first, say "I don't remember" or "I don't really remember" then proceed to recount something with a wealth of detail and inventiveness and the dreamiest of voices.

Again, the sacra/mental and monomythic trinity, yes: to invent and to dream and to remember as the three parts that also intervened—like those meddlesome fairy godmothers or wicked stepmothers—in fictional lives and real works of art. In those stories that warned you to never forget that everything told therein would always be voluntarily or involuntarily modified by the teller. And that then it would be modified again by the one the stories were told to. And, finally, that all of that would be more or less hidden from both by the living dead who reside in each and every story or by one who was born dead and lived to tell them.

Three parts transmitted at three o'clock in the morning, in the real dark night of the soul. In the three stations of Dante's *Commedia*, in the three knocks demanded of a ghost to duly identify itself. In that trio of vocalists with a band name that he liked so much, The Ink Spots, singing that song— an old song but one of those songs that never ages, an old-timey song, which is not the same thing—that he whistles now under the moon and that sings about "my echo, my shadow, and me." In the three parts/movements of *2001: A Space Odyssey*. In the three verbal tenses. In the debated three sections of the triune brain.

Three parts—inventing and dreaming and remembering—that came together in a single and total great thinking part that couldn't stop thinking. The recounted part and the part that recounts and will recount and was already recounted. The narrated and written and read part. Three parts of *déjà vu* subdividing into *déjà vécu*, *déjà senti*, and *déjà visité*. Recounting names and places that changed or blurred or evaporated into what was invented and dreamed, but that were so much harder to alter or to conceal or to disguise in what was remembered. Everything that could be excused—in the affirmative or the negative—with an "I forgot" or an "I don't remember."

You invented something to make it real and you dreamed something only to, in the vain attempt, discover that it was impossible to recount it with precision. But, in the end, the version that imposed itself was that of the memory, even though you remembered—inventing and dreaming—with your eyes closed and your mind open and looking forward.

The memory was the last thing used and the first thing put in writing, remembering—in the very act of writing it—something you just recalled even if it only happened or was happening seconds before.

What you remember—unlike what you invent and what you dream— requires some responsibility and implies certain obligations.

Names and dates and places, for example. And book titles and film credits. And all the things that people no longer bothered to memorize, because they were always a click or two away from remembering them.

He rejected that: the deceptive shortcut, the external memory aid. He continued practicing the theory of using his own memory: remembering was the most personal act a human being could do and he preferred that it stay that way. He preferred the truth of being wrong and the error of being right. The departure and the return and the parentheses, yes. The parentheses of the brief or prolonged delay between departing and returning; leaving something in free fall only to catch it a few days later; evoking the concentric circles of the target and not the straight line of the arrow. Everything that might blur in the present but that you couldn't deny had happened and that, amid doubt and uncertainty, kept happening as part of the now. Something that wasn't an invention or a dream, even though, on more than one occasion, it'd corrected the one or altered the other.

Ghosts, yes.

But this time and in this part, he decides that names will matter.

Unlike when he invents or dreams, now—when he remembers—he'll try to be precise.

More or less.

Thus, places like Sad Songs.

Names like The Girl Who One Night Fell Into a Swimming Pool and He Whose Name Must Not Be Mentioned.

Titles like *National Industry* or *The Impossible Story*.

Places.

Names.

Titles.

Words that are, also, like living or dead stars that serve (*Time is an asterisk . . . Same as it ever was . . . Here comes the twister . . .*) to orient or disorient you as you traverse the windy desert of a whole life to be remembered and dreamed and invented.

Like this:

First and to begin with, the title.

The title was like the airplane: somewhere to climb aboard so that everything could begin to climb.

Next and immediately thereafter—back when he still wrote, back when he still had something to tell—came the flight crew.

And only then did he—the passenger—come aboard, sitting down and fastening his seat belt. And sinking his claws into that little glass bottle the flight attendants offered him along with headphones and an eye mask and a little scented towel to wash his hands, stained with ink from answering absurd questions on the forms they made him fill out. A bottle covered in words like those colorful glass spheres that, as a boy, he played without really playing at staring at. Those little spheres with something inside resembling bewitched petals or seeds in suspension that, with luck and under the right conditions, he thought, would grow into blossoming trees where you could move around among the branches. Spherical words of others to be appropriated. Words that were nothing but possible epigraphs that he collected for some increasingly improbable future use. And yet, to have epigraphs was to have *something*: epigraphs had always been the eye of the keyhole of the door to a house to be built or taken by storm—or the explosive detonators that opened the door—that he wanted to enter and from which he'd been expelled. Epigraphs were the more or less strange moles on the faces of strangers you know all too well. Moles always benign in just the right spot. Moles not to be excised but tattooed—in small font—on your face to improve it, to make it more attractive. Moles on *beauty marked pages* courtesy of the kindness of strangers you knew as well or better than many of your more or less loved ones.

And so, for example—now, in the desert and the wind, making memory—he chose one of those epigraphs.(And—with a Bingol face but nowhere to insert any epigraph anymore—he remembered that it was from one of those joyously devastating stories by an author who'd kept him company from when he was a kid right up until that writer's advanced and late death. Someone who'd always been at his side, even though—pretty much from the moment he burst onto the scene and garnered the constant company of readers and worshipful rereaders of his work—he'd stopped publishing and cut himself off from his colleagues and the whole "little literary world." That writer who'd opted to disappear of his own accord and, unlike him, hadn't been forced to by circumstance. And it was in honor of and out of obedience to that desire and discipline that he usually avoided saying his name in vain or out of vanity.)

And the epigraph extracted but not remembered—because for him there was no need, it was unforgettable—came from one of the most melancholically joyful stories that man—so invisible yet omnipresent, like the omnipresent echo of that Beatlesque ultrasound (his stories were, in general, very sad; but reading them produced that joy you only feel when you finally find a kindred but far better written sadness than your own)—had written. And it was also, yes, a terrible and terminal sentence and very much on the *having-read-the-book* level. In it, someone told someone else that "The worst thing that being an artist could do to you would be that it would make you slightly unhappy constantly." A quote that he would type as a kind of automatic screensaver—materializing like a message from another dimension—whenever he paused too long in what he was writing, back in days when he still wrote without pause.

And the quote was accurate. But the quote's author hadn't had such a bad time of it after all, once he'd become an artist. True: the man had enclosed himself inside himself, he'd acquired the reputation of insufferable mi*zen*-thrope, and ended up deaf to all voices besides those of his characters. But he'd also lived for many years, more than comfortably sheltered in his bunker by the millions in royalties he raked in off his books that kept selling, generation after generation, almost miraculously and despite the exponential growth within the global population of the fakes and phonies he so despised.

But yes, it was true, that almost centenarian in the rye hadn't lied: because once you were an artist there was no going back—"slightly unhappy constantly"—and that's how you would move through the world from then on.

Through a world that the most famous character created by that exwriter (or, better, ex-published-writer, because they say he kept writing, just that he hadn't the slightest interest in publishing) had denounced as a total sham.

A world overflowing with fake people and "phonies": a term whose literal mistranslation into Spanish was, nothing happens by chance, used all the time now to refer affectionately to those new members of the family: "*telefonitos*" *móviles*, or mobile "phonies."

Turn upeth, ye phonieaddicts, the volume of thy ringtone.

And the Spanish idiom "*estar hasta a coronilla*"— meaning "had it up to here"—had taken on new and dreadful significance: *coronilla* refers to the "crown" of the head and nowadays people were recognized more by their *coronillas* than by their faces, always conversing with their heads bent, as if praying, as if their screens were siddurim or breviaries.

And, oh, he'd heard of couples that, instead of exchanging rings or vows exchanged phones as a form of absolute of intimacy, a way of being stripped totally naked and offering up all the good and all the bad of themselves. He'd been shaken when he'd heard about couples that were, actually, twenty couples, branching out telephonically into many others, thanks to something called polyamory, artificially incubated on sites for "hooking up," without the responsibility of feelings, but, at the same, writing on their profiles that what they wanted most was to find "the love of their lives." And feeling that, luckily, they now had the apps to ceaselessly search—like trying on new outfits nonstop in a megastore—until they decided, never entirely sure, to settle for the one that felt right and use it for a couple of days. And to trade it in for different one before the time for free returns elapses. Residents, most all of them, of a new world that was no longer his.

His was a world through which to move dragging your feet and with your head held high thinking about how to begin. Or thinking about absurd things that might end up being *useful* down the road, already en route, moving through that world that remained forever young, the world of his childhood, because that was when he'd decided to become what he was now. A world in which he'd thought about things for the first time that he hadn't stopped thinking about since. Things like—some of his favorite and recurrent ideas—"Isn't it good that human beings and dinosaurs didn't coincide in time and space and were separated by millions of years." Or "The death of Dracula at the end of the book has no drama and occurs in a handful of lines, as if merely fulfilling the final requirement of a long and complicated plot." Things to which were added—in the ultrasonic voice of thought—other things like "That's one of the reasons film was invented: so cavemen and Tyrannosaurs could play together and so the vampire count could dissolve, run through by a stake under the sun, dramatically and in slow motion." Random things like scattershot fragments that never completely come together when you dream or when you can't fall asleep.

And he didn't say or question all of this when he dreamed or suffered insomnia, no. And it wasn't a coincidence, he thought, that—even in the most plausible and realistic and *waking* dream—one of the ways to know if you were dreaming was to try to read or write something there, on the other side. It cannot be done. Impossible. You might believe you were reading in dreams, but you could never write in your dreams. Ergo, there was nothing to read there. Because nothing that you put in writing with eyes closed would make any sense if you could read it or write it with your eyes open. Yes, so it is, 'twas ever thus, and it was good that it was so, but it was no mean feat: there was no better way to escape from a nightmare than to attempt to read or to write and, oh, slipping into another nightmare, into the sweetest of nightmares, thinking that you would never be able to write *like that*, to be read *like that*. The same thing happened with the memory of dreams, always remembering to forget. That's why you had to write dreams down quickly, inventing a memory of them for yourself upon waking, before they dissolved like salt or sugar in water. And the thing is that in dreams there was no clear direction or precise sense; apart from the dreams dreamed in the great horror novels he read when he was little. Novels with lethal lovers coming back from the dead or killer clowns smiling up at you from down in the sewers and offering you a red balloon. There and then, in those oh so true fictions, diffuse dreams reassumed their ancient mythical nature as precise instructions and clear warnings. And you didn't question anything, because in that place—awake and dreaming of sleeping—it made no sense, because you knew that any answer would probably be another question. Or the same question as always and as never. The question with no answer, the one he asked himself now, after swallowing a handful of pills meant to keep him awake and alert. Pills that not only keep you from closing your eyes, but also erase every conjugation of the verb "to blink" from your memory.

And, of course, that question was: "What were you dreaming?"

Now, on this last night of his story, he has chosen not to dream. Now he has chosen to be like an invasive spore, like a speedy hooligan-hadron, sneaking in to contaminate a foreign laboratory. To be like one of those rolling tumbleweeds tumbling by in front of him right now and rolling up onto the rusted and poetic skeleton of a savage and detectivesque Chevy Impala or a Camaro that someone left out here before striking out for nowhere.

Now he says to himself that you never choose what you dream, like how what you remember of your dreams are but fragments that come to you whether you like it or not. One wasn't the *author* of one's dreams. One was the *reader* of one's dreams. And, likewise, one wasn't the author of one's memories: one was the *editor* of one's memories. To remember was, in a way, to dream while awake. When dreaming, one was invented and created and when remembering, one invented and recreated oneself.

"We spend our lives rewriting ourselves so we can reread ourselves," he says to himself in that desert under the stars and in silence. And luckily the giant green cow seems to have fallen asleep and has stopped speaking to his brain from inside his brain where now other possible epigraphs are being quoted.

"A dream is a creation of the intelligence, the creator being present not knowing how it will end" and "Another strange thing about dreams is that, unless one immediately seizes upon them, thinks them over and relives them, one does not remember them. A dream is not so much our own as a story composed by others, because while listening we are never as passive as while dreaming. Yet, beyond all doubt, we create the dream ourselves. *We create without being aware of it*, that is the extraordinary thing about a dream" and "Still dreaming, I noted that there are no antecedent facts in a dream, every-thing is action, there is no repetition—a pattern of evocative art."

All of the above had been jotted down by a writer, another writer, in his diary. A writer who committed suicide so that—though he didn't know it at the time—he, many years later, could add him to his collection of crystalline and spherical epigraphs. A suicidal writer he'd only read one book by—the book from which he'd extracted those random quotes—and so, because he'd read so little of him, he didn't dare remember or feel worthy of invoking his name, because if he did, he'd just be embarrassed by how little time he'd devoted to reading him, though he didn't let that stop him from harvesting epigraphs from his book (yes, he was like that, he did things like that). And he'd remembered the writer's name just a few days ago, while reciting that song lyric that goes "one of these days I'm going to cut you into little pieces" just as the song let loose and seemed to go crazy. He'd remembered it when he read it in the pages of one of his biji notebooks, almost suicidal himself, but, in his case, the model of suicide was limited to putting himself in poten-tially deadly situations. Suicide due to proximity, en route to that distant desert on the outskirts of Mount Karma, in Abracadabra.

(He remembered it when he read that suicidal writer—and he remembers himself remembering it and rereading it in one of his notebooks—telling himself that few things are more consoling for a potential suicide than a successful suicide. Someone who "took his own life"—that elegant way of not saying "killed himself"—and that to him had always sounded akin to taking off your clothes or ridding yourself of some annoying or cumbersome thing. And it occurred to him that suicides were death's true writers: they chose the style and time and place. Suicides who we wanted to believe irrational were, in reality, beings absolutely logical in their behavior: they weren't afraid of the brief instant of death but of the long, drawn out happening of life. And it also occurred to him that, in real life, someone's reasons for committing suicide were often not all that clear. In non-fiction, suicide almost always tends to kill the wrong person; while, in fiction, suicide tended to be committed with absolute clarity of intent and as a favor to the author, who almost demanded that sacrificial death, so he could mobilize the surviving characters and send them off in different directions. The immobility of the suicide victim post suicide set everything and everyone else in motion. In fiction, suicides—like coincidences—always had a *raison d'être* for their *non-être*. And if the suicide victim was a writer, even better: the best of both worlds. Imagining that writer whose observations about dreams he quoted as if he were remembering him on that agonizing and hot day in August in 1950, on the point of erasing himself or putting the final period on his life, in room number 346 of the Albergo Roma in Turin.)

Hotels were cities' epigraphs: outsiders to be appropriated, strangers to be recognized, and, like deserts, they were all connected by a secret trans-border passageway (he especially liked the ones that, in city after city, due to their proximity to terminal train stations, chose to call themselves Terminus, which, in the first place, always made him think about the end of so many things and the during of so many journeys). And he let go of the memory of that Albergo in Turin, sitting in room number he-doesn't-remember of Hotel La Nada, which was actually called Hotel La Cornada and was once a hotel for bullfighters; but it had been eons since those neons had all lit up on the hotel's façade, and now, La Nada, a sad joke, on the saddest of Mexico City, D.F. nights, on the last leg of his last journey.

That'd been just a few days ago, which is why, to tell the truth, it wasn't yet something to be remembered (fragments, instants, moments) but to be reproduced, so it didn't yet require a typographically different voice.

In fact, none of what'd happened to him in Mexico required putting the engines of memory into drive. For him, Mexico had always been unforgettable. Even before he went there. Mexico the country and Mexico the city always functioning—ever since his childhood, so healthily contaminated by the Mexican imaginary, by masks and skulls and telenovelas—like his equivalent to the rabbit hole or mirror that Alice fell down or passed through on her way to Wonderland. (And, yes, all of a sudden he remembered that one of Vladimir Nabokov's—the author of that book that he was now finally reading and burning page by page—occasional jobs had been, before breathing the light of life into his Lolita, to illuminate, in Russian translation, Lewis Carroll's nymphet, under the name Anya. And notwithstanding the name on the passport, the White Queen always said the same thing to Alice and to Anya: "It's a poor sort of memory that only works backward." And, ah, he remembers too that Dolores "Lolita" Haze was conceived in Veracruz on Charlotte Becker and Harold E. Haze's honeymoon and that . . .) And so now, as if enveloped in fog and advancing in retreat, he thinks that it's not that he's been happy in Mexico, but that he was Mexican in Mexico. Because Mexico Mexicanizes all foreigners and foreignizes all things Mexican and that's why English and American songwriters always insert the word "Mexico" in their verses—that whole "goin' down Mex-I-Co way"—when they had nothing left to sing or say. Mexico was like a kind of Rubber Cement, perfect for bringing together the scattered pieces—fragments, instants, moments—of a collage. No place better to bring it all together than scattershot Mexico. No place more apropos than Mexico the incomprehensible (he'd read somewhere that Yucatan descended, etymologically, from the Mayan *Yuk ak katan* ["I do not understand your language"] or *Ci u than* ["I do not understand you"] or *uh yu hthaan* ["listen to how they speak"]) to wind up comprehending everything. And the irrefutable proof, for him, was Anthony Quinn, someone who today would no doubt be harshly judged by soft millennials—the ones who believe that their recycling doesn't just get mixed back in with the trash when it's taken away—and condemned to death for his compulsive and out-of-control cultural appropriation: a Greek dancer, an Arab sheikh, a Jamaican pirate, a French impressionist, and a Ukrainian

Pope, a filmography that ended up—when he finally donned the skin of a Mexican revolutionary—coming off as fairly implausible, almost as implausible as that sprawling city suspended over a lake of pyramidal ruins.

He remembered it (remembered this and that) in an airplane hurtling forward, but suddenly landing in a hotel and, after all, weren't airplanes like immodest flying hotels?

In airplanes you missed hotels, in hotels you missed home, and at home you missed airplanes.

And in all of them, in every language, he'd felt like an *extraño: a missing person* nobody *misses* when he finds or loses himself *à l'étranger* as a *strano*.

And, sure, right, okay . . . Not *every* language; only the languages that *The Impossible Story* had been translated into: his last book, which was *also* ignored by foreigners when it came out, but suddenly—and for all the wrong reasons—it was on the lips and in the eyes of everyone and in all the newspapers and on all the news shows in the city that he'd just fled to come to this desert.

The book that *was not*, as he'd fantasized while writing it, the equivalent for him of what the *'68 Comeback Special* (that TV show that nights before he'd seen on a commemorative rebroadcast at a theater in Abracadabra to kill the time that was killing him) *was* for Elvis Presley. (And, oh, he thought when he thought about it, how was it that such comparative, referentially-maniacal examples of ceaseless, serial remembering occurred to him. Maybe that's where his block and drought came from. From the perverse paradox of a geyser constantly but barely concealing the impossibility of writing, because, when he couldn't write, he was always thinking about how everything he was thinking might be useful when it came to writing and, oh, all that nothing hanging up in the air, half water and half vapor and almost nothing solid. And, please, where was the button (the other button, the button of a particle de-accelerator) he could press—given that it was impossible for him to charge by the minute or by the hour or by the day, like taxi drivers or lawyers or party planners—to stop thinking *like this*. Besides, he'd never really been that interested in Elvis. Among The King's contemporaries, he'd always been far more attracted to the blinding sunglasses of Roy Orbison and the voyeur glasses of Buddy Holly and could someone explain to him why—you have to see it to believe it—frames and lenses are so irrationally and unjustifiably expensive, eh? What he *liked* best about Elvis is that he'd died sitting on the toilet and reading a book about the face of Jesus Christ and the Shroud of Turin. It didn't seem to him a bad way to die. There was no death more personal than that: reading in the bathroom; though, perhaps, he would swap out the book for a better one that, please, in that moment, let the book not be the, for him, impossible to read *Ada, or Ardor*.) The flammable Elvis who went in and out of the doors of his memory. Elvis whom he remembered as long as it helped him remember and, for that reason, a few more minutes of Elvis. And so Elvis, now, on the screen on the seatback in front of him on an airplane: Elvis in a Las Vegas ravaged by yellow radioactive winds, but still singing about how he can't help falling in love, while two different model and generation blade runners fight at his feet.

What he'd done in his last book (unlike that not-yet-described but aforementioned almost-robotic reboot of Elvis, wrapped in black leather and with the look of a Terminator arrived from a retro-future to be reinvented in 1968, the same year that *2001: A Space Odyssey* premieres and The Beatles begin to break up with the turbulent whiteness of *The Beatles*) wasn't a rehash of everything he'd sung up until that point so he could be relaunched into a supposedly better future while reprising past successes to later say goodbye with "If I Can Dream." (A future that, in Elvis's case, in the end, wouldn't have time to take place. He remembers that, after that, Elvis had had a good spell: the glorious single "Suspicious Minds," a couple of great gospel albums, and the formidable *From Elvis in Memphis*. But then his despotic manager—fearing he'd escape from him—took him to the golden cage of Las Vegas and, later, Elvis had offered himself to Richard Nixon as a "federal agent at large" for the Bureau of Narcotics and Dangerous Drugs to thereby combat the vices promoted by the new rock 'n' roll. And, after a few days, he'd insisted on becoming an "undercover agent" for J. Edgar Hoover's FBI. And he'd gotten fat singing "Amazing Grace" night after night, in a cape and a sweaty Las Vegas loop until he crashed in Graceland.) No. His thing had been something else. Nothing at all of a reprise. Pure original and unprecedented reinvention. Something that hadn't occurred to anyone, something that hadn't occurred for anyone. He'd set out to accelerate all his particles—to shrink yet expand himself—inside a hadron collider, to transform himself into the sybaritic and shivaritic Great Rewriter of All Things in the Universe. And so, the epic on Elvis's sneering lips—the gesture of one who remembers what he once was and wishes to be again—had little or nothing in common with the rictus of disgusted resignation on his face: something far more akin to the fragile disdain on Bill Murray's mouth (like someone tasting something very bitter), someone he'd been told, more than once, he resembled. Which was like bearing a resemblance to no one and to nothing, he thought. Bill Murray's was a face void of expression but overflowing with meaning. And the closest thing he had to a flammable and tyrannical Colonel was the demanding flame-enveloped ghost of his sister Penelope. And so, Elvis exploded physically so he could be in all places, while he only succeeded in imploding creatively so he would no longer matter anywhere and no longer write voluminous books—or books of any size—and wind up vanishing, going out of print. Like how the now-ever-ready-and-available-in-every-physical-or-virtual-record-store Elvis was vanishing for him, to no longer appear in his memory, except in his incarnation in one of his parents' many ad spots that were floating around on YouTube. The one filmed in Caesars Palace: his father as a sinuous Elvis and his mother as a spasmodic Ann-Margret, sponsored by the same brand of whiskey as always. The two of them like the paragon of the cool couple sailing the world aboard a sailboat before they became airborne fashionista guerillas.

So, *all shook up*, in the lobby of that Mexican hotel not remembered but, yes, unforgettable for all the wrong reasons (a hotel whose category isn't rated in stars but in meteorites and that, nevertheless, wasn't like that cosmic and Louis-XVI hotel where Dave Bowman arrives at the end of *2001: A Space Odyssey*), where they're selling postcards of the hangings and painting the passports brown.

A hotel that—unlike the hotels of Manhattan, where maybe they think it's a way to keep guests from throwing themselves from the heights, driven mad from trying in vain to figure out how to get those modern-design faucets or those not-so-smart-but-putting-users'-smarts-to-the-test TVs to work—has windows that *do* open. And that, when he opens them, he can't help but wonder (the same thing he wonders in hotels with windows hermetically sealed like the windows on an airplane) whether the altitude would be high enough to . . .

And, in his room (here all the rooms are small and have such low ceilings), the almost child-sized bed like a riotous bullring after the final climax of a bullfight (the woman he just met down in the bar and who, as he got to know her much better, had been like a bull between the sheets and had just left, though not without first—damn the evil hour he met her—cleaning out the contents of his wallet) and the TV on like the equivalent of post-coital cigarette for someone who never smokes. And there, on the screen that wasn't big but enormous compared to the screens people have surrendered themselves to these days—screens that'll soon be the size of a pupil—he saw again what he once saw in CinemaScope: a version of the first man throwing a tapir bone into the air and the bone climbing and climbing into the African sky. And he already knew what would come next. Because he'd seen it so many times. And though he's seen it so many times he was, once again, as always, fixated on that channel, waiting for the miracle of the most formidable cosmic ellipsis and millions-year transition in the entire history of film. And just before the terrestrial bone mutated into space metal, the miracle was interrupted with a commercial break. A spot for mobile phones. *Smart* phones whose offer of intelligence presupposed that they were there to make things easier for their *dumb* immobile users, but, actually, all they did was make life more complicated: they got users hooked, made them suffer so many failures and crashes, drove them to desperation when they got lost, and made them long for the good old days when what they lost were people and not telephones, which were always in the same place, at home, awaiting their return to ring or ringing on their own, like the most loyal and, yes, efficient of pets. And he can't believe what he's seeing, what he's *not* seeing. And the commercial was informing the viewer that there is more sophisticated technology inside that tiny device than what took man to the moon for the first time, not realizing that what matters isn't *how* you do something but *that* you do it. And then more ads, minutes upon minutes of things to be bought and to sell yourself to.

And for a moment he considers masturbating in homage to one of the shopping network girls to distract himself from all of that. But then he thinks, also, that maybe there are hidden cameras or double-sided mirrors in the room, so he can't even pull that off: nothing of *petite mort* and with eyes tightly shut (like Jorge Luis Borges and Ezra Pound in those famous photographs and, agh, could there be something that, please, for pity's sake, wouldn't make him think about something more or less literary?) and there he stays: matador *matado en* La Coronada.

So, better, OFF and lights out and the moist stains *à la* Rorschach concealed, and candles lit: those colorful candles with images of saints and devils and burning satanic virgin skeletons for conjuring curses, but good for nothing when it comes to giving his damned soul and possessed brain a rest. His brain that *pulsated* like one those disheartened brains floating in jars in cheap yet disturbing movies. His demented brain incessantly composing sentences nobody hears much less reads; because—though he can't stop reciting them as if they were blowing in the desert wind—he's no longer going to put any of them in writing to recite later.

Sentences written one by one in order to, later, also, be read one by one: pondering each word and considering them separately and not just thinking about how one led to the next. Sentences that occurred to him with each drink until the last drink of the night (which is the first drink you regret the next morning).

Sentences not like a succession of linked train cars but like a procession of roaming locomotives.

Sentences as long as hole-riddled mezcalero worms that, when you read them, you know where they begin but never where they'll end up or cut off.

Sentences that—when he had the strength, less all the time—he scribbled in a biji notebook so they wouldn't escape him; cutting off their tails so they wouldn't die but regenerate and grow even longer still with the impetus of the semicolon: one of his favorite punctuation marks (a punctuation mark that he probably deployed in an incorrect and indiscriminate way, making the excuse that he'd never found a precise and convincing explanation of exactly how it was supposed to be used) and one that for some time now idiots had been using to add a complicit wink to the end of their stupid—brief in length and short in understanding—texts.

Sentences durable as prayers to be recited while thinking about how writing long was like reading and how writing short was like writing (and it was clear that what he liked best was to write reading) and how he should insert that idea somewhere if he hadn't already, right?

Sentences like orations ("¡*Órale!*" the locals exclaim to indicate agreement or surprise, directing an imperative form of the verb *orar*—to orate—at the spirited spirits), like the orations delivered in Mexico for the dead, who always give death the runaround and never fully die, so that the living can feed off their ever-lively memory on the night of the Day of the Dead.

And, oh, the temptation to die in Mexico. Like Steve McQueen. Like Joan Vollmer. Like Neal Cassady from—according to the report of a forensic scientist using quasi-sci-fi jargon and possibly overwhelmed by the condition of the organism he was examining—"general congestion of all systems." Like Leon Trotsky, whose fresh corpse had been viewed in a morgue in Coyoacán by the young and as yet unpublished Saul Bellow, who'd traveled there after growing bored of the "weary, stale, flat and unprofitable Chicago" in search of "barbarism, color, glamour, and risk" and, no doubt, already thinking that someday he was going to put all of it in a book; because, for Bellow, everything in the rough draft of reality was to be revised in fiction. Like so many other dead foreigners, many of whom he'd documented for that book he'd been commissioned to write.

Because to die in Mexico was to achieve the most immortal of deaths (usually accidental deaths, deaths that confirmed the idea of death as the definitive and deadly accident) and to have a post-mortem and phantasmal homeland under the most *lindo* of *cielitos*. To die in Mexico was like living forever anywhere else in the world. In Mexico, the expression "*sentirse de muerte*" took on its full and true meaning (the only way to stay alive and kicking in Mexico was, indeed, to almost kick the bucket every so often), which amounted to feeling better than ever.

And going back to that place he could no longer go: back in his "good old days," he'd figured out how to bring together the best of both worlds: he'd written short, yes; but he'd written short *a great deal* and *at great length.*

He wrote as if all those fragments were pieces of a puzzle to be solved. He wrote as if they were colliding accelerated particles to be thrown into centrifugation inside a system of electromagnetic fields. He wrote first to see later what happened or *didn't* happen and how it all was transformed into nothing more than a hurricane of everything. And so, all those sentences like wind in the curtains.

And the open windows and his room in Hotel La Nada are on the second floor; neither very high nor very low. Windows specially conceived so words could leap from their ledges, like Acapulco's famous diving cliffs, where (he remembers, he remembers so many useless things, because at some point he thought they might be useful for his books) the Olympic swimmer, Johnny "Tarzan" Weissmuller—born in what is now Romania and baptized Johann Weißmüller—was buried. And—more information of the kind that keeps on accumulating in his mind like corrupted files—who asked lastly and willfully for, as his coffin was being lowered into the earth, that yell of his to be played three times, like a 21-gun salute. A yell that was actually recorded by an opera singer named Lloyd Thomas Leech (another version points out that it was Weissmuller's yell, but reinforced by superimposed recordings of violins and hyena howls) and that he once saw tattooed in the form of pentagram notes on the ass of a girl who tended to release that same shriek every time she reached the highest branches and strongest swinging vines of an orgasm. Yes: "Aah-eeh-ah-eeh-aaaaaah-eeh-ah-eeh-aaaaah!" on cliffs to be looked out on from windows and off which those divers hurled themselves with knives between their teeth to hide their disdain for all those tourists with lungs full of Acapulco Gold smoke and, ah, again, the golden throat of the *hound dog* Elvis (he'd expressly forbidden Elvis from returning, but, of course, suspecting that you couldn't give The King orders) in that bad movie and jumping off La Quebrada. All those divers *always on his mind* and resembling daggers leaping from the hands of gods with too many and little-used consonants in their long names to crash several floors below, at the doors to the netherworld called Mictlán. And once there, no doubt, he liked to believe, before jumping, praying to their patron saint the same way he prayed to Ella, to his Faustinian Morelian Saint of the Swimming Pools. Telling themselves that all those gringos, inflatable as duck-headed life preservers, who watched them and threw money at them, would never feel anything close to what they feel, falling through the air as if ascending.

And in that way, *¡órale!*, orating orations and sentencing sentences, other things—style was nothing but everything that was left on the shore to be picked up when the tide of the frustrated and shipwrecked and drowned went out—occurred to him.

And out of that and right there, *ahí mismito*, in Mexico, a good idea had come to him that, well, wasn't entirely his, but it occurred to him to remember it and put it in writing. An idea with style and in his style: the subterranean dead watching the living on TVs with ghostly screens. And he put all of that in a book he'd been commissioned to write, a book where he put so many other things that belonged to others but that he made his own. (And that was the one thing Penelope had forgiven him for the least out of all the unforgiveable things he'd done: that he'd stolen her beloved Lina—and that performance that she'd written and directed and starred in at a bohemian bar in Abracadabra—her Aztec netherworld televisions, her MTV, her Mictlán TV: her death not by stray but perfectly aimed bullet, from the rifle of a sniper at the behest of the psychopath Hiriz Karma, when she discovered Lina on the property, at the fatal hour, on the morning of the matrimonious interruptus of Penelope and the comatose Maxi Karma. And, later, Hiriz—now a raving-lunatic nun-theologian, who in her recorded sermons said things like "Hell exists to make Heaven more heavenly" and "God created the world and here's the world. What other proof do you need of God's existence?"—had started the fire that burned down the monastery-asylum Our Lady of Our Lady of Our Lady . . . where Penelope had perished. *Hiriz, Or the Ire*, and, yeah, sure: all of that sounded like the incomprehensible and impossible synopsis of one of those venomous, tropical, thousand-headed serpentine soap operas. And, OK, he'd put a good part of the vileness of all of that in that Mexican book he'd written on commission. And he'd also put in crazy Penelope's demented family of in-laws. And the aforementioned Joan Vollmer and William S. Burroughs who, hey, had already been of great interest to him long before the beloved martyr, Lina, probably even knew who they were.) Yes, *sua culpa*: unlike the Nabokovian John Shade in *Pale Fire*—and to the indignant desperation of his parasitic fanboy Charles Kinbote when he saw and read that everything he'd told him about his crazy kingdom had been ignored in the composition of that long and sad and pastoral poem of the afterlife—he *had* gained from using all that material that *was not* his. All of that material that *had been* Penelope's, but that was now part of one of his books. Because something that'd happened to someone else could be his to put in a book. Nobody owned reality, but you could take possession of it if you turned it into fiction. And again: he was not, like John Shade according to his creator, "by far the greatest of all invented poets." Much less, unlike John Shade, could he be cited as an example of loving and creative familial stability. But he had been far more attentive than the author of those pale and fiery nine hundred and ninety-nine intimate, elegiac verses. And he'd listened to and read and watched with great concentration everything Penelope had sent and told him about her Abracadabran odyssey on Mount Karma. In fact, he'd been *very* attentive. He'd *paid* a lot of attention. And he'd *borrowed* all of it with no intention of ever paying it back. (He'd been, again, like the Saul Bellow who, already an octogenarian, had challenged the political-*correctos* to show him "the Tolstoy of the Zulus . . . I'd be happy to read them." That insatiable and disagreeable Bellow—Bellow who liked telling a story about how, when "a wise man is asked the difference between ignorance and indifference? He answers, I don't know and I don't care"; Bellow who had written in a letter that he could have created a much better *Lolita* from the point of view of the nymphet and whom Vladimir Nabokov hadn't hesitated a second to rate a "miserable mediocrity"—who, ever vengeful, was always ready to take revenge in writing, and whose mega-biography in two volumes he'd recently read, after verifying, of course, that when he was four years old, Bellow hadn't had anything happen to him that remotely resembled what'd happened to him on that childhood beach. Almost two thousand pages delineating the map of a world that no longer existed, he thought as he moved through it. A time when intellectuals and novelists and essayists were the kings of creation and had some influence on the nature of their world. And he always remembered, and remembered again when he read about Bellow's life, that line from Genesis that went "There were giants in the earth in those days." And so— reading Bellow's life which was also Bellow's work—he'd been moved/ depressed by traveling back to that forever-lost victorious era. A time that would never come back, when writers and intellectuals moved across the surface of the planet like triumphant deities, gnashing their teeth and devouring with their eyes and ears everything that took place around them. Now, not so much. Now, they were all past-tense dinosaur fossils in a museum—dinosaurs like they used to be: gray and featherless—that visitors barely glanced at and on whom, though they themselves were always facing forward, everyone turned their backs; because all they cared about was capturing them in a selfie that neither had nor has nor would ever have anything to do with those other far more inspired forms of *self*-revealing that were Augie March and Moses Herzog and Artur Sammler and Albert Corde. All of them piloted by Bellow's memory, functioning for its master as a "terrible engine" used to judge and keep in custody "all the dead and the mad" because "I am the nemesis of the would-be forgotten." And there, in the Bellow biography, the words of one of his many alter egos, Charlie Citrine, confessing with pride: "I did incorporate other people into myself and consume them. When they died I passionately mourned. I said I would continue their work and their lives. But wasn't it a fact that I added their strength to mine? Did I have my eye on them in the days of their vigor and glory?" And no, of course not: none of that was literature of the I or autofiction. Bellow's novels weren't even novels of ideas. They were, rather, ideas of the novel. An exquisite alchemical process, a dark and dazzling art: taking the cells of reality and throwing them into a cauldron and making something sublime and bewitching out of them. Interlinking those cells in fiction. What had Bellow's genius been? How did it work? Easy to see but almost impossible to achieve: Bellow took—took by force—people worth remembering and turned them into unforgettable characters, leaving behind their empty husks and tattered clothing. Bellow—who understood his novels as "letters written by a secret personality"—turned tiny *real* people into mere footnotes of the fictional giants they'd inspired. And so, the falsifications replaced and became more indispensable than the originals. Bellow was not a biographer and so he wasn't obliged to respect the underlying fact over and above the imagination of the form that he relied on to relay it. Because what importance could all his ex-wives and ex-lovers continue to have? And people like Isaac Rosenfeld dying at his desk or Allen Bloom succumbing to AIDS or Delmore Schwartz—who'd written that poem he liked so much, with that line that went: "What will become of you and me (This is the school in which we learn . . .) Beside the photo and the memory? (. . . that time is the fire in which we burn.)"—collapsing at the doors to a hotel of ill repute, his heart broken, taking out the trash on a sordid street in Times Square? What was the point of them even having existed after a character as real as Elias Zetland died at his desk or one as real as Abe Ravelstein succumbed to AIDS or one as real as Von Humboldt Fleisher collapsed at the doors to a hotel of ill repute, his heart broken, taking out the trash on a sordid street in Times Square? And Bellow's initial brilliance and final malice, of course, was that all those character-narrators of everyone else—Bellow's own alter egos above all the rest—didn't reduce him, but, to the contrary, increased his power as a writer and intellectual on this side of his books. Every so often—he'd read this in that colossal biography of the colossus—one of the friends Bellow had vampirized had commented on their discomfort and even fury with the process in question. To which the writer responded: "I thought you would be excited by the fact that I found myself inspired to rest my hand on your shoulder and remember you in writing before taking off for the moon" to later add, with an epiphanic gambler's wink, a "Why can't we all forgive each other before becoming inoffensive?" And one renowned critic had justified his im/mortal snares: "The number of people hurt by Bellow is probably no more than can be counted on two hands, yet he has delighted and consoled and altered the lives of thousands." Bellow with the alibi and excuse—like one of his characters and another of his transparent mask, Moses Herzog—of being "a prisoner of perception, a compulsory witness." And how well—so well—he'd done it: isn't that what mortals were for, always ready and available to be more or less immortalized? Wasn't that better—to be cleaned up or dragged through the mud, either way—than passing through the foul world without leaving any trace beyond the obvious letters on that cliché of the gravestone? Wasn't it better to end up as dynamic and nutritious *good material* than as nauseating inanimate decomposing matter? And so, Bellow—who, clearly, hadn't been the only one; there were also the extremes of the symptom, namely Marcel Proust everywhere or Vladimir Nabokov above all in *The Gift* and *Pnin*—taking notes on and rating his contemporaries after chewing them up and digesting them in his writing. Bellow, who went around stealing personalities and anecdotes—like Iris Murdoch, his female and British counterpart—to make them his own in his work, as a form of ambiguous love or unattenuated vengeance. "I'm going to get you!" was Bellow's favorite threat. And the great revenge he took against any offenders who'd dared to cross his path, committing the crass error and unforgiveable blunder of attempting to block the progress of his runaway express train, was to track them down and catch them and put them in a book in his own way and semblance and according to his own imagination. It didn't matter who they were or the degree of influence or importance in his life. Children who were problematic because they were children and ex-wives for the simple reason of having been wives and lovers he seduced—ugh—by reading them his books in bed for days on end. Intellectual foes, because they dared disagree with his ideas or—like at one point he accused Stanley Kubrick and Arthur C. Clarke of doing with their *2001: A Space Odyssey*—for trying to replace not scientific/technological but humanistic dramas like *Othello* with "that." Students of the activist/hippie variety, because they questioned him when he was teaching his exceedingly well remunerated and masterful classes as "resident celebrity" at multiple universities. Reichian psychoanalysts, because they didn't offer interpretations in line with his will and taste. And even one waiter who'd given him bad service in a favorite Italian restaurant or for having dared refer to him as *Signore* and not—as Bellow corrected him at the time—*Professore*. Every so often, Bellow also portrayed someone's best side—in general a spouse who, though new, was already on the brink of being traded in for another—as if he were thereby awarding them a medal for some act of bravery in combat for his side and on his behalf. And so, Bellow, living off the living and honoring the dead—immortalizing them in his books, yes, but never letting them rest in peace—while simultaneously dancing on their tombs with a shovel in hand instead of a cane. And, finally, Saul Bellow on his deathbed: wondering and doubting "Was I a man or was I a jerk?"; but also, of course, convinced that he'd been a great character nobody but him would be up to the task of putting in writing, and better that way, better that way, better that way . . .) For good or ill, all he'd done was the dirty work Penelope hadn't dared do. An almost heroic act, his, a form of redeeming in writing everything Penelope had suffered live and in person. Art had, throughout history, always been the Great Healer, right? And so—not in that spirit, but, yes, almost convincing himself it was in that spirit—he'd carefully watched the video files that Penelope sent him as attachments to her increasingly hallucinatory emails from Mount Karma. And he'd cannibalized both—her words and images—with ravenous appetite, but, also, with admiration and gratitude for gifts received. And all he did was change (because he wanted to respect Penelope's original material, but *also* because everything was already there and because he wasn't coming up with anything of his own anymore) the family name. And attenuating ever so slightly the unreal reality of the crazy clan with glimmers of post-apocalyptic and existential dystopia. And above and beyond everything and everyone, to all of that, he'd added his distant yet ever proximal childhood perception of Mexico. The Mexico that he traveled to in his mind as a boy and the Mexico that welcomed him with a tumult of volcano-shaped sombreros and luchador masks and dancing skeletons and late-night telenovelas and shots fired into the air, always trembling from all the earthquakes.

And, yes, he also added a Proustian tumor (which ended up being anticipatory and, yes, the peril of certain graces is that they're often accompanied by disgraces) and a space boy named Estrellito, drifting in the memory of He Whose Name Must Not Be Mentioned.

And, finally, the part that was his and only his, invented and dreamed yet so unforgettable: he'd added Ella to that already explosive mix.

Ella as a singular kind of diver: falling into and rising out of the blue and chlorinated waters. Ella like a saint offering her quantum and physical approximation of what she termed the "Multidimensional Terrorism of Swimming Pools." Ella who devoted herself to searching for and discovering the definitive swimming pool as total landscape, as *Imum Coeli*, as the bottom of the sky: the perfect site for ancient Greeks and future extraterrestrials.

And it was so easy to feel immemorial and memorious and Hellenistic and cosmic there, in Mexico. And, alien, yes, but never a total foreigner. (And, there, he also remembered that other writer who'd passed through Mexico or whom Mexico had passed over. He remembered that other writer because nothing reminds a writer more of another writer than a writer. Writers—*true* writers—were like singular, specialized cells. Singular but, in a way, interlinked, yes: interlinked and bound together forever by kindred, gestaltic nerve endings. And he remembered that other writer, because he'd just finished reading one of his stories. And the story was, for that reason, far more important than the reference to the volcanic and always-on-the-brink-of-extinction name of the man who'd written it. A story included in a book with a title that came and was derived from a religious hymn, intoned by the fishermen on the Isle of Man as they cast their fishing lines into the sea in memory and honor of those other fishermen who were fished in Tyre. A story named "Strange Comfort Afforded by the Profession." And the story—another one of those stories that he hadn't read before he'd started writing in a way that was quite similar to the way in which that story was written—was about precisely *that*. Not about a plot but about a pattern: about the way in which the name of one writer inevitably invoked the name of another writer. And about how *that*—*that* aspect of the profession—comforted and consoled, in a strange but effective and agreeable way, writers who first and foremost were readers. There were fewer of them all the time. They'd been eradicated like marine species asphyxiated by the floating plastic of a growing number of writers who didn't consider the act of reading part of their profession. And, in that story, one after another, the author mentioned writers—Poe and Mann and Nabokov and Proust and Gogol and Fitzgerald and Flaubert and Eliot and Gorky and Baudelaire just to name a few of the writers invoked in the story— as if freely associating ideas via free stream of consciousness, in a universe where every notion and reflection could only wind up at a name on the cover of a book, because that was its natural and inevitable destiny. Strange comfort afforded by this profession, indeed. And something that, if you think about it a little, could end up functioning almost as an antidote to that *slightly-unhappy-constantly* thing from that other writer he didn't name and can't stop remembering: the realization that you were just one among many, but you weren't alone in your loneliness. And yet, yes, the author of that story had come to a very bad and very lonely end: not a suicide but pretty close, "death by misadventure" the medical examiner openly concluded in his initial death certificate. Before that—in the story that was only published in a posthumous book—a writer was walking through Rome. And the writer looked for and found the house where the poet John Keats had died, John Keats, who, before dying, had left in writing an inscription for his gravestone—according to his followers, who attributed his death to the effect of bad reviews "in the bitterness of his heart" and to "the malicious power of his enemies"—that read "Here lies one whose name was writ in water." "*Mente Meravigliosa quanto precoce mori in questa casa*," it read on a commemorative plaque by the door. And the character/writer/narrator in the story quoted a terrible line from a letter from Joseph Severn—one of the witnesses present for Keats' death throes—specifying that "his knowledge of anatomy makes it tenfold worse at every change." And—reading this and thinking he could feel the tumor that was inside him—he said to himself that there are few animals who know more and better their internal anatomy than writers. And there, from that line scribbled in that letter and quoted in Rome, his mind leapt to that other room in that other hotel he'd already remembered: to Albergo Roma in Turin. To that other writer confronting death with the eyes and the name of a woman, lying in bed. Lying down like he was lying down, thinking of the eyes of a nameless woman he'd renamed Ella: a Spanish pronoun meaning she or her but also just a good name. That writer and him, both lying down, together but separated by time and space, bound together by the unhappy condition of being writers bewitched by women. Both making a gesture, with neither words nor writing. The other was there, he couldn't see him, but he could read him, someone about to commit the "shy suicide," the suicide that followed a final note in his diary that read "Not words. An act. I won't write anymore": opening one by one and mixing with water and drinking twelve envelopes of powder for sleeping and never waking, not far from where there lay the sacred sheet of the most starry-eyed and suicidal sacred specter in all of History: the ghostly sheet of that other lost boy.) And remembering Mexico and its ghost reminded him again that in Mexico everyone was a medium. Everyone spoke for you and about you with the Holy Ghost and with the not-so-holy ghosts and with those ghosts it was better not to trust. The Mexican spirits who showed their faces and skulls out in the open and couldn't understand the asinine schtick of going around under a fucking sheet. Because, yes, it was totally un-Mexican for one of the most frequent manifestations of ghosts to be that of appearing and acquiring body and mass under a white, earthly sheet (could it be the same sheet they use to cover a dead body and the one they lift so the living can identify the dead who no longer have anything to do with the living people they once were and no longer are?) and to pull the blankets and quilts off sleepers who slept on unaware of what was being done or made or remade.

Mexican ghosts that crooned and cackled madly and danced and wept and donned bright colors and existed. Ghosts shot into the air. Ghosts that were what lives in the smile you only smile when you remember a dead person you love more and more with each passing day. Far more even than when that person was still alive, less alive than he was now, when he smiled and sang to himself "Tender is the ghost / The ghost I love the most" and made a list of ghosts the way he made lists of winds and deserts and epigraphs and airplanes and sentences and books and cities and movies and bad jokes—that always seemed great to him—and fragments, instants, moments.

Ghosts that you had to believe in first if you wanted to become a ghost later.

Ghosts that weren't black and white or color photographs: ghosts that are like black and white photographs lovingly colored in by hand.

Ghosts that—like dead beloveds, like ex-lovers who remain there forever, wandering about, returning in dreams or insomnias, and who sometimes caress you in the darkness or scratch you by the light of the moon, half Hamlet and half Ophelia—existed. a while back added to their list of universal clichés—intended to convince people who want so badly to believe—a "I see a phone, a mobile phone . . . I see something very important that's been communicated to you or that you've communicated with a mobile phone that is a . . . now I see it more clearly . . . an old iPhone that you forgot about or from which you erased very valuable information or where you saved a photograph that was very important for you."

Ghosts that, sometimes, speak slowly and sweetly, like adults addressing children and, yes, the dead—even if they were born very young—will always be older than the living.

Ghosts that always tended to have such a hard time communicating in a clear and simple and direct way with the living, and instead went around leaving cryptic signs and ambiguous messages or needing the help of intermediaries who, in most cases, when they weren't frauds or charlatans, seemed to always have some kind of mental issue (and if ghosts existed, why wouldn't ghost phones also exist, he wondered many time; a ghost phone with which to communicate with your ghosts and whose line never went *dead*).

Ghosts that never came with clear instruction manuals: impervious to sunlight and silver bullets and ancient spells; and all of them different, each with their own rules to obey or disobey.

Ghosts that you had to know and acknowledge and, in the end, understand.

Ghosts that, for that reason, are simultaneously the past of who they were when alive and the future of who they'll forever be when remembered by the living.

Ghosts that for Stanley Kubrick—filming and reinventing *The Shining* to Stephen King's despair—were optimistic creatures because, in the end, "If there are ghosts then that means we survive death" and that, in a way, life didn't end but continued even if only to terrify the living.

Ghosts that were like stars at midday: they were there even though you didn't see them, waiting for night to fall to rise from their beds and don their sheets.

Ghosts that writers like Charles Dickens or Arthur Conan Doyle or Victor Hugo didn't hesitate to believe in—afflicted, perhaps, by a supposed mental pathology known as fantastical paraphrenia, whose symptoms involved an excess of fantasies and that were nothing but the symptoms of privileged inspiration that they could never be cured of—because, after all, they'd made thousands of readers believe in the solid and legible specters they'd invoked in their writing.

Ghosts that were not antiquated but vintage entities initially designed for a different world than the world of today because they—as Edith Wharton said so well—"require two conditions abhorrent to the modern mind: silence and continuity."

Ghosts that haunt their old haunts, guided like birds and fish and elephants by the power of the most nostalgic and mnemo-cartographic of energies.

Ghosts that were orphan forms adopted by the familiar imagination.

Ghosts that—according to some theoreticians of the immaterial matter—are nothing but "emanations" of memory itself: not a haunted house but a haunted palace. Calls of the unconscious: don't forget it, don't cover it up with a sheet, the way you cover something you no longer use or that no longer works, because here it comes, rattling those chains it will never—no, not ever, never ever, not even when death do you part—feel free of. And no: it wasn't a dream, it wasn't invented.

But, he supposed, unlike what you dream, when you're awake you do more or less decide what you want to remember or what you'd rather forget, just as you chose to invoke one ghost or another. And, also, what you choose to remember out of all of that too much that you wanted to or wished you could forget. And, sure, it's true that salvation almost always resided in something you remembered (something you learned), but there were also times when survival depended exclusively on what you chose to forget.

And so, there are evasive maneuvers, ways to escape that prison without bars or limits that is the memory and that—even in flames or ruins or bombarded by some degenerative illness—is there forever. (Never fully forgetting, always remembering something because—as the Mexican writer Sergio Pitol, who he'd run into at a Mexican book fair, sharing a look of horror and panic at being there, the look of someone who asks themselves questions without answers to what they're doing there, surrounded by that multitude of people who the rest of the year didn't even look at a book from a distance—"Inspiration is the most delicate fruit of memory.")

Again, with his past fallen to pieces, he remembers that he's said it before: to invent is to remember something yet to come. To remember that something already happened is to dream with eyes open. And oblivion is to remembering what insomnia is to dreaming: a superpowerful anti-power, a potent impotence.

So here, like when he invented or dreamed or wrote (after all a writer was just someone who directed or attempted to direct his dreams to turn them into inventive and precise memories), it made sense to say that memory is alive and that dream is the ghost.

And, between the one and the other, the memorious medium mediating between the median and the mean. And so, warning by way of introduction, all of it will happen "Somewhere in La Mancha, in a place whose name I do not care to remember" and, for that reason, remembering it constantly but not mentioning it, thinking, erroneously, that *that* was forgetting. The omnipresence of that absent name that, centuries later, multiple localities would attempt to lay a claim. And, so, writing and always remembering that you write to forget: extracting a given memory and putting it in writing to convince yourself that something that already happened is happening again somewhere else, corrected, invented and dreamed and remembered better. And written better. And reading and being woefully aware that you'll forget the majority of the words you've read in the past (even the most beloved and admired), but, also, knowing that's why you put them in writing: to preserve them, to be able to remember them in the future, so that, in that way, you can live and relive them when you reread them. In the end, that was the only thing that counted: what was recounted.

Everything had a past, even the future: everything that might one day be written based on what was happening. Writing as memory's tool, because when you read you remember. And you did so knowing full well that the effect was residual and never faded. And that, on more than one occasion, something you fearlessly read so long ago and believed lost forever, would suddenly return and nail itself to the palm of your hand: giving new significance to your lifelines, to your fate, to the end of a book that only now revealed its true and full meaning. Everything that you read that somebody else wrote and that, now, informed you that it had a story—once again—to tell, to recount, over and over, until it understood and possessed it.

The recounted part—made up of inventions and dreams and memories—which is the only thing that counted, the only thing that mattered in the end, somewhere in Sad Songs or in Abracadabra, in a place that he couldn't forget.

And, just below, what comes next, what already happened.

What's remembered, here, is the contents of a life, something that happened and is still happening.

There it is.

Don't forget to shake before opening, which is nothing more than remembering.

A life more dead than alive (so different from the liveliness of Bellow's life, though Bellow had been dead for years) and yet, still breathing.

A phantasmagoric and long life, like a prayer nobody answers.

His.

Again, once more, there he goes and here he comes, just a few days ago, flying again.

He'd just left an airport to board an airplane the way one slips into a dream (and he doesn't remember having ever dreamed that he was flying; but he does remember having dreamed many times that he was flying in an airplane and, also, he remembers that in airplanes he invented many of the things that would later land in his books: airplanes were, for him, the lab and the experiment at the same time and in the same place, a location that never stopped changing location, in the air).

He was boarding another airplane in a series of airplanes with the unmistakable and increasingly unpunctual airborne cadence of the nonlinearity of anti-time.

An airplane is an airplane is an airplane.

In an airplane.

He was in an airplane—this airplane—that was the kind of airplane that never get lost in the air with the frequency that cars are lost on earth. In an airplane that contains fragments of all airplanes; like in those Beatlesque medley-suites where you hear something you already heard, but in different way and with a different beat: picking up speed but dragging its feet, with lots of delay for guitars solos, soloing, hanging on the high notes on high, after a first and last and only drum solo.

And he wonders if Freud ever patented the Ulysses Complex. Something that might be defined as the compulsion to turn even the shortest trip into a lengthy odyssey. Not free and associative and expansive auto-fiction but focused and turbulent airplane-fiction. Yes, what that final celebration in the Parisian chateau-hotel owned by the Guermantes had been for Proust (which, he'd read, was "something much more valuable than an image of the past: it offered me as it were all the successive images—which I had never seen—which separated the past from the present, better still it showed me the relationship that existed between the present and the past; it was like an old-fashioned peepshow, but a peepshow of the years, the vision not of a moment but of a person situated in the distorting perspective of Time") was what this last airplane—containing all previous airplanes and destinations and already foreshadowing what would come next and where he would end up—was for him.

In reality, a few eternal minutes ago, he hadn't left somewhere and hadn't entered anywhere.

The whole thing took place in a nowhere: a tunnel. The boarding process, again, for him, irrefutable proof that the human race wasn't made up of relatively evolved beings but of infra-organisms incapable of lining up in an organized way according to seat number, opting, instead, to, all at once, rush their departure gate, as if on the other side, instead of an Airbus, awaited the last helicopter out of Saigon.

But that was already in the past.

He was already in his seat with his seatbelt fastened ready for whatever came next. The feeling of occupying a space inside something half stage and half auditorium. The suspicion that you're an actor with only one air-line to recite, but it was an important line, vital to the plot. The answer to that eternal question that wasn't to be or not to be—though almost equally transcendent and existential—but: meat or pasta or chicken or fish?

He'd written and described and lived through this situation too many times, indeed. But it was a situation—climbing aboard an airplane that itself is about to climb—that never ceased to fascinate him. And every opportunity he got to live it and almost die of it and interpret it was like a new debut and premiere. A successful revival. A new variation on a classic and irresistible melody that, even though you know it by heart, you can't stop whistling with new arrangements. Accepting that at some point before too long, at least and if you were lucky, boarding time would be followed by departure time. The slowness of passengers filing in and the predictable surprise that their carry-on luggage never fit in the overhead compartments. The despotic courtesy of the crew. The closing of the doors with that pneumatic sound and the order to turn off, at least for a few minutes ("Please, we know it's so hard, but we implore you, okay?"), all "electronic devices" or to switch them to what's known as "Airplane Mode."

And there they all were (human beings who, if you thought about it a little, were also electronic devices that could be put on "Pause" or into "Sleep" mode) suddenly not really knowing what to do with their thumbs. Seated in rows, facing forward, in silence, as if at mass. Thinking there was nothing more different from a phone turned on than a phone turned off. Suspecting that the danger presented by keeping their phones on during takeoff was a lie (and not even guessing that it was a way to maintain sanity among the passengers), but also that it was very likely that the whole God thing wasn't entirely true either. And, of course, again, there was a great deal of liturgy to this whole ceremony. There, up front, the flight attendant signaling with her arms, in a sort of ritual and aerobic dance, demonstrating what was being narrated and dictated by a voice over the loudspeaker. And he knew perfectly well that nothing about those . . . tricks for a more certain survival? . . . made any sense or served any practical purpose. And the only thing out of everything the flight attendant did that had anything of a didactic, irrefutable truth was the brusque manner, accompanied by that whip-like sound, with which she drew the curtains separating the infernal purgatory of Economy Class from the celestial paradise of Business and First Class.

And yet, there were the credulous and the optimists: the fans of *Lost*, who for several years never stopped to wonder how it was that so many people could've survived a plane crash only to end up, in the final episode, in some kind of mental church or something like that. And again, yes, like at church, there were those who gave their full attention. And there were those who—also like at church—didn't even look up, thinking about anything else, perhaps out of pure superstition, telling themselves things like "If I don't know exactly what to do in the event of a tragedy, that tragedy won't ever manifest to test me . . ." Likewise, at one point he'd been convinced that the best way to conjure catastrophes was to put them in writing, to turn them into fiction and thereby deactivate them as nonfiction. To make them, in that way, more comprehensible and even logical when putting them in writing and imagining them as products of the imagination (with the inevitable and implacable clause not in fine but perfectly visible print that, yes, if they were well written, that the way they were told justified their telling) and that in that way the gaseous and airborne and in constant suspension and suspense *Once upon a time . . .* always imposed itself over the solid and unsuspenseful *There once was a time.* And yes yes yes: he'd always had a real problem with reality. For him, reality wasn't life but just the opposite.

In any case, some of them—him included—have never thought as much about death as they do now. About the possibility of a Great Beyond (he'd read that Vladimir Nabokov had referred to that territory as *potustoronnost* or ПОТУСТОРОННОСТЬ: a noun derived from an adjective to attempt to delimit that which was only found on the "other side" of all things and that, according to his widow, Vera Nabokov, had been The Theme that "saturated everything he wrote": and so, in *Pale Fire*, for John Shade, conversing with Charles Kinbote, nothing was less surprising than the fact that "Life is a great surprise. I do not see why death should not be an even greater one."). Airplanes were very good for that. Concentrating on the possible existence of a God of everyone (of whose presence or lack thereof, Vladimir Nabokov claimed to have information as privileged as it was confidential) or, in his case, the permanence of personal *holy ghosts.* (And—among and above them all—was the ghost of his little but immense sister: Penelope in his head, like an ache, like a demanding migraine, like the tumor of a tumor. Dead Penelope more alive than ever for him and whom he sometimes thought of as one of the vengeful specters in those terrifying and highly-exportable Asian movies: the long and wet and scarlet hair falling over the face in black and white. But at other times, Penelope appeared to him as the helpless suffering soul who, if you got too close to her, had the ability to detect your weak spots and did nothing but circle them in red pen until she perforated the page. Him, thinking of Penelope and Penelope speaking with the deafening secret voice of the dead. A voice only heard by those the dead want to hear it. A voice on a secret frequency, like one of those sounds only dogs or his Uncle Hey Walrus could hear, at the end of the final song on that one album. The echoing of those Penelopesque things that might come from the mouths of spectral characters in her books. Things like the things Penelope said. To wit, hearing them, in her voice, Penelope speaking, speaking to him: "The dead of Death and the death of The Dead. Death which is the problem and solution at the same time . . . When someone you loved and still love dies, it's as if you breathed in their death and Death entered your life. Death: the only thing that all the living have in common. There. In the air that surrounds the dead person. Their last breath being inhaled everywhere. Contagious. Like a germ. Like a bacterium. Death whose clothes is a patchwork of the dead. Death who's not an intruder but the magnetic center where all the things of this world will end up, but that, first, gets inside you and lives there. And so, though you're alive, you're dying all the time and thunder and lightning and . . .") Outside, in the night, on the other side of the ovoid windows more suited to a submarine than an aircraft, it's raining, as if it were the first day of the Flood, as if he were inside a haunted ark.

And—when the airplane begins to move, first slowly, traveling kilometers before finding its position on the last of the runways, and then the brutal acceleration and the takeoff—he readies himself to enjoy that which, lacking a better name, he has taken to calling The-Improbable-Moment-That-Inevitably-Takes-Place. The drops of water on the airplane window suddenly tracing horizontal lines moving backward and disappearing and drying up from the speed (and he remembers one of his grandmothers saying that dying and going to heaven must be something like that: "All your tears vanish as you run and run faster and faster and ascend and ascend higher and higher toward the Kingdom of Heaven." And it made him sad to tell her that if it was called "The Kingdom of Heaven" it was because up there, also, there would be vassals and slaves and different levels, not of life but of death). That magical instant when tons of metal and plastic and flesh and bone and fuel detached from the ground. Suddenly, inexplicably even though it'd been explained to him many times, once again, he's flying. He's soaring over the storm and he opens his eyes and there outside a perfect sun is shining.

His name, on high, as high as he'll ever be, is 3C.

In First Class, courtesy of accumulated miles and overbooking. Back there, behind him, on the other side of that curtain, groans and snoring and gaseous eruptions and crying babies can be heard. There are ever more people in the ever more asphyxiating air of airplanes. The democratization and socialization of the skies where everyone flies for a handful of crumpled bills and dresses in the same clothes they wear at home (the nomadic equivalent of the sedentary autofiction where everyone wrote about themselves without first thinking about whether or not they had something good to tell in a good way or if actually it would be good for them to get out of the house and go somewhere far away) just so they can take long-distance selfies to keep persons known and unknown in the know. Another of many errors of prediction in the literature of anticipation and with little or nothing to do with the enviable floating solitude of Doctor Heywood Floyd aboard that space shuttle, dancing a waltz en route to the space station, his pen floating in an empty cabin. Now everyone went into the heavens without having to die first! Everyone had the power of flight! Everyone flew everywhere all the time provided that it was cheap! And they did so forgetting where they'd been as soon as they returned home. And not remembering—every time they submitted themselves to those unsafe safety measures—how they wouldn't be allowed in with a two-liter bottle of water or perfume, how they had to remove their jackets and belts and shoes, how they had to place any metallic object in the tray, how they had to remove their laptop from their luggage and send it through separately. Forgetting all of that and thereby slowing everyone else down; because what they really wanted was for everyone to be aware of their persona and that they were going to be flying and spending the whole flight walking the aisles of the airplane wearing florescent athletic attire with matching slippers and stretching and contracting, convinced beyond all logic that touching the tips of their toes with the tips of their fingers wasn't just a historical achievement, but that, in addition, it was good for them. And back there they were all already starting to get loaded on in-flight booze and when they landed they would keep right on drinking and doing everything they weren't allowed to do at home and where's the closest McDonald's, please.

And those familial tribes of orthodox Jews (all respect to them, though he was the least orthodox of Jews and only went into synagogues when it was raining) who didn't hesitate to take his space by force for a few hours. That seat that was so difficult or expensive for him to obtain, beside one of the emergency exits, was now overwhelmed by all of them: getting up over and over to pray, unsteady and taking turns, men and women, leaving their babies on the floor and at their feet as they went to the bathroom to then recite whatever was appropriate upon coming back out. Maybe that prayer that goes "Blessed are You, Lord our God, King of the universe, who in wisdom has given form to man and who created in him many orifices and hollow tubes . . ." And what irritated him most was the state of the little portable books from which they read those prayers: the cover printed on the same paper as that of the pages and pages folded and stained with what appeared to be infantile effusions. And then he felt so tempted to pull out his brand new copy of *Ada, or Ardor* (specially acquired to see if this time, on this trip, he'd be able to read it, if it would allow itself to be read by him) from his carry-on and to recite over and over that line that goes "Pure Time, Perceptual Time, Tangible Time, Time free of content, context, and running commentary" as if it were a singular and unappealable commandment. And when, at last, he complained to the devout followers of the Halakha, but who appeared to have no regard at all for his person, they looked at him, their eyes wet with proud humility, and said they were praying for him too. And he responded that they shouldn't worry about his soul, that if they could keep their asses out of his face as they bobbed and swayed that would be enough and he would consider himself blessed by Jehovah and as if he'd already reached the Promised Land though he was high in the sky. And he told them that it was bad form to turn an airplane into the home of a single cult; because up there they all wanted to believe in the same thing, in the same brands. That Boeing or Airbus had done right by all of them and that, as such, nothing bad would happen; and that, if something were to happen, that whole thing of bending down and putting your head between your knees, as if praying the most contortionist of creeds, would actually do some good.

And yes: when he was a kid, he'd lived through the last days of a time in which, when you boarded an airplane you donned your best finery and manners, as if you were one of the few, privileged guests invited to a party in the clouds. Years when flying was a rarity, an exception, a moment to remember and never forget. You traveled to see and touch things that previously you'd only seen in movies or in photographs or in books, and prior to that, in precise prints or illustrations or paintings or in detailed novels, in intermittent chapters interrupting the action with almost documentary descriptions.

Now you didn't even have to move: you could, via the internet, flow down the invisible river of cameras that recorded everything everywhere and if, in the end, you opted to move, it was only to be able to insert yourself there: in indiscriminate photographs with your face strained by the effort of extending that arm, holding up a stick with a phone affixed to the end of it. And the person always foregrounded with the landscape or the historical site as a secondary, background element broadcast live to stoke the envy—but also to arouse pity with imaginary diseases or to invent suicides or to seduce someone long distance—of all those people who had nothing better to do than to follow what everyone else was doing. Gone were the days of the delicious torment of looking at slides upon returning home: when every click was considered at length, when every sight was like a prized possession collected on a secret safari, when what garnered prestige wasn't your face, but the pyramid or the cathedral or the wall or the skyscraper. And oh, that marvel that were the pages of contacts to be examined under the magnifying glass of a not private but personal detective. And no: nobody was all that moved anymore when they received those postcards that marked his childhood. That childhood that kept sending him telegrams that he, always waiting, received in the most unexpected moments. That childhood that had two opposite but complementary faces, on the same A-side, like the childhoods of McCartney & Lennon in "Penny Lane" and in "Strawberry Fields Forever": the one evoked realistically and in detail and the other diffuse and as if through colorful fog. Exemplary example: the Earth, blue and white and brown and round, floating in space and photographed from the moon for the cover of *Life* magazine—the way at one time we all floated inside our mother-ships with our whole past yet to come—and provoking in children and adults of the time that vertigo of knowing that they were there, inside, but seeing it all from the most outside of outsides. (And he saw *those* photographs in *that* magazine after watching the broadcast of the moon landing on television and saying to himself "I want to write something that feels *like that* to read, that is seen *like that*." Something always intuited but never expressed. Something deserving of that *nasapplause*: that emotional applause broadcast on TV, but as if in a movie, from the NASA command center at Cape Canaveral. And, of course, his beloved Teacher of Artistic Activities had assigned them a composition based on the success of the *Apollo 11* mission. And he'd turned in something featuring a timid selenite who spied on the astronauts but never revealed himself and in which he pointed out that returning home safe seemed far more admirable to him than getting to the moon and, oh, he'd felt like such a writer when he'd written that. Meanwhile, Pertusato, Nicolasito, of course, had gone for something emotive and full of poetic images about "navigating an ocean full not of starfish but of space-stars" and had won over everyone and beaten him in the competition.)

Now, the only vestige of that old magic of traveling that persisted was in the ever fewer planes that maintained First Class in Business Class, like an inexact recollection of what that experience had once been. There, that expectation of "I'm going there, but in the meantime I am here" still prevailed, survived. And the sense that "I'm comfortable and have plenty of leg room and a selection of movies to choose from, though most of them aren't worth choosing."

And surprise: on this flight someone has had the simultaneously inspired and obvious idea of packaging *Blade Runner* and *Blade Runner 2049* together. And he says to himself that, yes, he's going to re-watch the first one and watch the second one for the first time; though to tell the truth, this is the only place he sees movies anymore, up in that nowhere air, between *departure* and *arrival*: movies he'd never seen before and would never see on terra firma.

Maybe he got that feeling in First Class (that feeling of going somewhere, of transcendence, of being part of a chosen race) because, in the event of a plane crash, statistically, the people sitting in the seats closest to the cockpit had the lowest probability of surviving and continuing to accumulate miles. In first class, you boarded the plane first and you deplaned first and you died first and no problem there: because the key was in the hierarchy, in that *first*, which made you more acutely aware that, at any moment, all of it could come crashing down because of some minor mechanical failure that not even the fatal orange memory of the black box would ever reveal.

And that's where he was now.

In first class, a first for him when flying (and praying that he never arrive; that something happen along the way) to a different country. An ancient foreign country where it wasn't just that they did things in differently, but that they did things he would never do, no way, not now not ever. And they'd been doing them forever. And it was very clear to him that it was the kind of foreign country where it was really easy to lose your passport (or for your passport to run out of space on those little pages covered with impossible-to-decipher entry and exit stamps) and to stay there forever, adapting or not (probably not) to those immemorial different things (a more or less elegant way of saying that you were violated, upon entering or exiting, whenever you crossed the border). Things the locals had been doing since back when they ripped out hearts, still warm and beating, sank their teeth into them until they broke open, and then spit them out down the side of a pyramid. That's where he was heading, pulsating like an offering, like a human sacrifice. A go-between. A meddler. An intermediary. A medium between the ghost of his sister Penelope and the zombies who tormented her while alive and condemned her to the raging fire at the wuthering heights of her vertiginous madness. Penelope whom, now and forever, he doesn't want to remember, but . . . (Penelope appearing first as a purely sonic and monolithic and black and wordless aura that mutated into a piercing, helterskelterish scream—"Look out! 'Cause here she comes . . ."—calling him "Bad Little Brother" and commanding "Don't take a ghost's name in vain." Penelope—in one of her many madhouse monologues, on one of his visits—referring obliquely to their parents and her son and explaining to him that "M.R. James, who dedicated so many great stories to ghosts, when asked if he believed in their existence, answered that 'I am prepared to consider all evidence and accept it if it satisfies me.' And James Matthew Barrie, the creator of Peter Pan, wrote that 'The only ghosts, I believe, who creep into this world are dead young mothers, returned to see how their children fare.' . . . That's not my case, I fear, though there's nothing I want more. And, now and forever, that wasn't our mother's case either. Her ghost is probably wandering through discotecas and vernissages and fashion shows . . . And both James and Barrie make an understandable yet unforgivable error: the error of assuming that ghosts can understand and predict the feelings and actions of the living and that they're able to leave a clear and unquestionable trace. Especially if they didn't leave one when they were alive or if their actions were impossible to explain, going here and there, losing their breath, a breath they never imagined would be their last . . . No: ghosts just magnify the flaws of their living counterparts and death is the great, omnipresent absence. The ghost is the most complicated of all monsters: because it's someone who comes back to you. Someone you knew when they were alive— ghosts of strangers hold no real interest, because they weren't real for you while they were alive—and someone you, perhaps, loved or hated to death. That's why ghosts are such volatile matter, ectoplasmic nitroglycerin. A hypersensitive reactant. Like one of those effervescent pills that instantly fizz and bubble when mixed with the water of the living who will end up drinking them. And so, better not to bother them or invoke them with a Ouija board, though therein lies a dangerous tension, a perilous temptation, a love tinged with hubris: the desire to bring someone back who can no longer be seen. Someone who, capable of being far away and beyond death, has the infinite tenderness to stick around to look out for the living, always so needy and demanding. And those are vital desires that ghosts feed off of. The living are fuel for the dead. The dead who are the true and vociferous silent majority. The dead who, when they die, like imperfect ventriloquists, appear to almost force the living to say, 'Such is life' when really the dead think that the living should say 'Such is death.' And then, on the basis of that misunderstanding, the living begin to think up more than improbable inanities like 'He or she is on high now . . . reunited at last with his or her beloved X, watching over us' when nothing interests the dead less than the living or the dead who were once alive. The never-fully-acknowledged *raison d'être* of the Afterlife is so people can have somewhere to go where they don't know anybody . . . The master-less dead whom the Victorian resurrectionists considered their property; because a dead man without a family could only belong to himself, but he lacked the voice to assert his will, the will that came after his last will. The dead who, in a letter, Thomas Jefferson said, almost accusatorily and unjustly and erroneously, 'are not even things' and possessed no personality or will at all. Just the opposite, the dead are those who are—not *that* which is—always above and never below all the things of this world. In the end, the same thing happens to the dead as happens to the living: it's not entirely clear that they're the one or the other. That they're dead or alive. The dead who don't look like they're asleep but who can't wake up. Which isn't the same thing . . . It's not the same thing . . . And the living who don't let the dead die, who don't let them rest in peace. The living are the dead's alarm clocks because they never stop remembering and rereading them. And so, in the end, when they wake up, tired of not being allowed to die in peace, a dead person is a ghost. And they tend to be in a bad mood, of course. And, contrary to what's commonly believed, they don't come back to get revenge for something they suffered while alive, but for how insufferable the living are making death for them. So it's best not to think about the dead too much. Not to overfeed them, because ghosts can get really overweight and that would be unhealthy. It would be like giving them indigestion with the impression of memories that don't correspond to what actually happened, with too much added sugar and artificial flavors and colorings, making them shine brighter than they ever really did. That's when ghosts rebel against all that cloying sweetness and turn sour and bitter and vomiting and vomitific. And so, better, let them go wandering, so thin and translucent, on their way. On their way, far and wide, through the elliptical time of ghosts. That time that is also the time of dreams and of those dreams that are books. Books that, according to the wise Arabs, should never be written at night because they'll be dictated by specters; books that, in ghostly fashion, drop from the shelves and fall open to that page with that one paragraph that explains everything. And, maybe, that's why ghosts often use books, indicating pages and lines and words, to communicate with loved or hated ones or to frighten the strangers who've moved into the house that once belonged to that ghost. That's why, letting them go, not binding them to our memory with those same rattling chains. And only reproaching them for their absence once in a while; because paradoxically the best ghost is the one that never comes back. Like Heathcliff blaming Cathy. Accusing her of abandoning him. Reproaching her for not coming back from the dead to torment him and, in the end, only doing so on the last page of his life . . . That may be the only way to keep ghosts at bay. To make them feel guilty. To let the ghosts of the dead know that, when all is said and done, they're really not all that important and that they've surrendered and retreated in defeat. Or, on the other hand, who knows, to make them feel omnipresent and in-demand until they get sick of coming back, of having to be everywhere. Even on the bodies of the living, like that amethyst bracelet that Charlotte threaded together with the woven hair of her sisters— dead and in the ground yet always on the surface—Emily and Anne: writers far more interesting than she was but whose stories and memory now belonged and were reduced to her version of things as, no doubt, I'll be reduced to yours, heavy as it weighs on me, though it'll probably weigh more on you than on me, my Bad Little Brother . . . Ah, better to leave in peace those who don't rest in peace. Better to think less about the ghosts and more about the haunted house. The ghost is the author, but the ghostly mansion is the work. What has value, what matters, what contains and conjures . . . how do you put it . . . the memory palace? . . . It's no coincidence, I think, that the novel isn't called *Heathcliff & Cathy*. The novel has the name not of people but of a house, my Bad Little Brother. The novel is named *Wuthering Heights* and that's why it never occurs to the protagonist-lovers to leave that place, to run away together so they can be happy anywhere else. It's the same for me. I can't escape that book. And it'll be from there, from its rooms and the surrounding moors, that you'll hear me when I'm no longer on this side of things. Unlike Cathy, I am not Heathcliff, no. I am *Wuthering Heights*." And when Penelope started to get explosively heavy like that, he—who believed that a lively longing to believe in ghosts wasn't the same thing as fighting to the death to believe in ghosts—could only think about switching her off. About disconnecting her red and blue mental wires, with a "Don't talk to me about ghosts, I was born clinically dead and, thus, having been to the other side, I know far more than you on the subject, and that's why you're dying of envy over my first death, baby. And furthermore and better: I was born just before midnight—almost like the also-memorious-of-his-childhood David Copperfield —and died precisely at hour 0 and came back to life a few minutes later . . . And so, I came into this world first as fiction and then as reality and later all of that became a great personal story, which is something like the best of both worlds . . . Can't beat that, can you?" Then—to tell the truth, the part about the temporal coordinates of his birth was pure invention; but his parents weren't there to question it and, after all, the job of a writer was to "improve" reality, which he sometimes thought of as *feality*, and "When the legend becomes fact, print the legend" and all of that, right?—Penelope finally went quiet, withering him with a Cathy glare and a Heathcliff silence and, for once, she had nothing to say. A brief victory for him that he would proceed to undermine because he'd had too much to drink and to snort, spoiling the whole thing by following it up with a "And even though you won't believe it, I ran into your dear Emily Brontë there, and she told me to tell you that you'd totally misunderstood her book and that it was fine with her that it was Jane Austen and not she who appeared on the ten pound note, because Jane Austen's books sold more and better." Then Penelope smiled at him disdainfully and he—with the accelerated part of his brain that still reasoned somewhat proficiently—said to himself that he'd never needed the services of a good editor more than when he argued with his sister.)

But now, Penelope (yes, it was easy for her to point to her work as a key and decisive space; because the bewitching characters in her books were, for her millions of fanatical readers, more alive than their own parents) was dead. And Penelope was another one of his ghosts. And how did that the thing go that he believed in and that Vladimir Nabokov's Timofey Pavlovich Pnin didn't believe in. Ah, yes: Pnin didn't believe in an autocratic God but did believe, dimly, in a "democracy of ghosts" where the souls of the dead were organized into committees in perpetual session, supervising the fates of the living. If this were true, then, for him, Penelope was the most autocratic of ghosts. Penelope, who'd never confessed what she'd done as a girl. And Penelope, to whom he'd never confessed that he knew all about it, that he'd heard her little voice on the other end of the line. And that he'd been the one who'd actually carried out what it was she thought she'd done for all these years.

(He, back then, on the other end of one of those Bakelite-ish and heavy and stationary and immobile telephones that no longer exist and that commanded so much respect when they rang—and the ring of one of those telephones was never exactly the same as the ring of another, you knew when the phone ringing was your phone, unlike what happens now, you weren't always bringing your hand to your chest or pants' pocket, as if attempting to acknowledge a heart attack or an erection, every time a mobile phone with a ring that sounded like any other mobile phone, all of them sounding the same, rang—that you never picked up the receiver before a ring finished ringing. And nobody dared to interrupt its calling voice, as if that telephone were another adult. One of those immobile and slow-moving telephones that, as you dialed *that* number, gave you time to reflect and to wonder if you really wanted to make *that* call, telephones on which conversations were ten times shorter than on the high-speed and mobile phones of today, on which people repeat the same thing ten times, communicating in spirals that swallow their tails to spit out their heads. Telephones you only looked at when they rang or when you wanted them to ring. And, oh, those thrilling races to get the phone—hearing them ringing from outside the apartment, inserting the key into the lock—because your phone wasn't always with you, because you didn't go everywhere with your phone. And only barely making it before whoever was calling hung up on the Other End from where, just maybe, That Call from That Person was finally coming. And no: there was no way to know for sure, but there was so much passion in that wish. The voice and never the image of That Person you'd been hoping to hear for hours or days as long as centuries, and then, clutching that oppressive tube of the receiver and playing with that cord that curled around on itself like an elastic spring and yada, yada, yada. In any case, impossible to know in advance if it was in fact the voice you wanted to hear—strange and metallic yet unmistakable—or some other voice you had no desire to hear at all. Or if it was one of those occasional technical mishaps where you overheard a conversation between strangers and in which you could choose to intervene, to their surprise, like a god or a devil or a ghost in the machine. Now, not so much, not anymore, and he'd never allowed himself to own and plug in that fallacy known as an *answering machine*, disingenuous down to its misnomer name: because it neither answered nor responded to anything; it just listened and recorded, and better to avoid returning home to hear all those people reciting messages with the diction of schoolchildren. And the idea of long-distance phone calls no longer existed and neither did—he'd learned recently—the whole thing where if you hung up before three minutes elapsed, it made it impossible to for your call to be traced. Or the certainty and the protocol that good or bad news had to be communicated out loud in a living voice, one person at a time, and without the help of synthetic emojis or group threads. And before—if you didn't get the person, because people weren't always right beside their telephones—you called friends and acquaintances until you communicated with the person, actually communicated with them. Before you had to be insistent to get in touch. And, ah, the kind of things that occurred to him in flight, flying. Oscar for the Best Ominous and Fateful Telephone? Easy. That telephone at the beginning of that great Proustian-Fitzgeraldian gangster movie, *Once Upon a Time in America*. There, that gangster who says all he's done in recent decades is "go to bed early" and that he can't turn off the green light of his first love which is his last. There, he remembers, Jewish mafiosos and opium instead of aristocrats and madeleine, and holes and ellipses in the walls of the story, and that smile at the end. And that telephone ringing and ringing and ringing—all the time, all times at the same time—throughout the years and the crimes and the betrayals and the guilt.)

Yes: he was guilty of causing Penelope's guilt, the guilt was his and only his. The guilt was his, but, first, the idea was hers: instructions from Penelope to orphan herself that he'd put into practice the day before that day. The guilt of that day, a day he'd thought about ever since, every day. As if he were rereading it and correcting it but was never able to skip over (*efface expunge erase delete rub out wipe out obliterate*) it. The day of Christmas Eve, a day he remembers the way you remember something dreamed or invented. Though, really, in the end, he and Penelope hadn't done anything but advance the natural revenge children inevitably take against their parents: the revenge of surviving them. And their parents hadn't *really* been parents when all was said and done and to begin with, right?

And yes: most kids suffer a trauma of varying impact when they "discover" that Santa Claus and the Three Kings are actually their parents. They—he and Penelope—weren't particularly affected by that. But they did get sick and tired of being so tired and sick of their situation. (And he remembers perfectly the terrible moment when he and Penelope looked at each other in silence but deafeningly aware of it: they had no other choice but to accept that their parents weren't . . . parents. Or, better, that their parents weren't capable of being parents. That their parents— who was it who wrote that children were like priests and parents the heavens above?; who *hadn't* written, because he no longer wrote, that children could end up losing their faith and stop looking up?—were parents that didn't function properly or that functioned more poorly than the majority of parents or that, even, didn't function at all. That their parents—parents as that immediate and initial and proximate and omnipresent-in-their-absence version of *others*, of the *others*, of *everyone else*—made them think, think badly, that children always inherit their parents' darkness and that, every so often, maybe, with any luck, something of their light. That their parents—like *hard* and not at all *tender* Fitzgeraldian characters, almost always dancing "Let's Misbehave" wearing an "Ain't Misbehavin'" face—were cold-hearted and unconscious amateurs in that capacity. And that, for that reason, the two of them were degraded into something that wasn't what it was to be somebody's children, but, rather, something more like orphans in bad company. And that was why, so they could accept themselves as pure and solitary orphans, their parents had to be "ousted"—one Christmas morning—from that role they occupied with no right to or talent for it, like those apathetic Santa Clauses sweating into their suits in the heat of the Southern-Cone summer.)

And he can't stop thinking about Penelope (trying not to think about something is the same as trying not to breathe: you can only do it, at most, for two or three minutes), because, for him, the tender yet ever so tough ghost of Penelope isn't one of those chain-rattling ghosts, but, more or less as she herself said, one of those ghosts that enchain you. And so, maybe because he doesn't have a haunted house where he can go or to which he can return, her ghost accompanies him on airplanes and in hotels and in deserts.

And, yes, he was someone with so little spirit for anything.

Sometimes he even got the feeling that he'd become invisible. That he was no longer there for anyone. But there he is now. Inside an airplane. An airplane is never a house. At most, an airplane is one or two hallways. An airplane (the last flight, the finale of all his long oceanic flights and that's all folks: farewell to his airborne life, because he hadn't even bought a return ticket) is nothing but a container inside a container inside another container and on down until they close the top of the final container of your coffin so you can face the earth or the fire. Life is the container. One of those thermoses, cold on the outside and hot inside. Full of alphabet soup. Letters to be organized so you can read them as if you were drinking them. But the letters won't stay still because of the turbulence and they spin around on themselves in the thick stew of your memory and change schedule and destination, as if on those notice boards in provincial airports that still go *clack-clack-clack* with the sound of masticating skulls. Letters informing you about *arrivals* and *departures* and *cancelled* and *delayed* or saying would you be so kind as to make your way to the company's nearest counter, where they invite you into a special room and there you're informed they have something to tell you. And that something, needless to say, is going to change (*efface expunge erase delete rub out wipe out obliterate*) your life forever, the way only death can change life: something that first you'll think is an invention and then a dream and that later will become something to remember forever and never forget.

But now he—always readying himself for an emergency landing or a sudden increase in altitude—is above all of that and all of them.

Waiting for nothing, nobody waiting for him.

He's closing his eyes, telling himself it's all just a dream someone has invented, so he can keep asking himself how—after everything that'd been invented and dreamed—to go on, wishing to, at last, come to the end, to the FIN at the bottom of the last page or to the THE END filling in the final frames, to the "how to end" once and for all, for good or ill, for everyone?

Inventing that you remember what you dream?

Revisiting and interpreting the past as if it were one of those dreams that you invent as you tell it?

Being fully aware—between vanquished and victorious by certainty—that with inventing and dreaming and remembering you have the three possible modes and forms of confronting a story, true or not?

I invent, I dream, I remember, and, then, I exist?

Finally opening your eyes to remember everything you wanted to forget but couldn't?

Not what you imagined and what you slept through but what happened?

What happened and keeps on happening because you remember it?

The invention in the moment of inventing it?, the dream recounted as it was and not as it is reinvented upon waking?, the memory as something you need to believe in as reality to keep from succumbing to idea that you dreamed or invented it?

What—to go further but still in the vicinity—other people remember about other people, as if they were reading them, and what, though partial and inexact, is equally worthy of consideration, adding points of view to the complete vision of the self-portrait?

What you read to escape from the real and what you wrote to stop running away, and spinning around your own axis, and widening your stance to better stabilize yourself, and to take careful aim and to fire and to hit the fucking reality of things right between the eyes with the biggest of all bangs?

One thing was certain: sooner or later—if you didn't protect them as you should—memories wound up taking on the consistency of dreams. The same silhouette of those amorphous shapes where the things you chose to remember by inventing them upon waking blurred into what you decided to remember or not to remember as an invitation to interpretation when you opened your eyes. And it was then that you ran the risk that your imprecise and ever-revisable memory palace (a museum with paintings and sculptures changing location or being elevated to great halls or downgraded to tiny basements) would turn into, merely, a room with a bed in the middle, cordoned off in a way that, in this case, didn't indicate "do not cross" but "do not leave."

(And in his museum he'd remembered to hang an unforgettable and oneiric painting that he saw for the first time in a book from his childhood titled *Mi museo maravilloso*. A painting by René Magritte. That Belgian—that intermediate and alternative way of being French (or of being born in his now nonexistent country of origin)—painter who'd become so popular in the homes of the great intellectuals of the '60s and '70s. A painter Paul McCartney was a confessed fan of and from whom he'd "borrowed" that green apple to symbolize the discord that led to The Beatles breaking up. And Magritte, also, in the bedrooms of the children of the intelligentsia of the time, functioning as a cool form of protest against the imperialist ducks and mice of Disney. And maybe because they assumed that those oneiric paintings—like the also frequently hung canvases of Dalí and Rousseau and Chagall, whom he detested—induced sleep in their children. Made them fall asleep earlier and granted their parents longer and whiter and more lysergic nights. There, in Magritte, those men wearing mushroom-shaped bowler hats preceded, but combined so well with, the melodious military uniforms of *Sgt. Pepper's* and *Yellow Submarine* and with the lysergic aviator helmets of Peter Max and—closing the circle and with him exiting the circle of his childhood—with that faceless deserted man wearing a mushroom hat in the Yuma Desert inside the cover of *Wish You Were Here*. And he also remembers when his Uncle Hey Walrus, pulling one of his many, many practical jokes, altered the order of the songs on the cover of his copy of that Pink Floyd album—an album that, obviously, was really important to him—by pasting a new list over the original, so that he thought "Welcome to the Machine" came after "Have a Cigar" and not the other way around. In any case, the Magritte painting that'd so intrigued him as a child was called *La celfdes songes* and it belonged to the series *La Trahison des images*. There, dreams as the tool to betray or to reinvent what you remember seeing or having seen. The most well-known painting from the series was the one that depicted a pipe but warned that it was not a pipe: *Ceci n'est pas une pipe*, it said there in the exquisite cursive of the school's top student below the detailed and unquestionable figure of a pipe. And the figure of that pipe that wasn't a pipe connected directly to the figure of the boy that was Pertusato, Nicolasito. The protocol of taking attendance in school required last name first and first name last and "nay, pardon me. I fall into my country's habit of putting your patronymic first," Count Dracula said to "Harker, Jonathan," recently arrived to his castle. Pertusato, Nicolasito, who always raised his hand even when he didn't know the answer, leaning on his reputation and past successes in other lessons and on other occasions. And so it got to the point where he didn't need to study anymore, because the teachers stopped calling on him, because they took his knowledge for granted. Pertusato Nicolasito as that student who rubs all his classmates the wrong way and whom they never challenge with a teasing but friendly "Want me to tell you 'The Story of the Good Pipe?'" to which the response was, generally, "Okay," prompting the immediate rejoinder "I didn't ask you if it was okay with you: I asked you if you want me to tell you The Story of the Good Pipe." And, ah, there was no right answer to that infinite question and that story never ended and never began. And his reasons for disliking Pertusato, Nicolasito had to do with his other stories, with the stories Pertusato, Nicolasito wrote. Stories that Pertusato, Nicolasito brought to battle in their "composition duels," almost always besting him with his clarity and sentimentality. And he—later on, when everything seemed to take a progressive turn—liked to remember Pertusato, Nicolasito as an exhibitionist *à la* Keith Emerson or Rick Wakeman, while he preferred to define himself and *to sound* like a subtle and elegant version of Pink Floyd's Rick Wright: Wright as the true hero of *Wish You Were Here* and—nothing happens by chance, everything is connected, like how all those songs melted into each other amid voices and machine sounds and laughter and radio broadcasts and desert wind—*Ceci n'est pas une boîte* was the title under which Pink Floyd had released, in 2011, a monumental commemorative "immersion box" of that album that he hadn't stopped commemorating since it first came out. One against the other, comparing and competing during "free time" or on "optional assignments" at school—inspired by their Teacher of Artistic Activities, whom he always thinks of in those bewitching capital letters and never in the common and almost vassal-like lowercase "señorita"—reading their "open-subject compositions." Texts meticulously composed in school notebooks with—if they were the ones with better quality paper—the surnames of heroes of Independence on their hard covers. Or in notebooks with the soft covers and almost transparent pages and—to compensate for the humble nature of their materials with the pride of what they might end up containing—brand names like Art, Inspiration, Success, Ecstasy, Glory, or Hallelujah. But that wasn't true: Pertusato, Nicolasito was good at what he did. He was corny and manipulative, sure. But Pertusato, Nicolasito was better than he was with his "experiments." Pertusato, Nicolasito was very good, the very best. And it was as if Pertusato, Nicolasito could tell The Story of the Good Pipe without needing them to ask him to first: the story of a good pipe and the risks it took to stay lit; while he had probably come up with something about the horrible deductions of Sherlock Holmes's pipe, or something like that. And he wondered—to stop remembering all of that, to distract himself from his memory—if the Good Pipe from the story was Magritte's and if it was truly a pipe. Or if it was not a pipe. Or if it was a pipe without being a pipe. Because Magritte himself had explained—dismantling the poetic and pathetic duck test of James Whitcomb Riley—that "The famous pipe. How people have reproached me for it! And yet, could you stuff my pipe? No, it's just a representation, is it not? So if I had written on my picture 'This is a pipe,' I'd have been lying!" Though his favorite Magritte was a lesser known work. Again: *Key to Dreams*. And, over the years, he'd traveled as far as Munich to see it in person. And then, there, he saw it again with the X-ray vision of children. The painting was divided into four panels, like a postcard of one of those cabinets of curiosities from Renaissance Europe. And it depicted four images that were probably well acquainted or even close friends with that pipe. And, beneath each one, the same handwriting expanded on the correct mistake: a woman's handbag was titled *The Sky*, an open pocketknife was categorized as *The Bird*, a tree leaf was labeled *The Table*, and—on the bottom and to the right—a bathroom sponge ended up as *The Sponge*. But, as with the pipe that wasn't a pipe, the sponge wasn't entirely a sponge: you couldn't get it wet and clean with it. Years later, Magritte had expanded the series with six additional squares among which a hammer was identified as *The Desert*; and here he was now, in a desert, but he felt more like the nail than the hammer. And Magritte had elaborated on his ideas regarding the relationship between image/word and its constant and implicit betrayal in an edition of the magazine *La Révolution surréaliste* with "Looking at them, the differences between words and things, between the spirit, our body, and our ideas, get complicated. BUT TO SEE THEM, WE MUST BE THERE. To deny them would be to deny the spirit." There, then, Magritte rose above the Freudian interpretation of the dreamed and went beyond that cat in a box or that tree falling in the woods. Magritte bet on something far more, yes, revolutionary: a new order that didn't even seek a meaning or reason for being. Memory, he thought then, functioned a little bit like that, though not in such a radical way. Memory was subtler and more disciplined than the free will of dreams. In your memory, a fleeting passion could be recalled as the love of your life, an unconfessable crime as the solution to a complex problem, a book you once dreamed of writing as an unrealized nightmare—"*Puis-je appeler ce livre un roman?*" Jean Santeuil asks before becoming Marcel. "*Ceci n'est pas un roman*," they answered from the shore of an oceanic beach, but without that meaning they weren't going to let him try his thing—and, lastly, as an airplane being held up to an airplane, to an airplane painted inside a square below which it reads *The Memory*.

To another airplane.)

To this airplane.

To this airplane where, now, those who are reading (he spies on titles coming and going from the bathroom) appear to only be reading factual and testimonial and autobiographical books. Literature of the I and autofiction and, yes, this-novel-is-not-a-novel but a recreation of something reality already created and all of that.

Books for people who thought reading something that hadn't happened was a kind of scam and who, as such, only wanted to know about things that, having already happened to someone else, might also happen to them.

Hope so, hope not, hope maybe who knows.

But meanwhile and in the meantime the important thing was to read something *true*, ignoring—or preferring to ignore—that true art always resided in the invented part of all supposedly true things. And opting for something hypocritically true like those supposedly real lives promoting themselves on social media, where you have to photograph yourself reading the same book that everyone else was reading.

And he hated that.

And he hated it so much that—even at some point in the composition of *The Impossible Story*—he'd been afraid that he was drawing dangerously near to those beaches. Or he worried—even—about revealing himself to be a great resenter of the whole phenomenon; because the truth is that he did have a great true story to tell (the story of how his parents met their end), but he didn't dare tell it, because . . . Though right away he told himself no and made an excuse for himself, convinced that his thing was very different. His thing was, always, Literature of the I's or Auto-Friction. It was as if he'd taken one of those confessional and testimonial books and thrown it into the vortex of a hadron centrifuge to accelerate its particles and have it reemerge shooting off in all directions at the same time, to end up telling not a story that was true but a true story. Interlinking cells. Putting one thing in on one side and having it come out as something else on the other side. A mutation. Like in *The Fly*, like waking up transformed into a sacred scarab among blasphemous cockroaches.

And walking in the air—inside the airplane, outside wind of stars and desert sky—he had to bite his lip and almost cut out his tongue to keep from screaming about how misguided and lost all those readers were, reading writing that, for him, was unreadable. The sadness of their supposedly realist and clearly aimless readings. And feeling so tempted to almost howl one of those gyratory diatribes and luddite philippics that, here above, would incite the tasers of undercover officers (he could swear that one of them was sitting in 33A). Lame rants that, there below, in the depths of the hell of his profession, had, for some time now, made him into someone very (un)popular at seminars and book fairs and literary festivals. Making him, once again, an inappropriate and terrorizing freak, advancing in reverse and buzzing around his own shit and making an annoyance of himself in everyone's ears, needing to explain them to explain himself.

And so—and even though, from the dawn of his times, he'd always been so bad at mathematics—he'd always had very clear and well calculated the equation of DREAM + MEMORY = INVENTION. And he'd always thought that, if you were lucky, such a formula could give shape to literature, to fiction as a way of life. To a *This is not real, and yet . . .* To a, yes, *Based on a True Story*, but only in the sense that everything you wrote was true if you'd invented and dreamed it first.

And in that way—if you were luckier still and achieved a noble and exact result—get to feel the Nabokovian "thrill of diabolical pleasure that you have in discovering that you somehow cheated creation by creating something yourself." And—again, Vladimir Nabokov—doing it "for the sake of pleasure, for the sake of the difficulty," because "I have no social purpose, no moral message; I've no general ideas to exploit but I like composing riddles and I like finding elegant solutions to those riddles that I have composed myself," aware that "anyone can create the future, but only a wise man can create the past."

And so, not dreams making reality but reality making dreams and faithful dreams that become the most unfaithful of realities. After all, reality was increasingly unfaithful to reality. And it was suffused with uncertainties. With avatars, with the promises of compulsively lying politicians, with slogans, and with marketing-advertising jargon, and with post-truths.

And—again—there were more and more writers given over to writing novels that were ever more autobiographical and ever less personal and that, in their affinity for realism, were completely irreal: because it was impossible to know and to understand everything about your own life and all its environs (he'd read somewhere that Woody Allen never gave the full script to his actors, unless they appeared in all the scenes, because he thought that knowing everything that happened and would happen would turn their performances into something even more artificial than what a character playing a person already was). And yet, everyone insisted on *this is how it happened* as an interesting sales pitch and seemed not to recognize that thing that Oscar Wilde had once ironized when he said "I hate vulgar realism in literature. The man who would call a spade a spade should be compelled to use one." Novels that seemed overly concerned with not being novels, with being closer to nonfiction than fiction; forgetting that the first great modern novel had as protagonist an old man deluded by chivalric novels who, as it turned out, didn't know how to read novels, because he needed to believe that they were true. But, of course, that was a great character and not a minor author. Yes: now, on the other hand, there abound Quixotesque writers, forever accompanied by their complacent Sancho-readers. Writers who'd discovered that what they'd really always wanted to be were characters worthy of being written in one of those—a genre one of Nabokov's fraternal narrators considered "by far the worst kind of literature yet invented"—"biographies romancées." And he can only imagine the disgust and disdain all these *autobiographies romancées* would provoke in Nabokov, like that kind of almost-disgust provoked by—as he points out in the preface to the English edition of Дар / *The Gift*—all those who don't hesitate to exclaim "ah-ha" and then immediately "identify the designer with the design." And, from his enlightening pulpit at an American university, Nabokov had insisted: "Literature is invention. Fiction is fiction. To call a story a true story is an insult to both art and truth. Every great writer is a great deceiver, but so is that arch-cheat Nature. Nature always deceives. From the simple deception of propagation to the prodigiously sophisticated illusion of protective colors in butterflies or birds, there is in Nature a marvelous system of spells and wiles. The writer of fiction only follows Nature's lead . . . The mind, the brain, the top of the tingling spine, is, or should be, the only instrument used upon a book. A wise reader reads the book of genius not with his heart, not so much with his brain, but with his spine. It is there that occurs the telltale tingle even though we must keep a little aloof, a little detached when reading. Then with a pleasure which is both sensual and intellectual we shall watch the artist build his castle of cards and watch the castle of cards become a castle of beautiful steel and glass." And Nabokov had gone even further and said he hated "the tampering with the precious lives of great writers" as well as the "the rustle of skirts and giggles in the corridors of time," and had demanded "the plain truth of the documents . . . That, and only that, is what I would ask of my biographer—plain facts, no symbol-searching, no jumping to attractive but preposterous conclusions, no Marxist bunkum, no Freudian rot." And Nabokov wasn't at all pleased by the persistence of all those "researchers" who insisted that his *Lolita* had been directly inspired by a *true crime* that took place during its writing and that had involved a twelve-year-old girl, Sally Horner, kidnapped and taken *on the road* by a vulgar pedophile who had little or nothing in common with his exquisite degenerate. Yes, and so it was: for Nabokov, reality was nothing but the point of departure. The period and new sentence and new paragraph and on and on. Or the ellipsis that followed *Once upon a time* . . . The challenge was to go beyond that ellipsis, to escape that suspense, and to never ever stop.

And so, here and now, turning a deaf ear to the recommendations and instructions of, for him, the master of all masters, these novelized and tampering and rustling and skirt-chasing and giggling bad students' autobios starred in books that were written, sure, but weren't writing. Books that, he suspected, readers increasingly preferred because they increasingly believed in the first person over the third person, without understanding that the best first-person narrators in literature (Ishmael or John Dowell or Nick Carraway or Humbert Humbert and Charles Kinbote and—right you are, Penelope— Mr. Lockwood and Nelly Dean and Isabella Linton in a letter) were always the most unreliable. More unreliable even than those, in their day and not too long ago, scandalous veracious liars who'd sold their fictions—stories of young addiction and child prostitution—as their own loser lives to earn themselves loads of money and fame.

And that was why these readers of supposedly true things felt they got more out of reading nonfiction than fiction, similar to how they really liked it when people explained what classical music pieces *were about*: Death calling at the door in the opening measures of Beethoven's *Symphony No. 5* (and to go with the flow, to avoid getting electrocuted by their so self-satisfied ignorance, he explained to them that the disco version of the first movement told the story of an overdose in Studio 54 and a lot of them took him seriously; but first he had to explain to them what Studio 54 had been and who Andy Warhol was and . . .); and the overwhelming joy people experienced every time they heard what came to be known as the ode to "joy" at the end of the *Symphony No. 9*; and being able to imagine the seasons thanks to Vivaldi and the divine state of God from love of Bach . . . And in that way they could appreciate the complex process by which they came to select the best and most stupefying jingles for their Twitter notification ringtone and all of that. They wanted to be told little stories so they could retell them later. They weren't interested in literature but in being able to say they were interested in literature and—like proof, like someone repeating an alibi—having a couple anecdotes to regale people with at parties. Better than reading James Joyce was to know the story of James Joyce's crazy daughter. Or the tale of the one exceedingly-interesting-for-how-uninteresting-it-was *en société* encounter between James Joyce and Marcel Proust, which was better than reading Proust.

And so everything, for them, had to have a reason to be real. A reason that was figurative and never abstract or open to multiple interpretations. They needed the official and verified version of all things and even better if it was about or bound up in a story "of overcoming." And so too they convinced themselves that the bastard nonfiction was working for them while, reading pure fiction, they felt that, in a way, they were doing the work for the writer. That it condemned them to doing forced labor for others. For beings they could never fully trust who, sometimes, gave them the feeling that they were lying to them or trying to confuse them with flourishes of style that they perceived as expressions of mockery. Nonfiction, on the other hand, *normalized* the figure of the writer. And made it more exact and more honest. Nonfiction turned the writer into a kind of didactic informer/summarizer, into someone *real* but, at the same time, someone with a certain air of shamanic guide. And the symptom became, for him, even more toxic when a writer started writing about other writers and what those writers had written. Because, of course, it was far more useful and convenient to write about what you hadn't written and about what others had written. It was something *true* and you could present it as your own just by virtue of repeating it and elevating yourself as a kind of manager/master of ceremonies of somebody else's work: literature of the unrealizable I-want-to-be-like-that succumbing— almost right away and desperately and pathologically—to the irreality of the I-think-I-am-like-that. (And, yes, he'd once fantasized about writing a novella about Herman Melville's father: a beautiful loser, walking across a frozen Hudson River to return to his family and die among them amid deliriums and with his young son seeing it all and taking notes and thinking of the whiteness of the snow and the ice that'd struck down the author of his days and who'd once described him as "very backward in speech and somewhat slow in comprehension" and yet with a gift for understanding "men and things both solid and profound." Melville who had said that thing about how "The wonder-fullest things are ever the unmentionable; deep memories yield no epitaphs.") Though he'd known for a while now that if there was something even worse than being an exwriter it was being a repeater: a false recollector, a great rememberer of the external, a chronicler of the other, a lost traveler, a soulless spiritualist, and a body-snatching graverobber. The noble and personal and first and authentic version of repeaters were, of course, fathers and mothers telling their small children other people's stories, making them somewhat their own, with their own voices and alterations and additions. But the people who turned that into a profession were nothing but repeaters for adults who, though they already knew how to read and did read, remained not mature readers but childish listeners. A professional repeater was like one of those opportunistic and parasitic fish feeding off excretions from the bodies of leviathans or—sometimes even offering a small hygienic service, but just so they could polish up some author sidelined by passing trends and the advancement of philistines—like those little birds that feed by cleaning the teeth of crocodiles. Or they would go around like those preachers who feel a calling to foreign evangelizing, to the fiery preaching of the sacred texts of others, knowing themselves to be dull, and suspecting that they would always come crashing down from up on their tiptoes when their scandals or lies were revealed. Or they would shake and spin as front men of cover bands, receiving applause not intended for them, but better that than nothing. And they offered testimonials. And they were political. And correct. And they spent their time promoting something that'd happened because of their words and blather, feeling like masters of History and convincing themselves that reading something written by others and retelling it later was the same as having written it; when really all they did was present something they'd never asked permission to borrow as part of their own story. (A professional public repeater—exception made for Bob Dylan, reorganizing the words on the sign of that pet store in London to turn them into the lyrics of one of his songs back in the *Blonde on Blonde* days—was the most smarmy and fraudulent and false way to *not be* a lonely rereader. To not even be what you were when you wrote and reread your own work, over the years when nobody else could read it yet, until, at last, you considered it ready to be known and acknowledged by the eyes of others: true readers and not readers of what was true.) And so, the profound pretentiousness of those superficial yet ever-welcome volumes, penned by people who'd fallen prey to the temptation of believing that that was the way to elevate themselves, with those exceedingly (dys)functional collections of miscellaneous texts and thunderous manual labors; cannon fire aimed at the fodder of readers who didn't actually read except when it came to reading about what they should be reading (just reading titles and synopses of the books everyone is supposed to read; as if blindly obeying a tour guide who points at the leaning tower of Pisa but never at that straight yet secret street by which you could walk to it and disregards alternate routes, opting only for the obvious grand boulevards) and, then, in the most Instagramable of instants, taking a photograph of the judgable cover of that book or a selfie with it in their hands and that's as far as they needed to go and would go, stopping there and coming back down; minor volumes compiling the behind-the-scenes footage of exemplary lives (the *interesting* lives of a hermit pianist or a memorious Jesuit or a saintly soldier or a multiple-choice test inventor) and back stages of masterpieces (movies with disobedient computers and nostalgic androids or the album of an almost disbanded band or tenderly vampiric and wuthering novels) hoping to benefit from false proximity, like someone who hangs a credential around his neck after a concert to see if at last, in that way, he can associate himself with something. Because for indiscriminate and indiscriminating fans it was far easier to mistake the gatekeeper for the property owner and to identify themselves with something—so the oracle assured them—that was real, authentic, with something that or someone who *had been there*. And, ah, it was so comforting to feel you were getting that food fed directly into your mouth, those tales of celebrities or, better yet, those existences offered up as "secrets" or "for insiders." And they were served up—summarized and condensed and seasoned with some aphorism of dubious efficacy—as if in Tupperware, books processed with the help of Google (because the truth is that, in the majority of cases, the chef/delivery boy hadn't read them either and merely learned the ingredients of the recipe and in many cases hadn't the faintest clue about what they were pretending to know with such refinement and taste). All of them condensed into the same easy-to-chew-and-digest mush, like when you were a kid who couldn't read yet and had to have everything told to you by a maternal or paternal voice. Better that and like that, because—again—they already had to listen to enough lies at work and on the news and in their families and in their own heads.

And so, the people who wrote those real things or those things about real people appeared to fulfill their social function—a dysfunction—after all: using the blues of others to distract people from their own blues. And without too many complications or experiments (another of the favorite strategies of these fabricators of testimonials and addicts of the ephemera of others for concealing the ephemerality of their own chronology was to, also, devote entire volumes to their own parents in order to, beneath distracting layers of cloying affection and supposedly clinical excavation, be able to keep laterally talking about themselves and with a kind of barely subliminal "that's where I come from, son of Kal-El and Lady Greystroke." And thereby continue to strengthen their own myth with more Literature of the Me. And no: he hadn't written a single word about the story of his parents or why what happened to them had happened because . . . because . . . because he couldn't tell any of it without sinking further under and drowning. And because, hey, the story of his parents was too good to be true, to be made true, to be brought out and paraded down the catwalk of the new collection of *prêt-à-porter* brand Unbelievable Yet Real, for the brief astonishment of people who are dazzled, oh so easily, by little mirrors and colored stones). And so the solitary desk mutating into the full bar table where everybody who passes by is invited to take a seat with a "Come hither, O stranger, I have a life to tell you that'll probably change your life." And they limited themselves to telling it and didn't concern themselves with how it was told. Style didn't matter, because reality had never had a particular style of its own. Reality was multigenerational and unisex. What mattered was the sensibility, the sentiment, the feeling. Thus, pure catharsis and confession and pose and publicity of the personal. Everything that, for a while now, tended to land on the shortlists of the literary prizes deemed the most prestigious simply because they came with the largest stack of bills. Prizes where predictability had been imposed over logic. And what was predictable rarely had anything to do with what was fair. And he thought about how all of *that* was bad: how *that* wasn't literature, how *that* was *something else*. Something that seemed normal and appropriate but wasn't, it'd gone astray. Something that led—he was never able to understand it, it always seemed so strange to him to decide to differentiate yourself in that way— many people, more all the time, to try to be different people without ceasing to be who they were. To retouch and correct themselves the way you correct and retouch and, in a way, falsify an original, without necessarily improving it or having a good reason for doing so. Or to transform themselves, like one of those paranoid abductees in movies with aliens who still look the same as always but no longer are who they were. And could there be a special effect more simultaneously economical and terrifying than that, than that special defect? They were *others* playing at *something different*: The Thing and the Body Snatchers. A radical shift in the established order wherein everything appeared to proceed as it always had. A supposedly new genre that gave off a foul odor and was disconcerting in the way of someone you know but suddenly no longer really recognize because they have a new nose and a strange mouth and eyes that no longer blink after excessive tightening and stitching. Something like plastic surgery. Suddenly—and as if it were the most normal thing in the world—skin from someone's ass appearing on their face. A badly scarred and solipsistic degenerate genre that was all the rage, sought after by publishers and pursued by agents. And for which—when honoring it with accolades as they did more all the time—they should design customized prizes. The Premium Ego. Or the Prix Moi. Or the Shopping List Prize. Or the Premio Io Sono Io. Prizes specially conceived of to be given to what he referred to as "books with training wheels." Training wheels like the ones on your first deceptive bicycle that fool you with false balance and keep you from falling but, at the same time, prevent you from going fast or taking risks. Bicycles on which to learn to (ah, that verb from his past and his now nonexistent country of origin, which amounted to delaying arrival, to not concretize, to lie, to speak a lot in order to say very little) "bicycle" but not to ride a bicycle. Training wheels like all the convenient historical references—military regimes and narcos and civil wars and *du jour* persecutions and gender violence—that those personal anecdotes always leaned on. And if he (as more than one person had suggested and recommended, this or that editorial voice, time and again, insisting on the idea, telling him "Look at everything your beloved and admired Roger Waters did—and listen to how good it turned out—with his daddy who died in WWII") were finally to write the book about his disappeared parents. And if, in addition, in doing so he were to confess the secret detail in the tapestry of that night and . . . If he did that, he would, no doubt, be transformed into a new and far superior Céline, into a *maudit*, an accursed writer cursed even by other accursed writers, without that keeping his book from becoming a bestseller as impactful as it was fleeting. But no. He—maybe to expiate his guilt in an aesthetic and stylistic way—wrote what he liked to think were "books with no hands": like when you rode a bicycle—a bicycle without training wheels and even without brakes—and you let go of the handlebars and let yourself be pulled downhill with only the help of acceleration due to gravity and with a "Look, Ma!" on your lips (though neither his Ma or his Pa were there anymore, they were elsewhere, so far away, with eyes closed, eyes that he'd made close forever).

And strangest of all, he thought and wondered: if their lives—the lives of all those writers of the living—were *so* interesting and *so* thrilling, why hadn't it occurred to anyone else to write about them? In any case—these days and until someone started a new trend and modality—readers followed these auto-authors with the bovine docility of tourists getting off the bus for a quick and guided visit and back on the bus again until the next stop. All of them, with audio-guide headsets and saying to themselves, barely under their breath—like many and too many morons said to themselves in front of paintings by Jackson Pollock or Mark Rothko—a "Hey, I could do that too." All those people who thought that *thinking* about writing a book was almost the same thing as writing it. And then, of course and fortunately, never even attempting it and much less accomplishing it and opting, instead, to sign up for a class on "How to write novels based on true events" or "Tell that story you didn't know you had to tell!" only to drop it after two or three sessions and sign up for another one on taking the best selfies (one of them, the first one, showing them leaving that workshop of true fictions never to return with an emoji of indecipherable expression, sticking out its tongue and crying at the same time).

And yet, many were those who dared to launch themselves into the auto-approach, like drunks in a karaoke bar, or like those people who climbed up on rickety stages to sing those out-of-tune covers at summer festivals, because the band (only slightly more in-tune themselves) handed them the microphone for a few minutes so they could destroy a hit whose original version was already destructive. All of them convinced that autofiction was something like auto-tune: it made you sound deceptively in-tune though forever mechanical and monochord, no matter the volume of feeling to be sung and told. All of them the kind of specimen who only read books that—again—were really "true." And those who didn't hesitate to think everything was autobiographical and, after all, their own lives were very interesting *too*, because a lot of those lives that got published weren't all that interesting, right? And so, vicious cycle of addicts. Thus, the kind of undesirable who not long ago approached him at an event saying first that the host had told him "that guy over there is a writer" and then saying "my story would make a great book" now—moving on from the state of "people have always told me I would be a great writer"—starting to think of writing it themselves. And some of them even attempt it. Which for writers like him was a relief in the immediate sense (because they left him in peace for a while), but a hassle in the medium sense (because, for some strange reason, for the mere fact of having confided in him their dream now made reality, from then on consider him a kind of literary godfather with the obligation to read their rampages). And nobody was immune to that strain of influenza and he'd read some-where that 60% of the people surveyed in a recent BBC survey considered the profession of the writer as the best of all possible professions. Who were all those people? Where had they come from? What did they think it was to be a writer? How was it possible that many of them even allowed themselves to give advice about how to write a book when they'd never written one? Who was their role model? Someone who wrote romantic novels with vampires and sadomasochists and vengeful hackers? Some Nobel Prize winner with the airs of autumn or winter Latino ladies' man, strolling through literary festivals and spouting off impossible inanities like "in *The Metamorphosis*, Kafka was already anticipating the horrors of Nazism and the Holocaust when men were treated like cockroaches" without even stopping to think that Kafka had died something like a decade before the Führer came to power? One of the multiple new avatars of inclusive and combative and righteous nonbinary multi-sexuality? Or, of course, the inevitable auto-champion with supposed historical awareness and political commitment to the great causes and a compulsive drive to interpret the multiple signs of their time? Did any of the people surveyed have even the vaguest notion of how and off what an average writer scraped by? Who knows . . . In any case, suddenly everyone felt that they were writers just because they had a phone or a blog, similar to how, he thought, in the Far West, anyone could go out into the street and play at being a gunslinger just because they had a Colt; only that, in that scenario, many ended up justly executed with a bullet between the eyes in a dusty street at high noon. Although many others, out of pure luck or lack of justice, hit their mark. And, as chance would have it, they became legends. And he was convinced that everyone who went out and bought those books by the hundreds of thousands had fallen victim to a virus/spore in their pages, read the way you drink a supposedly magic potion. And that, if things went on like that, soon there would be offices that processed permissions authorizing (or not) your story to be told. Or meetings of auto-fictioneers anonymous where they would all gather to tell each other not about their lives but about how many weeks and months and even years they'd gone without fictionalizing themselves and to receive the emotional applause of their partners in crime. The ones and the others dreaming, in vain, of one day being able to get into their own fiction-auto; of inverting the equation, of accelerating the fiction out in front of the braking automobile of the self; of being able to entertain themselves first and then entertain others, like Charles Copperfield Dickens and Jack Eden London and Philip Zuckerman Roth and John Garp Irving had done before, traveling from their own lives into art that was for everyone. And, oh, the ecstasy attained by those self-drivers when one of their autofictions won one of those increasingly poorly written prizes. Nothing, they thought, could beat that: being awarded, simultaneously, a prize for their work and, also, for their lives. And he watched them walk up to podiums to accept awards. And things occurred to him like why not have a book of stories—an anthology that compiled all these drivers without a writer's license—titled *Auto-Fiction*. A book that would be narrated entirely by automobiles; with stories that would have brands instead of titles; where what you would hear were the multi-ethnic voices and engines of Ford and Renault and Rolls Royce and Porsche and Ferrari and Volkswagen and Honda (all of them narrating their lives and trajectories in first person, of course); and that, please, let them all end up running over their authors who were crossing the street without looking both ways first; leaving them crippled and out of commission and beyond all possibility of repair and bound for the scrapyard and the junkheap and doomed to the rust of oblivion.

And, sure, one time, in an interview, he'd said the following:

"The work is memory and memory can only be what the religious call soul. But it's something that doesn't go to heaven but rots on Earth; though it's also something that could be re-recorded over the memories of those yet to come. In an ideal order of things, in a world far better than ours, everyone would be obligated to write a diary or a memoir or an autobiography or, at least, a journal of random impressions. Thus, in that far better world and in that ideal order, everyone wouldn't only know how to write. In addition, we would be good writers, lucid in tackling our own story and—going over it day by day, revising the good and the bad—we would learn how to improve it and correct it before coming to the end, before it was too late. We would be better people and, as such, better characters." But—warning—he'd made this statement before the outbreak of this self-referential epidemic and he'd said nothing there about how all of that should be published and read by others. His idea was that it would be a personal exercise, to enlighten yourself in private, by the light of a candle and not going around turning on all the lights and appliances and opening doors and windows and *open house* and free tours and assorted herbs and powders for all.

Even "professional" and "renowned" writers tried that drug to see how it worked for them. Some of them had gotten tired of—every time they published a book—having to explain over and over, like someone talking to problematic children with learning problems, that they weren't the protagonist. And that everything they wrote hadn't happened to them even though they'd made it happen. And so, many of those who until recently wrote novels and stories—even of his own generation—now tread lightly or reclined completely in novelized memoirs or, better, *no*-vels. Suddenly, all of them had their past very present as if their future depended on it. *Something* had happened. Suddenly, those who until recently claimed to have "a life made for a movie" now had "a life made for a novel" praying in secret and aloud for it to then be turned into a "a life made for HBO or Netflix." (He remembered that once, not too long ago, the head of a cultural supplement had told him, almost in tears, that he'd received orders "from above" to give more space and attention to books by authors with "interesting lives," because "the books themselves were no longer of much interest." The idea was that if a writer hadn't had a good life he probably didn't have a good body of work, understanding the latter to mean something "attractive" to tell.) And on like that until even one of his older colleagues—a writer he'd always respected during his youth—had published a "brief yet exquisite memoir" about his grandfather during the civil war, always ready to return to the battlefront. He'd run into him not long ago and asked him why and what for. And the man—now in the middle of what he assumed was his last decade on Earth—had responded with, he had to admit it, the class and wit that characterized a good part of his body of work: "Because it's easier to paint naked people than clothed people . . ." he said. And then the man had paused to take a long drink from his red vermouth (it was that fall when everyone, including him, seemed to have just discovered that drink, opting to have in his house the most popular and cheapest brand instead of all those "artisanal" varieties, too heavily edited for his taste; because with the third glass of vermouth came the sensation of wandering through an oily orange fog in which you didn't get lost but you did convince yourself that you were and, oh, the excitement of feeling lost when you were writing only to, all of a sudden, find *something*) and continued: "You know, those folds in the cloth, those shadows . . . That's why people learn to do portraits copying nude models . . . And, of course, every so often a genius comes along revolutionizing what is supposedly simple and comfortable, elevating it to the complexity of the unique and unrepeatable: the successive self-portraits of Rembrandt, Nabokov's *Speak, Memory*, and, oh, that moment in that book, my favorite among many when it comes to the autobiographical, when General Kuropatkin shows the young Nabokov what the rough sea is like by organizing and disorganizing a bunch of matches only to, years later and fallen into disgrace, reappear in the shadows of a bridge, asking the writer's father for a light and the flame of that match reminds Nabokov of those other matches and, yes, the same fire, the fire that never goes out, the fire that never stops burning, illuminating what was and what is and what will be . . . Then again, as you know: when you get older you start thinking about and doing things you did when you were starting out. Including crying about anything and losing control of your bodily functions . . . Supposedly you're wiser, but that's not really the case. Unless wisdom is nothing but the absolute awareness that you can no longer carry out certain basic tasks . . . The same thing, my friend, happens with the practice of literature . . . It has its grace and its disgrace: before—above all in your first book—you spent all your time highlighting that something had actually happened; now, on the other hand, you have to spend your time clarifying that this hero or this villain isn't you, that you never did or thought things like that, though you have thought about them in your writing."

And yet—justifying them or not—the truth is he even preferred it when they tried to gain readers and positions by prostituting themselves grace-fully and writing noir novels with female detectives or historical sagas set in the Middle Ages. He preferred them among cadavers and cathedrals—they seemed less decadent—than trying to come back to life in the comfortably morbid cult of themselves. It seemed more noble to him: going around rob-bing the tombs of others was better than sitting there rocking your own cradle. But they weren't even recalling: they were re-cutting. And pasting. And they weren't creating: rather they were recreating in their own image and semblance, trying to convince people that everything ran through them, that they were historical when, really, they were just hysterical.

And they were doing it (whatever it was they were doing) at increas-ingly young ages. And at an increasingly faster pace, as if they no longer had enough time or strength to invent or imagine anything beyond themselves and what surrounded and ensnared them. And they put it in writing with *minimal* phrasing; as if they were afraid the past would escape or forget them or were thinking that if they didn't remember something quickly they would be immediately forgotten. And they tended to be short books, easy to man-age and—so there could be no doubts it was of them and about them and for them—displaying their own faces below the title, on the cover and not the jacket flap: in photographs with an expression of having just had the most narcissistic and self-satisfying and amorous and appropriate of orgasms. Books that were written—and he couldn't understand where the entertaining challenge or demanding fun was in all of that—in the same way their authors spoke. Comfortable books seeking comfort. Books of warm fluff or, at most, cool black latex, supposedly perverse yet fit for any fantasy. Fleshless books with no soul. Embalmed books. Books undead yet not alive. Books always more narrated than written.

There were more narrators and fewer writers all the time, he thought. And it was clear that the ones and the others weren't the same: a great writer wasn't the same thing as a great narrator (one great narrator was replaced by another great narrator without any great difficulty and they were many; while the few great writers were irreplaceable and went on accumulating forever and were forever there if called upon). The books of great writers spoke a single language all their own that was very difficult for others to learn and master. The books of narrators of varying stature, on the other hand, all chattered in the same tongue, spinning out sentences as if composed by functional yet dispassionate automatons. Sentences like "He spun on his heel and turned his back on everyone so they wouldn't see his diabolical smile." Descriptions, instructions, situations, and little more. As if they were directions in the screenplay for a movie that would always be better than the book. Flimsy and light-weight things of little substance that the authors justified in interviews with a shameless and proud and even messianic (as if hoping for the same effect achieved by the omnipresent absentist Jehovah at the time of the cabalistic *Tzimtzum*) "the reader shouldn't be distracted by the figure of the writer and what I aspire to is for the author to disappear into the story I tell." But, oh, the truth was there was never anyone there to disappear; and, at most, the "story" that "author" told was to writing what counting to ten was for a mathematician. And, besides, he wondered, if what they aspired to was invisibility, why were they always out there posting and exhibiting themselves on social media, documenting each and every one of their public appearances and even things like the unexpected death of their canary, as if they were miracles or historical events. Yes: there was neither personality in their personas nor writing in what they wrote (some were even proud of the fact that "my style is that you don't notice the style" or, again, "to vanish behind my characters"). There was no trace at all in what they wrote of what they'd read before and nothing in their previous work that deserved to be read later. To say that style was the absence of style (not to mention being proud of it) was to him as idiotic as stating that justice was the absence of injustice. Because for him *style* was synonymous with *truth*, with *essence*: that thing that had always been and would always be there: because trends changed and passed, but true style would remain. That style that was deep inside you, but that, nevertheless, required you to go out into the world to find it and rediscover it. That thing that was unique and individual and nontransferable, like one of those roundtrip tickets that were nontransferable but that, even still, could be communicated and shared with everyone when you told them about the trip; and if they didn't understand or appreciate it, fine, that was their problem or their loss. And all of *that*, that risk and challenge and conquest, was what—proud of their humility, yet knowing that they had never and would never possess it—all of those people who wrote those false things claimed they were renouncing. Those things whose only style was not having any style and whose only correctness was political correctness. And whose creators claimed they'd struggled so hard to attain that *clarity* and *simplicity*. Is that why they struggled? Is that why they wrote? To be simple and clear there was no need to write, he thought. To be *like that*—to write in that way—you didn't need to write you just needed to speak. And you really didn't need to read those pages. Clarity and simplicity should be the starting point and never the finish line. And you really didn't need to justify them, as their creators always did, with a Chekhov in their mouth, like a plastic rose between the teeth of one of those touristic and exceedingly artificial and contrived flamenco dancers. They were texts that weren't even bad, because they had never set out to be good. They were, simply and clearly, indeed, everything that they'd never aspired to be. Texts that he submitted to a test he deemed infallible and beyond all debate: looking for and never finding a paragraph that deserved to be turned into an epigraph in someone else's book; never a glimpse of a line worth chasing down and catching and cuffing with quotations marks as you reread it and read it its rights to not remain silent.

And again: he loved epigraphs. Epigraphs were like the complimentary nuts given out by airlines. He couldn't stop eating them. One after another, they were never enough, they always left you wanting more.

He considered the epigraph a literary genre unto itself, a kind of vampirism that didn't consume but fed. Epigraphs were like the perfect cabalistic writing that gave rise to the imperfect homunculus. And that, at the starting line of those first pages still thirsty for everything, offered a boost of energy as you set off down the road of your own story. And, yes, again, another of the many criticisms often leveled at him: his books had too many epigraphs. Too many for a lot of people and too few for him. And one of the most painful moments of writing his books had always been that of throwing multiple epigraphs over the edge, promising them a place between the covers and in the machine room of his next book and, yes, his first great exposure to epigraphs had been in the massive crew of them, functioning more as a kind of unofficial boarding prologue, in the opening pages of *Moby-Dick*. (One of the most recent epigraphs he'd discovered had come from George Saunders, in *Lincoln in the Bardo*, where it counseled that "One must be constantly looking for opportunities to tell one's story. (If not *permitted* to tell it, one must think it and think it.)" And he said to himself then: "Right, so it is, one must always be there, like a prompter for oneself in the orchestra pit in the theater of one's life." That place where—one of Penelope's favorite moments in that movie they saw when they were kids—a shot will then ring out. That scene in which, just before the bullet, they ask a variety artist—who claims to know and remember all of it—that oh so compromising and fatal question about a secret organization. And he, then, there and from there: conducting and prompting with a rhythm all his own, not caring that what's represented there resembles something so far away and so foreign. And epigraphs were the starting shots that came from elsewhere, telling you, get out of here and go do your own thing.) But, of course, there was a precondition, a matter of honor and dignity: to be able to use those epigraphs—to make them your own and assimilate them as part of something that was yours—first you had to know where they came from and how they'd gotten there. You had to read them not on their own or in one of those convenient and deceptive compendiums of quotes organized by theme, but within their own vessels and variety shows. To appreciate them in their precise context before being able to appropriate them and write them down and bring them somewhere else, to a diffuse and distant place, a place so far removed from their origin, forcing them to come aboard a flight to someone else's destination.

None of that mattered (and he was going back to the thing from before, spinning around like a whirling dervish, asking the flight attendant for another little bottle of whatever to help wash down those high-altitude nuts) to those who, clearly, were only interested in blindly quoting themselves in the most masturbatory of encounters and re-encounters with themselves and their followers. And they were happy occasions without too many exigencies. The important thing was that some people made other people feel happy, that they didn't demand too much of them, that they didn't tell them things like "Read a lot" or "Read books that are complex and that question everything you believe in" or—one of his favorites—"Reading is like surviving the most spectacular plane crashes and to come walking out through the flames with a smile on your face." Which, sure, was a little too much, a little extreme. Because for their followers—the ones who clustered around all those rapid recollectors and facilitators of the difficult—one random phrase that functioned as a mutual excuse so they could feel good reading and writing "things that had happened" was enough. And so, readers of the true went around quoting Jean Cocteau and his "Literature is a form of memory we don't remember" or "Literature is force of memory we haven't yet fully understood" (or something like that; because his admired John Cheever had once claimed to be the inventor and principal propagator of that false Cocteau quote) without really knowing who Cocteau was or what he'd done and wondering if Cocteau was that guy who went around sailing and sinking on TV.

Of course, they didn't know who John Cheever was either. Or Dante Alighieri (who, if you thought about it a little, had already been making auto-poetry or poetry of the I, right?) Or Henry David Thoreau or Henry Miller or Thomas Wolfe or Jack Kerouac (who once explained his dogma to William S. Burroughs, which boiled down to "a novel is only a memoir with the names changed") or Philip Roth or so many others who'd recounted their lives so long before, singularly and without worrying about feeling like they were part of a lineage or a genre or a trend. They had, yes, "heard" something about Philip Roth. Above all after he—a few years before he died—had announced he was retiring from writing after having enjoyed "some pleasure in this life" over and over and recognizing that his work had been precisely that: "Making fake biography, fake history, concocting a half-imaginary existence out of the actual drama of my life is my life." (Roth, about whom, he'd read, on his insomniac and sexless nights—because Roth had also renounced that—passed the hours by picking out a particular year in his life and going in reverse and returning there to revisit it, month by month, like a pilgrim of his own story, marveling at what was still *there*, within reach of his memory, as if it were waiting for him to remember it.) And no: they *did not* care that they knew next to nothing or that they weren't in the know regarding anything, much less what it was that sustained the private scaffolding behind the public pleasures of a writer. Because with that line of Cocteau's, oh so useful for his devotees (and, *yes*, they knew who the very popular and a little too clever for his taste Karl Ove Knausgård—that writer of selfies whom he'd stopped reading the same way he moved to get out of the frame and not appear as an involuntary guest in all those tourist selfies, with that stick held aloft as if it were an unjust jousting lance in the most Dark and not Middle but Mediocre of Ages—and Sheila Heti and the, indeed, quite talented Edward St. Aubyn were, though they only became aware of the existence of the latter after the miniseries with Benedict Cumberbatch in the role of Patrick Melrose), was enough and more than enough to get them to those one hundred forty or two hundred eighty characters or whatever it was (never enough) that they used to tell the universe not that they were reading him but that they had read about him, about them, about their lives more than their work.

And all of them *were* aware of who the memorious Marcel Proust was and had been; but of course they hadn't read him (or they'd read, at most, the opening section of Combray as a kind of satiating aperitif). To tell the truth, what they liked most by the Frenchman—whom, given the choice or the ability to rewrite him, they would prefer as an online influencer rather than an influence *sur la page*—was his famous *Proust Questionnaire* to which the writer had originally responded in a *confession album*, belonging to one of his many female friends whom he adored platonically and studied obsessively to later use in a coded rewrite, changing the sex of the loves of his life in his work. They liked—because it was an unmistakable sign of being someone— to be given that questionnaire so they could answer it; reading the responses of others who'd taken it first, thinking over each of their answers as if the whole thing were about the best grade out of everyone who took it. And they hadn't even realized that it'd been Cocteau who, on the occasion of the publication of *Du côté de chez Swann* in 1913, had offered what was, for him, the best blurb of all time for a book: "It resembles nothing I know and reminds me of everything I admire." Or that it'd been Cocteau himself, on November 18th of 1922, who'd called Man Ray (whose name *also* reminded them of something, yes; was it a brand of sunglasses?) to have him bring his camera to 44 Rue Hamelin right away. To that place Cocteau would later recall in his memoirs, comparing it to Captain Nemo's cabin, that place where he told Man Ray to come and take the last photograph of Proust: the one and only photograph taken of him right after he passed away. There, the dead man in bed, sheets drawn up to the tip of his chin, bags blooming under his closed eyes and—outside the frame but if you brought the photograph close to your ear you could hear it—the oceanic manuscript of the rest of *À la recherche du temps perdu*, making waves across the mantelpiece above the fireplace. At that time, Cocteau thought that pile of pages "was still alive, like watches ticking on the wrists of dead soldiers." (He owned a Proustian watch, yes. And he'd had on his desk, before all of it burned, that Man Ray photograph framed alongside another photograph of the Frenchman. The two photographs inside the same frame. The first photograph separated by a few centimeters but many years distance from the last one taken by Man Ray. The other photograph, taken by Paul Nadar, was that one in which Proust was still almost a child, looking at the camera. Serious, as was customary at the time, because it was very difficult to hold a smile throughout the long period of exposure each plaque required. And that's why nobody was smiling in old photographs. There, the very young Proust, chain and watch in his breast pocket, with the almost-transparent shadow of a first moustache already floating above his lip and perhaps saying to himself that maybe, in that moment, he wasn't all that interesting, but, oh, already thinking "just you wait, in a few years, I'll recall what I was like in my youth in order to turn myself into someone immense and you'll see, you'll read . . ." Not Literature of the I but Literature of the I, You, He/She, We, They, Everyone. Literature of someone who knows immortality is only achieved if, first, a person turned himself into a persona, a personage—into a character. And if that whole thing about how the brain kept living for a while after the death of the heart—as recent experiments with freshly dead mice had demonstrated, revealing symptomology that could be extended to human beings, the brain activity of the mice continued for a while after their last heartbeat: knowing they were dead and recognizing themselves as ghosts, recalling their lives already from the other side and contradicting the Latin etymology of the Spanish verb *recordar* [meaning to remember], which could be boiled down to something like *to repeat with the heart*, turning the whole act of memory into something not mental but emotional and, yes, decidedly *rechercheiano* —were true, then it was possible that *that* final photograph was remembering *that other* first photograph, he thought, thinking about what Proust was thinking.)

And it was clear that what really seduced all of them—all those who never gave a thought to such things and who didn't know or barely knew who Proust and Miller and Cocteau and Roth and Kerouac were—when they read the memories of others wasn't so much the remembering but the being remembered. And so—alive, but with so little pulse, and no longer wearing watches on their wrists or in their breast pockets as if they were medals, because now phones were specially designed to make you waste time—they spent their time posing for pictures immobile as statues. The idea—the not necessarily good idea—was to be impersonal personas. Better yet, now, if you were a woman and a victim subjugated by a system ruled by patriarchal men. (And the current best-seller was *Oppressed, Ensnared*. A memoir of assault and incest that a female author claimed to have suffered at the hand of her father for nine months of her life: the nine months of her own gestation. The author recalling down to the last detail how her father showed her his genitals, there inside, floating in amniotic fluid, every time he made love with her mother: "His cock like a sword, cornering me against the wall of the uterus, at the level of my mouth and my eyes and my pain, knowing that, if I were to scream, nobody would hear me and that all my kicking, rejecting the monster, would be interpreted as a sign that all was well, that I was, simply, a 'restless person,'" it read there.) And to be protagonists of plotless yet ultra-personified novels, following in the wake and style of Elizabeth Hardwick and Renata Adler and, at the moment, of Rachel Cusk or Jenny Offill. Minimalist novels about spontaneous pregnancies or sudden divorces. Or oceanic novels about that slap a teacher once delivered or that fingernail that came to life one summer, which they considered unforgettable and worth remembering for everyone, but were actually just the equivalent of the torture of the unhurried and unceasing dripping of a faucet you can't shut all the way off and can't help but hear all night long. Or the already classic my-father-loves-me-more-than-he-should or my-mother-hates-me-because-she's-jealous-of-me or something-dark-I've-felt-since-I-gave-birth. Or—at most, as a concession to something outside the self, something outside themselves—the only thing they were interested in was to seek out and discover some secret family history, to reveal it to the world as if it were evidence for their hypotheses about how all of that really, truly, actually happened. The great uncle three times removed who lost his mind in the Bataan Death March or who helped design the Ho Chi Minh Trail. Or the cousin who was born at Woodstock or died at Altamont. Or the neighborhood where they grew up (the name of the place tended to be the title of the book, thinking that one word said it all and that place, as such, instantly acquired the mythic quality of Atlantis or Xanadu or Valhalla). Or the always-available family members who died in civil wars or at the hands of terrorist groups or a military dictatorship. Or the mystical friend who committed suicide. Or genius children. Or—a classic of the deformed form—the babies they'd had who drove them crazy or the babies they hadn't had who also drove them crazy or who, even more interesting, depressed them with a strange kind of depression: a depression that paralyzed them for everything apart from writing about that depression. (And it wouldn't be long now, he said to himself, before they would all end up blending together, their stories becoming fused and confused like those dance-club remixes where a performer propped him or herself up by *featuring* a special guest who added nothing but their name and voice, convinced that more was always more irrespective of the quality or the need for them to work together except to be partners in that one crime: burying a song alive or profaning a deadly lived experience.) All of that leading to—better that way, according to marketing departments at publishing houses—short books, light on pages. Distilled down to what they liked to believe were haiku sentences and bonsai chapters—but with a cadence closer to that of a Twitter thread replete with idiotic memes—in order to inspire the kind of respect that miniatures inspired just because they were small.

And if they couldn't count on being somebody worth recounting, then they had no choice but to invent themselves; at which point they turned to fiction—at least for a while—in the most tortuous and almost embarrassing way.

Or even worse: stealing (borrowing without asking permission first, blowing up entire family relationships, delighting in their expansive and sweeping and vengeful wave of maliciousness, but without the talent or grace of Saul Bellow) someone else's skeleton and putting it in their own closet. And then bringing it to light with a prestidigitating *presto!* to the horror of its legitimate owners who thought it stored away under lock and key and suddenly find themselves reading it in a line like "'I've never told anyone what I'm about to tell you and no one can ever find out about,' I was told by a man I'd always believed was my best friend, but now . . ."

Or better/worse yet: becoming part of what—in the wake of the success of *Uber Driver*, a remake of Martin Scorsese's modern classic—had come to be known as Uber-Lit: the novelization of what passengers told their Uber drivers.

Or—spinning around in the contaminated air—going even further without having to move all that much and winding up writing something in which they confessed that, in truth, their last, highly acclaimed factual book was pure lies. False meta-nonfiction and, seeing themselves cornered, shouting out a "Duchamp!" as if it were a smoke bomb so that, before too long, all was more than forgiven and reassessed and, once again, celebrated as a (de) formal ploy.

The important thing, anyway and in any case, was to be there and to make an appearance and show themselves. Suddenly, they didn't only want to just present themselves but you had to put up with their whole family being projected up there, like one of those sadistic slideshows people showed after returning from vacation. (All of them like the equivalent of those people who paid for a ticket to a concert not so they could hear their favorite artist sing, but so—howling in the audience from the first to last verse of the night—their favorite artist could hear them holler their songs back at them. Thus the tactic adopted by Bob Dylan long ago of deforming his classics to the point that they became unrecognizable to his fans, so he could sing them on his own and in peace; the same Dylan who, not so long ago, had interrupted one of his shows to, irritated, rebuke his audience—their phones held aloft, filming him—with a "Should we play or pose?")

Fictions of the I? No! They were nonfictions of the I! They were auto-nonfictions! An absurd prestige given to what was supposedly authentic, what'd happened on this side and now was on the other side. And playing with all of that perhaps as a kind of subterfuge, concealing the fact that what they wanted and needed and claimed was a work of autofiction was actually an unconfessable and guilt-ridden work of self-help. Something that leapt from the psychoanalyst's couch to the patient's computer. Like those movies that were *based on a true story* and that, in the end, in the closing credits, used their final minutes to reveal the faces of the real people (informing you what did or didn't become of them), after a couple hours of watching their more or less believable characters. Something, he thought, like what'd happened with shopping malls: in the beginning, they were a place where you could go to find everything quickly in a euphoric "shopping destination experience," a place that had everything from family-style restaurants to cinemas showing the latest summer blockbuster in cool air-conditioned atmospheres. But, soon, the entropy of all of that was degraded into a blasphemous sanctuary, into a place where pimply adolescents got together to do nothing, unemployed prisoners of their own free time, overweight and with their noses buried in junk food, addicts of opiate serums and anabolic cocktails, and caravans of the elderly who'd lived past their expiration date, going round and round on their multifunctional wheelchairs through circular hallways and nostalgically contemplating the impossibility of escalators. All of them coming and going amid increasingly vacant and ghostly stores, everything on sale and singing the nomad blues, because of the rise of sedentary online shopping and, yes, bookstores had been the first of those businesses to close their doors. The last of the stores to close down had, no doubt, been that small shop with the palm reader or Tarot thrower or I Ching seers always ready to predict or to reveal—again, always the same, ace up the sleeve—an "I'm seeing here that you will be a great writer"; never an "epidemiologist who will rescue humanity from the spores of the next great virus" or an "expert in the acceleration of the most divine particles." No: the possibility of writing was something that was immediately believable for any unsuspecting dupe (because didn't they already *know* how to write?) and they went out of there, so satisfied, transformed into something like literature's Manchurian candidates, always ready for their minimal yet accumulative literary magnicides. The shopping malls that'd corporatized the first physical manifestation of the invisible internet: there, everything you didn't need dressed up as everything you didn't know you did need. Now—on the other hand but with equal though even greater compulsion—people shopped online: the internet (and everything that got cooked up and made worse there) like the memory palace of unforgettable and unfulfilled desire. While shopping malls were now the not-so-virtuosic ruins atop which the virtual had been built: all those different brands creating the same product: the mobile phone as the package and container of the universe in the palm of your hand and at your fingertips.

(Then he remembered the truer than true words—another possible epigraph from one of those names that always accompanied him and reappeared, like fireflies punctuating the darkness of his nights—of, once again, John Cheever. Cheever asking, "Is forgetfulness some part of the mysteriousness of life?" or answering "It seems to me that any confusion between autobiography and fiction is precisely the role that reality plays in a dream. As you dream your ship, you perhaps know the boat, but you're going toward a coast that is quite strange; you're wearing strange clothes, the language that is being spoken around you is a language you don't understand, but the woman on your left is your wife. It seems to me that this not capricious but quite mysterious union of fact and imagination one also finds in fiction." And him, there, remembering that line about a ship aboard an airplane, now overhearing the passenger in 21A explain death to the boy sitting next to him. "Death is like a ship that vanishes on the horizon. All of a sudden you stop seeing it, but it's still there, sailing.

It's the same with the dead and that's what happened to Grandpa: we don't see him anymore, but he's still there, floating in our memory." And the boy in 21B looks at him and asks: "And what happens if that ship sinks?" And he stops paying attention to all of that so he can refocus on tossing more lines between quotations up into the air, as if they were aerodynamic airline almonds, opening his mouth so they can land there inside. "But are not all / Facts Dreams as / soon as we / put them / behind us," Emily Dickinson had written. "Real is good. Interesting is better," Stanley Kubrick instructed his actors, the same Stanley Kubrick who'd recorded his own real breathing while suffering a powerful cold to insert in those very interesting and realer than real scenes, with wordless astronauts inside space suits in *2001: A Space Odyssey.* A lack of eloquence and sensitivity and humanity that'd outraged Ray Bradbury—who crosses paths with Philip K. Dick only once, in a bar, and diagnoses that every so often "you meet people and you realize they don't like being alive"—when he first saw that film, which seemed "terrible" to him and that, in his opinion, didn't stand a chance pitted against Steven Spielberg's *Close Encounters of the Third Kind*, to his mind the best science-fiction film of all time and, also, the most realistic; but that was a film that'd always unsettled him, because he couldn't help thinking that after the final credits came the part of—surprise!—the unexpected anal probe/invasion/exploration of the enlightened Roy Neary by the light centuries of the light centuries. And, again, Vladimir Nabokov—arched eyebrow and twisted smile—had said it better than anybody: "It is strange, the morbid inclination we have to derive satisfaction from the fact (usually false and always irrelevant) that a work of art is traceable to a 'true story.' Is it because we begin to respect ourselves more when we learn that the writer, just like ourselves, was not clever enough to make up a story himself?")

For him, all of them—those hyper-auto-realists calculating and writing themselves—were like clones, with that banal uniformity that airplane passengers acquire: different but all tightly secured by identical seatbelts. And seeing them and reading them, he suffered that nausea you feel confronting someone so concerned with their own authenticity that they end up making how artificial they are even more obvious. What in robotics is known as the theory of the "uncanny valley": the mistrust and fear produced by all things that weren't human but had the between pathological and functional need to be/appear just like humans.

And, oh, all of those people who weren't writers but needed so badly to appear like writers—serially and seriously assembling themselves, as if on an assembly line—were so busy telling themselves that nobody else mattered, because why read others when you can write about yourself, why invent others when you could falsify yourself.

For him, on the other hand, reality had always been something more akin to gasoline: it was good for getting you places, but it had no utility in and of itself, and you couldn't even drink it to quench that always-unquenchable, always-thirsty thirst.

And in this way, he thought, reality (classical reality, reality of everyone, of shared History and not each person's history) was becoming an antiquity of the future. Something many people (so concerned in the present with their pasts as if that was where their futures lay) preferred to think of—to conceal the terror of understanding themselves as passengers of yesterday—as retro or vintage. Reality was, for them, merely the uninteresting realities to be spread, like the sparks of a forest fire where so many trees burned, trees that would never now become that paper doomed to be replaced by the cilice of screens.

Thus, also, the compulsive addiction to the latest model of the gadget of the day. To being up to date and present in the present. At one time it had been enough to get a new car or a new house or even a new partner. Now you had to change *everything*. Modernizing was like not aging but—paradox—submitting yourself to the latest update that was up-to-date for less and less time and aged out of utility more and more quickly (and forced used-up users to become inexpert experts of increasingly rare and untreatable technological bugs in something that all of a sudden was barely less than an attention-demanding relative and significantly more than a cyclothymic pet and thus the carapace of the disheartening iPhone like the turtle shell and the Twitter notification like the canary song). And, from there—from those screens that you had to update day and night to be able to project yourself—they broadcast themselves, convinced that they were being seen and heard and read everywhere and all the time. Followed from afar in false proximity by followers giving out likes and little hearts (there was no longer any value placed on that sophisticated and rare emotion of liking and disliking something at the same time) and always wanting so badly to share everything—look but don't touch—they had to post so that they never truly shared anything with their "like"-happy followers. Because the important thing wasn't what enthused you, but to be an enthusiast who enthused everyone else's hunger for enthusiasm. The importing thing was to post yourself posting. And what you posted became secondary and was quickly replaced by the next post.

And so he—who neither took nor posted nor shared photographs—had recently been accused of talking about himself all the time, because, yes, he wasn't constantly clicking and posting his life. And so, it was enough for him to tell one or two things that'd happened to him—and that nobody had seen on social media, where he had no presence and refused to have one—at a gathering for him to be considered an insufferable narcissist and compulsive self-referencer. To top it off, he expressed himself in words and not in photographs (at most, he sent emails every now and then that were rarely replied to, because everyone had gotten out of the habit now that they were used to just responding with a thumbs-up). Absolute hubris on his part: you had to listen to him and to imagine instead of seeing what he was explaining . . . Describing something that could be seen/shown was a lack of respect and a waste of other peoples' time and was so outmoded. (How did that old but ageless song by The Kinks go? "People Take Pictures of Each Other"? Yes: there the storyteller voice of Ray Davies singing with the voice of Ray Davies. With the same voice that in another song promised "I'll remember everything you said to me." That voice that wanted to forget now what before it'd wanted to preserve forever and almost horrified by how people never stopped taking pictures of each other. Pictures taken almost by force. The ones and the others, incessantly taking pictures of each other just to prove that they really existed. And closing with—over a playful melody and after freezing the listener's blood with the certainty that true love that would stay with you forever wasn't photographable and, if you tried to capture it, it would always come out blurry—an almost sighing "Don't show me no more, please . . ." And that other Ray Davies song—off the same album, *The Kinks Are the Village Green Preservation Society*—about the forgotten art of, again and again, turning the pages of a photo album, a "Picture Book," with all those people smiling at the camera "to prove they love each other, a long time ago." Pictures in a book and not on a phone, yes. And he'd always remembered, yes. But he'd never forgotten to avoid taking pictures while traveling and of his travels. He didn't do it because he didn't want to share them. His travels were his and only his and nothing interested him more—being unable to rely on the memory-aid of his own postcards—than how they were transformed into something else, into travels of another kind. Into *voyages extraordinaires*, far more precise in their precision when it came to being selectively or capriciously recalled: the hotels he slept in intermingling with the hotels of his dreams, his unpunctual flights taking off just as he decided to check in for them.) And those photographs were stillborn and their residual power lasted but a click. Pictures that—unlike true photographs, from before, photographs that were carefully considered—didn't seem to grow younger as those who took them grew older and looked at them over and over to remember what something that no longer was had been like. Or never looked at them, because they were for others, for everyone else, to look at. Snapshots, yes, that sooner or later would disappear or be impossible to "recover" (that memory would be impossible to recover) when all hard drives went soft forever. Pictures of meals, of landscapes and of trips, of jewels and of cars, of the celebrities people bumped into and the ones they, shrieking, chased down and captured. Pictures of all the material matters they'd experienced in person but via a third digital eye, like a finger in their eyes and not in their foreheads. And, every so often, pictures of more or less loved ones they're always kissing or hugging with almost strangling and vampiric fury, arms aloft and in their hands a phone (and more than once he'd wondered how he could start the rumor that it'd been discovered that every picture subtracted five years from the life of its taker to see if in that way, maybe . . .). Yes: you had to provide—for yourself and everyone else—constant and irrefutable proof of your existence. And, at the same time, you had to reinvent reality, making it attractive and enviable and worthy of being shared nonstop, as if it were historical when actually it was just hysterical. A reality of their own that wasn't necessarily realistic or (un)worthy of an irreal realistic novel where everything seemed to fall in line with the discipline, as efficient as it was predictable, of a military march.

There was a time when you had to *work* to impose your own existence on everyone else: you had to do *something* before you became *someone*. Now it was enough—or so a good part of humanity had been led to believe—to have a "social media profile" without really having do anything or even leaving home. You no longer had to do anything but exist.

And so, in his experience, out of all his contemporaries who called themselves writers and who "didn't want to appear locked in their ivory towers" (becoming reality posters and influencers—always ready to rate or take down second and third parties, always bad influencers; it was clear that the Web hadn't invented hate but it had *ensnared* it and wrapped it up like a quick and easy gift to be sent anywhere free of charge—not through peoples' style of writing but through the millimetric documentation of their own non/existences with blog-tweet dissonance and the pathological and desperate and deceitful passion of being your own biggest fan) barely 25 percent of them had anything to say or write about all of that. The remaining 75 percent, he was sure, shielded themselves (some with more heteronyms than Fernando Pessoa, which they used to worship/electrocute themselves) behind their public reality, presenting it as part of their private reality. And as far as he (who recognized the symptom immediately, because some time ago he'd lost the ability to invent and dream, but he had no desire to conceal his drought by watering his barren lands with stagnant water) was concerned they did that and put that out there because, simply, nothing—or nothing irreal and original and personal and theirs and only theirs—occurred for them or occurred to them. And, yes, in more than one interview back when he used to be interviewed regularly—more regularly than he was read (so they could ask him to repeat over and over anecdotes about his encounters with Bob Dylan and Ray Davies or with that legendary filmmaker/painter and founder of the exceedingly experimental Páramo Pictures, whom he'd come to refer to as The Living Deadman: a man he'd been friends with during the his final years, a friendship that had turned him into a kind of appendix to the legend of the man's brief and fragile life and invulnerable death and expansive and powerful body of work) and because they considered him "clever" and "funny," but not now, never again, never ever—he'd described himself "a writer profoundly engaged with my own irreality." And over and over he quoted Vladimir Nabokov and his "Reality is overrated" and Marcel Proust and his "There is no enemy more skillful than reality" and Saul Bellow when he criticized writers who didn't hesitate to indiscriminately embrace every just cause simply because they were writers, writers who suddenly looked more like "actors who behave like writers . . . Art itself is secondary now, for the public rejoices in artists rather than in art."

And then he asked and asked himself whether, really, there was any way to be more authentic and purer and absolutely realist than to create a new reality. That was a *for real* realist writer: someone who took something irreal and made it real. And unlike all those writers who went around preoccupied not about the real but about the realistic. A true realist had the mission of pointing out everything that was irreal in day-to-day and night-to-night life.

And something he was *very* sure of, something that seemed *so* sad to him, was thinking of the possibility of a writer, unpublished and a genius and outside all recognizable coordinates—maybe someone called to write the next *Tristram Shandy* or any other story where the past is so clever it's never allowed to catch up to the present—tired of being misunderstood by publishers, telling himself that, in order to finally get published, the best thing to do was to set all those "strange things" and any "personal and unmistakable tics" aside. Heeding the warning of André Gide: "The public acclaims only what it already knows, what it recognizes; if you set out to do something new, that public gets upset and won't make things easy for you" (and likewise, though mistaken this time, Samuel Johnson declaring that "Nothing odd will do long. *Tristram Shandy* did not last"). And that writer becomes convinced it would be better to write something *of the moment*. Something like the Great Novel of the Illegal Immigrant Deported After Thirty Years of Living in the USA Who Climbs Back Over That Wall to Be Reunited with His Family, Etc. And he wrote it. And it was a hit. And with the fame and prizes that writer would remember his beginnings like a passing fever, like something that, fortunately, had passed and had never really happened to him. Something that had been replaced by and for him by the overvaluation of the current and the real and of the novel as primary material and device that had to "concern itself with its time" and all of that. And doing all of that with consideration of and appreciation for and attention to the figure of the reader, a reader that he and his work never had apart from himself and a handful of others that never exceeded the fingers on one hand.

And he always remembered those two notecards from *The Original of Laura* where Nabokov made reference to how "all those writers were stunning mediocrities" and how "they were supposed to 'represent an era' and that such representants could get away with the most execrable writing, provided they represent their times."

Whereas, for him, what was outside of time and place and reality was something that revealed far more about an era and a culture. That's why he thought that you had to dedicate present and the future to recreating—to recreating, to reinventing—the past. That thing that'd already happened (the truth is that prophets always bring up terrible news from the past that nobody wants to remember; and so the people who listen to them in the present deceive themselves and become convinced that they're predicting future events), but that seems increasingly unbelievable and hard to accept in the here and now. That's why, in addition, contemplating the past—first rereading it and then rewriting it—is only bearable if you dress it up in the nostalgia devoted to something that'll never happen again but that, having happened, keeps happening and changing depending on the voice of the person reinterpreting it. (He'd written something about all of this in one of his own books: "Nothing is more useless than a writer with an infallible memory. A writer with a good memory doesn't remember anything because he doesn't forget anything. For a writer, forgetfulness and the ability to forget are indispensable gifts. A writer constructs his work first by making himself forget and then by unmaking his memory. A writer must forget everything he wants to tell and find out not how it happened but how what happened will happen." Or something like that.)

And he got all mixed up thinking about all these things that he thought about, because he could no longer put them in writing, while in the earbuds the flight attendants had given him, Bob Dylan sighs and sings that song once sung by a crooner with an intact voice or by a pianist in black and white. A song to kill immortal time (and that in its original version included a couple introductory verses with allusions to Einstein and the Theory of Relativity and to a third temporal dimension) while everyone wants to leave that place they return to over and over. That thing about how "The fundamental things apply . . . As time goes by . . ." and how "It's the same old story . . . A fight for love and glory . . . A case of do or die." And that song was followed by another of his favorites and, hey, when did Paul McCartney record a version of "We Three (My Echo, My Shadow and Me)"? What would his Uncle Hey Walrus have thought of this? His "P." devoting himself to doing versions of standards from the school that he and his three friends and Bob Dylan (who was also singing Sinatraesque songs now) had helped destroy, when they no longer needed other people's verses, because they were writing and singing their own. Songs that were theirs, personal, impossible to separate from their personalities but, nevertheless, with no obligation to be strictly autobiographical, with no mandate to tell their own stories in their songs (and that's why, in his day, Bob Dylan insisted over and over and without anyone believing him that the pained and spiteful and vengeful album *Blood on the Tracks* had nothing to do with his then-in-process divorce and a great deal to do with his appropriation of some stories by Anton Chekhov and with singing and storytelling as if he had "yesterday, today, and tomorrow all in the same room").

But the song he was listening to now was something else. A different song about the three parts of loneliness: echo and shadow and me. One of many songs written by people who didn't know how to sing and who knew they would never be singing them in public. Because there were other people for that: singers who did know how to sing, but didn't know how to write the songs they knew how to sing. A song that for him had always been the closest thing there was to a complete writing workshop in the span of three minutes. A writing workshop where all you were taught was to memorize a verse that sang about how much a few words could contain. An immensity singing: "Imagine the book you would like to read and sit down and write it and that's all I have to teach you and now go home and good luck." But really imagine, all the way, without limits; looking at yourself in the mirror, but no, just at your eyes though with your eyes closed, imagining everything that could be seen beyond your eyelids. Something that, yes, had a thing or two to teach many of those hyper-egoistic auto-fictioneers about the borders between what happened and what could happen even though it hadn't happened and about the limits you had to come to know and to acknowledge before even starting to think about putting any of it in writing.

Not long ago, in a Michael Ondaatje novel, he'd read and underlined the following: "I suppose there are traditions and tropes in stories like this. Someone is given a test to carry out. No one knows who the truth bearer is. People are not who or where they think they are. And there is someone who watches from an unknown location . . . Remember that. Your own story is just one, and perhaps not the important one. The self is not the principal thing."

Yes: the basics and the same old story and the question of to be or not to be. And my echo and my shadow and me. We three, we're alone—"we're not a crowd, we're not even company," as the song sings—but living in a single memory and wondering "What good is the moonlight, the silvery moonlight that shines above? I walk with my shadow. I talk with my echo. But where is the one I love?"

Reality—that thing that both he and his favorite writers considered over-rated and that even experts in quantum mechanics were beginning to consider a kind of agreed-on hallucination—was, ironically and paradoxically, built out of equal parts invention and dream and memory, out of volatile matter that never stopped mutating.

Reality that Vladimir Nabokov—in his epilogue to *Lolita*—defined as "one of the words which mean nothing without quotes."

Reality was the echo of a shadow that you cast across yourself.

Reality that didn't always measure the same size or weigh in at the same weight.

Reality that expanded or contracted with no fixed pattern or predictable rhythm.

Reality that wasn't a whole or complete thing but fragmentary and unfinished and far from perfect.

Reality that could sometimes be found, compressed, on the TV news: in those brief seconds of silence and delay between the question of the anchor in the studio and the answer of the weatherman there outside, live and direct.

The poor guy trying to inform everyone that this was going to be the perfect storm, while wind and rain slammed him around the frame of the TV screen. There, far away but within reach of the hand holding the remote control, his smile tense and dripping, wearing the did-you-really-need-to-send-me-out-here-to-tell-you-that-the-weather-is-shit-and-it's-best-you-stay-home face. And, nevertheless, there are still those fools who go out and smile for that news channel's camera, as if to say, "It's scary out here" and then proceed to take selfies in front of huge waves or colossal tornados, probably thinking that they'll hold still to keep from coming out blurry in the picture and won't pull them out to sea or up into the sky. And he looked at them thinking: "Oh, ah-ha: that's precisely how I feel, really, truly: frightened and suicidal and stupid and wondering what am I doing here and why did I venture out against all odds and prognostication."

Reality that—contrary to what was almost always thought—hadn't begun with the Big Bang, but 100,000,000 years before the first light, with a dark radiation of the darkest depths, setting an empty stage with neither actors nor performance, like an avant-garde retro-narrative, until the conditions were right for the first, titanic stars to come onstage and shine, stars that, like his own parents, died so young and did not leave behind good looking corpses.

Reality that could last a whole night: that night that belonged to him and to Penelope and to Uncle Hey Walrus when—more characters than people—two children and their uncle went looking for parents they would never find. A vast night in which, as some poet said, men are so small.

Reality that, it was said, was something you only glimpsed out of the corner of your eye or—nothing more and nothing less—that was right in front of you.

And so he closed his eyes to better perceive it, as it really was.

And he understood that reality was, in the end, what one chose to remember of it.

And that that was never that much.

Most of reality dissolved in the air of oblivion.

The real part was—just and only—real in part.

And warning: a lot of what comes next could be introduced with the words "He remembers a dream he invented once . . ."

It's no coincidence, he thinks, that they referred to those inventive and dreaming and remembering books as "memoirs." Plural and not singular because memory is multiple. Memory is not one thing. And it changes depending on the mood you're in when you invoke or evoke it, often, under the influence of multiple memories memorizing the same event from different angles. And there's a distinct possibility that all the people who're praised for their "good memories" really—especially as they got older and had to hide the despair of forgetting things and needed to reassert themselves in front of acquaintances and strangers whose names they were not entirely sure of— are nothing but inventors and liars, claiming to perfectly remember things that never happened. And that was why the construction of what's accepted and studied as History (Histories, plural, was the title, στορίαι meaning "approximations, investigations," in ancient Greek of Herodotus) was actually built on rickety foundations and quicksand and temperamental seismic fault lines on top of which everything moved and nothing stayed still, which was why all of it could come crashing down at the most imprecise and unexpected yet most pondered and anticipated moment.

The same thing happened with all those fictions that pretended to be "a faithful reflection of the moment in which they were conceived" and all of that. Yes: all those writers who called themselves realists and were always so concerned with reality always made him feel some combination pity and disdain. To him they seemed (and he remembers that at some point he promised himself he wouldn't use—the same goes for the expressions, frequently reiterated in his work, "special defect" or "special effect"—the image of weathermen as a comparison for anything; but, of course, their forecasts often failed and missed the mark and the true purpose of umbrellas was not to protect you from the rain, but to be forgotten somewhere and never found when they were needed most) like, again, those suffering men and women on the TV news. Live and in person and out there under the open sky, shivering and shaken. Like you had to see them out there—so elemental in the fury of the elements, beaten down in the downpour, blown away in the wind—to know that outside thunder was rolling and lightning was flashing.

For him, back when he still wrote, the pleasure resided and was found in just the opposite: in creating something new, something that'd never been there or never happened before. Or that'd been there but had never been seen *like that* before. Something different and unknown and, yes, most definitely unsettling and difficult to assimilate on the basis of a theretofore only intuited, as if in a dream, familiarity. And so, for that reason, it was something that counted on writers—or at least on some writers—to recount it and to make it count. And for them to make it real no matter how unbelievable it seemed to be, because (was it the hyper-realist Émile Zola who said it?) in the end and when all was said and done, all writers were absolute and complete realists in their own eyes, in their way of seeing reality. Something that—sure—might end up having little or nothing to do with the reality of others or with that version of agreed-on reality everyone acknowledged to keep from going crazy. After all, that vocation or drive to make the things of this world strange (to superimpose their own singular reality over them, like that kind of varnish that revealed more of what it was protecting) never endangered the continuity and diffusion of the, for him, badly named realist novel. Because as he'd always thought and said on more than one occasion: there were no storylines more irreal than those of *realist* novels, so organized and detailed and reliant on dramatic timing. Because the experimental gestures of the avant-garde, paradoxically and possibly, strengthened all those storylines that were "like life itself." Because their *abnormal* books—without wanting to but at the same time not putting up a fight—did nothing but revitalize all those "normal" anecdotes and make them all the more attractive and gratifying And, that was why, it was highly likely that small multitudes had fled from his books toward the books of others (something that would never occur in the opposite direction). All those possible and subsequently impossible readers (maybe scared away by the reviews of his books, which were appreciative and even laudatory, but also always confessing they were exhausted by the journey the books had made them take), as if they were throwing themselves from the windows of a burning mansion, shrieking and running away from his books. Books that were "difficult" and "excessive" and had "too many pages" (and he'd read that in more than a few of the articles dedicated to them and he thought "The only thing that doesn't belong in this book is you, you illiterate . . . and let's see if for once you dare to point out exactly which pages are excessive") and considered "experimental" because they weren't full of dialogue or descriptive passages; because their characters didn't have names; because his sentences—which paid more attention to what the author thought about his characters than to what those characters were doing—were long and overrun with subordinate clauses; because they were full of quotes and references to *other* books and *other* writers they hadn't read (which provoked, indistinctly, a feeling of guilty inferiority or of proud superiority for not having wasted their time); and because every so often inside them there occurred a never entirely justified and not even all that risky— always with a safety net—typographical pirouette.

Yes, he confesses, it was him, he did it: he had a lot to tell, a lot to recount, because, for him, there was a lot that counted. So yes: too much work and they all ran off to realist novels, somewhere they felt a bit more at home. Thanks—you're welcome—to him. Because nothing was less interesting than a writer's writer to people looking for reader's writer.

And his explanations that writing *like that* was natural and easy for him, while writing "simply" or "classically" was like an impossible-to-cross abyss, were all for naught. So he watched them all run off into the sunset. Wreathed in his own fire, atop the highest tower, screaming down at them— with something that seemed a little too close to embarrassment for them but also a little for himself—about how could they not see that Art was difficult not because it wanted to be difficult, Art was difficult because it wanted to be Art. Or something like that. The kind of thing he tended to say and that, he thought and wanted to believe, sounded inspired, but, also, no doubt, worn out to all those who've long since struck out for greener pastures; to those who'd already gone elsewhere, somewhere, they were convinced, they would be treated better. And where they would be told about things they could identify with, things they could recognize, things that made them feel that they were characters worth narrating too, things that had nothing to do with the things he was now repeating over and over again, like a crazed weatherman, broadcasting from an airplane flying through the most perfect of storms, a storm based—really, truly—on a true storm.

His *The Impossible Story* ("a book of good faith," as Montaigne had quipped about his own book; a labor-intensive read for everyone else, yes, but with the perfect and unquestionable alibi of, first, having cost him a great deal of labor to put in writing) had been, of course, one of those "excessive" and "difficult" books. And, also, one of those books that was pleased and resignedly happy to be just that, to be precisely *like that*. (And he remembered what rock critic Robert Hilburn had said about how—once the golden age of the '60s had passed—rock bands had divided into those who made active music and those who made passive music. The passive artists of the '70s were all those frequent and modulated bands—Toto, Boston, Foreigner, Kansas, Styx—offering up a sound with no mystery and no doubt and ready to be played nimbly and comfortably; while the active artists—people like Elvis Costello, Talking Heads, Patti Smith, and The Clash—took the gamble of saying something different instead of going for the reflexive and automatic commercial success. Music that was more memorable and memorizable. And the same thing—similar parameters—could now be applied to literature, he thought.)

And he would bet anything (though nobody would take the bet since the result was as obvious as it was immutable) that nobody in this other plane was reading one of his books, just as nobody was listening to The Kinks in their headphones. Not even out of curiosity about the sudden and catastrophic resurrection of *The Impossible Story* in the realm of politics (and he preferred not to remember that now to, inevitably, remember it again when he didn't want to remember it, but at least, for now, he could avoid going into detail). Maybe, probably, the closest thing to that book of his—not in terms of style, but in terms of proximity—was one Penelope's gothic deliriums. Copies of which he *had* detected all throughout the cabin: because Penelope's publisher had chosen to print her book covers in phosphorescent ink, which gave them an almost supernatural glow in the half-light inside the airplane. There they were, there was Penelope: in the soft adolescent hands of readers (taking adolescence as that age—*adul*escence—that now spanned almost half a century). And he was so moved and a little frightened that Penelope's fans always read her in the organic format and never electronically because, they sighed, "that way we can touch her better." And that, still, none of them were interested in reading supposed truths, but just the opposite. Because Penelope's readers read to go elsewhere. And good for them. And, so, along the way, they'd convinced themselves that they loved the dead Penelope more than they loved their own barely alive parents.

And, yes, so, the idea—his—was that *The Impossible Story* would be the first of three books (trilogies were in vogue) that would end up being a single book that spoke one language but changed tone when inventing and dreaming and remembering. But never renouncing its idiosyncrasies during the long ascent, so that readers—finding themselves on the summit—would discover that they were in the mountains, that they were *one* mountain, that the mountain had climbed the mountain. And he'd invented and dreamed so much about that moment and coronation at the greatest of heights—though he would never arrive—he relived it now as the most unforgettable of memories.

Enumerating all of the books, the one book.

Books that were hard to describe—and to write—but recognizable from the opening page.

Books in which the protagonist wouldn't be him but in which he would be those books.

Books that were like an elephant, like Hannibal's elephants that once scaled mountain passes and, true, very few of them survived crossing the Alps, but they tried.

Books with elephantine memory, yet never renouncing the even more expansive amnesia of fish.

Books so voluminous and deafening and trumpeting and tusked that they were never "set free" via that absurd and passing trend of bookcrossing and would never be locatable via a *site* in the hollow of a tree (like empty bottles or used condoms), because no tree could hold them. And because he wanted his books to be of the take-no-prisoners variety: not capturing anyone and definitely not setting anyone free, forcing all comers to read them point-blank and as if they were in flames.

Books that for him signified an end of all of that, so he could start over with all of this and feel something like that epiphany Saul Bellew had in Paris—in 1949, after publishing his first two books that were so contained and disciplined, not knowing how or where to go from there—watching the city employees opening fire hydrants to let the water run; and then the sound and the sight of the water running across the cobblestones made Bellow think he would write something like that, because he needed to write something like that: something uncontainable and torrential and liquid with full "freedom of movement." And that sight reminded Bellow of a childhood friend, named August, who, when they were playing checkers, liked to yell: "I got a scheme!" And, yes, all of a sudden he also had a scheme, a map with an X on it. And that shift had worked out really well for him and—even though *The Impossible Story* had something of that unmistakable style where ideas melted into actions and thoughts into events—it hadn't worked out so well for him. But no one could take away the gains of his clever scheme, even if he had wound up lost and collapsing like an alpine pachyderm with no space left in its memory for everything it wanted to forget.

Books that nobody would make it out of alive but as if revived, transfigured, different from how they went in, asking themselves the unanswerable questions of where had they gone and what had they done there. Because it wasn't that he wanted editors and critics and readers and translators to suffer, no; but he did want them to be fully and absolutely aware, in their own bodies and minds, of everything he'd gone through in writing those books. That it be more than clear to them that he'd devoted years to that book to which they'd dedicated a handful of hours. And that, as such, he was far more exhausted and run ragged and that the payment he'd earned writing it—if it were distributed to him over the period of employment—was even less than what they would receive for skimming it and, if they were literary critics, handing in the often unfair judgement of a few horizontal lines. (And, yes, the guy in charge of the failed audiobook version of *The Impossible Story* had disappeared a few pages into the recording and they were still looking for him or they said they'd found him naked and talking to himself and running along a beach, along a different beach, but a beach that was the natural extension of that beach from his childhood. A different—yet the same—beach that soon, terminal, would go up in flames, he thought then.)

Books that bore no resemblance to that philosopher's stone of the species that all the new alchemists hoped and aspired to write. ("The key to success is to find a book that's written for people who don't like to read . . . A book that looks like a book, but that, really, is something else," a young publisher had once, with a conspiratorial wink, confessed to him. One of those disturbing and almost-adolescent publishers whom—on his insomniac nights—he imagined as those frenetic a-go-go dancers on musical TV shows from the '60s and '70s, a scenario wherein, without a doubt, writers were like the dancers cautiously twisting inside cages that hung from very thin chains. That publisher was a meticulous and clever producer of those increasingly success-ful book-toys, so gratifying to possess and so unnecessary to ever open, because they were made to be looked at and not to be read. One of many publishers who—with their apparent satisfaction and *unspoiled-monster* self-esteem—barely concealed the panic of gam-blers betting at random. For a while now, the publishing world had been one of the few markets immune to all the prognostications of the so-called *coolhunters*. It turned out to be impossible to predict what would be the next global success, just like—thanks to climate change—it was increasingly complex to anticipate a sunny tomorrow and, no, enough about weathermen, right? Although it was also true that one of the movies that he would have liked to have written starred Nicolas Cage in the role of a TV weatherman who dreamed of writing a science-fiction novel and who was looked down on by his father, a literary titan and winner of a Pulitzer with the face of Michael Caine and . . . The instant hit was just as likely to be a brainy essay by an Oxford intellectual as it was to be the sexual deliriums of a Nevada housewife hooked on antidepressants. Anything was possi-ble. *Thing*—not *book*, much less *literature*—being the operative word. And the publisher added: "The reader should never have to rise to the author's level. It's on the supplier to meet his customers where they are. And the reader is the customer and the customer is always right. Your books, for example: they're like climbing Everest with no oxygen and no Sherpa and no training. I think I heard you compare them to a mountain or something once, right? Well, that's just it. The problem is that, in this landscape, you're like the Yeti: you never show yourself, no one knows if you actually exist or why you're out there running around, in the rare event that you deign to come out of your cave . . . And so you scare people. And leave them feeling cold. And thirsty.

Because didn't you also say something about how literature is like a desert that has nothing in it because everything fits and only the bravest venture out into its shifting dunes and quicksands? Sure: the young master is like Lawrence of Arabia: a glorious bastard who likes his Al-Nefud because it's clean and has no sponsored kiosks and no palm trees along the road where you can stop and rest. But Lawrence was a madman and I don't know if you know this, but Peter O'Toole hated every minute he spent on that filmset out in the desert. And O'Toole always said that only God and lunatics love the desert . . . But let me tell you: straight up literature is the driest of all deserts. And it's a deserted desert where only once in a great while a fleeting vision blooms. . . But, of course, you don't write children's books or TV or film screenplays or essays on soccer or politics and you don't even connect with your readers on social media . . . And let's not even start on your radio show, as brief as it was unforgettable . . . That thing you read about the girl of the swimming pool . . . Wow . . . Debut and adieu . . . It seems like the books are all that interest you! And what books! Especially that last one you published, that kind of concrete block that, if it fell on your foot, would probably leave you limping for life . . . What was it called? . . . *The Impossible Story*, right? . . . That book is what makes the story impossible to read, ha . . . It makes no sense to put in all that work and—maybe without realizing it—you were even calling yourself out with the title: this story is impossible to read, ha . . ." And he, hearing all of this, had neither the strength nor the desire to tell the young publisher that he'd made the same joke twice in a matter of seconds. And that maybe that was a consequence of too much retweeting. In any case, the publisher didn't realize it and went right on with his rant: "Because, even if they do rise to the challenge, readers will only reach the summit if they haven't frozen to death or been buried by an avalanche along the way. And what's the reward that awaits them if they do make it to the top? Nothing but turning around and starting the agonizing and anticlimactic hangover of the descent, with no one to talk to, because they're unlikely to find other readers of your books in the vicinity, someone with whom they can feel complicit and share opinions with and swap selfies with your book in hand. These days people read so they can post that they're reading. So there's nothing for them to post about your books except that they failed to read them. And there's nothing people like less than feeling like they failed. It's not fair to give so much for so little in return. Books shouldn't be as hard to read as they are to write, my friend." And the thing that bothered him most in that whole tirade was the "my friend" at the end. But the title of that book, *The Impossible Story*, had always given him pause. And he tried not to think about it. But—again, more details coming up, he can't help remembering it, after all, it was the reason he'd been on multiple airplanes and was now out here in the desert—its title had recently come back with a vengeance, when it became the punchline of a lame joke between lightweight politicians in heavyweight combat. A joke that opened the door to his flight/expulsion and, without a doubt, more on that after these not-so-commercial commercials, commercials that his parents would've hated. Commercials for the anti-commercial *The Impossible Story*. And so, he preferred to think of *The Impossible Story* as—a far worse and more self-flagellating title—*The Last Book I Wrote*. And then to add—could there be an emoji for this? or one of those GIFs that looped a short fragment of something, for example, Robert De Niro at the end of *Taxi Driver* bringing one bloody finger to his head, pretending to shoot himself and "pfffffff"?—an "Oh God!" An "Oh God!" with the tone and intensity with which atheists and agnostics think about *That* and about *Him*. Those nonbelievers who say, "Oh God!" far more frequently and with greater suffering devotion than the true believers who really just believe in the existence of *Something* or *Someone* who listens to their confessions in order to forgive them all their failings. While the nonbelievers who take His name in vain—with that moan, with that "Oh God!," which is far more deeply felt and agonizing than that of the devout millions who consider Him an "imaginary friend" accompanying them from childhood until the end of their days—are actually invoking His unnamable absence. Believing beyond all shadow of a doubt that no one is listening, that nobody's out there, that the Holy Ghost won't be knocking three times to make manifest the Second Coming after the first and last leaving and won't be coming to the rescue, like an avenging angel from a comic book. And that, also, it's virtually and virtuously impossible and unbelievable that someone who is thirty-three years old would still have twelve or, better, eleven really good friends to invite to a last supper; because people only have that many friends during the undiscriminating and unreflective and ultra-affectionate years of childhood. Though, soon, almost right away, some of those great friends ran away or rejected the person of the host for reasons that weren't hard to understand. There isn't anybody out there, no. There is *nOh God!* and, at most, it had to be acknowledged that believing in the properties of holy water wasn't all that different from putting your faith in homeopathic tinctures. And so the emphasis of the expression, when expressed, was put more on the *Oh* than on the *God!* And *The Impossible Story*—which had signified for him a kind of brief resurrection and irrefutable proof that the line separating Icarus from the Phoenix was very thin—had been a book that belonged, without a shadow of a doubt, to the *Oh God!* genre. One of those books whose true subject was to point to a Great Beyond that no longer had anything in it, and, at the same time, it was one of those books you really had to believe in to be able to read. A book that fervently believed in not believing. Or in believing in nothing but books like that book. Books that you had to read to believe. Beyond that, the void. The only thing that *was* there, the only thing—alas, he lamented—left in all that antimatter was publishers with good ideas. Publishers were the new writers. The young publishers—carefully watched over by the older and eternal titans who never deprived themselves of nostalgic bacchanals—who always lived the wild and partying lives lived by writers at the beginning of the twentieth century who now lived the domestic and rather opaque and even depressing lives lived by publishers at the beginning of the twentieth century. Role reversal, indeed. Changing of the guard. And the first of those ideas, for present-day publishers, was why be a writer with nothing and nobody when you could be a publisher and have multiple writers to play with as if playing Candy Crush Saga. And oh oh oh God: he was even coming up with mobile-game imagery and metaphors and the truth is he felt more comfortable with . . . uh . . . with the weathermen on the TV news. And before long that same publisher—leaning on the bar in that supposedly legendary restaurant always frequented by the local intelligentsia, a place with an Italian name that'd always looked to him like it'd been decorated by Austin Powers's idiot brother and that, in recent years, had even been reinvented as a venue for launching and celebrating all the books that were derivative of and paid tribute to and were sometimes even direct-descendants of the geniuses and figures who, upon arriving from the New World to conquer the local literary scene, had been known to entrench themselves there for a few unforgettable years, divine and more ambidextrous than left-handed, amid gin and tonics and bloody marys, more *morts-vivants* than *bon-vivants*, before their inevitable victory—had proposed a project he considered "ideal" for him. "Because Dylan is like God for you, right?" the publisher gave him a full-toothed smile. And proceeded to explain his proposal, baring his fangs all the while and, yes, publishers had better teeth than writers because they ate better and did more biting. The thing was that, not long ago, in one of his few more or less public appearances, Bob Dylan—an almost pathological cinephile, habitually stealing lines from films to insert in the verses of his songs—had compiled a list for the American Film Institute of his one hundred favorite films. And the young publisher had the idea of putting together an "instant book" that looked at each of the films in question as well as their more or less transparent or oblique connections to the songs the songwriter—who, in addition, had just been awarded, amid true controversy, the Nobel Prize for Literature—wrote. And he—a Dylanite who believed in all things Dylan, closer to the "Oh, Bob" than the "Oh, God"—was interested in the project. And it even made him feel a kind of enthusiasm he hadn't felt in a long time. And he wrote an impassioned prologue and went so far as to compose texts jam-packed with quotes and allusions and footnotes. But his nonfiction was rejected for basically the same reasons as his fiction. Too complex and "excessive." And "you use three pages to say something you could say in three sentences or maybe, better, not say at all." For the publisher, his piece contained "too much information and

too many references," it was "too cult" and "it would scare away potential readers who would feel left out or, possibly, inferior." "Okay, so you
mean just like what Bob Dylan does and the effect he produces, right?"
he said by way of defense, with the absurd pride of a realization that
only dawns on you as you say it. Then the publisher looked at him
with pity and was silent for a few seconds, probably thinking about
how he could turn his rejoinder into a tweet. And then he said: "Yes,
but Bob Dylan is Bob Dylan. And Bob Dylan has Bob Dylan's fans."
And he didn't know whether to hug him or spit in his face for having
had the merciful tact not to add but just think—and he read it like a
subtitle across the young publisher's chest—a "And, also, Bob Dylan
has Bob Dylan's talent." And to alleviate the awkward moment a little—though the ice was already irreparably broken for the worse and
he'd been dropped into the freezing waters of a bone-chilling conversation—the publisher, seeing how horrible he felt, gave him another
pitying look. And offered him the following words, as if they were . . .
as if they were . . . as if they were a towel soaked in warm and viscous
and greenish soup—and where did he come up with these metaphors,
clearly he was touched by the darkness and few were the people who
could read his mind without uttering a curse or a *vade retro*—like
what that girl in *The Exorcist* vomited. Sure: he thought like one possessed, he thought in tongues, in too many tongues. But the words he
heard next were the blow that finally finished him off and came from
the mouth of someone who, for him, could only have been possessed
by the spirit of diabolical times: "Maybe it would be good for you to
talk to this booktuber & influencer I know, so she can explain to you
once and for all how all of this works. . . I'm sure you've heard of her.
She was the one who tweeted out all of Proust using inclusive language, because in her words: 'Proust became the first great feminist
writer when he transformed the men who had inspired certain characters in his novel into women.' And, sure, she's not particularly
bright when it comes literature, strictly speaking, and someone had
to explain to her the real reason why Proust did that. But the girl is
an absolute genius when it comes to self-promotion. Her new thing is
sharing mini-clips in which she dramatizes *The Odyssey* with a

Funko Pop doll . . . Plus, I must say, she's really nice to look at; but don't tell anyone I said that, for the times they are a changing." In that moment he realized that the constant fear defenseless or easily-offended readers end up feeling when they read—publishers already admitted without a shred of guilt or remorse that they thought more about readers than they did about writers, more about the reading than about the writing; or maybe it had always been like that, but he'd preferred not to see it and definitely not to read it—stemmed from something that was now a generational problem. From an insurmountable shift in the way people looked at the world and sought to understand how it worked. Because when he was growing up, all he wanted was to be shown what he didn't know. And the more arcane or inaccessible or difficult to track down, the better. Having someone reveal to you how much you *didn't* know didn't make you feel powerless, just the opposite: suddenly you found yourself more excited and alert and on the prowl than ever. Now—with the availability of almost everything via online search engines—finding stuff out was so easy that the eroticism of information that belonged to a select few had been completely lost, from the foreplay of the search, to the climax of the discovery. And that's why, for a lot of people it was enough and more than enough to watch some kid narrate a book with truly moronic diction and syntax and, as such, far more "complex" and "difficult to understand"—for all the wrong reasons—than his own. And to pay attention to him and act like remote-controlled robots. And so, in its day, in 1831, the publication of Victor Hugo's *The Hunchback of Notre Dame*, had provoked universal interest in a cathedral that at the time was in ruin and nobody was really paying any attention to and that'd even been considered for demolition. While the fire that burned that jewel of global tourism in 2019, had been the direct cause of the book climbing up to the highest bell tower of Amazon France's sales list. What happened in 1831 had been thanks to literature and had fixed the book's historical permanence, what happened in 2019 was the result of a catastrophe and would go down in history as nothing more than another hysterical and fleeting Internet phenomena and there they all were, in front of the cathedral, weeping but not letting that keep them from filming the fire with their iPhones. Things have changed, like Bob Dylan sang in that song, disillusioned at how things had changed, while interrupting his shows to lash out at the people recording and photographing him with their fucking phones, threatening them with a "We can either play or we can pose. Okay?")

Books whose subject was as exhausting as it was inexhaustible. The most transgressive subject of all in times that were dragging along and flying by. Books about reading and writing. About reading and about writing and about reading it all again when you could no longer write, when you became both victim and victimizer of a terminal or interminable block. Books that—contrary to the objective of that publisher he was just remembering—would never be liked by everyone in the world. And that's what it was all about and what those books were about. Because not everyone liked to read, much less to write (even though now everyone read and wrote more than at any point in human history, but did so more out of obligation than for pleasure, more to keep from feeling left out than to feel something inside). And he didn't want everyone to like him because, well, he didn't like everyone. (Once—an appropriately aerial analogy—he'd read the transcript of that public dialogue that came from a famous live discussion between John Gardner and William H. Gass, in the late '70s. Gardner, convinced that the novel had the obligation to be something morally inspiring and not so concerned with experiments and avant-gardes, had come at Gass with a "For 24 years I have been screaming at him, sometimes literally screaming at him, saying 'Bill, you are wasting the greatest genius ever written to America by fiddling around when you could be doing big, important things.' . . . Our definitions of beauty are different. I think language exists to make a beautiful and powerful apparition. He thinks you can make pretty colored walls with it. That's unfair. But what I think is beautiful, he would think is not yet sufficiently ornate. The difference is that my 707 will fly and his is too encrusted with gold to get off the ground." Gass—as addicted to lists as he was—was someone to whom many people now attributed the responsibility and the privilege and, on occasion, the unforgiveable sin of having coined the term "metafiction" and someone who was convinced that the artistic and the moral didn't always go hand in hand. And Gass—who in that moving preface to his *In the Heart of the Heart of the Country* had addressed the conflict between the voice of the brain and the voice of the heart when it came to weaving together a story someone would read and hear and who had specified, nostalgically, that "Literature once held families together better than quarreling"—had even admitted that the force that drove his writing was the force of hate. And he'd even defined the past as that coat you toss onto an armchair as you come inside, but that, invariably, you have to put back on to combat the cold of the present and the future when you go back outside. So Gass patiently listened to Gardner's accusation and then responded: "There is always that danger. But what I really want is to have it sit there solid as a rock and have everybody think it is flying." And when he read that, he'd started clapping and the book had fallen out of his hands.)

Books that, every time he started writing them, made him feel the same thing an American paratrooper—whom he met and interviewed for an article in the magazine *Volare* a long time ago—told him he once felt. A soldier who'd participated in D-day, flying over the beach, a different beach that was the same beach, at Normandy (being in an airplane inevitably led one to think of other airplanes in the same way that being in love forced one to evaluate other love stories), and who'd said with the strangest of smiles: "When I jumped out of that airplane, I felt that I was not only leaving the plane behind, I was leaving behind everything I'd been and done in my life up to that point. I felt that, all of a sudden, everything was ahead of me, including the rest of my life and, maybe, even the beginning of my death. And there I was, falling as if I were ascending, as if pulling off a simple yet impressive stunt, thinking about how the only difference between the living and the dead was that the living weren't yet dead and the dead had once been alive, floating in the void, but with both my heart and my head bursting with love."

Books written for the love of art and that took no time at all to discover that that love was never entirely reciprocal. That art (as well as the infinite jobs adjacent to all things literary that "agents or cultural movers and shakers"—always with a salary of their own from some foundation and/or government office—would ask him to do "out of the kindness of his heart" and "so he could be part of a great project" without offering any kind of material or economic remuneration) wouldn't love him with the same intensity and surrender with which he loved and loves and would always and forever love art. That art would acknowledge him as its lover, yes; but would never concern itself with rewarding his love, not even so that everyone else would acknowledge it, at least somewhat; so that they would value and respond in some small way to his work; so that they would love him as if, yes, by the art of magic. And in that way make him complicit in being and not being and being again, in being cut in two to then be reunited, in returning to terra firma after floating through the air.

And he'd said once —in a rickety auditorium more empty and less full all the time—that writing (and he liked to think that his last book had been, yes, one of those few solid yet soaring rocks longed for by Gass) was like doing magic, but without ever entirely understanding the mechanics of that magic. In writing—entering into a tumult of false bottoms and trapdoors to wind up emerging with your own thing—you are half expert illusionist and half ingenuous volunteer, exposing your delusion but letting yourself be locked in a cupboard and run through with swords, or levitate, or vanish. Going to write—going everywhere but, magically, never leaving your desk—was for him the most sane and precise and omnipresent way to put into practice going MIA and, at the same time, to pull off a great sleight of hand: because when you wrote you disenchanted loved ones and enchanted loving strangers. And—unlike what happens with professional magicians—when writing you don't distract people with a lot of talk and don't have a beautiful assistant to distract them either. No: when you write you work alone and in the darkness and madness of art and you do all you can and give all you have and doubt as passion and passion as vocation and all of that.

Now, he'd lost all his magic—and there was a dearth of passion and an abundance of doubt—and had no idea how to find it.

Now it was the magic and the act of making it that'd vanished. The illusion and trick of inducing it.

Now he was no longer an illusionist or a delusional volunteer: now he was just disillusioned.

Now he'd exhausted his power of enchantment (and he'd never found it all that surprising that on the posters of magicians from the golden age, the magicians always appeared surrounded by demonic and never angelic assistants; the magic of literature *isn't* white magic *either*). And things no longer occurred to him in the place where the most and best things had always occurred to him: crossing wide avenues or washing the dishes. (And he'd read once that the same thing happened to Agatha Christie: that, she said, "The best time for planning a book is while you're doing the dishes." And, yes, the perfect crime was a kind of spell and, at the same time, it could only be truly perfect if nobody realized that it was a crime except for its physical author who was always dying to tell somebody that he'd created a dead person. Likewise, he thought, in the theory and the practice of literature, what was most perfect was something that never revealed its perfection. For him, perfection—like reality—was overrated. Something whose strategy and structure were only visible to its author and, to everyone else, it would remain a question without answer until the great reveal of the how and the why and the to-what-end it'd been done.)

Now, nothing here and nothing there, on the page.

Now, paginated.

Now, he didn't write.

Now he knew in his own flesh and writing what Vladimir Nabokov had wanted to say when he wrote that "the future is but the obsolete in reverse."

Because now he had no future, now everything he had was behind him.

And—having gotten over that first moment of dumb and self-indulgent euphoria when not writing could be understood as a work of art in itself, like an invisible installation—now he knew the false euphoria of the retired soldier who, unlike a skydiver in the air, can go in reverse and retrace his steps. Sure: he'd survived no man's land, but, back in the trenches, he couldn't describe it, he had nothing to recount but the melancholy of still being alive while feeling deader than ever. And discovering that the watch on his wrist had stopped, that the glass covering the sphere had been broken, that one or two of its hands had fallen out along the way, and that neither the tick-tock of a manuscript nor a mantel on which to set it awaited him. Nor posterity. Because he wasn't dead in the white snow but alive and covered in mud. He was an undead soldier, one of the *marching dead*, stranded on a beach that wasn't historic in any way. And with nobody to come in a little boat and find him and bring him back home where they would give him more ammunition and provisions and a few days leave before sending him back to the front.

Now he couldn't even shut himself in a hotel, thinking that there he would write his masterpiece (and there, besieged by winter and hounded by his own ghosts, end up writing the same sentence over and over again); because that'd already been done by the failing character in a masterpiece by a very successful writer; and because he couldn't even come up with a single sentence to repeat and repeat and repeat.

Now—like HAL 9000—his mind was going and he no longer had any great enthusiasm or confidence in the mission: now he was afraid. And the song he had to sing wasn't that one about Daisy and a bicycle built for two. The song was that other song—a dancing song, but one that spent a lot of time thinking as it danced—where you heard, in that fragile-old-man voice with which Fred Astaire and Gene Kelly sang, even though they were young and lithe at the time, that line that went "And it keeps coming till the day it stops."

Now he—a one-time practitioner of the theory and practice of the most inexact of sciences—knew how the most exact and prodigious mathematicians felt, aware from their first additions and subtractions that their gift, like that of top-models and athletes, had a brief shelf life. That their variety of genius would give them at most ten or fifteen years of formidable ideas and wondrous results to, sooner rather than later, pretty much by the time they reached their fourth decade on this side of things, be replaced by the banality of repetitions or variations on preformulated formulas. Or, if they chose not to accept that, even by the incalculable madness of meaningless signs floating across the blackboards of their brilliant minds, where the chalk always made that fucking sound that kept them from thinking about anything but that fucking sound. The punishment that, yes, inevitably, came concealed behind the curtains of a reward: there existed an entire ancient and vaguely spiritual school of thought that defined genius as one of the many forms of madness; that claimed that singular inventiveness was unequivocally interwoven with the most ordinary psychosis. And now even neurobiologists were beginning to acknowledge that there's something true to all of that: a lower number of dopamine receptors or something like that, he'd read in one of those scientific magazines in which he understood next to nothing, but which he always found inspiring, they always gave him good ideas in the days when he still wrote or, sometimes, even more or less plausible explanations regarding the fact that he no longer wrote. (Could something like that—as his admirers/critics claimed—have been what happened to Nabokov, on the last leg of his journey, after *Pale Fire*, with what were, for many, the already too Nabokovian and self-referential *Ada, or Ardor*, *Transparent Things*, *Look at the Harlequins!*, and the death-interrupted *The Original of Laura*? In any case, the Russian had greatly extended his shelf life when, in the middle of the equation of his life, he'd switched languages and turned himself into an American writer, right?)

Now he knew up close the vital and mortal difference between a fish in the sea and a fish on the hook. And—unlike so many of his fellow writers who said they'd "left literature and fiction behind because they no longer enjoyed it or found it interesting"—he could neither fool himself nor lie to everyone else: it was fiction and literature that'd abandoned him, because it no longer found him interesting much less enjoyable.

It'd been, yes, an at once gradual and rapid process. Like one of those devastating illnesses that demand respect and immediately inspire terror: because their surname—generally a double surname—would be known, but their given name, and much less their nickname, would never be revealed. And even if it were, it would soon be forgotten (and once a specialist in the matter, in gray matter, had told him not to worry if he started to forget names and things: the thing to worry about was to no longer worry about forgetting, in other words: the truly alarming thing was to forget that you forgot). And so, the first thing to go forever were round ideas, immediately replaced by angular and uneven objects and the false hope of a final improvement and intensification. Suddenly, everything he saw out of the corner of his eye and read in passing appeared useful. (And at some point, thinking it might be a way to delay the inevitable, it occurred to him to rewrite rather than to write. To pay homage, mashup, those evasive maneuvers. Homework assignments, for example: set out to write the great family-guerilla novel of his now nonexistent country of origin with—for him, the great subliminally Latin American political novel—*American Pastoral* by Philip Roth as guide. The same thing had happened to him with another subversive foreign novel that he thought of importing and nationalizing: *Under Western Eyes*, by Joseph Conrad: a writer who had always struck him as overrated, but, even still, full of good moments, like when the old German, Stein, counsels Lord Jim with a "In the destructive element immerse!" Which was good advice for a character—and, sometimes, even for a writer as long as the writer knows how to swim and has some plush towels and a hot meal waiting for him when he gets out—but not for a reader, he thought at the time. And that was why so few people immersed themselves in the destructive though not at all elemental *The Impossible Story*, in which a writer who wasn't him—even though, in *real reality* he *really* had attempted it—fantasized not about ending but about reformulating the whole world, triggering a devouring black hole inside a Swiss particle accelerator and merging with the God Particle and coming back as the Great Rewriter of All Things and the Author Ex Machina who was no longer an exwriter. And he wondered then if those grandiose and messianic ideas came to him because the initiating and vengeful ghost of his own *National Industry*, his first book and his one "success," was demanding or tempting him to return to the adventures that'd been so successful when he'd first ventured out. In any case, he soon realized that they were all overly ambitious projects and he couldn't take them on, because he no longer had any ambition to project himself in any direction.)

And so, all he did—as if moving with the inertial impulse of the last gasses in an almost-empty combustion engine—was fill notebooks to overflowing with scattershot scribblings that, of course, just *had* to be part of a great design that, any one of these insomniac nights, would stop resisting and reveal itself in all its glory and oh so complex simplicity. And so he went around deceiving himself and everyone else with a "Oh, I'm writing the best sentences I've written in my life." And even sometimes, at some party, he would recite one of them from memory—like he'd read that a wandering Truman Capote had done in the days of his almost inaudible *Answered Prayers*—as if trying to write a book every time he opened his mouth to then close it with a period and new paragraph. Almost imagining those sentences printed on one of those little postcards (with his photograph) that were being sold in those bookstores that were selling more lit-gadgets (cups and posters and bookmarks and pens and erasers with writers' faces on them) and less literature all the time. And sure: at random and on their own those sentences sounded fine and he liked to call them "those sentences of mine." Sentences like prayers, prayers that prayed as if ascending to the ceilings in search of glory. And they were long prayers, like a creed. But they were prayers that nobody answered or understood if he tried to bring them together in a Te Deum. Brilliant and immoveable lines (here comes another one) impossible to move, like heavy pieces of furniture that couldn't be brought into harmony with the whole of a living room and that, as such, he'd been abandoning and covering up with the most ghostly sheets so they wouldn't be so frightening; meanwhile, in the bathrooms, hung towels that were desperately soft but never dried anything much less offered any warmth after you paddled around and submerged yourself in "the destructive element" and, in the bedrooms, in the drawers of the bedside tables, lay those cold sex toys with batteries rusted from lack of use. Yes: the last few times he'd attempted to approach literature and fiction to exploit it and to penetrate it, he hadn't lasted more than two or three minutes, five at most, before finishing. Then a moan and, embarrassed, he'd stood up, left behind the impotence of his type-not-writer on his ex-writing desk, and let himself fall onto his mattress like one of those damsels of classic cinema: picking up a little speed and taking tiny trembling steps and throwing himself facedown, sobbing and sighing and blubbering "Never again . . . Never again . . . Enough of all of this . . ."

Now he'd lost all confidence in the genre and in the certainty that attempting to write a novel was nothing more than the physical expression of an irreducible faith in the idea of an ending as a solution: that things came to an end, that everything existed in order to reach that final round period.

Now he was all ellipses with no trace mystery.

(Now he remembered the words of the *maudit* Jean Rhys—who, like his *maudit* sister Penelope, had submerged herself in another *maudit*-sister, a Brontë sister, only to rise again from the depths—about how Tolstoy and Dostoevsky were "great rivers" who fed the lake, yes. But that there were also mere trickles, like Jean Rhys herself, who also contributed their work to the volume of the great waters. It didn't matter how many liters. "The lake matters," Rhys explained to her interviewer. "All that matters is feeding the lake. I don't matter," Rhys concluded, drunk and with her wig twisted and on backward and lapping up the last drops from the rim of her glass.)

And now he—drip-drop-drpfff—had nothing to offer, not even a mere trickle; now he suffered, contained on the other side of a dam with no hole to *not* plug with a finger. There was no need. Because there was no reservoir. It was like he was dried up. Desiccated and alone and thirsty in the sun. That water that he'd once almost drowned in as a boy and a nextwriter—that liquid fire of words and plotlines—was the water that'd run through his fingers, always stained with ink and now erased by the erosion of the desert sand. Now he (as someone had once said, to a girl ready to be murdered and wrapped in plastic, on his favorite TV show) was "The Great Went." The Great Went or The Great Already Gone. Something that wasn't going anywhere and that could only spin around on itself (which *was not* the same thing as dancing while it all "keeps coming till the day it stops") with the deceptive inertia of a twirling *trompe-l'oeil* top.

And so he went in and out of bookstores, tormenting himself with all those new books that never stopped being written, gathering there, as if to talk among themselves. And, he could feel how a silence, between compassionate and terrified, fell over all of them—perhaps because it was possible that whatever he had was contagious—when they saw him approaching and read that he was arriving. (To, going no further, that bookstore where he often ran into Enrique Vila-Matas. Sometimes, in that same bookstore, he saw Vila-Matas in the company of that other writer, the one from his now nonexistent country of origin. The one who looked a little like Ringo Star but less well maintained. And to whom he felt irreconcilably similar in multiple ways and senses, beyond the decisive difference that the man in question always seemed happy and had no issues continuing to do his thing and—on top of all that good fortune—had even, he'd read somewhere, won a couple of those *interesting* prizes recently. That man who, on more than one occasion, was accompanied by his wife of many years and his son, that boy with the glasses with the hexagonal frames who, he'd also read somewhere, was the one who designed the covers of that man's books. And sometimes he was even there with his editor, who he'd been working with for decades and with whom he got along very well. And he wondered how one did or accomplished *that* and whether all of *that* was even possible. And it was clear that, yes, it was possible for a lucky few: to be happy with a wife and a son and an editor and writer friends; and to write *like that* from the certainty of that certain happiness instead of from the always *maudit* and lidless eye of a hurricane whirling with rancor and frustration. And maybe, who knows, he, in some multiverse *à la* DC or Marvel, would be part of all of that. And he would feel a little like he'd felt not long ago, for three hours, in a movie theater, watching the final installment of *The Avengers* . . . People in the dark uttering "ooohs!" and "aaahs!" and laughing and crying and—would it be *really* pathetic on his part to confess and admit that, in that moment, he missed and envied more than ever the experience of having a son to share all of that with?—the wonder and surprise of experiencing again *that thing* it'd once been to "go to the movies": stepping out of your life to enter a confined physical space where the screen was right there in front of you, enormous and exciting, and that screen entered into you and gave you the feeling of being part of something that was *also* part of everyone, surrounded by complete strangers recognizing each other in that shared feeling . . . A communal and primitive and eternal experience. An interconnection of accelerated particles. Maybe having a family was something like that: to be a freak and fan and nerd of something that simultaneously belonged to and owned you. Having something unique that so many others had . . . Being a writer wasn't the same. You're a writer and, sure, you form part of a tradition. But writers weren't capable of killing or dying for another writer the way many were, indeed, capable of doing for child. At most, writers killed to gain readers . . . And he'd learned all of this about that other writer, because he'd attended two events, at that same bookstore, featuring the man in question: one where he was in conversation with Vila-Matas; and another where his latest book was presented by his editor. And now that editor was no longer there, but, in a way, it was like he would be there forever. And there was Vila-Matas, who wrote nonstop and kept winning prizes, those "real" prizes that he'd always wanted to win so badly. Vila-Matas, who'd spent a long time—in the shadows, off to one side, not ignored but, yes, misunderstood by his contemporaries—doing his thing until his thing caught a break. And who, years ago, had written an entire book—one of his most successful books—about the symptom of the washed-up writer based on the figure of Herman Melville's Bartleby and on the figure of Melville himself—who'd ended up a bureaucratic customs agent, scribbling shitty poems on the backs of forms—and on so many others who'd preferred not to and not to be: "The disease endemic to contemporary letters, the negative impulse or attraction toward nothingness" and "the literature of the No" or something like that. And, oh, it was so easy to describe with great beauty the horror of the disease raging outside from inside "a home forever" when you were healthy and immune to the paralyzing virus . . . And no: Vila-Matas—out of pity or because he didn't make the grade—hadn't included him in his company of writers. And in general he limited himself to wordlessly greeting him, separated by tables or book-shelves, as if they were on opposite ends of a bridge enveloped in fog, lifting a finger to the brim of the imaginary hat of an imaginary spy, of that spy who Vila-Matas had once drawn/dedicated to him in one of his books. But there was no possibility of exchange. Vila-Matas had no interest in entering the oppressive nation in which he was suffering. And he, of course, didn't have the necessary visas or stamps to cross over to the democratic and liberated side of things, where Vila-Matas continued to do whatever he wanted, what he'd always done. But he didn't fool him, they didn't fool him, he couldn't fool himself, there was nothing romantic much less personally epic in all of that: nobody chose to stop writing, in every case one was *written off* because one had stopped writing. And the saddest and most tormenting thing of all: one stopped writing, yes, but one never stopped thinking about writing, about what one would write if one were able to put it in writing.)

And, yes, his idea for those books that would never be, books that would be one with *The Impossible Story*, was that those beyond-long books that he invented and dreamed would be like rereading something that'd been rewritten.

Books that were written but yet-to-be-written, yes.

Books that slid in like the green blade of a knife to be stained crimson in the hearts of people who read the same books everyone else read.

Books that were read like the practical and hurriedly scribbled marginalia in the screenplays of bad movies that somehow, inexplicably, ended up being produced and premiered and shown on television to comfort all those people who, as if in a trance, were unable to find what they really wanted to read. For them—all those amnesiacs, asleep and sleepwalking—he daydreamed of alarm-clock books, books that would give them back the ability to dream and to invent and to remember. All those zombies with such short attention spans (a couple hundred seconds, a couple hundred characters), no longer hungry for brains but voided of brain activity, hypnotized by books that offered the ease of reading as their only virtue.

Books that would reacquaint them with mobilizing stillness and pull them away from the banal magnetism exercised by the books that attracted people because they were trendy, from the magnet books. And doing so with the thundering and insistent sound of burning pages, of pages that burned one by one and sent readers leaping out of their beds, engulfed in flames.

And, of course, it was no mean feat to convince all of them that the pleasure was in the difficulty and that in the practice of making an effort resided the theory of the payoff. Most resisted or gave up in defeat. Yes, again, he could imagine all of those terrified people, more spectators of "visual" books than readers of written pages: shrieking as they circled through the ferocious forests of his prose, lost and tripping over roots, their hair getting tangled in the branches, searching for a clearing of pages less covered in letters. And at last, escaping the dense vegetation of his pages, finding sanctuary in reasonable and well-aerated banzai melodramas with bonsai IQs and plastic and rubber curlicues, where, at meals and in bed, in the company of characters "you could identify with" who spoke with the efficiency of automata—first you and then me and with the assent and enthusiastic support of editors and agents and marketing directors—they would, again and again, revisit Latin American dictatorships or European civil wars/transitions/crises or (new-old flavor) border walls. Short volumes that seemed to take place, all of them, in third-rate wax museums where the figures encased and enclosed in wax rarely resembled (though it wasn't odd to mistake Chaplin for Hitler or vice versa) their flesh and bone originals beyond their obvious features. And so, for that reason, you had to read on small signs who those dubious effigies lacking all mystery were supposed to be because it was impossible to tell who they were at a glance. There, the historical novel thinking that something historical automatically made any novel and its characters and heroes—like happy prisoners inside fish tanks or dioramas, the kind that lit up when you pressed a button so that, then, the figures would execute basic mechanical movements (opening and closing eyes, nodding or shaking heads, lifting or lowering an arm) while playing the recordings of solemn voices projected in the background—historic. Voices reciting historical clichés and marble and bronze and sepulchral phrases in a language that the people who said them, in their ephemeral historical moment, never spoke when alive. Novels that for him were like the homework assignments (so impeccable, in laminated folders, with stickers and passages underlined in ink of multiple colors and, in days before Photoshop, traced images) of students, more clever than inspired, whose only gift was that of an excellent memory: they knew the lesson and could recite and write it in the guttural voice of a writer of familial and political and continental sagas. And, sure, they—cerulean replicas to put on display of Pertusato, Nicolasito—got good grades and good reviews and the best seats on airplanes and the best rooms in the best hotels and the best—best in terms of prize money—awards for which they were always "invited to present themselves." Awards that gave certain publishers the sense that they had the green light to steal the winning authors from other publishers, like a gallant clash of pirate galleons at high sea, always with the tacit consent of the author who—like a fainting damsel in distress, with one eye ever open and alert—feigned surprise when the pirate publisher came aboard after they'd left the door ajar and the lights on and the manuscript sitting out on the bed so the pirates would have no trouble finding it and carrying it off like plundered loot. (When it came to dreaming of awards and of those dream-awards someday coming true, he'd always preferred the surprise awards that seemed to fall from the sky like unidentified flying objects: awards—not won but awarded—presented to the author. Awards far more presentable than the ones you had to present yourself for. Generous and fair and judicious awards. And then he remembered that idea for an award—he thinks Felisberto Hernández had come up with it—that revolved around the creation of a secret honor, awarded at the beginning of a promising career, that the recipient wouldn't know they'd received. The award would be given by a sort of top-secret organization with an absolute commitment to the cultivation of good literature, an organization that would watch over the awardee and—behind the scenes—take charge of "writing" him a perfect life: choosing him just the right partner, facilitating his purchase of an ideal home, seeing to it that his children received the best education, and even making sure he won one of those awards you didn't have to submit an unpublished manuscript for to be considered: awards for a job well done, not for a job yet to be done and let's see how it goes . . . Anything he needed to excel as a writer. And—only after a full life and fertile body of work, on his deathbed—informing that writer that decades earlier he'd been the winner of that award, which the public would only learn of in his obituary: the Post Prize or something like that. And he'd even fantasized about a multimillion-dollar prize, the Mortem Prize, which, to win, first a writer had to die. And in that way become one of those many rediscoveries that came far too late for the recipient. But thanks to which, for a while, that writer who'd been ignored while alive, would become the best dead writer of the year. Or better yet, another: the most economically well-endowed award in all of history, the Nevermore Prize. Awarded to those terrible "prestige" writers in exchange for them signing a document that made them swear to never write and/or publish another word for the rest of their lives: and so it was a humanitarian and almost euthanasic award that brought to an end the agony those writers said they suffered when they embarked on the writing of those incurable and painful and terminal and supposedly transcendent fictions, and, oh, yes, of course, again, fictions that were so engaged with their time.) But he—as it concerned just or unjust awards—almost couldn't care less. And—when he lacked the energy to lie to himself that he didn't really care about all those medals and awards pinned on other people's chests—he repeated to himself over and over again that, after all, they'd never given Vladimir Nabokov a National Book Award, though he'd been nominated seven times (going so far as to submit, at the behest of his publisher, when he was nominated for *Look at the Harlequins!*, "the ghost of an acceptance speech" composed with equal parts emotion and irony and where he stated that the true award came when the printed book that he'd put so much work into first arrived to his house, but also that, when he opened it for the first time, he experienced the punishment of finding "a fatal error"). Or a Pulitzer. Much less a Nobel with which they'd canonized mediocre Russian salads like Boris Pasternak or Aleksandr Solzhenitsyn (and he'd always admired so much that Nabokov never played the always-winning and clear-eyed "Victim-of-History" card, to thereby take, somewhat deceptively, medals and regrets and diplomas and apologies from everyone else in academic casinos and in winding circles of power where—at long lunches of cultural attachés whose only function was to attach long lunches to their expense accounts—they swapped awards for their respective protégés who, of course, always wrote *national* novels). Awards and books like the ones that'd earned fame and fortune for his arch-nemesis and infra-homunculus. The man who wrote books that—like the unpronounceable and Nordic names of products offered by that colossus of home-furnishing and decor—were impossible to remember and not mistake for each other, chairs for tables, beds for dressers, bookshelves for bookcases.

But, oh, *his* IKEA was unmistakable and unforgettable.

And exclusive.

And the responsibility was, in large part, his; because he'd been the one (in better days and probably in the confusion of ingesting controlled substances at some wild party) who had, in situ, given and bestowed upon him his blessing and a blurb that'd aided in the publication of the debut book of that man who, at the time, claimed to be his devout admirer and humble supporter.

Or at least that's what IKEA said on those nights back when they first met.

Then—almost immediately—it was something else.

Suddenly, IKEA, wrapped in his Byronian capes tailored on Savile Row and his fabulous and flamboyant head of hair maintained using baby panda hormones—"If possible, bisexual pandas," he specified—filing by like a triumphant general who'd never needed to go to battle, because nobody would dare oppose not what he was but what he represented.

IKEA weaving from the beginning his web with arachnoid dedication and smooth-operator skill.

The newcomer IKEA interviewing an old literary lion or IKEA himself being interviewed by the newcomer of the day and, then, by that old literary lion.

IKEA and those essays he wrote about "important" and "committed" and "engaged" and "literary" issues that always gave the impression that what he did, more than think for himself, was lean on the quotations of others and a sprinkling of nineteenth- and twentieth-century classics.

IKEA—always on exhibit and ever the exhibitionist—as one of the first writers to obsequiously sign up for an app that allowed readers to read what he was writing as he wrote it, "that way they can learn about the vacillations and certainties and advances and retreats of a true artist in the very moment of making capital-A Art."

IKEA who only liked to write books that were liked.

IKEA who cared more about connecting with the reader than with the writer, who was him.

IKEA as the convenience of supposedly high culture standing on tiptoes on a stage of ready-made phrases (when it came to his political postures and composure, where everything was black and white and no gray; IKEA never missed the opportunity of a natural catastrophe or social cataclysm to offer an opinion or to make appearances with big names at book signings) from which to declaim digestible more-common-than-sense common sense and with no regard for the proximity or real knowledge of the actual victims or victimizers.

IKEA who belonged to that abundant and avaricious brand of benefactor convinced that their mere presence was beneficial, and so he attended events and posed for group photos—in the first row and in the center if possible— and thereby considered his moral debt paid and his invisible yet decisive offering made.

IKEA playing at being King ONG (the Spanish acronym for NGO) and who was to the analysis of reality what one of those amusing and condensed TED Talks (as effervescent as they were evanescent, so brief and ostentatious, as illuminating as they were forgettable) was to the extensive study of any serious subject, because, he thought, if everything you learned in your life and had to show for it fit in fifteen minutes, maybe you don't know that much about it? Can *everything* really be synthesized and summarized? Wasn't there anything left worth dedicating hours of attention to the way people once did to novels as expansive as universes and not as fleeting as falling stars?

IKEA who was to literature what one of those superstar DJs was to music: he moved around a lot, smiled with all his teeth, encouraged his audience to jump around and worship him from down below, prostrate in front of his altar/booth. But any reader or dancer with a little common sense would see that that guy wasn't doing anything, that it was all predigested and prerecorded over loops of other artists that were subliminally identifiable and, as such, gratifying. And in that way, making the people who heard or read them feel smart just for recognizing them, helping them to feel that they were recognizers, not wanting to see that IKEA's thing wasn't talent and much less genius but just being in the right place at the right time. Or maybe IKEA was a genius; but a perfect genius of mediocrity and always ready—like how authentically genius geniuses tend to have a few valuable talented followers—to be praised and emulated by increasingly numerous and cheap mediocrities. Which—once you accepted the fact that, after all and in the end, IKEA's thing was just one more in a long list of irrefutable proof that this world wasn't fair—wasn't all that grave and was entirely predictable.

IKEA who was riddled with infinite defects but who ameliorated them with an absolute and singular certainty that he had none at all.

IKEA who was like the student athlete and king of self-promotion (with successive SHE-IKEAS as devout and royal cheerleaders) in the worst of all high schools that lasted a lifetime.

IKEA who'd named his dog IKEA (in order to feel like he was giving himself orders and being obeyed and so man's proverbial best friend would bear his name).

IKEA even pretending to be being a little gay (not openly so, but someone with a confused and ambiguous sexuality: someone far more interesting, because he could be gay if he was given a little push) when the president of an award jury to whom he'd been introduced was a famous gay novelist, not hesitating to ask for advice and guidance through his anguished confusion.

IKEA who transformed himself seamlessly into a seductive dancer of Caribbean rhythms (IKEA, of course, had taken classes in tropical steps so he could stand out among all his motionless colleagues at those frenzied book-fair parties. And he'd even invented a step—the Ikeíto—that became popular when it was adopted by a hot and rhythmical and hip-shaking popstar—who sang in a strange language that, supposedly, was Spanish—for one of her soft-porn videos) when the time came to sashay out onto the dance floor and seduce the widow of some Boom writer who ran a foundation that was founded in that writer's name and that offered the most generous of fellowships.

Between one extreme and another of his multiple occupations, IKEA always came back to him to tell him—taking prideful delight in his confessions, cracking up—about his adventures and accomplishments, as if considering him complicit in his intrigues and even the mastermind of his shenanigans. In a stupidly inspired way, he thought, IKEA now considered himself a Captain Kirk and he was something like his Mr. Spock: someone to affectionally and even somewhat respectfully mock. Yes: IKEA was one of his characters who'd gotten out of control. And it made him feel really guilty and uncomfortable because that was exactly the thing—a creator losing control of his creation—that Vladimir Nabokov had found so contemptable, a sign of extreme and unjustifiable weakness in a writer. Something foolish and undignified.

But at this point he'd accepted it.

Now he was just another—in his perverse and twisted way—of IKEA's many readers. Except he didn't read IKEA's books, he read IKEA. And reading him, he couldn't help but ask himself a question all writers ask themselves at some point in their life and work. That question: "How could I have come up with something like this?," but with light modifications in its DNA turning it into a "How could I have been part of bringing someone like this come into being?"

And maybe most interesting of all: the species IKEA belonged to wasn't anything especially surprising; because IKEA was nothing more and nothing less than one among many in the literary ecosystem. A free soloist. A climber who caused vertigo. An expert in the gripping and tension and fixing of ropes and pulleys and harnesses en route to his summit. But it was always somewhat surprising which peaks IKEA set out to conquer, the low points he reached on his ascents.

The seat of honor that IKEA—who'd now spent a couple decades transcending what in the beginning he'd imagined would never be more than a *flavor-of-the-week* status to wind up consecrated as a classic and permanent and always conveniently citable fixture on year-end *flavor-of-the-week* lists— occupied now was a unique landscape.

Nobody had ever gotten there before.

So far above and so far removed and with so little genius and so much talent for appearing ingenious.

And a year ago, IKEA (sordid details on the horizon) had pulled off the absolute and definitive feat: coming back from the dead.

IKEA had returned, more powerful than ever, to be consecrated as the first living-posthumous writer in the history of literature.

There was even the possibility—he'd thought from time to time and these days considered it a certainty—that IKEA had sold his soul to the Devil in exchange for his glory. And that the Devil—generally portrayed as a distinguished violin-playing libertine and an elegant and sophisticated lover of the arts and artists—must've said to himself that acquiring such an uninteresting soul was an excellent deal because it boosted IKEA's power. He was launched back into life as a sort of weapon of mass destruction or like one of those pandemics that escape from a highly classified governmental facility and lay waste to everything, but, at the same time, succeed in making the ever fewer masterpieces still in the vicinity more noteworthy and deserving of appreciation.

Thus, IKEA satisfied the needs of increasingly inferior readers while the stronger and nobler ones sighed in winter quarters and frozen castles, dreaming of epic adventures and, occasionally, even making them come true.

And IKEA also functioned as a variation on the Darwinian: his was the survival not even of the unfittest (there, in being unfit, was something of inverse greatness) but of the somewhat-less fit. (Another less scientific possibility, also supernatural, but far more personal, was that IKEA was the reincarnation of his ancient and first ink-brother and duelist in school writing competitions. The electrifying and electrocuted

Pertusato, Nicolasito: *mente meravigliosa quanto precece mori questa scuola*. His first dead body that, there, in that little coffin, had been reassembled to resemble a puppet that'd lost its inner ventriloquist. Never to dream again but looking "like he was sleeping," as those who dream of dying in their sleep say, the best possible death. And he could never understand all those people—people who when they sleep resemble dead bodies, but dead bodies that haven't been made-up for their wake: open-mouthed and pale-faced and mussed hair and the look of being soiled by nocturnal emissions—who said they needed to see the body so they could believe and accept the person had died: wasn't it enough for them to never see that person alive again? In any case, Pertusato, Nicolasito dead by accidental electrocution—though he did feel somewhat responsible for the tragedy—in the ruins that once surrounded his first school. Gervasio Vicario Cabrera, colegio n.°1 del Distrito Escolar Primero, before it was demolished at the orders of the maniacal Military Junta, so they could land in the *Guinness Book of World Records* for the length and width of an avenue in the now nonexistent capital city of his now nonexistent country of origin. The dead Pertusato, Nicolasito as a person to be reincarnated as one of his characters. As another one of his characters. As . . .)

IKEA who was always wearing a mask that ate away at his face but was a mask of his own face.

IKEA who'd achieved a level of pathological self-satisfaction only comparable to that of someone who masturbates while fantasizing about himself masturbating.

IKEA who was a kind of nocturnal and diurnal emission of the Boom. And the Boom (which he'd never believed in, maybe because at the time his now nonexistent country of origin hadn't contributed its own superhero to the whole deal) was like the machine in *The Invention of Morel*: it repeated the same thing over and over notwithstanding the passing of the years. And now the Boom was accused of and condemned for being machista when, really, to his mind it'd always been one of the most feminist moments in the history of literature: because the Boom had been the life and work of the all-powerful and empowered literary agent Carmen Balcells; all the others were just loose puzzle pieces and pre-consecrated writers. And (on its own the Boom was one thing, a thing that was about writers and books, while what he'd christened the Gaboom was something else entirely, a kind of mythical and almost-hysterical mysticism, the Gospel according to "Gabo" and his gang, which was destined to be preached throughout the city over and over, by the mouths of people who, for the most part, had never met or even seen García Márquez, but who never hesitated to take his nickname in vain), sure, the Boom was a good and efficient invention designed in its day by inspired or clever inventors. The problem was the people who were left in charge of maintaining it. IKEA was one of them. One of the many *boomitivos*, as he called them. A child and an abortion and the hangover from all of that and, at the same time, something uncomfortably close to one of those tribute bands, working unnecessarily to keeping the memory of The Beatles or Pink Floyd alive; because it was clear to anyone who could hear that nobody had forgotten or would soon forget the originals (and it would be better if they got a different occupation, because now there were these *live* holograms of the *dead* originals and, who knows, maybe before long they would algorithmically synthesize the novel Jorge Luis Borges never wrote or Francis Scott Fitzgerald's finished version of *The Love of the Last Tycoon* or would recover Herman Melville's last and lost *Isle of the Cross*). Beyond all of that, IKEA—who never missed an opportunity to refer to himself as a "humble follower of those titans"—always with a Macondo on his tongue, a Santa María in his heart, a The Cathedral on the table, and a Terra Nostra at his feet. IKEA devoting praise to his forefathers and totems and—as they died out—referring to their successive survivors, as one predecessor after another fell, as his all-time favorites. IKEA now, again, whenever he got the chance, publicly interviewing the last survivor at the party: a preserved conservative, with a face that looked more and more like the Grinch who stole Christmas, editorializing with sermons in Sunday papers about a world more flat than round, spinning more and more to the right, and without any of the reactive intelligence or malice of the more reactive than reactionary Saul Bellow in his final years.

And, of course, he wasn't among them, among the writers IKEA admired. And vice versa.

He didn't count at all for IKEA, except as a kind of first-person, inaugurating witness and, for that reason, worthwhile; but in the way you consider that mad relative locked in the basement or attic "necessary." And yet, he always wondered: was IKEA his friend? Maybe not: because over the years, a writer discovers—with a combination of surprise and inevitability—that almost all of his or her friends are writers. And that, for that reason, they didn't function like everyone else's friends: friends were, in ideal terms and for the civilian population, the director's cut of the family. The chosen logical family imposing itself over the obligatory biological family. But the writers' writer friends were something else. A writer became friends with another writer for reasons not strictly emotional. The result of that connection should have led, inevitably, to an inspired friendship worthy of being put in writing and read. Friendship as alliance, writers as allies. And then, almost right away, you learned that a writer who was considered good couldn't be friends with writers who made him or her look bad. And if things went better for those good friends who were bad writers than for you, everything got complicated and very strange. And then the friendship turned into something else, into something that only went one in one direction: into an unreflecting mirror, into an unfulfilling wishing well, into that ambiguous bond that completely united the mere spectator with the performer. It was then that you learned that what you'd always really longed for and aspired to was only and simply to have friends who were readers. Many of them. A million friends. But, nevertheless, knowing he wasn't interested in IKEA as a writer (he didn't seem any good to him) and nothing interested him less than writing like IKEA (though he would have enjoyed his fortune and privileges), he remained tied to his life, to his work, and to his persona. And, obviously, IKEA *had* to feel the same way. In his way, IKEA came close to being, maybe not a friend, but, yes, an accomplice he could maybe count on. Or a privileged witness. Someone who was always there and who'd even come to his rescue in a sticky situation: IKEA had covered his bail and lawyer fees when he came to get him out of a Swiss jail after everything that happened there. You know the story, it came out everywhere as a piece of "local color" news: his odd little number in the particle accelerator in Meyrin, Geneva, where he locked himself inside and pressed buttons to, first, cause an electromagnetic pulse that would render all electronic devices on the planet useless, and then to become one with the universe and be transformed into an omnipotent deity capable of rewriting the fate of all men in his image and semblance, and, above all, with his literary style.

But, of course, the whole thing went awry.

And a good bit of his rant from inside that hadron centrifuge, captured by the microphones of the security system, had been taken up with railing against and condemning the creations of others, including IKEA.

(Even still and maybe for that reason, IKEA never stopped suggesting odd stunts and indecent proposals to "relaunch your somewhat slow-motion career." Like, for example and assuming he would never come up with anything himself, writing a book comprised of the continuation—or, IKEA specified, not even that, because new addenda and new conclusions and "new endings" would suffice—of his very successful literary debut: *National Industry.* IKEA's, and almost everyone's, favorite of his books. IKEA even suggested a possible title—"I'll give it to you if you name and thank me in one of your lists of acknowledgements where almost everyone, living and dead, makes an appearance except me, man"—that admittedly he'd found kind of charming, if in a silly way: *All Told.* Or, also, proposing frivolous extra-literary farces: "I came up with the following: I punch you in public. Like Marito did to Gabo. Think about it, all these years later, people are still talking about it . . . Of course I would have to be the one to punch you, so there'd be some mystery. If you punched me, there wouldn't be any enigma or curiosity to the whole episode: everyone would assume the motive was the rancorous envy of the master surpassed by the apprentice . . . But if I take a good shot at you, everyone would wonder why, what'd you done . . . You would become a much more interesting person and people might even read your books again, to try to find some hidden clue about the whole thing. I could even make a statement like 'That bastard did something to me no writer could ever forgive.' Or I guess it would be better to go in another direction; nobody would think it had anything to do with some kind of aesthetic offense on your part or in your work. Nobody's interested in those things, there's no morbid fascination to them . . . I promise not to hit you too hard. In fact, we could practice it first. A great show. A literary happening that'll interest people far more than literature . . . And they'll film and upload it to YouTube and . . ." Hearing that, he made a counteroffer to do it on a much bigger scale: "How about, instead of you punching me, I shoot you in the face? And then I tell everyone that you asked me to do it and made me promise I'd never reveal the reason why, or something like that." Then IKEA had given him a strange look, with one of those smiles of his that always seemed to be looking for someone with a camera to capture it and post it and immortalize it. "The things you come up with, man . . . I'm not surprised your books never work . . ." IKEA smiled. And he added: "As a last resort, we could always spread the rumor that you've got some rare and terminal illness, to see if some jury for one of those farewell awards takes pity on you and . . . But there's no guarantee: you know, juries tend to be made up of writers and writers, apart from not being good people, never loved you all that much and the imminence of your death probably wouldn't move them all that much.")

And yet, in the end, IKEA *did* love him.

It was possible he loved him far more than those he considered his aesthetic peers. (And IKEA even made surprising and really affectionate gestures; like when he showed up with a mint-condition first-edition copy of *Conclusive Evidence*, Nabokov's initial version of *Speak, Memory*—and maybe he should point out here that, for writers, getting your hands on certain first editions is a lot like what holding Greek vases adorned with pictures of Odysseus's journey home (after so many unnecessary stops along the way just to have a story to tell) is for archeologists—and IKEA had given him a note that read: "As you'll see, even your oh so admired Russian allowed himself to touch up his own past.") But why? To what end? Again: sometimes it seemed like IKEA needed him in the same way ancient Roman generals needed a slave accompanying them during some post-victory parade, so his company was like that small hammer (the desert for Magritte) in that Chekhov story that's constantly banging on the door of a happy home. So that the slave with his humility and the hammer with its tock-tock reminded the happy and victorious people of the fleeting and desert-like nature of glory and the brevity of the good life. And that's how he imagined himself: clad in a humble tunic alongside the resplendent and golden armor of IKEA; not exclaiming but muttering a "I'm Spartacus . . . I'm Spartacus" and caressing a divine and thundering Mjölnir-sized mace.

And the truth was that a lot of people—including both his and IKEA's Wikipedia entries—also considered him IKEA's "creator" or "discoverer." For them, first and foremost, he'd been IKEA's "mentor" who had, also, written some very "strange" books. And the facts were indisputable and, possibly, would rob lines from his ever closer and briefer obituary: he'd introduced IKEA to his publisher after reading a couple of his early short stories that imitated his own with something that was neither cheek nor naiveté, but rather, he realized later, something perfectly calculated to pull him into IKEA's service, thinking he was doing him a favor.

And that was why, years later, that same young publisher, with a trace amount of residual guilt for having canceled his piece on Bob Dylan, had proposed he be the "curator" of a "memorial-volume" dedicated to IKEA. Because back then, a year before, IKEA (along with his "muse and partner and soulmate" SHE-IKEA) had been left for dead, after the small plane he'd been piloting had been devoured by the riptide of an oceanic storm. Because, according to that publisher, IKEA was "more beloved and missed than ever by his readers; they're buying even more of his fun and engaged and committed novels, novels that always impart some deep lesson without robbing you of the gratification of a quick and easy read." And then his latest and last literary agent almost went down on his knees and begged him to accept it, because "it's always good for people to see you." But that was the same agent who had, *also*, been the one who not long before had suggested that he switch over to writing fantasy under a pseudonym and that "he think of an alias with a lot of initials, because that's what worked in that realm: J. R. R. Tolkien, C. S. Lewis, George R. R. Martin, J. K. Rowling . . ."

And he'd had no choice but to accept the invitation to that funeral. Not out of financial hardship. Penelope's will had insured that due to his rather decorative labors as her executor (a renowned literary agency had decided to take her on as their only client in order to manage the volume of translations, reeditions, film adaptations, and merchandising), he would never want for anything, but, at the same time, he would never have anything extra. Penelope had made him the prisoner of her memory and legend and work (a detail that, no doubt, would take up even more space than IKEA in his, again, ever briefer and closer obituary and, oh, he would die for a good obituary). So there he was: with everything paid for but master of nothing.

And so, contributing to IKEA's funeral rites would, paradoxically, pull him out of the tyrannical and comfortable orbit around the always-blazing moon of the incendiary and subsequently incinerated Penelope, who'd burned her own house down and, along with it, the possibility of any posthumous pages, etc. (IKEA, who, one night, having had one too many drinks, had laughed: "It was funny, that thing you said in your talk . . . the thing about choosing 'Models of Fathers/Writers.' And the possible options: 'The man who, in a housefire, rescues his son,' 'The man who, in a housefire, rescues the manuscript of his novel,' and 'The man who, in a housefire, rescues his son, gets him to safety, and then goes back into the flames to rescue the manuscript of his novel and dies in the attempt and leaves his son an orphan' . . . But didn't you wonder why none of the young writers sitting at that roundtable at that festival laughed with you? Or why they all smiled at each other, laughing at you? The answer is quite simple: none of them have manuscripts to rescue; because if they did, they would be digitalized or in the Cloud or pieced together from blogposts or Twitter or wherever anyway; because why would they care about their children if they aspire to remain children for the rest of their lives, man . . . And why would they care about the health and safety of manuscripts . . . Manuscripts are heavy, and they shit and piss on themselves and wake up crying in the middle of the night and don't let you sleep." And then—and the truth is he'd liked that bit about manuscripts as insufferable infants, and he promised to write it down and steal it—IKEA had confided in him that "let's see if you finally get it: these days, the work matters less and less, man. What really matters and is valued is the life. Being more than doing. The key is to have perfect control and to post a daily edition of your own biography and that's what social media is for.") Besides, he thought, it would give him a chance to—between the lines and in code—get back at IKEA. To reveal some terrible thing IKEA had told him as if it were worth sharing. To throw his quotes back at him like daggers in rants that would sound spontaneous but of a masterful and malicious and calculated elegance and turn IKEA into his own executioner, while he, feigning sorrow, would talk about how much he already missed the sound of his voice and his wit and . . .

Of course, he couldn't come up with—nothing *came out* because nothing *came into* his head anymore—a single thought about IKEA.

Fortunately or not, a few days after negotiating the assignment, IKEA turned up alive.

But before that, before his unexpected resurrection, IKEA had already been the recipient of a big prize and there was even talk of the possibility of, for the first time ever, awarding a Nobel to someone who died that same year, though IKEA was more alive than ever during the months he lived as a dead man. (An idea that he remembered having years before. But, of course, not to apply it to IKEA, but taking a longer view, retrospectively, and awarding it to names like Kurt Vonnegut or Leo Tolstoy or Marcel Proust or John Cheever or, of course, Vladimir Nabokov. After having taken advantage of that recent and scandalous blank year to clean house and put everything in order, the Nobel committee should have turned around and awarded a group Nobel to all those writers who'd deserved it as much as or, in general, even more than many of the past winners. That was the kind of wit he brought to the table when responding to editors of culture sections or literary supplements back in those Octobers when they still asked him about all of that, because he was so "clever" and "funny." A righteous Nobel that righted all past wrongs, yes. A Nobel that would be more than an occasional and comical concession made to the supposedly great writer of an economically disadvantaged *republiqueta* so that people could better locate it on the map for the next couple weeks. A ghost Nobel awarded to the lively ghosts inhabiting the Ouija boards of their authors' books. On some insomniac night, he'd thought of taking it all even further: awarding the Nobel not to writers but to the characters they created. To be *truly* fair. To have the work—in the purest and most absolute sense of the word—be rewarded and to have the life disappear. The free individuals over the subject. To give it to Anna Karenina, to Faustine, to Adam Godley and his son, to Fuckhead, to Isabel Archer, to Nathan Zuckerman, to Geoffrey Firmin, to Dolores Haze to share with Humbert Humbert who was, in the end, the second writer of that nymphet. Or going further and better still: give the Nobel to the best fictional—but impossible not to believe in—writer. Give the Nobel to Cide Hamete Benengeli, to David Copperfield, to Martin Eden, to Sebastian Knight, to Sigbjørn Wilderness, to Jack Duluoz, to Kenneth Toomey (who'd won it in his own novel), to the agonizing Bergotte, to T. S. Garp, to both Clarence "Clare" Vawdreys, to Carlos Argentino Daneri ex aequo with Carlos Oribe, to Richard Tull, to Gustav von Aschenbach, to Webb Gallagher "Buddy" Glass, to Kilgore Trout, to Emilio Renzi, to Charles "Chub" Fuller, To Bradley Pearson, to A. N. Dyer, to Marcus Ahearn, to the Jorge Luis Borges who wrote in the stories of Jorge Luis Borges, and, of course, to John Shade. And he was very sorry—apologies to all the ladies in the trenches with scissors held aloft—but lying in bed with the lights off and his eyes half-closed, he could only come up with masculine characters. And, fine, they could create another Nobel for the best wives of writers and give it to Vera Nabokov, always and forever, year after year. And even a prize to all those Zeldas dancing around out there. But he didn't think that would please the Amazons. So he begged them to listen to him—madam justice and ladies of the jury—and to understand that his omission wasn't a result of machismo or misogyny or sexism, but, just the opposite: all the possible female candidates had been devoured by Penelope and her Tulpa sisters, who were extremely close to him, writing from the Great Beyond of the moon. The radiation emitted by Penelope and her creations prevented him from even remembering other women writers and other written women, and it's not that he felt all that bad about it, but he was a little worried that he should feel bad about it.)

Anyway, IKEA's position as engaged international celebrity committed to all humanitarian causes wasn't the position of many secret writers who might actually be dying and probably would benefit, career wise, from meeting their end. IKEA didn't need that whole thing where death got translated into being discovered or rediscovered and showered with prizes, which made certain writers far bigger than they ever would have been while they were breathing and going to the bathroom to read while trying to hold their breath. (And, oh, here come all those walking dead from the other side: the unfinished texts, the random pages getting herded toward the corral of posthumous books and the cages of the living-dead and the self-satisfaction of letting morbid readers rewrite a writer as they saw fit and not even suspecting—subjugated by the somewhat unreflectively elevating scent of mausoleum—that there was nothing easier than writing a great unfinished novel, that the hard part was finishing it, that what was really important out of those thousand pages was the last one, to live to write it, to accomplish the goal of all fiction and not to get distracted by the metafiction that surrounded those products unfinishable for reasons of force majeure. And the widow and friends and publishers going here and there and everywhere invoking the writer's name, but not in vain, because they were paid handsomely to do so. And all of them barely able to hide their happiness at getting the chance to act so falsely sad because that living monster was no longer with them, writing and getting under their skin with his erratic moods and temperament, sure, he'd been alive, but he'd also been killing everyone else.)

Again, this hadn't been the case with IKEA, who'd been rescued on the shores of a beach that didn't appear on any maps and, of course, with the perfectly opportunistic manuscript of his "drama of self-discovery," written in squid ink over the course of months on the leaves of a carnivorous plant.

Yes: IKEA hadn't gone to a desert island with someone else's book to read, he'd come back from one with a book of his own to be read. It was titled: *Live*. And now multiple libraries around the world were fighting over who would get to exhibit it in their glass display cases and it'd topped best-seller lists in both the "normal" edition and in the "deluxe" limited and facsimile and signed format.

Then, claiming to be "traumatized by the experience," IKEA had given up literature for a while; because he was never one to miss out on a trend and always tried on all the emperor's clothes.

IKEA signed on to that whole giving-up-writing thing. And most importantly: to *announcing* that he was giving up writing.

IKEA made his announcement wearing a somber expression at a well-attended press conference. The guilt over having survived his beloved during the emergency landing after a lightning bolt struck the Cessna with his signature adorning tail rudder was guilty of prompting his retirement. And he hadn't recovered "and I may never recover" from what he'd done to survive that tragedy (sordid details closer and closer) and all of that.

But pretty soon (a week or two later), IKEA discovered that what happened to him was no longer news. That nobody cared if you gave up writing while you were still alive and hadn't even reached the age of the young Arthur Rimbaud (on the other hand, he'd said as much to him once, IKEA was sure Rimbaud had kept on writing, somewhere in Africa, among rifles and lions, and that the poems he wrote were so bad that he'd decided to amputate them along with his leg). Not even if, when it came to leaving it all behind, you were named Alice Munro or Philip Roth, who never stopped giving interviews—which is pretty much just writing aloud or via dictation—to remind the world over and over that "hey, listen, is there anybody out here? I want you all to know and to tell the world that I don't write anymore, that I've left writing behind, but that doesn't mean you should stop writing about me, please, right?"

And what did IKEA do to work his way back into everybody's mouths and microphones and screens? IKEA had come up with a stupidly ingenious or ingeniously stupid idea (in other words, emblematic of our time) and had once again summoned the media to inform them of some "shocking news."

IKEA told the assembled microphones and cameras that his deceased but never forgotten and forever present—"because, as you know, she's part of me"—beloved had appeared to him in the middle of the night. And she'd done so to "beg me to write again, not to feel bad on her account, I'd only done what she would've done in my situation, she was fine where she was now, and please, I had to take up my pen again to illuminate my darkness and, along the way, the darkness of the world." And that, moreover, she'd "begged" him to keep her memory alive in the following way: writing, one day yes and one day no, from her perspective; that IKEA be, also, a female IKEA and, in that way, he could be a "trans-hermaphrodite-bicephalous writer."

And everyone wept and applauded and thus, also, IKEA was further celebrated as the first alternating transgender writer from beyond the grave and was consecrated as the icon of the new feminism (all those girls who, upon reading *Sophie's Choice*, said there was no doubt or dilemma to be resolved there, that the solution was quite simple: she should've kept the girl and not the boy) and, along the way, turned his deceased companion into the best-selling author she was never able to become while alive.

Before long, in any case, IKEA was already dating Clavicle Rothstein (another successful Latin American writer, famous for her "unsettling" fictions and ready to be the latest addition to his swollen list of muses ever hungry to catch their big break) and he didn't seem to remember much about his previous "beloved sister of blood and ink." (And he'd always been surprised and baffled by the idea of writers or actors or screenwriters or musicians shacking up with members of their own species. Was it possible they didn't know that they could never be happy being with people who were already in another relationship, a relationship with their art? Having once fallen into that trap—into living with someone—he'd come to think that the best woman for him would be a kindergarten teacher or an expert gardener or something like that.)

And what'd IKEA done with his dead beloved, with her mortal remains, on that desert island?

Sordid details coming now:

IKEA had eaten her.

IKEA—who first and foremost and when all was said and done was nothing more than a literary cannibal—had survived on that island on the delicious and nutritious and well-fed flesh of his beloved.

And behind IKEA, in his wake, nothing grew and everything withered, but, at the same time, he kept right on expanding (and, yes, he couldn't help but fantasize about how IKEA hadn't limited himself to eating a dead woman, but how he'd also killed her first, in the name of Darwin and the survival of the fittest or the most prolific). Nothing took up more space than nothing. Following in his stellar streak of stardust came paddling—dreaming of making it on their own—all those once friends or generational colleagues or co-national writers who'd surrendered or gone over to the enemy. Or who—like IKEA, whose only possible and enviable virtue was discipline when it came to his writing schedule—wanted to think of the writer's desk as the relatively close relative of the office worker's.

Fixed hours, established rituals.

The supposed merit that the mediocre tend to lean on, he told himself, having never been able to systemize his work. And he excused and explained himself with the idea that the people who worked *like that* did so because they knew they weren't all that inventive. Because they would never venture out into the chaos of undisciplined yet true creation. Because when they wrote they weren't creating but just *describing*. And, later, giving predictable interviews where they always talked about their plots but never (because it was nonexistent) about their style. Interviews where they explained their methods (often offering them in well-remunerated writing workshops they taught) and provided answers increasingly like the artificial answers of beauty queen contestants. Yes: they all wanted world peace. And they said so in clear and simple sentences as concise as the concise sentences they wrote. Again: small size (understood as artistic brevity and not as suspicious smallness) had acquired an automatic prestige similar to that of Zen koans and haikus, no matter that, many times, when you read it, the sound it made was not that of one hand clapping but that of two hands opening the cheesy slap of a Hallmark card (and he, mediating between different forms of genius, agreed that the contemplation of a pond could afford as much pleasure as the sight of an ocean; which did not change the fact that the ocean would always be an ocean and the pond would always be a pond while most puddles would never be ponds or oceans). And so, one after another, sentences following characters who talked a lot but said very little. And who *never* read *anything*, because they were too concerned with being read. And with having their concerns (about their country, about their generation, about their family; what true writer would ever be concerned with those things is what concerned him) concern those who were concerned with reading them.

Oh, all those colleagues he'd once known were for him like something that no longer existed. They weren't mathematicians or carpenters' wives, but pretty much: some of them were just scraping by writing political thrillers (or some other bricolage-formulaic genre). And others had finally achieved the excellence of the love of flighty and unfocused online readers, embracing the mediocrity of raising themselves up as some kind of new-age prophets. And so they presented themselves as writers who'd renounced the fictitious to focus on the true and the historic and the social. And they took pictures of themselves with their cats or sitting in front a chessboard where they had quickly staged an impossible and supposedly brilliant match. Or in front of their suspiciously well-organized bookshelves that made one wonder which was the furniture, the bookshelf or the books it held up and contained and sheltered, whether it was a library of authors or an authored library (in ideal and just terms, he'd always thought that, really, writers should have to pose not with their backs to their bookshelves but *behind* their bookshelves with the books out in front of them, their faces barely visible in that narrow gap between the top of one row of volumes and the shelf above). And they did every interview they could and said—like backstage prompters for a scene they were no longer able to participate in—everything nobody else was saying about them. And in that way, after insisting so much on it, almost coming to believe that all of it was true through the arrogance of repetition. Their thing was the comfortable role of divulger/facilitator not of literature but of literariness. Latching their little last names onto big last names and in that way dreaming of the false positive and infection due to proximity. Quoting themselves to be quoted in a product to be consumed in small capsules and placebos of what they believed and that they believed in. Pages like magic potions to—with the help of Wikipedia and things written by others, without ever acknowledging it, because everything-belonged-to-everyone—convince themselves and everyone else that they had the cure for the ills of the world, including the lack of literacy of the people who sucked down their sugar pills, thinking that was the way they would become more cultured. Yes: to describe the book to them so they needn't read it. To be facilitators of the complex. And thus, all of a sudden, they had something to discuss over top-shelf dinners and at underground parties (that new kind of conversation where everyone talked at the same time and nobody listened to anyone else, because that's what they'd grown accustomed to doing online, so alone but believing themselves accompanied, thumb tap on the screen and thumbs up). Or inventing writing workshops where—like those addicts who "recover" by petting horses—they taught you to stare at a copy of *War and Peace* until you "felt you'd read it."

Others—perhaps the most astute or the most practical—had repositioned themselves as "consultants" or "cultural movers and shakers," and he'd redubbed them The Mob-Dicks: a mafia of whale egos and small-fry spirits who found it perfectly fine for writers—unlike athletes and actors and musicians, who were always paid small fortunes to show their faces or to be the center of attention—to travel the world for nothing, a nothing that consisted of being given the opportunity to be writers in public. And it was taken for granted that writers would do almost anything for free. At this rate, he thought, pretty soon writers would be getting recruited and volunteering without hesitation to be guinea pigs in the testing of new medications or to be launched into deep space, when they'd exhausted the option of appearing in documentaries on absurd subjects they knew next to nothing about or, even worse, on other writers, knowing that they would like nothing more—disinterestedly yet feeling oh so interesting—than to talk about what happened to them, which was actually just what had stopped happening to them. And those gangsters organized book fairs. And festivals (he'd known writers who appeared to be addicted to them and even had a lover at every festival they attended on rotation, like sailors going from port to port, on tours more never-ending than Bob Dylan's; because nothing seemed to frighten them more than being alone and at home, having to write, when it was so much easier to be a writer without having to write). And seminars. And *conferences* where some of them, to attract attention, shot pistols into the air or started weeping in public or (a gesture that to him, again, seemed somewhat contradictory and inexplicable like that of . . . ah . . . those TV weathermen going out into a storm in order to warn everyone not to go out into the storm) showed everyone their tits to denounce the objectification and reification of the female body. And round-tables that lacked all the epic of Camelot and that did nothing to establish the actual differences between Arthur and his noble knights and the more-or-less voluntary and talented squires who'd just shown up to the tournament for the first time. All of them—especially the squires; maybe because they'd been "brought up" in a world where social media had made screen-addiction limitless and unrestricted and of similar importance—seemingly under the impression that there was a single and uniform level when it came to jousting. That there were no levels or hierarchies, that everyone was equal, that there was no good reason not to get together for group photos beyond aesthetics or friendships; because it was really all about "sharing opinions with colleagues in a fruitful and enriching dialogue." And connecting with the public that always included some psychopath who stood up to announce: "I have a three-part question" and then proceeded to tell his life story, while he thought to himself "invented part, dreamed part, remembered part." Or that other one who asked, "What are your books about?" and it took him a great effort not to say "At one point they were about being written. Now they are about being read." Or some patriotic idiot would get up, one who—no matter his or her nationality, omnipresent with different faces and ages and sexes—asked him, invariably, who his favorite writer was from whatever country they happened to be in, as if a book's birth certificate mattered at all. And he answered—over and over and in his different incarnations—that, for him, *Bullet Park* or *À la recherche du temps perdu* or *Pale Fire* or Анна Каренина or *Slaughterhouse-Five* or *El sueño de los heroes* or 金閣寺 were all written in the same language and had been born in the same place: Masterpieceland.

And supposedly you went to those places, to those "literary festivals," to "connect with readers." But—in ideal terms—the truth is that, for that encounter to be fruitful or to make any sense, he thought, it would have to be staged like this: him at a table, writing, and them (in varying but diminishing numbers) in chairs reading one of his books. In other words: that he meet them in the act of reading and they meet him in the act of writing. The practice of theory and the theory of practice in synch. And that in that way—naturally and all at once—nobody would find themselves faced with the frustration of asking, please and in vain, any questions (if possible not in three parts and including question marks and inflection) on behalf of the audience that the writer would have to answer. Because, clearly, he would be too busy writing codes for all of them to decode. And now that he thought about it: wouldn't it be far more logical and interesting if, in the final minutes of the event, he was the one who asked questions of his supposed readers and learned what all of them thought of him? That he even demanded proof that they were actually there because they'd read his books and might, even, find themselves obliged to describe them to him? But no one ever came up with anything *like that*. And, when he had suggested it, they gave him strange looks, looks that said they were suddenly realizing they'd made a mistake when sending out invitations. Or when deciding whom to invite.

Yes: he'd never been much for the likeability movement; more than once he'd said, "I like writing more and more and like being a writer less and less" (and he'd always thought that comedy smelled much better when you were cooking it up than it tasted later when you ate it); and he suffered a kind of cosmic-existential anxiety upon entering a hotel room, knowing he was surrounded by other writers. Writers who—he knew this too, because he was also one of them—might be good or bad when it came to writing, but who he knew beyond a shadow of a doubt were, every single one of them, what many people would describe as "bad people." Profoundly egotistical beings who only thought of themselves, because what they did they did alone. And, like him, apocalyptic and destructive people convinced that to create a world of their own first they had to destroy everyone else's world (there was a publishers guild, associations of translators, unions of screenwriters; but as far as he knew, writers hadn't even bothered to get together to collectively fight for their twisted rights, because nothing mattered to them less than their fellow writers unless—with an icy smile just before going up to share the same stage—they found out that someone else was paid more or less than they were to participate in the same event).

And he—having to choose between being a truly good person or a possibly good writer—had opted without hesitation and putting it all on the line for the latter. He'd risked it.

And so, he knew it well, he was a horrible person: an enriched miser, an endangered and dangerous man.

Someone with a lot of hate to give.

A person who'd broken the world record multiple times for all the times he said, "I'm sorry," and all that sentiment of regret had turned him into a person full of sentiment. In other words: a re-sentfull person.

And he'd only become fully aware of it—of how bad he'd been so he could be a good writer—when he'd stopped writing, when he could no longer write, like someone who only becomes conscious of how sick he's been after recovering his good health.

And, as by way of excuse, he liked to believe he'd always been a little bit like those charmingly villainous characters from fiction; like the "heroes" of Martin Amis or Saul Bellow or J. P. Donleavy or Bruce Jay Friedman or Joseph Heller or David Gates or Mordecai Richler or Kurt Vonnegut. (Catastrophic catastrophists and unpresentable presences all. Hatable beings so beloved by him and to whom he'd wanted to pay homage.

In a kind of, what in interviews he described as a "national thriller of manners" that he thought of—and he repeated it over and over with the enthusiasm of a used-car salesman in those same interviews when his first novel came out—as a continuation of the irreverent spirit of his stories in *National Industry*. In that novel there appeared, again, a lot of *desaparecidos*. And he'd even, very much à la Bellow, cannibalized multiple characters from the *mondo* of advertising and the underground planet of his parents. He wrote that book at full speed, in one week and based on a dream. And he called it *Samizdat*. The title was—as was appropriate for that kind of novel featuring a sensitive bastard—the name of the protagonist who made and unmade everything in his vicinity. And at the time, he thought of that book as very commercial and that it would return him to his initial fame and shower him with riches. But no, never again: he'd gone off the rails, and that train had passed by, and that train had run him over.)

On the other hand, good people were generally bad writers. At most, if they were lucky, they were decent storytellers and even sold well and, for that reason, won those well-funded-and-obviously-and-calculatedly-orchestrated-among-publishers-and-agents awards. That's what bad writers were good for, bad writers who, often, were overly concerned with being considered good people: to advance a few spaces and harvest praise and get translations and medals, hanging in the aerodynamic slipstream of the closest IKEA derivative (the uncommon fake good person who wrote authentically badly and for whom things tended to go exceedingly well) in their home countries, which were generally going through all kinds of crises. Taking from there everything of the very little there was to take and, if possible, making the leap to the publishing headquarters of the Empire to be considered—for fifteen pages of fame—the latest in an infinite line of more or less interesting indigenous writers. Someone ready to do their little number that, with any luck, a lot of luck, would bag them the four or five numbers of an advance courtesy of some compassionate advancer. All of them taking advantage of the open field while the good writers were maliciously occupied and distracted killing each other off.

And the phenomenon of social media had done nothing but increase this effect exponentially: now the good bad writers didn't even have to go to bars or book launches to cordially insult each other. They could do so right from their desks, even duplicating themselves with new personalities and aliases to thereby fire off insults and put-downs from multiple mouths at the same time and, oh, what a beautiful thing (personally, he'd never gone that far, he had no interest in wading into the online swamp; he wished no ill on any of those writers he recognized as colleagues, but he couldn't handle things going *too* well for them either).

Yes: writers were bad people, because you had to be a bad person to write well, to write thinking only about what you were writing and not caring about anybody or anything else. Once you accepted that, you could try to be pleasant and kind and even generous; but, in the half-light of your own abode, the dark truth gleamed bright and forced you to squint your eyes and avert your gaze.

And to wonder once again what you were doing there: in a hotel room always too close to or too far (never at a reasonable distance, maybe a result of the sadism or masochism of the organizers) from the literary festival of the moment. Wondering why all those little trips weren't given to writers at the beginning of their careers—and not in the middle or at the end—after one of those "wise juries" concluded that there was something there: a promise of great things that, no doubt, would soon arrive and would be in better health if that young writer were sent out as soon as possible to make the rounds and find inspiration at festivals the world over.

Unpacking and opening his laptop with the almost weightless movements of an astronaut in the void, hoping that space would somehow fill up. Turning it on like someone assembling—reassembling—a memory.

And there was the screensaver he'd chosen: the red eye of HAL 9000. That other computer, for once and in that case, hooked on humans and not, as happened now, the reverse: everyone addicted to never forgetting to increase the memory of their phones and tablets. That eye watching him watch it throughout his sleepless nights while he remembered that—in the discarded footage from the scene in which the astronaut Dave Bowman lobotomizes the computer saying don't be afraid, it will be just like falling asleep—HAL 9000 almost sobbed "Well, I have never slept . . . I . . . don't know what it's like." And Bowman answers, without stopping what he's doing with the screwdriver, that "It's very nice, HAL. It's peaceful. It's very peaceful."

And he neither had peace nor did he rest in peace.

And the idea of that cycloptic screensaver had at some point seemed amusing to him.

Not anymore.

Now it was nothing but an enervating and disorienting rejoinder. And it caused him a displacement similar in intensity—but with nothing of its grandeur—to that experienced by the astronaut Dave Bowman almost at the end of *2001: A Space Odyssey*, arriving to that final dwelling place in the far reaches of the universe (he'd once toyed with the idea that that Versaillesque suite was really another one of the many cages in the Tralfamadore zoo where the optometrist Billy Pilgrim was also being studied) after traversing a space full of stars, many more stars than a five-star hotel and, oh, an "I'm Afraid, My Mind Is Going" hanging from doorknob outside. (And he left that room so similar to so many other rooms, thinking he was there for the love of art and without getting paid anything and so tired of the fact that after so many years art didn't love him a little or, at least, wouldn't just totally ignore him and leave him in peace and not force him to accept this kind of invitation. And with all that despondency, he headed at top speed to the hotel bar to get loaded on tequila in the company of Eli Cash or some other writer who, like him, felt on the brink of the most spontaneous of combustions. And he went to poorly-attended panels where, he remembers, the moderators of the day asked him things like who his favorite living author was and he answered with things like why didn't they ask him about his favorite living books, books that could've been written centuries ago, taking into account the fact that, for him, the majority of writers living today were parenting stillborn books. Or, if not, insisting on that silly game of getting him to name names and affinities and phobias, which book of another writer did he wish he'd written. And, then, he told the story of the masterfully composed notice supposedly published in the newspapers of the time by the reoffending and tripolar Antarctic explorer Ernest Shackleton to recruit comrades in adventure. A notice considered perfect by the most qualified of advertising scholars, the one that all advertising copywriters wished they'd written. A notice, that, in December 1913, everyone swore they'd read, but that actually never got published. And then he told the audience that something similar had happened to him with some of his favorite books: when he reread them, when he risked the dangerous expedition of going back there, he'd discovered, with an icy chill, that they were not at all the books he remembered; that they were other or no longer even were. That they didn't seem all that good to him and had been far surpassed by the rewritten memory of those books. That in that way, somehow, he was now a kind of a coauthor of those books; and that, as such, he'd improved them at the cost of proving that they were worse than he remembered. Or he explained that there were also books that seemed to remain intact and untouchable in the face of any revisitation. Thus, the proof as unsettling as it was immoveable that nobody reads the same book two times, that nobody reads the same book twice. And—as a one-time response to that question they'd asked him about what book by someone else he wished had his name on the cover—he concluded that, the mature pleasure of having read that favorite book by someone else imposed itself over the rather adolescent desire to have written it. And that, confronted with the agony of writing *Moby-Dick* or *À la recherche du temps perdu* or *Pale Fire*, he now opted for the joy of being able to read them with pure, unadulterated pleasure. So they should devote themselves to writing books of their own that honored and celebrated the reading of the books of others. And, with any luck, their own books would end up making them wish that somebody else had written them, so that they could read them: that they wound up liking something they wrote so much when they read it that they wished they'd never written it. "It's something that, luckily, falls away like a first skin with the loss of certain literary innocence, when you don't hesitate to point, with the pride of agitated hormones, to this or that masterpiece as a text you would've liked to author. But as the years pass you realize, with wisdom and maybe resignation, that, if you'd written them, you never would've been able to enjoy reading them as you should . . . Because the best reading is for everyone else. Not for the author but for the reader. The reading from outside and submerging yourself page after page until you feel you're part of it. Always and forever . . . And that is the only certainty: you start really writing—for good or ill—*like yourself* when you finally realize that you'll never be able to write *like someone else*. The same thing happens to great songwriters: they resign themselves to the fact that the songs they like best are too hard to learn and so they compose others in their own way and to suit themselves. And then, when you least expect it, all of a sudden . . . Style. A Style of Your Own out of the fragments of others. And that's great: because in this way, instead of having innumerable possibly well-meaning yet false-all-the-same versions of The Beatles or of The Kinks, suddenly you *also* get the accomplished final perfection—arising from the initial flaw of a bad-and-failed imitator—of XTC or The Soft Boys or The Go-Betweens or The Replacements." Or, for him, any of those other "cult" bands that he liked so much because they felt so close to him in the whole "I could have been a contender" and as perfect musicalizers of the small cult of his persona and writings and . . . "To sum it up: what each of us has to do is nothing more and nothing less than write as well as we can and be happy because others have written far better than we ever will," he concluded. And, almost in a whisper, added: "In fact, there are books of mine I would've preferred to read and not to have written . . . And there's nothing I would like more than to discover that reading one of my books made someone so happy that they would never ever want to have written it . . . If all goes well, if he or she matures and ages as he or she should, that writer and that reader living inside the same body and, at first, living an oh so teenage romance in which they feel and want to be identical, but, with time, the one will grow apart from the other, waving in passing every so often, missing each other but with little interest in finding out how time has passed for the other. If they insist on the childishness of being Siamese twins forever, they'll end up fighting a duel or being chopped apart with an axe." Or he revealed to them that he was there "for the love of art and free of charge and so tired that, after so many years, art didn't love him even a little or, at least, completely ignore him and leave him in peace and not force him to accept this kind of invitation." Or he confided in them that they shouldn't have confidence in those writing laboratories that sold placebos of something that would never be an exact science and whose only grace ran through uncertainty, through writing while reading yourself without really knowing what would happen on the next page, through embracing and never letting go of the pleasures of the antitechnological in technological times. Or he warned them that "The two books that are hardest to write are, always, the first one and the next one. The first, because you think that you won't be able to do it; and the next one, because you think what is or what would be the point of continuing to do it"; while he thought that now, for him, his next book would be like his first book: the worst of both worlds, Sisyphus's stone in the Underworld or, less mythical and more pathetic, Laurel & Hardy's piano on the stairs at Silver Lake; and that between one and the next and at the end of all of them he was left so alone, like one of those radio-aficionados under a night sky pierced by stars, trying to tune in something, anything; a voice, a melody, a cry for help or assistance. Or he told them that same thing he'd said before: that writers were like bonsais who dreamed of being oaks; and, sure, okay, there was always some clever guy in the audience who commented that there were bonsai oaks; to which he responded that he wasn't going to waste his already wasted time arguing about botany with someone who was unable to understand what he was trying to say; and that, in any case, looked at like that, his line was even sadder and truer: a castrated oak that would never reach its natural height and power due to so many factors outside its control and in the control of others and yet, even still, the oak couldn't forget to remember what it could've been but wasn't and never would be. Or that they should know that one of the unmistakable signs that someone was a *true* writer was that they had readers who were certain they were going to hate what that writer had written even before having read it, but who felt obliged to read it anyway so they could *truly* hate it. Or that they shouldn't fall prey to the easy and automatic temporal temptation of the youthful tech-dystopia—nothing attracts tech zombies more than a zombie-tech novel—because nothing goes out of style faster in writing than youth and the zombies that come next only want to bury older zombies alive and to the death and to plant headstones in the mode of lapidarists for their entropic novels. Or that they should be very careful when playing the generation card—and that they should understand that their own generation wasn't the only generation, there was also the one that came before and the one that would come after—that, before long, is always a losing card that nobody wants to read or that gets lost in the mail or along the way. Or that they should never equate automated casual sex with automatic wild talent. Or that they should take off running when approached by political-familial sagas with titles like *The Faces of the Masks* or that marketed themselves as . . . uh . . . oh . . . *novels of their time*—as if there were a particular time to be novelized—and that opened by comparing a city to an anthill. Or that they should accept that a writer didn't have to belong to or be of the place where he or she happened to be born; that, in any case, the true nationality of a writer is revealed more by the place the writer chooses of his or her own volition, or, even, by some place they passed through along the way, even if they were only there for a few days, because of a personal choice or a random accident. Or that they shouldn't lose their way and should be aware that, to advance in their work, they would have to enter into the most disorienting and disjointed of worlds: a world that appeared to be assembled as a series of desynchronized concentric spheres that demanded that writers think like publishers, that publishers do their job in the manner of literary critics, and that critics be given, on more than one occasion, the right to feel that they were the true writers of what others had written. Or that they should take great care to not end up becoming those supposedly admired cult writers who were nothing but elegant and creative ice skaters, confined to their frozen circle or glacial rectangle beyond which they were absolutely inept at any task and let's see how they manage to go buy bread or the newspaper while wearing those skates almost as sharp as suicide razorblades. Or that they should watch out for something even worse: becoming a writer's writer's writer's writer. Or, to all those who came up to say that they also wrote and thought they wanted to be writers, he offered the warning—even though, oh, how he hated all sports analogies in the realm of literature—that they should never forget the fact that many people think they want to be boxers until they have to fight people who are totally and absolutely convinced that they want to be boxers. Or that it was far nobler and more epic to lose by K.O. fighting for a style than it was to get an O.K. win by points with something merely plot-driven and functional. Or that they not knock themselves out by thinking of their own book as just another accessory *à la* Barbie & Ken—believing that it is more important to be a writer than to write, taking more pleasure in being than in doing—to be carried around in that same little plastic hand that held a tennis racquet or a watering can or a frying pan. Or that they should keep their guard up in the presence of those writers—more or less seers in the land of the half-blind—who only mentioned Chekhov or Babel or Kafka's fucking diaries and that, in general, ran writing workshops akin to those third-world subterranean sweatshops that exploited minors useless for everything apart from, due to the smallness of their hands and brains, obeying like robots and inserting microchips into gadgets for the elite to use. Or that a lot of the time the whole thing about standing on the shoulders of giants just meant being dandruff. Or that they should always keep in mind that quote by Vladimir Nabokov about how there's only one school where you could learn to write and that was the school of talent and that, oh, talent is not something that can be taught; though there are techniques that help you better appreciate that talent and to find out that you have it or, far more likely from a statistical standpoint, that you don't. Or that they should not lose sight of the fact that they were living in times in which intelligence was the most undervalued thing in fiction and imagination the most overvalued. Or he gave them a choice, Dylanesquely, to *play* or to *pose*. Or that they should always keep in mind that if there was any ambition more unstable than that of wanting to be a writer, it was that of having wanted to be a writer. Or to those who said they were thinking of starting to write he recommended that that they spend more time thinking about reading; that they understood writing as the more or less disobedient daughter to be trained by that mother that was reading; that they thought more about writing than about publishing; that they thought more about writing the lives of others than about putting their own lives in writing; that they thought more about writing without a safety net than about writing on social networks; that they thought about how they could think even more than they were thinking; that they thought about *this* and not about *that*. Or that they thought about whether that almost addicted-like and automatic tendency to write about their childhoods wasn't just a misdirected fear of the future. Or that, if they were to use some autobiographical episode in their fictions, they understood that that moment, from then on, would always be part of their fictions: transmuted, abducted, given up like a hostage you no longer even consider rescuing, more written than lived and, if everything went reasonably well, entering—to never again be a part of their past—the eternal present of their books. Or that, he almost dropped to his knees and begged, they avoid what he'd come to call Driving Parent Syndrome: that recurrent scene in all juvenile fiction that recalled that parent—saint or lunatic or beast or genius—behind the wheel of an automobile bound for the easiest and most convenient of domestic epiphanies for someone riding in the backseat and, listening to the always cordially tense conversation between parents, taking shelter in that misunderstanding that people say things in the safe movement of their vehicles that they would never say in the seismic stillness of their homes, while checking their WhatsApp account and, ah, why don't they all crash, flip, burst into flames, and die, eh? Or that they should stop being so conservative and obvious and so young and so in love with themselves and take the risk of hating themselves a little or, at least, of feeling somewhat ridiculous. Or he implored them to, please, regain the time and wisdom of the past and become, once again, the seasoned readers of yesteryear who knew perfectly well and right from the start that everything a created character said and thought and did was NOT, necessarily, what his or her creator did and thought and said, and, for that reason, that character did not have to be likable or rouse the sympathies of all those readers sedated by overexposure to online profiles where everyone wanted to be sympathetic—to like and to be liked and to be likable; and, yes, all of this is called *fiction* and there must be some reason why that is and was and will be the case. Or to not go and immediately Google the causes and reasons for everything: that NOT knowing the reasons why, for example, asparagus is one of the few foods that immediately transfers its smell to urine could lead to something far *wiser* and more interesting in fiction—like in the old days, when people invented explanations for everything they didn't know—than the instantaneous and exact scientific explanation within reach of their fingertips. Or to be able to see that the fact that they had Twitter accounts that were similar/unified in their look and design to those of Barack Obama or Madonna or Salman Rushdie didn't mean that they were similar in their accomplishments or that, even less, that the democratic/anarchic availability of a tool like that didn't give them the automatic right to go around cyberspace, demanding explanations and taking prisoners to force confessions in the name of free speech or unrestrictedly pointing accusatory fingers at people far better known than they were; and, in any case, he pointed out to them, engagement and commitment and thirst for justice would not last them more than forty-eight hours, because there were so many new causes to take up or denounce. Or he clarified for them that literature was not one of those playful *escape rooms*: if you actually went into it, there was no way out, there were no tracks to follow or solutions to find, no escape hatch to open when they discovered that there was only room to be novel or Nobel there inside; that there was very little space for those already seasoned writers lost out in that open yet suffocating intermediate and gray room in which it was very difficult to breathe if you weren't the fleeting flavor of the week or the forever consecrated indigestion. Or that the practice should always come before the theory and not the other way around. Or that—if they weren't convinced by all the above—they should devote themselves to more fruitful endeavors; like designing and commercializing a fragrance named Ex Libris or Biblios with the vanillaish and earthy scent of the organic polymer known as lignin, that unmistakable smell that books give off as the paper and glue and typographies degrade and that is never entirely the same, because there are more inks in a mathematics text book than in a collection of sonnets; and, yes, there was nothing left to imagine, because he'd found out that a company called Smell of Books already sold a spray containing bibliophile essence to spray on e-readers and tablets. Or he pointed out to them that it wouldn't be long before virtual reality would be virtually indistinguishable from their real realities and that, meanwhile and in the meantime, a good novel—that other world of one's own that every writer should aspire to—offered far more and better consolation than any of those gamer consoles, because you always came out the winner of the game of any book you picked up. Or—if they managed to make a name for themselves—he begged them to ignore the songs of those siren-harpies asking them for texts alluding to great catastrophes of reality like terrorist attacks or virulent epidemics or auto-quarantining, further intensifying the contagion of autofiction and *autobiographies* and the propagation of plague-ridden and contagious *zoombies* of Zoom; he implored them to flee the immediate and the instantaneous as subject and to seek out something timeless and placeless, something that was everywhere at all times; and, please, that they not sign up for little online classes where they were instructed to compose poetic texts based on "personal files—photographs, emails, letters, text messages, notes, drafts, shopping lists, expenses, search and web histories—to create an automatic description of the I, coming up with dynamic forms of using personal objects, data, and accumulated information to compose poetic texts." Or he begged them, though he wasn't without guilt here, to not give birth to novels narrated by historical characters and no no no: there was nobody out there waiting for the interior monologue of the unborn and knifed baby of Sharon Tate or the rant of the ice axe buried in the skull of Leo Trotsky, right? Or he clarified for them that it wasn't the publication date of a given book—its place and time in the history of literature—that mattered, what mattered was the moment in which one read it. Or that, much less, should they go around trembling because their characters had taken control of them in the same way that actors claimed to be possessed by the intensity of the roles they had to play, losing sight or gaining blindness regarding what it actually meant to act or to write: to be someone else for a while in their lives and forever in their work. Or he suggested to them that they start by deeply reading and studying all those writers they wanted to be like; but—once they were already published writers themselves, maybe somewhat similar to their most-admired favorites—that they devoted themselves from then on more to reading and studying all the writers they would never be similar to but who were no less admirable and, paradoxically, more favored precisely because of that insurmountable distance; and only then to return to their first heroes and, rereading them, to ask their eloquent silences if they'd been in any way worthy of them, of their radiations, of their toxic influence and their healthy influenza. Or he warned them that the true classics were the ones, after having read them so many years before, you remembered next to nothing about but that at the same time made you remember absolutely everything; and that Starbuck wasn't the same as Starbucks. Or he pointed out to them that they shouldn't take the whole Canon thing and the slots to be filled on the shelves of their libraries all that seriously, because the whole Canon thing was really contrived for people who didn't read or for those who wanted to read only what was necessary to feel *well-read* and so they needed those training wheels on the bicycle of universality because they couldn't pedal their own Canon and main-tain the most personal of balances, no hands, at top speed and, every so often, fall down and crash with a smile of pleasure and pain at the same time. Or that they shouldn't limit themselves to only reading their contemporaries just because they were their contemporaries and always deemed "great" to thereby guarantee their own and recip-rocal "greatness." Or that they shouldn't just read the dead authors they wanted to be like or the living authors they wanted to like them. Or that they shouldn't start writing because they thought they should be celebrated just for doing it but because they needed to celebrate everything they had yet to read by writing. Or that they not succumb to the-exceedingly-juvenile-yet-now-for-all-ages sin of thinking they were revolutionizing something just by swapping one letter for another, making a language that had always had space for everyone supposedly more inclusive and, worst of all, thinking that the rest of humanity had the obligation to change along with them; something so absurd and outside of time and place that it was like the equivalent of the most Aquarian hippies from back in the day demanding that even their cancerous grandparents soak themselves in LSD in order to change the world. Or he begged them, in the name of their generation, not to break indiscriminately with the past, that there was *something* there, something interesting; that their generation was, probably, the last one to read the same books when they were growing up that their parents' and their parents' parents generations had read; that that chain shouldn't be broken, that there was a reason you begin with a *Once upon a time* . . . and not with a *There was a time* or, even worse, a constant and elastic and self-referential *There is a time and another time and another time* . . . He suggested that they not succumb to the arrogance of saying "no one gets it" when what they should do is humbly get up and say, "I don't get it" and, oh, there were ever more of the former and ever fewer of the latter. And he explained to them that there was no need for them to post a comment in reaction to everything they read; that most of the time there was nothing to say because it'd already been said in what they just read; that the relationship had always been that of reading what someone else had written; and that there was no reason at all for them to leave a comment down below, but always feeling so far above, about what'd been written, a comment that, generally, would never be read by the author being commented on. Or that whenever anyone said that thing about how "a picture is worth a thousand words," they should come back with a "okay, fine, so then tell me that a picture is worth a thousand words with just one picture." Or he talked to them about the horror movies he'd seen as a kid and almost screamed at them like a mad scientist: "Read like Dracula and write like Frankenstein! Read with unquenchable thirst and write using only the best parts of everything you've read!" Or—if they made him—he would read some especially cryptic fragment of his own work, warning them that "Reading yourself is as disturbing and unsensual as dancing with your own sister; but a really ugly sister; a sister who doesn't excite any perverse fantasy, but, to the contrary, an unrelenting desire to be an only child; a sister who looks nothing like my beautiful sister, and all of you already know who she is, because she's the only reason you've come to listen to me, right?" Or he suggested that they immediately start a book club where they would exclusively discuss books that everybody hated "with a passion that seemed a lot like love." And he begged them, if at some point they found themselves obliged to respond to one of those surveys of the "Most-Important-Novels-in-History" variety, to always clarify that they were "The Most Important Novels in My History." And most important of all: they had to demand to be paid for their participation, as if it were an article they were writing, "because surveys were the formula cultural supplements used so the party could be free for them and so that, every so often, they could come in under budget that week." And perpetuate that absurd and supposedly beneficent idea that culture should be free, that books should be given away and read without the author receiving any payment and, if they were going to be *that* generous, wouldn't it be more logical that, ahead of culture, they make food and lodging and healthcare free? And the host/moderator would get unsettled listening to him and look at him, again, as always, with an odd expression as if to say "We like to keep things simple here and I was just asking you for the title of a book, preferably a well-known book, so that then the audience could go out and buy it at one of these stands and . . .") And all their nerves and anxiety and worry about maintaining their position and the space they occupied and their ecstatic status as cultural functionary. It was clear now that everything ran through maintaining your position on the deck and—if you didn't have access to the bridge—at least you were relieved to have gotten out of the engine room, away from the scorching heat of the boilers, into which guest writers were thrown as fuel or into whose flames they hurled themselves for next to nothing, a couple photographs or a few drinks. And so, the "organizers" of disorganized conferences stared at their carbonated-ink-stained hands and felt so lucky to be sending out these invitations and not having to accept them, like someone casting nets into the sea, convinced they would catch something because there were more fish hungry to be fished all the time. And every so often those organizers published something themselves to keep their bibliography fresh; but their main task consisted of cajoling library rats to go here and there in exchange for plane tickets and hotel rooms and food vouchers and, if they were lucky, some scattered applause to boost their egos and maybe even a fling with some groupie or colleague as desperate or depressed as they were: with those illustrated girls or written boys who had no interest in their pasts and only wanted the future of appearing in a future book, inspiring in someone else what they couldn't in themselves. It was easier. More convenient. And more exciting; because when a writer told a reader that he or she wanted to know everything about him or her it was—for many, but not for him, whose automatic reflex was to distance himself and to run away—something far more erotic than saying I love you or I want to make love to you. It was like saying "I want to make you."

He'd gone from one to the next like a succession of Vietnams, where it was always Groundhog Day, until he could no longer take it or was no longer "summoned," which was pretty much same thing. So, he'd faced the facts and then gotten the hell out of there blowing it all up behind him (really blowing himself up, like one of those suicide bombers) and getting himself definitively expelled from Boomlandia, just as he was now being expelled from Stepmother Land. And he no longer had anywhere to touch down (his passport was stamped with too many stamps) and he didn't have much time left to adjust to those places before being ejected again. For a while now, his sense had been that he was forever departing and never arriving as he invoking that great quote from J. Robert "Shiva" Oppenheimer about how "The optimist thinks this is the best of all possible worlds. The pessimist fears it is true."

But he wasn't thinking about any of those things anymore.

He was already far past all of that.

After so much time trying futilely to write, now he was going to move on to the practice, to living it, so that maybe, later, somebody else would write him, pointing him out, up in the sky and thinking that what'd happened to him might make a good story.

So, now, ever further from all of that. Enough plotting out the same thing over and over: plotting out his resentment of others and his disgust with almost everything that had to do with his occupation and goodbye to the anguished diatribe of lightning and thunder.

At least for a while.

And to keep on flying through the blue and cloudless sky, in that airplane of the airline known as YesterdAir. His favorite airline whose particularity was to always travel, no matter the destination or the shortest distance ("Oh, I believe in YesterdAir" was its jingle/slogan as obvious as it was inevitable), in the opposite direction of the hands of a clock. In that way the aircraft regained its lost time, writing lines in the air, long white lines streaking across the deep blue that, if the sky were a book, would fill entire pages without a single period, only commas and semicolons in sight.

YesterdAir's inflight magazine was called *Get Back* (and he always got a free upgrade when traveling on this airline, because at one point he'd been a contributor to the magazine's pages, after years spent writing for *Volare*, his first job, courtesy of his "discoverer" Abel Rondeau, whom he'd always considered immortal, but who'd died not long ago, struck down, perhaps, by the scandal surrounding his exploits at Switzerland's CERN, where Rondeau had sent him to write an article he never planned to write because he couldn't write and because his objective inside the particle accelerator had been far more ambitious than to write a light travelogue in sentences far shorter than the ones he used to remember such things). And YesterdAir's frequent-flier miles (and he had many of them waiting for him to travel and a final boarding pass courtesy of *Volare*, that he was using now, for another pending article never to be written with the destination of a giant necropolis and a couple of ghost towns) program was called *Solaris* and had the slogan "Get back again." And the airline didn't advertise with any of those typical "high flying" ads that Nabokov considered his private *bête noire* and that depicted "the snack served by an obsequious wench to a young couple—she eyeing ecstatically the cucumber canapé, he admiring wistfully the hostess."

YesterdAir preferred, instead, to offer a different kind of melancholy.

For breakfast, they served madeleines with Bergotte tea or various infusions (and then he remembered, he'd written it down somewhere, that the meaning of *breakfast* referred to *breaking* the night's *fast* where sleeping or waking dreams chewed or imbibed). And they offered yellow liquor of Elstir and one of those cool and pricey designer mineral waters "from one of Hades rivers"; and its name was Lethaeus, and, when you drank it, it provoked "a mild and relaxing amnesia of pains and anxieties." And they sold duty-free harmonious Vinteuil perfumes and flashy Charlus watches. And all the flight attendants were named Odette or Celeste and the pilots' surnames were always Saint-Loup or Agostinelli. And the pillows and blankets were always embroidered with the words "Semper Memento." And in the most first of classes, the most exclusive individual cabins offered the luxury of having the plastic of their partitions lined with sheets of cork.

And now, in his headphones, he heard a song from an album by Ray Davies (who once, ever so gentlemanly, had invited him to afternoon tea and to one of his shows in Manhattan after testing him to make sure he was as big a fan of him and his work as he claimed) and he tapped the prancing beat with his feet and followed the sad lyrics in his mind. And, as tends to happen with the great songs, it sounded like it had just been written and was perfectly suited to that time and place. And in it, Ray Davies's voice—always so well-traveled yet so fresh; the voice of a vanquished victor, perfect company for a weather-beaten suitcase covered in stickers from places he would never see again—warning anyone who needed to hear it that "West to east / See the night turn into day / Move so fast / Too bad that you can't stay . . . You're always on my mind / And I can't tell you that I'd / Willingly follow you / To the end of the earth."

And, yes, he was a man with neither origin nor belonging but with Ella always on his mind. Not thinking of following her to the end of the earth, but yes, now, thinking of her on his way to the end of the earth.

And, also, thinking of Penelope.

And of The Son of Penelope or of The Son: of He Whose Name Must Not Be Mentioned and who sometimes, to try and diminish his importance, he preferred to think of in lowercase letters and with a somewhat casual air, with a better not to even think of his name, right? Or not? And believing, in vain, that in that way he could reduce his power and influence and memory; but knowing that, in reality, he'd never be able to elevate him to the diminished He Who Must Not Be Thought About. Or, much less, He Who Finally And Forever Has Been Forgotten.

Because he thought about him more than ever and remembered him better than ever.

And he was why he was where he was and was going where he was going.

Because when he managed to conceal his face—or hide himself from him—the memory of the boy's small hand in his own big hand (a perfect fit, like Cinderella's foot in the glass slipper) came back with greater power and presence. And then, once again, he would hear his voice in the conversations they used to have. Conversations that were so different from the typical and spasmodic and free associating (It's so hot-Home-Death-Jell-O-Batman) conversations people tended to have with children and that, also, had a lot in common with the way he wrote his books. But his conversations with The Son of Penelope—who, if he'd ever devoted himself to writing, would have been an eighteenth or nineteenth century novelist of the experimental variety—always revolved around on a single topic that they wouldn't let go of until it'd been fully researched and exhausted and then it was never spoken of again, as if they were crossing off items from a list of various interests and assorted curiosities.

The Son of Penelope had been, yes, something magical.

A *changeling* who lacked the final half of that legend: because he—that boy with the flaming hair—had been taken without anybody being left in his place. All that remained was his powerful and incorporeal memory. A memory that could be altered slightly but never too much. The memory of He Whose Name Must Not Be Mentioned was precisely the memory of He Whose Name Must Not Be Mentioned. And no rewriting or re-remembering could improve it.

Not like in the case of the Penelope's parents, who'd been and were also his parents; but whom he now evoked more with the profile of characters than of people, more personas than persons. Parents who—disappearing, making them disappear—had functioned for Penelope and for him like Joan Vollmer for William S. Burroughs and Syd Barrett for Pink Floyd: the one and the other had disappeared so that, in the wake of their disappearances, the people left behind could reappear as artists, as true writers, as serious musicians.

Their shadows had cast lights.

And he and Penelope had *grown up*, indeed.

But now he was an anomaly of the system (an exwriter) and an orphan with no descendants and now, without even a sister; though Penelope was always hovering over his shoulder with her wings spread wide.

He was a *rara avis* nobody said anything about anymore except, if he was lucky, that he was a curious case with interesting plumage. And that was all. Just an accursed writer nobody bothered to curse. A name (though his popularity when *National Industry* came out had landed him in his now nonexistent country of origin's best crosswords) almost unmentioned now and popping up every so often in a laconic or bumbling conversation or on a list of enigmas nobody cared about solving: because it was more annoying than complicated to accuse or exonerate him of the crime of not fitting anywhere in the puzzle. And his work was read even less now; because among its lingering side effects—according to the critical and revisionist prospectuses of academics—were the brain-busting migraines and nausea and dizziness triggered by the design of a piece that didn't quite fit, a piece like that one room it was better to never enter; because you didn't know if you would ever make it out of there once you sat down in that armchair and opened those books.

And now, there he was. And there was little or nothing he could do but look out the windows, look into the distance as the distance looked back at him.

And there was nobody sitting beside him on this airplane. Nobody to not talk to and absolutely everybody with whom to talk to himself.

Though sometimes (not many) he had to admit that interesting things could be overheard and that the respiration of airplane air could even bring inspiration.

One night, on another airplane, flying in the opposite direction that this one was now flying (he hadn't been able to get a ticket on YesterdAir for that trip, a trip with the more-than-final destination of a particle accelerator), he had a conversation with another passenger. A man sitting beside him and, as if in a trance, speaking in whispers like—he always thought the same thing—people speak in a church (a church already in the heavens but that at any moment could go with the Devil straight to hell). Around him, many of the other travelers were sleeping, sunken into that profound somnolence triggered by the limited use of their mobile phones, which they touched (because someone out there had bothered to do the work of counting) between two or three thousand times a day, the number of times (because someone out there had bothered to do the work of counting that *too*) that not long ago they touched their faces. Whereas now they all touched their phones to take pictures of their faces. And they'd already made videos of the clouds out the window, which had suddenly darkened as if by the art of magic, simulating a false night that aligned with the time of the place where they would be landing hours later and, at the same time, hours later. And they'd already taken pictures of the food on their tray tables. And of their faces in the airplane's bathroom mirror; but, oh, they couldn't post all of that pressing content to their social media profiles yet without paying extra; but what was great about all of that was that it was free, that it happened almost like the silliest of miracles. So, they crossed themselves (some with the laziness of people swatting away flies or picking at left over pasta or chicken) praying in low voices, but more than ready to release a scream into the sky if the plane plummeted earthward. Consoling themselves with the idea that—if someone suddenly shouted "Allah is great" or the pilot warned them of "a little problem"—they would be granted the last wish of switching off airplane mode in order to call their more or less loved ones, feeling suddenly that they loved them more than ever and that they'd never been farther away. Falling and then thinking about how, when people scream, all of them scream in the same language, in the Esperanto of the scream; and about how everyone understands each other in a scream, that there would be no need for the screams to be translated by the flight crew, who would, also, be screaming, though perhaps in a more orderly and systematic way, having been trained to scream inside flight simulators and . . . But nobody thought about any of that but him, someone who'd become a specialist in thinking about what people thought about in airplanes and had at one point even put it all in writing, in pages upon pages that, for many, due to the excess weight of their ornate gold incrustations, would never get off the ground.

But, again, there were more sleepers who believed in letting themselves be carried away to a place without reason or humanity or genius than there were sleepers who believed that if they shut their eyes something horrible might happen when they weren't looking or were looking elsewhere or if they let their eyelids drop. Sleepers who struggled to sleep at sea level (the melatonin in their nervous systems had already been absorbed by the blue glow of little screens; the light like the light at bottom of a swimming pool where everyone but Ella, no doubt, would quickly drown while searching for an app that would remind them how to do the butterfly or crawl stroke, an app that would allow them to recover everything they'd lost to the past—an *appast*). There, asleep in the skies, they closed their eyes, rocked by the funereal lullaby of a possible plummeting crash, so better to neither see nor feel it.

He wasn't like that; he didn't belong among the former or the latter.

And for more than one and a thousand nights he'd opted (or that's what he liked to believe) not to be a member of the majoritarian union of the unconscious who had that disturbing gift for falling asleep in public and in private. And he wasn't affiliated with the syndicate of the aforementioned fearful sleepers who fought against the machinery of drooping eyelids as if with sight went life or death. All of them committed to the magical thinking that nothing irreparable could happen if they were alert and on guard. If you paid attention, they told themselves as if self-hypnotized, you wouldn't end up inside a black box: no technical error or American skyscraper or French Alps, would prevent one of those landings where everyone clapped like seals, perhaps believing that they were just as instrumental to the whole endeavor as those men and women who clapped in the Cape Kennedy control rooms. (And he remembers the clapping pleaded for from the audience of *Peter Pan* to resuscitate Tinker Bell; clapping/device robbed from *A Midsummer's Night Dream* and *The Tempest* by the genius thief William Shakespeare, who'd described memory as the "warder of the brain" and it was to Shakespeare's memory that Borges had dedicated one of his last stories, revealing it to be a somewhat inattentive and arbitrary sentry of its wards; Shakespeare who'd been born, he'd read in Nabokov's *Transparent Things*, in the same year that mining for the graphite used in pencils was "discovered." And let's clap for all of that. And then the humble mortals in the auditorium would feel somewhat like gods, actors, characters: beings believed in and to whom oaths were sworn and who now—call them Prospero or Puck—were being asked to help by clapping, for they too were part of the show.)

He, for his part, moved around as if floating inside airplanes.

Long airplanes (airplanes that spent a long time in the air) were, for him, his bardo and his bushido and his true airplane mode. His living death and his death in life. His to be and his not to be. His neither sending nor receiving. His during between a beginning and an ending. His *on air* broadcast.

And so, in recent days he'd been accepting his increasingly sporadic job offers. Jobs not to be a writer in private but to play a writer in public and not the kind of job that would ask him to put on a show in front of everyone, because if they did, he'd drop all the cards when trying shuffle them. Taking a job on terra firma to be able to enjoy these nowhere hours, this weightless transit, this detachment from time spinning the time-zone schedules. His *free flow of consciousness* swerving into *free flight of subconscious* aboard ideal vehicles for rethinking your life like in one of those novels that unfolds over the course of one day that's like an eternity. There, millions of millimeters above sea level, he was like a Leopold Bloom floating *over the volcano* and *seizing the night*. There, he was quite modernist, but not at all modern. And he still didn't understand and had no interest in understanding how airplanes flew. Better like that. Letting himself be swept away by that ignorance helped him accept the many other things he didn't know about the work-ings of the universe (like the most intriguing of all for him: how did the speed of light come in through eyes to ignite the brain; like the one that interested him least: how the voices in telephones traveled along fiber "optic" and not sonic cables now, and why this change from the auditory to the visual had been made) and allowed him to feel so masterful and powerful in the humble art of arranging random words in the air. Words that, as someone had written, you had to pull down from the clouds to put on a blank sheet of paper. (In the air, he remembers *another* airplane aboard which he was reading *Henderson the Rain King* by Saul Bellow, and he can almost see himself there, long ago, underlin-ing that paragraph where the protagonist is delighted at belonging to the first generation to see both sides of the clouds: the top part and the bottom part; and to experience the realization that, previously, people had only dreamed "up at them" while now you could dream up and down at them; and that this new ability would help his contem-poraries accept the idea of death with greater ease and less struggle, there above, for a few hours, experiencing that body-out-of-body that people who died and lived to tell the tale claimed to have experienced for a few minutes.) For a while now, not even that. He didn't dream in any direction. And much less had he understood the death of his ability: the *off* of his *on*. Because now he didn't understand how one *didn't* write *either* and, even less, how he once believed that he understood how one *did* write (had someone already come up with the idea of offering a writing workshop for *not* writing or, better and more socially valuable, for convincing students to devote themselves to anything but writing? If not, he thought he would be the ideal candidate to "teach it"). **Now, just inertia and speed and seatbelt fastened, because when you fly you've got to tie yourself down to keep from flying away and because your body will be easier to identify if it stays strapped to its seat** (just to be annoying, to complicate the catastrophic task of identification, to turn himself into the "mystery passenger" at least for a while, he always tried to change seats during the flight). **Now, looking ahead and, every so often, standing up to go on short rectangular strolls** (always taking special pleasure in the part when he walked backward while everything was moving forward, as if he were Mr. Trip, his fetish-talisman toy that traveled with him everywhere) **that led him from the aisle by the bathrooms to the passageway by the kitchen in the back, where flight attendants with dilated pupils and grinding teeth took refuge. And he looked at them and wondered if flight-attendant jetlag was different from passenger jetlag. And he thought that yes, without a doubt, that flight attendants' connection to jetlag must be the same as medical examiners' connection to dead bodies: a cold intimacy.** (And he'd read once that jetlag happened because the soul or whatever it was—it's recently been proven that in the air and over a long distance, the brain's frontal lobes retract—always moved more slowly. That it trailed a few meters behind the body, bound to it by a kind of filament. And that the speed of airplanes delayed it even more. Several hours and thousands of kilometers. And that's why nobody was exactly themselves thousands of meters in the sky. And that the malaise you felt crossing oceans of clouds and rearing horse latitudes and for several days after landing was the result of that *soul-delayed* distance that rendered you more soulless than you already were. Until you regained a certain normality with that same relief felt when reencountering your soul, as if it were a suitcase left behind at your departing or connecting airport, rotating in false circles around those conveyer belts, and only arriving to its destination, somewhat disordered after multiple inspections, a few flights later.)

But, yes, every so often he had the luck of finding—in the seat next to him—a stranger worth meeting. Someone who told him something interesting that later he could write down in one of his biji notebooks, sitting on the toilet full of blue liquid, in a cubicle of plastic and light, barely wider than a coffin, trying to convince himself he could use everything he'd been told in the air, in the nonplace of some part: in the terra more or less firma of one of his books. Or, better, when he wrote down what he heard, it would of its own accord generate that written part, that place where he hadn't traveled for so long.

(And he remembers that then the man sitting beside him had looked at the book he was holding unopened and unread for years. But always brandished. A book-shaped book still functioned as an intimidating shield or vampire-repelling cross and still offered the best dome of silence to prevent conversations with strangers from starting up. Wielding a book in public gave undesirables desiring interactions with strangers the impression that those strangers might be dangerous or, at least, unpredictable. And so it was best to leave that person alone to his perversions. On the other hand, phones and tablets seemed to make the people sitting beside you even more loquacious and intrusive, to the point where they even had the audacity to touch other people's screens with their fingers. But the truth was that the book he was opening pushed him away too. Always and forever. The book was *Ada, or Ardor* by Vladimir Nabokov. A book that had rejected him again and again. But a book that he kept insisting on reading, as if it were a marriage proposal or job offer or—having never been superstitious and always disdaining generalities like black cats and broken mirrors and ladders and 13th days—a singular (and, as such, worthy and believable and closely personal) belief that would bring him closer to a divinity. There he stayed, in the opening pages, which he almost knew by heart at this point, of the novel in which Nabokov—not satisfied with having already reinvented the United States in *Lolita*—recreated the entire world. A novel that he knew everything about, but still couldn't read, even though he tried on every trip he took. And that was why he even bought, as a form of optimistic and hopeful expiation, a new copy and different edition for every trip, to see if this time yes, maybe on this flight . . . But no: sometimes he didn't even get past the family tree at the beginning, which frightened him so much that it almost made him blackout—that word that had always intrigued him because it included a *black* and a *lack* and an *out* and, yes, that was the kind of nonsense that occurred to him when it came to words that he could no longer write but couldn't stop thinking about, as if he were reading them—like the family trees in the opening pages of those *sword & sorcery* tomes, enumerating dynasties even more incomprehensible than the Karma dynasty. And he rarely got past that "Hue or who? Awkward. Reword!"— which sounded to him like a direct order from the other side of all things— at the end of Chapter 1. Or—at most, the furthest he'd gotten, the last line of Chapter 19—that "Ought to begin dating every page of the manuscript: Should be kinder to my unknown dreamers." And it was possible—he could barely admit it to himself—that his inability could be connected to the fact that, in *Ada, or Ardor*, Nabokov seemed, for the first time, to acknowledge the existence of higher beings, risking measuring himself against Leo Tolstoy and against Marcel Proust and against himself. And he did so by availing himself of an optical-technical device where the protagonist-lovers—who their creator, surprisingly and unexpectedly altering forever the perception of the novel, described in a letter as "rather horrible creatures" who had nothing to do with possible versions of his Vera—bound together by an indomitable and joyful love outside time and space, comment from the future on what's happening in the past and what readers are reading in the present and stop, stop, enough, too much, mercy . . . And yet he was calmed by the ever so familiar weight of that book, worn down by his insistence yet always new in its various incarnations, accompanying him here, there, and everywhere.)

And now, again, once more, yes, at last, Ada burning, in flames, reading first and then burning its pages, one after another, with no more airplanes on the horizon and in that pure horizon of all deserts and alongside that majestic green cow. In the desert, the horizon was where you were, always, and there he was, waiting for the horizon to come galloping even closer, riding an immense green cow and throwing pages of *Ada, or Ardor* into a bonfire,

now. (Before, he'd never been able to read *Ada, or Ardor*, though he'd tried so many times with so many different editions. Including a first edition hardcover and a first edition paperback that promoted the novel, deceptively and Lolitaesquely, as "The New Best-Selling Erotic Masterpiece." Multiple copies with typographical designs on their covers that opted for a solitary *Ada*, without the *or Ardor*, like the first Made-in-the-USA edition. The most recent, on the other hand, dispensed with the comma in the title and even omitted the subtitle that followed the colon: *A Family Chronicle*. And sometimes he thought that whatever was to blame for his own inability to penetrate that book had something to do with that absent comma and that omitted subtitle. And he and his work were like that discarded comma or that ardent "family chronicle," extinct and without descendants: something that had been but no longer was. Other covers were *Ada*-orned—yes, thinking about Nabokov made him Nabokovian in the worst possible sense—with automatically and obviously butterflied designs. Or with the faces of hieratic women. And he didn't judge that book by its covers, but all of its pages *did* judge him, accusing him of making it the only novel and only thing he hadn't read by that author. One of his favorite authors whose work he'd otherwise read in its absolute entirety. Letters, journals, lectures, reportage. He'd tried again and again. He'd even read a book about the book and had visited, on multiple occasions, a blog maintained by one of the most devoted Nabokov scholars—because, yes, he had to acknowledge that, though few and far between, there were *some* valuable blogs, dedicating all their passion and obsession to writers like William Gaddis or William H. Gass, whose work had never received such attention and focus back in the *unplugged* days—and that delved into every nook and cranny where his words cavorted. And he'd even spent a weekend lost in a demented sci-fi saga in which the characters from *Ada, or Ardor* were teletransported to Mars to stage a revision of the *Iliad* for some androids who were unsure whether the best style/form to carry out such an endeavor was that of Nabokov or that of Proust or something like that. But, again, he could barely get through the first fifty pages of the novel. Which was why, for a while now, he would open it at random and just read isolated lines from the pages he happened to open to. As if it were the Bible or the I Ching or one of those fires in which ancient shamans glimpsed the meaning of the universe.) **A bonfire like the one in which he was now burning the pages of *Ada, or Ardor.*** (And so, random and disordered paragraphs until one day, he thought, he would have read the whole book in every possible order. And then, miraculously, he would understand everything, the way you understand something that had always been there, in plain sight, but that you only see later. Meanwhile and in the meantime, he thought he was finding oracular messages, personal instructions, phrases that might have come from fortune cookies or from casting unloaded dice or sacred coins onto the ground. Things like "Destroy and forget" or "Revelation can be more perilous than Revolution" or, again, that, for him, simultaneously cryptic and crystalline "Hue or who? Awkward. Reword!" Or fragments that even seemed to align with those from his own past, almost functioning as better-executed sketches of what'd already been clumsily painted. Like that passing allusion to a comic called *The Goodnight Kids*, in which two young siblings, Nicky and Pimpernella, shared a bed where they read until they fell asleep and that now, tossing that page into the fire, he couldn't help but take as a distant but complicit wink at the comic strips about the strange and ephemeral and failed masked superheroes/luchadores: *Nightmare and Sleepy.* Insomniac guardians he'd desperately searched for in second-hand bookstores and collected as a kid along with the adventures of that immortal, with his antiquarian squire, asking, "Is the past as dead as we believe?" Or the reference to demented voices in the plumbing leading to the invention of the exceedingly expensive "hydrodynamic telephones and other miserable gadgets" like—though it turned out to be unbelievably prophetic—the "instantogram." Or that description of Aqua's mad and Zelda-Fitzgeraldian circulation through asylums "from Scoto-Scandinavia to the Rivera, Altar and Palermontovia . . . from Estoty and Canady to Argentina" and whose symptomology—described in the first and oh-so-flammable pages of *Ada, or Ardor*—reminded him so much of what had happened to Penelope; because, as with Aqua, "Her disintegration went down a shaft of phases, every one more racking than the last; for the human brain can become the best torture house of all those it has invented, established and used in millions of years, in millions of lands, on millions of howling creatures." And, of course, that whole thing about the "Texture of Time" recited into a recorder and transcribed by one Van Veen on the way to Montreux. That great idea—he'd read in an interview Nabokov had given while writing it—regarding the practice of writing a novel full of vicissitudes and joy sprang from a theory posited in an essay located near the end of that same novel. From that essay that included that paragraph that he came across every so often and that referred to the "Tender Interval" between two beats in the rhythm of time as that "gray gap" which is the only thing that gives any meaning to the notion of Time: that parenthesis between one memory and the next in which you seem to catch your breath so you can keep on remembering as if you were breathing.) Yes, again, sometimes he had the feeling that perhaps, in random and disordered lines, he'd already read the entirety of *Ada, or Ardor*. And that now all that was left was the chance and obligation to put it all in order. And that, maybe, that would be a new form of writing that mirrored the way Nabokov had written the book, using notecards that he combined and shuffled like playing cards.

Reword and Revelation, indeed.

That illusion didn't last long, of course.

And so he set down the exuberant and for him incomprehensible *Ada, or Ardor* and focused on its complementary counterparts that—he theorized—were books that could only have been written knowing that that alternate space-time family saga was before or behind them.

So he devoted himself to *Pale Fire* (1962) and *Transparent Things* (1972).

The first—for him, without a doubt, the most fully avant-garde and successfully experimental novel, in structure and form and humor, in the history of literature—was like an extract to be expanded while the second was like an extract to be contracted. The first already announcing the second—skipping right over *Ada, or Ardor*—when, in its final pages, the poet described the poem that occupied the central part of the book as a "transparent thingum."

And once read, both turned, for him, the unread, by him, *Ada, or Ardor*—through what he *had* managed to read of and about it—into an ultra-mega purge-detox of all extremely Nabokovian things: something the subject had to pass through to shed the adjective its own last name had become—like a wild-colored butterfly. Something it had to pass through so, once and for all, everything would pass through everyone. Then, at the end, afterward, perhaps inspired by his duel with a bothersome biographer, Nabokov had invited the crypto-autobiographical *Look at the Harlequins!* (where Nabokov's alter ego, the enigmatic Vadim Vadimovich N. or VV, was an alternate version of him, a bit like his detractors imagined him, glimmers of pedophilia included) to the farewell party, a book that functioned like an unplanned encore or like a collection of demos and rarities and B-sides.

And he thought about all of this, reading, facing forward and down but his eyes moving left to right; feeling somewhat perverse because, oh, for some time now, there was a danger that some ferocious female might spot the name Nabokov on the cover; because it was more than likely that, seeing it there, they would start screaming that the man reading that monster was an apologist for pedophilia and sexual assault. Especially if it happened to be the woefully misinterpreted *Lolita* (in recent days, its protagonist had been elevated to the alters of martyrology and its author rewritten as a degenerate character-narrator), whose single formidable and admirable flaw was that of being the one true and paradoxical Great American Novel (Lolita was the small white whale for that mad captain Humbert Humbert), written by a fiery/incinerating Russian in the middle of the Cold War, whose manuscript, at one point, despairing, Nabokov had attempted to burn.

And so, for a while now, he'd been carrying around Nabokov books carefully covered in brown paper; paper of the same color as the bags used to hide small bottles of shameful and guilty and tormented spirits, to be drunk and emptied on streets where you were always frozen and on the rocks.

And, yes, he warmed the insides of his brain with those other two supernatural books by Nabokov. Someone who was very occupied with and preoccupied by the supernatural, by the Beyond (by the *postustoronnost*). An interest that was more than pertinent and entirely inevitable for anyone who considered himself a storyteller because, after all and in the end, he thought, nothing intrigued the teller of stories more than what would no doubt come later but which is entirely unknown because nobody has gone there and, from there, put it in writing so it could be read on this side of things. And so

Nabokov, in work, returned over and over to the landscape of the Other Side. Nabokov didn't buy into the psychoanalytic interpretation of dreams but did believe that, at the end of it all, there was something more than eternal sleep and eternal dreaming.

And his most supernatural novel was *Transparent Things*, which was also—to compensate for his struggles with *Ada, or Ardor*—the Nabokov book he'd read the most times.

Transparent Things that, according to what its author said in an interview, has an incorporeal being as protagonist, a writer recently deceased, evoking the difficulties that ghosts have when it comes to perceiving the world of the living and to rest in the present without sinking into the past through the transparency of living beings. "It's a very funny novel. But not for everyone."

Transparent Things had always been and was still one of the books that he described as his "books-to-be-read-in-motion." Portable books, books of paper and ink. Books that—unlike screens—knew and let you know at a glance how far you'd come and how far you had left to go. Traveling books that had the precise length and exact weight to be read between the departures and arrivals of those planes or trains around the continent for work, heading to universities or festivals or book launches. One hour going and one hour coming back—or an hour and a half or two or three, at most—and those were the perfect books not to read but to reread among the clouds or on the rails: *Slaughterhouse-Five* by Kurt Vonnegut, *Oh What a Paradise It Seems* by John Cheever, the "Combray" section he'd excerpted from the first volume of *À la recherche du temps perdu* by Marcel Proust, anything by Denis Johnson—anything that wasn't *Already Dead* or *Tree of Smoke*—where you could rediscover lines like "I have more to remember than I have to look forward to. Memory fades, not much of the past stays, and I wouldn't mind forgetting more of it." Or something by Penelope Fitzgerald (though he tried to avoid the delicate tremors and elegant ellipses of the latter, because their exceedingly strange perfection and distance from what he did made him think of subtle derailments and gentle free falls so far beyond his reach and capability). Books whose endings he knew and that wouldn't leave him in suspense in the event of some unforeseen incident. Books that, for him, were the equivalent of those bibles (bibles where you could read that thing about *Remember not the former things, nor consider the things of old* and about how *The past is forgotten . . . behold all things made new*, but, also, that other one about how *We may be through with the past, but the past ain't through with us* or something like that) with covers laminated in bulletproof steel that American soldiers carried over their hearts when they disembarked on beaches or parachuted out of airplanes during World War II.

If the trip were longer and crossed oceans or hemispheres, he just took several of those books with him. But, beyond all possible combinations, *Transparent Things*—a book in which, on the other hand, you traveled a great deal and in multiple directions over the course of many years—was the only fixed and omnipresent title.

The brief and medullary *Transparent Things* was a book that the writer Mavis Gallant had described, gracefully but inexactly, as "a small mock replica" that Nabokov had constructed after "having spent his life building the Taj Mahal." And, yes, it was one of his favorite books. And he almost considered it his (not one of his). To the point where, every time he came across it in a bookstore, he bought it again (along with the obligatory new edition of *Ada, or Ardor*) out of the most despicable and wretched of motives: so that one less person in the world would be able to read it. For him, *Transparent Things* was the closest thing to that alien monolith in *2001: A Space Odyssey*: the infinite wisdom of a supermind condensed into something that the capacities and IQ of mere mortals could grasp. Imperfect beings like its protagonist, the serially and "monstrously in love" in spite of himself editor, Hugh Person. Someone who was always asking himself if anyone would remember him when he was no longer there and never daring to answer no in the face of the imminent and dark transparency of death: the most transparent of all transparent things "through which the past shines" and ends up being reflected not in a light at the end of the tunnel but in the vision of the "incandescence of a book" engulfed in flames. And so this singular book was narrated by the mysterious and plural and translucent (as in invisible) voice (or could it be many voices springing from one mouth?) of the living dead, making itself heard and swirling through burning hotels and snowy funiculars, a voice for whom all the living and opaque things of this world were made so clear and transparent. A book that he'd read so many times now that he almost had it memorized—and that now, more than read, he watched, like someone who no longer sings but absentmindedly hums an unforgettable tune—so he didn't even need to take it with him. But still, it was always good to have it, in his jacket pocket where it easily fit along with his passport and boarding pass, successfully functioning (just like the failed, for him, *Ada, or Ardor*) as a wall between his seat and the next. A book whose opening lines—cutting out the whole "Hullo person!" bit to increase the liturgical dimension—he recited at the outset of every trip with the same devotion with which others whispered prayers, putting themselves in the hands of supernatural beings. Beginning with "Perhaps if the future existed, concretely and individually, as something that could be discerned by a better brain, the past would not be so seductive: its demands would be balanced by those of the future" and closing with "More in a moment." But it was clear that that "More in a moment"—which, he thought, would function as the most perfect of epitaphs on that final page that was one's headstone—alluded to something far more transcendent than a simple moment. It was a moment, sure, but the kind of moment that contained—that had *within* it—the crossing of the Rubicon, that countdown, the instant he saw Ella dive into a swimming pool for the first time and those minutes of his childhood when and where—after almost drowning—he suddenly knew how to read and write.

It was one of those marvelous moments.

Or otherwise—more in a moment—he warmed his hands with *Pale Fire*: a book whose form was the book's plot (perhaps inspired by Nabokov's obsessive and demented system of footnotes for his translation of *Eugene Onegin* by Alexander Pushkin) and where Nabokov rubbed the pain of a poet's verses inspired by the death of his daughter against the visionary blindness of a stunned reader to make sparks fly and lightning flash. *Pale Fire*—its title taken from Shakespeare's *Timon of Athens*, where reference is made to the moon stealing its pale fire from the sun—again arousing in him the suspicion that Shakespeare's true and secret artistic project had actually been to write the most quotable of quotations. And that—to conceal his true intentions and distract from his authentic and exceedingly conceptual aim—he'd subsequently embedded them in plays. But—he was almost certain and completely conspiranoid—the *true* work of Shakespeare resided in those lines he sowed, first free and then captive, that throughout the centuries readers would pull out and harvest (the same thing happened with the Bible, another quote machine, whose lines were often elevated from epigraphs to titles) to write them on covers or as epigraphs or to be uttered by one's characters, suddenly speaking with the voice of the most immortal dead.

And in *Pale Fire*, the dead were also the ones who wrote and corrected and clarified in the shadows. And it was even possible that, in *Pale Fire*, it was a happily dead daughter who was dictating the poem to her devastated and still living father. There, the murdered John Shade's verse number 143 warning that "A thread of subtle pain, / Tugged at by playful death, released again, / But always present, ran through me" and perhaps referring to his daughter: the aficionado of spiritualism and suicidal romantic and drowned and ultimately "domestic ghost" Hazel. Hazel sinking beneath the waters of a lake while her parents watch television—a show called *Remorse*—and returning as a crimson butterfly. And there, also, the evocation of a "tin clockwork toy" belonging to the poet when he was eleven years old. Remembering watching it walk between the legs of a chair and under a bed and experiencing the sublime and black night distributing itself between time and space, with blood in the caverns and the mind in the stars and John Shade, epileptic and elliptically, remembering his own prehistory and anticipating every tomorrow. (A toy that he, inevitably, couldn't help but superimpose and make play with his Mr. Trip, the little wind-up traveling man from his childhood. Was there anything more deliciously chilling than believing that, sure, a great writer has written something for everyone to read, but—every once in a great while, almost never, once in your life if you're lucky—that, *also and in addition*, he's written it for one and only one reader? He felt that *there*. And he felt it even more when he learned, from a biography of Nabokov, that he'd been a lover of toys all his life. And so he'd felt fully within his rights to meld John Shade's toy with his own, with his adored and forever-companion Mr. Trip in order to wind up the toy with the same twist of his wrist, as if springs and gears were connected beyond time and space.) And he recited that stanza from memory as well as the demented and explanatory note of the possessed/obsessed Charles Kinbote remembering having seen that toy "on a shelf, between a candlestick and a handless alarm clock." And, automatically, thinking it'd belonged to the phantasmal daughter of the dead poet. But Kinbote had immediately received the explanation from Shade that that toy "was as old as he was" and that "he kept it as a kind of *memento mori*—he had had a strange fainting fit one day in his childhood while playing with that toy" and that "never mind, now the rusty clockwork shall work again, for I have the key." And, sure, Shade's toy was "a little Negro of painted tin with a keyhole in his side and no breadth to speak of, just consisting of two more or less fused profiles, and his wheelbarrow was now all bent and broken." And his, Mr. Trip, was a traveler, with a hat and jacket, carrying a suitcase. And it wasn't broken, but it was dysfunctional: it didn't move forward, but only backward. (And when they found out, his parents had offered to exchange it, but he refused authoritatively and without hesitation: because a toy like that, as it was, going in the opposite direction, in reverse, was unique, for him and only him. And years later—he only realized it recently and how was it possible he hadn't seen it before, how did making something so visible invisible work, how did he not remember it from the first time he saw it?—he said to himself that the man with the hat and suitcase in the desert, on the cover of Pink Floyd's *Wish You Were Here*, looked *so much* like Mr. Trip. He looked *so much* like Mr. Trip that might have been Mr. Trip.)

And both books, *Pale Fire* and *Transparent Things*—functioning perfectly, but, also, always looking back, revising the past, walking backward and seeing everything with eyes in the backs of their heads—were perfect for constant rereading (and Nabokov understood rereading as the only possible form of reading and a good reader as a rereader). And they were ideal for traveling: just the right number of pages and composed in brief chapters or entries. And they were so pale and transparent and solid and burning and between their pages he slipped the bookmark of a notecard on which he'd written another Nabokov line—taken from his diaries, from a section titled *Notes for Work in Progress*—that read: " . . . one little push and down the white and handless face of time . . . oh, lightly we shall slide."

And then, yes, as if obeying, propelled by that little push, he focused—going backward while that other YesterdAir flight kept moving forward—on what for a while now had become his favorite thing to read: his old planners (from two or three decades ago, their pages yellowed and brittle as papyrus) that, with the passing of the years, now, read almost as if they belonged to someone else, and left him wondering what might come next, what could've come before, like autobiographical and forgettable pulp novels.

Planners—like encyclopedias, maps, compasses, phone books, almanacs, and calendars, the marginalia and almost everything used to orient you in life; all those species rendered extinct by the arrival never to leave of those increasingly immobilizing mobile phones—belonged to a rare mixed and mestizo genre. A blend of novel and memoir and song where all that's recalled are convoluted verses and detached memories and a black and white group photograph depicting you standing beside someone whose nickname you remembered but whose last name escaped you: things that at the time were deemed unforgettable and that now were just fragments and tatters and random rooms with doors you'd lost the keys to. Used and full planners were a cross between autofiction and autobiography and nonfiction, swerving toward pseudofiction with the help of forgetfulness as unforgettable editor. A fragile yet elegant and exceedingly personal foundation (handwriting as the one trait beyond falsification) containing what'd happened and what you thought was going to happen and what didn't end up happening with the liquid syntax of dreams whose script you were never entirely able to decode the next morning, or the next thousand mornings. And there, in the end, the names and numbers of so many dead people so much harder to erase on paper (that kind of funereal rite of passage when, every year, phone numbers and addresses were passed onto the next year) than on screens. On those superficial surfaces where a click was enough to cross someone off or prolong their existence in your memory, external but all its own, though so easy to lose due to carelessness or an error or forgetting all those passwords that you had to type in like magic words to be able to access names and addresses and phone numbers that nobody could memorize anymore (it was also true that Socrates had already been warning us about the danger of "writing," about the act of reading instead of reciting, which would obviate the agreeable and noble obligation of memorization; though we only know today that Socrates thought that because, subsequently, Plato put all his opinions in writing). And he reread his expired planners and wondered who—around June of 1991—was that *E* he'd enclosed in a circle between exclamation points. Or where that place called X that he had to be "no matter what: at

03:30" was. Or what exactly he'd meant by: "Pick up delivery and send out / active elements / *The Recognitions* / Fake prescription; and why this was printed and that was in cursive and the rest was in ink of various colors.

And so, every so often, he picked up one of his old planners at random. And going through it, he discovered that the time that'd passed, like those broken and motionless watches that nevertheless told the right time twice a day, had returned (in the words of the pale yet fiery academic on a campus in New Wye, Appalachia, in an *apparatus criticus* of someone else's poem that he considered almost his own) his "calendric correspondencies," making the dates and numbers from back then turn back into the numbers and days of today. And he wondered how it was possible that the First World university publishing houses (heads up, literary editors! here, maybe, was the next phenomenon to exploit!) were no longer devoted to the cataloguing and storage and transcription or facsimile reproduction of the planners of great writers. Or even studying the subject of Litplannerology in which, for example, the planners and notebooks of Francis Scott Fitzgerald ("Forgotten is forgiven") are crossed with those of Ernest Hemingway ("When it's right you can't remember. Every time you read it again it comes as a great and unbelievable surprise. You can't believe you did it. When it's right you never can do it again. You only do it once for each thing. And you're only allowed so many in your life.")

Reading your own planners was like anticipating the past, he thought.

And, along with them and with his biji notebooks and, now, one of Penelope's notebooks, another notebook always traveled with him. A notebook that hadn't been his but that now would belong to him forever. A notebook belonging to He Whose Name Must Not Be Mentioned. Round and childish handwriting, zig-zagging orthographical errors, but most important of all: a rigorously wild imagination. Something he could no longer count on. There, characters like the horizontal and forever-bedridden Camilo Camito Camoncio; or Pésimo Malini, the worst magician in the world (whom, the boy had told him, a classmate named Fin had "stolen" from him); or his conspiratorial hypothesis about the secondary yet decisive omnipresence of Samuel L. Jackson in so many movies; or that theory that he'd presented in his kindergarten and that'd gotten him in a bit of trouble: it wasn't that— contrary to what was believed—Santa Claus and the Three Wise Men didn't exist but that they exploited long-suffering parents and forced them, year after year, to buy their products while fighting among themselves like the capos of two families of mafiosos. Creativity that he liked to think (the biological but comatose father of the notebook's owner, Maxi Karma, had had literary pretensions, but they'd only been that, pretensions) The Son of Penelope (who, sure, was a little freak; but what kid wasn't if you compared him to an adult, to a "mature person") had inherited from him by osmosis. And on the cover of the notebook and inside a label, a title that he'd always considered perfect and enviable and even worth appropriating without asking permission first: *Master Advice of a Man Who Sleeps on the Floor.* (And just a few days ago, as he was making his escape, he'd added this notebook and several of his biji notebooks to one of Penelope's notebooks on whose cover it read *Karma Konfidential.*)

But he—wondering if among the characters of He Whose Name Must Not Be Mentioned there was room for the appearance of his own Cerdic, warthog prince and bastion of the Porkyngs Oynk-Oynk dynasty, whose exploits, intended to help the boy fall asleep, had accomplished nothing but to make him stay wide awake—hadn't yet arrived to the dangerous point of opening *Master Advice of a Man Who Sleeps on the Floor* to see what it held inside. He still hadn't reached that point of no return on his one-way trip. To take the plunge of going inside, fearing turbulence no oxygen mask could assuage. And for that reason he opened his carry-on where he also carried Mr. Trip: that little tin traveler who'd been accompanying him, wound up, since his distant and wild childhood, walking backward. And he took out a planner from somewhere around the halfway point of his trajectory, when he'd already been turned away at the doors to Ardis, in Demonia, Antiterra more than once. And he glanced at the cover of his current edition of *Ada, or Ardor* (this latest one belonging to that crop of Nabokovs reissued by Penguin in the '80s, their covers adorned with the paintings of Richard Lindner) before closing it again.

(And then his airborne and strapped-in seatmate, looking down at the book, had said to him: "Ah . . . The Russian . . . I remember that The Russian wrote somewhere about how people who fall asleep on trains and snore with mouths open and eyes closed were like those shameless cretins who shit with the bathroom door open, offering up the fragrances of their bowels to the world . . . And he was right, he was right . . . Especially the ones who snore with an irregular rhythm, who snore unpredictably. You know: a snore and then silence; and just when you think it's over, all of a sudden, a series of grunts that make you think the guy is having a heart attack. And on airplanes the phenomenon is even more unpleasant than on trains: because there are more sleepers. Fortunately, like me, you're not sleeping. The Russian either. He was an insomniac. We surveilled him from outside his house. We took pictures of him in his study, writing standing up, scribbling strange words on those notecards of his. At one point, in 1961 I think, we snuck inside when nobody was home and stole a few of those notecards and gave them to our best codebreaker and the poor guy had a nervous breakdown trying to make sense of something about an assassin from a nonexistent kingdom being hired to kill someone in the U.S. and, of course, we all thought of the president and . . . A friend of mine, an FBI agent, pretty much lost his mind while assigned to the Russian. He got obsessed and wouldn't stop following him. And so he had to be "deactivated." Last I heard, he'd even followed The Russian to Montreux, on his own dime and not under orders. And he stayed there. And the guy even got a job at the hotel where The Russian lived, and hung around until his death, flitting around him, captivated by his light until his light went out. And even then, he stayed, circling The Russian's statue, getting tourists to buy him drinks in exchange for stories about him . . . Until he died and his son took over the business of telling stories about The Russian . . . We were there too, we spied on The Russian too. And we even considered recruiting him. But it wouldn't have done us any good. He wouldn't have been any use. He wasn't a spy and wouldn't have made a good one . . . All he did was disparage his fellow writers and countrymen and hunt butterflies, which sometimes he chased bare ass naked along ravines and up mountainsides. I got assigned to him for a while. I posed as a journalist named Shape and The Russian insisted on taking me butterfly hunting and we hiked up Mingus Mountain, with him repeatedly promising that we were going to see wondrous things and that I should be ready for some fantastic specimens and "winged nymphs of the woods." And he stripped off all his clothes without a second thought, as naturally as someone removing a hat and tossing it aside. I must admit, I'd never seen nor have I seen since a man so outside our world and so inside his own. I didn't know then and don't know now if that kind of solitary independence inspires fear or pity or admiration in me . . . The man appeared to exist only for himself and for that time and that place. And at the time I said to myself that he probably didn't pay attention to anything but the matter at hand and what mattered to him: himself . . . The Russian wasn't even aware that his beloved son—a somewhat unstable yet charming figure, as only one who brings together and practices the vocations of racecar driver, opera singer, and Russian translator could be—worked for us on occasion as liaison officer, helping to catch possible deserters. He was never all that dedicated to our thing or to his thing and, probably, only accepted our proposal out of fascination and because we covered his *bon-vivant*-with-famous-father drinks and dinners . . . But, as I was saying, there was The Russian. Naked and with his net aloft. But that day there was nothing there. Nothing to see or to chase or to capture. And he started crying. Seriously. The Russian cried in front of me like one of those people who don't cry often, but when they decide to cry, they really cry. They cry in sobbing bursts. His face was a mask of tears. "Laugh . . . Laugh . . ." he kept repeating, shooting death stares at the cows while his wife, Mrs. Russian, said things like "Did we really come all this way just to have some cows look at us?" The Russian couldn't stop crying and then I caught sight of a butterfly and ran after it and caught it and offered it to him like someone trying to console a child by with a piece of candy. The Russian looked at it almost with disgust and said: "A cliché with wings . . ." Then I understood. Immediately. The Russian had made me. To him, I was just a cliché with a double identity. A commonplace of the genre for someone beyond all genres, who looked down on all clichés, but—nobody is perfect, not even him—ignored the fact that a cliché was, really, a story worth telling over and over again. Something that'd been told many times before becoming a commonplace. And no longer just—as I was for The Russian—a banal insect. And I didn't see him again because The Russian would no longer see me."

The man sitting and speaking beside him—he spoke as if he were delivering a report after a more or less successful mission—was one of those octogenarians who appear fossilized more than aged. Blue eyes of an almost liquid clarity, close-cropped hair, skin taught across his skull, like a well-preserved mummy or some pharaonic writer like, here he comes again, William S. Burroughs. By the third whisky, the man had identified himself as "a retired intelligence agent, who every so often, still did some consulting on delicate matters and sensitive material . . . You know, the perfect candidate: the wisdom of experience and the age of one who could be sacrificed if things went awry . . . The kind of specimen you allow to retire, sure, but *also* always keep within arm's reach, just in case, because you never know. Even though I've got a leg full of shrapnel from a shootout along the Perfume River or from an explosion near Estación Mapocho, either way; but that leg always sets off the metal detectors in airports the world over. It doesn't matter, it's no big deal. I'm like that operative in bad spy novels—the ones that depict the job as something exciting and advonturouo and not as it really is, as a particularly torturous form of bureaucracy—who turns out to be the disillusioned traitor and always winds up getting executed by his idealistic disciple with tears in his eyes . . . But, ah, that's not my case: because what's the point of being a traitor in a world where no one is loyal." The man took a long sip from his drink and continued: "You say you're a writer and I suppose your profession must be a lot like mine: spying for decades and then, sooner or later, a young novelist comes for your head and your legacy, right?"

And then the old man had told him that they, the ones in the Old Guard, "The Good Old Boys," never referred to their workplace as the CIA—"initials for journalists and outsiders," he grunted—but preferred to call it "The Outfit." Or The Organization. Or The Group. Or "The Company." Something like that. And then he'd apologized with a "True, I suppose that for a writer we're not as interesting as our British counterparts . . . or even the Russians. They, in novels and movies, always seem to have private lives, personal touches, they play the piano really well or quote the classics while strolling down corridors of universities more august than ours where they all met in their youth and, oh, that omnipresent homosexual subtext . . . And, if they get bored of all that talk in those libraries and pubs, they have all the silly elegance of their Bond-brand escapades that never work out as well for us . . . We always come off as reasonably efficient robots . . . Or as batshit or broken machines, like Jason Bourne . . . Our thing is corporate paranoia, while theirs is neurosis with artistic derivations . . . But believe me, we have better memories, and our files are better organized. And we desert far more infrequently, because we never swallowed the whole romantic spirit of Communism thing and all of that."

And then the man had told him "something that, as a writer, will probably interest you." He confided that, during the hot years of the Cold War, they evaluated intelligence reports, categorizing them as A, B, C, D in terms of the level of trust they had in the source and as 1, 2, 3, 4 in terms of the veracity of the information. And so, A-1 equaled an absolute truth worthy of full credit and a D-4 an unattenuated falsehood from the mouth and in the words of a wacko or an enemy. "Throughout my long career, I never came across a single A-1 and I only ever read a handful of D-4s," the man told him with one of those straight-lined smiles, like a slash between his lips, like the slight smile of a cowboy contemplating something quite amusing. And, making the ice cubes dance in his glass, he added: "In nine out of ten cases, we were aware that the informant was somewhat trustworthy and the information somewhat true. The final ranking of like 90% of the data studied was C-3."

Indeed, that was what most mortals and most readers understood reality to be: a little bit C and a little bit 3.

And there he was, sitting in seat 3-C.

And so, then, the whole thing—which had barely concerned him before—ceased to concern him at all. But there were matters that did unsettle him and the man, whom he didn't hesitate to dub, automatic writerly reflex, General Electric, kept right on talking and drinking. And saying things like "The truth is all spies are narrators, storytellers . . . That's our primary occupation. And that's also why we used to

even recruit young writers from writer's workshops and funded literary magazines, so they would give us inspiration and help us when
it came to telling the tale. Think about it a little, think about kings
and ministers and dictators and presidents. There, in their offices,
after a long and boring day of meetings and signing documents.
When night falls, those men or women pour themselves a whisky and
order: 'Quick! Bring me my spies!' And the spies tell them supposedly
true stories. More or less real. Or, if not, if they don't have any to tell,
they make them up on the spot. Like jesters and fools and fortune-
tellers did so long ago. And, even before that, those interpreters of
the dreams of Julius Caesar whose—as I learned at Yale, where I was
first recruited by The Company—function, as Suetonius pointed out,
was to calm the spirits of the divine emperor. And so, if the man
woke up in distress because he'd dreamed he raped his mother, they
offered him a 'Fear not, Caesar. What you dreamed only means that
you will end up conquering the Universal Mother—the whole world' . .
. I'm not making this up, it's true. If you don't believe me, you should
read all those essays about the origins of the MI6 Circus: what the
recruitment officers valued most in the classrooms and hallways of
the best British universities was that their future spies were excellent
'raconteurs.' That was more important than their marksmanship or
physical capacities or brain power."

And, oh, hearing him, he knew he was in trouble. Because he had
to be *very* careful when supposedly real people started sounding and
thinking exactly like him through less or more fictitious characters
who so closely resembled the ones he'd once given voice to in his
writing. Characters he no longer sees or hears on the page, because
he no longer writes them. And so—*warning! warning!*—he feels like
he's begun to *write them* over people. As if he were tattooing them
and then reading them aloud and—for some not at all surprising but
yes secret reason—sooner rather than later they all started talking to
him about mobile phones, about phones that didn't yet exist when the
telephones, motionless and immobile, of his childhood rang.

Thus, then, that passenger, General Electric, sounding like this:

"It's odd . . . The way things have changed. We never could've anticipated what happened . . . The paradoxes of History, plot twists, and twists of fate . . . We spies devoted our lives and vocations to extracting and implanting information from and into everyone else. Using torture, blackmail, indoctrination, and bribery. With no concessions and no restraint. Because people didn't want to give or receive it. Whereas now, it's just the opposite: people never stop narrating their lives, down to the tiniest detail, taking pictures of everything they see, pinpointing where they're going and where they're coming from and where they are, while incessantly drinking coffee from those pods that flood their blood with aluminum, but it doesn't matter, because those coffeemakers are so photogenic and enviable and *postable* right? They all seem to live to be seen and no longer feel alive unless they're getting views and likes. They don't need or want anything but for everyone to know everything about their private lives. To be exposed. To show themselves. To post it all on the Web. That place whose name itself should be a warning: a nowhere that's everywhere and where we trap ourselves. But that's not even it. They confess everything of their own volition and happily collaborate for nothing. They're ready to do anything just to be looked at and listened to. They're like those insufferable children reciting poems in the middle of the living room for their families. There's no longer any need for the sadistic interrogations or the *femme fatales* or the improbable gadgets *à la 007* or—another lie that everyone has believed—the truth serum. Now—when it comes to the latest generation of spies—all you have to do is give one of the most expensive mobile phones to your rivals and to sit and wait . . . Everyone exposes him or herself, everything is exposed. To its radiations. There's no mystery. All hard and real work consists of reading through and filtering out so much toxic bullshit, so much private pollution. Because now everyone is more than ready to believe anything: *fake news* but, also, *fake oldies*. Everyone is ready to either have the past rewritten or to rewrite it themselves. It's a dirty job but someone has to do it, ha . . . And I suppose there's something good about it . . . I suppose there's some kind of social-psychological benefit to having millions of people who weren't doing anything with their lives suddenly feel they're doing a lot just by spending their time looking at and showing themselves on a screen as a kind of antidepressant . . . Though, of course, it's also the end of all mystery . . . Imagine if mobile phones had been around in Dallas '63. Today we would even have—or maybe we would have nothing, because everyone would've been too distracted tweeting 'you'll never guess where I am and what just happened'—Oswald's selfies in the Book Depository window and thousands of videos from all possible angles of that exploding head and Jackie showing us how to exit a convertible out the back; though the truth is she wasn't trying to flee but to recover the piece of her husband's skull that held in his brains, what was designated the 'Harper Fragment,' using the last name of the person, Billy Harper, who found it lying in the street, in Dealey Plaza the next morning, while walking his dog . . . And even the exact GPS coordinates of those supposed gunmen on the Grassy Knoll who, while we're at it, didn't exist and, even if they did, they weren't ours, I can guarantee you that. And though you might not believe it, I read this new refuted theory a few days ago online: it was *also* untrue that Jackie—sick and tired of his infidelity—had, after the first shot and just in case, injected JFK with an untraceable poison, taking advantage of the confusion, choreographed down to the last detail by Jackie herself, who'd demonstrated her keen attention to every detail when she'd redecorated the White House. Though I must admit that I really liked Donald Sutherland's bit in *JFK*. Clearly, it was all a conspiranoid delirium. But I really liked the idea of one of our guys, some Mr. X, as the ultimate clean copier of the dirty past and, no doubt, one of the best presidential raconteurs, spinning stories for multiple presidents before sending them to bed with a glass of warm milk and a ultrapotent sleeping pill . . . And we would probably also have, courtesy of those same phones if they'd been commercialized at the time, pictures posted from on that film set where, under Stanley Kubrick's direction, they falsified the moon landing, if all that nonsense had been true . . . And, believe me, if it had, it would've looked far better and more realistic and the possibility that the whole thing was a lunar *mis-en-scène* on Earth would never have occurred to anybody . . . And more than one person involved in the whole Watergate

scandal would've implicated himself via tweet . . . Because it's clear
that the finger is quicker than the neuron and shouldn't there be an
implicit-explicit prohibition against tweeting for all operatives while
in operation? Shouldn't a tweet be considered a crime of subconscious
exhibitionism? Shouldn't all government officials or private executives receive an electric shock every time it crossed their mind that
Twitter was the ideal medium for expressing an opinion? But beyond
all these details, the most important thing, again: then, like now,
there wouldn't be any mystery. Everything would be visible in all its
banality and everything would be recorded. There would be no space
for the fictitious within reality and for us to be able to believe in the
unbelievable, to be able to accept as fact things that're not facts . . .
And that's it. It's over. Without a doubt. Everything is revealed. In the
instant. Instagram. That site where people exhibit the most important
moments of their lives to have them judged by complete strangers
and where they realize that the pictures of their domesticated animals arouse more tenderness than the ones of their wild children.
And I've read that one of the new ways to tell if someone is really
depressed is if they post selfies in black and white and without any of
the filters that make them look more attractive. In other words: showing yourself as you actually are is the same as being on the brink of
suicide, while showing yourself there in full color with the features of
a cat or dog imposed over your own face is a sign of absolute happiness. And everyone's hooked. Snorting instagrams not with their
noses but with their eyes. Over and over. Without a doubt . . . Without
going any further, I learned a few days ago that there's only reliable
proof that two people were actually crucified in the Ancient World.
One Yehohanan, in Jerusalem, in the first century; and another body,
nameless, recently unearthed in Italy, near the Po River delta. That's
all, those are the only two. And yet—and this should be especially
gratifying for you and your colleagues, I suppose—there are many
thousand-year-old literary sources claiming that thousands of people
were crucified along the roads that led to the Empire's capital or
along the ridgelines of its colonies . . . And—already knowing what
your answer would be—I wonder: Isn't it far better to live in that

creative and recreative uncertainty? Isn't it far better to wonder about those improbably interesting things than to get answers to so many unquestionable inanities? Isn't it far better to make an effort to remember than to film something that you'll never see again and that, knowing you've already got it recorded on your device, your memory will forget within hours? Isn't there something fun and exciting about there being no record of some unbelievable thing that happened to us and that, when we describe it, nobody believes is real and we have to try to convince everyone that it happened, not by lying, but by telling it better every time? Isn't it better to remember than to record? . . . All those people with phones aloft, viewing everything through screens . . . Maybe, I think, it would be better to record everything with your phone and then put another phone in front of the first phone. And in that way you would see everything as you *actually* saw it when it happened: not with your eyes but through a phone. And to be able to say, 'I swear I saw it with my own iPhone' instead of 'with my own eyes' . . . And they say there's no greater punishment than being 'blocked,' being cut off from that celebration of idiocy . . . For us, that would have been a reward. Because we needed the shadows and invisibility. We wanted to go unnoticed and to devote ourselves to spying on everyone else without leaving a trace or being followed. Now everyone just wants to be seen and to add more and more followers; they want to be *followed*—can you believe it? . . . It's an epidemic. The moment when everyone turns into everyone else, into the same thing. The Grand Mal of the twenty-first century . . . I have a grandson . . . He's a great kid. A genius. A different kind of genius . . . A *new* kind of genius . . . He wouldn't have lasted half an hour in the field, in my good old days. But that's all a thing of the past and he's prepared for a different kind of mission for which I'm not suited . . . My grandson is just twenty-one and he's already considered a master of his craft. The craft of getting people hooked on the new form of drugs and alcohol and cigarettes: everything that you consume and that consumes you via phone screens . . . The phone as the thing that eases the anxiety of being phone addicted. The phone as comfort when your girlfriend leaves you or you lose your job . . . My grandson has explained to me that mobile phones are the new paralyzing weapons, that they're the technological evolution that has brought about the involution of the human being, hurling them from the heights of the crossword puzzle into the abysses of Candy Crush Saga: real nourishing letters supplanted by fake sugary sweets. An Omega Point headed for the most Alpha of flatlines. Something very fast that has made man slower and clumsier at moving through and connecting with and perceiving everything around him beyond that screen. You think it's always at hand—the latest trend is to hold it as if it were an unctuous piece of buttered morning toast and speak unctuously into it all day long—when really you're in its hands. And it's so disturbing to see lovers in the street who used to put their hands, both hands, all over each other and who now only do so with one hand, because they're holding their phones in the other. The same phones they'll use pretty soon to break off their long-distance relationship and to block each other so they won't see at a distance even though they are so close. The phones that, when taking a picture or making a video, force you to stretch out your arm in a gesture that recalls a Nazi salute. It's no coincidence that even homeless people who have nothing to eat still have mobile phones. Have you seen it? Begging for spare change so they can pay for data? Somehow, they get them and keep them charged—no longer asking for coins, but just for permission to use an outlet—and that keeps them calm and doped up . . . And there are also those lunatics in the street who used to go around talking to themselves—once lunatics and now just idiots—and now just hold a dead phone up to their ear and scream and are so difficult to differentiate from the supposedly sane people who're doing the exact same thing . . . And, oh, all those people who die in absurd accidents because of their mobile phones or who die sacrificing their lives resisting a mugger, trying to save their mobile phones, as if they were their greatest loves . . . Or who try to have an accident and to be filmed in the moment of the accident so that later people will give them a thumbs-up . . . Or when an accident happens in front of them and instead of helping those involved they opt to film them . . . And I've even seen a sign in a hotel that said: 'In the event of a fire, follow the instructions for evacuating the building and don't waste time filming with your mobile phone' . . . Seriously, I'm not making this up . . . People walked down the street blindfolded or drinking detergent or putting cockroaches on their faces or stuffing condoms up their noses to pull them out of their mouths or sticking firecrackers up their asses and setting them off or being driven to suicide for the love not of art but of YouTube . . . And I've even heard of kids taking naked pictures of themselves and sending them around the Internet to attract pedophiles just so they can get more likes . . . Farewell to the nineteenth-century romanticism of someone throwing himself into a volcano with a broken heart: now they all tripped and fell in because of their unstable and stupid desire to take risky selfies . . . Or because of some wild and idiotic self-destructive impulse . . . The only advantage of this whole monstrous trend is that now almost everyone has a picture of themselves on the day of their death, because they take pictures every hour of every day, ha . . . Wasn't it a lot better when phones were used to communicate bad news but not detonate bombs? . . Oh, all those phones that, now, whenever they ring in a feature film or on a TV show, make you bring your hand to your own phone. Automatic reflex. That never happened with the telephones from before, in the movies or shows from before. Now phones are calling you all the time. Telemarketers call you. Some even working for competing telecom companies that your telecom company sold your data to so they can call you at any hour, offering to sell you their soul while you tell them they should give you their home phone number, so you can call them in the middle of the night to discuss that new offer for a new model of mobile phone . . . And in exchange for all of that, phones also make it possible for you to communicate in fewer and fewer words . . . How nice . . . So you can write something short because there's no time, because you have to write something else right away, something even shorter and better and without parentheses or subordinates or dashes. And if possible without even any letters: a photograph and one of those little yellow faces or little clapping hands . . . Meanwhile, TV shows drag on for years and years and feature zombies and people who don't know they're dead. Shows that're more demanding than a girlfriend or a kid. And there's already an entire generation of parents challenging a generation of kids to a 'Spend less time on your phone and more time watching TV,' not realizing or unable to assimilate the fact that their kids watch TV on their phones. Scolding them with the same tone that, when they were kids, their parents used to tell them to stop watching TV and go read a book . . . But there aren't many of them either. Because they, the parents and even the grandparents, have been abducted too. Phoney-Snatchers, ha. And sometimes I understand not attraction but the advantage: now all those families who can't see or hear each other have the perfect excuse to sit around the same table, all together, not seeing or hearing each other, because they're all busy seeing and hearing other things on their phones, always on the table, just how we used to set our service weapons on the tablecloth next to the bread and a glass full to the brim with single malt . . . I remember my wife, may she rest in peace, though I doubt it . . . She and I cordially hated each other for decades. It wasn't a pleasant situation, it's true, but at least it was a vital and self-aware hate and, in its way, committed and almost loving. We hated each other to each other's faces . . . Now, there are almost no emotions like that. Now, there are almost no emotions of any kind. There's no longer that kind of love where nothing is secret yet everything is confidential. People fall in love and fight through screens and aliases, sometimes without even having met each other and . . . Hate is an emoji now. . . Something inserted quickly at the end of something read even more quickly . . . Something that's nothing but admitting the defeat of no longer being able to fully express anything with words and needing the help of a little, in every sense, symbol . . . Something that lasts very little time and has zero emotional sustenance, because what matters isn't slowly reflecting but quickly flexing. To be there. To show up. Loving and hating with the same finger and in the same way . . . And the cigarette after making love has been replaced by the tweet after anything and everything . . . And something tells me that the person who signs his messages with the alias Oliver Tweet never read the Dickens novel . . . Or at least never read that opening that I like so much, the one from *A Tale of Two Cities*: a historical novel but one with a handful of opening lines that would work perfectly in any time period or, even, for the autobiography of my covert life that I'll never write, because I signed a document promising never to do so . . . And, ah, the pages of a book that you read before falling asleep—the pages that lowered your eyelids in slow motion so that the blinds of your dreams could be raised—now are the same as spying through the keyhole of Instagram on the exhibitionists and liars who leave the door to their lives wide open and . . . But as I was saying: my grandson is what's now known as an 'ethical designer' at one of those multinational tech companies whose name isn't relevant . . . Or maybe it is . . . But I'm not going to say it . . . And my grandson tells me that the time to worry about book burning has already come and gone. What should worry us now is neuron burning in a society that spends its time distracting itself from long and deep and serious reading. We're headed more toward a *Brave New World* than a *1984*; but the powers that be are interested in making us think of *1984* as the only possible dystopia while they slip a *Brave New World* in through the backdoor and through the phones that are always right in front of us . . . And my grandson's thing is funny. His specialty . . . Did I already mention it? . . . My grandson is what's called an 'ethical designer,' ha . . . Because his profession consists, basically, of exploring the limits of what can be done—or going past those limits without anyone knowing or authorizing it, the way we crossed from Vietnam into Cambodia on Operation Menu—when it comes to the manipulation of data and, though you may not believe it, not long ago I saw a documentary about that war, about *my* war, where at the beginning it had a disclaimer regarding the inclusion of 'images that could negatively impact the viewer's sensibility'. . . Can you believe that? . . . Is it really necessary to warn people now, just in case, that the footage of a lost war won't be particularly edifying? . . . Are young people really that fragile? These days, my grandson, in a Cupertino bunker with brightly colored walls and surrounded by an array of gadgetry, is devoted to illuminating the algorithm of memory and pinpointing the parameters that could turn the act of remembering into an exact science.

And accordingly, distill it down to scrupulous equations without any scruples, until they achieve results inalterable in their power of corruption. And in that way, when all those Xs are revealed, being able to implant there what they want to seem unforgettable to the masses and to determine everything to be forgotten or not clearly remembered. To control the memory of the species to thereby be masters of its future. A new much cleaner and covert form of invasion. Specifying the hidden points of the past and locating the most porous of borders—and passing through them via secret passageways and trapdoors—when it comes to the hacking of brains. Making everyone think what you want them to think and remember. A uniform and targeted idea of the surrounding world and universe. Convincing everyone that they're finding something when really what they're searching for is predetermined by the stimulation of neurotransmitters via dopamine, making them feel that, typing, they are annulling the stress of the hormone cortisol . . . Or something like that . . . But one thing is clear to me: this whole thing about post-truth is just the tip of the iceberg, my friend. And our minds are passengers on the *Titanic*. Everything is totally FUBAR and FUBU and SNAFU and SUSFU and TARFU and An Imperial FU and you know what those letters stand for, right? Military jargon to very quickly describe a capital catastrophe. A black op that died on the operating table and, suddenly, in plain sight. I wonder if there's an emoji that would give them a face. Variations on one idea: FUBAR or *Fucked Up Beyond All Recognition* . . . And there's some grace to the whole thing. Or, better, disgrace: we achieved the technological capacity to store everything and for nothing to be forgotten in exchange for yielding and surrendering a neurological capacity with ever less ability to remember something. And, yes, we're talking more and more to ourselves. Or to strangers. Thinking we're all connected . . . The idolaters of hyperconnectivity have won the battle while we isolationists have retreated to our winter quarters . . . But the war isn't over yet. For every action there's a reaction and—you know what I'm talking about, you're a writer, you read and write on your own—the game is still afoot . . . And speaking of excess communication, I fear I've said too much, am I right?")

And *warning! warning! warning!*

And turbulence zone.

And oxygen masks.

And loss of cabin pressure.

And there, everyone, enumerating sins as if rereading them.

And there was no need for him to confess, because his crime had been committed in plain sight and where everyone could read it: almost nobody spoke aloud in his books and everybody was thinking all the time. And when they spoke, they did so thinking (his books always took place inside his characters' heads; and were about everything that might enter and exit those heads). And there was hardly any dialogue expect when, for example, two dinosaurs appeared to discuss how long it would be until the meteor came to wipe them all out.

No, it hadn't been an easy life, his life as a writer.

Anyway, he didn't write anymore, he was extinct, with no clear front and all rearguard. His stories were history, they were the stories told by skeletons remembering when they had viscera and were covered with muscles and skin.

A long time ago, creating his books had been like going to wage successive battles where he was taken prisoner only to rise up, revolting against that hard-to-put-in-writing foe and, at last, vanquishing it and narrating it. Making it his own. A truce-less war he—in theory and after practice—finally returned from changed, wiser and more experienced. A war he fought so he could live to tell the tale.

Now, as was the case with General Electric, all his great offensives were behind him, in the rearguard. And he (like one of those veterans who claimed to feel the arms and legs they no longer had), entrenched in his studio, only practiced the discipline of incessantly thinking about what he could write and what battles he could fight, if presented with the right conditions and if those Tartars ever came galloping in from the far reaches of that desert he'd traveled to with no return ticket. There he was, waiting, as if not wanting to admit he no longer waited or hoped for anything. Simultaneously on high alert and at rest, fantasizing about the moment of hearing and, once again, obeying the order *"À l'attaque!"* (for some strange reason, he always heard it in French and as if coming from a thin-lipped mouth beneath a waxed and musketeerish moustache). Then, he sighed, potential books like an explosion in the instant of explosion. Like shards suspended in the air, like more or less accelerated particles or like cells interlinked that—depending on the mechanisms of the conflict or the quantum mechanics—didn't exist until they hit home and acquired some form, some beauty. Ideas that came to him, all of them, composed of discomposed fragments. In *that* font. Like the impossible future of a past that never took time or place.

And he didn't even read anything new.

He didn't read young and voracious authors who—so concerned with their present—never imagined that their time on this planet and on the "literary scene" would be brief and fleeting. And, much less, could they guess that the seed of their own annihilation already resided inside them—in that fast-aging newness. Ephemeral youth was always the landscape where enduring wrinkles came to camp out. But, meanwhile and in the meantime, they all come together to mutually dedicate their books to one another (they cared so much more about their own dedications in the present than about the epigraphs of others from the past) only to—due to "aesthetic differences," thinly veiling the bad blood of professional jealousies or failed flings—eliminate those dedications in subsequent editions and swap them out for new ones and . . .

He didn't read them anymore, but, perversely, he did enjoy—with a dash of sadomasochism—observing them. They were so fertile and productive and prolific and always publishing. And yes, he'd read the messages that a good number of them periodically sent. Emails. His email address was so obvious—name & last name & @ & .com—that everyone had pretty much open access to it. And so, he got flooded with messages where, after a couple lines of empty and disingenuous praise, they always asked him for something. And young writers—maybe feeling they had a right to it, because at one time he'd also been a young writer for whom being a young writer had gone quite well—asked for *so many* things.

They asked him to read their unpublished manuscripts, as undesired as they were undesirable (leaving them for him —as if he were some kind of fucking Santa Claus or one of the goddamned Three Kings, always there and ever ready to read their wish lists all year round—in the mailbox at his house or in his email inbox without checking or asking his permission first and making sure to say in their message that "I've been meaning to read your work," not caring at all that they were subverting the natural and hierarchical order of things: the absolutely unknown writer should have to read the fairly well-known writer first, not the other way around). Which led him to wonder if the same thing happened to, for example, pediatricians: children dropped off by parents at the doors to their offices, demanding an immediate and free checkup and, it goes without saying, a perfect diagnosis. And at some point he would run into them and they would ask what he thought of their manuscript, the one they'd sent him, and at first he'd made the mistake of telling them that he never read unpublished work by people he didn't know, which earned him their hate—always freely given—forevermore. But a while back he discovered a far better and more efficient approach: he told them that what they'd written was a true masterpiece, that it was so good and so transcendent that he'd had to stop reading it, because he was afraid it would give him writer's block.

And he read the latest newcomers as if from ever further away in time and space. He flipped through their pages, standing in some bookstore and was surprised (never too surprised) to find that what they'd re-created and passed off as supposedly innovative was just—especially those with transgressive avant-garde pretensions—more of the same as always. And when it came to the local writers, there was the added aggravation of having to carry around on their backs the greatest neo-post-meta-modern freak in all of History (that strange and singular body, outside all time and space known as *Don Quixote*), turning their efforts at novelty into clumsy and quasi desperate tantrums. All of it got so old so fast, especially because of how all the possible permutations—on the covers of their books and birth and death certificates—of antique signatures and stale surnames like Gómez-Aquirre-Fernández-Molina-Ríos-Galíndez-Pérez-González-Ruiz-López-Ramírez-Díaz-Hernández got mixed together and confused in his memory (among them were a mediocre couple, alcoholics both, parents of a pair of kids zombified by their phones, he referred to—one of his characteristic good bad jokes—not as Scott and Zelda but as Zeldo and Zelda).

They asked him to find publishers for their manuscripts.

They asked him to write blurbs for the jackets of their soon-to-be-published manuscripts (one of them even went as far as to specify that "I don't need you to worry about the plot, because I already have a blurb on that; I would prefer that you refer to the quality and originality of my novel").

They asked him, later, to introduce them in public, though they hadn't read his books and certainly hadn't attended their launches (because it was all about getting him to read and praise them).

They asked him—radiating *selfie-shness*—to let them take a selfie with him.

And they asked him for secret formulas and top-secret codes—they were that childish—for getting prizes and fellowships and trips awarded to them and not to or for their manuscripts . . .

And he marveled at their ferocious voracity and constant activity. All of them going here and there, bouncing frantically off the walls until they shot out a door and onto a stairway that, they thought, only went up. All of them shiny and new and completely unaware of their planned obsolescence (the very idea of being a young writer implied that sooner rather than later said idea would cease to be a good or viable or sustainable one; and that only a very few among them would be able to make the transition to being just writers or, harder still, to penning one of those hip books as fleeting as summer storms or, practically impossible, one of those few classics that would never go out of circulation) and that, coming up behind them, there already echoed the ultrasound of a new generation of young writers who would very soon arrive to their world to replace them and declare them old-fashioned and outmoded after so many late nights out. All of them so unaware that youth was that place that you always left behind and never returned to and that the actions of youth always and due to inertia contributed to the decline of those who, ever older and ever less valuable, understood youth as a form of novelty and of pure and almost-impossible-to-realize promise. All of them failing to imagine that in an ever-nearer future they would be nothing but an in-person participant at an academic seminar where, over and over, they would pay homage to some immortal dead (and as such unable to offer and counter them with his own version of things) writer they'd barely read when they were far more concerned with writing and telling about themselves than with telling and writing stories.

Meanwhile, it was clear that, as writers, they'd been born into a different time than he had. A time when the literary vocation was better—or worse—described as a literary career.

When he was starting out, there were no literary festivals, no trophies, no fellowships, no translations (translations for which foreign publishers applied for subsidies that would never be awarded to him to write the very book that now they wanted to have translated), no residencies, no earnest petitions or historical manifestos (and wasn't there something absurd and irrational about collectively signing something you hadn't written with a bunch of people you had no relationship with or with whom—you only discovered when it was already too late, when the document had already been made public and was being debated until the next cause to defend or oppose came along—you had no desire to be related?) like autograph books everyone scrambled and elbowed to sign, no lists of "best writers under 39" (and he always wondered when someone would be brave enough to attempt a list—far more interesting and definitely riskier—of best writers over 40), no stories published online becoming fevered "viral phenomena" and leading to million-dollar advances for a first books that, of course, never sold as well as anticipated and ended up triggering a chain of firings at publishing houses and suspensions, until further notice, of any future contracts. They hadn't even had any readers but each other—the writers of their generation, completely ignored by those of the previous generation—meeting up in bars to face off in happy and desperate duels.

And yet there was one way in which today's writers were like him: almost all of them had decided not to have children (at most, he'd toyed with the idea of literary progeny, some kind *alter-hijo*, like Martin Amis had been for Saul Bellow; a child-fan to be chosen from among all those who chose him: the most talented and most handsome, but, warning, one who was never more intelligent than he was). But these days they had different reasons for not wanting children: he didn't want to be a father while they wanted to remain children forever. To be their own children—instead of having children who would make them miss out on an invitation to some festival—and to spoil themselves until they reached the age when they would once again be using XL-sized diapers and dragging themselves around, lonely but not alone.

And he could even see how the whole polyamory thing as a supposedly liberating excuse (something that, naively, they believed had just been invented, ignoring the whole free love thing from the Swinging Sixties and the Swinger Seventies, without going any further; and he couldn't help but feel unsettled thinking about how, when they sat down to listen to The Beatles or The Kinks or Pink Floyd they would, of course, convince themselves that they were making some big discovery; and maybe all that frenetic partner-hopping, he thought, was the direct result of the radiations of so much zapping around different platforms to watch interminable TV series that often never concluded; and, oh, maybe they didn't realize that by disregarding infidelity as a dramatic or comedic stimulus they were, also, dispensing with one of the great literary themes) was nothing but the cool new way to spread love for another around among so many that it would never exceed the voltage and intensity of the love they felt for themselves. And so, love for another would never distract them from focusing on their road to fame and to everybody loving them (or, what was almost the same thing these days, convincing themselves they were famous and that everybody loved them because that was the answer they got from the screen, the magic screen of their phone, which incessantly told them they were the most beautiful and talented and that Snow White was a tale that had to be interrogated because Prince Charming didn't get consent before kissing her and waking her up and there were all those dwarves exploiting her for domestic labor and . . .).

And in the beginning, sometimes, he even tried to help them.

And to offer them advice and contacts, seeking (sometimes, he had to admit) some kind of attention for himself in return when they were on an editorial committee or even the occasional carnal exchange with one of those—not necessarily talented but definitely beautifully featured—good girls aspiring to be a bad writer.

But what really made him proud was when they sought him out—and not someone else like IKEA—as a mentor. Until he realized that they only wanted him because—they thought—he'd *discovered* IKEA and had contributed to making IKEA into what IKEA was today (and, not to mention that, now, he was *also* "Penelope's Brother"). They wanted him so he would magically transform them into IKEA. They wanted a Merlin because they wanted to seize Excalibur and rule Camelot. But nothing interested them less than being that bewitched bewitcher, lovestruck and sleeping and lying in Brocéliande forest. They weren't attracted to true magic but only to the epic trick. And, of course, they knew nothing about the decadence and fall of the legend and kingdom, because they'd read nothing about it and had only seen Disney's festive adaptation or those recent and absurd and digitalized adaptations that always stopped in the moment of maximum Arthurian glory.

They didn't care about the past.

And the future was next week.

They lived in a present of ambitions and calculations and conspiracies where everything was prizes and agents and translations and fellowships and even aristocratifying medals.

And he couldn't blame them, they were born like that: programmed for that, with an app on their hard drives that he'd never had. Because it was true that it was all there for the taking and in their names. Again: none of that had existed when he was starting out. Not even the notion of the "young writer"—something the success of *National Industry* helped formulate—because there was no need to think about it and because the marketing gurus of the publishing world hadn't come up with it yet. Because, back then, the great writers—who also sold well—were still young and full of energy and projects that ran the gamut from the great continental novel to the utopic planetary manifesto.

(And again, he remembered that, for a while, with the eyes of an alchemist, he read what all those voracious newcomers sent him with true interest, thinking that it might end up being useful. One of them he never actually met—"your biggest fan"—sent him daily links to each and every mention of his name on the Internet. And yes: every so often he surrendered to the temptation of venturing out onto that quicksand. And he clicked on that sequence of blue letters and numbers. And he let himself sink down up to his waist in that mud or Jell-O in order to find out what was being said about him by the people who still followed him and the ones who'd never stopped coming after him. And he even did so happily and hoping to discover, out in that shitstorm, some noble creature. Someone who wasn't necessarily and obligatorily already "the top of the tree"—an expression, for him, first foreign and then local that he'd appropriated and rewritten as "the lightning rod of a skyscraper"—as a writer when he or she was starting out, but yes, at least, a reader with baobab roots. And he was surprised a little and then not at all that it was so clear how the self-referential inclination of the new generation of writers—forming and deforming themselves on the training grounds of social media—had deforested and wreaked havoc on a good part of the landscape. How these days almost every first book was woefully autobiographical and all of that and not how in other times when the autobiographical in debut works tended to be nothing more than the festive fertile terrain where exotic seeds were sewn. Now no, now not so much. Now the need to tell your story had been imposed over the desire to be a story-teller. More *alert-ego* than *alter-ego*. Ignoring that thing Francis Scott Fitzgerald had said about how "You don't write because you want to say something, you write because you have something to say." Every-thing produced by those chronic chroniclers came from or leaned on or climbed up onto the shoulders of dead family members or suicidal friends or physical maladies that were always terminal or exotic and never something common among writers like hemorrhoids—per-haps the literary *grand mal* par excellence. That plague—*ofa·lím* in Hebrew; but that the uptight correctors of the Old Testament preferred to diagnose as *tejo·rím*, or tumors, which had no particular reason to reside in the anus—God used to punish the Philistines: a category that also served to describe individuals lacking any artistic sensibil-ity and of exceedingly banal spirit.)

So, now, he no longer answered them and deleted their messages without reading them. And he wondered how it was possible that the National Geo-graphic Channel hadn't yet made them the subject of a documentary like the ones they tended to do on strange tribes covered in tattoos (and, yes, many of these young writers tattooed famous quotes on the napes of their necks or the faces of writers on their shoulders so they could feel even more literary; so they could publicly proclaim that they'd laid not only their minds but also their bodies at the mercy and disposal of art). Few times had he met a species more ambitious in the broadest sense of the word: they wanted everything and, out of everything they wanted, the thing they seemed to want least was to write. The ambition of the work didn't seem to matter at all, what really mattered, completely, was the lust of the life. And they seemed not to have understood why—it was no coincidence—in the final pages of *Fahrenheit 451* those memorizers of books were only dedicating themselves to the preservation of works of fiction and not to their authors' biographies. Yes: in the end—if everything went wrong and what was and had always been true became unmistakably clear—there would still be the comfort that readers were more interested in the persona in front of the person than in the person behind the persona.

Now (a little ashamed of himself; because when he was starting out, he'd looked down on all those consecrated writers who said they only reread the classics) he only devoted himself to writers who in general were dead and far away in time and space. Or, better, all his attention was reserved for and focused on the books that were the most alive, the immortal books. Books that—as time passed—had become the authors of the people who had written them. Books by writers that used to be read but that almost no one talked about anymore. And that definitely didn't get referenced on screen for the fascination of readers who didn't read much anymore, but who loved watching so called booktubers, with their peculiar diction and syntax, blather on for five or six minutes about new and ever so fleeting and ephemeral of books, making a lot of noise and with a high-pitched voices, cloudy eyes and dilated pupils.

And he thought—far from the practice, deep in the theory, furious as only those who only theorize tend to be—more about this kind of thing all the time. You never know more about something—about a vocation or a love— and understand it better than when you stop practicing it. Then you can only sort of remember better and better, but, also, in a way that resembled less and less, yes, how all of that *actually* was and happened.

"To invent" was a divine, two-faced verb where the features of dreaming and remembering melted together.

To remember was like rereading and revising yourself but blocking out what you didn't wish to see (after all, lying was a form of wishing) and simultaneously clarifying what in the beginning you only suspected.

To remember was like reading yourself already knowing what was going to happen, but, even still, ever ready for the surprise and wonder of discovering paragraphs and scenes that in their moment were overlooked or underappreciated or left by the wayside.

And to write was to remember into the future and to read was to predict into the past.

When you read—as if shot point blank by a projectile that opens a third eye with which you suddenly see so many theretofore invisible things—you remembered something that hadn't happened but that, all of a sudden, did happen. Something that from that moment on is and was something that took time and took place. Something that you could remember, but that also—with any luck or if it was worthy—would never be forgotten.

And for someone who wrote something that others read, the situation was even more complicated: everything happened first and you then you wrote it afterward, even though it may never have actually happened to you. But if it was something you happened to think then it was something that had indeed happened to you.

Again: it wasn't a simple life.

The greatest and never-surpassed investigator of all of this—his hero, another among many—had been Marcel Proust. A Jew, yes, but also The Great Resurrector.

Proust understanding The Past as a religion to believe in, because you never died there, because The Past always returned and you always returned to it.

Proust as the writer who had managed to write a work that wasn't a place where you went to live—which in itself wasn't easy to achieve—but was something far more complex and admirable: a work that came to live with you.

Proust (from whom he'd learned and understood that what was really interesting wasn't autobiography as fiction but fiction as autobiography) had understood it all very clearly and had known just how knowing he was, even if everyone considered him a frivolous dandy. Those who knew and claimed to have suffered him would have never imagined that his Combray would end up renaming Illiers (fiction imposing itself over reality as nonfiction), that his face would adorn T-shirts, and that his name would be cause for metafictional winks as much from the burning gaze of Vladimir Nabokov as from the cool eyes of one of the least sexy Bond Girls named Madeleine Swann.

And, of course, nothing of what suddenly was forever had really been that way even for a moment: the famous madeleine had actually been a small piece of toast, and from there, from that teacup, to infinity and beyond and coming back forever altered by the space-time radiations. The trick was to ramble far and wide and to change yourself by living all times at the same time (he'd felt something similar listening for the first time to the music and reading the lyrics of Bob Dylan's very Proustian and multi-temporal "Tangled Up in Blue") and not settling for the brief and easy act of the everyday X-ray, clumsily and hurriedly synthesized. Days (de)forming a line online. In that place without a map but in all places where anyone could become globally famous for a quick minute after paying the price—within everyone's price range—of intentionally playing the fool, falling down stairs or filming their cat or their baby or their baby strangling their cat or their cat smothering their baby's last breath. Very expensive cats and babies; the kind that look like they've been mummified by ancient Egyptians, yet still alive and meowing and wailing for the cameras. Adorable degraded to adored. Or vice versa. All of them there—including the invisible individual behind the camera—so that others could ineptly and quickly read and see and comment. And let them know how much they liked whatever it was they were doing with a thumbs up (the same thumb that once had been used to stop a car and hitchhike anywhere was now the thumb used to stop yourself and go nowhere), before moving on to some other post from some other person, time dissolving into itself, wasting time.

And when was it that people had decided that they would rather become "famous" for being incredibly stupid than to not be famous and just be a normal person? he wondered.

And Proust had explained it (Proust always explained the noble form of the symptom provided that it could be nobly narrated; that way of sliding from one moment to the next like a succession of screens) before heading out in search of what'd been lost. Preparing to track down the modalities and mannerisms of an age that'd been let go. An age that Proust endeavored to regain, turning stories into History, having himself photographed all the time and always with a silly expression and a lunar pallor or posing for that vampiric oil portrait with an enticing orchid poking out of his buttonhole never to wilt.

Proust had written: "The day comes when we realize that tomorrow cannot be different from yesterday, for tomorrow is made of yesterday."

Or something like that.

He didn't have the book on-hand at the moment to check.

What he did have was a watch he'd bought many years ago.

One of those watches "like the ones from before" and that every so often stopped ticking and you had to give them little taps on the glass of their faces, as if getting their attention so they would make time keep passing and marching out to the front it would never reach, but, even still, catching fire down in the trenches and getting wounded crossing fields of barbwire. (One of those watches that hadn't yet leapt from wrists to telephones, dispensing with the analog hands that, he'd read recently, had been removed from the walls of classrooms, because many of the students, more all the time, didn't know how to read them anymore. And so they got really stressed-out during exams because they didn't know how much time they had left to answer all those questions whose answers they didn't know, because they couldn't remember. Because their ability to remember had been atrophied by servers and search engines that, really, had turned them into lost servants. Students like the ones that once looked at him—back when every so often he'd dared teach a class to some "creative" graduate students—as if he were crazy or a being from another planet when he told them that, in the aristocratic novels of the nineteenth century, the nobles paid a special employee, a so-called *clockman*, to come to their homes once a week, generally on Fridays, to calibrate and set the time on all the many clocks in the house, which had been functioning without any problems or need for "updates" for decades in bedrooms and living rooms and halls. And then he explained to them that the presence of these secondary characters in those novels had the primary importance of, often, situating and fixing the action in a time that, sometimes, ran away from and escaped the characters who didn't know they were being read by their readers. And he also told them that that was how Vladimir Nabo-kov had detected the difference in the times—though they *transpired* together—of the simultaneous couples Anna/Vronsky and Kitty/Levin in *Anna Karenina*; thus insinuating that the different classes of love—happy or tragic—accelerated or slowed down the action. An idea that Proust, after Tolstoy and before Nabokov, would make explicit when he postulated that "The time at our disposal each day is elastic; the passions we feel dilate it, those that inspire us shrink it, and habit fills it." And so—he explained to his students who seemed more irreal to him all the time—the fact that *Anna Karenina* wasn't *as* realist of a novel as was thought helped make it possible to consider it, as Nabo-kov did, the best of all novels. As long as—he thought and said to his students—you ignore that small "flaw" that, at the end, Pierre Bezuk-hov doesn't appear to save the tragic heroine, rescuing her from the train tracks. And, of course, none of the students got his bad Tolstoy-ian joke. Anyway, it was more than clear that his very occasional students—he was invited to those "prestigious master's programs" that paid next to nothing more and more sporadically—preferred to live in a time when the clock was just one of many functions on a telephone that needed to be updated and traded in for a new model almost every year. And so, they never even stopped to think that it wasn't particularly productive to spend years of their lives following the twists and turns of dragons flying across the skies of absurdly named kingdoms week after week *either*. Whereas they felt fully in their right to regard him with faces that seemed to say, "so that's all a life of reading and writing books is good for: being able to discuss some bullshit about old watches." And, yes, *that* was all he was to them, looking at his watch, wondering how many minutes as long as centuries until the end of that class for the classless: something old and outmoded.) And so he glanced at his watch—which hadn't yet died and which didn't need to be updated all the time—that he'd bought when passing through Illiers, a town about one hundred kilometers from Paris. A place that, in 1971, had been renamed Illiers-Combray in honor of the most illustrious child who'd ever vacationed there.

He'd arrived to Illiers-Combray somewhat disappointed—last leg on a

Proustian pilgrimage—after having gone in and come out of 102 Boulevard Haussmann, near the Arc de Triomphe. That was the location of the apartment where Marcel Proust had shut himself in a room lined with cork panels to recreate his universe. A place now occupied by the offices of a bank where the employees looked up wearily at the visiting tourists while a guide showed them some laminated photographs so they could "see how it all had been." A guide who, after a few minutes and pointing to the exit, offered them a madeleine of almost synthetic pastry and wrapped in plastic and so un-Proustian, taken off a wheeled cart like the ones used to transport files. He, at least, wanted to ingest it right there. And he put the whole thing in his mouth and almost choked and felt absolutely nothing. No epiphany.

So, he went to the nearest tourism office and made inquiries about how to get to Illiers-Combray. And—fearing the worst yet still in need of an antidote for the prior frustration—once there he would not be disappointed.

In Illiers-Combray (which for him immediately became Combray-Illiers) everything was as it should be, as it had been and as it would always be. The church and the forking path in the nearby forest, one path leading to Swann and one to Guermantes. And the historic house where he bought his watch and rediscovered, with some astonishment, the smell of his maternal grandparents' house in Sad Songs (his own perfectly preserved "village green," the smell of earth hanging in the air among sacred trees taller than cathedrals, the smell of *vitreaux* light passing through the pine boughs) at the same time that, beside him, an old Indian tourist exclaimed "Grandma Anjali!" her eyes welling with tears and one of those smiles you only have when you're seven years old.

They had all come there—it was clear—to go back.

There, the house that once had been the house of the book's Aunt Leonie and was now Musée Marcel Proust/Maison de Tante Léonie where author and character coexisted. And he'd wondered then, in front of the sign at the entrance to the town that read "Illiers-Combray/Le Combray de Marcel Proust," if a writer had ever gone further or reached greater heights than that. And probably not: it was not common to have everyone else's geography mutate into your own geography. And to have your childhood bedroom become a museum piece. And to have all the bakeries near your house compete among themselves for who could sell the true madeleine that sent you traveling back in search of lost time. (Though the title of Proust's novel always struck him as incorrect, imprecise: time was never lost because it was everywhere, there, as immoveable as the monolith in *2001: A Space Odyssey*. What was lost, on the other hand, were all those primates—the men and women—jumping up and down all around it and whimpering and grunting and touching it with reverence. They were what was lost. Time didn't pass, what passed where those who surrounded it, knowing they were cornered and wondering what time is it, how much time was left, what had happened and what wouldn't ever happen.)

And there, in the house-museum or in the museum-house, the watch. The watch he saw in one of the glass display cases in the gift shop was a limited-edition watch with a white and numberless sphere and—with spiraling text shrinking smaller and smaller as it closed in on itself—that first line from *À la recherche* . . . where the narrator announced that he was going to bed earlier and earlier, not to sleep but to remember.

Like him, but absolutely not like him. That was the one way in which he could feel similar and akin to Proust, he thought.

In going to bed early.

But, once there, while Proust remembered his family and his time, he could only remember his family all the time.

And he'd read somewhere (or he'd written it, it didn't matter anymore) that at all literary fiction answered to two basic motives and could be synthesized in two movements: the family and the journey.

And sometimes—as had been the case with his flammable and finally aflame sister Penelope—you went on a journey to flee your family.

Now he, in his memory, embarked on the righteous trajectory back to where he'd never been and remembered something he'd once underlined in a novel by Richard Powers about how there are only two possible stories: the two most ancient and elemental; the only two you would ever read; the one where the future came to beat the past to a pulp or the one where the past leapt on the future to strangle it.

Now—back to front and front to back—he moved forward going back.

Now he was on his way to see the Karmas: another family that—by way of Penelope—was also somewhat his.

Penelope had lived with them and eventually fled after getting impregnated in a somewhat unusual way. And she'd had a son by a comatose Karma she'd suffocated before making her escape. Nobody could deny that, as source material, it was full of possibilities.

And he'd written a book between parenthesis (again and once more, a book he'd been commissioned to write, a book about Mexico City, D.F.) in which the protagonist-family had been freely and directly inspired by the Karmas.

And he'd never actually gone there, to Abracadabra, to Mount Karma, to see the Karmas for himself. And yet (and unlike what happened with the romantics in the eighteenth and nineteenth century, when every journey turned into an almost immediate book about that journey of which there was little evidence beyond random souvenirs to keep the journey from being forgotten) he remembered that place and that clan perfectly. Because he wrote them and he read them while he was writing them. In that book of his, so many years ago, about a crazed and crazy-making familial sect, which was none other than Penelope's in-laws.

The book that—instantaneous and fragmented and fleeting—he wrote in Mexico and finished on the Day of the Dead (wondering how it was possible there was no Day of Feeling Almost Dead) as little kids chased him through the streets asking him for money to buy little sugar skulls that dissolved in their mouths (and he wanted so badly to kick the little skulls of those little kids with insufferable voices specially trained to torture tourists). Kids who finally caught him and left him penniless when he stopped to by a local newspaper, the paper itself yellow and almost translucent, as if it'd been printed on eyelid skin. He couldn't help buying it when he read, on the front page—next to an illustration depicting a group of people looking up at the sky with expectant terror—the formidable and all-caps headline *GRAN COMETA Y QUEMAZÓN: EL MUNDO SE VA A VOLVER TODITITO CHICHARRÓN*, which, in English, would be something like: *HUGE COMET AND SCORCHING FIRE: THE WORLD WILL BE TOOOTALLY CRACKLING* And below, information about how "The world is ending! We're toast! Going to get fried! We're asking for it!

To be turned to ash! A great European astronomer recently predicted. This horrifying catastrophe will be foreshadowed by a massive comet that will appear in the coming days. This malevolent asteroid will collide with Earth and cause massive breakdowns of . . ." And the news was accompanied by another almost caricaturized illustration in which the comet was represented by a colossal man free falling and enveloped in cosmic radiance. (A meteoric man at whom the moon stuck out its tongue and, seeing it, he said to himself: "Someday I want to be exactly *like that*." And, years later, he thought if he were to merge with the hadrons dancing in a Swiss particle accelerator he could *like that*: to be an annihilating Shiva.) And it took him a few minutes to realize that what he'd bought wasn't that day's newspaper but one of those old prints—illustrated by the catastrophic and skeletal José Guadalupe Posada, for newspapers from the end of the nineteenth century—that were sold at the newsstands and bookstores around El Zócalo. And he cut it out and folded it carefully and tucked it away (along with a square notecard from an unfinished novel and a page from a magazine impossible to read in its totality) and used it thereafter as a random book-mark in his successive and indomitable editions of *Ada, or Ardor*.

And then he—for whom the idea of his personal Apocalypse as something everyone would experience had struck him as attractive and even righteous—began to burst out crying and laughing with tears streaming down his face. And so he went back to his hotel to keep writing his own end of the world, in the final section of that novel he'd been commissioned to write.

He wrote it as if in a trance and emptying bottles of mezcal and biting drowned worms and thinking about things like how mezcal was to tequila what bourbon was to whisky. In a hotel room in which he took long show-ers, long *duchas*. ("Duchamp!" he laughed like a madman; and he got into the shower with his mouth full of mezcal that he didn't swallow because—as he'd read once in an interview of David Lynch that had been conducted during the filming of the god-awful *Dune* with its gigantic worms at the Estudios Churubusco in that same city—that way he wouldn't let in any of the water of Moctezuma's Revenge which would envelope him in fevers and diarrhea.) In a hotel room that he only left at night—larval and almost slithering through the serpentine streets of D.F.—to, as if he had one hundred feet, find more worms and more bottles at a nearby mezcalería, which had once been a garage. A place to accelerate or crash, being waited on by the second most beautiful woman in the world—her name was Pupa, she said with the flicker of a smile—dressed in a T-shirt that appeared to be painted directly on her torso that said, "Don't Be a Coocoon: Be a Butterfly." (And how is it that little bottles of mezcal aren't offered in minibars or on flying voyages through wormholes where the worms look like gigantic kaijus? he wondered.) And someone in the mezcalería was singing in Náhuatl "Ça tontemiquico ahnelli tinemico in tlpc ye antle nel o tic ytohua nican temictli." And he—on his fourth or fifth tall and skinny shot glass—could suddenly understand that tongue, which wasn't a dead tongue but a tongue with its tongue sticking out. A tongue that sounded like grasshoppers, more sacred than scarabs, rubbing together their little back feet that, unlike cockroaches, they were never missing. And he translated and hummed "It's not true . . . No, it's not true . . . That we came to live on Earth . . . We came here only to dream . . . We came only to sleep . . . Nothing we say here is real . . . It's a dream . . ." And he said to himself that that could only be the voice of the hummingbird god Huitzilopochtli: the resurrector of fierce and plumed Aztec warriors transformed into those little birds like the ones he already felt *comic*ally circling his head and his bottles, hunting for the worms swimming in the alcohol ("I wanted to drown my sorrows, but the bastards learned how to swim," the voice of Frida Kahlo said to him, bursting from the plumbing in the bathroom of his hotel room, dripping off of that little wormy moustache of hers). Or, maybe, it was Tepoztecatl, one of four hundred Centzontōtōchtin: divine rabbits and minor spirits, protectors of drunks, always between sleep and waking. And, once again, he said to himself that, when it came to choosing what to believe in, he would never understand the success of monotheism in the face of the far more fun and varied polytheism. That wide open space where there was almost one immortal for every mortal; a move that later the Vatican had clumsily attempted to emulate with the profusion of saints and the multiplication of the Virgin Mary as if they were bread and fish. It was against that—against that sacred and supposedly pagan (though really far more vintage and with better special effects) joy—that Cortes and his discourteous friars had fought in these streets that were once canals, thinking they had won. But no. The ancient gods still flew through the air, heavy with broken neons and the stench of syncretic foods, of that limitless city, laughed at by maps that were always blurry is if in a perpetual earthquake.

And so, then, he commended himself not unto God but unto the Gods.

Unto all those ancient gods who were far more attractive and proximal and ever ready to interact with and even *believe in* their worshippers (who could choose this one or that one as if they were different flavors or had different functions and abilities depending on what you needed in a given trance) than the modern singular gods: always absent and promising returns that never materialized or even contracting in on themselves to leave more space for man and yet occupying the greatest heights of the Hit & Faith Parade. But the only more or less mystical and epic thing that came to his aid was a fat man stuffed into a bereft suit of broken plastic intended, in vain, to be that of Iron Man and topped off with a cowboy hat and around whose neck hung, atop a divine belly, a car battery with two handles. The man had offered him "volts" to "cure his hangover" so that he could keep on drinking, as if he were just getting started. And he had grabbed ahold of those handles and felt the ghost of electricity howling in the bones of his face and running through his body until it sang in his brain—accompanied by a riot of golden trumpets and mahogany guitars—that line that went "*Que te vaya bonito.*"

And in that way, *bonito*, he walked out of there: way up high already and—with a vast nostalgia invading his mind—so far from the land where he was born.

And so, before going up to his room, one song and one last stop in the hotel bar to mix—and mixteca—what came before with what would come later. His Sad Night, his Saddest Night, indeed. And to attain that state of dis(grace) in which—deserted and jetlagged—he felt again as if he were remembering all of it at the same time and as if time were *tangled up in blue* and weren't passing, but without that meaning that it had stopped taking place. Like those proverbial and never proven final seconds of life in which your whole life flashed before your eyes. Thinking too that it was possible that what you really saw in the moment of dying was everything you *didn't* live, everything you could've lived if you'd made the right choices. And that it was from *that* that hell or purgatory or heaven or all three states at the same time was made, and that all of it kept on expanding until it acquired the indolent parsimony of the centuries. Zen Buddhists probably had a name for that state. Something comparable to the "already dead" of the bushido of the samurais before they ran into battle, not caring about dying in combat; because he who fought was already dead and, as such, invincible. Something *like that*, but in the ethylic version and for warriors who went running out and, full of sake, whipped out their katanas, seeing double and convinced they were facing double the enemy. Should he call it *barshido* maybe? Something that happened to the people in the bar who asked for one more round (that round that you could never put an exact number on, but that was always mathematically and precisely one round too many) balancing almost gymnastically atop the bar and already thinking about things like how the barman looked an awful lot like a Latino version of Peter Lorre and who now threatened him with a volcanic *"You are no a de wrider, you are a de espider, and we shoota de espiders in Méjico"*? Should he maybe go back to Japan to find out if something like that existed?

(He'd been translated there. Just one of his books. And, if Andy Warhol had postulated that thing about how everyone would get their fifteen minutes of fame—temporal fraction that now, thanks to social media, had mutated into everyone being famous for at least fifteen people—the truth is that, in Japan, he counter-postulated, everyone, absolutely everyone had a fan club, but they didn't know it. He'd been to Japan, once, for a few days—a few fragments, instants, moments— to launch his book and give a talk. And in Tokyo—during an epidemic of dangerous mosquitos, the Imperial Palace gardens closed to visitors for fear of outbreaks—he'd visited a metro station. The Shinjuku Station of the Chuo Line, the favorite line of suicidal people who maybe understood suicide as a superpower to be used just once in life and in death. The curving blueprint of that station prevented putting up those doors/barricades to prevent jumpers. A station where, as an almost magical form of protection, the walls had been covered with mirrors so that very depressed or very euphoric people could see themselves there and take a second to reconsider before making that definitive decision. Though he'd thought that seeing yourself like that and in that place, reflected in all your ruin or desperation, could only have the effect of convincing you that nothing made any sense but to take that one step forward and down. And there, at the edge of the platform, he'd put on his suicide face—a face that looked better and better on him—and leaned his body slightly and reverentially forward, to see if the other passengers would look at him with worry or if they got nervous. But no, not at all. Maybe it would've been different if they'd known he was the brother of Penelope, who, of course, was more beloved in Japan than in any other corner of the universe . . . And in Japan, the sushi-chefs stared at him at first—as if they were diagnosing the needs of his appetite and palate—and served him nothing more and nothing less than whatever they wanted to serve him and refused to make him anything he would've actually liked. And he'd even conversed with a cat that meowed at him in Japanese so he didn't understand anything it said but was sure it'd been *something* very important. Probably an explanation of the, for him, inexplicable mystery of why the Japanese people in animated drawings and manga comics always had such round and wide eyes. And in Tokyo he'd experienced an earthquake in an oscillating bookstore on a building's sixteenth floor. A bookstore and building from which they'd been evacuated amid giggling and bowing via the stairs and he ran down thinking that his life was an earthquake that kept repeating and in which, ah, he wasn't sure that it was good for his mental health to feel, for those few days, like he'd gone to live in a Haruki Murakami novel, he thought at the time.) **He had more than enough, he thought now, with his telepathic green cow.** (Though more than one of his critics—as praise or condemnation—had, at some point, connected the invocations of Ella in his work with the phantasmagoric women whose tits Murakami couldn't stop looking at/describing . . . The truth is that Murakami had never interested him all that much except that one very short yet immense story in which—if he was remembering it right—a young couple discover that they're perfect for each other and, for that reason, they decide to forget each other so they can experience the miracle of meeting all over again, but . . . Likewise, from the very first time he'd gone there, he'd felt that his place in the world was Manhattan. And he felt it again whenever he found himself back there. But he no longer had the stamina or the money to live in Manhattan, in the unrealized dream of his youth.

That Manhattan where Central Park burned for forty days and forty nights after some imbecile tried to capture "the perfect sound of tree leaves burning for an ASMR to post on Facebook" and the employees at The Strand were no longer what they'd been and had ordered him, almost despotically, to spell Nabokov for them, so they could look him up in their system and he responded by saying "I can, but I shouldn't." And Paris—where as a writer they'd loved him more and better—was now so busy fighting against the increasingly numerous and terrifying narrators of Islamic terrorism. Those individuals who, for him, were so confused. Because why would anyone dream of and long for a Heaven where seventy-two virgins were waiting for you? Who in their right mind could expect to find any pleasure in the supposed reward of having to instruct so many inexperienced girls whose age and physical appearance were, moreover, never specified? Wouldn't it be far more gratifying to just select, at most, a trio of the most passionate and experienced and beautiful courtesans to screw you like you'd never been screwed before? Anyway, there they all were, measuring the greatness of Allah, meeting in massive gatherings on every full-mooned night, in the deepest depths of a crater, where once upon a time the Louvre had stood.) But all of that was a long way from Mexico, on whose Pacific coast, he suspected, mutant Japanese monsters vacationed when they weren't stomping on pagodas and nuclear powerplants or fighting against those gigantic robots whose pilots were interweaving their memories. Better like that, the conversation with the monk-barman exhausted (more monologue than conversation; he'd told him about his whole quaking escapade in Tokyo), he decided to quickly return to his room with the drawn curtains. And to open them—not the curtains, but the new bottles without labels, because it was the worm floating inside that identified and personalized them—to dedicate and consecrate them in sips and bites to Tláloc, Mesoamerican god of the celestial waters and Lord of Tlalocán, heaven of the drowned. The Aztecs didn't have a God of Those Who Almost Drown and Thereby Discover Their Literary Vocation. And so Tláloc was the closest thing he had left. And so, in his name, he filled himself with maguey hearts distilled to mix with the blood of his own heart until it found a disheartened beat like the thump of sacrificial drums atop pyramids. (As a boy, he'd gone from late nights of black and white TV with the monsters of Universal to mornings with brightly-colored demons of the pre-Columbian netherworld. And in fifth grade of elementary school at Gervasio Vicario Cabrera, colegio nº1 del Distrito Escolar Primero, he'd excelled in that subject while, at the same time, in perfect synchronization, all possibility of understanding and appreciating the world of mathematics and exact sciences—when it suddenly incorporated commas and letters between the numbers—was snuffed out inside him, as if it were a mysterious and faraway civilization.) **And now he, in situ, went through their names and properties and plumages, so many years having passed for him, a mortal, and barely a few thousandths of a second for those eternal deities. And, in front of the bathroom mirror** (that cruel and early and late mirror; the first one you see and the last one you see every day, reflecting the un-anesthetized truth with a combination of vanity and humiliation like that felt by ballet dancers and martial artists as they practice with mastery that thing of theirs which, they know, will never be entirely theirs), **he greeted himself the way the ancient Maya greeted each other. He looked at that face and accepted it as it was, acknowledging it with sounds that reminded him of the guttural invocations of the priests of Cthulhu. One said "In lak, ech" ("I am another you") and the other answered: "Hala ken" ("You are another me"). And no: it wasn't autofiction or fiction of the I. It was something else. It was something truly true. And neither the you nor the I in him could close their eyes. There they were and there he was. Unable to sleep. Outside the window it was December and it was Atemoztli—the month of waterfalls of the sky according the Culhua Mexica solar calendar—and a golden independentist angel unfurled its wings atop a column in the middle of the Paseo de la Reforma promenade.** (And him—another space-time leap—deforming himself and feeling like the insomniac H.P. Lovecraft's oneiric traveler Randolph Carter. Going down the Stairway of Deep Sleep, sliver key in hand and headed for the providential Kadath, in the readings of his hallucinatory and hallucinated childhood and those unforgettable nights—with that one especially unforgettable night—that he would give anything to forget. Yes: he longed for absolute oblivion for that horror story; because it seemed to be made not of words but of *horror*:

Horror with telephone—telephonic horror that already presaged that telephonically horrifying scene from David Lynch's *Lost Highway*—with Randolph Carter getting a phone call from the depths of a tomb. A call that concluded with "YOU FOOL, WARREN IS DEAD!" A call that he couldn't help make resonate with other dead people and other telephones and with another *fool* that was him and another *almost-dead* man that was also him. Yes: Lovecraft and all those tormented souls of his who went mad from reading, from opening impossible-to-close books. And Poe and Stoker and Matheson and King & Co. From when he was a boy until he was a young man, he got addicted to the greats of the horror genre, perhaps seeking to have them instill more fear in him with their fictions than he'd already felt and still felt in his non-fiction. Of course, it didn't work. But he continued and continues reading them and maybe, who knows, one of these days . . .) And he was still there: writing and fearing and betting that any one of those nights a great fright would provoke in him the shock of a cowardly but functional and welcome amnesia. And then acquiring the power to forget something—to forget *that*—to be able to remember it in another way and in another genre and as if from outside. In third person. Not as it happened but as it should've happened. Amnesia as the problem that solves all problems. Saying "I don't remember" was like saying "Better not to think of such things," "Let's change the subject," "Look to the future," and all of that. And, if none of that worked, then find a way to assign it to and write it for someone else.

But not yet.

There was still time, though less and less.

And so back then he flew not to—as he was doing now—visit it, but to reread it, to rewrite it, changing its last name.

That family.

Back then, at least, he could still write.

Abracadabra. Mount Karma. ("That most distant of places, that place you come to just before reaching the point where you begin the return trip, but without ever turning back, always advancing," Penelope had answered to his what-and-where-in-the-world-was-all-of-that.) So he chose to stop asking and to sit with all of that (with Penelope's notebooks and videos and their conversations, which were like those of a Kurtz who'd made it back from Vietnam) and limit himself to traveling in his mind.

He imagined them—the family and the house and the city—and he put them in writing (consulting atlases both real and imaginary; at the behest of an editor; for a collection of books on megalopolises; and he'd been assigned Mexico City, D.F.), but somewhere else. And so it was that, more than landing, he'd crashed in Mexico City. And from there he was cast adrift. Clutching a (another) strange book that functioned (applying the verb "function" to books, as if they were machines, had always produced in him a combination of disgust and fascination) far better than he could've hoped.

And Penelope—like Cathy and like Heathcliff in her beloved *Wuthering Heights*—had never forgiven him and had promised to have her revenge; but also, from that wrath, thanks to him, Penelope the writer had been born.

Enter-Exit Ghost. His private ghost. The ghost of Penelope.

Here she comes.

Penelope first as the frontwoman of the tuneless and paracultural The Showers (their thing was to sing good songs badly, but with the joy of someone singing in the best shower ever, with those psychedelic bathroom acoustics) in the underground nights of the capital of his now nonexistent country of origin. And then Penelope captaining that oh so *novelty* female version of The Rolling Stones: switching the gender and intent of all the Englishmen's songs—examples: "(I CAN Get) Satisfaction" and "Under My Heel" and "You CAN Always Get What You Want" and "Paint It Pink"—and calling themselves The Drowning Stones, in honor of the stones in Virginia Woolf's pockets, pulling her under the River Ouse.

Later—taking cover in her beauty and in being the daughter of their legendary mother and, last but not least, thanks to a brief engagement with a producer at HBO—Penelope in an infanto-feminist mashup of Johanna Spyri and George Lucas titled *Jeidi Knight*. And a starring role in the pilot episode of *Lauren Canyon*: a never-filmed TV series, recounting the adventures of a female detective in 1970s Los Angeles who dreamed of becoming a confessional and intimist songwriter *à la* Joni Mitchell and her derivatives

(Warren Zevon was supposed to be the creative consultant, but died before he could, without that preventing him from throwing himself at Penelope multiple times first. And he'd always respected Zevon: he was one of the few truly well-read rockers, capable of paraphrasing Arthur Schopenhauer with a "We love to buy books because we believe we're buying the time to read them").

Then, Penelope as a "high-profile" and amateur (a term that'd acquired negative connotations when at one time it'd been the most positive thing you could be: writing for *amour*, for love of art) novelist with her "blog-novel hyper-text alternative-historical lit-comparative" *Jesus Christ & Heathcliff: The Missing Years*. There, Penelope "researching" the absences of both subjects, before they returned to blow everything up and send it all flying through the air (and including photographs of the devout elderly during their Holy Week processions/recreations stopping along Christ's Road to the Calvary to take a selfie with the poor man who was already waiting in vain for a Good Samaritan ready to help him, as well as different varieties of cinematographic and televisual portraits of the demonic hero of *Wuthering Heights* championing Clive Owen in his day).

And throughout all these incarnations, of course, Penelope had never ceased to be Penelope. That was the key, his sister had explained. Changing without ceasing to be, but ceasing to be all the time. Like The Beatles, who never stopped changing and were so different—hence their multigenerational success—that they appeared to accompany all of humanity throughout the four stations of life, he thought. Thus, he theorized, Ringo was childhood, John was adolescence, Paul was mature family life, and George—who for obvious reasons seemed more and more to be the most interesting of the four—was that sweet bitterness and delicious resentment only attained in old age. Harrison—paradoxically the youngest of the four—had always been, from the beginning, the oldest.

But really Penelope had "learned" that thing about constant change as a means to becoming more and more yourself from reading a David Bowie biography, where it explained that the multimedia musician came from a family rife with the psychotic-schizophrenic gene. Grandmother and mother and aunts and, most especially, his mother-in-law Terry. Bowie was certain he carried that form of madness in the blood that circulated through his brain. And for that reason—out of fear—he'd decided to "professionalize" the symptoms across successive incarnations and multiple aliases: to keep that gene there, free and at the same time imprisoned. Getting out in front of the illness by taking advantage of it and mutating it into something good and on his own terms and in line with the times. Multiple personality as singular artistic credo and successive albums as sonic electroshock. Bowie never stopped reading and toured with a good part of his library and before that, when he was young, he went everywhere wearing one of those mod parkas with deep pockets and a book poking out just far enough so you could read the title and author and feel so interesting. In that way—reading, searching books for different personas that could work for him as new personalities—Bowie had found a way to be forever Bowie through serial metamorphosis, yes, but accepting himself as someone whose true pleasure and genius ran more through the act of *unmaking*: ceasing to be the person he'd been to make room for the other person he would become.

And Penelope felt *like that*.

And so Penelope finally became a universal phenomenon, worshipped by cold eyed and burning-hearted gothic fans for whom her life of invisible recluse made her omnipresent in all places at the same time without actually being anywhere. As had happened with Bowie in the last years of his career: not being there was the definitive yet impossible-to-define personality. Penelope's great achievement from the point of view of publishing marketing, he thought, had been not that of bringing a new life into this world but a new death. Her own. And not only her real and singular death but all those many other possible deaths that, though imaginary, weren't any less true. If living once is to die a thousand times, then Penelope had died once to live millions of times inside her readers.

So—from what he felt and saw—the truth was that Penelope didn't have much to complain about or to reproach him for.

But, yes, he had stolen her story.

He'd stolen it the way so many writers before him had appropriated others' lives to make them their own.

He'd written that novel on commission based on the lived experience of his sister, who, at the time, hadn't known how to see what was interesting about the hideousness of living with the Karmas and believed that literature began and ended in *Wuthering Heights* ("A book written in a state of dis/ grace," according to Penelope) and, at most, in the sisters and brother and father that Emily Brontë surrounded herself with.

He would've liked to enjoy that naïve yet solid reductionist and synthetic capacity his sister had. And the ability to convince herself that everything entered into and emerged from a single book where everything came together and everyone fit. He could've saved himself so much time and so many lists and so many quotes and so many references . . .

But, to tell the truth, Penelope hadn't been the only one to think that way. Many had been the priests and worshippers of Cathy and Heathcliff. And— again—even his once-worshipped H.P. Lovecraft (an author Penelope had always disregarded "for showing and describing everything and for constantly evoking the two things I hate eating most: shellfish and Jell-O" and because "Cosmic horror? You know what the truest cosmic horror is, Bad Little Brother? Waking up on the last day of your life not knowing that it's going to be the first day of your death and that then and almost immediately everyone but you will be aware of what happened . . . Do you remember that last picture taken of our parents just before they embarked on their ultimate lunacy? The one taken by that paparazzo who followed them everywhere. And what always strikes and intrigues me about that picture is the absolute calm on their faces. Something happier than happiness in their eyes and smiles. I never saw them happier to be who they were and to be together. Could what their expressions reveal be the relief of sensing that soon they would no longer have to go on or the ignorance of not knowing the novel of their lives was coming to an end, but feeling that you always had to show your best side just in case, *por si las moscas*, in case there be flies, in case there be scorpions, in case there be monsters?") had made reference to Emily Brontë's book, which was also Penelope's book. Lovecraft—in an essay as tentacular and amorphous and slippery as his gods—had postulated that *Wuthering Heights* was "quite alone as a novel" and a "symbol of a literary transition" and "marks the growth of a new and sounder school."

And he read those words standing in an airport bookstore (Lovecraft was, yes, the kind of writer who'd been really important to him a long time ago and who he only ran into now in public places, like a close acquaintance from the past you're not entirely sure you want to see again and yet . . .), looking for anything to distract him from a new and fruitless attempt to scale the increasingly precipitous and, for him, impassible heights of Demonia, in Antiterra, with Ada. That Lovecraft essay was a kind of appendix to the exploratory and sinister *At the Mountains of Madness*, a title that would work well for a biography of the two of them, of him and Penelope, he thought. (And he remembered all of that and, in truth, it was nothing more and nothing less than another way to remember Penelope, to not be able to stop remembering Penelope. Because Penelope—who wasn't resting in peace because she wouldn't let him rest in peace—was everywhere. On bookstore shelves and in movie theaters and on TV screens. And he's found himself obliged to live for her because he lives off her. Penelope maintains him. Penelope who, on facedown nights, appeared to him, like that man on the cover of *Wish You Were Here*: spectral and wreathed in the fire that had engulfed her, reaching out her hand. Her half psychotic and half cyberpunk rant spit out between grinding teeth, biting off her words, like the petals of an immemorial chrome-plated flower with too many thorns, to—"She's coming down fast! . . . Yes, she is! . . . Coming down fast!"—tell him things, so many things. But—"tell me tell me tell me"—never offering him *the* answer. Things like: "I'll tell you the only way you're anything like your beloved Nabokov. The same Nabokov who—after outing him to his father—repeatedly ignored and wrote off his gay brother who died in a Nazi concentration camp; who disparaged many of his contemporaries with pretty asinine claims; who let those unforgivable pictures of him wearing boxing gloves be taken, which didn't stop him from heaping scorn on the boxing-buffoon Hemingway; who was probably a barely repressed pedophile; and who abducted and enslaved his son and his wife, a wife he cheated on with a poet he, probably, had another child, a child he never even acknowledged or got to know. Do you know how you're like him? In that, like Nabokov, you're an insufferable person and think you're better than everyone else. Just that Nabokov, with his work—which is just the color mauve, his favorite, washing over a wondrous and privileged brain with nothing much to say or tell beyond a few exceedingly private jokes—managed to convince a few people that it was all true and that maybe he'd even recreated a world in his own image and semblance. Whereas you, well . . . *Pobrecito*, now you're nothing but my perpetual plus one . . . People see you and automatically think about reading me . . . I'm going to tell you something. Do you know why you could never read *Ada, or Ardor*? For the same reason that I can't stop reading or reciting *Wuthering Heights* over and over in my mind. The doctors and psychiatrists say it's "toxic" for me and have prohibited it; but I don't need to see it to read it anymore. Just like Cathy says to Heathcliff, when he snatches away her books, I tell them in her voice and words that *Wuthering Heights* is written in my mind and imprinted on my heart and they'll never be able to take that away from me . . . Because I live in and through that book . . . I live in *Wuthering Heights* . . . I move through the rooms of that biblical tragedy that also has two parts, two testaments, and above everything and everyone a fiery god ready to do anything to make his will be done in the heights as it is in the storm . . . Oh, but let's get back to your thing: you can't read *Ada*—I read it and I did so just to get under your skin—because happy families and incestuous passions between brothers and sisters are *not* our thing. Our thing is self-destructive families, my loathsome Bad Little Brother. Together, you and I can only make hate, never love . . . And we're so sad . . . All things familial have their merit and there's nothing more familial than sadness. And yet ours wasn't a very familial family, was it? . . . We just want all families to be as sad as ours. Not *sadder*, because that would be asking too much . . . And yet . . . A family in which first the parents abandoned their little children in a forest and later it was the little children who returned from that forest and . . . My son . . . The forest . . . The sea . . . And I don't remember the night our parents went missing or that other night my son went missing . . . But telling you I don't remember means I do remember them, yes? or no? . . . And this is how I am now . . . And this is how we are. We're all that's left. Lonely. Alone. You with your little tin traveler and me with my little wooden soldiers. Playing games nobody else can play because the rules are too twisted . . . Convinced that, contrary to what people think, the future is immovable, and the past does nothing but change and can be altered in any other realm of reality except for in the one we want most to enter or to escape from and never return to. We're like Cathy and Heathcliff—I won't make use of another simile here that would include Ada and Van, to keep from torturing you further with everything you don't know—in that chapter in the novel, spying at the window of the Linton mansion and witnessing a perfect-family scene, the kind of scene we never had in our family. There, Cathy and Heathcliff watch the same thing but see it in different ways: she sees what she wants, and he sees what he hates. The same thing happens to us with our perception of what was and what's yet to come. But we no longer have a future and who wrote that thing about how "The future is already here—it's just not evenly distributed"? . . . If that's true, Bad Little Brother, it looks like we came out losers in the distribution; because it's easy to think that we have too much past and that, for that reason, we already have enough . . . Whereas others . . . Do you remember the last time you read or heard the phrase "the twenty-second century"? It's not used, it serves no purpose, it doesn't work. The twenty-second century is the same as the twenty-first century: part of the present. We don't have a future in the same sense that our grandparents had one. We no longer have that unattainable and solid and distant and futuristic "Tomorrow" that they enjoyed and longed for and that we even briefly touched with our fingertips during our childhood. What we have now is, merely, tomorrow, tiny tomorrow: little and in lower case. Soon there won't be any frontiers or the feeling that you're approaching or have gone *elsewhere* . . . It's already happened, if you think about it, with nations and products: more the same one to the next, consuming the same things. Next will come a homogenous similitude between all times until they melt together into a uniform time. *All together now* . . . And so, the future is right there and no further and so close. Trembling. Looking over its shoulder and trying in vain not to let the fraught and flying present catch it and bite its skinny fragile-ballerina ankles. While the past, more or less the same thing: it's harder and harder to fix or capture in pictures or, harder still, in an encyclopedia entry, because encyclopedias are almost nonexistent now. Their entries approaching the exit. Encyclopedias take up too much space and nobody is interested in owning an *I Know Everything* because they know that anything they could want to know is already out there, invisible, zipping around on fiber optic cables, online. The past too. Now the past is composed not of encyclopedia *entries* but of encyclopedia *portals* that change all the time and are posted with pins and hung up on cables and electrical currents that could be cut off at any moment. And so, sooner rather than later, the past will be turned off so a universal amnesia can be turned on, where nobody will remember anything as it actually happened. And, oh, call me paranoid; but you must know that paranoia, if you domesticate and train it, is the most useful of virtues. And that it will always play in your favor renamed as *intuition* . . . And now I *intuit* everything . . . Including the arrival of that moment when we'll look back at the past like a movie whose ending we won't know but whose beginning we won't either. And there we'll be. Facing the room of our own past, but without the key to open the door . . . For that reason, in the meantime, we rewrite it in our memory or we deny it. A kind of training or rehearsal for The Great Forgetting. But, oh, terrible and sadomasochistic paradox: we have to think about what we don't want to think about in order to tell ourselves that we never want to think about it again. And I remember and don't want to remember that I played at that with . . . with . . . And I don't want to think about that. I don't want to remember that. And that other thing either. And I don't want to remember him. But I can't. I can't forget or stop thinking . . . And if someday that supposed singularity between man and machine occurs, sign me up, as long as it includes a *Delete* button. But I don't think that will or can be achieved . . . What will always separate the human being from artificial intelligence won't be the ability to remember everything but the inability to ever completely forget . . . But I digress . . . Thus, because I remember it perfectly, I almost can't remember what we did to our parents anymore . . . I don't need to remember it because what we did was unforgettable . . . Ah, yes, The Great Secret we shared but experienced separately and that I have only now, here on the Other Side of things, been able to fully put together. Bad Little Brother: you should know you have to die to be able to experience certain things. Now I know what happened. All of it. Now I know that back then I was not alone. . . The Great Secret that you knew all along and that I only knew in part, damn it, how well you kept it. The Great Secret that we didn't keep but that kept us: The Great Secret as our one true Mother and Father Land.")

And, oh, he found Penelope's monologues so articulate, but they left him exhausted. It wasn't like she was just speaking them, but like she'd memorized them and enhanced them with information she'd only gained access to after death (that "what we did to them" after spending years of her life thinking "what I did to them"); and like she'd written them down first and, after reading them over and over, she were reciting them with that shimmering sadness only aspired to and exuded by the sanest madwomen.

The kind of sadness that'll never become happy so that it can become sad again.

The kind of sadness that was only more sad or less sad but never happy.

The kind of sadness that, if you were to sing "Happy Birthday" to it, would only hear the word "Birthday" preceded by some dark, white noise, blacking out the first word because, of course, there was nothing happy about another birthday, another year gone, no matter how generously everyone not born on that day attempted to convince you to the contrary. Because—if everything went just right, right off the bat, if you were lucky and had all the fingers on your hands and the toes on your feet to later be able to count the years—you were born crying and came into the world head down, after floating in and breathing liquid for nine months. And the rest of your life was nothing but blowing out candles. So, truly, was there anybody out there happy to be out there?

And so, Penelope (the same Penelope who, when she was a girl, got indignant with her classmates who "confused *brand* with *product*: one of life's basic errors that would subsequently lead them to confuse love with being in love" and who also said "*chicle*" instead of "Chiclets" or "chewing gum") speaking to him from beyond the grave, speaking to him in a long and drawn-out way, like wind through the crags. Penelope not asking him to let her in but—unlike the ghost of Cathy in *Wuthering Heights*—bursting into his room, kicking open the window and proceeding to jump up and down on his insomniac bed.

(A bed that he'd imagined as a device of steampunk aesthetic that moved around on rails. And that included bookshelves and gigantic Persian pillows known as patifolia atop which odalisques and eunuchs had once reclined. And a sound system that played "Spent the Day in Bed" on repeat with Morrissey's voice saying that thing about how "I'm not my type, but / I love my bed . . . I spent the day in bed / It's a consolation when all my dreams / are perfectly legal / In sheets for which I paid." Or allowing him to hear the voice of Nabokov reciting that poem of his where he marvels at the mobility of his bed with a "On certain nights as soon as I lay down my bed starts drifting into Russia." That Russia to which he never returned except in his imagination, on poetic nights of gesticulating trees when the rain on the roof sounded like the unwinding of a windup tin toy traveling backward into the past because that's where the sun was waiting.)

Yes, he'd fantasized about staying in his bed and never leaving and taking shelter in the embrace of his pillow and his blankets thinking that there, at last, he would be safe. To be like a dying Louis XIV but without the adulators fluttering like moths and fireflies all around him. "And so to bed," Samuel Pepys and all of that. But soon he'd read one of those always suspicious and oh so creative studies for which, mysteriously, there was never a lack of funding (unlike what tended to happen with the search for cures to popular and terminal illnesses) and that claimed that staying in bed was more harmful than smoking, that it caused a 25% acceleration in the deterioration and dysfunctionality of the body. And that staying there too long submitted the organism to the same destabilizing stressors experienced by astronauts in zero gravity (above all if, as in his case, the bed was a solitary one) in addition to cooking the body not at a slow burn but at a low heat in an ecosystem of various rabid bacteria and germs that, in his case, appeared to have mostly affected his nervous system and neuronal activity.

In bed—before being driven out by a mob like the ones that come bearing torches and looking for the monster at the end of the movie—he'd passed the time imagining absurd products and demented brands that, at the same time,

were quite logical and even possible. (Flashbacks of his sparkling and brief life in advertising, like those of a marine sunk neck-deep *in the shit*, after returning from several tours in Vietnam. Possible products that he wrote down in one of his biji notebooks specially devoted to such pollutions. To wit: † A brand of Dante sleeping caps, like the ones that always appeared with him in busts and portraits; Dante who'd divinely rhymed that bit about "La terra lagrimosa diede vento, / che balenò una luce vermiglia / la qual mi vines ciascun sentiment; / e caddi come l'uom cui sonno piglia." † A hyperactive and sleepwalking stuffed lemur with always-open eyes and hypersensitive pupils and in *2001: A Space Odyssey*, the daughter of Heywood Floyd—the actress was one of Stanley Kubrick's own daughters; could his daughter actually have been that sick during the development of that project?—asks her father to bring her back a live lemur from his travels as a gift just after they got their wires crossed and, another great anticipatory feature in that film, she also asked for the gift of a telephone, as kids at the beginning of the twenty-first century tend to do, in days when their parents still demonized Coca Cola but found it perfectly acceptable to immobilize their children with mobile phones; children who when having their little friends over no longer ask them "Want to see my room?" but "Want to see my tablet?" A stuffed lemur that would serve as a pet/companion for all those exhausting and finally exhausted sleepless children. Selling the patent for that stuffed lemur to Perky Pat, Inc. so they could insert a spy chip in it. An integrated circuit that would absorb the wants of the infants and the terrors of the parents and vice versa and subsequently transmit them to a central headquarters to be centrifuged and distilled into consumer profiles. Consumers for whom the deep-sleeping teddy bear no longer has any use except as an object of hate and envy, tearing out its colorful glass eyes beneath eyelids furrier than eyebrows, eyelids that close all on their own when you lay the bear down and open when you sit it up; the opposite of what happens to him: insomniac in bed, asleep at the desk. † Writing a book for children to read to their parents—and not the other way around and illogically as has been the case up until now—and fall asleep while reading it; because nothing wakes a child up more than having someone read to them to make them fall asleep. † Designing—with the help of a programmer—a videogame in which G. K. Chesterton's dragon faces off against Augusto Monterroso's dinosaur. † A screenplay for a parody/homage/critique of Spider-Man, set in Bangladesh and with a young hero who's unable to fight villains, because he's too busy spinning cloth in one of those enslaving sweatshops that produce clothes for the big brands of the First World. † A measuring device that calculates the royalties paid to the author of a book not on the basis of the number of copies sold but on the book's positive impact on the psyches and lives of readers. † The Proustophone: a telephonic device and a number to call to connect you with your own memory when you wanted to remember some forgotten thing or to recall something with absolute precision and intensity. In the same way that Proust, in his day, used the théâtrophone to listen to operas and plays without leaving home—a kind of aural and personal YouTube—the Proustophone would help you to regain lost time. And also bring to your lips—as Proust describes in his novel—that kind of smile you smile when you know the person listening can't see you smile. And to hear the voices of the living as if they were the voices of the dead and, as in the case of that call the narrator receives from his grandmother, the voice of someone on death's doorway coming through that "supernatural instrument before whose miracles we used to stand amazed." † The silliness of something that could well be called TwEAT: a food that would be uploaded to the Instagram account of the person eating it in real time with every bite taken and, oh, he'd come up with that ridiculous idea when he found out that the noble Henry James, late in his life—long after supposedly regurgitating that line always attributed to him, the one that goes "Tell a dream, lose a reader"; but that neither he nor anybody else seemed able to locate anywhere in his work; and wouldn't it be great if that line were a collective dream, something dreamed by all his readers but lost?—had become a follower of the doctrines of the then famous Horace "The Great Masticator" Fletcher, who recommended that you chew each bite thirty-two times before swallowing it, an exercise that, perhaps, had influenced the

composition and dictation of those long sentences of his late style. †
The algorithm for an app called What?app that gave you the opportunity to feel like the heroines of golden age Hollywood in that black and
white that looks nothing like and has nothing to do with the black
and white of real life. Majestic leading ladies on enormous screens in
colossal movie theaters back in days when nobody in the seats reflexively brought their hands to their own phones whenever a mobile
phone rang in the movies, movies where the mobile phone oftentimes
had more lines than a lot of the actors. Bringing, instead, their hands
to their foreheads, arching their backs, fluttering their eyelids, and
sighing a "Oh, I wish I could forget all of it." And doing so. Amnesia,
voluntary or otherwise, that the plotlines of so many romantic dramas or tense thrillers or romantic and tense Mexican telenovelas fed
off. Ingenious novelty that would soon be forgotten, but, at least this
once, selling exactly that: the ephemerality of the memorable. An anti-
memory-aid. An app where you could write down everything you
wanted to forget. A technological paradox. A Wikipedia in reverse.
Writing down everything you didn't want to remember and, in the act
of remembering it, forgetting it forever, following that dictum of Edgar
Allan Poe about how "If you wish to forget anything on the spot, make
a note that this thing is to be remembered." The "appeal" of the app
would be that, every so often, it would purposefully and functionally
block and "lose" all your stored data. And, in that way, you could
blamelessly forget, dumping all the blame on the invention. Quickly
and cleanly. And, oh, he would be his own most loyal customer, never
forgetting how to use and operate that tool for instantly forgetting
without a bad conscience. The success of the application, he told himself, would be guaranteed because it would strip away all the appeal of
something that'd been perfectly natural and unplugged for millennia,
turning it into something programmed and electric, delivering to its
devout and imprisoned users another dose of that same forgetfulness
that led to the cemetery where phone numbers and addresses and
birthdays and titles of movies and books and paintings they once
knew by heart—not because they were within finger's reach but
because they were within reach of their brains—had gone to rest.

Everything that at some point you reread and rewrote and rewatched and reorganized and reexamined and repainted until that external thing became part of you, something that you climbed up and down from with a healthy fear of falling whenever you wanted to. And, yes, that whole thing about uniform memory-making had always struck him as a kind of dictatorial dystopia, whereas the making of oblivion seemed more democratic and even utopic.) But, oh, again: he came up with all these inventions, but his inventiveness was never sufficient to sketch out a plan for *something* that—at three in the morning or at one hundred-twenty in the week—would function as a switch to switch off Penelope. Something that would deactivate and unplug her memory, speaking to him with the tone of an ancient translation.

Penelope whom, though he no longer wrote (he who was first a next-writer and then a writer and now an exwriter), he couldn't stop thinking about, now more as a persona—as one of his characters—than as a person.

Penelope who lingered on but was no longer there. Or she was there, but dead, after burning in a fire at a deluxe monastery for lunatics set by a lunatic loonier than the patients. A crazy nun and Penelope's sister-in-law, the sister of her short-lived husband who got stuck at the comma of a coma and whom Penelope brought to his final full-stop.

But Penelope (her mortal life had ended so her long and immortal death could begin) was survived by his memory of Penelope. And, more than anything and almost anyone, Penelope was immortalized by all books she'd written that were still there, everywhere. Modern books based on the nine-teenth-century dynamic of a trio of future novelist sisters, outside of time but deep inside of that ancient space of mists and moors. And Penelope (a young writer, yes, but *different*; one of the few and truly singular young female writers who die too soon so that, suddenly eternal, it's never too late for them) had felt like one of them: a specimen of an extinct species and, at the same time, an evolved organism anticipating what was to come. Like Neanderthals confronting Cro-Magnons. Or was it the other way around? Or was it actually that they hadn't disappeared but melted together into something new?

The best of both worlds in any case.

Thus, Penelope was classic and modern. A museum piece and lab experiment. "I'm the most futuristic of brontësauruses," Penelope had joked, knowing that she wasn't the species headed for extinction, that was him, her brother: a maximalist and even retro-avant-garde writer who was increasingly difficult to read for newcomers or those who, at this point, would never come. Penelope, on the other hand, took the world by storm. Penelope was impervious to the rapid mutation of trends. Penelope sold even more than the adventures of the chronocyclist Jim Yang by Peter Hook(ed). And she never even had to kidnap a child and, besides, she was a woman.

And so, it was likely (it wasn't likely, he'd already checked, or was that on another flight?) that in that very moment multiple passengers on that plane, under the beams of their overhead lights that illuminated far more than they appeared to, were reading the luminous living voice of the dead Penelope.

And on the back covers of her books that picture that would forever adorn posters and postcards and T-shirts: Penelope wearing a T-shirt she designed herself. There, over breasts with pointy, almost accusatory, nipples, the broad face of Heathcliff from the prints of Fritz Eichenberg and Clare Leighton, a pin stuck in the cheek of the vengeful lover above the legend "Gothic but Punk!"

Penelope who, with her words, accompanied her young readers in escaping the fear being afloat thousands of meters above the ground. All of them moving their lips as they read her, as if they were praying and feeling, yes, that "it's like her books transport me to another world." Thus, her fans, the *penelopíadas* (as one literary critic had dubbed them), being swept away on one of the adventures of the photophobic terrorist and frozen Amazon and moth lady of their dreams, Stella D'Or. That defendress of darkness *à la* Thunberg (but better written and prettier and more inspired in the voltage of her beliefs), obsessed with light pollution and firing off invocations like: "First came the torches and then the lighters and now your mobile phones— those instruments of torture and self-torture for people to whom everything seems interesting but who aren't interested in anything—to illuminate the sacrifice of the martyrs in the *circus maximus*. All of them condemned for having wanted to regain the darkness of the gray night and the voice of the stars. The true voice of the stars, of the stars that, though dead, illuminate far more than all those blogs now abandoned yet still out there. The stars in the sky muted by Earth's silencing lights. The light of dead stars is the most luminous of all. The light of something that's no longer there and yet keeps on shining. The light of dead stars that, like the past, already passed away, but that still glitters in our memories. And everything passing is not the same as passing everything by." (And, okay, sure: he'd added that bit about mobile phones and blogs when he reread it and parodied it and abducted it and took it for himself, for his writing, which wasn't really for anyone anymore.)

Or hunkering down in the lunar spaces of the lunatic and electromagnetic Tulpa sisters, their tunics tied with hallucinatory Van Allen belts.

Or accompanying the little extraterrestrial dAlien, who only wants to go home, and who knows perfectly well that "The majority of shooting stars—know this, earthlings—are just astronaut shit, burning up as it comes into contact with the atmosphere; and so, you already know what I'm going to say: you're wishing your most fragrant and personal wishes upon the fecal matter of very public personas." (And it's funny that the keening and gyrating Kate Bush—someone Penelope hated/admired so much for her song "Wuthering Heights" and for having reclaimed Emily Brontë as a totem before she had and for physically resembling her idea of Cathy so much, and, if all of that wasn't enough, for having been discovered by Pink Floyd's David Gilmour—ended up recording an entire album, *The Tulpa Transmissions*, inspired by his sister's cosmic characters. And he always remembers how, for a while, there was an urban legend that Penelope—between one asylum and another, like Nicole Diver in *Tender Is the Night* and before bursting into flame in that final monastery—had booked, for herself, one of those jets that fly up to the edge of the atmosphere. To thereby—according to one magazine and one of those reporters who enjoyed, as he did, maniacally firing references off into the air with psycho-encyclopedic compulsion—"gain access to definitive solitude, to the exorbitant orbiting isolation of Bowie's Major Tom and Elton John's rocket man and Harry Nilsson's spaceman, of the space psychologist Kris Kelvin in Stanislaw Lem's *Solaris*, of Kubrick & Clarke's David Bowman in *2001: A Space Odyssey*, or of the literary DJ Walt Dangerfield in Philip K. Dick's *Dr. Bloodmoney*." At the time, he'd asked Penelope if it was true, the thing about her "trip to the stars beyond the clouds where the blue of the sky at the outer rim turns to ultramarine," and Penelope said: "Don't be an idiot, Bad Little Brother. I don't need that. I feel completely and totally and perfectly and absolutely alone everywhere I go: in a bathroom or in a stadium full of people or at one of the numerous events with innumerable readers for my first book.")

And, sure: he'd read a few of Penelope's books when they came out—not all of them—first out of curiosity and then to try to understand what the key to her appeal and her success was and, he only admitted this to himself, to see if he could figure out how to reproduce something like that.

But no.

Nothing.

Here.

Nothing.

There.

And, before long, nothing even where everything he'd ever written once had been.

His books had been very different. From those of Penelope and so many others. Not really working for and not all that attractive to the "great reading masses," but—unlike what happened with the books of William Gaddis or William H. Gass or Robert Coover or John Barth or David Foster Wallace or so many others—they weren't of any special interest to the always-protesting academic chapels of his own language, because they didn't "fit" into any of the preexisting theories, because they were uncomfortable and troubling. (He'd read all of them, all of those also "excessive" North Americans, like he was visiting a succession of specialists, as if seeking an "explanation" for what was happening to him. He wasn't looking for a cure, because he had no interest in being cured; rather, he was looking for something that would help him live and write and even be better read in the light of the suspicion that he, like He Whose Name Must Not Be Mentioned, had also been a *changeling*: someone who'd been swapped out for someone else and so, now, in the United States, a writer who'd been born in his nonexistent country of origin and adopted, was gaining renown writing testimonial novels in Spanglish about the life of an immigrant in Manhattan and was winning all the most important prizes with books with plots so easy to recount whenever anyone asked what they were about.)

His books, on the other hand, more than recounting discounted.

They were books that wanted to feel like all those other novels written back in the good old days (good days only for literature, to be sure; for everything else they were bad days, days when it wasn't even worth asking what day it was) by writers from his now nonexistent country of origin where being from there ran through feeling like being from everywhere and nowhere at the same time. Novels that never renounced the feeling of short stories. Novels that were fragmentary, elastic, atomic, mixed-breed, like beasts in a bestiary, episodic. Novels insistent on being singular and unique and outside all tradition to end up being part of a tradition comprised—justly and paradoxically—of unique and singular novels. Then and there, writers were like freewheeling members of the shattered body of a blood brotherhood, made up of orphan novels with neither ancestors nor descendants. And whose family tree was a horizontal trunk riddled with holes you could go in and out of to count the concentric rings in the wood. A trunk covered with moss and embroidered with the comings and goings of laborious beetles and deadeye scorpions in an always-burning forest in whose center stood a library both fireproof and foolproof but not entirely forgetfulness-proof (the spines of the library books bleached by the sun; especially the ones with red or yellow lettering. Or the books in those pornographic pictures where naked women were made to look like sexy librarians and—already in his adolescence, another unmistakable sign that he was doomed and damned—he was more interested what book titles could be spotted behind all that bare skin. There: pale and faded, and yet, when you took them off the shelf, to remember them, on the front and back covers, those same reds and yellows remained bright, as if the time hadn't passed for them). A family tree with neither branches nor roots. So different from everyone else's trees (including the one from the opening pages of *Ada, or Ardor* that always made him so nervous every time he tried again, in vain, to prune it). Because the truth is that behind a good part of a human being's genealogical curiosity isn't the desire for a better future but the longing for an illustrious past. And that's where that impulse comes from that is the same for all those people who believe in reincarnation provided that they're the ones who get to be the new vessels for Cleopatra or Napoleon. Or for John Lennon: always so functional, first warning that "The dream is over . . ." to soon thereafter again become the most comfortable and easily imaginative, naïve, and utopic dreamers of a better waking world you could only gain access to with the help of sleeping pills. All of them convincing themselves with a desire more demented than mad that they were come from some mythic place deserving of those dynastic diagrams.

Whereas he didn't want any of that.

He wanted neither ancestors nor descendants.

He wanted to begin and end in himself.

He didn't want to create a school and didn't need an alma mater to be proud of.

He dreamed that his inventions (his serious inventions and not the inventions he wrote down in that biji notebook) were, yes, "one-of-a-kind" books.

Books that made you ask are we there yet? And the answer was that there was no "there" to get to; and what it was really about was focusing on escaping, on finding the exit. From that place where, supposedly, books described reality and only reality, to leave it behind—further still—forever.

His were books that—if they'd been graphic novels with superheroes tormented by the potency of their own power—would feature one Bildungsro-Man: an aspiring warrior who would never see any action, because he would always be reflecting on and recalling his origins and his (de)formative years. A titan always on the verge but never quite ready, because he knew that in his own genesis, his own origin story (always the most interesting part in the life of any superhero; always far more thrilling than the successive and interminable duels with archenemies and psychoromances), he'd already faced everything worth fighting against and overcoming. And so, Bildungsro-Man would never go anywhere, always preferring to stay in his fortress of solitude thinking about going in search of lost time.

His were—he liked to think—books that became conscious first of the act of writing and then the challenge of reading, as if they were dangerous stunts to pull off high in the sky with no net down below.

They were books that, when he finished writing them, he felt a relief like that of having a tumor removed (and he'd always been unsettled by the fact that a tumor could be "benign"; a tumor was a tumor, period; something to be removed, excised from the body of the text and the text of the body, right now, without delay). He felt that very brief happiness that made him realize, within a few days, that what'd been removed wasn't a tumor but an organ: one of those important and vital organs that don't come in twos. And that now inside him was a hole and it was home to a void. If you'd never done anything like that, you couldn't even imagine how it felt to know what you wanted to do, to figure out how to do it, and then to do it. That limbo where, then, after such certainty and assurance, there was nothing left to do but—like someone waiting for rain in a drought or a letter in solitude—to figure out what you wanted to do again, to do whatever it was and whatever it had to be. Then, in that intense white zone, he only begged to once again fall ill with the emergency of a next book. He prayed to have another tumor grow inside him and branch out far and wide in his body, like a dark shadow, like the calligraphy of ink spilled in a glass of water. An inverse and negative and benign version of that other tumor he'd invented for his **Karmatic Mexican book** ("A big tumor on the median line that's destroying the pituitary gland and the optic chiasm and adjacent zones and extends on both sides toward the frontal lobes. In the back, it's starting to come into contact with the temporal lobes, and toward the bottom the diencephalon or forebrain . . . We don't really know what it is. It's unprecedented. We only know that it's growing at an alarming rate and that the consequences of its activity seem to be, based on the tests we've been running, not a progressive destruction of neurons but a mutation of them. They're different cells. It's as if the tumor were eating them like a parasite and, once they were digested, turning them into something . . . new. New neurons. Hypnotized neurons. This has been causing a progressive disappearance of your memory as you've previously understood it and its replacement with another kind of memory. A form of memory that I'd dare define as Absolute Minimum Memory. Your brain has been discarding data accumulated over the years faster and faster until little by little it starts emptying out and . . . We can't say for sure, but comparing our observations of the latest X-rays and your behavioral patterns leads us believe that, in the end, you will concentrate on a single memory, using the total capacity of your memory for the one-size-fits-all of an entire life. The tumor has already ravaged your memory systems in the temporal lobe. Which, we expect, will cause a progressive inability to record and recall new experiences. Everything indicates that, for some impossible-to-pinpoint reason, your brain has opted to rescue a single memory from the shipwreck of your past. The same memory over and over again. A small fragment of time elevated to the level of eternity. Something like meditation in certain Eastern religions, but in a permanent and irrevocable state . . . Thus the risks of the magnification of a small event that, growing to unexpected dimensions, modifies reality and tailors it to its needs. A new way to understand what's already happened based on a random and minor accident that changes the way we see the world. Tripping over the uneven flagstone of a hotel patio, for example, and it unleashes a torrent of sensations and memories. I think what's going on with you is a little like that. Something caused one cell to wake up and for that cell to wake up another cell and on like that until . . . For that reason, if you let me, I've taken the liberty of defining your illness for an article that I'm writing for a technical journal as Combray Syndrome," a neurologist explained to the protagonist in the pages of that book that was his but that he'd robbed from Penelope. And, yes, clearly, of course: he—who'd written and invented that tumor whose diagnosis was just a coded confession—hoped, when the time came, to have perfectly clear what, given his case and pathology, his one unforgettable and inerasable and memorious and minor yet absolute memory would be).

And this is what he was like afterward: "healthy" and "cured" but empty, dancing around his apartment like a naked Jeff "The Dude" Lebowski. His dick like the end of a deflated balloon to be inflated. Clapping and reciting in whispers (he'd never been a good reader of poetry, but in this case, he was attracted by a title that felt like it was his, like it was intended for him) "His Toy, His Dream, His Rest," by the dreamer of songs and *fleuve* poet John Berryman: "The conclusion is growing . . . I feel sure, my lord . . ." Or sing-shouting, in call and response mode, asking and answering, that bit that goes "Well who's that writin'? / John the Revelator / Who's that writin'? / John the Revelator / Who's that writin'? / John the Revelator

/ A book of seven seals / Tell me what's John writin'? / Ask the Revelator / What's John writin'? / Ask the Revelator / What's John writin'? / Ask the Revelator / A book of seven seals." And, for obvious reasons, omitting—the way you pass by in front of an open window—that other verse from that same and very well-known anonymous song in a different version where it gave the order to "Seal up your book, John / An' don't write no more / O John / An' don't write no more."

But, of course, one John didn't want to learn anything from his insomnia because, obedient, he'd already written everything he had to write. And the other John offered no response to his prayers from azure beaches of Patmos.

Who's that writing? What's he writing? What had he stopped writing? What conclusion is growing? Who knows what and who it would be.

One thing was certain: it wasn't him. He had nothing left to reveal. And he definitely didn't have seven sealed files to open and then compose the end of all things and witness the final point of the verdict of the Last Judgment.

There had been, yes, seven parts in his last book.

He'd decided to do that based on a desire to discredit and contradict one of those manuals/cookbooks about the seven basic plots in fiction (a manual he'd once seen in the trembling hands of a poor kid, on an airplane; one of those kids who wanted to be a writer, because what he really wanted was to be read) and on the memory of the lyrics of that song, near the end of Pink Floyd's first album (where you heard the instruction: "A movement is accomplished in six stages / And the seventh brings return / The seven is the number of the young light / It forms when darkness is increased by one. / Change returns success / Going and coming without error. / Action brings good fortune. / Sunset, sunrise").

Seven files to be opened—in the most sundown of sunrises—like seven seals to be broken and ridden apocalyptically around.

And all he had to draw on for it was the recollection of his version of that biblical woman, bathed in sunlight with the moon at her feet, walking across the water of a swimming pool. And the memory of the boy who would fight the dragon, riding on a princely wild boar and who was more *lost boy* than *changeling*, vanished somewhere between the forest and the sea and taken to the most hellish of heavens, while he recalled both of them from his purgatory.

And a time came when that comatose blank zone between one shadow and the next and one book and the next—expanding in ellipses that no longer intrigued anyone—ended up devouring everything. Not with the operatic epic of an Armageddon but with the most personal emptiness of a sentence vacated of everything done to date for having committed the sin of taking the Lord's name in vain and offering toxic testimonies and contaminated evidence.

The truth, the whole truth, and nothing but the truth? How could anyone in their right mind demand something like that of a writer? There's no place. Or time. Order in the court and abandon the judgment you lost, auto-fictionalizers.

And for him and in him there was nothing left.

Nothing but that phantom itch where there's no longer a typing hand (but not fooling himself, that was just a spasm across the keyboard) as a kind of last vice of what he once understood as his literary vocation. That vocation that wasn't really a vocation but a constant. Something that all human beings had. A gene that could be activated, or not, at will the way someone turns on a light upon entering a house, more or less aware that it's a light they'll never be able to turn off again and that, as such, they'll have to pay a lot for using all that electricity. The need to tell stories or the folly of telling stories. Something that, really, you didn't choose but that in the end you gave up—in truth, the true calling was that of not being a writer—when you realized it required too much effort. And so, many potentially great writers ended up being formidable joke-tellers or gossips. Whereas others opted to be great readers. The human species was divided, in the end, between those who told stories and those who needed to have stories told to them, as much be able to fall asleep as to stay awake.

And he wondered once if women, after being pregnant, felt the same thing when they gave birth: that emptiness surrounded by viscera that'd moved to make room for something that was no longer there and that now, sure, was outside, but it wasn't what it'd been. It was no longer just part of them, now it was part of everything. Could a baby be for them like a book they'd finished writing so others could begin to read it? And that now the book, on its own, could rewrite itself as it saw fit, just as every reader would understand it in their own way and from their own perspective and could offer opinions about how the newborn resembled X or Y or Z?

And, yes, on more than one night, in the kitchen at a party, amid dirty plates and glasses where the corpses of cigarettes floated, some mother had confessed to him that the ecstatic climax of nine months with that welcome invader inside her had been followed by years of disillusioned disappointment (*that* was the true "postpartum depression") caused by that incomprehensible extraterrestrial, there outside. You were only a *true* mother during pregnancy, she explained. During what was more another dimension than a period of time when a woman's hormones danced the Charleston and anything was justified and always the fault of others, including that thing that was tap dancing inside her. And that even justified such, to him, absurd behavior as proclaiming with an inexplicable pride that she didn't want to know if the baby was a boy or a girl, as if it were a game, a surprise, making the absurd excuse that "all I want is for it to be born healthy," because it was being born into a sick world; when really she should be anxious to know absolutely everything about that boy or girl that would come into the world to kill her a little, and, at the same time, to make her immortal: that supposedly tender disinterest that actually revealed an absolute indifference and that was as stupid as reading a detective novel without wanting to know who the killer was. After that, there had only been awkward situations and . . . But all of that seemed to him an exceedingly banal comparison, a crude simile: the thing about having a kid and writing a book and what was the other one? Ah, yes: planting a tree so you could climb it and never come down or so you could hang from its branches as the crows pecked at your eyes.

And, oh, his books laughed and swelled with that delicate and intoxicatingly putrid scent that almost nobody would dare accuse certain flowers of giving off, but his books, that was another story. And sometimes they withered. And they didn't let him sleep and in that wakefulness (and in the impossibility of dreaming and freely associating) came the substitute of memories like waking dreams.

But having a child was very different from writing a book. Even an only child who never really was only one child. Because even an only child was many children. They were successive and different versions of that same only child as he grew up and—contrary to what people thought or wanted to believe about a manuscript—not necessarily better in subsequent iterations. (He'd seen them, he'd *felt* it in them. In the adolescent children of others. In their true and ferocious faces masked by other supposedly inoffensive faces, vegetarian faces hiding carnivorous faces and what they truly believed about their parents. That disdain. Like something that radiated in invisible yet powerful waves. And if he could perceive it, he couldn't even dare imagine how that silence would upset its legitimate creators, its masters who suddenly were nothing but slaves to be mistreated: they had taught them to speak and to walk and to eat and suddenly they were just some idiots for their children, for those who had once shit themselves and been so afraid of the dark. And, oh, he'd once seen a man walking down the street, talking to himself, with hair forever stuck in the exact instant of being stuck by the lightning bolt of the years, and he'd heard people, when they saw him pass by, saying things like "His son committed suicide . . . he hung himself in the basement or the attic . . . And up until that very night, he'd always seemed like the happiest kid in the world and . . ." He imagined himself, then, in the cliché of the lost child's bedroom. Sniffing clothes and little shoes like the saddest-faced hound. Turning things over, deciphering old toys, looking at drawings against the light, seeking the secret code. The explanation for what would always be inexplicable. Responding—whenever he was asked how he felt—with a "Don't you understand? I don't feel anything. I don't have anything to feel or to feel for . . . Can you leave me alone? Can I go home now?" Yes: kids were like boomerangs that were hurled away only to come back and crash into the people who'd thrown them. And if you managed to grab hold of them when they came back, well, the truth was it still hurt your hand to catch them. And he needed his hands to write or to remind himself that he no longer wrote.) And so, he never thought about having or being had by a child or children. Or he thought a great deal and put a lot of effort into not thinking about it. Because there were nights, even in the act itself of not making love while making love (as a method for lasting longer there inside, feeling less and less here outside), when he thought about that terrible second in which one spermatozoid won the race to knock first at door to the casino of an ovum and to break the bank. And about how, suddenly, everything started moving as if in the spin cycle of a washing machine: the roulette of the genes, the lottery of future disease, the uncontrolled randomness of new traits trading cards with the gestures of ancestors, the bad run of victorious hormones, the impossibility of confidently placing a bet on a given number. Cells interconnecting. And the certainty that sooner or later the house would always win and that the story would end up being told by someone else, someone younger, with marked cards and smudged notes, and with fewer books read than his creator and more regrets than Frankenstein's Monster.

He thought about how you could try to raise a child in the best way possible (which was impossible; the important thing was to be there, the unforgivable thing was to not be there), but you could never correct a child as you pleased: a child was a tormented and tormenting manuscript that, sooner or later, you would throw into the air in a scattering of loose pages and plot holes and outbursts incomprehensible to their author and first reader.

He thought that not having children was a far more authorial gesture than having them: putting a final period, that everything would end with him, that there would be no possibility of a sequel or spin-off (at most some kind of youthful prequel of himself or one of those occasional "imaginary adventures," which had made him so nervous when he was a kid, where Superman and Batman were married and miserable like that was some great transgression when, for him, what was truly bizarre was that all those defenders of justice had once been children but—maybe this was their real superpower—they appeared to only grow until thirty-something years old and then stop aging), that the story would come to an end with his end.

And to all those people who told him that they were thinking of becoming parents, he always told them that, before turning thought into action, they should read (above all if they had or believed they had what's known as "literary vocation") *The Shining*: that Great American Novel by Stephen King about family disintegration, marriage and paternity as the most combustible of states and feelings, and the Henry Jamesian "Madness of Art," that novel that was authentically realist in the way that only truly fantastical novels could be. That condition, like a great snowstorm, lashing all those writers they (Stephen King and Henry James, possibly the two writers who'd written most and best about writers) had written, fighting among and against themselves, or fleeing from readers and executors and critics, who they tried to slow down by laying down long sentences across the path behind them, like invisible ropes and at the level of the throat.

Or, if not, if after *The Shining* they still weren't entirely convinced to move on, he would suggest that they watch a movie called *Eraserhead*, with that sniveling and demanding fetus that, no, did not look like anybody (it didn't look like Pa or Ma) but itself. And at the time nobody knew how David Lynch created that little noisy monster with such a low budget (though numerous hair-raising urban legends circulated about it). To tell the truth, nobody knew much about what David Lynch was trying to do with what he did, though Lynch did say things that, to him, were of an almost blinding clarity. Things like: "Even if they're new ideas, the past colors them." And, of course, there were many (and he was sure that among the passengers on this flight there were a few) who tended to complain about how they didn't understanding anything about David Lynch's art. And he—who admired Lynch's audacity and his dreams—wanted to scream at all of them, asking if maybe they could explain how it was that that plane they were now traveling in stayed in the air and moved forward through space. Or why the sky was velvety blue and not red like those curtains that never stopped moving. Or why the pilot's voice over the loudspeaker, announcing possible turbulence, sounded like that of a dwarf talking in reverse. Or how it was possible that they were going to arrive to their destination at exactly the same time they departed their point of origin. Or what it was that caused—something about the air you breathed in airplanes?—people, without a shred of shame, to tell the most private and secret things in their lives to the stranger sitting next to them or to bald-facedly lie to them, saying things like "My job is too complicated to put into words, but let's just say that I'm working on something like the calculating the exact age of the universe." Why, better, like in so many other orders of life, like in love or in hate or in the most absolute of indifference (did all those people really have a logical explanation for why they kept sleeping beside that person for whom they hadn't felt anything for so long or why they kept playing with that kid who had nothing to do with them?), didn't they give David Lynch the benefit of the doubt and, in so doing, grant themselves the gratifying certainty of letting go and floating and flying, eh?

But David Lynch (he'd never seen anything by David Lynch on the menu of in-flight movies, maybe because Lynch's work was considered too disturbing and confusing by those who spent their time selecting what should be watched, there above, having determined that, at certain altitudes, people preferred light comedies or swift superheroes or historical dramas or disingenuous biopics with straightforward plotlines no matter how unrealistic or improbable they were) **had been explicit and clear that** *Eraserhead* **had occurred to him when he found out that his then girlfriend was pregnant.** (One of those girlfriends who was probably delightful in the early days. The kind of girlfriend who, on that first date, orders dessert first because "I don't care about saving best for last" and hours later, when you go out to buy croissants and leave her naked in bed and come back to find her up and making coffee, wearing nothing but that "So Many Books, So Little Time" T-shirt. And all of that seemed so adorable right up until the inevitable moment when, sooner rather than later, you discover that you don't like it that she wears T-shirts that aren't hers and stretches them out and you find it a bit irritating that she eats ice cream before pasta. And you realize that what you liked about her was the foreplay and the penetration, but never too deep. And suddenly, how was it that her farts sounded louder and smelled worse? And how frightening it was—if you stared into her eyes close up—that you could read her darkest fantasies in them and that those fantasies were even wilder than yours. Yes, she wanted to do more twisted things with your friends than you wanted to do with hers. And even worse, even more perverse: she wanted to have your kid, a sobbing little monster that would never let you fall asleep.) **And that was when—in that instant of cold fire, not because of the T-shirt thing but because of the belly growing under those T-shirts—David Lynch said to himself something he would repeat in his autobiography: "Oh, no, my life has ended."**

Because yes: you didn't *have* kids, you were *had* by kids.

Children took place then replaced: children took place for their parents in order to later—chronologically and spiritually—replace them. And there were even some kids who ended up writing books about their writer parents, leveling accusations like "My father spent more time looking at his books than watching at me . . . And when he read me bedtime stories and I was really tired, he wouldn't let me go to sleep until the end and whenever I started to shut my eyes, he would tap me on the head and say, 'No! You can't fall asleep just as the main character is about to board a plane and start describing the passengers' conversations!' and he asked me to summarize all of it at breakfast and questioned me to see if I'd really understood it and . . ." Kids of women who could also end up writing books; women who, in addition to leaving, always insisted on *explaining* why they were leaving. And threatening without much enthusiasm or credibility to "take the child" with them, but not insisting too much out of fear that the threat would become a bit too tempting for the defendant, a more than convenient offer, a punishment reward.

And, of course, the arrival of a child altered you, turned you into the most servile of deities. It transformed you into one of those competitive parents who, like Jehovah, ended up demanding the sacrifice of your child out of unspeakable jealousy upon discovering that people loved your child more than you and so you quickly called your child back to your side. Or it transfigured you into a kind of Lucifer obsessed with your child being the best and most powerful whose calling in life would be none other than avenging your own fall and defeat.

And he didn't want to be like any of them (though it always seemed to him that, in the moment of truth, the Devil was a far better and more devoted father than the absent God, whom you would never want to sell your soul to, because, most likely, you would spend an eternity haggling over it; and movies about the Antichrist were way more fun than ones about Christ; and few scenes had frightened him more than that one from *The Omen* in which Gregory Peck—already so far removed from the little rascal Scout in *To Kill a Mockingbird*—cuts a few locks of the little demon Damien's hair and discovers the 666 on his scalp). And it'd always struck him as very revealing that the great escape artist Harry Houdini was the son of a rabbi and also one of the most shackled cases of the Oedipus Complex in all of History. There was no escaping those chains, no way out of that water tank. No: he didn't want any of that for himself, he just wanted everyone to leave him peace. (Whereas, when it came to his work, he never wanted to escape: he wanted everyone to let him back in and to shut the door and lock it and throw away the key. He wanted to be his own spouse and his own child.)

Besides, if he were to become a father, he would be afraid of dying during the delivery.

So, why get in trouble or go looking for conflicts? What was the point? What was that movie where Bill Murray (again, he'd always liked to think that he looked a little like Bill Murray. That—not having been blessed with one of those coyote-faces, like Donald Sutherland or Alan Rickman or, yes, Bob Dylan—at least he had a Bill-Murray face. A face that was blank but awash in shadows and that contained everything yet to be done or undone. One of those faces on which nothing seems to happen so that, really, absolutely everything can happen, a face with the ability to expressionlessly express it all) shuts his eyes with annoyance, and says to his supposed and soon-to-die son that he'd never tried to contact him because "I hate fathers, and I never wanted to be one"? And what was that other movie where Bill Murray explained to a young woman—confused and far from home and lost, just like he'd been so many times, in the hallways of a hotel as big as the city in which it stood—that "It gets a whole lot more complicated when you have kids . . . The most terrifying day of your life is the day the first one is born . . . Your life, as you know it . . . is gone. Never to return"? (And, sure, he remembered that, in that very same scene, Bill Murray went on to say "But they learn how to walk, and they learn how to talk . . . and you want to be with them . . . And they turn out to be the most delightful people you will ever meet in your life." Though something told him that, there, Bill Murray was trying to get that pretty girl next to him on the bed to relax, without touching her, because he felt that she was almost like his own daughter and, also, a terminator who'd come from the future.)

And when he was upset by the slight and fleeting anxiety of having missed out on some experience that everyone claimed was indispensable for all creators—married life, paternity, family, the perception that nothing ended with you and that everything would live on in others—he'd opted to imagine it in a wealth of detail. Just like he imagined—it was easier and not as risky—so many other things that he would never be or do. Like surfing monstrous waves or learning Mandarin. That's why he was a writer of fiction and not nonfiction, right?

And so, he'd documented and even gotten dangerously near the eye of that hurricane and the mouth of that volcano and, at its edge, breathed in the toxic fumes and had been struck by the circular lightning bolts of that secret solitude of two soon to be blown up by the arrival of little boys and little girls of colossal appetites and gigantic needs.

And he'd even dated some single mothers who snuck him into their houses on the sly so their kids wouldn't know he was there. (And he had the disturbing gift of repeating the same sequence/routine that he'd starred in and lived through when he was a kid, but reversing polarities: when it was the daughters who snuck him secretly into their rooms, praying that their parents didn't notice that they were no longer their "pretty little princesses" but underbelly courtesans of knights of fortune.) And at one point he'd even been having "relations" with a mother and daughter at the same time, and it was great, but, of course, it didn't last long.

And, of course, without a doubt, no question about it: more than once, at those many conferences for Penelope's fans (and he still felt dizzy and out of breath remembering the massive funerals that were held for the incombustible but burning Penelope, memorials held far and wide and high and low all over the planet that'd dwarfed the already massive funerals of Charles Dickens and Victor Hugo: millions of Penelope's readers crying from the same eyes with which they'd read her, many of them online but present in body, socially distanced but united by the contagious virus of their weight), he had made good and efficient use of the line: "do you know who my sister is?" to procure some fresh and firm and crazy flesh.

Likewise, he'd been at the disposal of successive and beautiful and exceedingly intelligent lesbians who found him "fun every now and then" and told him that their time with him "reaffirmed their preference" and who also thanked him effusively for his "always interesting book recommendations." No gay men ever came onto him because he'd been considered a persona non grata after writing a story depicting a homosexual man as a kind of party animal, addicted to epiphanies, and not at all combative or committed to his community. Or maybe he didn't strike them as the type. Bill Murray and all of that. And animals were afraid of him, babies cried when they looked at him, nuns (even the rare pretty nuns) crossed themselves when he passed by, and his long and horizontal nights were a thing of a past to be invoked from the most vertical of insomnias.

That past in which he'd never truly fallen in love, whatever that meant (the thing with Ella was something on the other side of love, Ella had blown the house up only to open the door after), and where it'd been clear to him, on the other hand, that sex allowed him to pseudo fall in love. Sure: that kind of love might not have been a deep love; but it was—unlike supposedly romantic and spiritual and true love—a love that you could touch and see and penetrate. And—at times, for a few seconds—a love that could make him feel that it was possible to die from love, to die a *petite mort*, yes, but to die all the same. But it was a love of seconds, a collapse from which he was immediately resurrected. And from which, every time, he returned more convinced that his self-love was right. And that love, as everyone else understood it, would always be wrong for him. And, everywhere, eternally out of place and intrusive. And that that wasn't bad. Because everyone else's love wasn't true. It was a lying love. And it was a childish and dangerous love (Could there be anything more immature and risky than thinking that the best took place at the deceptive beginning when really you had to go look for it and not find it until the very end?) and, not in vain, that was why those very same lovers of love—all of them struck stupid by Cupid—didn't hesitate to represent it as a bare naked and flying infant, threatening to decenter the smitten by centering a bow and arrow. That was, also, why the ability to *fall in love* again required, necessarily, the ability to forget much of the previous fall so you could get back up and, in that way, fall again, thinking, like a distant yet forever nearby echo, that thing Maurice Blanchot wrote, that thing about how "You will never find the limits of forgetting, no matter how far you may be able to forget." The same was true of the infinite limits of love, he thought. And true too of all those dupes who claimed to be happier than ever because they'd just fallen in love (he approached them, especially at train stations and in airports, kissing one another as if their bodies were all mouth, to breathe in deeply the scent they gave off like the most romantic of vampires); which to him was like thinking that an internal hemorrhage was less serious than a superficial cut, because, after all, blood was supposed to stay inside the body, right?

And so—based on his own experiences—he'd developed a kind of sixth sense and X-ray vision for looking at other couples. Those so-called "perfect" couples.

Couples who laughed at parties to avoid saying things—those things that he could read between their teeth and on their lips, like HAL 9000—like "The important thing is not, as people believe in the beginning, to have simultaneous orgasms, but, over the years, to know perfectly what your significant other is thinking, because it's exactly what you're thinking." And then—he thought and knew—both of them would immediately tell themselves that it was better not to think about that. And then mutually send each other a kind of loving telepathic beam that would erase those ideas from their minds at the same time, the way you erase an email or block access to a social media profile.

Couples that most people found enviable; but in whom he could easily detect the hidden lymphoma, the metastasis of their lies. And nothing struck him as more simultaneously exotic and banal than a couple that was happy in public. Because he could see them as they were in private. He could depreciate them and appreciate the marvel of two people who stayed together and kept hating each other only out of and for and in the name of love.

Couples—avoiding all allusion to paternity or to its absence or to the obsessive evocation of his own parents or the even more obsessive observation of other parents and of their almost always incomprehensible habits—he always approached as if they were some kind of exotic species to make them nervous with awkward questions. Questions like how did they get to know each other and, then, when did they stop knowing each other. Questions like didn't they think—as he thought—that the human race had taken an enormous step backward when it became scientifically possible to know the baby's sex before it was born. And if the loss of the fun of that mystery (because even though parents almost begged not to know it, someone in the doctor's office always ended up revealing the secret) of not knowing if the baby would be male or female was now the closest thing to knowing a really important plot point in a novel in advance, before having reached that decisive chapter. (When it came to marriage, his role-model husband had always been Pablo Picasso: two of his wives lost their minds and the other two committed suicide, or something like that, he wasn't sure. But there was a very clear pattern of behavior in his partners: batshit crazy or suicidal, Picasso never had to leave them, voluntarily or involuntarily, they facilitated the transition.) He saw them and perceived how the elegant and figurative curves of their public self-portraits were transformed into the cubist angles of their private lives. The same thing—again—with their children, so gracious outside and so disgraced on the inside and the whole "Do you want to see the baby?" that they asked him in a voice at once tremulous and under-slept and deformed from speaking that cloying goo-goo gah-gah language, convinced that doing so made them more comprehensible to someone or something for whom a mathematical theorem sounded the same as an Elizabethan sonnet. (And him thinking then that if he wanted to see some hairless, demanding creature, convinced it was the center of the universe and with a true propensity for sudden tantrums, he already had himself, every morning, in the unanesthetized bathroom mirror.) And he wondered why and to what end they had those . . . yes . . . *creatures*. Because the inevitable question wasn't that "Why did you decide not to have kids?" that people asked him now and then, the inevitable question was "Why *did* you decide to have kids?" (He'd read somewhere that it was in that way—by reproducing—that the species went about purging imperfections from their genome. He'd also read that, if that were true, something wasn't coming out quite right in the practice of said theory.) And yet, hey, be fruitful and multiply. And later—in subsequent chapters of an interminable series—dressing them up in those immaculate little sailor outfits to conceal the tattered underwear of castaways. And it was then that those ex-babies were asked over and over "What do you want to be when you grow up?" Speaking to them the way adults speak to children: feeling forever young and ignoring the fact that the little ones thought they had always been old and prehistoric. And that they were all taking up too much space and time inside their childhood bedrooms where all they wanted was to be a little more alone. And so, the poor little things looked up with those almost-cartoonishly wet eyes at the enormous faces, there above: blinding them with smiles as fierce as interrogation lights, wondering what that whole being "grown up" thing would be like. Did it have something to do with their size, with their abilities, with their ambitions?

In any case, he'd known, always and forever, what he wanted to be when he grew up. And he'd already been it, even when he was really little and he started reading and writing before ever learning how.

And now he was and did nothing.

Now he was like a baby who'd never had a baby.

Who was it who'd said that thing about how "A writer is someone who can make a riddle out of an answer"? He couldn't remember, but he couldn't forget that—if that were true—he was now someone who didn't know what to answer when asked what he was. The until not long ago very simple and correct answer for him had devolved into the most difficult riddle of the most demanding sphinx. Thus—from no longer being anything—that thing about being an exwriter after having been a writer and a nextwriter.

So now he spent the hours imagining alternate destinies, variable trajectories.

And so, he preferred not to imagine that there was neither heaven nor religion nor countries nor possessions, but that—it's easy if you try—his kids and wife were the same, not as imaginary friends, but as family imagined from a safe distance, from the incalculable proximity of the imaginary.

An imagined family in which—for obvious reasons, out of respect for the unfathomable, to keep from falling into the obvious and absurd—Ella was never his wife and He Whose Name Must Not Be Mentioned was never his son.

His imaginary family had shifting and fluid faces. Faces of actors and actresses. Or it was based on a picture that caught his eye in some magazine at the doctor's office. Or it behaved like some family he encountered in passing for a few seconds on streets and in parks and that struck him as particularly "civilized." It took him little to no work to assimilate them and make them his own, to make himself belong to them so they belonged to him, for a time (never too long) that lasted as long as a fantasy never to be put (and that now he could never put) in writing.

Not for nothing and for something was he a "creator" and a "creative."

It was more pleasant and less offensive that way.

He especially liked to recreate himself in the scene of a final goodbye that would never take place, but that he didn't want to deprive himself of composing in one of the most-visited chambers in his false memory palace that remembered into the future and along an alternate route, like in one of those parallel universes where Batman and Catwoman lived happily ever after. Because, in his experience and as far as he knew, people without descendants tended to die suddenly and without warning. Because, maybe, he reasoned, without any watchful relatives to importune, it made no sense to stage a long and agonizing and exhausting (above all for everyone else) death, and so, better just a quick click, like someone vanishing in a column of colorful smoke.

So that was why he imagined for himself a farewell in more or less good and entirely close company. (Though to tell the truth he'd always anticipated a quick and solitary death: go to a hotel with a bottle of pills, empty the minibar that now nobody would pay for, turn yourself off slowly with porn playing on the TV, leaving his naked body there so the proper authorities would be sent to dispose of him and could touch his organs as they pleased, *do not disturb, please make up room*.) But in his fantasies, there he was: hypothetical husband and father, on his deathbed, dying before his time, as was befitting. Dying before his time yet at a ripe old age and almost identical to his son, as if anticipating the irresponsible and playful and time-wasting use of that popular aging app that will age too soon. Like in those movies where the same actor plays both characters and, sometimes, even the grandson. You know it already: rapid fade to black and in the next scene a new heir without a father behind him and his whole life ahead of him. Like in those family sagas prior to penicillin (people died all of a sudden; so they weren't obliged to put on all that unrealistic aging makeup) and all of that. And thereby avoiding the regrettable postcard of almost putrescent and Valdemarian progenitors clinging to the arms of their past middle-aged progeny: old men walking beside very old women and old women wandering next to very old men all of them quickly hooked on the modernity of their mobile phones; all of them part of a generation of pioneers: the first one that, statistically, was going to live far longer than people used to live; the first crop of older than old people who died, with their brains worn out from so much thinking and so tired of making so much memory, without even being aware that they were dying and reminding him of that ingeniously terrible quote by Oscar Wilde, who maintained that the primary duty of any gentleman was to dream: "The tragedy of old age is not that one is old, but that one is young."

And—he kept thinking, thinking about that quote—the tragedy was remembering perfectly how you had been and how you would never be again. And being reminded more and better all the time of that unforgettable paradise (sometimes purgatory, sometimes hell, but, even still, always better than the future-less present) from which you'd been expelled. (Though, at the same time, he was sure that aging *well* ran through being nothing like how you'd been when you were young. There was nothing worse than that, he thought: being the old version of the young person you'd once been. The old person *recalling* the young person so much, and thinking that, oh, better not to recall all of that. It was far better, he was sure, to be—for everyone—an amnesiac *new* old-person. Someone who was entirely different from the person you'd been and who didn't even allow for comparisons to that *old* new-person. Someone like him, who was no longer even able to recognize himself in the picture from the jacket of *National Industry* and who, forced to examine the good aspect of that whole phenomenon, was neither recognized nor pestered by unsettling ghosts of Christmases past.)

And sometimes—like now—all those people of advanced age traveling, *travelaging*, all together and in groups, on airplanes, smiling when said airplanes started to shake, because they're not afraid of imminent death because their death is imminent anyway. So, while we're at it, it wouldn't be bad to die there and then and to appear in the newspapers where, otherwise, they would never appear. All of them unaware of the fact that at a certain point in life you should only leave home when you're never going to return, because they stink up spaces that are too enclosed or too public (or maybe they know that perfectly well, but they take morbid pleasure in going around, in plain sight, reminding everyone that that thing that they're no longer waiting for is precisely what awaits all the rest them, to terrify the young, knocking at their doors in a kind of inverted version of Halloween Night). Some of them—the few, but for that reason the most unsettling—dressed to the nines and with shining smiles; like in those TV commercials, geared toward "the elderly," for paradisiacal retirements or medications to eradicate all erectile dysfunction and strengthen all orgasmic spark and, no, they couldn't be real: those were young people made-up to look old, he shuddered. All of them flying like disoriented gargoyles, searching fruitlessly for the eaves of a cathedral to find repose and take refuge. Old people moving so slowly due to the lawless gravity of dragging around so many memories and excess baggage that some of them opt to, better, not collect their luggage from the circumventing airport carousels of their brains and thereby live in a pure and weightless present. In a narratively ideal order of things, he always thought that progenitors should die when their kids reach legal adulthood or, at most, when they turn twenty-five years old. That way, he thought, if there was nothing left to do, it was better to just "multiply yourself" halfway down the road, after having lived your life and reflected a great deal on the few pros and innumerable cons of the thing. Also being able to opt, having procreated too young, for the somewhat reproachable "disappearing suddenly and mysteriously" only to reappear in the final chapter and then "bequeath a considerable fortune," having never uttered the psychotic favorite words of the parents of his generation who understood nothing about their role and responsibilities: "I just want to be your best friend." (When it came to the practical disappearance and theoretical reappearance of his forever-young father and mother, he and Penelope, clearly, had facilitated the former knowing full well that there was little to no chance that the latter would ever come to pass.) In this way, the ascendant descendant would still be full of zeal, with no ties to the past, ready to set off in search of multiple possibilities. An orphan, in the end, and more than ready to be adopted by life itself without having to bring along a whole lot of baggage. Free of entangling roots and with no obligation to make periodic visits to the increasingly ruinous ruins of the people who'd created him and from whom he'd fled with nothing but the clothes on his back. Better that way, he imagined himself then: paterfamilias on his deathbed but already ready to be embodied in the next generation and doped up with the latest-generation painkillers. Elegant and propped up on soft pillows and wearing a *robe de chambre* of the kind worn in classic comedy films based on plays by tycoons who appeared to never leave their bedchambers. And thus allowing himself the generosity of saying goodbye to his wife with a "Love somebody else, but—and you know them well and that's part of my legacy—somebody without my oh so perfect and adorable flaws." And asking his son to forgive him "for the trauma that all of this will cause you; but please don't let my departure pull you under, no, turn it into something valuable, make something alive out of my death, immortalize me with your memory." And some other sappy nonsense of the kind that almost brought him to tears.

Almost.

But five minutes of fantasizing about all of that was enough for him to discover something that he'd never stopped being certain of: he was entirely happy to live alone, without anyone who would cry over him for years and—most important of all—without anyone who would make him cry for decades. He would never be an old man *like that*, because he would never have anyone at his side reminding him of how little time he had left, that *that* was what it was to be old. Nothing interested him less and irritated him more than being "the author of the days" of someone else (really the coauthor), above all and more than ever because he no longer wrote. "Taketh away from me that imprecise and unpredictable mystery," he ordered and begged in his perfect isolation. And he obeyed himself. And he couldn't stop remembering what could happen to someone like him—bitter fruit of a perfectly dysfunctional family—if he got too close and felt himself drawn in by the gravitational pull of some imperfectly happy tribe of the kind that, every so often, demanded a propitiatory victim, the sacrifice of some "outsider" to be able to continue with their thing, with their people. (And he'd never really understood the foundational greatness of Chekhov; but he could never forget that disenchanted and old character from *The Seagull* who recalled, melancholically, that when he was young he'd only had two wishes: to get married and to be a writer. And that, of course, neither had come true, because those two desires—like opposed and irreconcilable forces—had wound up canceling each other out. And so, the only dream that'd come true for that man was, merely, that of having it made perfectly clear to him what it was that he'd never achieved. Then, almost instantly, the sound of the shot of that pistol that, according to Chekhov, if it was shown in the first act, had to be fired in the third, just before the final curtain.) A more than illustrative example of the above—and he always kept it in mind and had been so shaken when he read it—had been what happened to and what became of the poor intellectual and office worker and poetic nighttime rambler Leonard Bast, in *Howard's End* by E. M. Forster: the poor guy—abducted by the clan of disturbed Schlegel sisters and by the well-to-do Wilcoxes, and then stoically putting up with giggles and tinkling teacups and cakes so dry they're impossible to swallow—got crushed to death by a bookcase. By a bookcase that, moreover, wasn't even his own. Could there be a death more humiliating and shameful than that? Than perishing under a pile of unknown books, that haven't been read, and that no one knows which ones they are and much less if they would've been to the dead man's liking? Probably not. And then, before long, they all went back to being happy, having overcome the circumstantial complications. And nobody really remembered Bast anymore, not even the mother of his son.

For him, the absolute truth when it came to the subject of family and children was in that famous monologue from Woody Allen's *Manhattan*. A monologue in which, near the end, the protagonist, Isaac Davis, listed the things that made life worth living (Groucho Marx and Frank Sinatra and Marlon Brando and that novel by Gustave Flaubert and apples and pears painted by Paul Cezanne and "Potato Head Blues" and the second movement of the *Jupiter Symphony* and Willie Mays and, of course, the face of the very young Tracy), but at no time did he include his young son. Then there were people who pointed out this omission as a flaw in the screenplay and irrefutable proof that, when it was filmed, Woody Allen hadn't a clue about what it meant to be a father and, much less, about the fury of Mia Farrow. But he wanted to shout at them that no, that it wasn't true, that it was exactly *like that*, that Allen hadn't forgotten or not known anything: Isaac Davis had already contributed to bringing his son into the world, but that didn't, automatically and obligatorily, mean that he didn't love "Ummm . . . Swedish movies, naturally" more. Yes, parents of the world, better that you admit it, even if only to yourselves, he accused: you might love the pincers of Sam Wo's crabs more than your child's fingers; you might love an almost-adolescent girlfriend far more than that demanding and ungrateful little homunculus who had no interest in talking about *L'Éducation sentimentale* and didn't even understand the rules of baseball.

In any case, it didn't seem bad to him that all of that was a preoccupation and even a pleasure for others. (At a dinner following one of his book launches, John Irving, who'd been a father most of his life, from when he was eighteen and of multiple children with great age differences between them, had mentioned to him that, for a writer, one of the advantages of having children is that, all of a sudden, you got to remember your own childhood all over again, down to the last detail, through those of all your children; to which he'd responded by asking "And what's good about that? All I want is to forget my unforgettable childhood." And then John Irving had looked at him with a combination of disgust and pity and perhaps a bit of fear. And, yes, he thought that writers could be divided into those who discarded and accumulated and those who, like him, whenever they tried, in vain, to discard something only managed to accumulate more, with every fruitless attempt to become lighter and more of an orphan, going back and going forward. And, okay, fine, sure: toward the end of her life, the great Virginia Woolf recognized that, beyond what she'd written, she'd failed because she'd never had children; but, warning, Woolf was mad and she heard voices that, most likely, called her "Mommy" and asked her why she'd left them out in the dark and cold.) **And it didn't bother him in the least that all of that—parenthood, children—happened to other people** (and to that end, he had no problem at all that mothers nursed in public as long as those mothers weren't bothered by him watching them nurse in public). **He was delighted to have people multiplying all around him just so he could observe that whole physical-chemical process—the fusion of the affections and dysfunction of gluttons—from outside, always behind security fences, like a person who gets a kick out of watching someone else's house burn down. And who, in addition, allowed himself—without asking permission first—to take notes, to later be revised and cleaned up, coldly and hygienically, in the laboratory, bottled in the void that was overflowing with everything that occurred to him regarding something that would never occur for him.** (Did IKEA ever have kids with any of his ex-wives or with the one he'd devoured? Had IKEA really eaten his beloved? Was she pregnant when IKEA ate her? Had IKEA eaten the placentas of his children? He wasn't sure, but he should know. At one point he'd written that it was true. And he'd even seen it in the act of typing it: pictures of IKEA surrounded by blonde children that looked like they'd walked off the set of the *Village of the Damned* or *The Sound of Music* or out of the glossy pages of society magazines where irrepressible Catholic families pridefully showed off that they didn't know and didn't want to know anything about birth control techniques. But he was no longer sure about everything he'd given IKEA credit for. And maybe none of that was or had been like that. His biography—IKEA's—was foggy for him, and yet he knew his bibliography down to the last detail. And, of course, IKEA had penned the inevitable "modern young-adult classic" titled *The Imp of Aconcagua*. And he'd even written lyrics for an album of eco-ethnic songs to be sung by Anorexia when she broke up with her Flaquitas to transform herself into a director of progressive children's programs and in that way "raise the ecological awareness of all Latin American children.")

In summary, in broad summary: for him, women were a brief and intense yet fleeting experiment (like what rockers sometimes composed when they went to the wild environs of Morocco to beat bones and bang on animal-hide drums, because they couldn't come up with anything new in London or New York anymore), one that, if it went well, there was no need to repeat in the same test tube, due to issues of hygiene and toxicity. Children, on the other hand, were more complex and interesting subject matter, to be observed with protective eyewear that sometimes turned out to be ineffective and if you stared at them for too long—like an eclipse, like the eclipsed He Whose Name Must Not Be Mentioned—could end up blinding and damaging the eyes directly connected to your brain.

Children were time machines, but ones that only allowed you to travel forward and in real time. Minute by minute. And that made their parents far more aware of the time that was passing and passing to never pass again (and more than one of those parents had mentioned to him that the first thing you lost when you became a parent was almost all awareness of all the time when you'd been a childless child: distant childhood became clearer and came closer, yes; but you could no longer recover almost anything of all those years—that *terra incognita*—when you weren't exactly a child and not yet precisely a parent).

Children were also like those books whose genre was never entirely clear, because they encompassed all genres: horror, comedy, coming-of-age, romance, revenge, and, finally, those books that started out loving to end up hating. Children were, yes, books of very particular general interest. You could have two that were a lot alike, but never totally. And, again, if booksellers and librarians were rarely entirely sure what genre children should belong to, then their creators had far greater problems, never knowing what section to put their children in: philosophy?, religion?, self-help?, history?, poetry?, fiction?, essay?, comics?, children's, with those tender stories for kids where desperate parents "forget" their offspring in clearings in dark forests so they end up getting stewed by witches or devoured by wolves? Or one of those books that you buy without giving it much thought in an airport bookstore, thinking you would leave it behind in your hotel room before boarding your return flight, once you'd read and finished it, but, suddenly, unexpectedly and against all odds, you discover that it's one of those stories that has changed your life, one that you won't ever be able to stop thinking about, rereading, discovering things in it that on the first read, on that flight, had gone right over your head, higher over your head than all those storm clouds that, look out, here they come again?

And he always thought about books the way others think about children and about trees and about chainsaws and about terrible accidents, like parents forgetting their kids inside locked cars or like books that get left behind on airplanes or in hotels or that get burned in a desert after you've forgotten how to write them. (He even put some of them into writing on shoots of arboreal paper already withering and yellow around the edges, the color of teeth that've already bitten off more than they can chew and now are tired of chewing and now can only handle mash and mush.) And when he stopped, stopped making them, he started to think of books to think up, of future books: of the starting line of books where he stood, waving a kerchief or checkered flag, so he could wish them good luck and tell them to do the best they could without his help.

The thing from before: exwriter.

Demoted category. The medals of the nextwriter he was as a boy and of the writer he was in his youth stripped from the lapels of his uniform.

And so, now, he was no longer functional and efficient and a man of action like the professor vampire-hunter Abraham Van Helsing (and, again, he remembered himself, as a boy, reading *Dracula* under the covers and with a flashlight, his first *adult* book, "for grownups" and in the "original, unabridged edition"), but just one of those superstitious Transylvanian villagers with no names to distinguish the ones from the others. All of them crossing themselves at the beginning of the novel and warning the traveler Jonathan Harker that something dreadful awaited him in that castle that was in ruins and yet still included a well-stocked library. Frightened but, at the same time, so happy that an imbecilic foreigner has stepped up to have all the terrifying things that usually happen to them happen to him and who will distract the monster so he forgets to torment them at least for a while, until the next full moon that the children of the night howl at with their music.

And so, for a while now, he can only think up books that have already been thought of, as if they were children not to be procreated (because he can't) but perhaps to be adopted (though that verb remains an unrealizable fantasy). Safer, less risky and, if you don't like them, you can trade them in for different ones, they say.

He thinks—the way one thinks of being legendary and undead and unliving and ever-thirsty—of an impossible-for-him possible book.

A book that would contain thousands of pages whose Theme and Plot would be the invocation of that same phantasmagoric book.

Time and again, a book.

A book that was one yet, at the same time, three books: like those triple concept albums of the '60s and '70s, like The Kinks' *Preservation*, back when the people listening to them had sufficient attention span to listen to them all the way through (not like now, when there is barely enough time for a random song recorded and sold as a single, without context; a solitary song that you don't play or put on but that you download and consume and move onto whatever comes next by whoever else is in the vicinity). Long albums that you looked at and watched spin, analyzing the song order and composition, guessing at secret messages recorded in reverse, keeping it very clear that, there and then, it was all about the *long play*.

A book about the impossibility of writing that, nevertheless, couldn't stop being written.

A book that would be the book with the most writing on the subject of not being able to write.

A book that, in practice, would contain its theory and whose plot would reside in its style.

A book whose main character would be none other than the language the book spoke (one language but with linguistic variations and rhythms and phrases that distinguished what was invented and what was dreamed and what was remembered).

A book that would say everything anyone else might say about it later about itself first.

A book that—like the monolith in *2001: A Space Odyssey*—would contain the enigma and the resolution of its own mystery.

A book at once crepuscular and dazzling.

A book that would be like an outfit designed by John Galliano or Alexander McQueen for that model named Piva: impossible to wear out on the street, but perfect for strolling through the salons and gardens and catacombs of palaces inaccessible even for the reddest of deaths.

A book that would be the question to all the answers.

A book that would commit the perfect and pardonable crime and sin: proving irrefutably that lives have a logic and an order; that lives are, really, novels or books of stories; that they are born and die, yes, but between the one point and the other they begin and end multiple times and, sometimes, they close off their parts and doors by leaving them open; that, looking back, they discover that secret thread of fate correcting and redacting all sequence (*A* and then *B* and then *C*) into transcendent consequence (*A* and thus *B* and thus *C*) and thereby giving meaning to the past.

A book that would express itself like someone remembering and making memory with a *memory almost full*, but—unlike so many electronic devices— always with space to recall something more and to forget something less.

A book that would make readers wonder if they hadn't already been told that anecdote about Bob Dylan interrupting his show; if they hadn't already had the pointing statue of Christopher Columbus pointed out to them; if they hadn't already heard all that stuff about autofiction (adding, maybe, the detection of a virus that leaves behind neurological lesions in those who survive it and whose clearest symptom among the writers who contract it is that of being degraded from clean maximalists into dirty minimalists); or about mobile phones, or that other thing about a tourist in Illiers/Combray (because a single memory could work in different contexts, rising from the depths and going back down again, like a submarine periscope) to thereby hide everything that it didn't want to remember unless it was remembering to forget it.

A book that would be more behind than ahead.

A book with a lot of past invoked in the name of the future.

A book that would be autobiographical, yes, but that wouldn't be the *memoir* of a life and would instead be about the creation of its own style: its method and its way of being and making.

A book that would be written in the most first of third persons, because what it would actually tell—beyond its anecdotes—would be the way a writer invents and dreams and remembers. His mental process as if it were a language in itself. Examining the interlinking of its own cells (*cells interlinked within cells interlinked* and all of that). Following the path traced by the electric sparks jumping from one neuron to the next and heading down all the byways and bifurcations along the way. And on like that, until it achieved the blinding illumination of, having been everywhere, understanding that there was something terrible and marvelous in the idea that the most distant place in the world you could ever travel to or conceive of is, also, the closest: one step back, just behind you, going in reverse, like Mr. Trip.

A book in which not only would many things occur, but that, in addition, would make many things occur to readers as they read it. And would, in a way, turn them into writers too.

A book that would be like "Three Tenses," the famous novella written by R, referred to in *Transparent Things*.

A book that—like Nabokov's *Pale Fire*—would mutate its readers into its ideal and perfect readers: readers who, among exceedingly pleasurable growing pains, would feel they were writing the book as they read it and who, right away, would reread it. And that, before they even read it, when they were only on the first page (as Charles Kinbote warns and predicts in his introduction regarding the second canto of the poem), would already know what its readers' favorite parts were and would be.

A book that would drive its readers crazy and that—like what happened to the Nabokovite Brian Boyd with *Pale Fire*—would even force them to write other books about it, theorizing about the multiple possible identities of John Shade and Charles Kinbote and Botkin V. and Hazel Shade and about who the true author of the poem "Pale Fire" (all those pale and fiery lunatics eclipsed and stealing sunlight from the dazzling and true and undisputed author: Vladimir Nabokov, that perpetual rememberer, that—in the verses of the *preterist* and collector of old nests, John Shade—boy who was instructed and trained by his mother to first look at something and then immediately: "*Vot zapomni*":

Now remember. Vladimir Nabokov, over the years, selecting the opacity of apparently disconnected things, texture over text, to achieve the transparency of the unforgettable because "what can one do to remember all that? You have to link it to something else." And there was so much to remember and to write down and to decode of one's own past that, when it was done, "with interest, with amusement, seldom with admiration or disgust" and especially when it came to a "hypertrophied sense of lost childhood," you experienced "mild hallucinations") and the notes that accompanied and cornered and strangled it was. And that those other books would almost be like involuntary and possessed sequels to the first one, with footnotes clad in boots of seven leagues and one language.

A book that wouldn't be a *bildungsroman* but a *künstlerroman*, only in reverse: the story of a writer who, having reached the zenith of his development and with nothing left to write, would begin to fold in on himself (*efface expunge erase delete rub out wipe out obliterate*) as they say Jehovah did or like how they say that the universe will end up contracting in on itself at the end of time. And in that way, rereading his life and work, that writer would, also, proceed to rewrite it.

A book that wouldn't be a magnum opus but a magnificent working.

A book that would be (the adjective didn't strike him as unquestionably laudatory, because there were frightening and megalomaniacal monuments; statues whose true and ultimate *raison d'être* was to cease to be at the hands and ropes and cannon fire of those who, sooner or later, grew weary of having them standing there; those who, mysteriously, never seemed to intuit that being a statue also implied always ending up being toppled or melted or, in his case, going out of print) *monumental.* And that would include lines like this one, so that his detractors could quote it in their reviews.

A book that would follow the instructions in that letter from Franz Kafka to Max Brod in which he postulated that "I think we ought to read only the kind of books that wound and stab us. If the book we're reading doesn't wake us up with a blow on the head, what are we reading it for?" Or writing it, he added (and at one point he'd considered writing a short story where Brod *did* burn Kafka's manuscripts: really bad texts—including the terrible endings to novels like *The Castle* and *The Trial* and *Amerika,* leaving them masterfully unresolved—and only preserving the really good ones, the excellent ones, the ones that're well-known and that cut and wound and deliver crushing blows).

A book for which he would be, in his own right, a believing and skeptical medium. Someone invited to sit down at that table in whose center—instead of a crystal ball or Ouija board—would be a small screen where he could beg for letters out of which, from the tips of his fingers, would emerge concentric lines more personal than those of his fingerprints.

A book that would be about a book and whose first words would be "Call me Book." And that would be like one of the books Herman Melville aspired to write—after having started his voyage with successful titles, even though, as he wrote, "my only desire for their 'success' (as it is called) springs from my pocket"—and that, as he said in a letter to his father-in-law, who supported him and his family at the time, he wanted to spring not from his pocket but from his heart and for them to be written like "those sort of books which are said to 'fail.'—Pardon this egotism." Books that Melville set out to write immediately but that ended up arousing in critics of the day expressions like "intolerably unhealthy," "repulsive, unnatural and indecent," and "might be supposed to emanate from a lunatic asylum."

But now (*What's John NOT writin'?*) enough and more than enough of thinking about that book of books.

Because after so much thinking about it, it was as if he could read it.

As if he'd written it without needing to write it and he were reading it without it being there, as if it were part of that darkness where the world was in braille.

A book that—once it was done and after he was finished with it or it was finished with him—would force him to go into (or, better, to found) a detox residency for writers. (Penelope's ghost is flitting around here, again and always, and adds that "the truly good books are those that not only don't let go of their reader but don't let go of their author either. Emily Brontë let herself die when she realized she would never rid herself of Cathy's agony and Heathcliff's fury; but what you're proposing to establish would be nothing but a refuge for cowards, something worthy of an inept and mediocre Branwell Brontë—who erased himself from that portrait in which he painted himself next to his sisters, and he couldn't even do that well: because he's still there, repentant *pentimento*, still visible under the paint that covers him like a sheet, a ghost tormenting himself—and never an Emily Brontë, Bad Little Brother of mine.")

In any case, that book like a clean and well-lighted place where men and women would be able to kick the habit—pale and with hands trembling from so much typing and from giving it up, wrapped in bathrobes and prostrate on deck chairs, staring out at sunrises and sunsets that they no longer narrated—after so many years writing or thinking about a book or, like him, about a book in three books. Having passed ten years there inside so that ten years would pass by (asking himself, less and less sure, whether that thing he was writing was for him a dummy or a ventriloquist and then telling himself that it didn't really matter); completely addicted to that voice, injecting it and snorting it and swallowing it and smoking it. *Quickly. Quickly and slowly.* Like that other before him, locked inside himself and, also, locked inside by himself. Until he understood that it would be impossible to excise that voice that was already like a part of the byways of his heart and of the beats of his brain.

That voice that sometimes, like right now, he understood as a stand-up comedian. Standing up and moving up and down the aisles of an airplane. Silent, but ceaselessly thinking about and revising and refining his routine, aware that stand-up comedians are, by definition and occupational hazard, the great memorialists and rememberers: always making memory and remembering and starting off their jokes by looking back with a "I remember when . . ." and then proceeding to recount saddest episodes of their past in a funny way.

It was a voice full of voices, other voices that that voice claimed as its own for the simple reason of having once upon a time read them.

It was a voice that was far more than a voice: it was a voice that was an entire language.

And then, having mastered the one and the other (he'd mentioned this in an interview, back when he was still writing and could therefore allow himself the luxury and permit himself the hubris of imagining such things), fantasizing about completely giving up writing for at least a couple years: like someone sinking into a deep coma. And emerging from it voiceless and having to learn to speak all over again and thereby, in a way, becoming totally different from who he once was and had been.

And wondering if then he could be other, different, a new writer.

A writer who no longer dragged around the dazzling baggage of all those blind quotations, leaning on the crutches of what'd been said or written by others, cured at last of his referential mania that—he knew it—had been nothing but shield and excuse and evasion to avoid referring to his own thing, to his own story, to what he didn't dare tell. To the names he would never be rid of. To what he'd done and wished he hadn't done but could no longer put right. To everything that, being irrevocable, he could only think about and acknowledge as a good story and then . . .

Fantasizing, yes, of leaving in order to return and to bring back from the other side, at last, another personality and character, like someone being reincarnated as the person he never was. And to be closer to those other writers—Faulkner, Chekhov—he'd failed to read or understood in their moment. And who now told him that all was forgiven and that he could be just like them.

Or maybe not: because the protagonist of the miracle can never control the nature of the miracle that, it's understood, is the true protagonist. Maybe, in the most ironic of plot twists, he would become a writer a lot like IKEA.

Or even more perturbing and perverse: maybe he would decide to put in writing what everyone was asking for. The story of his parents. And the story of Penelope. And—they didn't ask it of him because they couldn't even imagine it—the story of what he and Penelope had done to bring about the undoing of their parents . . .

But no.

The world wasn't ready for such a confession. And much less to forgive something like that just so he could thank them for their compassion and understanding. And sometimes he toyed with the possibility of being forgiven without needing to ask forgiveness and that all the had to do was give thanks. He already admitted it: he was *not* a good guy; he was a bastard.

But things didn't work like that.

And thanks is given but forgiveness is asked for. It's asked for by the one who'll give it to the one to be forgiven ("Ask my forgiveness") or it's asked for by the one who wishes to be forgiven ("Forgive me"). And, if everything goes well, it's given more or less mutually. Few actions as transcendent—and simultaneously more ephemeral and instantaneously archivable—as asking forgiveness. It has about it something of a very simple and yet always effective magic trick (another magic trick, another number that he can no longer pull off or never really could pull off all that well or that he performed too many times): now you hear it, now you don't. And pay attention because, if you don't, you'll never be sure you actually heard it—forgiveness being asked for or given—muttered between clenched teeth or mumbled under the breath.

To err is human, to forgive is divine.

Asking forgiveness is neither the one nor the other.

Maybe that's why people asked for less and less forgiveness, it was offered in diminishing quantities (or with the immediate, unreflective flippancy of all online communication) and was found on the shelves with less frequency, while the fabrication of unforgiveable—not at all the same thing—trolls was being ramped up, he thought while failing to fall asleep.

Between waking dreams and sleepless nightmares never to be reveal. Between insomnias that—according to Proust—are what help you "appreciate sleep": that thing the body uses to measure time and that, in turn, has and takes its own time, until it can evaluate the activity of "Time, the artist."

And back to him came the pseudo-structure, the voice of the conscience, the unborn ghost, of that book in three books.

And those three books in one book. A book of his that in turn would contain other books of others and lives and works of illustrious rewriters of their own lives and bodies of work like Francis Scott Fitzgerald and William S. Burroughs and Bob Dylan and Marcel Proust and Emily Brontë and Vladimir Nabokov and . . .

And all of that was so much easier to move around inside the library of his mind and his memory than here outside on this side of things.

And so, he fantasized about putting it all there inside: about leaving nothing roaming free or yet to be corralled (at most a brief farewell-coda volume like the last novella Cheever wrote that was ideal for a short trip: a pure and quasi-heavenly happening with nothing of the hell side of the theory) and then riding off into the sunset. With his debt paid, having justified himself and done himself justice. Behind him only the murmurs of the fainthearted who would never forgive him for "having left," as if to be a writer from a particular place obliged you to reside and live there as part of "the local scene." (Once, IKEA had offered him a short, unsolicited lecture about how "it's so important not to cut ties with the place you are in and with the present, man. All your mentors and the writers you most admire are dead and aren't doing you any good when, really, you should be praising people who might still do you a favor in exchange for you referring to them as your maestros . . . And you never go back to where you came from. Big mistake. You've got to go back now and then, you've got to tell people how you can only think about that place from a distance, you've got to repeat over and over how much you miss certain streets and scents and sunsets and words. You know: that's all it takes and they'll all be happy and they'll be giving you national prizes before you know it, man." And he pronounced the word "man" with an odd emphasis and accent, as if sucking down an oyster, as if making his voice higher to sound younger, more young-Latin-American writer, tastier, *más sabrosito*. And he savored the word "prize" as if it were his favorite dish to be eaten again and again, *con mucho chile y salsa*.)

And not satisfied with that, having practiced his Nobel acceptance speech in front of the bathroom mirror so many times (the Nobel speech imagined in privacy was for writers the equivalent of those absurd and invisible air guitar solos for so many teenagers), he'd gone as far as composing and decomposing the critiques and reviews his creature would receive. Reviews he liked to describe as "Watson Reviews": the kind that, with intelligence and perceptivity, manage to explain Sherlock Holmes with a clarity and accuracy that the selfsame detective of detectives would never have been able to deploy to deduce himself. And he had to admit that, every so often, he'd gotten a review like that, penned by names who seemed to have understood him in depth and in form. But they were few and far between and, to tell the truth, nobody wrote like that about people who wrote anymore. Now, that kind of review was almost impossible—he wasn't the only one and they weren't like that only with and for him—because now reviews were little more than opinions with a rating or a certain number of tiny stars beneath a title.

Reviews that, of course, had little or nothing to do with the ones he'd gotten, deservedly or not, back when he was first starting out, in his now nonexistent country of origin. Or in his now adopted ghost land where—for all the wrong reasons—he'd even experienced a moribund revival related to his last book, *The Impossible Story*, for pretty sad, but, in a way, hilarious motivations (the kind of situation that never occurred to anyone, because it was the kind of situation that only occurred to him and for him).

Yes, the critics who were his contemporaries (many of them also writers and/or professors who'd fought against him with a combination of disdain and rage, over what'd happened to him and what he'd achieved with his lucky first book, *National Industry*) had been replaced by a new generation of critics who didn't have that problem. They were young and had none of that jealousy or resentment, because—they thought, they believed—there was still time for what happened to him to happen to them. And, moreover, they had so many writers their own age to hate . . . And so, the evaluations/devaluations of his work had gone down—above all in the cultural supplements of his now nonexistent country of origin—a road that started out with a "I don't like it" (because they defined themselves not by what they liked but by what they disliked and what, suddenly, they found so useful in that sense); followed by a "I'm not interested in it" and a "I don't care about it"; ending up with a "I don't remember it" only to, all of a sudden, offer a "Honestly it's not bad after all." (Whereas his MO was different and, he thought, better and more elegant: when thrown/asked about a name that he didn't . . .uh . . . care for, he opted to seal himself in the most hermetic of silences, he said nothing, transferring the responsibility of drawing conclusions and interpreting that emptiness full of possibilities to the person who'd asked. And everybody happy . . .)

The engagements with his work that he imagined, on the other hand, weren't obviously laudatory; but they seemed contaminated by both the good and the bad of what he did. As if the critics he invented for himself were intoxicated on and by his "same old" style, which, for good or ill, was so "instantly identifiable" and "chronically digressive." Disarticulated articles that ran the gamut from the easy and payment-free cult worship of his followers (who sometimes sent him amazing letters that said things like "I've rarely found a writer I admire so much still living. I write letters to the dead ones too, but they don't respond"; or who, even, recognized him and let him jump ahead of them in lines at big-box stores or movie theaters, a far superior gesture to that of being asked for an autograph, he thought; and, ah, he couldn't help shuddering whenever someone, glowingly, referred to him as a "cult" writer; because cultists end up occulting; because he remembered those lines from Saul Bellow's *More Die of Heartbreak* about how being a cult object was neither difficult to achieve nor something to feel that proud of; and that if you were worshipped by cultists, it was good to be fully cognizant of the fairly irrational nature of all cults and of how they usually come to an end to make room for the next cult) to the views of writers more than ready to be guinea pigs in the testing of new medications or to be launched into deep space—having tired of participating in documentaries on absurd subjects they knew next to nothing about or, even worse, on other writers, knowing that nothing would please them more than to talk (with disinterest but feeling oh so interesting) about what happened to them, which, really, was the same thing that'd stopped happening to them—to the absolute incomprehension of the majority of "serious" critics.

Oh, those reviewers had always been poorly paid, but, though it seemed mathematically impossible, they were more poorly remunerated all the time (among them, again, that writer from his now nonexistent country of origin, who he ran into every so often in bookstores, the friend of Vila-Matas, who seemed to have a suspicious talent for discovering a great new foreign writer every week—always made in the USA or the UK, never any of his compatriots or writers of the same language—with a kind of evangelical frenzy, as if he were howling out the recommendations he uploaded to his weekly column, and where did that guy's almost-desperate enthusiasm come from, why did he read so much, what was the name/brand of the psycho-stimulating pills or hypnotics that he swallowed with his breakfast?). Reviewers who—since the implosion of journalistic media, coinciding with those sporadic but increasingly lengthy and frequent economic crises—resignedly put up with martyrizing delays of up to three months to get paid and with the humiliation of transferring the rights to their work for fifty or eighty years postmortem or "in any other country or jurisdiction that may be formed in the future or for a term of extended validity in accordance with any new regulation subsequent to the signing of this contract" and all other kinds of madness only possible because the whole profession had gone mad. And, in case all that wasn't enough, the reviewers were reviewed themselves (generally amid virtual and not virtuo-sic mockery) by online reviewers. Reviewers with ever fewer characters and lines assigned to them and ever fewer digits on their invoices. And—totally spent—not even slightly interested in the kind of writer who, when you read him, showed you not just how he wrote but, also, how to read him; and yet still so predisposed to feeling that they were intrepid cultural defenders par excellence always ready to "discover" what was already in plain sight. Slippery cabals that, every so often, came to an agreement—of a more than dubious consensus (and always taking everything out of context, as if the material to be measured were pure present, beginning and ending in itself, with no past and ready to be forgotten just a few months later)—to spotlight and elevate, with a combination of hysteria and solemnity, a particular book onto the altars.

Without going any further, just recently, there'd been, with all of them kneeling at its feet, one of those excessively ornate central European novel-istic cathedrals, lauded with prayers and supplications, all seemingly cribbed from one another, like the most inevitable and inertially dominant domino effect, combined with that old habit of copying the work of the classmate at the next desk.

Or the postmortem consecration of that crazy Iowa farmer who'd left behind a thousand-page manuscript about his postmodern tractor that tore off one of his legs in an accident during spring planting, as the sun dipped slowly below the horizon, with no capital letters or punctuation of any kind.

Or a stint of militancy alongside some combative writer with a name like Krakatoa Chibcha Cheguevara-Smith.

Or the celebration with acclaimed scandal of the calculatedly transgres-sive diatribes of a Frenchman with the look of a *clochard* freshly clobbered by a bus that, not fully satisfied, backed up to run over his body again.

Or almost adolescently fainting at the feet of a Nordic giant who suf-fered the little that he'd gone through so deeply, exploring his existential inertia across thousands of pages, narrating absolutely every detail of all that nothing.

Or—at most and in last place, with something that that he saw as an infe-riority complex with respect to everything that came from the North and the West and a superiority complex with respect to everything that came from south of the Rio Grande—giving the intermittent and sporadic welcome to almost touristic and emigrant and colorful Latin American swallows. To those authors who, every so often, gathered—on the waterfront of the city he was now leaving behind forever—for a group/generational photo, at the feet of the statue of the "discoverer" of their lands (a statue that pointed out toward the horizon in the wrong direction) and asked themselves again about the hope that'd brought them to those shores (and whom, once that brief initial enthusiasm passed, they ignored until further notice; the whole rite recalling the grace and disgrace of that moment in *City Lights* when Charles Chaplin was lavished by a millionaire drunk every night only to be unceremoniously kicked out of that stately mansion the next morning). To those novels with lots of tits and ass and a picaresque hero of a kind not found on that peninsula of the ailing Old World, functioning like Viagra for tourists in lands both exotic and permissive for powerful monied visitors. And then to completely ignore them once they reached that little climax (which might even include the inexplicably coveted appearance on that TV show about literature to which, in all these years and after all those books, he'd never once been invited and whose host—a man who reminded him so much of the *nowhere man* Jeremy Hillary Boob in *Yellow Submarine*, banging away at his typewriter—pirouetted and blabbed around abandoned factories used as a set for discussing the latest young-adult dystopia). And on like that until the next swing of the bipolar pendulum of their shared—reluctantly and out of historical obligation—language. In general, he thought, this kingdom seemed to treat and take revenge against its one-time colonies in the same way that—between indifferent and scornful—the rest of the surrounding kingdoms treated it. (It was also true that there wasn't all that much interest from the other side when it came to what was written in the Old World in the same language, beyond the forced awareness that it was well worth it to pay attention to those who now had the power and the publishing houses and the contracts to be signed and the well-funded prizes and the almost always irrecuperable advances and who, moreover, paid for multiple rounds of drinks at steamy festivals and tropical book fairs.)

And on like that again until—once for, for the decades of the decades, amen—they got together again. All of them together, on both shores, howling beneath a circus tent, overrun with circus freaks, a "Gabba hey! We accept you! We accept you! One of Us! One of Us" transformed into "Gabo Hey!"

And on like that until they agreed almost telepathically on end-of-year lists, highlighting new books by wizened old heroes, who couldn't be dispensed with because they were indispensable, so that they could, then, go back to all their typical pursuits and flavors of the day and of the month and of the year and of the decades: the Civil War and the Transition, the City and the Country, Independence and Autonomy, the Realist Novel and Novelized Reality.

All that future material to be calibrated by those same critics who, with a complete lack of shame, opted to look the other way or cross over to the other side of the street when they saw him coming, in person or in writing (because everything that, once in a great while, they praised about the new tropics or the ancient empires was even more strictly rationed out when it came to anything imported from the south of the Americas and especially when it came to someone like him, who'd been cursed in his now nonexistent country of origin). Critics who—when it came to the species he belonged to—remembered to award a deathbed prize, quickly and just before the award became posthumous; then they felt they had the right and authority to be guests at the congressional funeral rites, because they'd contributed in some way and were offering a kind of spark to set that Viking ship ablaze. Critics who even confessed in writing their inability to process his work ("I don't get it," one of them had admitted; and he couldn't help but take that inability as the kind of definitive praise that tends to be heaped on books that were different and that make an impression and, after all, critics had said the same thing about *Moby-Dick* and about *Ulysses*, right? Which, at the same time, didn't stop him from imagining spitting on that individual from every possible angle and altitude, while simultaneously screaming at him "Am I making clear what I think of you? Do you get it or do you need a more detailed explanation? Do you get *this*?"). Critics like spiritualists: few were those who didn't lie and many were those who only said what people wanted to hear and read.

And so, when it came time for his periodical evaluation—his check-up that was more and more a check-out, with each book he published—they all went swinging psychotically to and fro, for a few meager, stammering lines, between cautious condemnation and dubious fascination. Striking him first to stroke him later while begging his forgiveness or, even, going so far as to point to him as the "exalted" evangelist of a "theology" where literature was everything and there was no room for anything or anyone else. And, in that, he (someone who'd given up everything and everyone in the name of reading and writing) was in full agreement.

He wasn't all that concerned with the hypothetical *No Future* and the already proven *No Present* of literature but with its *Yes Past*.

And, of course, *The Impossible Story* had been the drop not that topped off the glass but that broke the dam.

The Impossible Story had been somewhere between a howl of fury and a cry for help. The novel of a castaway on a sinking island with no palm tree, surrounded by an ocean full not of swimming sirens but of floating alarms. A compass-less map where everyone thought they were the treasure and wrote all about it, but no longer felt any need to read anything, because there was no time for that anymore, because they were too busy writing about themselves in hopes of getting found and discovered. A world in which everyone thought they were writers without first passing through literature; as if anyone who wanted to could go into an operating room and roll up their sleeves and perform an open-heart operation, based on what they'd once seen in a movie, in one of those medical thrillers, or on some episode of that series with the messianic and insufferable yet somehow sympathetic doctor. A landscape in which, mysteriously and not so mysteriously, the people who already had everything also needed, as the ultimate and definitive trophy, to have a book. To be the authors of it or to have it written for them. It wasn't really important how it came about. What was important was to have that primitive yet perfectly functional object and for it to have their names on the cover and for it to have them as protagonists.

And so, everything had been filled up with imposters and posters, ready to pay whatever it took to, also and in addition, be writers. To have a book, to be in a book, to be a book, aware of the fact that the expression/praise was still "That man is an open book" and not yet "That man is a turned-on tablet."

A book is a book is a book, indeed.

And he was a book; but he was a closed book.

And so he went around—around ever less festive, cut-rate festivals—making comments like "Don't you find it revealing that one of the most-famous magicians of his time and the best-paid magician of all time, given name David Seth Kotkin, didn't opt for a stage name like Xander The Uncontainable, but for David Copperfield? Get it? Could it be that you cannot see and marvel at the irrefutable fact that fiction is the great escape that'll always bring you back home? Fiction as that place where—presto and abracadabra—now you don't see you and now you see you somewhere else, everywhere else, without moving? And all thanks to books that open like doors, like an Open Sesame, so you can enter the cave of immeasurable treasures. And, sure, the idiot Kotkin said he'd chosen that alias no more and no less 'because I liked how the name sounded,' and yet . . . All of this to say that I know your tricks, that I can see with perfect clarity the double backs of your boxes and the threads and wires on which your false calling hinges and from which it hangs. You're not magicians, no. At best, you're nothing but volunteers from the audience to be cut in half or to disappear and never come back."

And—magic!—they read and wrote online with no control or filter, as if they were graffiti-artists working from a distance, but chewing on shoes and pissing and shitting on every lap. On the Inter*net* they were all venomous tarantulas. And they defended the right for nobody to have any secrets and for every private thing to be public.

On blogs and in tweets, they all suffered from Tourette's Syndrome. And they screamed in all caps riddled with orthographical errors. And they opined about everything they neither knew nor understood. And they condemned each other to hell as if they were diabolical, all powerful emperors. And they talked shit and were shit-talked and talked shit about being shit-talked. And they thought that that place was reality without realizing that it was, really, the most irreal place of all. And they were convinced that their pronouncements had some kind of authority, just because they were gratuitously—gratweetiously—accepted by a cybernetic algorithm specially designed to extract their preferences and then sell that data to multinationals that would design products especially desirable to their ever so unsophisticated minds. And there was something pathologically fascinating in the mechanics of the whole process: somebody posted a quote of somebody else, and suddenly everyone started howling at those words, convinced that their author was listening and paying attention to them, not wanting to think that everything was proceeding just as it had before, that none of them even existed for that individual at whom they were snapping and sticking out their tongues and baring their fangs to attract his or her attention. And there the hyenas laughed and the dogs barked into that overpopulated void, using fake names or aliases, accompanied by little circular pictures of the faces of Orson Welles or Hypatia of Alexandria or Jimi Hendrix or Carson McCullers, always the faces of people who were far more talented than they were and with far more memorable faces than their own, even for them. And they no longer felt the need to psychoanalyze themselves, (paying) to unload all their highlights and low-darks in private, preferring to proffer (free) psychotic stupidities like "I brought him luck because I insulted him a few days ago in a tweet." And then making excuses for their rants with that sputtering political catchphrase—"They quoted me out of context"—without realizing that the context was the Internet itself. And, oh, wasn't it a little odd that people—given the opportunity to be other people online—always opted to be worse people than they already were? And that, at the same time, they were all so hypersensitive and ever-ready to be offended or, if not offended on behalf of themselves, to get offended on behalf of someone who would or should feel offended? And that the comfort of their childhoods made it so the people his generation, by comparison, were almost kind of Dickensian? And that they were always ready to accuse and condemn and talk shit and call for justice that, apparently, was up to them to administer? And wouldn't it be nice that every time they talked shit/defamed/insulted/lied online they would have to pay a not-too-high fine in order to, in that way, suddenly demonstrate how you could clean up the environmental contamination and lower the rate of virulent contagion via those asphyxiating networks? Wouldn't it be great to scientifically prove that—like what people thought about photographs—every time you posted a tweet you lost a fraction of your suffering soul?

And so they came back without ever having left, all of them convinced they were *followed* the world over. And they reminded him so much of those sovereigns of next-to-nothing, on their little planets where there was barely even enough space for them, floating through the void and the illustrated pages of *Le petit prince*. And, of course, any reference to his work (to that inevitable "again, more of the same") included the inevitable and increasing particle of "better known as the brother of . . ."

But now, not so much.

Now, not even that.

And his profession didn't allow—unlike that of rockers and songwriters who could kill their uncreative time while making easy money revisiting their own work in those acoustic or symphonic horrors or in duets or, even, going out to rob the venerable tombs of others and sacred uncorrupted bodies in the Standard Cover Cemetery—you to rewrite your own books, changing the protagonists' genders or cutting out metaphors or adding lots of footnotes and comments. Or maybe it did, but he'd preferred not to notice.

In any case—he had to admit it, he'd admitted it ever since his first obligatory reading in his role as executor—Penelope's books were so much better than most interplanetary bestsellers. And he felt something a lot like pride every time his sister's books appeared to drop down the bestseller lists whenever one of those phenomena as frequent as they were ephemeral shot up.

Things like the "self-help memoir" of a Mexican drug trafficker—who'd been imprisoned in Russia and had become a three-star Michelin chef cooking in prison—titled *Archipelago Gluttony.*

Or that YA and sci-fi saga, *The Invaded,* in which the evolved pacifist aliens who'd conquered Earth realized what a bad deal they'd made in taking over and trying to improve our species, suddenly happy to be taken care of and to no longer have to do anything for ourselves (a plot that was a plagiarism/homage, he thought, of/to the old sci-fi pulp novels of Isaac Goldman that he and Penelope and their childhood friend—Tomás?, Tommy?, Tom?, the one he wasn't sure actually existed or if he'd invented him, the one who'd eventually became a composer of newscast soundtracks and of sonic-pastiche imitations for documentaries about The Beatles and David Bowie and Bob Dylan and Pink Floyd and The Kinks that lacked the production budget necessary to include the artists' original songs—had devoured years ago. And that now were all the rage thanks to some TV adaptation, until the next new thing came along, here it comes, there it goes).

Or the latest hit of new journalism tackling, for example, the comings and goings of a girl who, yes, was always *that* same girl at all the rock concerts—from Melbourne to Murmansk—filmed and appearing in multiple rockumentaries on the shoulders of a boyfriend who was always a *different* boyfriend.

Or that supposedly vile gore novel called *Fresh Flash Flesh!*, featuring anorexic but cannibalistic models whose only nourishment came from nibbling on the bones of their colleagues, because "the flesh of emaciated models doesn't make you fat."

Or some new alternative self-help system/program with mystical recipes for a material world. The latest incarnation in that vein was called *The Neptune Sublimation* and it proposed recovering the gills of "man's immemorial oceanic and submarine past." And it'd caused a disturbing rise in the number of drownings at beaches and in bathtubs the world over. And had sold millions among those who were convinced that dolphins were smarter than human beings and who, apparently, never saw a single episode of *Flipper* during their childhoods and never put up with that cetacean doing nothing but laughing with that insufferable laugh like that of a senile old man (not to mention the fact that Flipper couldn't have been all that bright, because he "acted" for free).

Or some Nordic detective novel with a title like *The Girl Who Failed to Understand the Instruction Manuals for Assembling Absurdly Named Furniture*, in which everyone's grandfather had been a Nazi back in the day and was still a Nazi in his free time.

Or all those quick-dissolving hip-cult codewords trumpeted by bleeding-hearted book-loving girls, wounded but never dying and always on the warpath (their writings always enumerating multiple self-mutilations and attempted gender suicides) pilgrimaging from sanctuaries erected to the broken verses of Sappho, passing through the mausoleums of Jean Rhys and Clarice Lispector and Leonora Carrington and Sylvia Plath and Alejandra Pizarnik, until they arrived to those witchy stories and that *no girls allowed* club in the mouth and thought-bubbles of Little Lulu as an alternative to the nymphet Dolores Haze. An explosive and depressing combination that convinced many of them that they could do that *too* (and it always surprised him that they hadn't yet "discovered" the martyr Joan Vollmer; though maybe she didn't interest them, because she hadn't left behind a full body of work but an empty hole, the one in her head; because really her work had been that of jumpstarting the work of William S. Burroughs and his irrealities; because she'd been more of an accessory to and collateral of the work of another: that bullet entering Vollmer's head—that orifice like a keyhole—had been Burroughs's starting shot). And so they wrapped themselves in those really hip T-shirts with the self-portraited face of the Mary Poppins voyeur and compulsive photographer Vivian Maier or, even, of unattenuated psychopathic mediocrities like Valerie Solanas getting raised up onto the altars of victims of machismo, because, oh, how they loved those (the most important thing was the bizarre life above and beyond the more or less freak body of work) stories of sudden success, built on word of mouth and key of keyboard. (And their boyfriends, in general, thought that Banksy or some other clever dude was the most revolutionary thing that had happened in recent times that were, of course, the primary and only times in which they generally didn't perceive, or did so only ever so slightly, anything prior to the year of their births all the way back to the paintings on the walls of the caves of Altamira.) And how did they fail to realize, he wondered, that the very few authentic cases with any true talent in that sense and format and story—but who rarely achieved the status of genius—had a single and almost constant Mephistophelian clause: almost none of their goddesses had known fame while alive or, if they had, they'd been acutely unhappy or seriously ill or . . . And so, they turned themselves—to see if maybe that would do the trick—into false and professional specters. Into pale weirdos and hieratic serial producers of fictions with a perverse air, but an air that never caught a fever or sent a shiver. And that read like the kind of thing Roman Polanski might come up with—and discard—over breakfast.

Anyway, these were thoughts that he stopped thinking almost immediately.

Because—beyond any singular perversion or sweeping trend—Penelope's thing went back on the attack.

And it took everything by storm—it took everything by storm, again, when his own work was already considered dated and past its prime—with all its ephemeral passion.

And Penelope reconquered first place with her neogothic deliriums and her heartbroken and invincible-brained damsels, supported by young readers not ready to die for her (because she was already dead), but more than ready to languish in her memory for all the eternity of their youths. Reading her books over and over. In a closed-circuit loop. Never moving on from her to other books by other authors (with the inevitable exception of *Wuthering Heights*), but returning to her. Penelope as Alpha and Omega and Genesis and Apocalypse. Penelope as Literature and Fiction and an inseparable part of their stories and realities.

Only once in a great while did a writer appear with such a capacity to possess his or her readers and almost turn them into characters in his or her body of work.

And only once in a great while—such was the case with Penelope—did a writer appear who would never disappear.

And, only once in a great while, could anyone, in hospital waiting rooms or at airport gates, be spotted still holding his debut—once a bestseller in his now nonexistent country of origin—novel: *National Industry*. An anomaly at the time that, in turn, turned him into an anomaly: his name like a disturbance to ignore in the literary system; because in its day, *National Industry* upset people, it was inopportune and startling, contradicting too many good theories with its, for many, bad practices. (And he wasn't paying attention, because you never pay attention to the words of pilots over the loudspeakers and in your headphones; and is it just his imagination or did this one just announce that "This is my last transmission from the planet of the monsters . . . The anomalies we believed overcome will recur again before long . . . Please, keep your seatbelts tightly fastened"?) And is it possible that the pilot has used the word "anomaly" in a very different context than he was using it? And—to distract himself from the turbulence now shaking everything—he thinks that, if he'd had a daughter, it wouldn't have been bad to name her Anomalía. A name that was so much better than Dolores or Esperanza or Angustias or Mercedes or Milagros or Soledad or Remedios with which irresponsible parents flagellate newborns until their deaths. A name that, on the other hand, in its ambiguity, worked just as well for raving lunatics as it did for drop-dead beauties or peerless geniuses.

He'd remembered then that Serge Gainsbourg line about how fidelity was better than beauty because fidelity lasted forever. And no: it's not that he considered *National Industry* an ugly thing; but he did consider it something that would always be a part of his biography. The specimen to be mentioned in summaries of his work and life alongside his parents and his sister ("One is irresistibly tempted to compare the strange longings and nauseous qualms that enter into the complicated ecstasies accompanying the making of a young writer's first book with childbearing," he reads on one of the pages of *Ada, or Ardor* as the fire reads it simultaneously). *National Industry* was irrefutable proof that *book* readers were ever more abundant than *author* readers: enthusiasm and interest and attention lasted and were valued only for a single title that everyone read no matter who was responsible for it. And in general, there was no point in proceeding to read that writer's previous or subsequent books (he, on the other hand, belonged to what appeared to now be an extinct species of reader and he'd always followed the trail of a life to the bottom and beginning and end of its work).

National Industry was also—with perspective—the uncomfortable reason why he never unquestioningly embraced the comfortable category of completely and absolutely unlucky. His triumphant past enhanced his present defeat. His early and glorious idiot savant—for many, thinking about him at that time, it wasn't a coincidence that the *idiot* came before the *savant*—impact had automatically conferred on him the label/category of "lucky." Especially when it came to his profession and, even more especially, when it came to a first book. And so, now, so many failures later, he wasn't even granted the victory of feeling like a total loser who might be worth rediscovering. He'd only managed to access the ambiguous and vague category of someone neither lucky nor unlucky: someone, complexly and simply, unlucky but with something like "Wild Thing" or an "American Pie" or a "My Sharona" or a "The Future Is So Bright I Have to Wear Shades" that he could always fall back on when it was time for the encore.

And the thing is that *National Industry* had stayed more or less alive, in suspended animation, with successive re-editions. Periodic comebacks that relaunched it as historical artifact with which, now, he had the inevitable love-hate relationship one tended to have with one's first hates and loves.

National Industry called out to him over and over, like Hamlet Sr.'s ghost to Hamlet Jr. saying "remember me" (and suddenly he remembered that the first translation of *Hamlet* into Spanish had been titled *El Hamleto* and, yes, those were the bad shores where he'd washed up, and it was by their direct descendants that he was now judged as "incomprehensible"), but, in his case, it wasn't that his first book was calling for revenge against everyone else but for justice for itself, a desire to do itself justice: *National Industry* was, really, not a murdered father but a firstborn and eldest son who refused to move out of the house where he was born and asked to be maintained in perpetuity and revisited over and over again, above and beyond all the siblings that came later. Siblings it despised and reproached for having stripped away the privilege of being the most-beloved only child. Thus *National Industry*, instead of holding up an empty skull, held up a full brain, full as only a first book can be, a first book that contained everything he'd thought about during so many years of thinking only about a first book and never a second or a third.

And the truth is that—with perspective—he'd gotten to the point of telling himself that it wouldn't have been bad to retire right there, to have ceased to be back then and almost at the beginning. *So long, farewell, auf wiedersehen, adieu,* saying goodbye to the grownups and going straight to bed after *National Industry*. One shot right in the bullseye and sufficient for the echo of its bang to reverberate forever. Like Grady Tripp had done with *The Arsonist's Daughter* or Antoine Doinel with *Les salads de l'amour* or Robert Sparrow with *The Philosophy of Time Travel* or Jep Gambardella with *L'apparato umano* or, of course (he wasn't going to argue with Penelope's ghost about the fact that her favorite author hadn't written more due to extenuating circumstances like death), Emily Brontë with *Wuthering Heights*.

Living off others continuing to hear that echo and, in every case, passing the years sketching the dreams of a second interminable magnum opus, offering up to those awaiting it only the most mysterious of smiles. Far better that, he thinks, than continuing to write and publish only to be, once again, like one of those perpetually debuting and previously invoked *one-hit wonders* of pop music: recognized until the end of time for just that one song with no attention paid to anything that came after (even if what they'd done later was far more interesting than that one goddamned catchy single that turned out to be inescapable and that they kept in reserve for the end of the show to sing through gritted teeth and choking back tears).

But no, he kept writing.

And he wrote different things.

Like his second book, *Sacred Memories*, which seemed to have been written almost in opposition to *National Industry*. So different and, also, so happily misunderstood and delivering recitations of the lives of mad saints and of the secret twin of Jesus Christ, with background music performed by the pianist Glenn Gould and, yes, praised be the clouds of cocaine atop which he wrote it like one possessed.

But, also, he had to acknowledge something about his debut: when he periodically looked back through it, maybe because it'd been written on a typewriter, the lines of *National Industry* had something immovable about them, a feeling that there was nothing to correct, that they were all precisely as they should be. (He remembers the strange and unpublished emotion that he'd felt, being an unpublished writer, every time that, in a movie, the protagonist-writer sat down and, like a machine, started typing unceasingly and at a breakneck speed—the way only actors acting like writers wrote—because something had occurred, because something had occurred to them. He remembers his first typewriter, back in the days when there weren't yet personal computers: a heavy Remington that was painted an almost hot-rod-mechanic pink and that, at the end of every day, he draped a cover over, the way you cover the cage of a parrot that repeats whatever you tell it or a ventriloquist dummy that you make say everything you don't dare say with your own voice. And at some point, desperate, he went so far as to wonder if the solution to the problem might not be in going back to writing on a typewriter like that one, like someone going through a process of reeducation: going back to the beginning, starting over, writing anew the way he once wrote. More slowly, but, also, more assuredly. Like, again, emerging from a deep coma that forced him, point by point, to learn everything all over again: to walk, to eat, to talk, to read, to write. But yes, he realized it almost right away: it was clear that computers had changed the way writing was done. And that, along the way, that golden moment of reflection had been lost. That instant

when you paused to calibrate what had occurred to you in the middle
of your brain before making it occur with the tips of your fingers and
the help of a machine seemingly as simple as it was indestructible.
So different from all those devices that suddenly appeared and took
desks by storm, but that, even in victory, broke down so easily or
lost documents without warning or had software that quickly became
dated and useless. Or, even worse, that self-destructed due to so-called
"planned obsolescence"—maybe to make them more like human
beings and their inescapable termination of service date—baked in by
their own creators, as if said creator were God, to thereby force people
to buy the new model, which they had to learn to operate and to love
and to take care of and to suffer every time it fell ill again. And, oh,
once upon a time an unplugged Olivetti could wind up accompanying
a writer—with minimal service once in a great while—throughout
his or her entire career with that *clackety-clack* that made you feel
as if you were floating and that reminded him of the *tap-tap-tap* of
Fred Astaire dancing across walls and rooftops. Now, the fear of the
white page was nothing compared to the panic of the black screen
and of all those horrible things that could happen because of exotic
viruses and various bugs that ended with you trashing the hard
drive. In exchange for all that fear—like one of those agreements
in fine print—it offered the palpable and typeable illusion of feeling
like a "real" writer, facing that clean and "finished" screen, as if it
were already the page of a printed book. An illusion that, to be believable, only required a wall in which there were a couple holes, like a
vampiric bitemark on the neck, where you could plug in the fangs
of a more or less portable word processor. Though for him, reading
on screens had always reminded him of the impossibility of painting with watercolors in the rain. But, yes, people used to think more
before putting something in writing, because it wasn't so simple—and
because it was far more tiring—if you had to type it all over again.
The arrival of all this exceedingly futuristic convenience—on the
other hand, one hand washes the other—had done away with pens for
crossing out and liquids for retouching and pages to be stored away.
Everything could be thrown up right in front of you, like a voracious

vomiting, without precaution or care, and worked over in the act of being written. The sentences in *National Industry*, on the other hand, were like prayers that didn't allow for any modifications. There was something about them that could neither be found nor attained in his subsequent books: far more gaseous and liquid and open to being changed and irradiated with constant gusts of inserts and additions.)

And so, *National Industry* never stopped pestering and reproaching him at least until, years later, he published a voluminous book of stories interlinked by the idea of farewells and the Great Beyond—his opus number 5—titled *Lives of the Dead*. After that, it was as if National Industry had, at that point, discovered that this younger but far more voluminous brother could give him one of those unforgettable beatings if he kept being so annoying and demanding.

And he wondered if any of his occasional fans could perceive the difference between *National Industry* and everything he produced thereafter: all of it far more electric, yes, but also far more electrocuted by its own excess, his fingers now in the outlet, anomalies of a different voltage but anomalies all the same and in the end and in the beginning and coming across the wire.

And thinking about all of this, he remembered something that he'd forgotten and that'd been said to him by that unforgettable anomaly of his romantic life—would he have married Ella?, would he have had a kid with Ella?, would Ella have loved him?—that was Ella.

Here and there and everywhere.

In beds and airplanes and deserts. Before and now and after. Ella's voice, which was the voice of the breathing of the universe. (And he remembered every word that came from Ella's encouraging mouth, all her beliefs unexpectedly childish for someone so wise. Ideas like, for example, if someone sent you the kind of postcard that can be bought anywhere, the sender invariably appeared half hidden but visible if you looked for him with a magnifying glass, in the picture on that postcard though you didn't see him at first glance, at the Coliseum or Big Ben or the Great Wall of China. And he, not satisfied with that, had even memorized all of her involuntary sounds: her physiological tics, her little coocoo sneezes, her pendulous snoring, and the grumbling of the gears of her stomach, sounding like the tensing of the springs of time. And, when Ella slept, he would even bring her fingertips to his ears so he could hear the secret songs—top ten greatest hits—and silent bells recorded in unrepeatable grooves of her fingerprints. And—when Ella was no longer there—he remembered Henry Miller's recipe for forgetting a woman: turn her into literature. And it was clear that Miller's recipe hadn't worked all that well for him and that he'd actually concocted more like its opposite. And so, since that time, Ella in all the pages of his different books. In Mexico, in Victorian London, in his now nonexistent country of origin, and even on another planet. Remembering her better all the time and even adding all those things that'd never happened, but that could have happened to his memories: variations, digressions, alternatives, anything that would make Ella endure longer in his memory. Was that love or was that something more, something beyond love, leaving love behind waving goodbye from the dock or platform? Was love just one of the many manifestations of the Darwinian survival of the fittest? The divine and unconditional love, the *agape* that an immortal god can feel for his mortal worshippers, the ἀγάπη? Was it something you put into your mouth whole and—more of Ella's sounds—made that unique and addictive and lovestruck sound that Pringles made when you chewed them; the same Pringles that the voice of that passenger had referred to on that airplane without knowing he was preaching the gospel according to Ella; the same Pringles whose characteristic shape was achieved thanks to a machine press developed by Gene Wolfe, an industrial engineer but also one of the greatest writers of science fiction and fantasy of all time, creator of the ancient and Roman mercenary Latro, who forgets everything when he falls asleep at night, but first puts it all in writing so he could read it the next morning, and of the torturer Severian, master of a perfect memory and of the sword named *Terminus Est*, and who was considered the Marcel Proust of the genre, with his always-memorious or oblivious characters, anticipating their futures and forgetting their pasts. One thing was certain: Ella was the girl who that one night fell into the swimming pool. Ella—after coming up from the depths—saying "down there, the sound of the outside world seems like it's been run through the lungs of a giant." And that "if it were possible to look down from above at all the swimming pools on the planet—the real ones and the fictitious ones, the ones that interest you, like those that belonged to Jay Gatsby and George Bailey and Ned Merrill—and to upload that data to a supercomputer, people would find that their shapes end up shaping first letters and then words and sentences and, finally, the secret novel of the world and, yes, I am its author." Ella, who'd explained to him what love was. For Ella, love was just "a language that you could only learn by listening but that everyone believed they spoke perfectly until, lost and disoriented in the foreign-ness of their feelings, they discovered that they lacked the key terms to accurately express themselves. And that they didn't want to have to go back, their baggage and money and heart stolen, understand-ing that they could try again, on another trip, but already accepting that they would never speak like native speakers. In any case, nobody was born speaking that language, but everyone died wishing they understood it." And, Ella continued, "I suppose that this is a little bit like what happens to you with your books: before writing them, you imagine them as perfect, but once they're read they tell you, don't feel bad, it's all okay, you did the best you could, right?" And then she'd proceeded to expound on the paradox that for something to be truly unforgettable first you had to try to forget it. And that it was much harder to forget than to remember. To forget, you had to dismantle the stage on which something had happened and convince yourself that none of it had been written and rehearsed and performed and condemned or praised by the public and the critics. To remember, on the other hand, was a selective task and it could be done in pieces and without worrying too much about significance and structure. Forget-ting is classic and meticulous while remembering is avant-garde and experimental. Remembering was free. Forgetting cost a great deal. And only then, after gesturing toward remembering some forgotten thing—like someone who dreams or invents something, correcting and improving and making it perfect—did that something assume its material condition that would withstand the passing of the years and distances, that would transcend time and space. "You almost drowned when you were a kid and you can't forget it. And you've spent an eternity rewriting and altering that moment, feeling that, for you, it was the beginning of all things. Whereas for me, forever afloat, there's nothing to do but to think about everything that never happened to me . . . As a girl, I was always intrigued by the way the irreal women of the royalty waved. Queens and princesses in distant lands, more distant than fairytale kingdoms. I saw them on satellite broadcasts. At baptisms and weddings and funerals. With that way of moving their hands, like dolls, as if in slow motion. They waved as if they were underwater. Like sirens and nymphs and sea monkeys doing sea monkey business, as if the television were an aquarium, I remember thinking. Then, as soon as I could, I didn't dive but let myself fall into the first swimming pool that came within my body's reach. Not because I wanted to be a princess, but because I wanted to be able to wave like that," Ella said, her words emerging, as if muffled, from the other side of a towel. One of those towels that in previous incarnations were kerchiefs, whose mission was to collect tears of laughter or pain or the uncertain tears of the always damp eyes of infants or old people. Towels that, when set aside, revealed one of those faces that made you wonder what it would look like—undrawn, freshened up, the same yet different, as if unmade to be remade—during the act of making love. Ella's face that, he knew, would never be entirely for him, his. And so he wanted it to stay there, fixed, forever, imprinted on that towel like one of those dubious holy relics, but this time, for once, true and irrefutable and worthy of worship; like the one in that Italian city where a writer thinking of another woman, his own Ella, began to compose the endeavor of his own death.)

He remembers that and he remembers Ella, on this airplane.

Sleepless.

Again.

Thinking about how little he liked flying and about how much he had liked writing scenes in airports and on airplanes.

In airports and on airplanes everything felt feeling and glowed as if enveloped in clouds. His airports at the so-called "golden hour" (that time when passengers wandered down their aisles, walking slowly and buying things they didn't need to the joy and pure profit of the airline) and his airplanes during the long gray hours when, again, they tried to sell the passenger anything they could.

Airplanes and airports were, for him, like the library in the detective story or the bunker in the post-atomic drama or the bedroom with cork-lined walls or that other planet where all the marvelous moments happened, as a kind of gift, to be seen all at the same time (locations and circumstances where it would've been so much wiser and simpler to confess right away or to breathe deeply and fill your asthmatic lungs with radiation or to empty them of oxygen).

His airports and airplanes, again, like Chekhov's gun: triggering locations where his characters, not pulling any punches, were unleashed to let loose even more and go down shooting and shot into the air.

His airports like—*very* bad joke—everything good the Wright brothers ever did devolving into something very *wrong*; because he wasn't afraid of flying but was afraid of airports.

His airports (those places where nobody was too disturbed to see someone crying like one possessed or running around like a lunatic or howling in tongues, at least until the explosive Muslims started detonating in-flight stalemates) like haunted houses and his airplanes like the ghosts that entered and exited them.

And him, obsessed, there inside (tray tables, objects and ideas in suspension, going up to come crashing down, three knocks, mouthless voices, and black boxes), had liked writing those parts so much. Describing the faces of passengers who paid close attention to the flight attendants' flight safety instructions or ignored them completely; but the ones and the others thinking about precisely *that*. And him thinking that they were the same passengers as always but always different though possible to classify according to stable constants. The ones who either say the phrase "You only have one mother" with relief or with regret; or the ones who, when installing doorbells on their front doors, either choose doorbells that can be heard outside when they're rung or doorbells that can only be heard inside the house and that make visitors wonder if they're actually working; or the ones who choose either to decorate their walls with paintings (or prints of masterpieces or posters) or with nothing but photographs of themselves and their relatives; the ones that can be divided into those who either pop bonbons without a second thought or those who take a little bite of them first to find out what's inside and, if they don't like it, set them aside, incomplete and unfinished.

And then he wonders whether those positions could be applied to attitudes for a hypothetical division between types of readers. Not like the one Nabokov came up with in his day (running the gamut from the banality of book-club members who needed to identify with the hero or heroine to readers who focus on the socioeconomic angle and prefer things like action and dialogue to the nobility of readers who had to have memory and a dictionary and "some artistic sense") but something more automatic: the ones who needed to have everything explained to them and the ones who preferred not to know *anything* before it happened.

And, of course, everything that occurred to him up there didn't amount to much but did take up a whole lot of space. A whole lot more space than was permitted, but he always found a way to sneak all of it in and bring it up there with him without the airline employees noticing. What he smuggled up there were, yes, the airborne parts of long novels where everything seemed to be up in the clouds and had nothing at all to do with those tiny flash fictions (flash fictions being the strawman that'd always struck him as the patrimony of brilliant fools like the contestants on reality shows who had to demonstrate everything they brought to the table in one minute and, often, it's not like what they brought to the table would last much longer than that anyway; and here a flash fiction occurs to him ready to not occur for him: "When the museum guard woke up, the dinosaur skeleton was still there"; and maybe lives are wide river-novels and obituaries, merely, weak streams that dry up after a couple of days, after a couple nautical miles like those and not aerial miles like these). Flying miles where he narrated absurd and ephemeral things for himself, like the space-time impossibility of having Glenn Miller's plane crash into Antoine de Saint-Exupéry's plane. All those parts that weren't very attractive anymore (they were more and more inconvenient and less and less gratifying), because modes of writing had degraded as much as modes of flying. The cheap tickets and the democratic capitulation of the skies. The heavy and indigestible light-diet airlines (something similar to what'd happened with computers and social media and blogs that convinced the masses they were professional writers and distinguished readers and qualified critics) transformed those once exclusive heavens into a hell, overpopulated with babies and old people and pets that in the past had been left on the ground, saying goodbye from the other side of glass doors, but who now accompanied their owners like additional prepaid carry-ons (and, oh, how he hated those moments in movies when dialogue and action between people was interrupted by the close-up of the family dog or cat tilting its heads and looking up at its master with a combination of shame and bewilderment and disgust). And it hadn't come into anyone's head—amid all the reboots and remakes—to send racing back down the runway that franchise that piled up ever more twinkling stars known as *Airport*, because nobody was scared anymore about the possibility of an accident during take-off or landing or midflight. Fear had assumed less special-effect-ridden forms (he also remembered "The Langoliers," that flying and kind of stupid novella by Stephen King; and did he really need to remember this *too*?) and now you had to endure interminable lines to get through security, never-explained delays, overpopulated airports and overbooked flights, bags lost never to be found (whose weight had to be calculated down to the milligram, to avoid paying demented fees, as if you'd broken some martial law), and it was always possible that some psychotic undercover onboard officer wouldn't like your beard and would beat you to a pulp in front of the rest of the passengers who, offering no help or protest, would just film the episode with their phones so they could express their indignation later online, alongside the exhibitionist exploits of artisanal assassins and speeding drivers and gang rapists and kids beating up other kids, so anxious to share their exploits they don't even stop to think that they might be seen and punished by the authorities.

And there was no longer any need for the anticipation of a catastrophe in which the airplane stopped flying and plunged in the most imprisoning and inescapable of free falls, because flying was, in itself, already a calamitous experience. And, oh, he still remembered how, in his childhood, flying was a magical and infrequent exception and as fantastical as the opportunity to make love standing up in one of those capsule-like bathrooms, places that, for him, never had the sexual appeal that many people say they feel and want to experience (for him, airplane bathrooms were always the sinister aerial adaptation of the Bates Motel shower in *Psycho*, a movie that he saw for the first time on television and whose ending—at the time, for him, unimaginable—had become, over the years, never more on the nose, The Mother of All Spoilers). And he remembered how, back then, travelers got dressed up to go process their passport (and combed their hair for the picture, because it was one of "the important" pictures, even though it always ended up looking like a grim and barely recognizable mini-portrait of Dorian Gray that they would try to look at as little as possible when checking to see if the expiration date had elapsed). And they were all so innocent and naïve that they even believed in that thing about nonsmoking seats and, oh, such long flights and only one movie, which was like Super-8 distracting you from the CinemaScope out the window (sometimes thunder and lightning and even the true fantasy of a demon walking on the wing). And back then you had to think so much and so carefully about what book (better something from the nineteenth century, with characters with their feet firmly on the ground) you would take with you high the skies, so that it could take you higher still and . . .

And yet, there they were, those parts free flowing and up in the air.

And he kept thinking about how he would write them if he were to write them: those parts that, for some time now, whenever he entered airplanes or airports, had given him the distinct sensation that he was being written with and within them.

In the very act of passing through check-ins.

Or of fastening his seatbelt.

Or of reading an article in one of those in-flight magazines like the ones he'd kept working for even after becoming a "published writer."

Or of starting to watch a movie you'd never dare watch on terra firma, excusing and distracting himself with thoughts like "Doesn't it seem perfectly implausible that the brothers who reinvented darkness were named Lumière?" And there, an inferior romantic comedy and/or action movie with a superhero tortured by his powers and differences who inevitably faces off against an interchangeable villain always obligated to proclaim that thing about how "I am the Destroyer of Worlds!" before being destroyed. (And he remembers himself as a kid and standing in front of one of those full-page panels in the comics of Stan Lee & Jack Kirby, thinking about whether all those intergalactic villains might not have studied together, at the same school where they had to go up in front of the class to repeat that same speech over and over.)

And a few times, like on this flight, discovering that on that screen on the seatback in front of him they were offering something that he needed to see even though he didn't know it consciously. Double feature, as he said before: *Blade Runner* and *Blade Runner 2049*, and more on that coming soon.

Meanwhile, he looks at that map as unrealistic as those anatomical diagrams where the different organs appear in different colors, clearly differentiated and separated by borders of humors and functions when, in reality, there inside, everything is mixed together and so exposed to what's on the outside. That map that charted the swift yet slow trajectory in the journey of his insomnia which he hadn't even managed to vanquish—unlike what'd been achieved and recommended in his day by Man Ray, photographer of Proust's eternal sleep—with the remedy of sleeping with a lead-loaded pistol under his pillow. Point-blank awake. Gaining hours and losing time. East to West. Thinking of this or that destination. Advancing in reverse. Now and there, him like the five-star platinum-top-max-VIP member of that exclusive club, at least as exclusive as that one where everyone got together to share figurative dreams: the club in which there's no longer anything to tell, beyond their expressionist and abstract lack of dreams (and it was clear that the success of the lack of clarity of the abstract is intrinsically connected to the time someone can pay attention to something they don't understand but would like so much to make some sense of).

There he is.

In the air.

On one of those false nights of flight. Flying nights that expand and contract depending on whether you're moving with or against the clock and when, as the hours pass, the airplane itself feels increasingly submarine. Envying those sleepers all around him who were like Proust's sleeping man—Proust again—who "holds in a circle around him the sequence of the hours, the order of the years and worlds" and who, upon opening his eyes and in a blink "consults them instinctively as he wakes and reads in a second the point on the earth he occupies, the time that has elapsed before his waking."

He could do it too.

Precise location and exact time.

But without the refreshing pause of sleep and all the time looking at that map there in front of him with that slow cursor/arrow signaling the advance and retreat of kilometers and marking how much time had passed since departure and how much was left before arrival. Dreaming while awake of the somewhat futuristic possibility of the induced sleep—the suspended animation—of all those cosmonauts, launched into the void for the long nights of light years dreaming about who knows what. (Because, for example, the *Apollo 11* mission had lasted—he typed it in and found it—195 hours, 18 minutes and 35 seconds. In other words: Armstrong and Collins and Aldrin—who during his childhood had coexisted with Curly and Larry and Moe—had to sleep up there. And to dream. Was there a record of their space dreams? Did they study that on space stations: weightless dreams or floating insomnias with a, yes, "space cadet glow"? In *2001: A Space Odyssey* it's noted in passing that astronauts don't dream. But he didn't buy it. Just the opposite. He thought that astronauts dreams *had* to be as *deep* as space itself. As deep as his were when he was five or six years old, an age when his dreams started to be reduced from spectacular Cinerama to diameters more appropriate for intimacy, though still in that little rocket-shaped bed and under those sheets printed with pure, day-less nebulas to be replaced a few years later by the sticky arabesques of his nocturnal emissions.) And he wondered how long it would be before airlines offered the service of resting in peace for the duration of the flight as precursor to future astral odysseys. Big pills for small but extended deaths in tourist class and business class and first class where the imagery and pleasure of the plot of what you dreamed would vary according to ticket price. (And he would pay to dream of Ella again, to dream of being with Ella, eating breakfast after a first night that kept repeating and improving. He and Ella talking about the way movies depicted dreams, almost always badly or unrealistically. And Ella telling him that, one night, Alfred Hitchcock woke up in the dark convinced that he'd come up with the best possible idea for a movie, the best story ever told and ready to be filmed. And that Hitchcock quickly wrote it down in a notebook and went back to sleep and the next morning, expectant, he'd read what he'd written there and all it said was *Boy meets Girl*. And then he'd thought that, yes, *Boy meets Girl* was the best possible story to tell. And he remembered a Girl and a Boy, a Young Man and a Young Woman, who once upon a time had reached out to him to ask if they could interview him on camera and tell his story and . . .) Though, of course, it could all go wrong and then there'd be crazed computers interrupting the maintenance of constant vital signs, the short-circuit and loop of an incessant nightmare and, oh, that paradox that'd he'd always found so disturbing: that one where every bitter nightmare yielded the sweetest of awakenings, when you realized that none of it was real and where the sweetest dreams—dreams that, according to Joseph Campbell, were the personalization of myths, myths that were public dreams, while dreams were private myths—were transformed into the bitter nightmare of opening your eyes and realizing that none of those pleasures were real. Or the somewhat paranoid idea that bitter nightmares or sweet dreams were nothing but the random and fragmentary pages with collage phrasing of the book that the unconscious reader was writing about the dreamer who once upon a time had been a writer but not anymore. And, hey, who could dare claim that dreams had no logic after spending a few minutes studying the supposed lucidity of waking life? (One of his recurring nightmares was that he started to write again, to write a lot; but that what he wrote weren't novels but—as a form of punishment for misbehaving in school, letter by letter and name by name, before that brief final scene/coda—the oceanic final credits and technical titles for big summer blockbusters. Another of his recurring nightmares was that he wrote a very short book, composed of brief paragraphs with big spaces between one and the next, three or four per page, like vengeful lashes across the back of an ex-lover whose real life would change forever, change for the worst, for being "the one from that auto-fictional novel," and that it was a big success and received ecstatic reviews and tons of celebratory tweets from his sisters of blood and fire; because his books had shrunken and because he'd sprouted tits and was a female poet and author of a book containing the verse *I contain multitudes*, but those multitudes were made up of her and only her, of replicas of herself. Another of his recurrent nightmares had to do with the existence of a book that would function with the mechanics of a dream but in reverse, like a dream of Mr. Trip: narrating a story in three phases that went from the deepest oneirism, unfolding in a world where everyone had lost the ability to dream—and, yes, *to dream* and *to remember* were the same thing in French, right?—and moved through a semi-unconscious fantasy featuring Penelope as protagonist, and culminated with the guilty insomnia and target in the night of a dark and timeless confession of the unconfessable.) Or to mistakenly be woken up too early, ninety years before reaching that distant planet, that planet of monsters, where somebody was broadcasting a final transmission enumerating dreams. A voice with the cadence of a midnight DJ where nights lasted centuries so that you heard "I dreamt Philip K. Dick was walking around the Civitavecchia Nuclear Station . . . I dreamt nobody died before their time . . . I dreamt that a storm of phantom numbers was the only thing left of human beings three billion years after Earth ceased to exist . . ."

Meanwhile, now and here he's still here and now. With little to dream and to tell upon waking. Just the crossing of an ocean and hours stretching out as long as days. Again, victim of another attack of that "radiant insomnia" Nabokov documented—in the pages of his diary, May 1974, after getting the help of a dose of Rohypnol, also known at the time as "the don't-forget-me drug"—when he was toying with the idea of a novel. And Nabokov wrote down in his diary dreams of the desperately messianic variety, the kind of immortal dreams of someone who knows himself to be increasingly mortal. Like this: "Dream: the solution of the supreme mystery which we learn after death is that the cosmos with all its galaxies is a blue drop in the hollow of my palm (thus deprived of all the terrors of infinity). Simple."

Years later, Nabokov would take notes for a very complex novel that—holding his breath—he'd barely started and would never finish, for reasons as decisive and "simple" as having ceased to breathe forever without first, convalescent in a hospital, his eyes full of tears, telling his son that a certain butterfly was already on the wing.

A novel that ran out of breath.

A novel disassembled in the typical notecards (him reading the photocopy of the reproduction of that notecard of that unfinished novel that he has with him along with a page from a magazine and that Posada print; that notecard with Nabokov's printed handwriting where he reads something that could well be the magic words of a disenchantment) and in capricious lists (random and capricious lists are the more or less secret language of people who can't sleep and for whom uniformly jumping sheep are of no use).

A novel whose plot wasn't entirely clear except that in the book someone was reading a book. And someone insisted on "the art of self-slaughter" and on "the process of dying by auto-dissolution . . . delicious dissolution!" a "purifying" suicide in slow motion resulting in the "greatest ecstasy known to man." Someone erasing himself appendage by appendage, starting with the nails embedded in his toes, as if he were melting in front of a mirror to later, maybe, with any luck, solidify again and be different and better.

A decomposed novel desperate to be composed in successive hospital beds (beds that, in his final years, Nabokov found himself going in and out of due to falls suffered chasing butterflies, to infections of the kind you only find and contract in the waiting rooms of doctors' offices, and, finally, to an incurable bronchitis caused by a nurse who left the window open on a cold night) as if in a "diurnal delirium."

A novel that—Nabokov said in one interview—he was reading aloud "to a small dream audience in a walled garden." An audience consisting "of peacocks, pigeons, my long dead parents, two cypresses, several young nurses crouching around, and a family doctor so old as to be almost invisible."

A novel "*without* an I, without a he, but with the narrator, *the gliding eye*, being implied throughout."

And, again, his eye hadn't been gliding for years.

His eye tripped and fell and now didn't even blink, flying above the oceanic night.

His He without ancient I, not erased but smudged and blurry and broken down into fragments, suspended in the oxygen-less air there outside. Suspended and in suspense and gone to pieces (but pieces that were unbreakable), on a final mission bound for a location known as Mount Karma in a place called Abracadabra, after stops in the dead Colma and the deceased Zzyzx and the departed Nothing: locations where he would feel as if he were eliminating deleting erasing crossing out canceling nullifying obliterating himself.

Until then and until now, on the inevitable occasions when he'd theorized about suicide, he'd always bet on a window. One of those windows that—say how you use them and they'll tell you what you're like—some people open to look at the sky and others to look down at the ground and to think about how if someone were to, if you were to . . . A window that always has two faces and two sides and, sometimes—on nights of ghosts and storms—faces looking in from the not incorrect but yes opposite side: a window with a view from outside looking in, a window looking from the past to the present.

A window in the greatest heights (he'd read somewhere that, all throughout time, windows were the consolation of fictions first person and that, maybe that's why, there were few things more primary and personal than sacrificing yourself after stepping out on a windowsill and jumping). It struck him as the right and most functional thing from a narrative perspective: precipitating like an event from a window down to your death after a whole life spent going in and out of doors (he'd always thought of the eyes of keyholes as even more private and particular viewfinders.)

A window in an airplane whose windows can be opened.

(He remembers, like that, the breaking news and later, not long thereafter, the story of that ghost airplane. An airplane that levitated more than it flew. An airplane on automatic pilot with the crew and the six passengers dead inside it, with no need to ascend into the heavens because they were already there, high the sky. The airplane—a private Learjet, with ten seats, headed from Lake Buena Vista in Florida to Dallas, Texas—had suffered some kind of depressurization. At more or less twenty-six minutes after takeoff, when they were flying over Gainesville, the pilots had stopped responding to the calls of air traffic controllers, and suddenly the airplane climbed to 45,000 feet, far above the altitude that big commercial airliners fly at and where one could only survive a few seconds because of the lack of oxygen. Then the jet changed direction sharply toward the northeast, and was immediately given an escort of six F-15 fighters: two were dispatched from the Tyndall base, two from the Eglin base, two from the Tulsa base; and he has all this information carefully written down in one of his many biji notebooks. The order was to shoot it down if

- 346 -

any surprising or dangerous behavior was observed. But no, nothing less surprising or inoffensive than a coffin with wings and ice on the inside of its windows, which that funeral procession of fighter jets accompanied—in its spectral voyage of four and a half hours over the states of Georgia, Alabama, Tennessee, Illinois, and Missouri, Iowa and Minnesota—until it ran out of fuel and crashed in South Dakota, in the agricultural region of Mina, to the west of Aberdeen. The TV had broadcast all of that live and direct and on the air: the mechanical exchanges of the military pilots, the lack of control of the air traffic controllers, the sepulchral silence in the cabin of the private jet, the angelic choir of demonic children in their schools singing "The Ballad of the Last Dead Plane." And for a few hours that anonymous King Learjet was as famous as *Flyer I*, as the *14-bis*, as the *Spirit of St. Louis*, as *Batwing*, as the *Enola Gay*, as *Air Force One*, as the *Spruce Goose*, as the oh so holy *Pope Plane*, as that airplane taking off from the Casablanca airport, as that other aircraft that arrives to an orbiting hotel dancing a circular waltz. And he'd been right there, in front of the screen, taking notes, thinking that someday, all of that might end up being useful to him, something he could use.) And now, opening that same notebook and looking for and finding those pages—where those names, models, altitudes, and places were specified—he understood that the only use they had was to help him remember better.

Before and back then, when he wrote all that down, he was still writing. And everything seemed to happen (everything had a barely secret meaning and a precise function, like in a puzzle with vaguely neuronal-shaped pieces whose design you came to recognize only as you got closer to putting it all together) so it could end up in one of those books of his where everything fit. Books that were vast and always contained more space. Books that were unfamiliar with the empty seat, but, also, with overbooking.

Now, not so much.

Now, not anymore.

Now, again, he is and remains an exwriter who once was a writer and before that a nextwriter and whose mind has suffered a pressurization problem. And now he's flying in suspended animation, out of inertia. Not dead but always thinking death couldn't be all the different from the place where he now floats and where the only thing that occurs to him is that nothing occurs to him anymore.

Now, never.

Now, never ever.

And yet he absolutely imagined himself—in the act of killing and crossing himself out and erasing himself (again that whole *efface expunge erase delete rub out wipe out obliterate*: that refusal to keep on playing and losing)—almost like the hero who sacrifices himself in an action movie, heading out to sea. Like Martin Eden, that sailor-writer from that book that'd made such an impression on him as a kid. The name that was also the title of that book by Jack London, his favorite among the adventurous writers of adventures from his childhood and who—it was clear—seemed to know much more and far better what his characters were talking about and writing about and experiencing. Far better and much more than was demonstrated by the books of Emilio Salgari and Jules Verne, who always seemed to be raving or over-imagining. And, in addition, *Martin Eden* told the story of something that he'd never read before. Another kind of adventure: that of someone who, having begun as an outside adventurer, decided to transform himself into an inside adventurer—into a writer. Someone who reread himself first to rewrite himself later. Someone who wrote while writing himself. Someone doing something so exciting and (he'd never liked underlining books, but it was when he read this one that he first picked up the habit of copying down quotes in a notebook, the eldest ancestor of his biji notebooks) where he read things like: "And then, in splendor and glory, came the great idea. He would write. He would be one of the eyes through which the world saw, one of the ears through which it heard, one of the hearts through which it felt"; or about how writing "was the conscious effort by which he freed his mind and made it ready for fresh material and problems. It was in a way akin to that common habit of men and women troubled by real or fancied griev-ances, who periodically and volubly break their long-suffering silence and 'have their say' till the last word is said."

Martin Eden—he knew right away—was a kind of autobiography in code of Jack London; but in no way was it fiction of the I. *Martin Eden* was a believable fiction and it went beyond where its author had ever been and even arrived to the suicide of its protagonist by drowning, contributing years later to the myth of Jack London's own suicide that never was. And so a novel rewriting the end of a life.

Martin Eden, a book he'd once received as a gift from Uncle Hey Walrus.

Martin Eden, a book that the always out-of-breath Pnin looks for and can't find for his son, because the bookstore employee knows nothing, has read little, and can only offer him another London—in his day, the best-paid and most-read writer in the world—book, the obvious *The Call of the Wild*. And then Pnin says, "Strange! The vicissitudes of celebrity!" And he was surprised that nobody was familiar with that book in London's own country, while in Russia everyone knew it and read it and almost considered it an instruction manual for the perfect development of the working-class artistic hero.

But for him, *Martin Eden* is nothing more and nothing less and above all the first book with a writer protagonist that he read thinking, surprised, that hey, a writer could *also* be the book's protagonist and, sure, in *David Copperfield*—another kind of crypto-autobiography, where Dickens, in chapter XV, anticipated the inventor and dreamer and rememberer Proust, with that window at the top of a staircase recalling another one from his childhood; Dickens who, on more than one occasion, proclaimed, with a combination of pride and self-pity, that "I remember everything, I can't forget anything"— there was also a bit of that. But not as much and never with as much power as in *Martin Eden* (he'd never read the act of reading written about with more passion than the way London did in that novel) where, step by step, you were shown the steps to follow to turn yourself into a character-creating character.

And then him—who at that point had already thought so much about being a writer—thinking that he would *also* like to be the protagonist of a book who wrote a book too, maybe that same book, as if it were his autobiography before his life had even been lived.

And then something clicks.

And he clicks one of those pens they give you on airplanes.

And he writes something down on the in-flight safety instructions.

And it's the first thing he's written in so long and the first thing he's thought to put in writing (it's the first thing he remembers having put in writing) in who knows how long.

And what he writes is *Man meets Boy*.

Him as and playing Him.

Him, suddenly decisive and definitive and capitalized.

Him, no longer the stationary Odysseus laying siege to the walls of Troy, but the Odysseus moving ceaselessly for a decade of trying to return home.

Him like the theretofore tone deaf and uninspired Caedmon waking up from that dream to recite the poem that God commanded him to compose—"Sing to me the beginning of all things," he suggests and orders—and which, of course, is a great poem, but it's not as good as the one from the dream that he failed to fully memorize.

Him inventing and dreaming and remembering and choosing to stop posing and to start singing and playing.

Him enveloped in music sounding like Ennio Morricone (and, yes, *Martin Eden* was the novel David "Noodles" Aaronson is reading in the bathroom of his adolescence, in *Once Upon a Time in America*, in that movie that's so sad and that ends with one of the happiest smiles in the history of celluloid: a smile that He has tried to smile so many times but never gets quite right, though maybe now, who knows, perhaps . . .)

Him, someone who's always felt, at most, like an anti-action anti-hero: the guy who gets killed in the first scene (but thereby sets in motion the existences of the protagonists). Or, better, who so far had been heard as the metallic and ex-machina voice-over of someone seeing it all from far away, like a distant relative you've heard of but never met.

Surprise: Him, suddenly, protagonist.

"I'm going to get me!" He thinks.

And He—with reddened eyes—thinks it both on last night's plane and in the desert of this first desert day.

And He thinks it while thinking about where He is.

Thinking about how—after all and despite so much complaining on his part—sometimes reality gives you a gift and approaches the truest irreality. The outside world becoming the inside world. Opening the door. Finding the thing that unlocks the lock and solves the riddle and hits the right note, in a word: the key. And leading you back to the *keyboard*: back to that board of keys and notes and riddles and locks to unlock.

At last, the unattenuated and irrefutable proof that *He was right*. That He was the master of the truth. That the fictions He wrote were there to correct everyone else's world and rewrite it better.

Him looking out the window of the airplane (and He'd already written something like this, something similar, with waves instead of sand dunes, in the last pages of his last book; and there was nothing left for Him to do but to wonder if that book—which he thought about for the first time in another millennium and when He was much smaller, when He closed that Jack London novel after opening it for the first time—that He already wrote and that was going to be three books that never were, hadn't been, after all, a proto- and auto-fictional fiction of the I, but, also, anticipatory and futuristic and autobiographical in how it jumped ahead in the story it told to what was going to happen to Him now) and seeing there below, in the desert darkness of lightless sand that he's flying over, the flickering point of a fire that He lights. And then imagining now what will soon come true: someone, Him, burning the last page of a book, of that book that always travels in his carry-on. Throwing it into a bonfire as if throwing a bone into the air.

A final page where, in the perfect farewell paragraph, it reads (and at last He'll read): "Not the least adornment of the chronicle is the delicacy of pictorial detail: a latticed gallery; a painted ceiling; a pretty plaything stranded among the forget-me-nots of a brook; butterflies and butterfly orchids in the margin of the romance; a misty view descried from marble steps; a doe at gaze in the ancestral park; and much, much more."

Some final lines on a final page where it rereads (and He rereads): "Not the last adornment of the chronicle is the pictorial detail: a latticed gallery (the house He's fled, pursued by torches and the roar of wild boars); a painted ceiling (the phosphorescent stars stuck to the ceiling of the room of He Whose Name Must Not Be Mentioned, painted the color of the skies of New York's Grand Central Station); a pretty plaything (Mr. Trip: his parents recalling and constantly reminding him that he must've been around two or three years old at the time and He stopped in front of a shop with the toy in the window and wouldn't stop crying until they went in and bought it for Him; while He, for his part, remembered that He saw it there and all He did was stand there pointing and staring at it wide-eyed, not crying, but smiling. Penelope hadn't been born yet, but, no doubt, her version was best of all, her own private toy story: the shopkeeper had come outside to see what was going on with that kid who refused to move from that spot in front of the window and—knowing that the toy was broken, that when wound up it only went in reverse, and that nobody would buy it—decided to give Him the toy for free and as he did so he said: "The two of you: together forever") **stranded among the forget-me-nots of a brook** (Uncle Hey Walrus's electricity-ravaged body floating downstream, scarcely a memory of what it'd once been); **butterflies** (Cornell, Ithaca and Montreux and particle accelerator and Swiss meadows and, first and foremost and when all was said and done, his grandparents' house in Sad Songs and, there, his little finger turning the dial of the old and heavy and immobile telephone that, like the chamber of a Chekhov-brand revolver, as it spun back to its initial position after He turned the dial by putting his finger in the hold beside a given number, sounds like a skull gnashing its teeth and chewing on bullets) **and butterfly orchids in the margin of the romance** (*Ada, or Ardor* and *Tender Is the Night* and *Wuthering Heights* and *Dracula*); **a misty view descried from marble steps** (Penelope in flames in the monastery of Our Lady of Our Lady of Our Lady of . . .); **a doe at gaze in the ancestral park** (Ella) **and much, much more** (And so many transparent things less. Speeding things that didn't exist back then and that, for Him, had been invented too late. And, hey, where had these fucking piece-of-shit mobile phones been back when He needed them most, when He needed to interconnect cellular phones. Why didn't they ring or why weren't they yet ringing on that night when they occurred to Him as if in a fever for which no science fiction had come up with a cure. When He imagined them with the desperation and anguish and euphoria with which the best ideas of anticipatory or speculative literature tend to be illuminated. When He wanted so badly—and with such power and terror and love—for the use of and familiarity with those mobile phones to have arrived a few decades earlier and to be holding one in his hand back then and to dial a number that He hadn't even had to memorize. Because it would've been enough to click on *Mom and Dad*. And how strange and not at all futuristic but really quite primitive and very much in the style of *2001: A Space Odyssey* those two forever-infantile words sounded to Him. Then, if that'd been possible, with one of those "smart" phones, He could've let Mom and Dad—who, without a doubt, would've been hooked on and addicted to and junkies of those phones—know that the military was coming for them, to get out of there and get away. If mobile phones had existed back then, He could've warned them that He'd given the government their exact coordinates and reported their absurd plans to the bad guys in the movie in rapture of unconsciousness—a condition He'd learned about reading a bad translation—and that He was so sorry and that now the soldiers were coming to capture them. Or He could've even sent them a brief message with no missing letters. Or a *Danger!* emoji or something like that. He could've let them know the soldiers were coming to arrest them, to disappear them, and, in the end, to throw them out of another airplane—not a ghost plane but a plane loaded with almost-dead bodies into that river that they'd sailed down so many times aboard the *Diver.* And having failed in all of that, but if those Proustian phones that allowed you to communicate with the almost dead had existed—phones that, no doubt, would exist, but, also, too late for Him—at least He could've promised them that He would've done, that He would do, anything to deactivate all of that. To be able to save them. To forget the plan that Penelope had come up with but that He'd put in practice. To rewrite all of that—that increasingly vast, miniscule, absolute memory—not with a happy ending, which would've been impossible given that it's his parents we're talking about here, but at least, yes, with a *to be continued* . . . raising anchors instead of sinking bodies. There they go, there they would've gone. Alive. Mom and Dad going, as always, and forgive me forgive me forgive me)."

And He—at the moment fragmented and snap-shot—seeing them from the air, from the air of a desert airplane fertilized with all his dead ghosts, the only passenger, flying against the wind, believing in the fluorescent glow of that glass of green milk from the visionary green cow that He now brings to his lips and drinks and swallows to return to an orgasmic future and hurl himself into a yet-to-come past. A past that He no longer fantasizes about altering, because, at the same time, any change could cause something even worse to happen or make something good that'd happened not happen.

So, better to accept what was and to focus on what's yet to come.

To write.

Him filling in the blanks on that immigration form that asks if you've ever committed a crime and good question and the temptation to put "Mr. Trip" on the line for his name and "nextwriter" where they ask for his profession.

The temptation to truly lie once again.

And then hearing or thinking He hears the voice of the pilot over the loudspeakers—interrupting the movie He's watching, in the moment when a replicant recites something about "cells interlinked"—announcing that thing about how "as we begin our descent . . ." About how soon, very soon, what went up will come down and then He will initiate his ascent.

And, then, the YesterdAir pilot (Bloch? Jupien? Norpois?) asking a question, not for everyone, but for Him and Him alone.

Asking Him if, now, He knows how to proceed, how to go about starting to write again, how to go on—once everything that has to happen has happened—and make it to the end; the end being, he remembers now, all that's left to come to pass, the last thing to become present and future.

And He answers the pilot—and answers himself—that yes, that He does.

That He knows that now, He knows that and much, much more.

And He calls to the flight attendant (Françoise? Berma? Gilberte?) and asks her to, please, serve Him up one final glass of milk from that colossal green cow before landing for the last time and forever.

And He gives her a smile.

(That smile.)

(This smile.)

More—much, much more—in a moment.

(*More in a moment*).

II

THE RECONSTRUCTION
OF THE FRAGMENTS,
THE ETERNITY
OF INSTANTS,
THE MARVEL
OF MOMENTS,
AND EVERYTHING THAT CAME BEFORE THAT,
AT THE SAME TIME,
IS ONLY REMEMBERED NOW

We do not remember days, we remember moments.
—CESARE PAVESE,
Il mestiere di vivere

[He] tried to dissect it into small enough pieces to store
away—realizing that the totality of a life may be different in
quality from its segments, and also that life during the forties
seemed capable of being observed only in segments.
—FRANCIS SCOTT FITZGERALD,
Tender Is the Night

A review of life is not an orderly account from conception
to death. Rather it's fragments from here and there.
—WILLIAM S. BURROUGHS,
Last Words

It's exactly my sense of existing—a fragment, a wisp of color.
—VLADIMIR NABOKOV,
Ada, or Ardor

Fragments are the only forms I trust.
—DONALD BARTHELME,
"See the Moon"

Go, get you home, you fragments!
—WILLIAM SHAKESPEARE,
Coriolanus

BY WAY OF BEGINNING WHAT COMES NEXT / EVERYTHING YET TO COME ABOUT WHAT'S ALREADY COME TO PASS

He remembers (and everything that comes back to him these days travels from the past to the present so secure yet so heavy with excess baggage, but beside him, ever lighter; and so he starts out remembering all of it in this font, but then proceeds to remember it like this, with this other typography) how he was when he started writing and reading and writing.

He remembers what it was like to smile the smile that always wrote itself across his lips whenever he opened a book and that continues to do so; because when you read you're forever young and forever how you were and how you will be: the timeless smiling age of the reader who writes and knows he has a beginning.

A *Once upon a time* . . . a yesterday-I-didn't-know-how-but-today-I-do-and-will-forevermore.

And then he remembers reading and smiling looking at the first words he put in writing: the first and the last lines and some parts in the middle, at random, of a novel written by someone else, but that now, reading it, was also his.

His parents' favorite novel.

Tender Is the Night by Francis Scott Fitzgerald.

He read them—those letters blending together into words—in that magic instant when, after almost drowning, there outside, he felt he knew how to read without ever having learned to read.

There and then he read: "On the pleasant shore of the French Riviera, about halfway between Marseilles and the Italian border, stands a large, proud, rose-colored hotel" and "One writes of scars healed, a loose parallel to the pathology of the skin, but there is no such thing in the life of an individual. There are open wounds, shrunk sometimes to the size of a pinprick but wounds still. The marks of suffering are more comparable to the loss of a finger, or the sight of an eye. We may not miss them, either, for one minute in a year, but if we should there is nothing to be done about it" and "Who would not be pleased at carrying lamps helpfully through the darkness?" and "Strange children should smile at each other and say, Let's play."

And, before closing the book and losing that ability that he would only regain, after weeks of intense practice, years later, he jumped to the last page and there he learned that "in any case he is almost certainly in that section of the country, in one town or another."

He remembers smiling and thinking: "Yes, now this is a good book."

And not long thereafter, though almost an eternity for someone at that age, and already learning the language of literature (still a child but already possessing that superpower, as if he were another person, with so many books yet to be opened like doors and so many doors yet to be closed and with so many lamps and smiles to light up, to go out and play in one town or another with no fear of the scars that always leave you wounded), he opened another book.

And he read.

And he remembers saying to himself that the beginning of that particular novel could, also, be read as a question on one of those *multiple-choice* tests that he was always having to take in school at that time, again and again, with no warning or comprehensible purpose and surprise! and the sadistic smile of the tender yet diurnal teacher of the moment when announcing the pop quiz.

And so, now, then.

It was:

A. the best of times and the worst of times;

B. the age of wisdom and the age of foolishness;

C. the epoch of belief and the epoch of incredulity;

D. the season of Light and the season of Darkness;

E. the spring of hope and the winter of despair.

F. All of the above.

G. Everything yet to come.

(*Instructions for the test-taker*: before answering, take into account that we had everything before us, we had nothing before us, we were all going direct to Heaven, we were all going direct the other way—in short, the period was so far like the present period, that some of its noisiest authorities insist on its being received, for good or for evil, in the superlative degree of comparison only.)

MARK WHAT DOES OR DOESN'T APPLY:

He remembers everything that he will remember (which is everything that he didn't forget, everything that already happened but comes back in fragments, instants, moments) here and now: on the edge of a desert of crazy diamonds, under the brilliant light and last breath of almost-dead stars. Stardazed after so many airplanes.

Pages torn from a book—another book after so many books—in one hand. Pages that he burns one by one and on which are written things like "he soon noticed that such details of his infancy as really mattered (for the special purpose the reconstruction pursued) could be best treated, could not seldom be *only* treated, when reappearing at various later stages of his boyhood and youth, as sudden juxtapositions that revived the past while vivifying the whole."

And a rifle in the other.

The last chapters of a novel he'd never been able to read though he tried so many times and the cold weight of a rifle he's going to fire for the first and last time.

Finally, the ending.

But the ending is inseparable from the beginning.

The ending is just the exact point when a long beginning concludes, he realizes.

He's gone so far back that now he's alone facing himself.

He remembers, yes, that back then, in his now nonexistent country of origin, it was the worst of times and, also, it was the worst of times.

He remembers that there (*Noms de pays: le nom*) everything seemed to be up in the air. As if someone had thrown it there for the pure pleasure not of watching it go up but of seeing it come crashing down; like a bone that remains overhead suspended in space, transformed into an artificial satellite that'll orbit the memory of the person who sent it flying so high from so far below forever.

He remembers that bipolar time (abundant and poor, paradisiacal and infernal, benevolent and malignant).

He remembers his childhood.

And, during that childhood, the point when tests in school mutated from the writing of more or less long and detailed answers (answers that explained or at least tried to explain what happened) to the *multiple choice* modality. From composing and structuring ideas and events to, merely, marking what you thought was correct with an X. To nothing more than choosing among multiple options, some of them patently ridiculous or that couldn't possibly be correct.

They were, yes, simple questions that left no room for doubt or a second option (and that, involuntarily miseducating, would have little or nothing to do with the questions he and his classmates would be facing as their bodies grew and the years they had left behind shrank as they went searching far and wide for answers to the test known as life. Years in which the right choices wouldn't be so fast and easy to see and mark and on to the next one).

They were questions *with* answers, because the answer was already written below: they didn't have to think it over and work it out, they just had to choose it out of the others with the certainty of knowing or the luck of guessing.

They were questions that everyone thought the same thing about unless they were wrong. And, even so, the ways of being wrong were limited and lacked all imagination and creativity for error.

They were questions that instantly died so the answers could be born.

They were reflexive and automatic questions.

They were questions like telephone poles alongside the road, poles that ceased to exist where the aimless and wandering desert or the cloudless sky or the cloud that covered everything—including desert and the sky—began.

And they were being left behind at breakneck speed.

That was the important thing.

To answer them quickly without overthinking.

Never before had he and his classmates rushed to answer questions in the present—good or bad—about what had already come to pass. The past was no longer a burden they bore but *a thing* they ran roughshod over. And really that saying, repeated time and again, about how something was *a thing of the past* no longer applied. Now, all of a sudden, it was more like the past itself was *a thing to be kicked*. Far away.

And, sure, you could argue that, at that point, their pasts were light and brief, yet, oh, *at the same time*, they suddenly found themselves forced to memorize that other past that was universal and stretching back thousands of years: geological ages and mathematical formulas and names of patriots and verb conjugations and dates of battles and the location of organs and geographical and scientific discoveries and last names of teachers. But they achieved it by the pure effort of memory and not the application of logic, and the whole *multiple choice* thing did nothing but intensify the symptom of that pleasant malaise. The headline was more important than the news, synthesis more important than exposition, simplification more important than complexity. It was, yes, the best beginning of the worst of times, times that (they couldn't imagine it; the science fiction they consumed at the time didn't aim that high or go so far so soon) would bring increasingly small screens and increasingly brief messages wherein orthographical errors would be allowed and even validated as a distinctive and inclusive feature of a new language! Times in which you would answer not by choosing between multiple choices but between little yellow and supposedly funny faces.

The whole *multiple choice* thing served, his teachers explained, to facilitate the students' education and lighten everyone's workload. And—thus the transparent joy on the faces of his educators—the tests were corrected almost as quickly as they'd been printed, with the help of a perforated stencil that quickly reported wrong answers and certified right ones without any need to reflect on them or discover a pattern of learning/unlearning in a given student.

Suddenly, they were all the same because they all answered correctly the same way or made the same mistakes when processing the choices that they heard as if someone were whispering lines to them from the sounding board at the foot of the stage.

For him and for his classmates the whole *multiple choice* thing was, at the time, something like a revolution. Something comparable to what the confirmation of the roundness of the Earth had been for previous peoples or, more recently, the coming never-to-leave of the birth control pill.

And, also, a novelty. (Although, he only found out about this many years later, the format was far from brand new. And had actually been created long before, in 1914, by a professor at the University of Kansas named Frederick J. Kelly, to then immediately be applied and thereby accelerate the recruitment forms for soldiers bound for the Great War which, on future tests, would be renamed in the correct answer/choice as World War One. And, oh, the paradox that many great "advances" very often came about primarily to be applied in retreats and attacks before, later, being applied to civilian life. Thus, again, the contradictory absurdity of summarizing and distilling a whole life, so it could be more quickly processed and sent off for a more than likely and quick death in the trenches of irregular design, defying the rectitude of all geometry or the neat order of sequential of lines of text. And, in the margins, the handwriting of a hierarchy of officers recommending greater care and discipline and a more proper use of the equipment the next time they had it, and attention! and present arms!)

And (at the time it wouldn't be long before his parents, leading a fashionista terrorist cell were *A. Executed, B. Murdered, C. Disappeared, D. All of the above*; and luckily there was no possibility of answering how and why they'd first been captured and who'd actually been responsible; because the answer would require too many pages and couldn't be thoroughly explained with an X. *Reported by their own children who could no longer stand them*) he remembers too that he said to himself without saying so to anybody else that the whole thing of answers being reduced to choices wasn't progress but regress. That, in that way, the answers didn't undergo evolution but involution, and lost all the characteristic and defining traits of the person who gave them.

Sure: it was functionally easier to answer them. But they were questions lacking all personality that yielded answers lacking any character. Undead questions and zombie answers. Questions that from now on, even though they all thought differently, they would all answer more or less the same and in the same way. And in a few, very simple words.

He knew too that, over the years, Kelly—already at his post as dean at Idaho State University—came to repudiate his Frankenstein's monster comprised of random parts with a "These tests are too crude and should be abandoned." And he acknowledged they were only appropriate for evaluating a small part of what was taught. And that their use and application should be abandoned as soon as possible, given the risk of turning students into beings who could only express themselves in short phrases and deficient definitions and marking nothing but one letter with an X. Which would train them to choose only when offered preconceived choices and not because of something they actually knew or believed. And that, in the absence of multiple choices, they would obey too easily and too automatically the one choice they were offered with the discipline of automata.

Businessmen and educators—beyond pleased with the simplicity of calibrating and evaluating—rebelled against Kelly en masse, deeming him a traitor to his own dogma.

And Kelly was fired from his position for being:

A. A revolutionary and anarchist
B. Inconsistent in his beliefs
C. Crazy in the annoying and inopportune kind of way
D. All the above

But the truth was that—sometimes and despite the prior digression—the correctness of the answers could vary according to the temperament or modus operandi of the person giving them without ceasing to be correct. Or that, even, none of the choices seemed right to the test-taker who would feel excluded and different and, sometimes, so happy and proud to find him or herself outside the parameters and norms. If that were to happen, then, just in case, the test taker—Kelly's unconscious revenge or anomaly in the system for identifying potentially volatile subjects?—would be advised to choose what seemed "most correct" to them.

Something similar, they say, happens with something you decide to remember.

Oftentimes it's incorrect.

Oftentimes you invent how something that's no longer clear to you happened.

Oftentimes the most correct thing is the thing you forgot.

And yet, decisions are made based on what you think happened, on what you decided to remember or not remember.

And so, many years later, he would come to understand the multiple choice method as the one most utilized when memorious and exceedingly private and intimate self-examinations are taken.

Thus . . .

. . . what come next are:

A. Inventions
B. Dreams
C. Memories
D. All of the above

And end of discussion.

And then, never again, he promises himself, will he stumble or fall into making use of such a device.

Starting then he would no longer have choices but absolute certainties. The return like a wild and passionate old-school cavalry charge, where answers had to be elucidated on a blank page without the aid of preconceived choices.

But promises are made to be:

A. Broken
B. Forgotten
C. Altered
D. All of the above

LISTS OF FRAGMENTS / FRAGMENTS OF LISTS

He remembers how, sometimes, option D. *All of the above* became something even more disconcerting, positing the existence of many correct possibilities and many possible corrections.

Sometimes, option D. *All of the above* become D. *None of the above*.

And so, for that reason, anything was possible.

Because then, the correct answer was outside. And you had to go out and find it without any help and only the false clue of everything that it wasn't, which, at the same time, was only a part: because there were many more things it might *not* be.

And it's with that kind of enlightenment that one experiences the true yet false electric shocks; like in those torture tests orchestrated by Stanley Milgram (had Milgram and Kelly been friends?). Tests where, sooner rather than later, everything ended up starting to be connected—with that total intimacy from which there was no coming back, through the pulses that beat inside cables and switches—in the way only victims connected with victimizers. The ones and the others always ready to kneel down in prayer to Stockholm and its syndrome.

And all those options as a kind of list.

His lists, yes.

To have lists was to have something.

Lists of everything, lists of anything.

Lists you wouldn't necessarily follow but that you would go along eliminating deleting erasing crossing out canceling nullifying obliterating as one by one you completed or discarded its items.

Lists that were useful and not like those inevitable and mendacious lists popping up during the final days of December in cultural supplements (and on which he always shone in his absence). Those countdowns triumphantly counting down the best of what'd been published that year when, really, they should, more humble and sincere, announce in whispers what the supposed "experts" had liked most out of the very few and very obvious (that they found themselves obliged to like) things they'd read in the last two months.

Lists that were like a map there was no need to explore, it was enough to have it and to promise (in vain) to go out and use it someday.

Lists that were an important part of his aesthetic and his style when he wrote and that now were lists of what he would never write (including those exhaustive and euphoric and often so criticized lists of acknowledgements and thanks at the end of his books and, ah, he felt so grateful to be able to write when he was able to write and so in debt to all those who, in one way or another, had helped him do it), and yet . . .

"Only connect," yes, E. M. Forster had instructed (and what was the name of that Forster story about the disconnection of an advanced, highly-anticipated machine much like the Internet that addicted all of humanity and rendered everyone completely and absolutely disconnected and gone to pieces and left their reality fragmented when it broke down?).

"Body, heart, soul, intellect, so we care ourselves into parts," Denis Johnson had enumerated.

"We see parts of things, we intuit whole things," Iris Murdoch had explained.

"But we are ruled by words. (Literature tells us what is happening to words.) More to the point, we are ruled by quotations . . . So much for the transmissibility of the past! Disunite sentences, fracture memories . . . When my memories become slogans, I no longer need them. No longer believe in them," Susan Sontag, the insomniac obsessed with dreams as inventive material, had offered.

"There is no complete life. There are only fragments," James Salter had concluded.

Fragments enlisted and listed and complete in themselves and at one point, for him, possible and instant epigraphs.

The fragments that didn't yet suspect they were part of a future collage.

The fragments inventions and dreams and memories feed off of; all of them speaking the sinuous tongue of the elliptical and nonlinear.

The fragments that were the conductive and uninsulated language in which the great sacred and religious texts were written.

The fragments as the form of communication whereby the faithful and devout learned to believe in gods even though they couldn't see them; because they didn't need to see them if they'd already been written, because they could been seen in the most sacred books of all the books, all of them sacred.

The fragments composing *A Thousand and One Nights*, the *Panchatantra*, or the *Kalevala*, where the gods learned to believe in humans even without, on more than one occasion, being able to believe in what those humans were doing, watching them all the time incredulously, fascinated by the strange ways they behaved and wondering if they'd really conceived these creatures who later, in turn, conceived of them.

The Cosmic Fragments by Heraclitus and there "It scatters and it gathers; it advances and retires," "Invisible (underlying) connection is stronger than visible (tangible)," "Death is what we see when awake, and what we see asleep is sleep," "Mortals are immortals and immortals are mortals, the one living the others' death and the dying the others' life," "A man in the night kindles a light for himself," "We do not act and speak like men asleep," "The waking have one common world, but the sleeping turn aside each into a world of his own."

The fragments that some scholars had divided into typologies of absolutes, implicated and ambiguous.

The fragments out of which are composed all the works of Shakespeare, that man who wrote almost everything he wrote so people could quote him as they pleased. All those ideas and thoughts first and only after—at least that's how it was for him—looking for and finding a plot (a plot oftentimes delirious or absurd and, in general, strange) to fit them into. And then the audience and readers took the inverse path, reducing his wholes into fragments. Into quotations more or less blind but always useful and practical and that make you look really good at parties or when you use them as titles or epigraphs for books. And he wondered if there was already (there probably was) an app that had all of Shakespeare organized and chopped up by subject so you could invoke him at your convenience: *WWW*, or *Will for Whatever You Will*. And he remembers that he read Shakespeare for the first time when he was very young. Attracted not so much by his mad comedies (he'd almost performed in one of them in a school play directed by his disappeared Teacher of Artistic Activities) but by their paternal ghosts and witches and skulls and by their star-crossed lovers and crazy young women, forcing him to learn the primary and primordial lesson that anything that starts off well can end bad, very bad indeed. And, also, comprehending that, in the end, true talent or genius was made manifest in the quality and greatness of those unhappy endings where all the characters ended up going to pieces.

The fragments in the leaping *Essais* of Michel de Montaigne's fall from a horse: reflections about almost everything that their author considers "badly joined marquetry" dissuading the reader from continuing already from the preface—almost like he had warned in the opening pages of his *The Impossible Story*—with a: "And therefore, Reader, I myself am the subject of my book: it is not reasonable that you should employ your leisure on a topic so frivolous and so vain. Therefore, Farewell." Fragments in which the maniacal and referential Montaigne complained all the time about his bad memory; but knowing that that propensity to forget is what really allows and obliges him to remember it in writing; citing accelerated particles of others in order to, leisurely and completely, be able to better explain himself to himself.

Fragments reconstructing themselves as "a funerary shrine raised to the light of my memories" because "we write not to remember what is lost, but to dictate what must be remembered" in the vivid and sepulchral *Mémoires d'outretombe* by François-René de Chateaubriand.

The fragments assembled by Robert Burton in his ever more expansive and, for him, paradoxically euphoric *The Anatomy of Melancholy*.

The fragments that Thomas Alva Edison understood the material of human memory to be made of: microscopic particles that floated, invisible, around us and arranged themselves into whimsical shapes. Edison called those particles "little people" and was convinced they came from the outermost outer space. And in a way, in his almost-poetic delirium, Edison's science wasn't far from fiction. Because it was becoming an increasingly solid theory that life on Earth emerged from microorganisms climbing aboard comets and meteorites and crashing into the surface of the planet to kickstart the machines and reactors of evolution. Wouldn't you know it: the terrestrials were extraterrestrials. From stardust they came, yes, but who knows if to stardust they would return. One thing was certain: evolution wasn't what it used to be and, to prove it, you just had to look to moments like the domestication of fire, or the mysteries of reading and writing being revealed, or the moment the first oyster was sucked down and it was discovered that *there* was *something* interesting just as it was decided that pearls would be valuable, alongside, now, the incessant updates inside microchips programmed to almost immediately go obsolete. Now, it was the machines that evolved, but just so they could break down better and more quickly.

The fragments that Ludwig Josef Johann Wittgenstein referred to in his *Tractatus* as the material "with which I have filled voids" but "I don't know what they represent and it is difficult to judge it now correctly."

The fragments ("the whole and the complete and perfect are basically abhorrent to us," Thomas Bernhard moaned) that helped us to endure the horror of something complete and unfathomable.

The fragments that were the (dis)organizable notecards Vladimir Nabokov used in preparing his books and for which "The pattern of the thing precedes the thing. I fill in the gaps of the crossword at any spot I happen to choose. These bits I write on index cards until the novel is done."

The fragments and "random things" that ending up composing the un-disassemble-able assemblages of Joseph Cornell's collage boxes.

The fragments that—according to James Salter in *Light Years*—transformed all of life into something inevitably incomplete and mysterious and inside of which "there is no form, only prodigious detail that reaches everywhere: exotic sounds, spills of sunlight, foliage, fallen trees, small beasts that flee at the sound of a twig-snap, insects, silence, flowers"; and all of that deceptively woven into two kinds of life: the one people believe you are living and the other life, which is the one that causes all the trouble, that life that you long to see.

The fragments that give deformed form to books like *Around the Day in Eighty Worlds* and *Último* round by Julio Cortázar.

The fragments that one of Donald Barthelme's characters said he trusted, while his author—in a parodic communique and with newsman diction—ended up communicating that he no longer trusted them, that in the future he would "seek wholes" because "fragments fall apart" and break all the time and informing everyone that "Endings are elusive, middles are nowhere to be found, but worst of all is to begin, to begin, to begin."

The fragments that were random lines from that composition book that bore the title *Master Advice of a Man Who Sleeps on the Floor*, written by He Whose Name Must Not Be Mentioned, The Son of Penelope, where it said things like: "Really, if you enter the castle you cease to see the castle (so it makes no sense to spend hours waiting in line to climb up the Eiffel Tower or the Statue of Liberty or so many other places that are for looking at for free from outside and not for going inside only to discover that paying to be inside only made it so you couldn't see them" or "Prize or punishment?: the toys children dream of are the ones that will only be invented once they're grown up. They'll be able to buy them, but they'll no longer be children" or "The dead are always complex literary masterpieces or popular bestsellers, depending on the type of readers the living who don't stop reading them are" "My mom is a little crazy and my uncle is a little sane. Who do they have left?" And guess which one of those lines is the one that he had invented and inserted there. Don't overthink it, it's very easy, just in case, in case you were wondering: it includes the word "literature."

The fragments in the telepathic voice of a majestic green cow that speaks to him and speaks to him and doesn't stop speaking to him in the desert and in the wind and under the most lunar of lunatic suns. Short phrases, immense ideas, with the cadence and diction with which he had once imagined the International Language of the Dead.

The fragments like archipelagos that, when viewed from high in the skies of a map, end up forming an entire continent.

The fragments like brain-breaking, migraine-inducing jigsaw puzzles that fit together into a single piece that you had to stare at up close until you fixed it in your memory, because, sooner or later, another piece would come along not to complete it but to complement it and . . .

Fragments to efface expunge erase delete rub out wipe out obliterate . . .

Then he—a boy at the time, a nextwriter who wanted to be a writer when he grew up; who never imagined he would be an exwriter because, arrogant, he was convinced he'd never run out of loose parts to tie together or choices to choose—said to himself that *that* was precisely and entirely what his work would be. *That* would be *his oeuvre* when his vocation was truly and fully realized, when at last he could read and write whenever he wanted and not just for a few minutes after almost drowning.

Yes, faced with the lack of any answer among the first choices, his thing would be to go out in the world or into his own mind to seek and find fragments. But long fragments, far longer than telegraphic *multiple-choice* brand answers. Fragments and quotes and parts and things and moments and memories fractured to—thinking about them a great deal, polishing them with that ferocity with which old people bring out the shine on the heads of little ones when they rub them—distract him from the rust he was covered in and from knowing himself broken, shattered, wrecked, only capable of moving forward in reverse.

And to organize them into lists.

And so, the referential mania from outside to avoid admitting the interior and self-referential suicidal tendency: because there was nothing more egocentric and narcissistic than the fantasy of crossing yourself out with an X. Something like what George Bailey longed for in *It's a Wonderful Life*: for everybody to forget him so, at last, he could forget about them and about Bedford Falls and about that fact that it was all his and only his fault for entrusting an uncle—who was very kind but, apparently, with an already quite advanced case of Alzheimer's—with the responsibility of making the deposits (and, oh, he was never not struck by the fact that Frank Capra's entire filmography revolved around the idea of money, and not love, as the true engine of the universe).

So, he thinks and hopes, maybe all those slices and splinters and fractions and random pieces (like those supposed relics of the cross of Jesus Christ, nails and wood that, if put together, would encompass a couple forests and span the Brooklyn Bridge) could end up configuring another kind of X. An X not to cross something out but to mark a precise location, a location to arrive to and once there . . .

Yes, assembling all those parts—*A. and B. and C. and D.* used up—into a secret model and finally achieving the goal and fulfilling the destiny of putting option X in writing. *Everything that occurs to you regarding what occurred in your life is fair game from here onward, even if you've invented it or dreamed it up, because from now on, when you think about it or write it, it's part of reality.*

And so, once the X he was bound for to dig up the treasure was clear (knowing that X would be a letter not just to read but also to reread), discovering what kind of reader he had to be first to only then be worthy of a treasure chest and of jewels and, maybe, even, not a Jim-"Treasure Island"-Hawkins style happiness, but an Edmond-"Montecristo"-Dantes brand revenge.

And, for all of that and all of them—that he would come to know almost by heart after having passed through their pages so many times—the kind of reader he had to be was a rereader.

Because to learn to rewrite what was yours, first you had to pass the test of becoming a rereader of everyone else.

THE GOOD REMEMBERER (A HOW-TO GUIDE)

He remembers that nothing is reread (and rewritten) more than the memory when it makes memory.

Making memory is unmaking reality.

Or remaking it.

And the symptom intensifies when it comes to making memory about childhood. "It may indeed be questioned whether we have any memories at all from our childhood: memories relating to our childhood may be all that we possess," Freud pointed out.

And so, sidelong glances and childhood as a construct only possible looking back, when you recall it and, at the same time and so much time later, invent it.

Because childhood, while it's happening, isn't childhood: it's just all there was and all there is. And its language—not a primitive language, rather a constant there-are-no-words—is the language of visions as fleeting as falling stars streaking for a few seconds across the night sky (indeed: everything in reality lasted less time than in fiction; and he always remembered that the epic gunfight at the O.K. Corral transpired in less than half a minute; that it'd been one of those moments of the "more in a moment" variety that Vladimir Nabokov referred to in *Transparent Things*). And so, the brief childhood ended up being nothing but the extended adult rereading of everything you remember of it as if in a dream.

"More in a moment," going in reverse.

But he remembered so much of his childhood and out of what he remembered was the memory of being fully conscious of his childhood as it was passing; because he'd been declared clinically dead when he was born and before he began to breathe and because there, as a part of his childhood, were the childhoods of the characters in the books he read, reminding him that that was where everything began and where nothing would end, because some part of childhood would stay with you, like a tattoo, until you were old and wrinkled.

The memories of his childhood were now, paradoxically, the old age of his memory: everything that he remembers better and better. Or that, at least, he recounts most and best and that—as such, though he doesn't put it in writing¬—he corrects most and best. And on like that until he gets the best possible version. The idea of his childhood as a melody that he practices over and over again (previously on the keyboard of a computer, now moving his fingers in the air where nothing is written) until it comes out of him and sounds perfect, with just the right tempo and precise breathing.

And so, he remembers how he almost drowned once.

He remembers how, at that time, he would've been about four years old: that last year of those long, long years that seem to be just one year with four long twelve-month seasons each.

He remembers that it was summer.

And that he saved himself.

On his own.

Without any help.

None.

From anybody.

His parents, he could hear them, arguing with each other, on the beach. Something about . . .

. . . which version of their favorite book was best:

A. The original with flashbacks
B. The subsequent version, reorganized to be chronologically linear
C. Both

But really this argument was nothing but the façade of another far deeper argument:

What's the best way for them to deal with their relationship:

A. To move on
B. To back off every so often
C. To go their separate ways

And he wasn't yet able to read the book's title and author—*Tender Is the Night*, by Francis Scott Fitzgerald, the tragedy of a marriage *fou*—but he already knew which kind of writing corresponded to the person and which to the personas—to the characters—even though he didn't know how to read yet.

He doesn't know how to swim yet either.

His parents were—to use one of those words that, over the years, he would never try to use except by its primary definition—*immersed* in their argument. And they hadn't even noticed that he was *immersed* in the water: his feet no longer touch bottom and his arms don't know how to paddle and he swallows water that tastes nothing like the water he drinks at lunch and dinner when he comes to know the horror of running out of the Coca-Cola that accompanied his favorite dish: a big bowl of alphabet soup.

His parents were completely ignoring the possibility of his death, the possibility that the answer to the test that he was taking out in the water would be, though correct, the worst possible answer.

But he—pulled by undertows or the sudden swelling of something that was neither river nor sea, at the mouth of that watery map—found a way to save himself and to make it back to the beach and, exhausted, flop down on the sand like a castle.

And then his parents looked at him without seeing him and said/ordered him to do something ridiculous, but something that, for him, all of a sudden, was logical and possible, "Why don't you go write?"

And then—he remembers it down to the last detail, as if he were reading it first to write it later—the power of that salvation gave him the miraculous and ephemeral ability (like a free sample of the future) to know how to read and write. Even though he hadn't learned to write or read; and yet he was still inhabiting that space where, because you haven't yet learned to do it, you're more aware than ever of the marvel of writing and reading. Even though he was about to cross the border into the age when—even the majority of people who never become writers or serious writers—people read and write the most: the childhood that reads childhoods during childhood. The age he was when he couldn't even dream of a future like the present, where people write and read (and reread because there's no longer any need to tell the same story that until recently they didn't know over and over again) more than ever, but where, also, they do so not with child-like voracity but with childish bulimia.

Reading and writing, finally being able to do it, was a rite of passage then, a step forward.

There he was then, confronting that mystery that seems to contradict all narrative logic: first you read and then you write, but also, as primitive and primordial as it might be to think it, at the beginning of time, there must've been a first writer so that then (perhaps right away, the same hands and the same eyes) there could be a first reader and . . .

And suddenly he understands: the first writer and the first reader were the same person, at the same time: someone who invented and dreamed and remembered in one act.

D. All of the above.

And he remembers that the entire miracle lasted but the brief eternity of a few minutes (he read some random lines and was able to string together a few words in the notebook where previously he'd only drawn pictures) before he forgot how to do it. But, fleeting, it was more than enough time for the Big Bang of his literary vocation to explode. Something like catching a glimpse from his crib—in the darkness of childhood and through a door left briefly ajar only to be closed again¬—of an entire adult party raging just outside, in the living room, but a party that was still impossible for him to attend and for it to attend to him. A party that in the future he would be invited to dive into headfirst and with arms open, into the embraces of book pages more open than the embraces of arms and, with great effort, to keep himself afloat and swim to the shores of so many desert islands, inhabited by so many characters waiting to be rescued and to rescue him.

To float reading, to sink writing.

First superficial and then profound things, profound yet always transparent things.

Because if you don't know how to swim, it's impossible to strike out into the unfathomable seas beyond the shore where the water comes up to your knees or to move along that descending curve in swimming pools where "you can no longer touch the bottom" and where Ella wasn't there as a life-preserver. He realized then that floating and breathing among letters (as happens with the Siamese actions of remembering and forgetting, of sleeping and waking, of inventing and imitating) also meant submerging yourself in them and swallowing them until you could swallow no more and discovering that you were made of water and ink. And, yes, you had to learn how to swim down below and to touch the bottom and to hold your breath and breathe deeply in the depths. But doing so knowing that, if you went too deep, at a certain point of no return, the human brain convinces itself that it has amphibious abilities and removes the diving suit and drowns, wearing the most superficial of smiles.

And he also remembers that word coined, again, by Freud—who understood remembering as "a dynamic, transforming, reorganizing process" and the "reminiscences," not just the personal and present ones, but also the historical and immemorial ones, as the culprits of all hysteria—in an 1896 letter to the biologist Wilhelm Fliess: *Nachträglichkeit*. Which could be translated as "retranscription," and that was used to understand a particular memory as one of those longitudinal cross sections of the Earth's crust with the different geologic layers representing "the psychic achievements of successive epochs of life."

In other words: mental health depended on the constant ability to revise and rewrite and excavate within your own memory, in the cemetery where only the living-dead are buried. The inability to adjust the past to the present and the fossilization of yesterday, Freud concluded, led to various pathologies and to madness from which there was no coming back.

And so, remembering everything just as it was—*D. All of the above*—wasn't a virtue, it was a defect and even a grave danger.

Likewise, first you *learned* how to read and, if you were lucky, only afterward did you *know* how to read.

THE GOOD READER (A HOW-TO GUIDE)

He remembers that he'd talked to a writer, Ricardo Piglia, about the nature of the "ideal reader" and about what Piglia had written in one of his books titled—perhaps optimistically, perhaps melancholically—*El último lector*, or *The Last Reader*.

There he wrote that "the reading addict, someone who can't stop reading, and the insomniac reader, someone who is always awake, are two extreme representations of what it means to read a text, narrative personifications of the complex presence of the reader in literature. I would call them pure readers; for them, reading is not only a practice, it's a way of life."

Later, Piglia classifies that kind of reader as someone who experiences and enjoys "a relationship between reading and the real," but, also, "a relationship between reading and dreams," and who understands that "in that double connection the novel has plotted its history." A "particular kind of reader, the visionary, one who reads to learn how to live" and who has understood that the novel "seeks out its themes in reality but finds a form of reading in dreams."

And then, both of them, he and Piglia, had remembered at the same time—as if waking up—something they'd read about reader typologies that'd been pinned down and labeled by a writer they both liked, though him probably more than Piglia. Because he liked that writer like an addiction, like a dream, like someone he couldn't stop reading and rereading and, in that way, inventing.

Not long after that conversation, Piglia was diagnosed with ALS and became perhaps the most "pure" of "last readers": with the help of hardware called Tobii (which Piglia described as having "the look of a telepathy machine," but reading that description, he was struck by the idea that it was another possible model of William S. Burroughs's Dreamachine), Pigla wrote his final books not with his hands, which previously would've held a pen or typed on an Olivetti Lettera 22 or a Macintosh, but with his eyes. Letter by letter until he formed first words and then sentences, staring at them fixedly as if seeing them and believing them at the same time that he created them.

Pigla—for all the wrong reasons that were tragic and unjust as only the dictates of the body, often riddled with errors, can be—had ended up writing as if he were reading: with the tips of his eyes.

And then he remembered that other device in one of Stephen King's most reviled and misunderstood novels (but one of the ones that he, who'd read all of King, liked most) that was written, according to the author's confession, on a base diet of cocaine and alcohol. In *The Tommyknockers*—one of several/many of King's novels featuring writers who were "in trouble"—there was also talk of an extraterrestrial "dream machine" that read the scattered thoughts of writers and arranged them and gave them meaning and edited them and transported them to paper without anyone needing to touch a keyboard. Something that was "more like dreaming than writing . . . but what comes out is unlike dreams, which are often surreal and disconnected . . . It's a dream machine. One that dreams rationally." And it resulted in perfect books. Not thanks to a writing machine—a typewriter or a computer—but thanks to a writer-reading machine that put writers in writing so they could be read. A machine for inventing and dreaming and remembering writers. And, yes, of course: it was the novel of an addict, the literary equivalent to the sounds of David Bowie's *Station to Station* or Fleetwood Mac's *Tusk*.

He remembered that and then thought about how, toward the end of his work and life, Piglia—writing with eyes wide open—hadn't managed to become the last reader but had been the definitive reader.

And he also remembered the other writer that he and Piglia had remembered simultaneously.

By way of introduction to his *Lectures on Literature*, Vladimir Nabokov—who understood Freud as nothing more and nothing less than a great fiction writer—had offered instructions for a perfect reader. Someone who for him—for Nabokov—could only be a constant rereader. Because Nabokov thought that to reread a book was to remember with greater precision and greater detail what on the first time through had seemed unforgettable and worth returning to. Rereading you didn't just return to the book to be reread but to all the other books that before, in one way or another, had led you to that book and to all the books that, later, that book had led you to. Books never stopped recalling books, remembering each other with affection and gratitude. Their authors, not so much, almost never. Writers tended to suffer amnesia of writers.

There, in those preliminary words, Nabokov advocated—insisting on his scornful distrust of all realist ambition—for a reconsideration of the great classic European novels as if they were "fairy tales." (In *Pale Fire*, John Shade and Charles Kinbote coincided on the perception of *À la recherche du temps perdu* as "a huge ghoulish fairy tale, an asparagus dream, totally unconnected with any possible people in any historical France." And the bit about "an asparagus dream" was an allusion for connoisseurs. Even though he might take it as a personal wink through time and space: because he'd always been obsessed with the mystery of how eating asparagus made your urine smell like asparagus. His favorite physiological mystery. And he'd even looked up its possible double meaning in a *Dream Dictionary*, where dreaming of asparagus was interpreted as the equivalent of a "prosperous neighborhood and servants and very obedient children." Ha. But he'd gone much further in his research into the possible origin of Nabokov's comment on Proust. And had discovered, with singular pride, in a stretch of the "Combray" section, the despotic and witch-like Françoise forcing the cook to prepare asparagus knowing she was allergic to it. And, yes, again: he would never not marvel at the faithful smell of asparagus in your urine after you ate asparagus, as if, smelling that liquid that flowed out from inside you, you were rereading that asparagus you'd already ingested down to the last detail.)

And there, in that introduction, Nabokov defended the choice of the artist to avail himself of real materials but only if, almost immediately thereafter, he used them to sculpt or to paint or to compose a world of his own where he would end up meeting his reader (the reader who would've already sipped from many of those original sources) and, there, they would come together in an embrace of mutual appreciation.

And how could a writer be sure that that reader was his, the one for him, the correct and right one, the one in possession of all the faculties to read and understand him better?

To answer that question, Nabokov—"One evening at a remote provincial college through which I happened to be jogging on a protracted lecture tour"—had offered several options on a *multiple-choice* test that, according to him, would serve to elucidate the qualities one must have to be a good reader.

Nabokov warned that "I have mislaid the list, but as far as I remember the definitions went something like this"; and that you had to choose four items from a list of ten (numbered and not lettered) that were the following.

A good reader:

1) Should belong to a book club
2) Should identify himself or herself with the hero or the heroine
3) Should concentrate on the social-economic angle

4) Should prefer a story with action and dialogue to one with none
5) Should have seen the book in a movie
6) Should be a budding author
7) Should have imagination
8) Should have memory
9) Should have a dictionary
10) Should have some artistic sense

And, of course, for Nabokov (who in an interview had already specified the three levels of reader: "at the bottom, those who go after 'human interest'; in the middle, the people who want ideas, packaged thought about Life and Truth; at the top, the proper readers, who go for style" which was nothing but the result of following and obeying the one true commandment: "caress the detail, the divine detail"), the obvious and inevitably correct answers were so clear and so easy to discern.

And so, the only possible biography for a writer, Nabokov had decreed, was the history of his or her style: not what occurred in the life of the writer, but what the writer did to make everything that occurred to him occur after finding his style.

Sooner—as in Nabokov's case—or later. Nabokov who—when *accused* of always writing the same book—patiently explained, as if addressing inferior lifeforms—that he'd had the luck of understanding and appreciating where his greatness lay from the outset and that, as such, there was no reason for him to waste time writing books that were always different, to see if, in that way, he could discover what or where that *je ne sais quois* was; like what happened to thousands of writers, to all those poor wretches incapable of understanding that "Artistic originality has only its own self to copy" and whom he pitied for being so wide-ranging and so uncertain and so unoriginal.

But, between confusion and despair, Nabokov—who, with disappointed satisfaction, kept on finding that his students almost always selected the heroes, the dialogue, and the socioeconomic—saw how the correct choices tended to be marked least.

And those were 7, 8, 9, 10: imagination and memory (a property that the writer considered "a tool") and a dictionary ("a dictionary the size of an elephant," he specified) and, of course, last but not least, some artistic sense.

DAGA & BIJI & LINGCHI

He remembers that, of course, he was always convinced he knew how to count from seven to ten. And, as such, that authorized and continued to authorize him—immediately and ever since—to make certain changes and adaptations to the texture of his time and reality. But—warning—always remaining fully cognizant of each and every one of the alterations that he made or had made.

"My sense of the past is vivid and slow. I hear every sign and see every shadow" and "I live so many centuries. Everybody is still alive" a colleague of his had written once, a Made-in-the-USA madman from the south, and with palindrome last name.

That writer who he'd gotten to know on a campus in the north, in a land of cornfields and motorcycles, where every night they'd emptied bottles with names on their labels and shot the air full of lead from inside pistols.

Hour after hour, like that.

Until many church-bell tolls became few, as few as the options on a *multiple-choice* test.

Until the disingenuous literature students (their prose so proper and predictable and full of heroes and dialogue and socioeconomic issues) and the almost fictitious and beyond perfect farmers (tractors parked by the door, rifles on the bar behind which were bargirls who, in their time off, starred online in so-called corn-porn and best not to go into detail about that) and the many-times-rewritten owner of a bar called Last's (appearing here and there in stories and on blogs) all went off to dream. And so tired of the excessively impassioned monologues and long sentences that the two of them wielded as if fighting a duel that would propel them along to the cold of morning.

For that reason (his perception of the past was similar to that of that other writer whom he never saw again until he read and reread him in the fragments of his books quoted in his obituary, which evoked a man telling stories of old men fishing on docks hoping to hook marine monsters or to be harpooned by terrestrial sirens with long legs and big tits in the name of love), he felt validated and valiant when it came to altering his story to make it not more real but more authentic and indisputable and, yes, to give it some artistic sense.

And some *style*.

And in doing it—in *re*doing it—he didn't lie but gave it all a sense it didn't have at the time.

He didn't break it, he fragmented it.

And so, to begin what'd already begun, he decided, he would have to replace those *As* and *Bs* and *Cs* and *Ds* with successive †s.

Simultaneously unifying and making the selection of answers more difficult.

Turning all the options into a single many-headed option.

And, thus, all of those †s to stab and pierce them.

The † as the typographical symbol he used to pin fragments down in the pages of his biji notebooks.

Notebooks that—for him—were the equivalent of those journalists' notebooks in American movies. Those spiralbound notebooks that—naively and admirably—everyone trusted and nobody questioned and that, supposedly and without a doubt, were irrefutable evidence of unforgetting memory. And, maybe, that was why nobody dared falsify or quickly scribble anything down in them a few minutes before settling scores in front of editors, in those always hyper-frenetic editorial departments.

Notebooks like sacred writings that, as such, ended up as impossible as they were unquestionable.

Notebooks believed in like sacred texts and amen and go with God.

His, also, included key annotations and decisive fragments recorded in situ, but that later, on more than one occasion, seemed to have lost all meaning or importance or, simply, seemed more dreaming than dreamed, they were incomprehensible, or he couldn't pin down what they referenced.

And, again, here they are and there he goes:

"The biji—筆記—is a genre of classic Chinese literature that appeared for the first time during the Wei and Jun dynasties, and reached peak maturity during the Tang and Song dynasties. *Biji* can be translated, roughly but more or less faithfully, understanding translation as a kind of slow-motion reading, as 'notebook.' The different items in a biji can be numbered, but, also, can be read in any order, opening a path for yourself, starting at anywhere and jumping back and forth or up and down or side to side. Beginning at the end and ending at the beginning. The idea is that, one way or another, each reader ends up discovering a story as unique as his or her reading. And a biji can contain curious anecdotes, the words of others, random musings, philo-sophical speculations, private theories regarding intimate matters, notes about others' works, and anything that its owner and author deems appropriate."

The †—he learned—was a typographical symbol also known by the name *obelisk* or *dagger*, terms that were both derived from ὀβελίσκος (obelískos) and from ὀβελός (obelós), and that meant "roasting stake" (and more Greek words of the kind that he loved, because he can see them but not read them; the only one he can write from memory and always standing up is αἱμορροῒς). Though that † reminds him more of the hand of an hour-less clock or, even, a different kind of stake, the kind used to skewer Transylvanian counts.

A symbol that in the beginning was represented by the ÷ and was used for the first time by the Hellenic scholars of ancient Greece as a mark of criticism on the margins and the shores of their oceanic manuscripts. Its "invention" was attributed to the Homeric scholar Zenodotus of Ephesus, who availed himself of that symbol to highlight questionable or incorrectly employed words or false or bastardized paragraphs in the manuscripts of the *Iliad* and the *Odyssey* and of their many more or less apocryphal derivatives.

A symbol that, later, early Christians adopted to indicate a pause of melo-dious sensual silence between the hymns of one psalm and another psalm.

Here and now, millennia later, the † has a typographical status slightly inferior to the asterisk. And it could also symbolize a deceased person (dead in combat, if it was a soldier) when it was positioned next to his or her name. Or it could mean extinction, or to label something that no longer functioned as obsolete. In Physics and Chemistry, the † was used to indicate a specimen that was in a state of transition or something like that: its particles acceler-ated and its cells interlinked and all of that.

And it was no coincidence that he liked that symbol so much, he thinks; because, when he put it down, it *also* reminded him of the key that wound up his little tin traveler.

What's more: he could even embroider it across the chest of his super-antihero suit.

Particleman!

Product of an "accident" in a great collider of swiss hadrons and all of that!

A mere writer mutating into a complex rewriter of the entire universe!

Meanwhile and in the meantime, he used the † to skewer scattered fragments and turn them into pieces of something that dreamed of being an invention.

There he was.

In hospital waiting rooms or at airport gates or in the waiting area that was that desert.

Throwing those little daggers with blindfolded eyes, (or with open eyes, like those wrathful eyes that threw knives in comics) and asking himself if it made any sense to do what he was planning to do and answering:

†. Yes
†. No
†. All of the above
†. None of the above

And in that way to continue using those daggers as if they were the daggers used by the earliest emperors in the most Ancient China (in other words, in that China that was ancient even before the turn of the twentieth century; though the ritual was later recovered for that outside-time-and-space war in Vietnam). Daggers sharpened for the lethal ritual of *lingchi* (凌迟；凌遲) or "death by a thousand cuts" (杀千刀/千刀万剐；殺千刀/千刀萬剮).

He heard the word *lingchi* for the first time from the lips of the exceedingly imaginative and memorious and encyclopedic and artistic serial killer Hannibal Lecter (he'd also heard the theretofore—for him—unknown name of Matteo Ricci from that same full-toothed mouth for the first time; and that's what good popular literature is for: for finding out about things that, in general, high literature doesn't concern itself with and that turn out to be so useful when launching yourself into the air to try to fly as high as you can).

And he read somewhere that it was also discussed in the never-read-by-him (not because he hadn't tried multiple times) *Hopscotch*, by Julio Cortázar (along with *Ada, or Ardor*, the other book that, for him, as a reader, wasn't illegible but unreadable, and he'd always thought that *Hopscotch* would be a great title for the memoirs of a cocaine or heroin addict; but in the case of Cortázar the truth is that his resistance worried him less than in the case of Nabokov).

The torturing ritual of lingchi was carried out using tiny daggers to small pieces of flesh were stripped off the body of the prisoner being interrogated. Difficult questions that demanded answers with no *multiple-choice* option, much less an *I-don't-know* or, even worse, an *I-don't-remember* option. Questions often leaving a blank page that found itself blood-spattered red. And so, thin strips were sliced off the interrogated body to, along with them, extract juicy fragments of information from the memory of the tortured individual.

One by one.

Painfully.

Like how sometimes it hurts to remember.

The punishment was doled out on three planes or levels: public humiliation (because strangers were invited to witness the torture); slow and painful death (no need to explain anything in this sense); and unbearable punishment beyond life (because, the supreme priests warned the condemned man, not even on the other side would he become a reconstituted "whole").

And it started with the arms and legs.

And it ended with the head, where inventions and dreams and memories resided, inventions and dreams and memories that, in the final death throes, were transformed into one, single thing: into inventions and dreams that were remembered and about which—autofiction!—the tortured individual would swear anything was true as long as they granted him the final mercy of letting him finish dying so he could begin not remembering.

Once, on the first page of a novel written by an air force pilot and *bon vivant*, as a kind of epigraph (but an epigraph by the author himself; which to him, such a fan of opening his books with a collection of the words of others, extracting epigraphs from them lingchistically, as if they were layers of ideas, had seemed to him a gesture of admirable and enviable pride: being able to compose perfect and quotable lines to introduce ones that wouldn't be quite so perfect or quotable but that you had to acknowledge as your own and as possible epigraphs for others) he had read that a moment came in life when you realized that it'd all been a dream. And that only the things you preserved in writing would have any possibility of being real, of remaining on this side of the ocean.

That was a little bit like—though not alone and manning an F-86 Sabre hunting MIGs, but merely one among hundreds, strapped into seat 3C inside the dilated intestines of an Airbus A320—he felt now.

As if he were so far from shore and with no strength left, as if he were cutting himself slowly, as if he were going under and almost drowning, as if he were fragmenting, as if he were dreaming himself deeply, because he'd lost his gift for inventing himself across the surface of reality.

And—cut and drawn and bloody and bound for a bottom from which there was no coming back with his pockets full of broken stones—here came another fragment about fragments.

A fragment that engaged and disengaged with his now nonexistent country of origin.

HIS NOW NONEXISTENT COUNTRY OF ORIGIN

He remembers that all of this happened a long time after so much time. All of this that, now, is interference, a white and sky-blue noise. An invasion, an insert, an unscheduled news bulletin from yesterday broadcast from the future to be tuned in right now.

Everything that lies ahead, now behind.

After that and before this.

Like opening an already-read book and suddenly realizing that in the middle of it was a part, another part.

A new part that he didn't know or remember and that, unexpectedly, was like something he was inventing in a dream in which he appeared reading a book and remembering.

A timeless part but with all the time in the world, because—from where he is looking at and remembering it—the past neither stays still nor is it always in the same place at the same time. And it's even possible that the past hasn't yet passed and that it has yet to come to pass in that and in this part.

There it goes, here it comes.

It already was, it soon will be.

Here it is and now is the time: because really everything—though it might not be real—happens in the moment it is told or retold.

It happens and it happened—of that he's certain and about that he can be precise—when The Democracy came back from that place where it'd gone without, honestly, almost anybody at the time being all that concerned about preventing its departure, hit and run, and off it went with only the clothes on its back, as night was falling.

And The Democracy must've done something for something like that to happen to it, right? they all thought aloud and said under their breath.

Again, people talked and wrote and theorized in practice—like had already happened during its too many previous absences—around and about The Democracy *like this*: with a capital D. As if The Democracy were a famous brand or a featured product or, better yet, a living being. A more or less intelligent organism, a family member you didn't miss until they were no longer there and had disappeared from all the places they used to frequent.

Someone who, though absent, seemed closer than ever.

Someone who'd gone (or who'd been told to go, for their own good) on a long journey.

Someone who, all of a sudden in their absence, was more beloved than anything in the world.

And, now, that someone was back. And, as tends to happen, they weren't as perfect and as fun as everybody remembered. And besides they came back accompanied by horrible allegorical songs that generally included an incorrect usage of the word "utopia" and by very strange people who made promises that were impossible to keep and ended up doing almost the opposite of what they'd said they would do and . . .

But it was better than nothing.

And it was better than everything that had happened in recent years.

The Democracy (though imperfect and full of nervous tics and with a bipolar and histrionic temperament; it reminded him a little of the main character in *Sunset Boulevard*, always "ready for his close-up") was, in any case, much nicer than the twisted and inhumane and finally-deposed managers and commissioners and administrators who, for years, had done whatever they wanted in the building or had made a mess of the home, orchestrating the tuneless and cacophonous disappearance of neighbors, going to war over barren borderlands with the foreigners from the embassy next door, and only concerning themselves with the maintenance of the soccer field that they had built on common areas of the property.

And a couple of presidents had already done or were doing their thing with The Democracy.

The first, who didn't complete his term, and who left (*left* was an omnipresent verbal form in territories where *being* was nothing more and nothing less than the inevitable but instantly superseded preliminary to *ceasing to be*) not because "he left on his own" but because "they made him leave," because they told him "you're gone." Someone who, on a tour through the south, probably gobsmacked by the whistling of patagonic winds and confused by bad advisors, had fantasized about moving the capital down there: reestablishing it in a small town called Sad Songs, on the cliffs where on full-moon nights the roaring of the sea lions kept the sea dogs from falling asleep in the beds on their ships and forced them to count oceanic sheep or made them dream of strange things, about things like changing maps and altering geography.

The second president came wrapped in ponchos and flags and hit-single marches and with his arms around a couple of dead and immortal and everhandy mummies (without hands the one, without one finger the other). And he said things like "Everybody follow me: I won't lie to you" while winking one eye with the face of a Turkish caliph and of a *truco colifa* (and, yes, the jargon he'd retained from his now nonexistent country of origin—in this case a Lunfardo slang term referring to a phony yet lovable madman—was, inexplicably, irremediably antiquated; and, for him, its words had acquired the faded, washed-out colors of certain TV shows and movies from the '70s and of the flag itself). And in that way, with a sleight of hand, the man had accomplished the peak democratic feat: putting a mild local tragedy on par with a tragic universal wound. And magic with illusion, but magic in the end. And only as long as it endured; intuiting that it couldn't last forever and that—as tends to happen in the most titanic fantasies—when events precipitated and started sinking there would never be enough lifeboats for everyone. But, in the meantime, everybody happy, for as long as that oasis that was the illusory and illusionistic value of the local currency didn't dry up. A value that nobody acknowledged outside the borders of that country (something similar happened with a good number of local writers) where everybody traveled to buy everything that was on sale. On the double. While they still could. Before they wouldn't be able to be able to anymore. And everybody knew that things couldn't go on *like that* much longer (and *like that* left and was gone and, like in those sagas of the fantasy genre, a frozen new age of shadows and madness and spiritual degradation and economic devaluation and presidents who presided just a couple of days before being replaced and more little marches and more Capital into the fray and . . .).

But, meanwhile and in the meantime, at the beginning of the last decade of the century and of the millennium and of so many other things, the first thing that everyone looked for in the morning—the way others looked for the meteorological forecast or the horoscope—was that fantastical currency value, to find out if everything would remain that irreal for at least one more day.

And, oh, at long last and after such a long wait, all those big important and imported rock bands who'd never come before came (among them, the Rolling Stones; who, from then on, came back again and again, satisfied and incredulous at the disproportionate adoration they inspired there, a passion they'd never aroused anywhere else; not even during their refulgent youth, now so long gone, like the lyrics to their songs—fine to sing but better not to think about). And athletes were elevated to the level of gods and talked about themselves in the third person singular. And taxi drivers talked to all possible persons (and, sometimes, kidnapped or decided not to kidnap a passenger based on how much they enjoyed conversing with them). And entire plural families landed in Miami, consummate hordes of invading consumers. And on television they broadcast candid cameras and jokes that weren't bad but terrible to late-night fits of hysterical laughter. And every so often, to keep from kicking the habit, the lame joke of some building blowing up and the tanks rolling out of barracks to take a little spin through the streets and someone dying in "ambiguous circumstances." And everyone insisting "never again" while wearing a you-never-know expression. And nobody was all that sure about where reality ended and fiction began in that country (his now nonexistent country of origin) and, yes, in remembering—more than in inventing or in dreaming—names mattered, served, functioned even to reveal the perfectly oiled dysfunction of the country.

A country about which—sometimes, in that place that was the rest of the world and that he'd taken to calling Abroad, without specifying customs or languages—people asked him if his country "pained him." And he—who'd left a long time ago and had missed out on the latest aftershocks of the same eternal earthquake—answered that "it can't pain you because you don't know how it doesn't pain you, because 'twas ever thus; so there's no difference between pain and not-pain. There's no before to the pain. And, of course, there's no after to the pain, nor will there ever be."

But that wasn't true. He didn't really think *that*.

That was one of those clever things he said in interviews (and he'd been, back in the days when he was still interviewed, a clever interviewee, perhaps due to the advertising DNA he'd inherited from his parents) so that it would—he could anticipate it and rarely did he fail in his predictions—be highlighted in larger text within the body of the interview, back in days when people still read the news on paper. A slogan, yes. One of the more deliberate and calculated and hierarchized ancestors of the undisciplined and massive and diuretic tweet.

Now—so removed in body and mind from what was no longer there—the truth was that, for him, his now nonexistent country of origin was like an amputated limb and a cauterized stump. A name that only poked out the letters of its head on the jacket flaps of his books beside his date of birth. And that, he was sure, would not be repeated when time came to—if his books were reprinted—add the date and location of his death, when he was already history, ancient history.

DREAMMACHINE, TRIPMACHINE, ETC.

He remembers that, during his childhood, in his now nonexistent country of origin, the parents of the intelligentsia had the custom of, on Saturday afternoons, taking their children to a cultural center that, at that hour, showed films for intelligent children. The same cultural center that, at night, mutated into an underground venue for surreal-lysergic bacchanals and where, just a few hours later, the parents (after depositing their children at the safe houses of resigned grandparents) returned make their own childish mischief.

He remembers that one Saturday morning the program consisted of a collection of early short films by the brothers Lumière. With a live pianist whose function was to give that silence some kind of cadence and who—back when he debuted, he learned much later—also helped to silence the noise of the very noisy early film projectors.

There, on the screen, workers leaving a factory, a train pulling into the station, cyclists on the streets of Lyon, things like that. And everybody seemed to be playing themselves and were all really bad actors. Almost as bad as the parents of the children gathered at that theater, who played really bad parents and who, actually, seemed more like children dressed up as adults, only thinking about how soon the children's part of Saturday would come to an end and night would fall so they could forget about all of that for a few hours and go out and play by themselves and with each other. Parents who, at those matinee functions, were wearing sporty and youthful attire like what they saw in North American movies set on campuses of colleges and universities, but who, in a few hours—*easy riders* and *emma peels*—would be dressed in patterns somewhere between hippy and sci-fi, with metal appliques and fragments of mirrors and crests and flags stitched onto their blue jeans and Greco-Roman sandals and wooden clogs and would be making antinatural movements and strange faces (he and Penelope spied on one such party that broke out in their own home, on a week night or on one of the weekends when their grandparents were gone on one of their poker tours). Very similar to those men and women in black and white and moving so quickly and silently on the screen. And worst of all was when all those silent and black and white beings, there in front of them, made of light and shadows, tried in vain to be funny. And it seemed that the sensation that they experienced then was the presentiment that that new medium would soon be abducted by stories far more complex than theirs and then they would no longer be up to snuff, they would no longer be worthy, they would have nothing to tell, they wouldn't be autofictional. Their reality, they suspected, would cease to be interesting and the fact of being filmed and projected would no longer, in itself, be enough. So they clowned around and looked at the camera and stuck out their tongues and laughed like mad while leaving work or entering gardens: to make a memorable impression in the worst possible way. The one thing that seemed more natural than all the rest is the one with the train and maybe that's why it frightened the neophyte viewers at the time it was made.

And he also remembers that the fragment that impressed him most—directed by Louis Lumière, just forty-five seconds long, filmed in 1895 and shown for the first time in 1896—was titled *Démolition d'un mur*.

Nothing all that impressive: a group of men (with Auguste Lumière in the role of *contremaître*) knocking down a wall.

And that was it.

And that was more than enough: because unlike Georges Méliès—that simple magician who was only interested in cinematography for its potential to enhance the supposed power of his illusions—the Lumière brothers were, already, men of film. From a literary perspective, the Lumière brothers were an influence and outdid themselves while Méliès was an *influencer* always concerned about seducing his audience.

The titles of the Lumière brothers first films were, as such, also their plots: and, sometimes, reading those titles took as much time as watching the short reels themselves. But, of course, at the time, everything shown on screen was novel. There was nothing unworthy of being shown, because everything was yet to be filmed. But, yes, any kid at the time had already witnessed, whether they enjoyed it or not, the knocking down of walls—a metaphorical one, yes, but a wall all the same—in the blueprints and structures of their families, where modifications were always being made so more people could come in, more new couples of fathers and mothers.

In any case, what interested him most as a boy was what the presenter/host of the "session for microbes" had to say—in one of those voices that adults mistakenly believe children understand better—before projecting the film. He told them that this had been the first film with involuntary special effects. Because, at one its first screenings, the operator had forgotten to turn off the projector when rewinding it. And so, to the astonishment of the spectators (among them the worker-actors themselves who exclaimed: "The masters Lumière are wizards!"), saw how that cloud of dust turned back into a wall and stood back up. Following that surprise, the accident spun off into the serendipity of a revolutionary discovery and from then on, the short film was projected and re-projected that way. Rewind and *marche arrière* and lost time was suddenly regained (and The Beatles had a similar happy accident with the recording of John Lennon's voice while working on "Rain"; and they would repeat it intentionally on "I'm Only Sleeping" and "Tomorrow Never Knows" and "Strawberry Fields Forever" and in some of their promo videos at the time, which his parents imitated in one of their ad spots).

And many years later, he saw *Démolition d'un mur* again in a documentary about the Lumière brothers. And he thought that that wall that fell only to stand itself back up was like the one invulnerable wall in his memory palace. The wall he'd never dared invent anything about. The wall that sometimes returned in his dreams, diffuse and as if shrouded in fog yet always *there.* The wall that only once in a great while did he dare lean his head against to remember. The wall that was his own Wailing Wall. The wall that was *that* night.

That Night.

And seeing the Lumière brothers' wall, he couldn't help but wonder if Marcel Proust had seen it in his day and—seeing that new form of trick-less yet tricky magic, artifice made artifice—if it'd caused *something* to occur to him.

When that wall had fallen for the first time, Proust would have been twenty-five, publishing the miscellanea *Les plaisirs et les jours*—which had that line about how "The paradoxes of today are the prejudices of tomorrow"—and telling himself that, maybe, it was now time to attempt something "more important." And the imminent artistic maturity of Proust was already demonstrating the eloquent knowledge that "For, although our memories are entirely personal, they resemble those estates which have hidden side-gates, which often we ourselves have not discovered and have to have opened by a neighbor, so that we find ourselves arriving home from at least one direction which we had never taken before."

In the memory palace, yes, and more regarding its blueprint coming up, remember to remember it.

And back then, it was also the infancy of those other homes, homes as external as they were internal and thus memorizable, homes elevated into other kinds of memory palaces: that of film and that of photography. And their primary function and application was eminently practical: they were memory-aids and memory-trappers, and, through them, yesterday was preserved, like one of those prehistoric mosquitos that still bite, though they're preserved in the amber of millennia.

And after all—heightening his suspicion that Proust had seen that wall fall—*À la recherche du temps perdu* was full of allusions to optical-technological (including the shop window of the Combray *optician*) and to celestial mechanics and even to previews of Einsteinian relativity. Very sophisticated ideas that seemed to oppose or want to compensate and perhaps apologize for the foolish glibness with which Proust tended to photograph himself among friends, racquet in hand, as if it were a guitar, off-key and missing the beat. But, there, acting the idiot, Proust actually thinking so wisely about how "Some critics now liked to regard the novel as a sort of procession of things upon the screen of a cinematograph. This comparison is absurd . . . the sort of literature which is content to 'describe things,' to provide nothing more of them than a miserable list of lines and surfaces, despite calling itself realist, is the furthest away from reality, the most impoverishing and depressing, because it unceremoniously cuts all communication between our present self and the past, the essence . . . it is precisely this essence that an art worthy of the name must seek to express."

And—it was all connected—not long ago he'd seen another silent film filmed in 1904. People going down the stairway at the Parisian church of the Madeleine at the exit to a wedding. Upper class guests (the wedding of Duke Armand de Guiche to Elain, daughter of Duchess Greffulhe and inspiration for the Proustian Duchess de Guermantes) and, among them, a man who didn't appear to entirely fit in. Out-of-place bowler hat (everyone else was dressed in strict *hauts-de-forme*), raincoat, and looking everywhere but at the stairs. The most qualified scholars didn't hesitate to identify that image as the first and possibly only one of Marcel Proust in motion. (And seeing Proust move there, so quickly and spasmodically, with that exceedingly eloquent cadence of silent film, he imagined a possible traveling Proust, ever restless and wandering the world over: books by Proust with Jules Verne plots and Tintin *ligne claire*. Thus he invented a Proust who fell, toppling down the stairs and hitting his head and forgetting his entire past, so all that was left for him to do was to construct a present, almost desperate in its restlessness, and an exotic and adventurous future. *Proust on the Moon, Proust and the Blue Lotus Tea, Proust and the Mr. Trip Affair, Proust and the Guermantes' Scepter, Proust in Sodom and Gommorah, Proust and Flight 714 to Combray* . . .) Yes: the experts recognized that hat and that raincoat; and they knew that Marcel and Armand were friends and that the former's wedding gift to the groom was a revolver with the childhood poems of the bride engraved on the grip.

And that revolver makes him remember—everything continuously connects looking back—the revolver with which William S. Burroughs effaces expunges erases deletes rubs out wipes out obliterates Joan Vollmer in a

Mexico City apartment (the whole disastrous and absurd episode would've been a great and somber Lumière-brand short film to be shown going forward and in reverse, he thinks) to thereby, he would say later, become a writer possessed by a demon blacker than black ink. Burroughs who'd read all of Proust during his brief and sickly and very odd and mismatched stint in the military (he spent the whole time in the infirmary, with a book in his hands and in front of his eyes) reading books that took place as far away as possible in space and time.

And he remembers too that he read *À la recherche du temps perdu* in fifteen days, in a hotel owned by a union of mimes (and, inevitably, everyone is a mime in silent film) and in absolute silence. Incommunicado. Proustituted and Proustified. With neither phones nor TVs and, along the hallways, the rest of the guests practicing being swept along by the wind, opening a window, pushing against a wall that was impossible to knock down, because it was invisible. There and in that way he read, so happy, about the little Marcel in anguish due to his mother's absence and not being able to fall asleep and waiting for one last kiss (Burroughs had a similar story about the nights of his childhood) and entertaining himself with the shadows of colors and medieval romances, of the treacherous Golo and Genoveva de Bravante, living in the forests and all of that, projected on the walls and ceiling of his room by a magic lantern.

The lantern was still there, more magic than ever, in the museum dedicated to the writer, he saw it, he saw it, he remembers perfectly having seen it, illuminated. He saw it after buying madeleines at one of several bakeries in Illiers/Combray that claimed to be THE bakery, when he went to the little house-museum of Proust, and the truth was it wasn't that bad, because it was all was there. Original furniture. Little bedrooms. Children's books. A little bed for an asthmatic boy who didn't suspect he was a long-winded giant capable of toppling castles. And, suddenly, the inexplicable mystery—rising with the falling of rain—of a scent identical to that of his childhood vacations in the original, patagonic nucleus of Sad Songs. And the whole thing wouldn't have seemed to him anything more than an epiphanic and exceedingly-groupie sensorial hallucination if, in that very moment, at his side, another pilgrim (because of her features, he could tell that she was Indian and because of her English, which she probably studied at Oxford or at some other supreme shrine to the language) hadn't sighed, after exclaiming a familiar yet already faraway name, a "How odd . . . It smells just like my grandma's house in Bombay, when I was a girl." The possibility that that house in Illiers/Combray—the precise location that'd inspired the most mature pages ever written on childhood—would somehow contain the universal essence of all childhoods produced in him one of those strange fearless frights, but that now, remembering it, allowed him one final inspiration. Another form—perhaps benign—of that tumorific Combray Syndrome that he'd invented for his Mexican novel and that now had come true. Something like a chill to seek refuge from in the heat of the magic of that visionary lamp that helped the young Marcel discover "the color of words" with "supernatural multicolor apparitions, where the legends were depicted as in wavering and momentary stained-glass window . . . Certainly I found some charm in these brilliant projections, which seemed to emanate from a Merovingian past and send out around me such ancient reflections of history."

And later, already a *perdu* addict but *retrouvé*, he moved on to *Santeuil* (that earliest projection of Proust and of Combray) and there, in its first pages, he underlined: "The presiding genius of memory which, more quickly than any electric flash can make the circuit of a globe and, no less quickly, that of Time, had set [Jean] back in the past without his noticing that so much as a second had elapsed. Electricity does not take less time to bring to the ear pressed to the telephone receiver the sound of a voice which, in fact, is many miles distant, than does memory, that other powerful element in nature which, like light or electricity, moving at a speed so vertiginous that it seems almost to be its opposite, an absence of all speed, a sort of omnipresence, is everywhere at once around the earth, at the four corners of the world where its gigantic wings forever quiver like those of the angels which filled the imagination of the Middle Ages."

And yes: the man capable of stringing together those words was *also* the man—according to his biographers—who was sexually excited by sticking women's hat pins into the heads of live rats or begging, on his knees, for a young man dressed up as a gendarme to decapitate chickens. Nobody was perfect and what mattered in the end was the originality of the imperfections.

And, yes, he remembers reading Proust (when he was more or less thirty years old) but feeling like a child again: because the reading of Proust infantilized him by increasing his intelligence (opening doors he didn't know existed); it returned him to a state of wonder and astonishment like when he first learned to read, but made him feel like a prodigy confronting something far more prodigious than he would ever be. And he remembers that Proust—"a perfect memory is not a great incentive to begin a phenomenology of the memory"—didn't just make him feel immensely small but also provoked in him strange and inappropriate ideas, a short time thereafter, on a trip to France.

There he not only visited various Proustian landmarks and went to pay his respects to the portrait of Proust in the Musée d'Orsay, in what'd been a train station, with that immense clock reminding visitors that they might move on but those paintings would remain right there. Signed by Jacques-Émile Blanche and better than any selfie. There, Proust glowed like a vampire too shy to go around biting necks and, oh, one night he dreamed he was the flower that adorned his lapel. He *also* went there to hire a professional in the "acquisition" of valuable manuscripts (alias P'tit Coco) to have obtain the corrected pages stored in the vault of the Gallimard publishing house: the sheets of proofs with multiple manuscript annotations and a collage of strips of paper with additions to *Du côté de chez Swann*. (The crime failed to get off the ground when P'tit Coco—who always ran background checks on potential clients—deemed him "unreliable and emotionally unstable, in addition to being the author of books that were too long and that would be a nightmare not only for their eventual translator, but, also for the suffering and patient partner of whoever had the misfortune of giving them a voice in another language.")

And, yes, he had one of those lanterns (his and that of his contemporaries had been the last simultaneously antiquated and modern childhood where toys still seemed so novelly vintage; first the Cine Kraft projector and then the slides in the View-Masters were nothing but updated versions of what little Marcel had, descendants that'd only evolved ever so slightly thanks to a little bit of electricity and a lot of plastic). But now he has another one, of a different type and model and with different intentions. But, also, excavating from among the ruins of the past. A Dreamachine like those of William S. Burroughs that—as tends to happen with a good part of what Burroughs does—emerged from his first contact with the ingenuity of his cut-upper partner in art, Brion Gysin.

And, again, nothing happens by chance: in the early '60s, Gysin was passing his days at an artists' colony in the French commune La Ciotat (at whose train station the Lumière brothers filmed the arrival of that train). And, traveling by bus to Marseille, Gysin has a "spontaneous hallucination" staring out the window at the setting of the sun through the lines of trees passing by on the side of the road. Stroboscopic effect—with that blinking, again, very much à la silent film—that could end up inducing a form of hypnosis and that, without falling entirely into a trance, allowed you, according to Gysin "to travel toward yesterday." Or something like that. The effect wasn't a new phenomenon: Saulo de Tarso had experienced something similar by ceaselessly blinking his eyes on the way to Damascus and Nostradamus liked to move his hands with his fingers spread apart in front of the full moon. Gysin then consulted an optician friend who told him it was very easy to emulate that effect at home: all you had to do was turn on a record player, set it to spin at 78 Rpm, remove the arm with the stylus and, in the center, set up a cardboard cylinder with regular shapes cut out of it and a 100-watt lightbulb inside. Watching it spin, staring at it, with your eyes closed, feeling its flashes through your eyelids. Gysin names it the Dream Machine (and patents it on the 18th of July 1961, in Paris), but, later, Burroughs edits it to Dreamachine. And he shares it with Ian Sommerville—his "systems advisor," a euphemism for lover—who also designs the "random-sequence generator" that will result in the inspiration/tool for the cut-up, that other form of collage. Sommerville, in 1966, will be in charge of installing duel Revox recorders in the London flat of Ringo Starr for Paul McCartney who would use them to record the voice of Burroughs talking to himself while staring at, unseeing, a Dreamachine. One of the visitors to the session—*just connect*—is Dan Richter. The mime—the only mime he loves and admires—who will be in charge of choreographing and executing the movements of Moon-Watcher: the hominid who suddenly evolves thanks to that black monolith, that form of hyper-developed Dreamachine, at the beginning *2001: A Space Odyssey* (Richter, also, was the person who, a couple years later, would take the photograph for the cover of the raging *John Lennon/Plastic Ono Band* where the newly unmade Beatle will primally howl, rejecting everything he'd invented and remembered and concluding that the dream had ended.)

"The world's only artwork you look at with eyes tightly closed," Gysin raved at the time.

And, yes, the idea that dreams are part of memory and vice versa.

Gysin connected it to the recovery of forgotten memories and—for many of the people who used the Dreamachine—its effect was something "like real dreams . . . very often people compare it to films. Well, who can say who is projecting these films—where do these films come from? . . . indeed the alpha rhythm contains the whole human program of vision. Well—that is a big package to deal with—and I don't think anybody particularly wants . . . Flashes of forgotten memories, as if you were receiving a treasure you were always owner of but never aware you possessed." "When you cut into the present the Future leaks out," Burroughs adds.

Burroughs—the least upbeat of the beats, the one who will never go out of style, because his imaginary comes to him from the future and he never danced to that already-ceasing-to-be bebop beat—spends hours in front of that strobe, in his room in the "Beat Hotel" at 9 de la Rue Gît-Le-Coeur, Latin Quartier (now an elevated four-stars hotel, but at the time class 13, the worst of the worst: hot water three days a week, monthly change of sheets, the only bath had to be reserved and paid for separately), and mentions the Dreamachine in *The Ticket that Exploded* and in *Nova Express*.

In 1986, upon learning of the death of Gysin, Burroughs turns it back on (or he makes Burroughs turn it back on, so that his words match the scene better) and says that, seeing himself ever more surrounded by the deaths of his friends and contemporaries, he feels more and more that he's living—and having more and more waking dreams about—in the Land of the Dead: "Everyone I see is dead. The only thing that bothers me about the Land of the Dead dream is that I can never get any breakfast . . . That's typical of the Land of the Dead, no breakfast."

The same thing happens to him now.

There are fewer and fewer hotels that include it (breakfast) and you have to go out hunting for coffee and toast and that orange liquid that has nothing to do with oranges. And his French is so bad that he's afraid of going into a Paris bar and ordering something, because all those waiters seem, always, to sadistically pretend that they don't understand even one word of Spanish or

English. What's more, the French have that disturbing and despotic mania of changing the original title of everything. And he'll never forget the astonishment and indignation of Uncle Hey Walrus when he found out that Paris movie theaters had released the movie *A Hard Day's Night* about/featuring The Beatles (maybe because the four of them went running through the streets, and that helicopter at the end, and those photographs from the air of London in black and white?) as *Quatre Garçons dans le Vent*. And worse and more blasphemous: the French had even dared to rename HAL 9000 in *2001: A Space Odyssey* as CARL 9000 (even though Penelope, probably just to play the contrarian, had never seemed bothered by *Wuthering Heights* being Francofied as *Les Hauts de Hurle-Vent*, because she also really liked how *Cumbres Borrascosas*, almost like Spanish castanets, sounded). And how did the rest of idiomatic humanity respond to all of the above? With a lack of energy or—for him—with too much elegance and subtlety: with all those pretty French girls always ready to make love with any foreigner in movies that weren't foreign, girls who always seemed to be named Chloé that was, really, a name of Greek origin.

So he remembers—he marked it with an X on his map/guidebook—that he was near the building where Marcel Proust wrote *À la recherche du temps perdu* (whose first translator into English, C. K. Scott Montcrieff, maybe as a kind of tepid reprisal and to the initial despair and subsequent resigned acceptance of the author, retitled the book more subtly with a verse from the Shakespearean sonnet as *Remembrance of Things Past* and it's first part, "Du côté de chez Swann," as "Swann's Way," the translator even going so far as to insert a dedication to his friends into it).

And he tells himself that near that bank office where Proust once deposited and put his memory in writing, without a doubt, there would be a more or less polyglot bar and, probably, a gift shop where he could expand his collection of useless Proustian trinkets. But no. None of that. And like he already said, already remembered: he left that place completely perplexed and with a mouth full of madeleine.

And he also—so many years after his magic lantern—has a Dreamachine. Not the one that Uncle Hey Walrus had assembled (maybe to try to stop barking or to bark louder than ever, at that point it no longer mattered to him) according to Gysin's instructions: Uncle Hey Walrus took the liberty of putting two disks atop the circular and spinning turntable. Uncle Hey Walrus's original copy and number 00018, of *The Beatles*, which has so many scratches that you almost can't listen to it and that, at the beginning of "Helter Skelter," repeats over and over that primal scream of "Yeah Yeah Yeah."

No, his Dreamachine is different and it's unique.

It's called Mr. Trip.

His perfectly imperfect toy that moves backward when it should be moving forward.

More a *Mnémomécanique* than a Dreamachine, he thinks.

Something that his parents bought for him when he was very little. Something they offered to exchange when they discovered that it was defective and he—he remembered or had decided to remember it this way—completely rejected the idea. Because he liked that it was *like that*: that it was unique, that it went backward instead of forward, because—he thought then, pure intuition—to be able to tell it, first you had to know how to go back, how to move in reverse.

And all that interested him, willing to kill himself for it, was to live to tell the tale, to find a way to tell it all, even if he lost his life in the process.

SEVEN: PLOTS, AGES, SINS, SOULS, ETC.

He remembers that once, on an airplane, he happened across a book titled *The Seven Capital Scenes*. One of those self-help manuals for writers or, worse, a treatise for those naïve and desperate individuals who were convinced, as a final option, that starting to write would somehow be good for them.

The book wasn't his, rather it belonged to a young man (whom, right there and from then on, he couldn't help but rename The Young Man) who recognized him, introduced himself, told him that he'd read his work and that he admired him and wanted to be a writer and . . . he asked The Young Man if he would lend him that book.

The voluminous essay (it wasn't one of those books that are easy to hold up in the heights, where, being up in the air, everything seemed to weigh more and not less) promised to illuminate the mechanics of writing stories and novels. To reduce them to simple equations, propped up on the exceedingly improbable—yet so enticing and seductive—theory that there only existed seven basic plots (just like there were seven capital or deadly sins or seven Shakespearean ages of man, being committed and represented over and over again, with slight variations, in a world that was nothing more than, like it or not, the stage of a theater with an audience of varying size in the auditorium. And audience sometimes applauding and sometimes booing and sometimes yawning and not understanding).

Plots that were repeated with small alterations in form but not in depth, from the beginning to the end of times and of books and of theater and of film and of television.

To wit, another *multiple-choice* variation, wherein all the answers could end up being correct or incorrect:

1) Vanquishing the monster
2) Rags to riches
3) The search
4) The comedy
5) The tragedy
6) The rebirth
7) The journey from dark to light

And that was it.

Or not: because he was missing the most important plot of all: Plot number 8) which, for him, was like the undesirable yet so attractive eighth passenger, devouring the previous plots one by one. The plot that asked itself what was happening and what can I do to get out of here and go over there, or vice versa. The plot that asked itself about the other plots as it assimilated and digested them. The metaplot inside of which everything else fit. The answer to the miraculous equation that would turn him back into what he'd once been—someone who wrote and who hadn't yet forgotten how to put that plot in writing.

Yes: he didn't need to know how to start writing but how to start writing again.

And there weren't many manuals for that. Above all in times when everyone was writing all the time about everything they were doing and thinking.

Everyone seemed to have gotten addicted to making memory, yes. To distilling and refining and cultivating and producing memory. Memory, all of a sudden, like a powerfully addictive drug, but a drug could be acquired and manufactured without a recipe or any overly-complex processes. Memory that got hooked on memorizing itself. You start out inhaling the smoke of faint recollections that produced stupid laughter and end up shooting your veins full of the hardness of what can never be erased, something that took your breath away and left you breathless between respiratory failure and convulsions, shattering your heart and frying your brain. And so, of course, nobody forgot anything, but, at the same time and simultaneously, nobody felt obligated to remember anything: addresses, phone numbers, dates of anniversaries various. All of that was now remembered by an external and artificial memory that didn't commit—according to what the psychologist Daniel L. Schacter had catalogued—any of the (also) "seven sins of memory."

Memory, whose final stage—according to Shakespeare in *As You Like It*, which he had to explain to somebody once was not a play about Facebook—was a "second childishness and mere oblivion / sans teeth, sans eyes, sans taste, sans everything . . ." after he went through and/or recounted the ages of the infant, the schoolboy, the lover, the soldier, the justice, and the slippered pantaloon. (Ages to which he allowed himself to add that permanent age for a writer that is the age he was when he published his first book. An age at which, in a way, the writer would remain imprinted and fixed until his death, whenever it came). And so, old age like that fast-approaching asteroid—that wasn't going to crash into him, but that he was going to crash in to—only to discover water and oxygen and life there, but, also, a rarified atmosphere in which you begin to forget everything you want to remember and to remember everything you want to forget.

Shakespearean ages to which Schacter counteroffered, memorizing the following sins:

1) Transience: the notable diminishing of retention with the passing of time, a diminishing that can bring with it a forgetfulness that sometimes can imply the literal loss of the information.

2) Absent-mindedness: a kind of anomaly (a name that'd always seemed to him a great name for an absentminded girl whose absentmindedness always brought trouble) of the memory that involves problems to the point

where attention and memory become interlinked. The common errors of this condition include losing your keys or your glasses or forgetting your commitments; because in the moment of the codification of the memory, you didn't pay the necessary attention . . .

3) Blocking: what happens when the brain tries to recover or codify information and suddenly a different memory interferes or intervenes. Blocking is the principal cause of the "on the tip of my tongue" phenomenon (a temporal inaccessibility of stored information).

4) Misattribution: what happens when the correct recollection coincides with the incorrect recollection of the source of said information. For example, a person who is witness to a murder after having seen a TV program might come to accuse the murder on someone who they saw on that TV program.

5) Suggestibility: when the memories of the past are often influenced by the way in which they are remembered and when only certain aspects are emphasized so that it can seem like a specific kind of memory, those specific aspects are often incorporated into the recollection, whether they happened or not.

6) Bias: the feelings and worldview of a person distorting the memories of past events.

7). Persistence: a failure of the memory system involving the unwanted recollection of disturbing or undesired information. This memory may vary, be it a small mistake made at work or a truly traumatic experience. And those persistent memories can lead to the appearance of phobias, post-traumatic stress, and even suicidal impulses.

And he feels that to be able to write you have to commit those seven sins and several more sevens besides:

The Kübler-Ross model when it came time to process the death of someone close to you, a person who wasn't you yet still very much yours. There were the stages of denial, anger, bargaining, depression, and acceptance; to which he added a sixth and a seventh stage: the between parentheses in suspense of the (*to be continued* . . .) and that stage of rewriting and rereading.

And the Buckman Protocol for communicating bad news, another seven stages: preparing the most suitable context; finding out how much the person whose life you're going to destroy knows about the thing; knowing how far the person wants to go when it comes to finding out about what's coming and what's already here; sharing information; responding to the feelings the subject then displays; planning the follow-up to the process; evaluating the strategies used. And he, again, adding one more. And locating it, actually, in first position, at the beginning of everything: taking off running as fast as you can to avoid being caught by the radioactivity of that expansive wave, running for days and thousands of kilometers and never ever looking back.

And the seven souls that the ancient Egyptians enumerated in their *Book of the Dead*, that they painted on the walls of tombs or the sides of coffins and that William S. Burroughs recounted, while staring at his Dreamachine:

1) Ren, or the higher and secret name that is the soul that first abandons the body in the moment of death and is in charge of directing "the film of your life from conception to death."

2) Sekem, or the energy and the power and the light to press the right buttons according to the orders of his director.

3) Khu or the Guardian Angel, the supervisor of shooting the film.

4) Ba or The Heart, often traitorous and unstable.

5) Ka or The Double, the only reliable guide through the Land of the Dead.

6) Khaibit, or The Shadow of the Memory and of all the past conditioned by the way in which you decide to remember or forget it.

7) Sekhu or the Remains, what's left, what turns out to be impossible to forget.

And it is perfectly clear to him that his present is nothing but a continuous and reread and persistent and blocked battle between Khaibit and Sekhu. And that he—to tell the truth and not to lie, at this point, woeful sinner—no longer dares to bet on the victory or the defeat of any one of them.

(UN) MAKING HISTORY

He remembers a quote from the beginning of a novel (*Lunar Park*) where the book's author (Bret Easton Ellis) quoted the beginning of another novel of his (*Glamorama*), and where it read:

"So I don't want a lot of description, just the story, streamlined, no frills, the lowdown: who, what, where, when, and don't leave out why, though I'm getting the distinct impression by the looks on your sorry faces that why won't get answered—now, come on, goddamnit, what's the *story*?"

And, yes: it was a good goddamn question.

And, at the same time, a perfect defense for taking apart a plot and studying its instants and fragments and moments and throwing everything that sounded or read as superfluous and even disturbing or irritating to readers over the railing.

Leaving behind just the bare bones, yes.

With no flesh to be removed by means of ancient and remote and eastern torture methods.

Anticipating the storm.

The problem with such a system and/or instruction was that such rules or intentions are not applicable when walking backward and making story (remembering; and you can't remember in a streamlined and no-frills way) is what it's all about.

THE AGE OF NOW . . .

He remembers what it's all about, yes.

It's all about fragments, instants, moments.

And, remembering that, he feels even more ancient.

He feels prehistoric.

He feels like a man from the caves where dialed phone numbers (numbers that were never offered irresponsibly, like cigarettes or candies, without requesting prior authorization from their legitimate owners) were memorized. And when, also, in the half light, stamps were licked to be stuck to envelopes containing multiple pages of what'd happened and been written to be read in the future. And you had to actually get up from the chair to change the channel (so few channels, in black and white, and yet the feeling that there was always something good to watch) and there was no such thing as that talisman that was the remote—but absolute—control that allowed you to watch a movie from the beginning, even if it was already underway, and watch it again and record it just by pressing a button.

Not like during his childhood, when favorite movies could take months or even years to be broadcast again and when, during those extended pauses, you re-projected them in your memory, changing details, altering scenes, improving them and, along the way, in that way, learning to narrate by narrating and remembering them (when, on the other hand, books were always there; books could be turned on whenever you wanted to read them again, to reread them).

Or during his adolescence, when you had to wonder what the name of the person singing that song that you just caught the end of on the radio was. And you always knew that you couldn't just get the answer in a matter of seconds or of †; but that it didn't matter either: because back then you still possessed that human yet divine superpower of *making memory* and not the deceptively all-powerful super-impotence of having others do it for you, externally, using the most artificial of intelligences. And most important of all: back then you weren't constantly aware that you could find out anything you wanted to know on a portable screen (back then, computers and the mental notion and spatial concept of the computer occupied and were the size of buildings, as colossal as they were top-secret), you had to leave the cave to go find it and hunt it down. Because a lot of what you wanted to know was far away, in other countries as unreachable as bygone times. Knowing too that it wouldn't be at all easy to track down and trap the information, that the answer to the mystery was like an elusive mammoth, always moving and difficult to corral. But also realizing that—having to hook it with the hook of a question mark first to later stab it with the spear of an exclamation point—it would grant you access to the most satisfied and proud and plenary of joys.

What was the name of that age when you weren't yet aware that it was the end of multiple ages?

The Age of Waiting would be a good name, he thinks.

Times when you had to wait for everything. Times when it was normal to wait and nobody got nervous because something was delayed for a few seconds. Times when, while waiting for something to come or something to happen, so many other unexpected things came and happened with vertiginous slowness.

Times in which those unexpected things turned out to be far more interesting and beneficial than the ones you were waiting for.

Now, not so much.

Now everything comes right now.

Now you know everything that's coming and everything that comes now is everything you asked for almost right now.

And, since it already came, you're now already wishing for something else to come right now.

Now, ready, set, now.

Now was right now and welcome to the Age of Now.

Because now you never wanted anything complete.

You wanted it in pieces.

You wanted fractions that were turned into reality on the spot, but that never managed to be a satisfactory whole, because—unlike its fragments and its instants and its moments—they were pieces that had never been part of a whole to be put back together. They weren't like the fragments of that broken vessel that—according to the *Tikkun Ra* in the Kabbalah—had once contained the Divine Light and the repairing of which was the duty and responsibility of the men to whom God gave space and time so they could find a way to illuminate the dark. All the space and all the time in the world and the universe.

But *those* fragments were not like *these* fragments whose only and diffuse and instantaneous objective was, in the Age of Now, to keep on feeding the desire to keep on wanting fragments.

. . . THE AGE OF WAITING

He remembers that before, then, in his childhood—in the last years of the Age of Waiting—people daydreamed so much more than today, when people are becoming insomniac sleepers, illuminated by the bluish light of screens.

Because back then you had to wait for everything.

Everything took longer to come.

And that was a good thing, because—he's said it before—in the waiting there was time to want. There was more time to focus and reflect on every one of your desires. There was more time to invent and to dream and to remember everything that couldn't be forgotten but that the power of the desire perfected and made even more desirable.

Desires resisted more but were more resistant.

Desires were more enduring.

Desires—again—took longer to come true during the Age of Waiting, but you waited for them to come true with greater desire.

Desires were more desirable.

Desires were like daggers drawn seeking somewhere to stab.

To remember and to sharpen and to stab:

† That "imaginary adventure" of Superman where his human identity was revealed, or he retired, tired of saving humanity over and over again, or he married the tiresome Lois Lane.

† That toy in the toy store that always sold out before your birthday rolled around or before you saved up enough to buy it and that, later, would probably never be restocked, because back then there was never much of one thing. Everything was exclusive due more to scarcity than to marketing, but exclusive all the same, and truly exclusive. Toys like those imported Aurora Universal Monster models kits, far more attractive in random pieces fresh from their boxes: before, perfectly fragmented and better than after, being imperfectly assembled (especially the few phosphorescent pieces: the hands and the claws and the fangs and the faces, advertised in running-blood letters with a "Glows in the Dark!").

† That *other toy*.

THE TOY.

His forever.

And, thus, the ecstatic happiness of holding that little wind-up, tin traveler with a hat on his head and a suitcase in his hand.

And what did it matter that instead of moving forward, that little traveling man moved backward? Because what really mattered was that that toy's defect made it truly unique. And that, moving backward, it'd come to him and him alone, waiting at the edge of the table to keep it from falling into the abyss, protecting it as if he, small, were one of those giant gods in the films of Ray Harryhausen with Jason or with Sinbad.

† Those voices (the voices of his grandparents, far from home, in the south, on vacation, in Sad Songs) giving the most obeyable order of all: ordering him and Penelope to go out and play every morning. To play outside. In that outside that kids who lived the rest of the year in the city were hard pressed to gain access to, apart from brief and controlled sojourns, like going from the bed to the living room. And their grandparents generously decreeing that he and Penelope (with sandwiches and thermoses in their backpacks) not return until lunchtime. And later—after a siesta whose primary function was to make them hope that that siesta would soon come to an end—"going outside" again. Until dinnertime (though, every so often, Penelope did "use" those naps, actually falling asleep, and, in his memory, his already immense little sister was so similar to one of those Balthus girls dreaming that people were dreaming of them). And in that way, running to that forest and to that point where the path forked, to the right the path that led to that palazzo imported stone by stone from Venice and reconstructed there and inhabited by a an "old crazy lady, crazier than she was old" coexisting with a hundred chickens that she dressed up in silky little doll clothes; to the left, the path that led to the abandoned house of a local caudillo, the doctor Carlitos Cisneros, who, one morning, had gone up in a yellow airplane and thrown down hundreds of copies of a private edition of a book he'd written, in which he recounted all the most unmentionable secrets of that place (not autofiction but airplane-fiction, with long and convoluted sentences and all the time and all of it as if he were "telling it to one Odetta"). And everyone who saw him fly that day claimed that, once he'd unloaded his cargo, Carlitos Cisneros did a few pirouettes in the air, scrawling "The End" in smoky white across the blue, and was never heard from again.

Or if not, arriving to the beach under a sun that seemed never to rise and never to set, always there. And on the shores finding things that'd been thrown off of boats or had drifted in from a desert island (one summer he was constantly gathering bottles with messages inside them, which he read as if they were chapters in a serialized novel, the story of an anonymous local who only dreamed of being shipwrecked and whom he and Penelope tried to identify while simultaneously rewriting and adding information and hypotheses regarding his identity, suspecting that, actually, it was all just one of the typical games of Uncle Hey Walrus). And, one windy morning, the unprecedented event of a whale washing up on the shore, beached and singing until it died. A whale that, with the passing of the days, was picked at by gulls and clawed by crabs until, swollen by the gasses of putrefaction, it ended up exploding when a curious party got too close and lit a cigarette beside it and the sound and the smell were smelled and heard everywhere.

And then, time extending like a someone stretching their muscles and the theory and practice of childhood being something that should take place outside, yes, because the future would soon be arriving with all the interiority of jobs and spouses and life indoors.

† Those favorite movies that—again, he insisted on it over and over—you had to wait until they were rerun on TV or rereleased in theaters to see again. In those immense movie theaters where almost nothing took place that was appropriate for children of medium age apart from the constant replaying of animated Disney classics, using increasingly-damaged and, yes, fragmented copies. Films with scratches, skips in scene, and the occasional and delightful (shrieks and giggles in the darkness) spontaneous celluloid combustion, while he made memories and inserted and projected in his mind the part that was missing or the part that he wanted to put right there, between the parentheses of that burning elliptical pause: Mary Poppins getting pecked at by penguins or something like that. Because home projectors were a luxury and copies of films were scarce and expensive. And VHS didn't even exist yet much less the possibility of typing in the name of a film online and being able to watch it right there and then. So, wanting so badly to be able to watch them again, awaiting their return, movies were imagined. You daydreamed them. You corrected and added to and improved them. And thus, in that way—counting the months or years until you would be able to see them again—you subliminally learned how to tell a story. How to narrate. And, from those versions—imprecise but entirely your own—you ended up achieving personal sound and a vision all your own.

And so too (advantages of the drought or scarcity of stuff for children/ youth, which shoved kids off in search of adult shores sooner than nowadays, when everyone appears to be trapped, at least until after their first divorce, in a Marvel/DC/*Star Wars* loop, wanting only to obey the bad boy and—like him—be the patricidal Kylo Ren when he orders "Let the past die . . . Kill it, if you have to") developing earlier on a personal and inimitable style that left no room for inconceivable yet all too real infamies. Like the animated and disanimating *The Emoji Movie.* He started watching it out of pure and morbid curiosity on one of his last flights. And within the first minutes of that horror, they were already talking, euphorically, about emojis—which, of course, had already, inevitably, been assigned their own special day on the calendar—as "the most important invention in the history of communication" for "times when nobody had the time or the concentration to type *real words.*" And then he couldn't come up with the answer when he asked himself if this was how it would all end; if millions of years of evolution and effort that led from the bison painted on a cave wall to the lettered lines of diverse alphabets were going to end like this: with the shapes of fruit and vegetables standing in for sex organs and tits and asses.

And, yes, there'd already been one of those always disconcerting scientific studies that demonstrated that emojis "altered the brains of their users," because said users were never entirely sure what they meant and whether they were "ironic or sincere" in what they expressed. And—seeing and hearing that—he made his exit from movie that was set in a city called Textopolis. And he unfastened his seatbelt and went to the bathroom to throw up, propelled by the fear that some clever screenwriter had already found himself dreaming of writing the Great American Emoji Novel. And had figured out a way to insert into that garbage something IKEA had once thrown in his face, as if it were a bone or a pile of shit: "Hey, man, you know what your beloved Nabokov once said in an interview? Someone asked him where he ranked himself among living writers. And Vladimirito answered: 'I often think there should exist a special typographical sign for a smile—some sort of concave mark, a supine sound bracket, which I would now like to trace in reply to your question.' What sign do you think the Man was referring to, man? To me it sounds a lot like an emoji, am I right?"

Luckily, nothing about the virtues of emojis was being discussed when he was a kid. There were no movies barely concealing their condition as subliminal propaganda for stupid smartphones or misapplied apps. The movies he saw during his childhood might have been crafted to make money, sure. But also to enrichen viewers. And, due to the lack of children's content, so many others (that was an adult world and not one geared toward children like today, a world where kids were exposed no problem to films like *The Poseidon Adventure* with its upside down world and its terrible deaths and its crises of faith) had become adult-movies-for-kids-of-his-generation-and-situation (and because his intellectual parents needed to be able to deposit them somewhere for a few hours while they went to liberate oppressed peoples or to betray friendships or to float in space). That'd happened to him with *Citizen Kane* or with *The Third Man* (he remembers that on one of his tours, at a Hispanic institute in Vienna, he'd met an old man, Herbert Halbick, who'd once been that three-year-old boy yelling at a terrified Joseph Cotton and who confessed to him, almost embarrassed, that he remembered absolutely nothing of the shooting of the film and that, every time he came across the film on TV and he saw himself there, it was like looking at "a ghost of myself"; and then he thought about how, yes, few things are more frightening than the sudden materialization of the child you once were and you have been). Or with *Lawrence of Arabia*. Or, of course, with *2001: A Space Odyssey* (and, oh, one of the last things he did with Penelope's son, with He Whose Name Must Not Be Mentioned, was take him to see a commemorative rerelease of *2001: A Space Odyssey* and he reminds himself to definitely remember more about that later on). Movies that back then didn't tend to make a run on TV (and if at some point they did, they were atomized by infinite commercials or with multiple cuts because of their excessive length), but that, at least, were shown a couple times a year at the projection room. In that room in the heights, on the ninth floor of the cultural center. A place to which he and Penelope returned over and over again while their little classmates preferred submarine documentaries or talking animals or comedies with French rabbis and gendarmes or Italian cowboys with fake American names or national commandos from his now nonexistent country of origin, training kids in order and respect for institutions and, yes, back then there wasn't much to do but watch movies.

Then and there, he and Penelope rode up in the elevator surrounded by adults who looked at them not really comprehending what they were doing there. And they, to further unsettle them, the one to the other and the other to the one, spoiled and spoilers, in loud and high-pitched voices, said things like "I must admit that this time your child costume is quite impressive" or "When we get out of here, let's not forget to swing by the church to ask for some food" or "Rosebud is the sleigh" or "Harry Lime is alive" or "HAL is crazy" or "Better for Mr. Memory [inspired by a real person known as William James Maurice Bottle and whose artistic name was Datas and who had the power to not forget anything he read and who when he died sold his brain for 2,000 pounds] not to answer the question about what The 39 Steps are" or "Don't forget to take your cancer meds" or "You'll see: our intergalactic pursuers from Urkh 24 will never find us up here."

So then—small but feeling ever bigger seeing those great films again—he and Penelope watched them closely, to remember them more and better, to forget them worse and less, to rearrange and reassemble them, to reread them in their own image and semblance.

COLLAGE AND (DE) CONCENTRATION

He remembers that, of course, he didn't remember those movies entirely or in their entirety.

He remembered scenes, moments, fragments, instants.

And sometimes they all blended together and an ape in the middle of a sandstorm was struck by the sudden appearance of a sled while keening zither music played or something like that.

And in school—in primary school, where one was first exposed to bodies of knowledge in a fractioned way, to simple parts of complex subjects, to the basic pieces—before you were shown how to draw, you were shown how to cut and paste.

Collage, yes.

And oh how they liked to say that French word there, in the classroom. Clutching scissors and tubes of white and viscous glue and small colorful squares with a metallic tint that made them seem futuristic and random magazine pages (pages that sometimes included photographs of his parents and, oh, the unspeakable—but suddenly stimulated and authorized by his teachers—joy of dismembering them, cutting both of them into pieces with scissors). And, he supposes, if he'd ended up a serial killer (one of those perfect and uncatchable monsters who finally gets caught because of something as stupid as running a red light), those collages of his (mother with her legs at the height or her ears, father with his head under one arm, sailboat burning in the flames cut out of a photograph of a forest fire) would have been tucked away in EVIDENCE-brand plastic bags to be studied by psychiatrists and Made-in-Quantico experts in criminal behavior.

Collage was, yes, the magic word and the password and the *Cut it, Sesame* and the *Pastacadabra*.

And saying it made them feel like artists, foreign, cosmopolitan, removed, and even like invaders and conquistadors and all-powerful mad scientists searching for some kind of logic in everything they (dis)assembled and (re)fixed, under the permissive gaze of the Teacher of Artistic Activities. A teacher who for a while and unlike all the other teachers of all the other classes, yes, allowed them to create without imposing any geographical limits or syntactical rules or mathematical formulas or national holidays.

The collage was an authorization to break with everything, an everything is valid reward.

The collage, where all of them were the beloved children of the chaos that preceded the inauguration of a new world that was all their own and personal and that they pasted and brought together by pressing the fragments down with the tips of their fingers onto poster board.

The collage was something as unto-itself as fingerprints or snowflakes (though not long ago he'd read about recent discoveries that were starting to admit the possibility that—in light of the finally admitted impossibility of producing a complete and definitive census across time and space, between yesterday and today and tomorrow—there exist fingerprints and pupils that are partially identical in different people; as if composed of parts of fingers, parts of eyes, like a collage, yes. Or maybe what happened was that lines and colors and shapes of prints and pupils and snowflakes were recycled and would become available again in the future, when they would be reassigned, when their users died, and they no longer touched or shut or melted).

The collage was making pieces out of something external (and, sometimes, pulling out fragments and epigraphs and blind quotations or ones you knew when you saw them).

The collage was to make something of your own out of the pieces of others.

The collage was to destroy while creating.

The collage was the mixed and simultaneous Tralfamadorian books in Kurt Vonnegut's *Slaughterhouse-Five* and the "millions of acts both delightful and awful" all of them occupying "the same point in space, without overlapping or transparency" in Jorge Luis Borges's "The Aleph."

The collage was fusion: such a sci-fi word, in days when the idea of the future still existed as something autonomous and unreachable and hadn't yet been, yes, fused to/with an already-futuristic present, into a kind of atemporal collage where both the retro and the vintage fit, but always as cutouts of the here and the now.

The collage abolished the historical while simultaneously intensifying it, blending time periods and styles (and he remembers one that he made back then and still has to this day: the painting *Rooms by the Sea* by Edward Hopper *collaged* with the great wave of Kanagawa painted by Katsushika Hokusai coming in through that half-open door and *VG 10!* in the qualified and qualifying handwriting of his invented and dreamed and remembered and always capitalized Teacher of Artistic Activities. A teacher who, before long, would "disappear" along with his parents, but who would reappear, oneirically, in his first wet collage: him falling between her spread legs to wake up with his pajama pants wet with something reminiscent of the glue he used to make his collages).

The collage was the noble and artisanal ancestor of the bastardized and industrial Photoshop.

The collage that—though it was originally Made in China a thousand years ago—was the modern French relative of the cut-up.

The collage that'd been, at the beginning of that century, the modus operandi favored by the surrealists, but that to him, really, seemed a better potential representation of his current fragmented reality.

The collage that to him seemed hyperrealist.

The collage that, as Robert Rauschenberg understood it, was pop before there was pop, for his *combines* and *gluts* while he erased (*efface expunge erase delete rub out wipe out obliterate*) a drawing by Willem de Kooning and titled it, in 1953, *Erased de Kooning Drawing*.

The collage in all those films from the '60s and '70s (especially *2001: A*

Space Odyssey, which was a collage in itself: three distinct parts that end up assembling one story).

The collage that was the technique used by The Beatles for the covers of *Revolver* and *Sgt. Pepper's Lonely Hearts Club Band* and for the interior poster with random pictures and scattered letters of *The Beatles* and to record/assemble songs-in-fragments like "A Day in the Life" and "You Know My Name" and "Happiness is a Warm Gun" and "Revolution 9" and the farewell medley on the B-side of *Abbey Road*. And, oh, all those voices and sounds and howls and laughter and alarm clocks and, argh, all those fucking phone conversations on the albums of Pink Floyd: that band that was ecstatically unhappy in everything they devoted themselves to and always on the hunt for the triumphal sound of absolute frustration with their surroundings.

The collage that was the sound resulting from all those four-track machines that they used to record all the best albums of his childhood. Four channels, one for inventing and one for dreaming and one for remembering and a final channel for blending it all together, as if they were the past and the present and the future and the resulting timeless time for mixing and remixing all the time.

The collage that, for his admired fragmentor Donald Barthelme (who also considered Rubber Cement "the most important tool of genius today" and who wrote multiple stories on the basis of pasting together pieces of different figures), was "the central principal of all art in the twentieth century in all media" and "in which unlike things are stuck together to make, in the best case, a new reality," which may also be something unto itself: "an itself, if it's successful." A sane representation of "anxiety" as "the central principal of all art in the etc., etc.," to thereby end up accepting that "the aim of literature is the creation of a strange object covered in fur which breaks your heart." And that for that reason, when the more traditionalists "called for more structure," to satisfy them and shut them up, "we brought in some big hairy four-by-fours from back in the shed and nailed them into place with railroad spikes."

The collage was the technique that, according to the insomniac poet Charles Simic (one of the few poets that he *got* and who once told him that he wrote blind and with the lights off, to keep from waking his wife and that, in that way, the following morning, he was able to marvel at the multiple possibilities offered him for tying those loose verses together), was "that art of reassembling fragments of preexisting images in such a way as to form a new image," and it constituted, for him too, "the most important innovation in the art of this (the twentieth) century."

The collage as the fragmented and philosophical discipline alluded to in the ardent pages of *Ada, or Ardor* that he'd set ablaze, wherein: "An individual's life consisted of certain classified things: 'real things' which were unfrequent and priceless, simple 'things' which formed the routine stuff of life; and 'ghost things,' also called 'frogs,' such as fever, toothache, dreadful disappointments, and death. Three or more things occurring at the same time formed a 'tower,' or, if they came in immediate succession, they made a 'bridge.' 'Real towers' and 'real bridges' were the joys of life, and when the towers came in a series, one experienced supreme rapture; it almost never happened, though. In some circumstances, in a certain light, a neutral 'thing' might look or even actually become 'real' or else, conversely, it might coagulate into a fetid 'fog.' When the joy and the joyless happened to be intermixed, simultaneously or along the ramp or duration, one was confronted with 'ruined towers' and 'broken bridges.'"

The collage that was his style and his Nabokovian "true creativity."

The collage that was, personally, his calling card. His real thing and his burning standard above ruined towers and broken bridges besieged by fetid fogs and ghost things.

The collage that in his books—and especially in *The Impossible Story*—was the direct and familial and close relative of *cut and paste* and *copy and insert*.

The collage that was, in essence, the essence of his profession: you cut up when you read and you pasted when you wrote. Or vice versa.

The collage that was the way in which he exercised his memory and his method for assembling a whole life, his own, but as if it were that of someone else. Discovering, with perspective and looking back, all those connections and lines. Uniting one fragment with another fragment that he hadn't noticed when pulling together the different pieces. And so, all of a sudden, that woman had a sun face and that house lived underwater. And at a certain point—as he'd written in one of his books back in days when he still wrote books, in days when he remembered how to write a book, how to begin and to stick with and to finish a book—he understood that "The memory, after all, is the experience, and the important thing isn't what happens to you but what you do with what happens to you" and *cut* and *paste*. And *save*.

The collage that was dangerous if you didn't use it carefully and responsibly and only after intense prior training with full knowledge of everything you were cutting up.

The collage that was like accelerating particles and interconnecting cells and all for the simple pleasure of making them collide.

The collage that was, for him, something as enumerable and enlistable as the desert: that blank-page landscape where you could stick so many solitary things that suddenly come together and become inseparable.

The collage that was, also—having become indomitable and impossible to corral; with that manner and those tendencies that (he couldn't have suspected it back then, clutching blunt-tipped scissors suitable and safe for children) would end up being sloppily and irrationally stuck and pasted together into the most characteristic formal attitude of the end of one millennium and the beginning of another—*zapping, sampling, remixing, linking, web-surfing,* and, finally, the hyperactive yet crippling Attention-Deficit-Disorder *way of life.*

The collage that, now, for him, was no longer the search for and focus on the whole but the dispersal and displacement of everything.

The collage that was something very similar to what he'd felt that morning on that childhood beach when he almost drowned and suddenly—as if a couple pieces of futuristic metallic paper had been pasted on top of him— he knew how and was able, for a few minutes, to read and to write and to understand.

Thus, continuing to believe in continuing to create.

Thus, understanding (or not understanding) everything in slivers and shards and fractions and details with no time given to contemplating the totality of anything.

Thus, the contemplative and reflexive calm of the all-for-one (during his childhood when there hadn't been screens where the universe was within reach not of your hand but of the tip of one finger, the necessary movement was in the shoulder, and the collage and its practice was absolute excess and self-absorption) had turned, in recent times, into the frantic and senseless spasm of the all-for-everyone. Into total lack of concentration. Into creativity as merely recreational. Into the original as copy. Into admitting that you couldn't focus your attention on anything for very long with, yes, once again, that one finger stuck in your eye.

And so it was that—coming unstuck from the pages—the slowness of the years turned into the speed of the smithereens.

HAVING FUTURE (AND NOT HAVING IT)

He remembers that back then, during his childhood, he already perceived that there was something *strange* in all of *that*. In—generationally—inhabiting the last futuristic childhood (because soon the future would be an inseparable part of the present; soon the future would be nothing more and nothing less than the next night of every day or, at most, the next weekend or, further down the road, the latest coveted model of mobile phone).

Thus, his childhood and that of his contemporaries as the last childhood where the whole future was still in the future. A childhood with imagined colossal computers and planets always inhabited by tentacular aliens and the most beautiful women in the most skin-tight outfits and interdimensional wormholes and wristwatches with screens on them used to converse with loved ones and to argue with beloved archenemies. A childhood in which the technological advances had something imperfect and primitive and beyond-the-grave about them. A childhood when, over the course of several months, they'd watched a delirious documentary called *Memories of the Future*, claiming that the gods of ancient civilizations had been extraterrestrial astronauts doing something akin to religious tourism on Earth.

And, oh, on this side of that big white screen, all that domestic and instantaneously primitive technology: the *clack-clack-clack*, like a grinning skull, of the first electric typewriters not coming to replace/forget the *clickety-clack* of acoustic typewriters; the saturated and washed-out colors of the latest-generation televisions (and that so-strange palette of the pale films of the '60s and '70s); the walkie-talkies that you couldn't talk on if you walked too far apart; the Polaroid-brand pictures (the ones that people would flap, thinking, who knows why, that they were accelerating their revelation) where everyone had the aspect of freshly-embalmed corpses with red Nosferatu eyes.

And the few battery-powered toys and the many toys powered by flesh and blood or by being wound up by the turning of a metal key.

Toys like his toy.

Toys like THE TOY.

And space was always outer and infinite and unexplored but to-be explored.

And the supposed and increasingly abundant irrefutable proof of intelligent life on other planets that that one little girl was always talking about, that one really ugly little girl with an old lady's name: Hilda, the daughter of some of his parents' friends, who were also models and who sometimes came over to visit, that horrible little girl who never let go of that dirty and smelly globe-shaped pillow, while saying things like "Roswell" and "Area-51" and "Planicie Banderita" (and much later on he read a story by that other writer who was born in his now nonexistent country of origin and who he often saw conversing with Enrique Vila-Matas; and the truth is that the story wasn't bad at all; and in that story Hilda—or someone very similar to Hilda, his Hilda—made an appearance; and it was around that time that he started to worry and think about things like alternate dimensions and space-time loops and all of that and all of those things referenced by the futurism of his past).

And, back then, everyone was still looking up at the paradox of an ancient sky with the same eyes as the eyes of ancient peoples. Because no teacher of basic natural sciences would dare teach any of that. And not until the first great frustrations and disappointments of his adolescence (coinciding with the arrival of the insufferable Carl Sagan and his turtlenecks who, nothing happens by chance, had really, really rubbed Stanley Kubrick the wrong way in his advisory capacity, while Kubrick was preparing to shoot *2001: A Space Odyssey*) would he learn that a good part of what you see from down on Earth could, itself, no longer see anything: because most everything that appeared there above was no longer actually twinkling or blinking, its eyes having already shut, though the worlds kept wheeling around. A good part of everything lighting up space was the ghost light of dead stars, things that were no longer there and that now were only inventions and dreams and memories.

The sky was full of unforgettable dead things and that was why the dead went up into the heavens. Yes, deep down, the sky, which was automatically associated with what was yet to come, was nothing but what'd already taken place and actually no longer existed up there in space.

And so, outer space was not all that different from inner memory. Outer space was now, really, also, the always internal past.

Now, decades later, just the paradox that the most futuristic thing ever undertaken and achieved by human beings had already happened more than half a century in the past, at the zenith of his futuristic childhood: going to and returning from the moon.

And they never went back to the moon, even though, paradoxically, any of today's mobile phones possessed technology multiple times more sophisticated than that of *Apollo 11*. Because by the time of *Apollo 12*—a mere milestone after the greatest success of the space race—people were already tired of looking up and they only regained some interest with the unlucky number 13, when there was the possibility (finally frustrated) that its crew would die out of orbit. But, subsequently, again, even the program's most recent astronauts broadcast down to Earth things like "How's it going for us? Well, all of this is really boring." And, of course, everything that happened with the *Challenger* and the *Columbia* was a big surprise, yes, but wasn't something that could be considered a lot of fun.

That was what'd happened with the what-will-be or the what-could-be: futurism was ever more remote and ever more a thing of the past. And even photographs of the Manhattan skyline that including the twin towers of the World Trade Center today seemed more of tomorrow than of yesterday (and he'd always wondered why, when it came time for the reconstruction, they hadn't rebuilt the World Trade Center exactly the same as the original or, at most, with one additional floor to thereby, with the palpable recovery of its memory, not do away with the memory of the attack and the fall of the towers, but do away with something that was unforgettable for the terrorists).

And, who knows, if extraterrestrials were watching Earth from another planet, as if it were an entertaining and disastrous TV show, maybe they also preferred to rewatch old episodes from their favorite series: reruns of past seasons where people still read unplugged books by candlelight and the air was cleaner and clearer and the telephones only rang a few times a day and people had to rush to answer their call (you had to go to the telephone, running, because fortunately, the telephone didn't walk around or sleep or travel with you) as if it were a crying baby with a cradle and a bedroom all its own and not a mutant that howls incessantly and that you have to carry around and hold in your hand all the time. Worse special effects back then, for sure; but far better feelings than later on, than right now.

And thinking about all of that made him think—a few days ago, flying in another airplane—of a possible idea for a novel not *of* science fiction but *with* science fiction. A novel with a melancholic extraterrestrial tuning in Earth and with lots of snowflakes, each of them different, like fingerprints (and, again, when he was a kid he was already wondering how they'd arrived to that certainty about the singularity of fingerprints: had they compared them all, including those of everyone who'd died since the beginning of History? Same goes for snowflakes: how could they claim something like that, that no two were the same? Especially after someone had told him that artificial snowflakes were all the same, circular and not hexagonal, and that that was why some skiers were very good on natural snow but not so much on fake snow and vice versa) And, in that possible novel, that made reference to September 11th, 2001 and featured two lovestruck young men, under the falling snow, but—unlike what happened in that one story that he wished so much that he'd written—not dancing or dying. And, of course, there—watching them from a window—he would insert a new variation of Ella and . . . And he asks himself why hadn't he obeyed that initial impulse—already felt in his childhood, after seeing *2001: A Space Odyssey* for the first time—to become a science-fiction writer (and thereby cater to and thrill all those rather undeveloped androids roaming around book fairs and festivals who, when they asked him "what his books were" and he said "Fiction," immediately asked "Science fiction?") A "genre" writer. Happy and secure within the clear and precise parameters of the chosen model. Not the futuristic or the space-operatic kind of science fiction, which had never interested him all that much, but classic science fiction, science fiction derived from that of Verne and that of Wells and that, in a way, ends up connecting to and biting the tail of the comet of the historical and realist novel that, sooner or later and always, wound up being read as a kind of science fiction in reverse and, hey, if even that fantasy for the brainless known as *Star Wars* took place in the most distant past, *a long time ago in a galaxy far, far away* . . . The science fiction that always took place in the present and functioned as a kind of black hole, drawing the light of tomorrow toward the here and now. The science fiction that didn't concern itself so much with projecting into the future—a reflex that'd become even more automatic with the blooming of atomic mushrooms and the uptick in postcards of the apocalypse—but accelerating the present with the help of characters literally ahead-of-their-time and often out of their minds. The science fiction that, paradoxically, authorized everything as valid (the future as a blank page) while simultaneously demanding absolute obedience to tradition. And science fiction was a genre, a literature, not *of ideas* but *of an idea*: all you needed was one good and original idea to build a book or a twenty-four volume saga on top of and to be loved and enriched by fans who would never abandon you after your first book and who would accompany you forever, to infinity and beyond. Readers far more interested in having you describe, in perfect detail, the exact composition of the atmosphere of Urkh 24 than in the diffuse orbits and absolute voids of the ritual of reading and writing.

Because, after all, *that* is what his books were all about: about the inexact, non-fiction—but nevertheless increasingly alien discipline—science of reading and writing; about another form of interplanetary voyage and cosmic mutation and interdimensional wormhole, but with far subtler and harder-to-describe technology. How much happier would he be if he'd embraced one of those ideas (Martians, time machines, mad robots, utopias and dystopias and entropies; subjects that, in addition, were far more adaptable and filmable and easier to illustrate in bright colors and blinding onomatopoeias) where all you had to do was follow the traditional steps, spinning off variations of a handful of clear and firmly-composed and preestablished arias.

But, now, not even that. And that excited drive to make contact with beings from other galaxies in a possible novel didn't last him long (though it did last him a lot more time than what he'd once devoted to a possible synopsis for a TV series with a comedian from a ghost club named Stan to be titled STANd. Or that other one with zombies that never got past the title: *The Living Bad*; and he wasn't even sure if it was a good title or just a/another bad joke). And even a name for an antihero that he found funny: Charlie Surf. And another name for a possible psychoanalyst detective: Jean Levy (the idea was that he was an ex police officer and profiler who moved to a small town and worked there as a therapist and ended up learning all the town's secrets and becoming the most powerful person in that place and for that reason people were always trying to kill him, over and over again, and that was the great idea: the detective was, always, the possible victim). And he'd even had a sinister idea, propping himself up on all those exceedingly successful and supposedly moving fictions of the Holocaust, with kids in pajamas and book thieves and tattoo artists and ballet dancers and orchestra directors and librarians and artists various (he'd always been surprised by the abundance of sensitive and aristocratic top brass Nazis who were big art lovers in all those novels and movies; or that indispensable scene where, amid the clamor of battle, everything appears to stop so that a soldier boy or a village girl could sing an ancient and devout hymn with an angelic voice). His idea features a Great Jewish Writer from Berlin. A writer Hitler is an unconfessable fan of. Particularly of his series of novels about the Karminsky family; few things gratify the Führer more than, over the course of decades, following a clan obsessed with social and economic climbing and the wretched quarreling and conspiracies of its members. For Hitler, there is something almost pornographic about reading them; watching them in writing, Hitler feels like a voyeur spying on a world foreign and contemptible to him, but, nevertheless, enticing and exciting. But the Great Jewish Writer hasn't written in years and feels his creativity is expended. The Great Jewish Writer is out of ideas and Karminskys seem exhausted and exhausting to him. They've reached a dead end, and he feels more trapped alive than blocked, like a prisoner between parentheses. And so Hitler—in the darkest shadows, like a sinister puppet master; responding to those millions of devoted salutes of raised and extended arms with the indifference of his own arm folded at chest-level, as if it were hard for him to do it, as if he was made uncomfortable by the mad love of his people—decides to provide the Great Jewish Writer with inspiration and subject and tragedy. And so—presto!—Hitler creates Auschwitz-Birkenau & Co. and branches various. The Final Solution for all lack of inspiration. And the Great Jewish Writer is sent there, to the concentration camps, so he can, yes, *concentrate*. Workshop! Arbeit Mach Frei! Creative Writing! Autofiction! The Great Subject! The Karminskys, agonizing in uneventfulness, were resuscitated to die with the vitality of those who know themselves to be part of History! Millions of nonfiction deaths to preserve a handful of fictional lives. And the Great Jewish Writer survived the Third Reich (Hitler had seen to it that the man suffered a great deal, but that he was never allowed to die) and then—beyond the fatal passing of a few Karminskys through the gas chambers and crematory ovens—he penned multiple despairing masterpieces. And he was beloved by his own as the great elegiac bard of his people and the forger of the just memory of the dead immortalized in his pages.

And within a few years, he wins the Nobel: an indisputable Nobel. And near the end of his life, Great Jewish Writer—who hasn't stopped producing novels and stories and essays about the horror of all of that, the Karminskys now far from the picaresque folkloric and part of the symbolic and sacred—is visited by the widow of a top brass SS officer who reveals the whole truth to him and shows him irrefutable documents and in the hand and handwriting of Hitler (obeying the last will of the psychopath? threatening to take the information to the press?) revealing the whole secret plot. Then the Great Jewish Writer realized that he wasn't just the author of the Holocaust, but that, in a way, it was far worse than that: the Holocaust was of his authorship. And, feeling so guilty, he committed suicide. The Great Jewish Writer committed suicide like so many other survivors of the Holocaust had done (but due to a motive that was very different than the typical survivor's guilt) and his passing was mourned by all, the world over and . . . But no, he couldn't, it wasn't possible to go that far. It was one thing to put up with the disdain or disregard of his colleagues and another thing entirely to open the door to let the hate of millions of people (many of them without the slightest interest in literature, but more than ready to call via Twitter for his execution, a ceremony they wouldn't hesitate to film on their iPhones and make it go instantly viral) come in to play. And it wasn't a *great* idea anyway. It was just a gray burst of black humor. An aftertaste—universal history instead of regional history—of something he'd done in *National Industry*, when everything was still ahead of him and he didn't feel any public shame, because that was the only way he could attenuate the shame he felt in private. *National Industry*, which, for him, had signified that thing that Fitzgerald warned about in his essay "Early Success": the reward of triumphing very young (and in a way foreshadowing that that, also, authorized premature failure, "the conviction that life is a romantic matter" and that "In the best sense one stays young"). But no. Because—Fitzgerald expanded—that was all just "an almost mystical conception of destiny" that ends up nullifying all "will power" and, in the worst cases, resulting in "Napoleonic delusion" seeking to recover that "eternal Carnival by the Sea." There he was now. Though not at the shore of the sea but at the edge of the sky. Flying in freefall. In his imperial and ousted exile to which nobody but him had condemned and confined him. Now everything was lengthily brief. And more rheumatic than romantic.

And it went by slowly at high speed. And nothing had happened in so long. Like here and everywhere and forever. Random sparks of what'd once been a forest fire or that'll cause a plane crash. In any case, he spent fewer seconds on that than were dedicated to the most down of counts or slightly longer than it took a freshly launched space shuttle to blow up.

He would rather—or fooled himself into thinking he would, lacking any options—be on the moon.

On the moon of his childhood, in his small but not waning room, on the waxing moon of back then. Concentrating on that seasick ocean there outside—out in the vast night in the vastness of the night—that he aimed to defy. Thinking childishly—and while his parents looked at him strangely and sadly every time they recorded an additional inch added to his height—about all that time ahead of him and about all that brief time behind him that was, nonetheless, ceaseless increasing, like a bathtub slowly filling to the brim and that, sooner or later, would be emptied of dirty accumulated water, sweeping away particles of his body through the plumbing, first to the river and then out to the sea.

And yes: there was something strange in the fact that back then, when your little friends howled "Happy Birthday" in your face, they were really celebrating—scientifically and exactly, mathematically—not the year that was beginning but the year that was ending. Yesterday was celebrated and not tomorrow. You'd completed one year but it was celebrated cumulatively with the others you'd completed previously. You were congratulated for another notch on grip of the deadly pistol of life and not for taking aim and firing at new targets and hitting the bullseye. And the person being celebrated was forced to reflect not on wishes for tomorrow but on unkept promises. Or on promises already broken, hidden, swept under armchairs and rugs, behind doors that would never open again. Doors sealed shut unless you forced them open, all alone and in the dark, lighting your way with the not-entirely-effective aid of candelabra, so hard to hold steady and barely illuminating anything beyond a few steps in front or behind you; like in that movie in which Dracula looks more like a tango singer than a vampire.

And when not singing the birthday song that wished you a "happy birthday"—as if admitting the possibility that your birthday could *also* be sad—everyone broke (he'd heard it for the first time at the party of a little imported friend whom he, like he did with Penelope, usurped many years later without asking permission for that novel on commission: a Mexican named Martín with telenovela-actor parents who his own parents had gotten to know in Acapulco, while filming one of their many nomadic spots) into that other far stranger Latin American birthday song, with those lyrics and that music, about King David. That whole thing about "*las mañanitas*"—"little morning serenades"—that were sung to "*muchachas bonitas*" but that were also sung "*a ti*" even if you were a *muchacho* and not a particularly *bonito* one. A song where if you changed the lyrics to "*muchachos bonitos*" would produce the disturbing impression that David, after having defeated Goliath, went around courting pretty little boys. (And one of the few things he had to thank his parents for—or maybe, actually, it'd been Uncle Hey Walrus—is that they hadn't hesitated to replace all of that with "Birthday" by The Beatles from the album *The Beatles*.)

In any case, the truly disturbing thing: the paradox that as you got bigger you had less time: that the increase in size simultaneously signified that you would be occupying that space for less time. And that if you were unlucky—or maybe if you were lucky, who knows, maybe the reward was in no longer remembering that you wanted so badly to be given the first last prize of oblivion—with the passing of the decades there began the deterioration of the halls and stables and basements of the memory palace. And that you were never going to go back, forgetting how to move there inside, while faces lost their names or names misplaced their faces to suddenly discover that everything had been covered with the heavy blanket of a dawn-less night. Wondering on one fine morning—*una mañanita*—that nobody would forget but you, who am I and where am I and where did all these strangers singing "Happy Birthday" to me come from and how can I bring this dangerous expedition to a safe harbor, an expedition from which few have returned, bound for the tropics of the bookshelf and desk or to the poles of the kitchen and bathroom and maybe, once there, remembering not the place you have come to but the place from which you parted. Breaking apart into fragments harder and harder to locate on the map of the memory of a life or in the blueprint of a story, with imagination and some artistic sense and style and with all the words in an elephantine dictionary as a compass to help you find not the elephant graveyard but your own tombstone.

MATTEO RICCI: AN INTRODUCTION

He remembers, once again, yes, exploring all of that: the idea of the past as a lost continent to be recovered. And, as he penetrated and delved into its jungles and oceans, trying to map it on one of the pages of his biji notebook. But not like a map, like a blueprint. The blueprint of a memory palace, following the instructions of the unforgettable Italian missionary and mathematician and cartographer but above all Jesuit, Matteo Ricci.

Matteo Ricci (利瑪竇, Lì. M dòu; Macerata, Italy, 1552 – Beijing, China, 1610); whose methodology he'd included in a story that he'd written many years ago, and of which he only remembered the figure of Matteo Ricci, not entirely sure how much he'd invented about the person to turn him into a persona, a character.

Matteo Ricci who'd proposed—as a method to keep from forgetting—the construction of a mental structure, of a forever palace (and whose teachings had also been adopted by Hannibal Lecter when it came to planning his menu and, in prison, telling agent Clarice Starling that "Memory is what I have instead of a view"). A place in whose different rooms you could go about organizing the different historical events within your private history as if they were objects and furniture.

Or, better, like museum pieces.

And he'd visited various exhibitions organized in that way. Monstrous and all-encompassing exhibits organized in a series of rooms dedicated, each one, to a milestone or event.

He remembered his visit to the *Stanley Kubrick Archives* (with a room dedicated to *2001: A Space Odyssey* where they were exhibiting the fetal Star-Child, the hairy Moon-Watcher costume, the ever-open eye of HAL 9000) or to *Pink Floyd: Their Mortal Remains* (with an entire wing dedicated to *Wish You Were Here* and the different photographic shots of that man in flames. And that other photograph of the swimmer in the sand. And the one of that kind of Homo Magritte of the Mr. Trip variety. And the one of that kerchief drifting in a forest wind. And the one of the diver in the lake. All inside the complex packaging of the album: a production developed, to the despair of the discographer, by Pink Floyd and the graphic designers of Hipgnosis Studio, who insisted on putting all of it inside a black case. With no band name or title. Opposite yet complementary to Richard Hamilton's white design for *The Beatles*. An idea to which, after a lot of negotiations, Pink Floyd agreed to the commercial concession of that sticker with the glass hand and the metal hand. And he'd heard of Pink Floyd fans who'd preserved their copies of *Wish You Were Here* intact, unopened. And that a few among them—a subgroup of fanatical fans—even refused and continued to refuse to ever listen to the record. And they kept it sealed and impeccable. Like on day one. And, from then on, they imagined that music that they never listened to. Unforgettable but impossible to remember. Absent yet omnipresent, as tends to be the case with all people who're no longer here, but who, because we wish they were, never cease to be. And who're there and are part of that absence that you cover up or deny or hide with the invented part and the dreamed part and the remembered part).

And he remembered moving down those Kubrickian Pink-Floyd-esque passageways: first in chronological order and, once he'd come to the end of both exhibits, turning around and going through them in the opposite direction, in reverse, like Mr. Trip, restaging the course of History to transform it into the ebbing tide of memory.

And, yes, the idea that the past could also be in front of you was also the credo Matteo Ricci preached. Something similar to what, several centuries later, would be attempted by academies like the Mnemosyne Institute of Philadelphia, where executives and politicians would go to strengthen the muscles of their memory (understood to be the substance they would feed off throughout their lives and careers) until they grew tired of remembering. Or to what would be sought, with more radical methods, by people like Brion Gysin and William S. Burroughs, developing the state of hypnotic awareness achieved with the help of the spinning Dreamachine. Or the putting in practice of what Vladimir Nabokov theorized in *Speak, Memory*: "One is always at home in one's past" only to, subsequently, confess that "I do not believe in time. I like to fold my magic carpet, after use, in such a way as to superimpose one part of the pattern on another. Let visitors trip." (And in one of the collected interviews in *Strong Opinions*, Nabokov had warned that: "I am an ardent memorist with a rotten memory, a drowsy king's absent-minded remembrancer. With absolute lucidity I recall landscapes, gestures, intonations, a million sensuous details, but names and numbers topple into oblivion with absurd abandon like little blind men in file from a pier.")

And Matteo Ricci, of course, possessed the irrational optimism of true believers and invited everyone to come aboard. And, please, watch out for the rugs and don't get too close to the end of the pier. And, yes, Matteo Ricci thought that control could be maintained over such a structure. And that it wouldn't sprout trapdoors on the landings of stairways or at the ends of corridors, like the ones the servants went in and out of like ghosts passing through walls. Coming and going. But not for that reason did he deprive himself of that architectural technique wherein the overstuffed palace chambers looked like framing and were surrounded by a circuit of empty passageways, by hidden borders through which to move more quickly, without getting your ankles tangled in the dense and deep carpets, advancing or retreating unseen and, as such, impossible to remember. Something like, he supposes, that narrow space that separates the cerebrum from the cranium and that, no doubt, would make wi-fi access and other forms of coverage difficult, leaving uncovered everything you would rather not forget but not remember all that time either. As if piercing a membrane, bound for another world, secret and distant and yet still part of this world.

The problem and its essence, of course, had to do with the idea that that space to be built had to be well-constructed and to not contain surprises that, even though you knew what corner you'd left or hidden them in, would never cease to startle and, sometimes, scare you to death based on a whole life or its most terrifying instants and fragments and moments. And then, oh, the line that separated the frightening Booo! from the sobbing Boohoo! was *so* thin.

And Matteo Ricci warned: "Since this entire memory system can work only if the images stay in the assigned positions and if we can instantly remember where we stored them, obviously it would seem easiest to rely on real locations which we know so well that we cannot ever forget them. But that would be a mistake. For it is by expanding the number of locations and the corresponding number of images that can be stored in them that we increase and strengthen our memory."

And so, the trick and the fun and the challenge—and not to cheat with obvious and predictable and perfectly memorable visions—was to deposit old memories in new rooms. To understand that the fear of forgetting is what makes one brave and unforgettable and unforgetting.

And it was in 1596—historians and theologians claim—that the Jesuit Matteo Ricci showed the Chinese how to construct a memory palace. Which didn't turn out to be simple. Neither for him nor for them.

The Chinese translator of one of his books had explained it to him once; but he didn't fully understand it and was immediately convinced that he would explain it incorrectly if he were to describe it, but he really liked the idea that there might exist something like what he *had* understood in that moment; understanding it, like so many other things, as something that might end up being of some use to him at some point.

And what he'd understood was that the Chinese didn't have the same perception/conception of the past that Westerners had.

To begin with, their verbs didn't have different times.

They didn't change in order to indicate that something had already taken place and was already there or had already been left behind.

The Chinese, on the other hand, represented the idea of the past by using context (or what the Chinese preferred to call "aspect"), adding words or temporal expressions equivalent to "yesterday" or "two hours ago" or "last week." And so time, for the Chinese, existed outside the immutable verb that, sometimes, was strengthened/temporized with the so called "Particle 了." An accelerating particle and an interconnecting cell that had nothing to do with the past in itself but with something finished and done. And something that could even be used today or tomorrow if you wanted to refer to an action already initiated and in progress and to be concluded in a set amount of time. And the graphic symbol for the "Particle 了" reminded him of one of those little hammers used to break the glass of emergency exits. A tool—a small sickle to go around cleanly and Lingchianally slicing off pieces of memory—to relieve all at once the pressure of the constant present and to give it a time and an age.

Or something like that.

And he thinks (almost tempted to replace the † with the 了 when he writes down something in his biji notebooks related to the past and the present), better that not too many people learn of the existence of that symbol. Because they would probably go out en masse to get it tattooed where their necks ended or where their asses began and would even call on their virtual but not at all virtuous gods to design an emoji to represent it.

In this sense, the Chinese were a little like Vonnegut's Tralfamadorians. Those extraterrestrials whose books (the paragraph that referred to them in the novel *Slaughterhouse-Five*, one of the novels that he'd returned to the most times, was the paragraph that he'd also quoted in his own books the most times) were all read simultaneously and not one after another. And that (Vladimir Nabokov wanted similar properties and virtues for his out-of-this-world books) had no beginning, no middle, no end, no suspense, no moral, no causes, no effects, aspiring to achieve and thereby achieving something formidable: the—as described in that favorite terrestrial book of his that, no doubt, would also be among his favorite extraterrestrial books—surprising and beautiful depths of marvelous moments seen all at one time. Moments seen more than read by readers who, when they died, remained very much alive in the past and in the present and in the future. Readers who'd always existed and would always exist and that could always be revived and, yes, reread in volumes deposited in the library of the memory palace.

And so it was that Matteo Ricci taught the Chinese to remember and to forget at the same time and to remember again.

Matteo Ricci instructed them to find that lost time, the indispensable misplaced yesterday, to use in the edification of a faraway present and a rapidly approaching future.

Matteo Ricci had explained to the Chinese that the size of their memory palaces would depend on the volume of what they wanted to remember.

Thus, the most ambitious structure—the most complete memory—would consist of hundreds of buildings. Infinite shapes and sizes. Streets and avenues. Parks and promenades. And a river into which at night—during sleep or insomnia—you could throw the inert matter of oblivion, the waste of amnesia, voluntarily or otherwise. And, also, open fields where you could leave pieces of furniture out in the elements so that anyone who passed by could take them and adopt them the way someone might adopt or kidnap someone else's child and even come to consider that child their own. But it wasn't easy; it wasn't simple. And on more than one occasion, what was discarded reappeared in its original location, as if by the art not of black or white but of sepia magic. And so, you opted to move objects that sometimes, were hidden under a bed or that changed locations, so you wouldn't find them or find them again (putting into practice what Charlie Manson and his clan did when, before listening to "Helter Skelter," they went into peoples' houses and didn't steal anything or cause any damage to the sleepers, but changed the location of everything, so the owners would be so frightened when they woke up, disoriented, in their homes. What was the name of that game Manson and his followers played? Oh, yes: *creepy crawling*. The unmaking of the memory of others and the redecorating of their memory palaces as a kind of creeped-out and creepy game). You went around creeping past lightweight artifacts or heavy miniatures that—though deteriorating—were still there and that, if they were missing, could be restored with new pieces, until they looked like they were newly fabricated yet different from how they'd been in the beginning.

The bigger the palaces "and the more there are the better it will be," Ricci said; though, he added, it wasn't necessary to start out by conceiving of colossal buildings. There was no reason to disregard the existence of modest little palaces or simple blueprints.

What's more: if you wanted to start on a small scale—forgetting at first the market square, or the hotel for memorious travelers, or the boarding house for forgetful passengers, always misplacing their passports and tickets, or the governmental offices where documents got mixed up—you could erect just an entry hall.

Or a modest wing.

Or a humble study.

Or, maybe, a room with cork-lined walls.

And even a dresser or a divan.

Or a very lively altar of the dead.

Or—as he learned to do when he was a kid—just one idea inside a little box. An idea that—when he let it out of there, like an intuitive and childish mnemonic device—he forced himself to put back together, going in reverse, as if he were Mr. Trip, until he reached its original source. The idea, when he was a boy, was to retrace that idea: first to outline it and then, walking backward, to proceed to take it apart, until he identified each one of the fragments that had ended up composing it. Step by step. In reverse. Until that past, yet regained, idea—after having been thought—began to think for itself and became part of the present first and, if everything went well, ended up projecting itself into the future. Like when someone who doubles back only to break into a run and launch the attack.

All these things—buildings, objects, devotions—were, actually, mental structures organized in the brain with the grace of an interior decorator. They weren't constructed with "real" materials, of course. But the true purpose of those imaginary yet solid constructs (that, like in act of reading, began, for Nabokov, with catching a glimpse of something that started off as a flimsy and unstable house of cards but that wound up being transformed into something solid, made of beautiful steel and glass as you moved into and through it) was to provide a place in which to store the infinity of concepts that make up the memory of human knowledge.

"To everything that we wish to remember," Ricci pointed out, "we should give an image; and to every one of those images we should assign a position where it can repose peacefully until we are ready to reclaim it by an act of memory."

And then Matteo Ricci—a Jesuit after all, sent to China with an exceedingly unforgettable mission—added, almost in passing, that you should reserve a VIP spot in the structure of the memory where you could hang a cross. And he always had an allergy to all religious creeds, unless they could be used as machines for producing fictions. And, even though all the Catholic orders of the Society of Jesus were what struck him as the most agreeable, the truth is that, when it came to Catholicism, the only order in which he truly believed and trusted was the Restraining Order. But it was also true that on those occasions that he sought refuge from the storm in one of those cathedrals—that for him were always like car washes where you could be cleansed of your sins and buy forgiveness—he felt envious of the blind faith of a religion that, paradoxically, offered up the possibility of seeing again as one of its miracles. There inside—in one of those other palaces of what couldn't be forgotten because it kept being repeated over and over to the point of exhaustion and martyrdom, breathing in that air heavy with incense and sweat from centuries of so much standing up and kneeling down and surrounded by all of those hardcore-gore-slasher effigies—more than once he'd felt jealous of all those who didn't doubt and considered themselves watched over by higher powers and felt the immensity of heaven (while all he felt was his own smallness; and how far away he was from any divine presence; and the certainty that only people who believed in heaven went to hell, because you couldn't believe in the one without the other, they were an indivisible pack; and that you could be a perfect and atheistic and agnostic son of a bitch like him and have a divine time on Earth and be a true and all-too-real hell for everyone surrounding you and anyone you trapped). Or who could justify their human errors or the horrible actions of others with a "Thy will be done," even when some of those same churches came crashing down on top of the faithful—all those vampires and zombies drinking and eating of the body of Christ—during the most well-attended masses. There was, of course, the possibility of "converting"—a move that sent him back into the realm of the automobile, the vehicle *tune-up*—but he didn't *believe* himself capable of believing in it. And the thing is that all those classic British writers who, on death's doorstep, decided to start crossing themselves, had always produced in him an understandable mistrust: you couldn't start praying only when you get to that point, just like you couldn't give up writing to reinvent yourself as a jazz (music that, for him, was the sonic equivalent of autofiction, and he'd never understood it and he suspected that, especially in its bebop and modern variation, it was nothing but a sadistic form of revenge black people were taking against the white race, forcing them to say over and over again, as they snapped their fingers like idiots, swaying stupidly, that they understood that racket so they wouldn't be considered racist) musician or a top chef or a plastic surgeon or a vertiginous tightrope walker: all professions with processes not all that different from the process of writing, he thought.

And so, he didn't hang a cross in any of the rooms of his memory palace; but he did hang a print of that portrait of Matteo Ricci, painted in 1610 by his "Chinese brother" Emmanuel Pereira, born Yuwen-hui or 游文辉 (the Chinese and Roman calligraphy that functioned as a frame for the watercolor was, as a kind of intervention, done by Matteo Ricci himself). And every so often, while wandering his rooms with a soulless sorrow, he stopped to look for him and there he was: Matteo Ricci with those almost medieval robes that centuries later would be adopted by space operas for their sagas with giant worms or villains with masks similar to those of samurais.

Matteo Ricci is there alongside a picture of his parents and another of his Uncle Hey Walrus with four of the most-famous and possibly most-beloved men of their time, of all times.

In his memory palace there's a whole room of pictures (he refused to turn people into things, into objects): so all his people were there: Penelope with

He Whose Name Must Not Be Mentioned in her arms and Pertusato, Nicolasito and the Karmas and even IKEA and, of course, Ella: dripping wet and pushing herself up with her arms at the edge of a swimming pool as she got out just so she could fall into another as soon as she was able. All of them orbiting around the room and around each other.

And it's a place he doesn't visit too often, because he's afraid that once he's in there he won't ever get back out.

Afraid, yes, because Matteo Ricci teaches you how to construct a memory palace but not how to destroy one (a far more strenuous and spectacular feat than knocking down one wall in a silent film), which is what truly interests him most: how to be able to bring down the beams in the roof of that one night of his childhood that played on *very heavy rotation* on MIND-FM— the transmitter/receiver of his head. Afraid that all those voices and faces would surround him and spin ever faster in ever smaller circles. Until they pierced his body and melted into him. Like the most accelerated of particles. The most interconnected of cells interlinked within cells interlinked within one stem that was him. Remembering what Marcel Proust had written about how "After a certain age our memories are so intertwined with one another that what we are thinking of, the book we are reading, scarcely matters any more. We have put something of ourselves everywhere, everything is fertile, everything is dangerous," and asking and answering himself "how can a literature of notations have any value since it is beneath the little things it notes that the reality exists (the grandeur in the distant sound of an aeroplane, in the outline of the belfry of Saint-Hilaire, the past in the savour of a madeleine) these being without significance in themselves if one does not disengage it from them. Accumulated little by little in the memory, the chain of all the obscure impressions where nothing of what we actually experienced remains, constitutes our thought, our life, reality and it is that lie which a so-called 'lived art' would only reproduce, an art crude as life, without beauty . . . The duty and task of a writer are those of a translator."

And so it is and so he thinks, with someone else's words, as if they were the seatbelt strapping him into a seat in which to dream (more furniture arrayed and arranged around his memory palace), aboard the most faraway and roaring and ghostly of airplanes.

PALACE SEIZED, LOST KEY:
THE NATURE OF THE CATASTROPHE

He remembers that the most important thing—what should never be forgotten for any reason—is not to forget where you left the key to the memory
palace. A key that looks a little bit like a †. Make multiple copies. At least
two. Always carry one of them on you. Always leave the other hanging from
a nail by the door, at hand and within view of the lock. Because, if you don't,
there may be trouble.

And, as an example, he always kept in mind, as a kind of antidote against
the catastrophic (above all aboard airplanes that at any minute could fall into
the water and sink), the story of that second officer aboard the *Titanic*. David
Blair. A sailor who was dismissed at the last minute, just before the ship
disembarked, and who kept—as a kind of keepsake—the key that opened
the cupboard where the binoculars were stored. And, already at high sea,
they couldn't open it and had to trust in the not-so-long view of lookouts,
without magnifying lenses, and everyone knows what happened next, soon
thereafter. Decades later, Blair's key—which was no longer his—was auc-
tioned off at 90,000 sterling pounds. And, when he found out about that, he
couldn't help but think that, sometimes, to appear you must disappear first.
And that certain tragedies are necessary so legend can triumph: because, if
what'd happened hadn't happened, with time, the *Titanic* would've been just
another oversized ship converted into a hotel or a museum or into a pile of
scrap to be recycled.

Yes: disappearance determined omnipresence, something or someone had
to cease to be to become unforgettable. Like his parents. Like Uncle Hey
Walrus. Like Penelope. Like The Son of Penelope saying, as they walked out
of the movie theater together, after seeing that movie about that ship, that
"When I grow up, I want to be an iceberg." Like Ella.

Few things were more immortalizing than death ("Our immortality is
made of memories and lies," William Gaddis once said to William H. Gass;
and in *The Tunnel* Gass had written that "There is history. There is history
remembered. Which is history too, the second time around").

And that was how the best mysteries-to-be-solved worked.

And his plan, now, was to solve a mystery and a disappearance.

So, he left his memory palace and, in an act of compassion, he carefully locked the door and threw the key into the gutter. He wasn't going to let some poor devil come along and think he could walk in and rob the place, at that hour and with the palace seized.

REDUCTION OF THE BRIEF

He remembers that—when he learned of the existence and achievements of Matteo Ricci—what interested him about Ricci's method was the theory but not the practice. Like in almost every order of existence, what drew him most to Matteo Ricci were his preliminary recommendations and he was going back to revisit them now with renewed and updated caution.

He told himself then that, in that way (initiating himself by getting accustomed to brevity and to the small; to remember with the aid of an astray or of a broom closet for the kind of brooms that would come magically to life and inside of which some progenitors would lock their offspring as punishment or lock themselves for the reward of a forbidden act), he wouldn't cause another effect than the one already being suffered by the kids who were learning to write inside the restrictive cage of Twitter. They would be the same ones who pretty soon would probably be at symposiums defending the haiku and flash fiction and the videophone as the most sublime and pure forms of Art. And they would ecstatically blather on about the aesthetics of Joe Brainard and Georges Perec in their respective *I Remember* (1970-1975) and *Je me souviens* (1978): two short books composed of brief lines, transcendent in their day but now degraded by their constant and ill-considered rebroadcast from and to and between phone screens or, even worse, by ever-more frequent ersatz imitations and clumsy knockoffs.

Lines like "I remember not very scary ghost stories, except for the dark they were told in" or "I remember not being able to pronounce 'mirror'" or "I remember the '*surface corrigée*'" or "I remember the 'displaced persons.'"

Lines and things that would no longer sound mysterious or inspiring or timeless or with all the time in the world or with 丁.

Things that read nothing like and had nothing to do with the final memories of someone undergoing lingchi torture or tormenting himself by reconstructing miniatures of his unfathomable past.

Things it cost them nothing to remember because they saw no danger in it, they saw refuge.

Things—emptied now of all personality and mystery and singularity—that, in their day, worked well and made sense.

Someone had called those two books—the ones by Brainard and Perec—"memory machines."

But that's not what they were, that's not how it was.

If they were memory machines, then, for him, they didn't work and were absolutely imprecise in their telegraphic precision.

Nobody remembered *like that* anymore.

Nobody made memory "by memorizing" anymore, like when people studied dates of battles and births and deaths of founding fathers in school.

Nobody remembered so clearly and cleanly anymore.

No, now memory (the little that was used of it) was white noise and black holes and star dust that had fallen over everything.

So, he preferred to put those books of Brainard & Perec closer to the category of compilations of fragmentary waking dreams but dreams all the same (because, again, to make memory was to dream and to invent). He felt that their respective *remember* and *souviens* were closer to those books of dreams where people like Graham Greene or Federico Fellini or Jack Kerouac or Carl Jung or William S. Burroughs or Robert Crumb or Willy Nebel wrote down tatters of their oneiric life.

And he preferred to leave them *there* too, off to one side.

And only reread them in that place in his memory palace where it was far easier to fall into a deep and fragrant daydream: the bathroom, that place where now almost nobody read books, preferring, instead, to stare at their telephones.

And yes: he spent a lot of time in the bathroom of his memory palace.

And he imagined it like that bathroom you never get to see in that species of cosmic suite where astronaut and infinitely displaced person David Bowman goes to grow old and to die and to be reborn at the end of *2001: A Space Odyssey.*

There, he read and reread those dream diaries that'd always seemed to him a little bit like one more among many forms of pornography: shameless in their exhibitionism and never reaching the orgasmic revelation of what the point of putting all of that in writing was. Human narcissism or quasi-religious fear? Because if the experts in that intangible subject always started out by acknowledging that the only thing they were consciously certain of was that people slept because every given number of hours they felt the desire and the need to sleep, it obviously wasn't clear to them what the function and utility of putting dreams in writing was.

Minimal uncertain certainties: when it came to writing down dreams, some were of the write-it-down-so-it-comes-true school, while others were of the write-it-down-so-it-doesn't-come-true school.

And both coincided on the write-it-down-to-remember-it idea.

But to remember what? The vague opened-eyed recollection of something that was already as if enveloped in fog and shadows and only experienced with closed eyes?

In any case, neither one turned out to be of any use to him.

Because what he wanted was to forget. To forget not a sleeping dream but a waking nightmare that he remembered in a full luxury of lush detail. And that, of course, he couldn't put it in writing. There was no point in confessing now something that had already happened and that, as such, couldn't stop happening.

He'd read once what Norman Mailer had written about how the "condition of memory, that painful place to which we return over and over because a fundamental question is still unresolved: something happened to us years ago which was important, yet we hardly know if an angel kissed us then or a witch, whether we were brave or timid."

He didn't have that good luck, he had that bad luck.

He hadn't a doubt, he'd forgotten nothing: witch, timid.

And it happened over and over in his memory.

That night and that other night and this night, the one that's been falling since the beginning of time.

EXPANSION OF THE VAST

He remembers thinking about how the difficulty, of course, resided—for a pure and definitive reader/rememberer like him—in choosing the room in his memory palace in which to put that night, That Night.

Maybe on one of the highest shelves of that other memory palace that was his library. His capricious and never-entirely-organized and unpredictable library that—for all those people who have never had one or the other—is the closest thing to an undomesticatable domestic pet. The kind of place and situation where you know the precise location of something and yet it is so hard to reach, because just thinking about that, up there, gives you vertigo. And you're a little bit afraid that, suddenly and without warning, it might bite or soil or ignore you.

His library.

His liferary, his biobrary

His autobiobrary (something in complete opposition to what'd recently been preached by an Eastern video-evangelist about organizing the harmonious household where, if you wanted to attain the most home-sweet-home of homes, there was only space for a library of no more than thirty books or, in any case, of books that were carefully selected by one of those trendy "library curators" on the basis of the personality of their owner who, of course, had no reason to read them, but, yes, to approve of the color of their bindings and covers and spines to make sure that they matched the color of the walls and furnishings). All those far more than thirty books—he read somewhere that thirty had been the number of books in the library of Leonardo da Vinci—that he'd read and, remembering, arranged in his mind according to the order in which he'd read them. And on like that, until it gave shape to an alternate autobiography.

Someone had told him that Thomas Jefferson divided his home library (which later grew into the universal Library of Congress) into three great zones based on the "faculties of mind" put forth by Francis Bacon: memory, imagination, and reason. Three main zones out of which, in turn, sprang forty-four additional subdivisions. At one point, he considered deploying that system, but, of course, the part about reason . . . In any case, he still dreamed that one day he would find the definitive order for what he'd read. And what he'd not read which was also there: thanks to the art of tsundoku, which made you buy books that you wouldn't necessarily read, but that you just had to have. To have them *there*, not reading them, but so you were able to read other books in peace. He could almost see it, with his eyes closed, like one of the many possible visions proffered by the Dreamachine and by doing—to stick with the rhythm of the beats—as Jack Kerouac had instructed when he said, "in tranced fixation dreaming upon the object before you" and "from the bottom of the mind" knowing that "the jewel center of interest is the eye within the eye." And always—here Kerouac is using the slang of the day to equate the tea drinker with the marijuana smoker—"Like Proust, be an old teahead of time."

All the books by everyone else but also his own, yes.

And, once they were organized never to be forgotten (because once they were there, he would remember them word for word), always leaving the door open and hanging, from its knob, a sign like the ones people hang on hotel room doors where it would read, in all caps:

DO YOU LIKE THIS LIBRARY

OF YOURS?

DON'T LET YOUR CHILDREN DESTROY IT!

And, yes, the children, the children who are—in a curious physical-temporal paradox— the ones from whom parents emerge from.

The children who give birth to their parents and who, on more than one occasion, dazzle and blind them.

And destroy their books.

PARENTS: A GROWING APART

He remembers that—because he can't forget it and much less lock its doors—his memory palace is surrounded by a big garden that takes and contains the shape of an amusement park ("amusement" being a word with a meaning that for Westerners is as ambiguous as "interesting" is for the Chinese creators of Chinese curses and Chinese tortures whom Matteo Ricci attempted to teach that no, you don't do that).

And there's no clear answer to why one gets on a rollercoaster: to have fun or to suffer, for it to start or to end, to say "I did it" or to think "I'll never do that again"?

And so he remembers the trip he and Penelope took to Disneyland with their parents who were, in themselves, like a *montaña rusa* (the Spanish term for rollercoaster, literally, in English, a "Russian mountain"), like a volcano of every possible nationality that you had to ascend slowly only to come plummeting down from its highest point at breakneck speed, fleeing the threat of an imminent eruption.

The first and only time their parents took him and Penelope on one of their escapades, because they realized pretty quickly something they already knew: they had a much better time on their own.

Or that it was less complicated to travel without children.

Or that, actually, their children—the children—were just secondary characters, only making an appearance in the great novel of their lives when a lot of chapters were already behind them.

He remembers the ad spot his parents filmed there, at Disneyland.

A new stop on their festive and somewhat desperate world tour sponsored by a brand of whisky. His father's great idea that he couldn't stop thinking about it because it was—from an advertising perspective—a very good idea. The endless campaign of a young and beautiful couple, adventurers, globetrotting on a sailboat named the *Diver* and docking in the most glamorous ports and (with very low production costs) starring in and filming and editing the footage themselves, which they almost immediately mailed in to be broadcast on the screens of TVs and movie theaters.

The good-for-everyone proposal (*everyone*, in advertising jargon, was reduced to the client and the agency and, in last place, the audience) had been accepted several years before. And ever since, their spots had won international awards and (being ads with no dialogue but with music playing in the background, carefully selected songs that inevitably became hits on the radio) were shown in movie theaters and on TVs the world over. And they'd made his parents if not celebrities then at least well-known characters who were even serigraphed by the true falsifier Andy Warhol (for a couple thousand dollars) in that spot set in countercultural Manhattan, where his father pretended to play guitar in The Velvet Underground and smiled at the look of deep disgust Lou Reed shot at him while his mother danced wildly with Edie Sedgwick and—scandal!—at one point her lips even seemed to brush against those of that falling and ready-to-fade-out superstar.

And so, most of the time, his parents weren't around, or they were coming or going.

And when he and Penelope asked them where they'd been or where they would be going, the answer was always the same: "Somewhere far away."

And for them—for he and Penelope—"far away" was an idea that, then and from then on, always had an unmistakable Andersen-Grimm-Perraultian resonance. Farawayland was the kingdom where parents went to think and fantasize—to invent and to dream—that they didn't have any children, to forget that they had children. Farawayland was the magical realm where their parents didn't remember that they had been and continued to be parents.

But on that one occasion, they took them along to Disneyland, of course.

Because they needed a couple children to film there.

There, their mother as Tiger Lily in a bikini more for the *lost men* of the Playboy Mansion than for the *lost boys* of Neverland. And their father as a seductive Captain Hook, playing at untying the knots of the top of their mother's bikini with his hook. And, of course, they were the *lost boys*. But pretty soon their parents realized that the idea of including those two children in pajamas waving from a window of the pirate ship didn't add anything to the spot. And it might even muddy/confuse the oh so *in* and *cool* image of the globetrotting couple that they'd been cultivating and that was enjoyed/envied by their fans and viewers who, no doubt, had children of their own who didn't even allow them a couple hours away at night to go to the movies. A turbulence that maybe, probably, would cause viewers to wonder uneasily and even disappointedly: did those children belong to the fabulous couple or were they just some kids who happened to be in the vicinity? Did the two of them want children of their own or did they just like to occasionally play with other peoples' children and all of that was just a fantasy? Were they able to continue traveling when vacation was over and their kids had to go back to school? Or would they find themselves obliged to add a couple of sedentary grandparents in future installments who took care of the children and waved goodbye to them from the dock every time they set off on another adventure, getting back to the good life? And did they really do all that stuff they did in front of their children?

It was clear that they were nothing but secondary characters in a novel not about love but about people being in love with their parents. And there was no space for them to be themselves. Because their parents didn't love each other, they were just in love with the idea of being in love. For them, love was nothing but a perfect and exceedingly commercial product. And they didn't look at each other, they reflected each other, as if they were mutual mirrors that every so often they kissed or asked who is the fairest of them all and the answer was always the same and it was always them and there were never *multiple-choice* options. And—their parents had promised to lie to each other until death did them part and that's precisely what they did right up until the moment when their children did them part from life—it was a false answer, a trick answer that they always fell for, because it was the answer they wanted and loved and longed to hear. And answer that—while other parents at the time dreamed of changing the world—confirmed them as parents who only aspired to changing partners. And not even in a definitive way: infidelity as a fleeting distraction, a brief parentheses, an unserious diversion that serviced to reaffirm for them the certainty that they were two peas in a pod and were made for each other. Separating for a while—which lasted the length of an ad spot for an inferior product—was for them the ideal way to be able to choose each other again, to reunite the way one returns to a classic and top brand: their own, not perfect, but, yes, one whose perfections and oh so seductive defects they already knew all too well. And, yes, there was a good reason why the Bible used the euphemism "to know" when it came to pointing out that someone had slept with someone else. And he'd always been convinced that the sexual chemistry between his parents had been of the atomic-physics variety: explosive and overwhelming and, why not, evangelizing for a cult that began and ended in themselves and in which they couldn't help but believe until death did them part and, faithful, they died together and in the same place and at the same time, in the storming of a department store or being thrown down from the heights of their Olympus over that place where that river opened onto that sea where there was a beach where he'd almost drowned only to resurface, clinging to his brand new and miraculous literary vocation. So . . .

Better not to complicate things, they decided. For them—and for so many of their friends—children should be spectators for their parents and not the other way around. Children were audience and not protagonists. And the, from the beginning, easy and quick and biological improv of *having children* was very different from the instantly sentimental and slow and prolonged-in-time-and-space lifetime role of *being parents*. And so, their next installment proposed a change of tack for the ship, trading it in for a space shuttle, emulating the sexy cosmogony of *Barbarella* with background music by Walter Carlos and his mother and father as orgasmic sidereals. And there wasn't even one child on that other planet.

So, at Disneyland they bought he and Penelope some of those little booklets with tickets for all the rides and even hired a couple of adolescents with mouse-ear hats and acne to watch and accompany them and who pretended not to hear when Penelope asked in perfect English if they could visit the frozen Walt and how long it would be before the park would add a *Wuthering Heights* attraction.

And he and Penelope read that sign at the entrance that said, "Here you leave today and enter the world of yesterday, tomorrow and fantasy." And, reading it, Penelope said, "Hah . . ." And even at that young age nobody said "Hah . . ." like Penelope.

And he wanted to visit the Haunted House so badly.

And Penelope was especially drawn to (though she'd never admit it) that promenade of international singing and somewhat disturbing dolls. But the lines to enter those attractions were interminable and in the end they settled for the ladders and hanging bridges of the Swiss Family Treehouse: the somewhat demented ecological/domestic construction of the sanest of families. A real and unsinkable family, no matter the shipwreck. All of them inseparable and together and with one common goal and one *raison d'être*: to be a family.

Then, he and Penelope climbed down from one of those fake branches made of concrete and reinforced steel, somewhat weak and very depressed: a condition that at the time was quite novel and *en vogue* in terms of its diagnosis in children, and that parents in general—and theirs in particular—preferred to process as fatigue or sunstroke or, already laying the groundwork for the next move, as "missing their grandparents."

And so it was that he and Penelope were put on the next, unscheduled—but suddenly predictable and inevitable—attraction of a big airplane that took them back to the un-amusement park of home. And so he and Penelope left behind the worlds of yesterday and tomorrow and returned to the world of today, of now, of then.

Without that hindering or frustrating the new fantasies of their parents who—perhaps influenced and disturbed by the childish atmosphere of the place they were coming from—when they got back, began to speak in low and giggling voices and to toy with the idea of doing something truly impressive that next Christmas: "Something that the whole world is going to talk about." And, oh, it was fascinating, even for him and Penelope, to watch their parents plotting something: the way in which they appeared to be intimately and almost supernaturally connected and in perfect communion. At those times, they truly were two peas in a pod. United and inseparable, like a two-headed organism (just as it was frightening to hear them fight; because the complete knowledge they had of one another enabled them to say the words that would be most hurtful, lightning and sparks, forest fire) thinking the same thing at the same time, the one finishing the other's sentences. Then, watching and hearing them together, in perfect synchrony, it was like getting on the most dangerous and terrifying tide of any tribulation—not amusement—park. Then, you had to put your tray tables in their upright and locked position and fasten your seatbelts.

It wouldn't be long now, yes, before the two of them would be the ones flying through the sky; not like Peter Pan, but falling, cast down from the on high.

But first, within a few weeks, their parents were already back in the capital, in what they called "our revolving port."

And they spent a few days at home and asked him and Penelope—almost ordered them—to invite some of their little friends over; because there was nothing their parents liked more than to throw them parties and drive them crazy and seduce them. And to know that they were the "favorite parents" of all those boys and girls who looked at them with dilated pupils (he had no doubt that Pertusato, Nicolasito was in love with his mother and that it was to her that he'd dedicated one of the maudlin and tacky poems that he read in class) to, when the sun went down, be sent home to their own parents in a state of hysterical vibration.

In Disneyland, his father had bought an album of marches by marine-composer John Philip Sousa and—at full quadraphonic-stereo volume—he made them all march through the hallways and rooms of the apartment and taught them to scream-sing "Dixie," not caring that it was a Confederate and slave-owning and southern hymn because "the important thing is that it's really catchy." (And "Dixie" was a song whose first notes he now, so many years later, always remembered whenever he heard the tweet-tweet of Twitter; and, yes, his father's ghost coming through the sound of telephones so that he would never be allowed to forget that it was with a telephone that he'd betrayed him.) And his mother had taken the girls to her dressing room and put makeup on them. And she'd filled them to bursting with sugar from candy and smoke from her long and skinny and in-vogue cigarettes (their parents smoked more like vampires than like bats and they thought that that whole thing of the casual smoker was an invention of people who were opposed to that great product that was tobacco). And she explained to them the truth about Santa Claus and the Three Kings (she'd never allowed him and Penelope believe in them because "we would never let some strangers and foreigners get the credit and gratitude that's rightly ours," their parents had told them, always unready to give up any starring role and, yes, they even went off to film in the relevant spots: first, one in which the *Diver* pulled into port near the North Pole; and then another where it docked at a subterranean desert oasis. And, in both, they came bearing gifts to be handed out, including, of course, bottles of the whisky they were promoting). And, of course, one of the kids ran off and hid somewhere and started crying because they didn't want to stop believing in all of that, at least not yet. And he and Penelope couldn't help thinking about what would happen in the next few years, with their possible girlfriends and boyfriends; with their parents abducting and possessing and seducing them (and he and Penelope probably also thought, separately but simultaneously, that their parents had to be stopped, shut down; that they had to take their parents down the way you take down the telephone off the wall and bring it to your ear to send out an

S.O.S. or, maybe, better, to give up their location and sink them). And there was, also, disturbing occasions when, with a sadistic and almost bipolar attitude, their parents completely ignored their classmates and little friends and, passive-aggressive, frustrated them almost to the point of suicide by making them wonder what they'd done wrong and why "their favorite parents" no longer loved them. And then those boys and girls—diminished, even littler than how little they already were—went home profoundly upset by the normality of their progenitors. And they shouted at them to leave them in peace, and accused them of "not being like other, cooler and more fun, parents" when they, after feeding them a healthy and balanced meal, insisted on reading them stories before they went to sleep. Stories with parents who never left and would never leave and who were always there and would always be there, accompanying them and saving them, like Liam Neeson in those movies in which he always transformed into a familial killing machine (and who will never be a kind of absent or inexplicable enigma, like those suddenly vacant pre-Columbian cities, like the *HMS Terror* or the *Mary Celeste*, like what may or may not have happened in the Dyatlov Pass incident). Because the children of forever-parents are children forever; even if later those children have their own children who—suddenly—turn them into grandparents.

Grandparents are a rewriting and a rereading of parents.

Grandparents—supposedly, in ideal terms, he thinks—were corrected parents, who sought almost desperately to make their grandchildren into the children they never had.

GRANDPARENTS: A CLOSENESS

He remembers that he doesn't remember much about his grandparents. Or that, yes, he does remember, but the ones are mixed with the others. The four of them get confused and blur together for him like different models of a single brand: city grandparents and country grandparents. And yet still difficult to distinguish the ones from the others. Old age makes everyone similar. And the four of them seemed so old to him even though it was possible that they really were not. But back then people—all he has to do is look at his photographs—aged earlier. Or, better, they got old faster; and, also, they died sooner and at a younger age and attained that ancestral form of memory more quickly. That memory that is also the memory old people have just before they cease to be old to begin to be new and dead and in which everything that happened seems to be happening again and all at the same time. There, everything that comes to pass and has yet to come to pass is the past: that matter made of love for what you never want to forget or out of hate for what you can't ever forget. The antimatter that was degraded to be corrected in dreams and inventions. The accelerated particles, the slow fragments, the marvelous and terrible moments, the cells interlinked where, suddenly, everything was connected to everything else and nothing was all that visible or precise.

What were and had been his grandparents' names? In what order did they die, the ones after the others, in a short period of time, as if turning off lights in different chambers of his memory palace? Was it important to remember, to remember them?

And, yes, even though, after their parents disappeared, he and Penelope spent several years with their grandparents (in the capital from March to December and in Sad Songs from December to March) and loved them so much (with that intensity of the Spanish verb "*querer*"— in addition to meaning "to love" also means "to want"—which, also, is quite atavistic and at times inexplicable), the truth is that their grandparents never struck him as great characters (because, unfortunately, the grandparents of their generation couldn't be true grandparents, but were, instead, a more wrinkled and responsible variety of parents when compared to their own children's inconsistency with respect to their grandchildren).

And he already wanted to be a writer; he was already a nextwriter.

And there is a time in the life of every nextwriter when there is nothing less interesting than not being a great character like the ones in all those books you can't stop reading and whose plots—in most cases—are their characters, their immense characters. And his four grandparents were, for him, at most, middling characters. And they didn't have any great story to tell (or actually they did, their possibly Nabokovian flight from the fire of the Russian Revolution and their arrival here, so far away, all of them on the same ship; but they never talked about that; that was like a huge closed-off room in the mansion of their memories, where he'd once caught site of his grandmother's passport with the exceedingly ornate stamps of the governor of *Sankt-Peterburg* where it read "*épouse du bourgeois*").

So—mixing them all together and highlighting their best traits and retaining the parts he liked best—he'd created what might be understood as his first great literary creation.

A Christmassy and Dickensian and Frank-Capranian solution: a magical character.

Take note, future biographers: Eames "Chip" Chippendale.

His movable/noble first and last names like a complicit wink for himself (and it was clear that he'd a knack for using movables—as in furniture—for nicknaming, because there was and there remained IKEA). Chip among the names of the furniture to be arranged in his memory palace. Chip like a solid and elegant and stylish piece amid so many digressive divans or armoires disassembled according to supposedly clear yet impossible-to-follow instructions.

Chip was, also, a result and direct influence of the books he was starting to read at the time after finishing *Dracula*. All of it, at that point, very *Rule Britannia*, and "God save Fu Manchu, Moriarty, and Dracula" sang The Kinks, glorifying the Victorian villain on "The Village Green Preservation Society." Books that came into his life through his eyes: James Matthew Barrie and H. Rider Haggard (*She!*, Ella!) and H. G. Wells (and there, in the movie that isn't bad at all, with that so-precise and Victorian-designed machine, the speaking and spinning books, the *talking rings*, of *The Time Machine* saved from the memory of the cataclysm) and before long Henry James and E. M. Forster and Aldous Huxley and, especially, Ford Madox Ford, who taught him the whole "unreliable narrator" in writing the saddest of stories (and who, with the passing of the years and the dwindling of readers' attention spans, devolved into unreliable readers: readers who were increasingly distrustful when it came to accepting anything that wasn't linear and uncomplicated and, yes, reliably narrated and with characters they could identify or feel comfortable with, good or bad and no gray area or vague nature, please, that's an order).

In his imagination, Chip was the owner of a bookstore and had once been a close friend of Sara and Gerald Murphy, his parents' heroes. The Murphys who—he explained, in his imagination—concerned themselves with leaving an inheritance (and naming him guardian) for the children of that "very funny" couple that they met a while back, in the last years of their lives, the ones who filmed commercials on a sailboat they had christened with the name of the protagonists of that novel poor Scott wrote and that they assumed were inspired by them or something like that, that couple they had their picture taken with at some party in the south of France.

Chip who publishes him.

Chip who raises him like his own son and turns him into a writer and stoically and gracefully puts up with the progressive madness of Penelope.

Chip to whom, sometimes, he made reference in interviews as if he were real and whom, nevertheless, he never put in writing beyond a few lines in *The Impossible Story*. And, yes, he's an ingrate (and swapping out and switching some letters, also, a disgrace) and so, nothing for Chip. And nothing for his grandparents of whom he has retained in writing a mere gesture, a mere phrase, the secret custom of dying their hair with teabags, those straight-line-mouth smiles more in their eyes than on their lips, the way one of them would always respond whenever he asked if they remembered this or that: "I would remember it perfectly if you hadn't asked me whether or not I remember it." Or the way they sat, holding hands, to "watch the radio": because they stared at it while listening to it, as if seeing what they were hearing, because radio was for them what television was for him: the invention of his generation. But, also, because on the radio they saw everything—including the colors—he couldn't see in those fuzzy and not-very-believable images (and that's why they listened to man's landing on the moon and "we saw it much more clearly than you did"). Or that impossible game they played with him and Penelope on long car rides: "Let's play don't think about . . ."; and then their grandparents (the ones from here or the ones from there, either way) said something which, automatically, they all thought about and then tried to remove from their minds, attempting to think about something else, which then became the next thing not to think about and on and on . . . Or, out of nowhere, that variety of entirely useless yet fascinating information like "I bet you don't know why people tie a knot around their index finger to keep from forgetting something. The obvious and correct answer is, of course, that they see the knot and remember why they tied it. But never accept the reflexive and obvious answers, my boy. You must look deeper to find a better answer. It turns out that index fingers have the speediest connection and most direct route through the nervous system to the cerebral hippocampus. The part of the brain where, they say, the capacity to make memory resides. So now you know and don't forget it: tie a knot on the tip of your index finger so you won't."

And, oh, there were so many times that he'd been on the brink of cutting off, lingchianally, both of his index fingers, to no longer have an accusatory and more-than-imperfect past there pointing at him. But he didn't have to go so heavy on the hyperbole either. And so he settled—as a form of self-flag-ellation—for one of those always surprising and painful, despite their small size and length, cuts to the knuckles or to the thin skin of the fingertips, from the treacherous blades of pages or those little yellow sticky-notes that he used to keep from forgetting something (something to-do) and that, inevitably, he only wanted to forget about once it was done. Cuts you were almost unaware of in the moment of the cut, but that, minutes later, there they were, as if at the turn of a page: a thin line of blood merging with the lines of ink.

And he'd cut his fingers so many times on the edges of books that cut deeper and better than razors that, he's sure, his fingerprints are not what they used to be. And, so, just a thread of blood and saliva scarring over and a pain too big for such a little cut (if he remembers right, it's F. W. Marnau's *Nosferatu*, that obligatory falsification of *Dracula*, where a derivative of Jona-than Harker cuts himself while inspecting the deeds to the properties Count Orlock purchased in Wisborg, causing the count's bloodthirsty and fanged mouth to water) and asking himself how and when it happened. Because he'd forgotten or hadn't noticed it at the time, but it ended up being impossible not to remember that it was there, cut and cutting.

POST-IT© & LIST & *

He remembers that time is a sharp and pointed and piercing asterisk (from the Latin *asteriscus* and the Greek στερίσκος or "little star," that spinning symbol that every so often he tries to pin down with one of his biji daggers so it'll stay still and stop flitting about like a butterfly); and he also remembers that he uses Post-it notes as if they were the sticky flypaper that hung from the rafters in the summer at his grandparents' house in Sad Songs.

He remembers that a Post-it—as so often happened—was only ever lit upon by chance, when you were looking for something else and didn't at all expect to find it. The Post-it, like one more among the many progenies of that variety of unexpected miracle known by the exceedingly literary name (like Anomaly, another possible name for the unstable daughter he'll never have or one of the many of the "girlfriends" he had had) of "serendipity." Serendipity, a neologism coined by Horace Walpole—derived from a Persian folktale that told of the comings and goings of the three princes of Serendip—and that'd blessed humanity with such fortuitous discoveries as penicillin and Viagra (which, as far as he was concerned should never have been commercialized, because it drove old people wild, old people who should've been devoting themselves to playing dominos or gazing at sunsets and who now were roving around on twilight sex-tours and, moreover, wanting to write about it), that spring thingy that can walk down the stairs, the pacemaker, the color magenta (which, if he remembers correctly, was one of the favorite colors of the synesthetic hearer of colors Vladimir Nabokov, and the most-used word in his books was "mauve," forty-four times), Corn Flakes, plastics, artificial sweetener, and his beloved Bubble Wrap, which more than once he'd wrapped around his suitcases at airports just so that later he'd have something to pop and detonate, in almost compulsive little explosions, in his hotel rooms.

The Post-it—he'd learned—had been created in 1968, when at the 3M laboratories they were actually trying to develop the formula for a beyond-improbable super-sticky glue that might even be used to bind the pieces of passenger airplanes together, replacing all those bolts and screws. Something to keep everything up in the air. Something a bit ridiculous and with little chance of getting off the ground, and fortunately, he thinks, they never discovered anything like that. On the other hand—fortunately—they did discover the composition of a subtly adhesive glue that was much better suited to affixing light and scattered thoughts, random things to remember and stick somewhere so they didn't get swept away by the winds of oblivion. Spencer Silver—their creator, with the name of a comic-book character—roamed the halls at 3M for years extolling the properties of that adhesive, without anyone paying him any attention. Until in 1974 a colleague, Art Fry (another great name and he liked a picture he'd recently seen of Fry—with a Post-it stuck to his now-wrinkled forehead, with the little drawing of a lightbulb going off on it—so much that he'd stuck it, with a Post-it and not a magnet, to his refrigerator door), thought to use it to keep bookmarks in place in his hymnals. And then more "Hallelujah!" than "Eureka!" (and one Alan Amron—a name that he didn't find all that attractive—proclaiming in the desert that 3M had stolen the idea from him).

And him, remembering all of that, asking himself why he remembers all those dates and names, why not forget about all of that. And answering in the low yet booming voice of someone talking to himself that, clearly, faced with the impossibility of forgetting what he really wants to forget—the guilt of that night—he's opted to bury alive, so very alive, that memory in tons of random information, to silence its deafening radioactivity, ever more potent and toxic, as the years and the Christmases pass.

And so it goes and so it goes on . . .

By 1980, Post-its had already become a healthy epidemic. And they were everywhere in various colors (though everyone knew that that pale yellow was their original, and thus true and authentic, color) and different shapes and sizes. The Post-it sticking but—unlike what happens in a good number of human relationships—not tearing when it came unstuck. Post-its remembering everything you didn't want to forget and that, once processed, could be crumpled up into a convenient and functional little ball of paper to be thrown and sunk into that cylindrical trashcan where, of course, so many novels that would never be written unfolded; and it wouldn't be long now before they'd be publishing an anthology of writers' Post-it notes, he thought, before not thinking about it anymore.

And the pleasure of writing something down on a Post-it, of ripping it off that little block, of sticking it somewhere with the feeling of having accomplished *something*, of unsticking it once its mission had been completed or it'd died in action, and of throwing it over your shoulder like throwing away something once unforgettable but not anymore.

The Post-it used by many artists as inspirational material and (he remembers when he read and saw it and imagined himself in one of them) by the editors of *Esquire* for, in 1989, an infamous and polemical and literary "Tree of Fame," putting all the famous writers from the U.S. in their place, from highest to lowest.

The Post-it as the perfect thing to lean on in the post-truth age.

The Post-it sustained something personal and important you didn't want to forget in the face of the supposedly clever and public and instantly forgettable tweet. The Post-it was the permanent and stable and reflexive Dr. Jekyll. And the tweet was the ephemeral and volatile and stumbling and trampling Mr. Hyde (and he supposes that, if he hadn't died and had gotten more addicted and further transformed, the wild and creative Hyde would've come to think that if he failed to drink that potion, he ran the risk of being transformed into the repressed and contemplative Jekyll).

And that's the way of the world: people are writing more tweets and fewer Post-its all the time.

And the fact that the communiqués of today's politicians are delivered through the electricity of screens and not through frameable paper only puts into evidence how they can say anything with absolute impunity, because, well, everyone was doing it. The tweet allowed and excused any statement without even obliging you to make an excuse later ("I can write the dumbest tweets tonight," because it's allowed and because nobody asks for genius from a tweet, merely and at most a touch of ingenuity or not even). And it validated the whole everything is valid thing, because the tweet expressed itself in the language of the instantly forgettable and no doubt he who tweets last tweets best and on to the next one.

The Post-it, on the other hand, was the un-masochistic yet simultaneously self-flagellating version of tying that knot around the finger of the memory while, there outside, everyone preferred to use that index finger to type-point, with bad manners and worse orthography because, yes, now errors in writing were considered features of style. Features that weren't particularly attractive, he says to himself; and from there too—serendipity of low, oh so low, voltage, the placebo of inspiration—the fact that he gets even by writing more and more Post-its.

Which brings him to a newspaper headline that he doesn't know if he should mark with a Post-it or cut out and hang with a magnate. Putting it there, on that cold door, and reading "The ExoMars lander crashed because it thought it had safely landed." And telling himself that he has felt like that for such a long time: more crashed than landed.

And looking for and finding a new Post-it and, better, thinking about the really important things in life.

Writing there "Need milk."

It's not a bad beginning for an endless novel, he says to himself, standing there, in front of the open refrigerator and next to the door that watches over the light of the I-don't-remember: the interior light of the refrigerator that turns on when you open the door (though he's not sure that, there inside, strange things don't happen with the door closed and that, when he closes it again, one of those disco balls doesn't start spinning and the different foods don't dance the Pixar-Boogie). The light like that of a nonviolent yet still terrifying interrogation—remembering that someone wrote "Helter Skelter" in pregnant-actress blood across that surface where others pin up faded photographs of loved-ones and old calendars and children's drawings with magnets—always making you ask yourself what you're doing there, what you're looking for, what it is you can't find because you already forgot what it was you were looking for and whether there might exist something called Refrigerator Amnesia. Something equivalent to that void where you know there was something but you don't remember what it was, but that, all the same, you remember that it was there: that there was something there that is no longer there and now is like shadows and smoke. Something very important yet simultaneously very forgettable. The memorious equivalent of a graveyard of memorious elephants: a magical and legendary place that, if discovered, would reward the brave explorers with the ivory of everything that'd been forgotten, with the skeletons of memory capable of sustaining the flesh and organs of everything experienced on the way to that final and dislocated dwelling place.

"Need milk," he thinks to stop thinking, for a few seconds, about everything he needs and he's going to keep needing and about the increasingly abundant lists (in his biji notebooks) enumerating all the things he doesn't have.

List-making, indeed.

The list as a special breed, as part of his organism, as a trait, and—again—as an unmistakable feature of his style and, no doubt, a more or less direct consequence of having gotten intoxicated on all those *multiple-choice* tests as a child. And he reverts to it because his style—though he's no longer able to put it in practice—is all he has left there inside, along with half a lime and a Tupperware container that's better not to even open to remember what it contains and to just throw it in the trash, like a Post-it with dangerous thoughts written on it.

Thus, his thing as an enumerating, an arranging, proposing a singular and, often, quite chaotic order.

The list—now—like the consolation prize for someone to whom nothing occurs now except for lists of things that won't ever occur.

The list as the best form of acknowledging the impossibility of organizing his ideas and, as such, the fact that the ideas he thinks best are the free and the associative and the multi-referential. The list that—in its relation to the Post-it—is the equivalent of Coca-Cola to Pepsi-Cola or McDonald's to Burger King: the same yet different. Toxic sugar and fast food. And both end up in the same place: among the leftovers that aren't worth saving so you can forget as fast as possible the hepatitis-colored enumeration of all those unhealthy and broken and unkept promises.

He discovered the *idea* of lists expressed as such and in writing at his grandparents' house, in Sad Songs, in a book assembled by the best-selling writer Irving Wallace and his two sons· *The Book of Lists* (probably the writer's way of putting a couple slackers to work so they could make a bit of money off their last name). And he learned that lists helped to relieve anxiety, to make you feel like you were doing *something* (even though you did *nothing*), and that the lists that worked best were handwritten lists. You remembered more and better if you wrote something out by hand than if you typed it with your fingertips. If you wrote your lists on a screen, you would forget them more quickly with the passing days, until more and more they resembled the diffuse and dissolving things written in dreams.

And so he memorized songs with the mechanics and functioning of lists. Like "Series of Dreams" by Bob Dylan. Or like "You're the Top" by Cole Porter or "Eclipse" by Pink Floyd or "Come Together" by The Beatles or "God" by John Lennon or "My Favorite Things" by Rodgers & Hammerstein or "Fifty Ways to Leave Your Lover" by Paul Simon or "50 Words for Snow" by Kate Bush. And he remembered having read that, in his final days, Saul Bellow, his memory already gone, stayed silent and smiled in public and, when asked what he was thinking about, he said: "I'm making a list of the things I've done and the things I haven't done." And he read too about the Russian psychologist Bluma Zeigarnik who patented the "Zeigarnik Effect": the idea that people remember unfinished things more and better than finished things.

And he also learned that, when it came to the hour or the minute or the second or the years of lists, you had to be humble and not demand or promise impossible things.

For example, never list something like "Write novel," something like "Need book" on a list.

NOTES FOR A THEORY
OF THE FABRIC OF MEMORY

He remembers that then he said to himself that, if fiction had turned its back on him, maybe he could tackle the whole nonfiction thing. The reality about the irreal. Devote himself not to writing but to writing about people who wrote. To be like one of those priests who've taken a vow of celibacy (when, really, they've just given up doing something they can't do anymore). And then limit himself to preaching the Good News, feeling like someone chosen by committee or someone more or less important just by finding a way to sneak into all the pictures. The gospels according to others, but, when all was said and done, sacred texts that were far better written than anything he would manage to write if he kept on writing. He had a friend at a radio station (one of those quasi-homemade broadcasts born of the technological boom that now enabled the existence of film festivals with films made on an iPhone and all of that). He wasn't so much a friend as an acquaintance (as the years passed he had more and more acquaintances and fewer and fewer friends), but he was somebody who, every time they ran into each other, didn't fail to tell him that "*National Industry* changed my life when I first read it" (and he, hearing that, couldn't help but think how unstable a life you had to have for it to be changed by a simple book, one of his books, and then he couldn't help but wonder if it'd changed his life for the worse). Then, during one of their encounters, he told that guy an "idea" he'd had. He wanted to "put together" a series on memory. He had a possible title that struck him as pretty clever and that, in turn, alluded secretly and personally to the little tin toy and fetish object from his childhood and forevermore: *(Re)Wind-Up My Mind*.

And his acquaintance/friend said that, yes, that of course, that that would be most welcome.

And he, at first, was even a little excited and started looking through his biji notebooks. To remember or not to remember. That would be the question. A personal exploration in his voice, but, also, so similar to that of all the hearers of names and places that changed or got mixed up or easily faded into what was invented or what was dreamed, but were harder to alter in what was remembered. An invitation to walk that tightrope—in the affirmative or the negative—that was also the fine line separating an "I forgot" from an "I don't remember."

And he could almost imagine his invisible-man voice, floating across the airwaves, hypnotic and seductive and perhaps transforming him into the closest thing to an incorporeal yet omnipresent being, as if he were (de)composed of accelerated particles that interlinked with the cells of listeners listening on the radio or on their cell phones. And that, in that way, his voice would be the voice of the free flow of consciousness and the unrestrained association of ideas stylized in his books, the books he'd written and no longer wrote. But a voice now amplified and replicated and explained by some of that nonsense about oral history and ancestral tradition so enjoyed by people with too much free time and too little awareness of it; but that actually barely concealed childish convenience that listening required less effort than reading. But maybe in that way, who knows, he would say what he hadn't yet been able to write and even fool himself with the idea that the word traveled better at the speed of sound than at the speed of light, of the light of a lamp or of a screen.

And so he started collecting different information.

And a variety of quotations. Vladimir Nabokov and Bob Dylan and Stanley Kubrick and Marcel Proust and, of course, the radial Kurt Vonnegut of *Mother Night*. Or newspaper clippings with headlines like "Your Memories Have Been Manipulated" and where it was explained how a university study (another one of *those* studies) had found that the memory borrows, without asking, moments from the present and inserts them into the past to make it seem more impressive. And that, in that way, for example, when you try to remember the precise instant years ago when you met a loved one, you couldn't help rewriting it on the basis of everything you'd been through since. Thus, also, all those supposedly repressed (but induced by the researchers) memories that suddenly surface amid sobs. The thing about, suddenly and so many years later, people discovering/remembering that their parents participated in an orgy where they worshipped Yog-Sototh or—the study detailed—finding that 16% of participants "swore they met Bugs Bunny (a Warner character) at Disneyland and 30% of them claimed, in addition, that the bunny was on drugs and licked their ears."

And he, upon reading these things, always wondered who funded this kind of research and, in this particular case, where the novelty lay. Because, in the end, reformulating what'd happened so it had a better narrative logic as it related to the rest of one's life was nothing more than the master's degree in the career of any more or less consequential liar: if said liar had managed to lie to everyone and to get them to believe all those lies, then all that was left was to take on the specialized challenge of lying to him or herself. And to believe those lies. There was no need for an experiment to elucidate something that'd been part of human nature since the beginning of time: if you didn't remember things that never happened, then you were failing at life.

But in any case—fooling himself more and better all the time into thinking that he was excited about the project—he started making one of his many lists. And he never expected to find himself obliged to make a list of his lists, even though the specia*lists* claimed that making lists is good for your mental health: structuring, ordering everything temporally, made you more efficient. But he knew the truth: lists were really false comforts and innocuous substances. Making a list made you believe that you'd done something (that you would almost never actually do) just because you *listed* it. Making a list was to make vain promises and to believe in the unbelievable. Maybe that's why he'd become a consummate expert in list-making, that was the closest he could get, at this point, to writing supposedly non-fiction fictions. Lists were a . . . how did they put it . . . ah, yes, that ever-so-witty expression for dimwittedness: a "mixed genre."

So he got down to enumerating different possible themes for each episode.

Episodes that would refer to mental disorders linked with the persistence or absence of memory (remembering it all or not remembering anything or remembering all of a sudden or the sudden intensification to maddening extremes of your own biography). To the mystery of why it was easier to remember bad jokes than good jokes (because what's bad is *not* forgotten even though the great peril of bad jokes was that many people, too many, take them seriously). To the final miracle of people stricken with Alzheimer's remembering everything, down to the most ephemeral and perfect and normal of presents, just before dying, thanks to something scientists had denominated (he liked the name a lot) "terminal lucidity"; something that, in the end, granted you the reward/punishment of remembering clearly that you were dying and that it was possible that soon thereafter you would begin to be forgotten or, what was pretty much the same thing, to be remembered imprecisely and unfaithfully, until you were swept up in that final rising tide of sleepiness, of sleeping more and more, until you never woke again. To those new Dutch towns/nursing homes whose inhabitants were all suffering Alzheimer's and, as such (apart from the supervisors and trained staff), no one there felt all that bad about having forgotten everything; because everyone there remembered almost nothing and in that way, paradoxically, the disease's advance was slowed. To calling things by their name and better to refer to Alzheimer's as cancer of the memory, no?, yes? (and to the memory of, back when he still wrote a lot, him wondering if that disease would offer him the blessing of a more or less extended period of time in which he would no longer be able to write anything but could read as much as he wanted; and in which he would enjoy everything—even what he was rereading —over and over, as if it were the first time, until the next first time). To those instances of "collective forgetting" into which, reflexively and automatically, an entire nation can end up slipping in order to continue existing historically and not become nonexistent history. To the possible interpretation of *Apocalypse Now* (a film he had always considered a big little brother to *2001: A Space Odyssey*: Kurtz was another HAL 9000 to be deactivated and Willard was Bowman), as if it were a trip down the Lethe, the river of forgetfulness. To the myths regarding the possibility of greatly improving your memory and the many methods for doing so that took no time at all to be forgotten. To the tendency of people to remember the beginning and the ending but not the during (in one of his biji notebooks he'd copied down a line quoting Ricardo Piglia on the subject: "What's the point, kid, of telling a story, if it's not to erase from your memory everything that's not the beginning and the end? Nothing between the beginning and the end, nothing, a plain, arid salt flats, between it and me, nothing, the most inhospitable vastness, between the victim of suicide and the survivor"). To insomnia as the door that leads to oblivion. To having something on the tip of your tongue, but, unable to swallow or spit it out, having it stay there, choked off as if in a trance, in the heart of the night. And to the people who manipulate others' memories as if they were those "targeted" surveys. To—again—remembering something that never happened ("My parents made me participate in satanic rituals when I was one year old," I swear). To the dolphins with one eye closed and half their brain awake and to that ancient but still living shark called *Somnius microcephalus* that'd been swimming—*nadaba y nadaba y nadaba en la nada*—in the nothingness of the depths of artic seas for more than four hundred years. To the enormous brains of elephants (with so much space for memories more frightening than mice) that allowed them to find their hidden necropolis and to the tiny instinct of salmon that bore them back to the place where they were born. To the great schools for the study of the memory (Hermann Ebbinghaus's at the end of the nineteenth century versus Frederic Bartlett's at the beginning of the twentieth century; or better not: because he didn't want to have to show his work and find things online that he would forget a few seconds after copying and pasting them). To the photographic memory and the auditory memory. To the memory that can be declarative and explicit (long-term) and semantic and episodic and hardworking and specialized (short-term) or (more long-term) arbitrary and insatiable and implicit and not declarative, where everything fits and is worthwhile even if it's not worth a damn. To the cerebral hippocampus and to the amygdaloid nucleus. To the different and best and generally voluntary and conveniently forgetful memoirs and journals and hybrid novelized variations of great writers (Nabokov and Dylan, of course; but also those of Frank Conroy and J. R. Ackerley and Mary Karr and Adolfo Bioy Casares and John Cheever and the Woolf brothers and Michael Ondaatje and Joan Didion (who'd said once that "Memory fades, memory adjusts, memory conforms to what we think we remember" and "We forget all too soon the things we thought we could never forget"; and proposed "playing" with a "close third-person" when it came to narrating someone, clarifying that "By a 'close third' I mean not an omniscient third but a third very close to the mind of the character" and, yes, the narrative persona as an inextricable tumor) and Thomas Bernhard and Frederick Exley and Primo Levi and Edward St Aubyn and Leo Tolstoy and Virginia Woolf and Vivian

Gornick, who'd already warned that "most people who are writing memoirs are not writers"). To the search for the exact recipe to make the madeleine from the first part of *À la recherche du temps perdu* (which, let's not forget, in the early drafts, again, was a banal and simple piece of toast). To the many ways in which memories are corrected and rewritten and to the need to forget the most crowded avenues in order to be able to save the most unforgettable passages (using here quotes from Douglas Coupland: "Part of accepting the future is acknowledging that some things must be forgotten, and it's always an insult because it's always the things you love"; and from Milan Kundera: "Remembering is not the negative of forgetting. Remembering is a form of forgetting"). To the reasons why, when you return to your childhood haunts, everything seems smaller than you remembered it (a theory regarding the shrinking of memories so they take up less space inside brains that are increasingly reduced in size or with increasingly airy chambers?) To the reasons why everything seemed to go faster as you got older (with the passing of time, time speeds up its passing, passes faster, as if it didn't want to be passed by or feel like the past, but, at the same time, arriving more quickly to the end of the race). To the reason why it is the brain that decides what to throw over the edge while it sleeps. To Funes the Memorious saying: "'I alone have more memories than all mankind has probably had since the world has been the world.' And again: 'My dreams are like you people's waking hours.' And again, toward dawn: 'My memory, sir, is like a garbage heap.'" To the ancient Roman scholar known as Bibliolathos or "the book forgetter" because he'd written some treatises that he could no longer remember. To that episode of *Black Mirror* in which the absolute and exact memory of an entire life is stored in a kind of external hard drive that you can consult whenever you're confronted with the slightest doubt, with results that turn out to be catastrophic; because it was good to forget certain things or to remember them in a different way (and about how being able to remember everything might end up bringing about the end of the desire or need to write anything). To the supposed impossibility of forgetting how to swim or to ride a bicycle. To the beginning of *Look Homeward, Angel* by Thomas Wolfe and that bit about how "But we are the sum of all the moments of our lives—all that is ours is in them: we cannot escape or conceal it. If the writer has used the clay of life to make his book, he has only used what all men must, what none can keep from using. Fiction is not fact, but fiction is fact selected and understood, fiction is fact arranged and charged with purpose . . . a stone, a leaf, and unfound door; of a stone, a leaf, a door. And of all the forgotten faces . . . Remembering speechless we seek the great forgotten language, the lost lane-end into heaven, a stone, a leaf, an unfound door. Where? When? . . . Each of us is all the sums he has not counted: subtract us into nakedness and night again, and you shall see begin in Crete four thousand years ago the love that ended yesterday in Texas . . . Each moment is the fruit of forty thousand years. The minute-winning days, like flies, buzz home to death, and every moment is a window on all time. This is a moment." To the German words *Fernweh* (which means "having nostalgia for places we have never been and that we long to know, but to which we may never be able to go") and *Eigengrau* (which could be translated as "brain gray," a color that wasn't exactly black but the color that people perceived in the absence of light and that, for him, was the color of oblivion, because sepia had always seemed to him to be the color of memory). To the different theories regarding "memory-aid" lists that, when you read them, don't make you remember what they refer to, they just make you feel so alone and abandoned. To that thing he'd read somewhere about how the first known list was dated to 3200 BCE and was in Egypt (and that it enumerated workers'—not slaves, as had been believed—excuses for missing work, while building the pyramids: illness, "He was brewing beer," "He got bit by a scorpion," "He was collecting stone for the scribe," and "His wife was menstruating"). To the other list of an ancient Sumerian king enumerating dynasties and floods. To the list of the 1,186 ships sent to conquer Troy in the *Iliad*. To the Ten Commandments. To the list of "things to worry about" and "things not to worry about" that Francis Scott Fitzgerald—after elucidating on a different ethylic list the conjugations of the verb "to cocktail"—enumerated for his daughter Scottie, including therein a "Don't worry about growing up" and a "Don't worry about the past." To how your perception of your own distant past ends up taking on the same texture as the evocation of a dream from the previous night: the past was something relived in the half-light and what you remembered of it were random scenes, the smell of things you couldn't clearly see, interrupted lines whose sense or senselessness could be interpreted however you wished so they meant what you wanted them to mean. To what Stephen King said about how "We think in a different way as children. We tend to think around corners instead of in straight lines . . . The essential and defining characteristic of childhood is not the effortless merging of dream and reality, but only alienation. There are no words for childhood's dark turns and exhalations. A wise child recognizes and submits to the necessary consequences. A child who counts the cost is a child no longer . . . The one thing about kids is that you never really know exactly what they're thinking or how they're seeing. After writing about kids, which is a little bit like putting the experience under a magnifying glass, you realize you have no idea how you thought as a kid. I've come to the conclusion that most of the things that we remember about our childhood are lies. We can have dreams where we redream things that are truer than what we remember waking. We all have memories that stand out from when we were kids, but they're really just snapshots. You can't remember how you reacted because your whole head is different when you stand aside . . . And, paradoxically, we'll never be able to forget all those stories that we were told or that we read or that we saw back then" (and, as it related to him, he feared that Stephen King wasn't quite right; even though King is a great writer of writers and of children who, when they grow up, will be writers who'll never be able to forget that terrible thing that happened to them when they were kids and so they write it over and over again). To the more than likely possibility that in the golden and novelistic nineteenth century—when everything hadn't yet been electrified and neither movies nor television nor telephones with movies and television had yet arrived and the past took its time in arriving to the present via newspapers, one day at a minimum, and so there was more time reflect on what'd just taken place— many people were scolded with a "all you do is waste your time reading all those books all the time when you could be living your life and being a ballroom cat instead of a library rat." To the lists of words made by the sailor who wants so badly to be a writer, *Martin Eden*, to increase and improve his vocabulary. To the lists of lovers and dreams of Susan Sontag: a fan during her youth, like him, of the initiating Martin Eden. To the amnesia of newborns (which lasts up until they're three and a half years old and allows them to forget all that time slopping around in their own shit and piss). To the genius minds devastated by the ends of their lives of Iris Murdoch and Saul Bellow, forgetting everything they'd read and written and concentrating, her, on constantly watching *Teletubbies* and, him, on *Pirates of the Caribbean*, over and over again, until the end, floating in that, according to Murdoch, "dark and boring place"). To inconclusion of all those TV series that begin but are canceled due to lack of audience, giving frustrated viewers the sensation that they dreamed them or invented them or that they barely remember them until, finally and in the end, they forget them forever. To the sharpened spatial memory of the blind, moving through their not haunted but spectral houses—they don't see it, but there it is and there they are, bewitched and bewitching those houses with their memories of them—with superior grace and precision than people who can see. To the theories about how every degenerative and amnesiac mental illness is rooted in prolonged insomnia of the kind where you can't do anything but remember to livingly kill the most living-dead of times (mentioning in passing that Winston Churchill only vanquished his insomnia the night after the bombing of Pearl Harbor and achieved "the sleep of the saved and thankful"); and, along the way, reciting that *Silvae* by Statius: "What fault or flaw has made me merit this, O youthful Sleep, most tranquil god of all, to be the only wretch unblessed by you?"; or those poems by Borges (whom he'd once run into and sent flying through the air on the street while chasing one of his Coke-Coliseum Girls) that wax eloquent about how "The universe of this night is as vast as oblivion, as precise as fever . . . In vain do I await the disintegration, the symbols that come before sleep" and how all of that "Is to count off and dread in the small hours the fateful harsh strokes of the chime . . . It is saying over fragments of paragraphs read years and years before." To Eugène Ionesco saying that "Most people, when they try to tell their dreams, interpret them, explain them, speak to them, intervene in them, remember them. The dream is a story or a situation that must be recounted in the most naked way or that should only be described. You shouldn't tell dreams, you have to try to describe them; the dream is not speech, it is images." To why people say "intermittent light" and not, better, more precise "intermittent darkness" and why not apply this last principal to what's forgotten, allowing the idea of the *damnatio memoriae*: applied to criminals and statesmen, but, also, to writers during the dictatorial correction regimes or throughout discontinuing editorial democracies or in the anarchy of the reading masses, always ready for novelty and with a proclivity for forgetting everything that already took place, even though it's still there waiting to be read and reread. To the doubt that yes, as a child, one remembered everything and, suddenly, came the original and sinful temptation to forget despite some traumatic episode: forgetting as something that's turned on so you can turn off. To the enumeration of recovered memories and lost memories as tools to frighten away those unforgettable ghosts in *A Christmas Carol* and *The Haunted Man* by Charles Dickens. To George Gurdjieff & Co.'s "Self-Remembering." To the invention of some absurd and incomparable clinical case; example: a writer who no longer writes gets a blow to the head that causes complete amnesia of everything he read and thus, every so often, he recovers memories of the novels of others—the story of a catastrophic marriage between a psychologist and patient, the story of a house on a paramo through which multiple generations of a crazy and cursed love pass, the story of a central European vampire who goes off on a pleasure cruise to London, to the revelatory and perhaps supernatural and pale and fiery transparency of certain things—as if they were his own and he writes them, and then he writes more and better than ever, and nobody tells him anything that makes him get depressed and lose the dream and forget how to sleep. To the song "I Can't Forget" by Leonard Cohen and to "Potholes" by Randy Newman and the so sad but luminous farewell of "Torneremo ancora," the last song by the great referential maniac Franco Battiato swept away by Alzheimer's (and how was it that none of his stuff, with his exceedingly particular English pronunciation, had made any mention of the *Hadron Collider*) and to all those other songs about forgetting and remembering whose titles and performers and authors would escape him and fade away but that he would never stop whistling in the most unexpected moments. To mnemonic exercises (and to the precursor of Simonides of Ceos, who was able to identify the bodies in a temple that had collapsed based on the places they had occupied at the banquet table, which, fortunately for him, he had withdrawn from early; a method subsequently adopted by Cicero to keep from forgetting his cutting speeches that had the property of cutting off the digestion of many). To the way in which his favorite stand-up comedians (Jerry Seinfeld and Ricky Gervais and Louie C. K. and Dave Chappelle) wove the different threads of a story together as if it were something random and improv, but that actually was coldly memorized, calculating down to the millimeter every idea and word until reaching the final period of the punchline. To *Rashōmon* and the different ways in which the same story can be told. To all those novels and films with sleepless secret agents who got hit on the head or who, voluntarily or not, participated in an experiment and forgot who they were or who the person they loved was and whose name was always on the tip of the tongue they used to kiss that person (including that movie that Holden Caulfield denigrates in *The Catcher in the Rye* without naming it, but that is clearly inspired by the demented and romantic and forgetful plot of *Random Harvest*). To the paradox that in so many cases, amnesia was the great narrative resource (like in *Captain Marvel*, another memory in the memory of that airplane he's now flying in) of having something to tell that couldn't be told because it'd been forgotten. To the melting clocks in Salvador Dalí's *The Persistence of Memory* ("Just as I am surprised that a bank employee has never eaten a check, I am amazed that no painter before me thought of painting a melting clock . . . And no, they weren't inspired by the Theory of Relativity but by the memory of a block of camembert cheese melting in the sun of a landscape of my childhood," Dalí said about his painting that, when he saw it for the first time, he thought that he'd imagined/remembered it being much bigger). To the fragmented/fractionated sequel to *The Persistence of Memory* painted and titled by Dalí—who according to Vladimir Nabokov was nothing but "Norman Rockwell's twin brother kidnapped by Gypsies in babyhood"—as The Disintegration of the Persistence of Memory. (And to how he and Ella would never forgive Dalí—with the consent of Alfred Hitchcock—for that absurd and implausible and exceedingly childish oneiric sequence in *Spellbound*.) To the different kinds of amnesia: the anterograde in which new events are not stored in the long-term memory; the retrograde in which nothing of what happened before the illness will be remembered; the post-traumatic, typically due to head injury; the dissociative, due to depression; the global and absolute, and cryptomnesia, where you think a memory is something new and not of the past, which is what happened to George Harrison when he wrote "My Sweet Lord" and, without being aware of it, recomposed "He's So Fine," written by Ronald Mack and performed in 1962 by the Chiffons, and put the song on the radio and compared it with the "original"; the post-hypnotic, which was denied Uncle Hey Walrus when he came out of his canine trance; the dissociative/fugue state, which led you carry out unplanned actions and to later be found wandering around somewhere and unable to remember how you got there; "source" amnesia, where you remember the information but not where you got it; unreliable amnesia, where you questioned your own memory, and the amnesia invoked with the help of bottles and powders and herbs; the lacunar, where you only forgot a single event . . . and the truth is that, faced with such a buffet of forgetting, he would try a little bit of all of them (but he would serve himself a big dose of the last one; so he could, in addition to forgetting that he'd forgotten how to write, *also* forget how happy writing made him, and, maybe, taking it all a little further, even the end without beginning: forgetting how to read; something like what happened to him after he'd been able read and write for a few minutes without ever having learned to read and write first). To—once more, he couldn't repeat it enough—the fact that maybe *that* was happiness: being able to read your own books as if they'd been written by others, having forgotten that you wrote them and thereby turning yourself into the definitive reader, into the perfect reader of yourself. To that idea that—Proust *dixit*, again—the memory was a kind of pharmacy or chemistry lab where the hand could stop and select at random a sedative drug as easily as the most dangerous of poisons. To the idea that all plastic surgery—that stupid form of editing—would only be justified for him if it also included in what it offered the ability for you and for others to forget that you'd been operated on and cut and pasted and how you'd once looked, before the scars. To how—according to the latest studies—every memory was like a small but visible mark on the brain. To how memories are sensitive, volatile matter. To how memories are particles in constant and increasing alteration. To how memories have made neurons burn. To how memories can make you forget everything but those memories. To the so-called "memory bump" that comes when a private memory is made unforgettable because it has been framed by some historical event and, yes, the always anecdotally interesting where-were-you or what-were-you-doing when . . . To headlines regarding scientific breakthroughs like "For the First Time in History, Scientists Have Made Time Run Backward" (but that, when you read the articles, you learned that actually they hadn't achieved anything, rather they "have opened the doors so that in the future . . ."). To why his had been the last generation to feel proud of having a good memory and to why you no longer had to have it inside you, because the entirety of memory was there outside, forgotten and remembered with a couple of clicks and awaiting (he'll see it soon on the seatback screen of the airplane) the payback of the Blackout that in *Blade Runner 2049* took place in 2022. To how it seemed to him that the whole global amnesia thing was already here, it was already happening little by little, like gums receding from teeth. And both the teeth and the events were going to precipitate into free-fall one of these fine mornings, when the big-data tech companies unplugged everything for a few days, unleashing chaos and a global mega abstinence syndrome. And that after an imprudent period of time, they reconnected everything, yes, but with the novelty that, starting then, you had to pay for everything and nothing was free, and the world would be divided into those with enough money to get high and those wandering around as if dope sick, moving their fingers, typing on an invisible keyboard, and no longer with any ability to remember how things were done off screen. Maybe then, after many years passed, certain neuronal mechanisms would be reactivated that would allow them to think and to feel disturbed by things like how strange it is that so many insulating precautions are taken when you get a simple X-ray and none are taken to insulate people from the radiation of all the mobile phones and tablets and, little by little, people would recover the automatic—in reverse but always facing forward—reflex of making lists, lists where so many fragments are listed, handwritten lists . . .

But, mysteriously—terminal lucidity?—he began writing something else. A kind of supplication/ode/invocation to his girl who, that one night, had fallen into a swimming pool.

A memorial to/of Ella.

A "This is a moment" like the one preached by Saint Thomas Wolfe.

And he liked it.

And he read it to the air, in the air, his first night on air.

And nobody understood any of it and, then, an urban and radioactive legend began to circulate about a girl (or two or three or several more, who, before throwing themselves into swimming pools, started a chat room named The Dead Swimmers) who'd committed suicide/drowned after hearing him read that, as if forced to dive in and not come up to breathe, driven by a kind of subliminal command woven into his words (a conspiranoid theory that, no doubt, General Electric would've had a good laugh at).

And—true or false, true—that was the last thing he wrote and it was as if he felt that he had nothing else to say, that he only wanted to say that, so they would hear him say it, all alone.

AH, LOOK AT ALL THE LONELY PEOPLE . . .

He remembers that he was happy alone.

And Penelope too. More or less happy. A Penelopeistic happiness, in any case; because, Penelope said to him, "Happiness is a lightning bolt, but then the thunder."

And that, more than anything and above all else, they were both *so* happy when they got together—so long after their interminable childhood—to show each other and demonstrate for each other how unhappy they'd been, to lovingly hate each other for what they'd done and for what they'd become.

Penelope, in that monastery-asylum where she penned her flammable pages and where she ended up burning to death.

Him, in that bed he barely ever got out of and that, when he did, it was only to experience the pleasure of going back to bed; telling himself that, after all, Marcel Proust (convinced of a "nestled relationship" between "Sleep and Time") had gotten under the sheets to, from there and without moving, leave the world; and that Woody Allen worked on his screenplays on a mattress; and that . . . The slight difference resided in the fact that Allen and Proust wrote a lot in bed, while he used the bed, basically, to think about how writing in bed was very uncomfortable, so . . . But it didn't matter and thus him there in his bed remembering that thing that went "Just go to bed now. Quickly. Quickly and slowly" but not who imparted that order yet obeying it nonetheless: a trembling jog and a bumbling jump and an almost graceful fall—falling was always the easiest—to end up prostrate in the exact center of his memory palace.

Under a glass cupola, in a circular room from whose nucleus—him, there, lying down but not resting in peace—radiated, like the rays of a black sun, throughout all those door-lined passageways. Passageways like in The Beatles' house in the melancholic Liverpool drawn and animated at the beginning of *Yellow Submarine.* That gray city where all those lonely people walked, with "Eleanor Rigby" playing through the sad streets. People who were truly lonely and aware that they were lonely and not deceiving themselves by sending dispatches of one or two lines out into the ether in order to feel more and better accompanied by beings as lonely as they were. In that movie that has almost nothing to do with The Beatles (and maybe that's why it turned out so well, and the four of them were the first to be surprised by that miracle). In that movie that frightened him so much as a kid (and he still felt the fear as an adult), during that sequence, while "When I'm Sixty-four," played, when The Beatles got younger and got older and got younger again, while adrift and sailing through the Sea of Time (the way David Bowman got older only to be reborn when he flew through the Space of Time). In that movie that he'd seen for the first time with Uncle Hey Walrus and that he'd come out of deeply moved by how, toward end, the wicked and defeated Blue Meanies were playing with the idea of going into exile in nothing more and nothing less than his now nonexistent country of origin. But before that, those doors leading to so many other places that were unforgettable or, which wasn't the same thing, impossible to forget.

Like that inerasable night when he and Uncle Hey Walrus and Penelope—alone in each other's company—traversed the city in search not of lost time but of their missing parents: the ones who had only a few hours left before they would disappear forever.

UNCLE HEY WALRUS / A DIAGNOSIS

He remembers that, actually, Uncle Hey Walrus wasn't his uncle; but that that didn't really matter all that much either. Uncle Hey Walrus wasn't his mother's brother, but it was as if he was. A false yet more authentic brother than many real brothers. Uncle Hey Walrus was the son of some friends of his mother's parents. The village lunatic or the village idiot. The protagonist of "episodes" (euphemism that encompassed both his mental issues and his occupational catastrophes) that, immediately, became supposedly funny anecdotes to be sung throughout the streets of Sad Songs.

Uncle Hey Walrus as "artist" and "bohemian" and "hippie" and, yes, as the years passed, he liked to think of him as one of the many great possible uncles of literature, but with none of the villainous characteristics (Creon, Claudius, Ebenezer Balfour, Ralph Nickleby, Tío Silas) that uncles in fiction appeared to favor. Really, Uncle Hey Walrus is, for him, much closer to Captain "Uncle Toby" Shandy: wounded in battle, living in isolation, obsessive not when it came to the history and science of military fortifications but yes when it came to the Battle of The Beatles, where Uncle Hey Walrus knew how to fight and lose triumphantly. And from whose front he returned changed forever and begging for people to give peace a chance not in general and for everyone but in the singular and just for him, begging that Fabulous Four to leave him in peace.

The voice of Uncle Hey Walrus explaining something to him that he hadn't asked him to explain, but explaining it to him all the same. Back then, Uncle Hey Walrus's voice was a voice that they (he and Penelope and children in general) found funny and adults—who considered Uncle Hey Walrus not a lost case but a case that it wasn't even worth it to go out and try to solve—found demented. Uncle Hey Walrus was a case that couldn't be closed, but an individual who had to be enclosed.

And so, after his return from London at the end of the '60s and "crazier than ever," Uncle Hey Walrus went in and out of different psychiatric institutions, as if he were one of those specialized and professional tourists who snuff out or light up stars in tourism guides. There inside, surrounded by padded walls, Uncle Hey Walrus saw the stars that were lit up for him, inside his head via cables and electricity and that left him talking, forever, in *that* voice. A voice that reminded him and Penelope so much of The Beatles' voices when they were having so much fun singing and recording their most fun songs. The voice on "Yellow Submarine" ("Full speed ahead, Mr. Boatswain, full speed ahead . . . Cut the cable, drop the cable"), the voice on "Magical Mystery Tour" ("We've got everything you need . . . Satisfaction guaranteed . . . And that's an invitation"), the voice at the end of "All You Need is Love" ("All together now . . . Everybody . . .") A voice like a retro lo-fi whisper: half staticky radio host and half fairgrounds preacher speaking in tongues. A voice that invited you to join in and that never stopped giving instructions. Uncle Hey Walrus's voice is the desolate version of that voice. The voice of someone who has heard those voices up close, too close; and that has been left ravaged and devastated by that proximity, like someone who stares up at an eclipse or stands in front of the expansive wave of an atomic explosion.

Uncle Hey Walrus was there.

Uncle Hey Walrus was a witness and returned to tell of it when The Beatles—The Beatles recording *The Beatles* and it's dazzling whiteness, like a colossal whale and like a tall fountain, barely a year after the colorful *Sgt. Pepper's Lonely Hearts Club Band*, because at the time, the speed of pop was frenetic and vertiginous—sang to the fall of their own empire.

So, back then, Uncle Hey Walrus sat him and Penelope down on his knees and said to them in *that* voice: "It's enough to compare the *yeah yeah yeah* in 'She Loves You' with the *yeah yeah yeah* in 'Helter Skelter.' It's all there. The complete story. The cry and the howl, the Alpha and the Omega and the beginning and the end and the beginning of the end and that end that has no beginning, children."

Many years and many compilations of The Beatles later—he confesses with no shame—he went up to the basement or went down to the attic to find the box of Uncle Hey Walrus's belongings to see if they might be of some use to him. Be useful to him. Something that would help him get the engines running (*full speed ahead . . .*) and get him writing again. Or, at least, something he could make a little money off of.

And he didn't find Uncle Hey Walrus's valuable memorabilia, but he did find his notebooks. His journal documenting his time at Apple and Abbey Road. And that, he thought, might make a good novel (and, of course, as he'd done with Penelope's Karmas, another appropriation: another novel not about ghosts but by a ghost, another novel for which he would be the most *maudit* of, yes, ghostwriters).

And something any publisher would find attractive, he thought.

Because The Beatles were never going to disappear as such, only separately. Because The Beatles would be getting together and breaking up until the end of the time, like in a before-birth and after-death loop. The Beatles were always and would forever be interesting. More interesting all the time. They were the musicians who'd sold most in the twentieth century, more than half a century after breaking up and ceasing to be. And the most desired and seductive. In their own way, The Beatles were un-dead. Were immortals. Were vampires: there was probably nobody alive who didn't have one of their albums or one of their solo albums (still Beatles even on their own) or at least one of their songs on heavy rotation in their memory palace.

There were a lot of notebooks belonging to Uncle Hey Walrus and he considered incorporating them as bonus material. To use and take advantage of Uncle Hey Walrus's multi-volume journal and his notes and observations as the foundation of a grand saga—or, at least, a novella—about his time at Apple and Abby Road.

The Beatles appeared in his pages first as Lennon, McCartney, Harrison, and Starr; then as John, Paul, George, and Ringo; and finally as J., P., G., and R. As if they dissolved in Uncle Hey Walrus's mind as they disintegrated as a band.

And so, reading Uncle Hey Walrus's notes, he came up with the title *The Beatles* (like that, with the *s* crossed out, that *s* singularizing the plural, Uncle Hey Walrus as The Beatle) for the story of his trip to London and his nights and days in the life of The Beatles.

Had Uncle Hey Walrus been something like Claudio, that young hippie and Vietnam veteran with vacant eyes and the air of a would-be Calvin Klein model who shows up at John Lennon's house in Tittenhurst Park while Lennon was recording *Imagine*? That guy who, in the documentary about the recording of the album, came to Ascot Studios looking for answers because, he thought, Lennon would have them? (And it was Lennon himself who explained to him there—almost in the kind of voice with which one speaks to child—that he had no message to offer him, but that yes, on the other hand, he could invite him in for breakfast.)

No.

Not at all.

Uncle Hey Walrus had all the answers.

He had too many answers.

What he needed were the precise questions so that all those answers would be the right ones, so that his notes would make sense and have some direction. What Uncle Hey Walrus wanted, desperately, was a *multiple-choice* test with a single answer/statement and, below, multiple question options.

And he expressed his desire in prose that was telegraphic, sure, but that had a lot of information to draw on. That phrasing cannibalized with the spasmodic diction of Uncle Hey Walrus and that nickname courtesy of the titles of two songs: the free stream of (un)consciousness of "I Am the Walrus" and the barks of "Hey Bulldog" with that line about how "If you're lonely, you can talk to me."

And all of that, he remembers, was due and thanks to something that happened to Uncle Hey Walrus.

At his birthday party, when he was turning ten, Uncle Hey Walrus was hypnotized by one of the guests and forced to go through the most obvious routine of the participant in the show, answering that call of "for my next trick I'll need a volunteer." And so, the hypnotists ordered little Uncle Hey Walrus to keep his hand raised; he convinced him that it was very hot (and he started stripping off his clothes to the panic and delight of the little girls that were there); and he made him believe that he was a dog. And, in that moment, the hypnotist had a heart attack and died right there in front of all the guests, parents and little friends (at one point he recounted the whole episode for He Whose Name Must Not Be Mentioned and maybe that's where the boy came up with his own useless illusionist, Pésimo Malini). And so the magician never gets around to un-hypnotizing the little Uncle Hey Walrus, who only comes out of the trance after three or four or five or six slaps from his father. But—it soon becomes clear—that, in some corner of his mind, the little Uncle Hey Walrus is still a dog: he has fits of howling at the moon, urges to lift a leg to pee on a tree, an impulse to stick out his tongue when food is put in front of him. And, most disturbing of all: already an adolescent, Uncle Hey Walrus loses his mind every time he hears *Sgt. Pepper's Lonely Hearts Club Band*, always at the end of side B, after "A Day in the Life." (Pretty soon, reading an interview with P. he found an explanation for all of that, for Uncle Hey Walrus's barking: The Beatles had slipped in a transparent sound of 15 kilocycles, only audible to dogs.) And whenever he heard it, Uncle Hey Walrus, alone among all people, got down on all fours (on hands and knees) and howled and began to spin around on himself, as if trying to bite an invisible tail. And so, when it came to that part, people who knew him stopped and removed the LP from the record player before that drawn-out note of multiple funerary pianos brought that last song to a close.

Years later, Uncle Hey Walrus travels to London and stands guard outside the door to the Abbey Road Studios. And one morning, he intercepts P. and tells him his story. And P. gets a real kick out of it and feels a little guilty and offers him a job doing "something" during the recording of *The Beatles*.

And that was how Uncle Hey Walrus became something like The Beatles' mascot. Their human dog, the best friend of those four men who never stop barking and biting each other. Into a Renfield, vampirized by his lords and masters and by all that music of nocturnal creatures. And there, among them, Uncle Hey Walrus ends up losing his mind. And he remembers Uncle Hey Walrus telling him about it (when he was recalling his time at Apple and Abbey Road, Uncle Hey Walrus seemed to fall under a spell, assuming the restrained and frigid diction of cold data, like a more or less close relative of HAL 9000) in a functionally dysfunctional voice. A voice so similar to those voices that were everywhere these days, speaking yet constantly failing to comprehend the commands people gave them, the voices of all those vibrating toilet seats and TVs—with that function that switched the image of classic films to the texture of modern video—and "smart" cars and "virtual assistants," which, ostensibly, had some use, but pretty quickly turned out to be totally useless. The voice of Uncle Hey Walrus's memory remembering that he was there, at those distorted yet ingenious recording sessions. That he was a witness. That he saw and heard all of it. And that it hadn't been—and still wasn't—easy to have been a part of that, to witness that collapse and that shipwreck of four people (four of the most beloved people in the world), who'd loved each other so much and who could no longer look at much less listen to each other. And who now recorded their tracks separately and in different rooms at Abbey Road, in a self-destructive yet hypercreative manner, sending each other little messages, more acidic than lysergic, from one song to the next. Thus an ultraviolent P. playing at being more J. than J. on the bestial and chaotic and screaming and primal "Helter Skelter" which, he said, he wanted to give the sound of "the rise and fall of the Roman Empire" (and no, it was no surprise then that Charles Manson had understood it as war cry and battle hymn and bloodlust). Thus, too, J.—who'd already distilled "the sound of the end of the world" in "A Day in the Life"—counterattacking with the orchestrated and elegant and dulcet lullaby "Good Night," which he was listening to now, closer all the time, with R.'s voice as if giftwrapped and floating in orchestral sweetness.

But the spirit of *The Beatles* was restless and every so often it went out to possess and challenge others with its psychotic ambition. To be doubles, to be more, to be so much and so many, to grow and to reproduce and to multiple and to fire off its concentrated egocentrism in all possible directions. The same thing happened with, again, Fleetwood Mac's *Tusk*. And—beyond the more or less achieved and obvious conceptual ambitions—with The Rolling Stones' *Exile on Main Street*, Led Zeppelin's *Physical Graffiti*, The Clash's *London Calling*, The Smashing Pumpkins' *Mellon Collie and the Infinite Sadness*, Guns N' Roses's *Use Your Illusion*, Prince's *Sign o' the Times*, Ryan Adams's *Gold*, and even Pink Floyd's *The Wall*. In other words, chasing down and catching a sound of sounds. Arriving to a place where everything is allowed in so that everything can be let out and risking being misunderstood in its day beyond its successful commercial performance—because, of course, *The Beatles* sold *a lot*—to only be glorified later on when people came to understand the solid structure concealed among its supposed fragments.

And *The Beatles* even managed to become—something that J. would have loved—an art installation/experiment: in 2013, the sculptor Rutherford Chang converted the Recess art gallery in Soho into a record store whose bins only included seven hundred copies of the first edition of *The Beatles*. The closing of the exhibition was the playing—digitally retrieved and rerecorded—of those hundreds of copies of *The Beatles*. All of them playing at the same time, starting out all together now, to—as the spins and revolutions unfolded—end up separating and distorting until they attained the category of, yes, pure white noise: the sound playing inside the head of Uncle Hey Walrus, he thought when he heard it, trembling.

The producer, George Martin, shuddered whenever some fan would come up and tell him that *The Beatles* was his or her favorite among all the band's albums and he never stopped insisting, until his final breath, that, out of that double album, they could have made one excellent album.

Lennon always considered it "my favorite."

Starr always felt it was "the most important for me personally" because that was when he left and came back and, he thought, played the drums better than ever, because, to get him to come back, they all wrote good lyrics and music and they were a band again like they'd been before, at least for a while.

Harrison arched an eyebrow and smiled a twisted smile and held one of his deafening silences to, then, limit himself to a "When we recorded *The Beatles* incredible things were happening in all of our lives."

McCartney—when they asked him if *The Beatles* wasn't too long, if there weren't too many songs, if it wouldn't have been better to exercise greater control over the chaos—chose to respond that "It wasn't easy at the time, no. But I'm not a great one for that, 'you know, maybe it was too many' and that. What do you mean? It was great. It sold. It's the bloody Beatles' White Album. Shut up!"

And he remembers that later—reorganizing, cutting, shifting, rerecording him, producing him—he attempted the exercise of being Uncle Hey Walrus: being him and writing him and giving him a more profound and serious and, yes, literary voice. A first person that, in that way, would remember him and be superimposed over what the electric shocks had made him forget and that would help him remember and make him feel that, if there was anything good about amnesia, it was that, fortunately, loved ones already knew perfectly well and had detailed knowledge of what the amnesiac liked most and what made him happiest.

Yes: they remembered everything he'd forgotten and now, for a few pages, he was Uncle Hey Walrus.

And so they (his family and friends) delved into his gray and as if petrified—like the forests and buildings of an invaded Pepperland—lapses in memory. And they brought all those colors close to him. Like offerings. Favorite books and foods and landscapes where they felt that he, Uncle Hey Walrus, fit in perfectly. And music that sang to his most private sentiments. And movies that he could watch over and over even though he knew them by heart before he'd forgotten them. All of that so that he—Uncle Hey Walrus—could enjoy it as if it were the first time. All of them dazzling. All of them classic but as if new. All of them forgotten but immediately unforgettable. (Well, not all of them: because often what truly was liked most was what was the worst thing that could be done, he thought Uncle Hey Walrus thought, a child of his time and part of his de/generation.)

And at bottom or at the top or in the depths—as if in a secret passageway—the breathing of that which, though it never answers when you ask its name, is called *déjà vu*. That which calls to you and tempts you with the idea that you already saw it and heard it and that it already was and that now it's coming back. Something to which you don't pay too much attention: because after all and before everything else since you were a kid they've taught you not to talk to strangers even if they look so familiar.

So better not to overly complicate things by trying to disentangle the mystery of how something reminded you of something. Better to relax and surrender to the happiness of what you don't remember but that turns out to be so instantaneously familiar.

And then, of course, for Uncle Hey Walrus, everything was as if he'd been reborn into a perfect, customized, ideal world. A world made in his own image and semblance from which all messiness and lack of grace had been removed by his guardians. Living there and like that, Uncle Hey Walrus thought, was maybe the closest thing to feeling like a god and to feeling what a god feels: floating amid thunder and lightning and floods, making light and unmaking darkness and forgetting everything you didn't remember.

In any case—they tell him that they told him before—his forgetfulness would pass. It would be a forgetfulness that, pretty soon, would end up forgetting to forget to begin to remember to remember. His memory would return, they explained to Uncle Hey Walrus, "like a rising tide."

And then Uncle Hey Walrus thought—he thought that Uncle Hey Walrus was thinking—about whether or not that would really be all that good: because the waves of his torrential past would end up destroying the few sandcastles he'd managed to build during his brief amnesiac present. And maybe, among those fragile and ephemeral constructions, there might be something indispensable and revealing for his future. Something that—having reconstructed his yesterday—he would no longer remember to forget the next time it came to losing his memory.

But Uncle Hey Walrus didn't have much time to think about other times.

And, then, again, the specter of the high voltage electricity howling in the bones of his face.

They strapped him down to a bed.

They put a rubber tube in his mouth so he wouldn't bite his tongue.

They shoved his head into a helmet with electrodes and bombarded his brain with volts (and not little volts) to give him, if not peace, at least a truce in all that war going on there inside.

And with the truce came the memory of the forgetting.

Remembering forgetting was a pause in the battle. Returning from the front, moving in reverse in the most triumphant of retreats.

And Uncle Hey Walrus came out of there with very little, almost naked: the whisper of his name, two or three faces, and the promise that everything would slowly fall back into place, the way the furniture in a memory palace gets rearranged following an earthquake.

But then Uncle Hey Walrus discovered that all of that was nothing but an arrangement lacking any logic. As if—after the quake—you concerned yourself first and foremost with organizing the silverware in a kitchen drawer rather than with standing up the chairs and table and putting new panes in the splintered window frames and sweeping the floor to keep from cutting your bare feet.

And so, there, random details that you have to chase down like fleeting mosquitos or immortal cockroaches. The problem resided in distinguishing which category this or that belonged to. And the issue was deciding with which side they aligned: expendable bugs or decisive insects.

And here they come.

Examples:

A paragraph from *On the Road* by Jack Kerouac (whom friends from his childhood nicknamed "Memory Babe" and friends from his youth "The Great Rememberer" because of his prodigious capacity to remember everything) that Uncle Hey Walrus learned by heart and that he read under the trees and beside the river, in Sad Songs, while dreaming of leaving that place never to return.

The print on the fabric of a shirt whose buttons fly through the air when a girl (her name?, her face?, was it the mother of his true-false nephew, who was fantasizing about it so much time later by putting it in writing?) tears it off him in the darkness of the school gymnasium while everyone else dances to a song with a chorus of which he only remembers the singer screaming the word "twist" and the word "shout." An old song in a new version and performed by a brand new band of four boys whose name or names he doesn't remember.

The feeling of going down a stairway, jumping steps, four at a time, with a lightness and elasticity in his body that now seems to him closer to that of a superhero (or a furry and four-legged animal) than to that of his own person, which, in the best of cases, could barely function as a shy and awkward double civilian and human personality.

The frightening taste of the food during his obligatory military service: a situation that he passed through quickly and at high speed, only to be discarded after a few days, after the first of his attacks, during one of those night watches, which had been, poetically, named "*imaginarias*" and where, yes, Uncle Hey Walrus began to imagine things, strange things and ugly things.

And everyone knows that, when Uncle Hey Walrus starts imagining things, that's when the trouble starts.

And so, once again, padded cell and straight jacket and flashes and sparks and thunder and lightning in his neurons.

But nothing has yet come back to his memory about the how and the why he ended up there. Dead zones and black holes and his memory like one of those maps of ancient explorers specializing in *hazardous journeys* that have too many blank spaces and—where the lines of rivers and mountains and cities end—the legend "Here be monsters" warning travelers that there's nothing more monstrous than the unknown, than the beyond.

And it's clear that what you don't know is almost always what's most interesting.

Which drives him to push onward.

Even though, in the case of Uncle Hey Walrus, onward is nothing but pills and precautions (the increasingly numerous bottles of dark pills under the light of the nightstand) while behind him the mystery grows like the murmur of people talking about him in low voices who move away and get quiet and look the other way when he turns around to give them a despite-what-you-seem-to-think-everything-you're-saying-is-perfectly-audible-from-over-here-even-though-I-can't-hear-it face.

And then, all of a sudden, there's nobody there.

And back in his parents' house, Uncle Hey Walrus knows that, yes, those are his parents, even though he doesn't remember them being his parents. Because he also knows that he prefers the parents of that girl from the gymnasium, because imagining that he's their son at least allows him to feel like her brother, and being her brother is better than nothing and, oh, she's in love with a boy from the capital and . . . He knows that they're his parents because they look at him in a way that only parents look at their children: with one eye full of love and the other eye full of fear. And Uncle Hey Walrus twirls around with no fixed direction like one of those long and between-parentheses sentences he was using to think about rewriting Uncle Hey Walrus. He lives between parentheses, like those sentences into which he was thinking of inserting Uncle Hey Walrus to see what would or wouldn't happen to him. Uncle Hey Walrus like the Beatlesque and sonic homo collage, moving *so tired* through what was once and still is his house, though now, all of a sudden, it looks more like a department store where every room is bursting with temptations and products and things that, right away and without fully understanding why, he wants to possess so he can, he understands then, bring their names back from oblivion, what to call all those things that call out to him to remember them, please, right? Also, Uncle Hey Walrus soon realizes, there are things that are missing, that have been hidden away in that amnesia palace. Empty spaces where previously there were presences that have since been removed to keep him out of trouble, so the past won't complicate the present and the future.

One of the suddenly blank zones are the walls in his bedroom. Empty now, but covered in white rectangles framing the nothingness. Spaces where the color of the walls seems slightly discolored and that, later, Uncle Hey Walrus will understand as future memories of something soon to come or something that already came and already passed: that blank and white cover of *The Beatles* that he only saw the sketch of before being sent back to his point of departure, as if he were hearing again a first song that starts with the sound of an airplane taking off or touching down.

There, floating, those omnipresent absences like the ghosts of paintings and posters that Uncle Hey Walrus can't remember, but that his parents took down the night before he came home from the institution so he "wouldn't get nervous." His *legitimate* parents, even though, for him, they're like bad imitations or like *body snatchers* who've come from outer space (they're not his adopted parents: the parents of that girl who arrived there, to the end of the world, fleeing the Bolshevik Revolution and who'd been brought up on romantic and adventurous novels where, again and all the time, someone "spun on her heel and turned her back on everyone so they wouldn't see her sincerely weep").

What is it that's gone missing there?

What is it that's omnipresent by omission?

What is it that, staring at the walls, he still can't remember?

Answer: the photographs and the covers of the albums of The Beatles and, on the bookshelves, all his journals, his not-biji but yes-beatle notebooks. *Beetle* and not *bee gee* notebooks. Also missing are his Winco record player and his records from the shelves (the doses of electricity haven't helped explain to him once and for all why those small singles that spin at 45 rpm have such a big needle in their center while the bigger long-plays that spin at 33 rpm have such a small needle) and, on them, the songs of The Beatles that drove him crazy or something like that. "I Am the Walrus" and "Hey Bulldog" that he sang at a scream (and that's why it didn't take long for him to be nicknamed Hey Walrus). Everything that his parents—his *real* parents, when they heard him howling and barking from the other side of the closed door to his room—had thought could only be the maddening sound of madness or of demonic possession.

His *true* parents who've done a good job and who've cleaned deeply and edited everything conscientiously but—as tends to happen with every endeavor you want to be or believe to be infallible—who make one small and massive and insurmountable error.

Because when he lies down, between the bed and the dresser that serves as a headboard, he finds a picture.

A picture of his, from his past that's one of those pasts that'll last forever.

One of those pictures that, for him, has the weight of something instantly historic.

One of those pictures that're the result of a random second, of a *click* that makes a *clack*. And that—once revealed—have the unquestionable air of something perfectly composed and planned out, when, in reality, they're the result of chance, of just the right moment.

There, in the picture, are seven men. Four of them appear lying on the floor of a recording studio, as if struck down by their own brilliance. He recognizes them at first sight. They are J. and P. and G. and R. Another two people appear there talking among themselves. They are producer George Martin and his sound engineer Geoff Emerick. And, in the background, half hidden amid a forest of microphones, there he is, Uncle Hey Walrus: plaid shirt (could it maybe be the same shirt that girl unbuttoned, what was her name and, oh, how hard it is for him to recover names after his time spend in that electric bed), alone yet surrounded by so many people, with the air of melancholic beatnik lumberjack.

And seeing himself there, revealed and in black and white, Uncle Hey Walrus can suddenly almost feel the vibration of the sound in his feet. Their sound. The sound they've imposed on and given to the sound of the world, changing it forever.

And, seeing that picture, his memory comes back and engulfs him like one of those waves that spins and slams you against the bottom and makes you lose all sense of direction until, at last, inertia pulls you back up to the surface and you breathe deeply to shake off the weight of those depths.

And he remembers.

Uncle Hey Walrus remembers that he got out of there and went over there.

They put him there inside because he couldn't stop going outside himself. Because he was "unstable" and "volatile" and "a danger to himself." And he remembers that that was the case because the "situation" had gotten "out of control."

And the "situation" had been "complex" for so long and, again, *All together now . . . Everybody . . .* Ever since Uncle Hey Walrus went to find The Beatles and had to be brought back when everything came crashing down. When to the crack in his personality was added their break-up (when The Beatles finally understood that all they needed was love, but that money couldn't buy it, and that they were going to carry that weight a long time) and they sent Uncle Hey Walrus home, as if giftwrapped. Once there was a way to get back home and sleep, *pretty darlings*, and do not cry: Uncle Hey Walrus tied up tightly with ropes and ribbons and, fixed on his face, the whole time, that smile of a saint possessed by the devil or of a sanctified devil, either way. The smile that you can hear even when you're not seeing it. The smile that made everyone who saw it want to weep. The smile that they erased with electricity and that now came back to light up his vacant face and his eyes that no longer cried but just produced what Uncle Hey Walrus described as "eye sweat" and that looked at the picture in his hand. The picture that he's holds now and stares at asking himself how this whole story is going to go on and then answering himself that there's no way: that this is as far as it goes, that he has blisters on his fingers, that he doesn't have the strength or desire to keep passing himself off as Uncle Hey Walrus in writing. And that his style looks and sounds nothing like that of Uncle Hey Walrus who, reading his notebooks, he writes like this and rereads here and now and . . .

HELTER SKELTER / TAKE 19

He remembers reading random pages of Uncle Hey Walrus's journals:
"May 30th - October 14th. 1968. All those books about The Beatles. How many are there? Too many, for sure. And I don't show up in any of them. Other people show up. Everyone else shows up. The acidic and lysergic Timothy Leary shows up saying things like 'I declare that The Beatles are mutants. Prototypes of evolutionary agents sent by God, endowed with a mysterious power to create a new human species, a young race of laughing freemen.' Memo to Timothy: The Beatles didn't create me, they destroyed me. They made me cry. *Cry Baby Cry* and *do not cry* and doing everything possible to forget everything people remember in those biographies and autobiographies. There, J. and P. and G. and R. The four of them recording. And always four different versions of a single day or night. *Hard* or *in the life*. Never *in my life*. Either way. If there's ever a doubt, stick with what R. remembers. He's the one who remembers the most and the best. 'I was impressed because he was laughing all the time,' R. says in an interview when they ask him about the Maharishi. Transcendental meditation that instead of bringing them together breaks them apart. It separates them. In Bangor and in Rishikesh. I go with them. They take me. I let myself be taken. They want me to *see*, they tell me. The light inside. They go in search of answers but forget to bring along the questions. Like me. R. is the first to come back because he can't handle the bad food, 'it was frightening,' he explains (and because he ran out of the cans of Heinz beans that he'd brought along and that I'd gone to buy for him). The Beatles fragmented and then the death of Brian Epstein, by 'accidental drug overdose,' drives them even further apart. (Brian who, days before his death, stopped me in one of the hallways at EMI and said to me: 'I don't know if you even want to think about this, but I wouldn't want you not to know: there's a place inside you, and there always will be, that'll never change

if you're twenty or forty or sixty years old. You'll always be the person you were there, then. Who you were and have been since the beginning. The problem is that you'll never know exactly where inside you that place is.') And so *The Beatles* won't really be an album by The Beatles. *The Beatles*, really, is an album not by The Beatles but by *The Beatles*: a far more imaginary band and with far lonelier heart than that of Sgt. Pepper. *The Beatles* could be titled *The Ex Beatles*: a double album of four soloists with unsurpassable accompaniment and yet . . . I think it's their best record. The change of perception regarding the creative peak of The Beatles as a sign of the times: first *Sgt. Pepper's Lonely Hearts Club Band* as the indisputable zenith; before long the revaluation of *Revolver*; or the farewell of *Abbey Road* and it's B side; and the purists who insist that The Beatles attained their greatest heights with *A Hard Day's Night* (their first LP to include *only* songs that they'd written) because, there, The Beatles were still in a state of maximum and primitive purity and hadn't yet been *Beatlified* as great artists and musicians of an entire era. But *The Beatles* is better. *The Beatles* contains everything that came before and everything yet to come. *The Beatles* as that exact and immovable and forever age that B. was talking about. Demo and rarity. All the previous styles and all the styles yet to come. *The Beatles*—nothing happens by chance—which is white, like that killer and quite clever whale in Herman Melville's novel: *Moby-Dick*—misunderstood and even condemned at the time of its publication, to later be canonized as one of the greatest *Great American Novels*—contained, when it came to form, aesthetics, and plot, everything that had come to pass, that was coming to pass, and that would come to pass: from the Bible to the work of the next avant-garde and why am I thinking about these things?, I don't think like this, now, it's like someone else is thinking me (and, yes, he confesses, okay: he was the one thinking like this while reading Uncle Hey Walrus's notebooks and sorry and he'll go away now). *The Beatles* by The Beatles as something spontaneous and scintillating after so many years of absolute control. Simultaneously remembering and predicting. And with that white and numbered cover (the first four are for them, J. claims number 00001 because 'he screams louder,' but it's R. who finally ends up with it; they give me number 00018). And there, on the cover, nothing but the name of the band (it was going to be called *A Doll's House*, but, in the end, luckily, no) after the colorful and overpopulated cover of *Sgt. Pepper's*. Design by Richard Hamilton (they only pay him £200, and everyone at EMI is delighted, after how much they spent on the sleeve of the previous record) who, also, suggested that each copy come stained with an apple core and a circle from a tea or coffee cup. They say no. Better pure white. But a white that gives away every stain and crack, making them even more obvious and impossible to hide. *The Beatles* as the instruction manual that not only forces you to disassemble The Beatles but also demands that you choose your favorite Beatle. And that—with all those songs, thirty?—you reassemble your own ideal album and discard the songs that you don't like now, but that, you suspect, you'll like a lot at some point, when you finally understood them. I am there and, obviously, it's not the best background music for a psychotic. I was there when that perfect Four-Headed Monster was reduced to four monstrous and blatantly flawed individuals. I saw it and I lived to tell the tale. I crack, break, fall to pieces. Four pieces. Everything collapses. Everything breaks down and here comes Magic Alex again with his inventions that don't work waving at the camera and saying, 'Hello to all my brothers around the world, to all the girls around the world, and to all the electronic people around the world.' Electroshock. Yoko screams. Electroyoko. They tell me she's Japanese, but I'm convinced that she's not a member of any human order. I'm sorry, I don't like her, always around. Pet and lady and mistress. And nothing irritates an intruder more than an intruder of the opposite gender. Someone or some of them (J. and P. and G. and R.) kick around the idea of buying an island and going to live there. *All together now*. To go be castaways. With no need to wonder what book to bring along because it'd be an island with a library (and why is it that people always ask you what book you would bring to a desert island when, really, what they should ask you is what book—water resistant—would be the best life preserver and would keep you afloat until you reached that desert island). To be masters of the ground they float on and of the sea they walk on. In their octopus's garden. Like kings but without all the complications or responsibility. Then, again, sinking. The screams. 'Helter Skelter.' I am there when P. accompanied by J. and G. and R. records its first takes (previously, he'd sung it at the end of a version of 'Blackbird,' with acoustic guitar and anticipatory paradox: a bucolic song in support of the civil rights movement leading into the laid-back but still menacing version of something waiting to be turned by a psychopath into the battle hymn of a race war). I think a lot of people are going to think J. is the one singing and screaming on 'Helter Skelter.' But it's P. who screams. He screams a lot. Why? Paul read in a Pete Townshend interview that The Who were going to release the 'raunchiest, loudest, most ridiculous' single ever recorded by a rock 'n' roll band. P., without ever hearing it, decides to outdo it and what The Who ultimately end up releasing is the smooth and polished and well-crafted 'I Can See for Miles.' By then, P. has already howled like never before on a track whose subject is falling, but whose performance keeps climbing and climbing. The first of his many takes: July 18th of 1968. The morning after opening night (I went, they took me) of *Yellow Submarine*. I can't forget the dates. I forget names and faces but not the dates. Names—memory theorists say—are the first thing to go, the first thing you forget or decide not to remember. That means something. I'm forgetting here, then, all mention of the wide eyes of Charles Manson and focusing, more and better, on the song and on the unforgettable names of J. and P. and G. and R. and on 'Helter Skelter.' Multiple versions. Frenetic and slow. Some more than twenty-seven minutes long. P. Screams more than J. and more than Yoko (whom I'll never call Y). Note: it's R. who—after 18 takes without stopping—screams the whole "I've got blisters on my fingers!" It's not J., it's not J. as many Beatles-specialists say. And R. gets tired of all of it and all of them and leaves the band and it's incredible how much Robert F. Kennedy, just before the Big Bang 2, looks like R. like R. looked like some years before. R.—at the request of and with apologies from J. and P. and G.—comes back. The song comes and goes around the studio until September. September 9th. *Number 9 . . . Number 9 . . .* George Martin isn't present and maybe that's why they all act like lunatics. G. runs around the studio with a burning ashtray atop his head. And a lot of people don't like 'Helter Skelter.' A lot of people love it. J. derides it maybe because P. is so J. on it. Others describe it as 'the perfect manifestation of a bad idea' or, simply, a 'drunken bender.' Wrong. 'Helter Skelter' is a good and very sober idea. 'Helter Skelter' is the cornerstone track on *The Beatles*. The volcanic sound of their dissolution. Divorce Album that foretells all those divorces of The Beatles' fans who fell in love listening to 'She Loves You' (on *The Beatles*, The Beatles are beginning to discover, almost stunned, that they can't stand each other but can't live alone; on *Let It Be* they don't even want to see each other anymore; *Abbey Road* is the guilty but final—and for that reason loving—first and last one-night stand, so they could remember each other fondly, with that iconic photograph crossing Abbey Road for an album singing that farewell line "Once there was a way to get back home," but not anymore, never again, all they can do is immediately go back across that street, in the opposite direction. All they can do is recover a past that took time and place only a few seconds before. The rest is pure imagination). Perfect soundtrack for childish parents taking their first dry runs at separately going to collect their inexplicably and precociously mature children (but, also, strong and advanced so they can survive in the crossfire and not perish in the friendly fire of their parents). Alternating weekends. Splitting up the books and records. Fighting over who gets vol. 1 or vol. 2 of *The Beatles*. Years of flying and forced landings and the Beatle-imperative to always be changing, to ceaselessly mutate at breakneck speed, which wound up frustrating more or less sensitive minds, minds that, of course, were far less talented than the minds of J. and P. and G. and R. All of them, young parents who stay up late, discover that the *revolution* is one thing and that to live *revolutionizing* is something else entirely. And—not to stop but yes to press pause on all those arguments—they go up on the rooftops to be alone, to break up, like The Beatles, who go up together, sing one last time live and in person, and go back down alone."

HELTER SKELTER / THAT NIGHT

He remembers that he—irradiated by The Beatles at a young age and hence the maniacal references and complicit winks and tics throughout his work so exasperating for some people—hears all of that in *that* voice. The voice of someone giving orders that, he knows, won't be obeyed because he's giving them to himself. In the voice of Uncle Hey Walrus who he hears, he's almost convinced, at moments on *The Beatles* (on "The Continuing Story of Bungalow Bill" and on "Revolution 9") and, he's more than convinced, several times on the eleven CDs that make up that *box-bootleg* that he bought at a shop in London: *The White Album: All That Happens in 1968*. (All of that material that, until not long before, had been illegal and that, awhile back, had been astutely and commercially reassembled by the artists and record companies themselves and developed into luxuriant and heavy cases to seduce fans nostalgic for all of what'd already been released and would never be released again as demos and alternate versions and conversations in the studio and copies of concert tickets or press clippings; as if, all of a sudden, the records themselves set out to remember everything that'd been forgotten. And, oh, he wondered how many more times he'd have to repurchase *The Kinks Are the Village Green Preservation Society* to convince himself that at last he finally had everything he'd never had and never would have: the unforgettable and total and absolute memory of something.) There, all those demos and sessions and rarities, "number 010 of a run of 500." There the voice of Uncle Hey Walrus and, at a particular moment in one of the many takes of "Helter Skelter," the voices of J. and P. and G. and R. shouting "Hey Walrus!" And he read more than one biography of The Beatles that asked what it was they were referring to when they shouted that and offering the most varied and uncertain of theories. None of those books—that he never fails to flip through every time they come out, going directly to the onomastic index—makes mention of Uncle Hey Walrus, settling, instead, on things like "at that time, the doors of Apple were open and the craziest characters that you could imagine were coming and going."

But nobody imagined Uncle Hey Walrus there and so he imagined him. On his nights of insomnia. Uncle Hey Walrus with them. He imagines it on *that* night. It's the night of December 24th of 1977. An austral summer night dreamy for many but nightmarish for him and Penelope for very particular reasons (but isn't there something of phantasmagoria and mass delirium about the fact that the Christmases there, in his now nonexistent country of origin, are always hot?), but that he remembers as if they were taking time and place in the middle of autumn and not in winter, because autumn is the season of memory and the sepia of fallen leaves is its color. There they went, there they go, here they come. He and Uncle Hey Walrus and Penelope. They just got off the train that brought them from Sad Songs. Penelope clinging to her copy of *Wuthering Heights* as if it were a life preserver and him clinging to his copy *Dracula* as if it were a cross made of long fangs. Looking for their parents who in turn had been possessed forever by that other novel of tempestuous vampires that is *Tender Is the Night*. Walking like they never walked before. Walking and encountering strangers on almost every corner, like stoplights that made you stop or sent you on your way, the way things were before, when people ran into each other on the streets and in cafes and bookstores, weaving together true and more enduring social networks. From the center of the city to the forests by the Planetarium, which looks like a flying saucer and which, if The Beatles had ever seen it (Lennon had joked about how the band's name had been bestowed on them by an interplanetary being riding a flaming pie: "Henceforth you shall be The Beatles with an a," it commanded them; and it was a dumb and graceless name, it was the only thing The Beatles had done wrong: naming themselves The Beatles), they would have probably tried to buy it to record their next album there. A *black album*, black like that night, its sky full of crazy diamonds under which they advanced, exhausted, he and Uncle Hey Walrus and Penelope like unidentified walking objects. He and Penelope knowing without Uncle Hey Walrus knowing that the two of them have done something terrible and that, yes, everybody has something to hide and the two of them do too (he has more to hide than Penelope, because he's also hiding something from Penelope), and he doesn't have a monkey but he does have that tin traveler that walks backward. And he and Penelope don't know but intuit that soon, by the next day, their parents would be history just like The Beatles. That his parents were going to be chased down and caught and separated and thrown down from a place far higher than the rooftops of Apple Corp. And they'll come to learn that "*Denn die Todten reiten schnell . . .*" or "For the dead travel fast . . ." as some Transylvanian villagers said to an English traveler who knows where he's going but can't even imagine what he's getting into.

But there's still—while his parents are still alive and heading full speed toward death—a short time left. A very short time. And now the three of them—he and Penelope and Uncle Hey Walrus—pass in front of the amusement park. And there's a strange structure there, a kind of conical tower with a slide spiraling around it from above to below ("That attraction is called Helter Skelter," Uncle Hey Walrus tells them, but talking to himself) so that, when you get to the bottom you go back to the top of the slide where you stop and you turn and you go for a ride and you go back up to throw yourself off again and so fast and don't let it break you into pieces and look out! And he's so tired and feels so alone, *it's been a long, long, long time* and how did he lose it and where did it all go and now it's time to say good night, good night everybody, everybody everywhere, good night.

ALONE / IN PUBLIC

He remembers that there was a time when, like The Beatles, he was also on tour. Going up and coming down. As if on a spiraling slide. Without rest. Until, like The Beatles, he decided to stop touring. Unlike The Beatles—who decide to retire from the stage due to material fatigue and existential weariness and exhaustion from all that hysterical screaming—for him the thing was that his performance dates became few and far between. The Beatles bade concerts farewell while he greeted being disconcerted.

But, yes, supposedly, writers are the most sedentary and nomadic of all. They worked in stillness but moved a lot in their own heads. Though suddenly—for a while now—writers found themselves obliged to go hither and yon to prove that they really existed. So people could see them and for that reason—more and more—didn't have to read them. Better, more convenient and less effort to listen to them speak there outside of everything they wrote there inside. And in that way not have to read them.

It wasn't always like that, of course.

At one time, spinning in ever smaller circles, he offered a story to Volare on the "mortifications" writers experienced *on the road*. (Could there be anything more humiliating for a writer who no longer wrote than to set out to write about the travails and discomforts of writers who were still writing and who, as such, had no reason to complain about anything?, he wondered then, notebook in hand, asking and writing down answers from writers he ran into at the time; feeling like one of those broken athletes who gets invited to the party to bring a bit of color and to make the people still on the track aware that, if they screw up, they could end up exactly like that: like him, like an exwriter between parentheses.)

Then he remembered John Updike—with that strange bird face, so prolific up until his last day, always in flight—sighing: "When I set out on this trail, in the Fifties, writers were not expected to promote their books, go on the road, or sign them, none of that. You were supposed to produce the books, and that was about the extent of your responsibilities. Now producing the books is almost the beginning of your real responsibilities, which are to get out and sell it." And Updike added: "If an artist had a set of opinions to purvey he'd be a preacher or a politician. A work of art, a work of literary art . . . is an attempt to make a kind of an object, with the mystery that objects have. You can look at it in one way, find another light, and see another. All of these breaches of [artists'] privacy are in danger of taking the art out of it."

And, yes, if you think about it, there may be no greater form of humiliation for a writer—for any artist—than finding himself obliged to explain, live and in person, as if defending a terrible crime before a court, what he does and what he did and what he hoped to do in private.

And Martin Amis referred to that strange phenomenon that began in the '80s with newspapers adding more pages to their supplements and needing to fill and cover them. And so, for that reason, the previously unthinkable and uncommon idea of having "literary writers" (beyond the typical "opinion" writers) take charge of reflecting on whatever to, soon, discover that those writers were starting to get "what they can't help but covet: not more sales, necessarily, but more readers" along with a certain status of public personality. Yes: nothing seemed more curious than a fiction expert writing reality. And, then, the collateral effect of an entire audience intrigued by "the business of creating fiction" (and also with the, for him inexplicable, curiosity about whether the specimen on display writes in longhand or has a magic word for summoning ideas) and from there, according to Amis, "the fact that every last acre of the planet is now the scene of a boisterous literary festival." The good side of this trend—Amis argued—was that it was something that forced you to break with your "habitual solitude" for a while. The risky parts of the deal were "the usual costs of conspicuousness."

Suddenly, then, writers submitted to the same radiation that the already veteran songwriters were submitted to by the arrival of MTV in music videos where they appeared in suits with epaulets and absurd lapels and running in slow motion and being stalked by girls who could be their daughters or granddaughters.

But in truth—he thought—the precise maneuver and bad habit came from long before. Its echo could even be heard resonating from the days when Greek rhapsodists and medieval jesters traveled far and wide to rhyme and sing. Though maybe it'd been Charles Dickens in the UK (who prescribed that "there's no foreign land that won't make of you a poet") and Mark Twain in the USA (who diagnosed that "The gentle reader will never, never know what a consummate ass he can become until he goes abroad") who professionalized the game and charged a lot and got paid well for public appearances, making speeches or jokes or even bemoaning the injustices of the world, to be celebrated in massive auditoriums overflowing with crowds.

But they, Dickens & Twain—exhibiting their inventions in public the same way that Edison and Tesla were doing at the time, as if writers were benefactors of humanity, which they helped make progress with their inventions and genius—were special cases, exceptions to the rule who, of course, hadn't had to deal with so many situations between bizarre and unpleasant.

And in one of his biji notebooks he'd been compiling impressions of those impressed upon.

The novelist Margaret Atwood warned that, along the way, the "mortifications never end." And the poet Simon Armitage explained it with a precision as enviable as it was experienced: "Literature offers endless opportunities for embarrassment and humiliation because it operates at that boundary where private thought meets its public response. Live literary events are the front line, the human interface between writing and reading. Sometimes the two elements mix, sometimes they curdle, and sometimes they stand like oil and water, resolute and opposed." For his part, writer John Lanchester describes the point (pointlessness?) with just the right words: "'Events,' as publishers call them—readings, festivals, signings—seem to have a tropism for disaster."

And all of that had gone far better for all of them and their work than it had for him and his.

So, in a way, he found something consoling about this general perception/suffering beyond the individual, where writers were like a product of radiation given off by readers, who, in a way, equalized or reduced all of them to the same uniform valence, irrespective of royalties and prestige.

But the truth is that the whole thing was founded on an error. And that error was the misunderstanding of wanting to meet the writers you admired, because you assumed that upon seeing them in person, you'd perceive something extra and essential not in their books: something that completed the experience of having read them. There, live and in person, you wanted to confirm the belief that the writer was "the real deal"; while what he or she wrote was just a kind of malodorous excrescence. Which, of course, wasn't true. The work was and should be "the real deal" and that was what readers should devote all their attention to. The author him or herself was just a distraction, an intermediary, the more invisible the better, a footnote and, on more than one occasion, almost an error: someone who should be read— listened to in letters—but never seen. If you wanted to meet a writer, the page was the best place for that never-blind date. And the repeated failure to perceive this obvious reality was the reason book launches tended to go badly. And the sad truth was that, when they went well, they tended to be very boring.

And there was, even, a possibility—in reality almost a certainty—that was even more bizarre: the fact that a good number of the people who went to see writers did so without having read them first (and they didn't even think about reading them after) and wearing the same expression of someone who is going to check out a used car. Hoping to be convinced that they're worth driving, that it was a good deal to buy them, that it made sense to read them and, then, leaving without purchasing anything, because, after all and in the first place, they don't even know how to drive.

Which, for him, was absolutely absurd. Meeting a writer first and (with any luck or good predisposition) only reading what they'd written later was like meeting an actor and only afterward seeing him on stage and then, when you ran into him again, not knowing if he were with the person or the character. With writers the same thing happened, just that, in most cases, people rarely went any further than staring at them for a while. Unlike what happened with actors or musicians, writers weren't *followed*; at most, people followed one of their books (one of those books that got lucky enough to "be successful," because success came to the book and not the creator) and then put them aside to follow another book by another author. Again: the truth is that the majority of attendees of literary festivals were there so they didn't have to read and to wash away the sin of not having read. It was enough to show up, take a selfie with the little figure of the moment (like one of those life-sized cardboard cutouts) and, if you wanted to be serious about the whole thing, to ask them to sign what appeared to be a school notebook, because "I haven't been able to find any of your books."

When it came to him, he'd learned back in his youthful and triumphant days—going around his now nonexistent country of origin hand-in-hand with *National Industry* and with *National Industry* in his hand—that the humiliations inflicted on writers away from their desks revolved around various recurrent situations worth putting on a *multiple-choice* test:

A. That nobody showed up at the venue

B. Discovering, without prior warning, that you were participating on a panel with a colleague you'd always hated (with that kind of hate that tends to be reciprocal) or would hate within a few minutes

C. That the only people at the event were people you didn't want to see for anything in the world

D. That there would be in attendance various/many lunatics of the kind who first tell you that this book "changed my life" to subsequently whisper "you stole my life to put it in writing" (once, on one occasion, someone committed suicide during one of his book launches, right there, blew off his head with a bullet, not necessarily because of anything he'd written; but the trick, for him, was convincing everyone else that that wasn't why, that it wasn't his fault)

E. That the person presenting and/or interviewing you hadn't read the book or that, to your face, they confused you with another writer, or asked you about all kinds of things that had nothing to do with the book that'd brought you there

F. That the writer was drunk to the point of vomiting or nervous to the point of nausea and ended up behaving in a very inappropriate way

If made to choose, he would have to check each and every one of the options because he'd seen them all happen and had them all happen to him. And then, getting to his feet and going up to the podium of the day and starting to read something (maybe it wouldn't be bad to do it with your back turned, like a mass in Latin, like Miles Davis's trumpet) that almost nobody was interested in or that would end up being almost incomprehensible to almost everybody (maybe a brief, but still intimidating and for most of the attendees, incoherent reflection on the relationship between Vladimir Nabokov and John William Dunne, based on a text previously written for another time and place) like someone who recalls something that didn't happen down to the smallest detail so that, suddenly, it has happened and, of course, yes, now F.

F. Amounting to everything that you want to forget and that—that being impossible—you correct, reinvent, rewrite and, through successive recollections, even end up attributing to someone else. To that other person that was still him, but whom he chose to put outside, as if he were reading himself for the first time and rereading himself later. As if he came across himself, walking quickly and nervously along the ravines of a literary festival and when he saw him—seeing himself—he thought, "I didn't imagine it would be *like this* at all." As if he were a character who didn't really work in the end, but, even still, he sends him out just to find the door by which to reenter, like an orphan astronaut locked outside of his mothership by design and whim of an artificial intelligence that's gone mad or only dreams and thinks of itself.

THE DREAM OF THE INVENTION OF THE MEMORY, ETC.

He remembers having read that the latest research on the subject (and he always liked that whole "latest research" thing, as if it were an "Extra! Extra!"; as if the never-entirely-clear results of experiments were weaving their way into the fabric of news, rumors, inventions, dreams, memories; and there he went again, floating in the most outer of spaces, knowing the preestablished stops on his voyage, but distrusting his own trajectory and even more the finality of his ultimate destination) seemed to suggest that there was no division between what encased the brain and the content of the mind, between the form and the content, between what you think and what is thought. In other words: there was no difference between the organ and what that organ interpreted, there was almost no distance between being asleep and being conscious, beyond a few miniscule chemical reactions.

Something like that.

And the truth is that he enjoyed having the most qualified and reliable scientific magazines to read those complex articles diagonally or vertically. And then later to rethink them in his own way, until all those new and precise discoveries more or less fit within his already fossilized beliefs. Nothing more useful than the supposed exactitude of the sciences applied to the inexactitude of literature, he postulated.

And so, he'd thought he'd understood—or, at least, he already believed in it simply because it was *useful* to him, it *worked* for him in/for *something*—that the membrane separating what you actually remembered from what truly happened was equally thin.

And so too, from a literary point of view, the memory started off being or wanting to be realist (there was never any doubt that the characters in books always remembered *exactly*; the only possible accident was amnesia) to end up being postmodernist.

Now and outside, on the other hand, the memory, at the same time, had so many styles and so many formal stunts. Now, the memory was like the quickest of quick sands into which you could sink (let yourself sink) to escape the shipwreck of the present. From that ship (the SS *Caliban*? one Gilbert Pinfold, as insomniac a writer as he, in the beach recliner beside him?) with all the furniture bolted to the floor so it wouldn't shift during the storm's trajectory. Now, the memory was a sea where waves always washed over good-byes and where the tides turned into the undertow of something you suddenly remember without remembering why you remember it, wondering if it was *like this* or *like that*. Now, the memory was the living territory where what was lived was invented. And the one and the other were instantly believed; because you needed and wanted to believe in the past like a kind of faith and dogma that, lovingly professed from the present, had some scheme, some beauty.

He remembers that—in the mid '60s of the past century and when he was in his mid-sixties—Vladimir Nabokov had read the essays of the innovative aeronautical engineer, revolutionary in the art of fly fishing, and philosopher sui generis John William Dunne. He'd written an essay about the relation-ship between the two of them—though they never met in person—to read at a seminar at the Nabokovian Cornell University, in Ithaca, New York.

Dunne (about whom Jorge Luis Borges had already written in *Other Inquisitions*, in which his "A New Refutation of Time" was also included; and maybe it was through Borges, though he'd surely deny it, that Nabokov discovered Dunne's ideas) focused on the nature of time and its connection to dreams in *An Experiment with Time*, from 1927. And he continued focusing on it in that book's various sequels and expansions: *The Serial Universe* (from 1934 and where you can read formidable lines like "Time is . . . but that is what this book is about"), *The New Immortality* (1938), *Nothing Dies* (1940), and *Intrusions?* (1955). Dunne—like the priest and theologian Pavel Floren-sky—maintained there that the substance of dreams was interwoven with episodes and images of the past and of the future mixed together in more or less equal proportions. And that—in the same way that it is the subsequently created believer who first names God creator—time didn't only move forward but that, in addition, it moved backward, from the future into the past, drag-ging along with it partial vision of things that hadn't yet happened, like the confused yet recognizable voices of the dead. Time inside of other time from infinity to the point of origin and contracting just as the universe will contract once it reaches its point of maximum expansion. And that all of this—the combination of inventions and dreams and memories—was only *experience-able* and possible to perceive and to see with eyes closed, sleeping yet so conscious of other things. And he understood—he understood very well—why Borges and Nabokov were interested in Dunne: his concepts were very literary, his work also functioned as excellent stories, worthy of distinction, and his theories were useful and inspiring to, among others, the fantasies of C. S. Lewis and J. R. R. Tolkien and H. G. Wells (whose masterful story "The Door in the Wall" was a kind of field test for Dunne's theories), who was Dunne's very close friend.

Yes: there are moments when science is the best fiction, until time mutates it into nonfiction.

Dunne called his "discovery" *serialism*, leaning as much on the, at the time, brand new Theory of Relativity as on the first formulations of laws out-side the law like those of quantum mechanics. And what Dunne discovered there was that—for practical and calming purposes, to keep from going mad or out of time—human beings had convinced themselves (just like when it came to adjusting reality to a collective and not a personal vision) that time was moving in only one direction. For mankind, time could only move forward, obeying the dictate of the tolling bells that the Church and the cathedrals laid claim to since the Middle Ages (as they'd also done with books and libraries) to thereby maintain power over the unpunctual illiterates who needed the sacred scriptures read aloud to them or to be reminded at what hour they should kneel down and prostrate themselves to hear those scriptures read and obey them unquestioningly. Time, then, like a predictable and obedient river and not like—based on what Dunne delineated—what it actually was:

an inconstant and tempestuous ocean where the waves and tides and eddies of yesterday and today and tomorrow come and go unceasingly. Time that passed—like the groundhogesque days of literary festivals that always seemed the same and for which he always dressed himself the same: upside down smile and gray blazer and black T-shirt and blue jeans, what he'd determined was his writer uniform like that of the most impotent of superheroes—fluctuating and going up and going down, all at the same time. And Dunne pointed out that it was during the act of dreaming (without mooring lines or compass and tied to the mast of the unconscious) when all of that more or less took place. And that it was possible to learn and separate the three times and, in that way, to conjugate them and use them as prophetic anchors for what was to come or as lighthouses illuminating what'd already come to pass and what you hadn't known how to see in its moment. And that—according to Dunne, reread and rewritten and retold by Borges—it would be in the moment of death that "we shall finally learn how to handle eternity. We shall recover all the moments of our lives and combine them as we please. God and our friends and Shakespeare will collaborate with us . . . So splendid a thesis, makes any fallacy committed by the author insignificant."

Dunne recommended recording dreams upon waking but not worrying about capturing them in their totality, rather, only focusing on the most significant episode: on the dreamed part where what was invented melted into what was remembered, on that key fragment. Once that decisive scene was identified, Dunne specified, the rest of the dream would begin to be remembered and it would even be possible to recognize its "anticipations" in the following days. The dream like a train. Like DreamTime Express where you pick a bunk in the right sleeper car—without thinking too much about the engine or about the dining car or about the caboose—returning home from the end of the line to the point of departure. "Reverse Memory": the kind of dream that, supposedly, you should have after something happened and not before. And that was already invoked by Dante: "'Ah, pray you (so may your seed find peace again)' / 'Unravel the knot that makes my reason fail,' I said. / 'If I hear you rightly, you seem to foresee / What time will bring, and yet you seem to deal / Differently with the present.' He answered me: / 'Like someone with faulty vision, we can behold / Remote things well, for so much light does He / Who rules supreme still grant us; but we are foiled / When things draw near us, and our intelligence / Is useless when they are present. So of your world / In its present state, we have no evidence / Or knowledge, except if others bring us word: / Thus you can understand that with no sense / Left to us, all our knowledge will be dead / From that Moment when the future's door is shut.'"

Time like rereading something that's never been read.

And again: Nabokov put the act of rereading far above the act of reading; he'd dedicated a poem to "a future reader" whom he could already read even though he didn't know him; he'd postulated in *The Gift* that "The real writer should ignore all readers but one, that of the future, who in his turn is merely the author reflected in time"; he'd written a story in English titled "Time and Ebb" in which time folded in on itself and "then nothing but a lone star remained in the sky, like an asterisk leading to an undiscoverable footnote"; and he would say farewell with *Look at the Harlequins!*: a very unfairly misunderstood final and *memoirous* novel/alternative autobiography with a protagonist—unlike his beloved Mr. Trip—unable to imagine that he was walking physically and corporeally backward through his world and his memory.

And Nabokov had experienced his first "unquestionable success" in the practice of Dunne's theories when he watched a movie (he didn't mention the title) that he claimed to have dreamed two or three nights before and in which there took place the visit to a museum and the director of that museum. A dream that has (though Nabokov apparently didn't remember this in his comments about the dream) multiple scenes from a story of his titled "The Visit to the Museum" written many years before. Or, then, discovering—confirming that he was right; and he himself had felt something of Nabokov's joy when he reread that moment—that in chapter four of *Pnin*, he's already *dreaming*, years before it was to happen somewhere else, of the mad flight of the King of Zembla across mountain ranges and continents in *Pale Fire*.

That Zembla—another kingdom by the sea—that, in reality, wasn't a place on the map but a state of mind: a dissociative flight, but at the same time an unbreakable and unforgettable geography. Zembla like an irretrievable past, but a past that, nevertheless, came back from the future to retrieve everything that remembered it. Zembla, which was far away but—taking some distance and gaining some perspective—increased the perception of the ache for what was and what would no longer be, but somehow would forever be, understanding that "the rest is rust and stardust."

Only what's remembered keeps on shining and illuminating; and that was how Nabokov opted to remember in his unsurpassable version of the subject in question, in *Speak, Memory*: avoiding the defects of the *memoirists* ("men who have too little imagination to write fiction and too bad a memory to write the truth," he noted in his story "Time and Ebb") and remembering only what he was interested in remembering in the way that, for him, it should be remembered. (Bob Dylan—many of his songs functioning like waking dreams—had used the same for his selective and spasmodic and intermittent memories in his *Chronicles: Volume One* which could have well been titled *Sing, Memory.*) Leaning on the reinvention of his past and its reorganization ("What interested me is the thematic lines of my life that resemble fiction . . . It is a literary approach to my past") into what he called "themes" in accordance with the way in which his life had been plotted out by "invisible chess forces" such that, by the end, all those themes melted into an "unrealistically real" whole, with the matches of the past already lighting the flames of the future. Or vice versa and with a gust, extinguishing the now so that the then could be lit up with everything yet to come, like some cells interlinking with other cells.

And so, Nabokov (who'd spent his entire life denying the possibility of oneiric interpretation as part of the unconscious and considering anything that originated with Sigmund Freud as a farce for the vulgar or credulous), nevertheless, found Dunne's precepts very useful. In them, dreams not as something nebulously interpretable but as something clearly legible. And nothing interested a writer more than something he could read. And so Nabokov decided to avail himself of Dunne's instructions as a foundation and method for the almost essayistic section, titled "The Texture of Time," of the novel that he was working on at the time, the same novel that, here and now, he was burning: *Ada, or Ardor.* A section that, finally, he read in the desert (a decidedly oneiric-chronological-inventive landscape that suddenly flared, like someone blowing softly on a match) and as he read, he was throwing the pages one by one into the flames, pages in which Van Veen was in the process of preparing his anti-Freudian lectures.

These hypotheses also drove Nabokov (who, after rejecting the "considerable honorarium" with "revulsion," had finally come around to writing a screenplay for *Lolita* after experiencing "a small nocturnal illumination, of diabolical origin, perhaps, but unusually compelling in sheer bright force" and that Stanley Kubrick [who was known to go to bookstores, close his eyes and choose books blindly because he liked them to surprise him and, if he didn't like them, no problem, he put them aside; and he suspected that Kubrick had always wanted to write a book, but had never pulled it off, a nextwriter who went straight to being an exwriter and thus his complicated and sadistic relationships with the writers he worked with and adopted like an ingenious rereader-rewriter, without pity and however he saw fit, writers like Jim Thompson and Dalton Trumbo and Terry Southern and Arthur C. Clarke and Anthony Burgess and William Makepeace Thackeray and Stephen King and Gustav Hasford and Arthur Schnitzler and, yes, Vladimir Nabokov] didn't hesitate to celebrate and manipulate and retouch as he pleased to the aggravation and regret and "reluctant pleasure" of the writer, only discovering it at the premiere in 1962) to keep a brief but substantial dream diary. A diary that would start off snoring in October of 1964 and that would stay awake throughout almost three months and was only finally published in 2017 as *Insomniac Dreams: Experiments with Time.* There, all the notecards that Nabokov slept with under his pillow and that, no doubt, were—with their whisper of words, with their flapping of phrases—what kept him awake. Notecards with that exquisite schoolboy handwriting and an exceedingly childish signature (the first signature of a boy already so self-assured that, no doubt, he never considered changing and adultifying it), but by that time already a master outstripping all other masters. A diary in which (the project managed to more or less lift the fogs of his intermittent insomnia, comprised of one hour of sleep and one hour of wakefulness with visits to the bathroom, for almost the totality of those ninety nights) Nabokov was able to pin down the "curious features of my dreams." Particularities like an obsessive perception of the passing minutes with multiple views of clocks, the appearance of complete strangers, "erotic tenderness," verbal details, "fairly sustained, fairly clear, fairly logical (within special limits) cognition," professional and vocational matters, "memories of the remote past (childhood, émigré life, school, parents)," and a great difficulty in recalling any dream in its entirety upon waking.

And yet, Nabokov managed to record much of what he experienced with his eyes closed: an argument with Edmund Wilson in a railway station about Nabokov's use of the word "upstairs"; a fit of "child-like" sobbing; a fierce and exceedingly violent fight with someone who tried to seduce his wife "Ve" at a dance; a conversation in the office of the director of a small provincial museum (museums as recurrent territory in his dreams) in which he, without realizing it, proceeds to exhibits of something that looked to him like insipid pastry but that turn out to be archeological soil-samples or something like that and, then, "I am now wondering not so much about the effects upon me of those (very slightly sugary) samples of soils but about the method of restoring them and what exactly they were—perhaps very precious"; the definitive horror of finding himself, without net in hand, in a train car whirling with marvelous butterflies.

All of that separate and blurring together in the room of dreams, one of the most inventive and unforgettably forgetful rooms of the memory palace.

DESK / TOMB

He remembers that then he said to himself: "This is a room. And it's a room that I shall now annex to my memory palace. Giving it a preferential location. A place to go to and to return to over and over. But I am here now and they're not asking me to leave."

And then, yes—once concluded the exposition on Dunne & Nabokov—he had the idea of locking himself there inside. Right there. Of cloistering and entrenching himself in there combining religious breathing with illicit panting. And, from there, to preach his credo with the passion of every last one of his molecules. And then he recited that thing about blood-black nothingness beginning to spin a system of cells interlinked within cells interlinked within cells interlinked within one stem and scion that could only be him.

But he said to himself that perhaps that would be to profane that sanctuary in which he found himself and one thing led to another. And then he thought about that particle accelerator at CERN, in Switzerland, not far from that other Nabokovian sanctuary that he was thinking about visiting soon. And associating freely but not that freely—because being in a place where one of his gods had worked automatically reminded him of another place of another one of his gods—he thought about Al Kooper, on June 16th of 1965, slipping into Studio A of Columbia Records at 799 Seventh Avenue, in New York City. Al Kooper going in there without anyone having invited him and clutching a Hammond B-3 organ that he hadn't the slightest idea how to play (up to that point, Kooper's instrument was the electric guitar) as if he were a shipwreck survivor clinging to a piece of driftwood. And then, out of pure intuition and audacity and chutzpah and desperation (like someone who never learned to swim but, sinking, floats and swims), Kooper giving birth to that immediately unforgettable riff on "Like a Rolling Stone." And (not long ago he'd seen a home video recorded from a recent performance in Paris, in which Bob Dylan took apart that song and put it back together again, one more time, stopping the band between choruses to sing solo, playing arpeggios on the piano like Liberace and, ah, he wondered then, what it would feel like—no doubt it would feel very, very good—to continue being *acclaimed* for something you'd done when you were so young, to be able to continue doing something like that after so many years, something that you'd done so much with for so long and that now seemed timeless and clearly it was clear to him that *National Industry* was not "Like a Rolling Stone") he was going to achieve something similar but with inverted polarity—destroying and not creating, colliding hadrons near Geneva—and he thought why not and he thought just because . . .

But right now, he was still in Ithaca. In an office at Cornell University in Goldwin Smith Hall. In what'd been Vladimir Nabokov's office during his stay here between 1948 and 1959.

He'd been invited to that university for some "Nabokov-related events." What he was going to read was titled *Mind Out of Time*: The Theme of the Double and Temporal Alteration and Oneiric Activity and Disdain for Reality in Vladimir Nabokov and Bob Dylan," and it referred to the relationship between the melodious Russian writer and the songwriter, applying, again, the hypotheses of John William Dunne, among many other things and better not to add anything else.

And—while he was at it and since he was there—an enthusiastic local scholar would be devoting a day to his work, putting special emphasis, of course and inevitably, on *National Industry* (and he'd already resigned himself to the idea that the best way to tolerate the inevitable was to think of it as something good, more or less).

But what really mattered to him was to be there, in Ithaca, where Nabokov had drawn up—as if he were a general—the maps and offensive maneuvers for the course of a course officially titled "European Literature of the Nineteenth Century." A course whose one unbreakable rule was that, if a student needed to go to the bathroom, they could only do so with a note from the campus doctor. A course renamed "Dirty Lit" by *The Cornell Daily Sun*, because, they understood, it took up turbulent issues like the free-falling adultery and skirt-hiking of Anna Karenina and Emma Bovary.

In here, in that office, Nabokov had written *Pnin* and *Lolita* and had started *Pale Fire*. In here, Nabokov had come up with John Shade and Charles Kinbote (Kinbote sometimes being *so* Nabokov, like when he reflected about how "We are absurdly accustomed to the miracle of a few written signs being able to contain immortal imagery, involutions of thought, new worlds with live people, speaking, weeping, laughing. We take it for granted so simply that in a sense, by the very act of brutish routine acceptance, we undo the work of the ages, the history of the gradual elaboration of poetical description and construction, from the treeman to Browning, from the caveman to Keats. What if we awake one day, all of us, and find ourselves utterly unable to read? I wish you to gasp not only at what you read but at the miracle of its being readable") and that whole thing about a system of cells interlinked within cells interlinked within cells interlinked. Outside, in the hall, someone—one "Philip R. Reilly '69 and his family"—had financed the idea of building a "Pale Fire Lounge" that celebrated the writer's time in these classrooms and hallways. Armchairs and glass display cases with first editions and some handwritten pages and reproductions of the different covers of the book on the walls. And by the door to the office (they'd told him that it was now occupied, as had been custom since the departure of the Russian, by, successively, the person of greatest seniority and lushest curriculum vitae; by an academic whose out-of-place name he made sure not to memorize and forget immediately) they'd placed a plain and fairly inelegant plaque. There, merely, it read a simple yet ominous *Vladimir Nabokov*, and added the two dates that framed and contained that space-time of slightly more than a decade when and during which the writer had Nabokovized several of his favorite authors and books for the local students.

But he—Nabokovite *summa cum laude*—was now inside. He'd gotten—almost on his knees—them to let him go inside and spend a few minutes alone. That office was, for him, the equivalent of the vision of that "tall white fountain" on the other side of a heart attack: the one that in *Pale Fire* the poet John Shade managed to glimpse, luminous and pale at the end of a tunnel, during the briefly eternal lapse of time in which he'd been clinically dead, after a heart attack during a lecture. On the other side of all things, in a state of *postustoronnost*, as he'd once been himself, during his exceedingly complicated birth that his mother never stopped reproaching him for. And he, of course, didn't remember anything of all of that or nothing of what'd happened to him in the moment of being born dying to be born once again. But John Shade—absorbed in contemplating that fountain—had understood that all of that was not made of human atoms. That the true sense behind that scene and vision was not part of the sense of mankind. And that, beyond all natural shams—like those where what you believe to be a reed ends up being a bird or a knobby twig ends up being an inchworm—that tall and white fountain was replaced by something very different. Something that could only be grasped by someone who "dwelt in that strange world where I was a mere stray."

And yes: he felt exactly like that.

With no need to be fully dead (because he was already a part-time dead man) but working more and more hours as a dead man. Not being dead but playing dead without wanting to be or play dead.

Someone with all the time—the dead time—in the world.

He was an exwriter.

And he was now, yes, somewhere he'd always wanted to come, one of the few places in the world.

And he'd read that thing about how the molecules of a person—their words and even the vapors given off by their imagination—remained, in a way and forever, in the places that person had inhabited and frequented. Not like a ghost but like a kind of echo of what'd once lived there.

And so he stripped naked and spread his legs and stretched out his arms and began to breathe deeply. Opening and closing and lifting and lowering his extremities like a frenetic and not at all divine and disproportionate version of that *Uomo vitruviano* drawn by Leonardo da Vinci. He was, of course, playing the fool. But he couldn't help himself. There was always a chance—he said to himself sweating after just a few seconds of starting his aerobic-atomic session—that *something* of Nabokov was still there. That some residual molecule of his time in that place—a sagacious suggestion of ever so accelerated particularities—was still bouncing zigzaggingly off those walls. And that it could enter into his organism through his mouth and be transformed into a new cell that would redeem all of his upon interlinking with them in the most curative and elevating of metastases.

To be, at last, Nabokovized beyond literature and closer to science.

And that later they would dedicate to him an article in *Nature* or in *Scientific American* or in *Wired* or, better, in *Analog* or *Interzone* (any magazine that wasn't *Volare* or *Get Back* would be fine with him, he didn't have too many aspirations in that sense).

A few minutes after he started his metaphysical gymnastic routine, they knocked on the door, but he, lost in his callisthenic clamor, didn't hear them. And they finally came in and found him immersed and uncorked in what, from outside, could only be the preliminary rounds of a satanic possession or a sudden and fatal heart attack. He opted to encourage the second hypothesis and brought his hands to his chest and let himself fall to the wood floor, faking cardiac-epileptic convulsions, or something like that. And he realized that, in a way, he was offering his own particular and unexpected homage to the also-struck-down John Shade—but a homage all the same—and he was taken to the university infirmary. And, to make his tribute to Nabokov and to *Pale Fire* even more obvious, he recited almost verbatim the words of John Shade to the doctor who attended him. The same words that the poet had said to his doctor when he was attended after his syncope and that he repeated for his readers in the poem: "I can't tell you how / I knew—but I did know that I had crossed / The border. Everything I loved was lost / But no aorta could report regret."

And he was fairly certain that the doctor who attended him knew who Vladimir Nabokov had once been and continued to be, but that he probably hadn't read *Pale Fire* (yes, maybe, *Lolita*; one of those books that, like *One*

Thousand and One Nights or *Don Quixote* or *Moby-Dick* you didn't actually have to have read to feel like you'd read them; books where all you had to do was hold them and give them a few pats on the back, as if they were babies you wanted to get the air that was making them uncomfortable out of; because even if you hadn't read them you'd breathed them in, they were in the air, their presence was more powerful than any possible physical-corpuscular sediment left behind by their authors; the work had greater atomic weight than any life, yes). But even still—and this was the irrefutable proof of the never-fully-explained mystery of the effects fiction exercised on reality—the doctor responded to him with the exact words with which that other doctor had responded to John Shade: doubting very much that, in the state he'd been found in, "one could hallucinate or dream in any sense. Later, perhaps, but not during the actual collapse." And he said it with a twisted smile, before telling him that there was nothing to worry about, that his heart or brain were fine, that what'd happened to him was a result of something he'd had for breakfast that morning or, maybe, a fit of hysteria. And that he wasn't the first of "the many fans of the Russian writer" to come in with "such extreme" symptoms. And he emphasized the word "Russian" as if it were an unpleasant taste and, yes, those were days in which a new president had once again wound up and set in motion the—more a dirty game than a broken toy—always-ready-to-be-thawed hot Cold War.

So he left the doctor's office to say goodbye to the university authorities who stared at him with the kind of stare of people trying to capture every last detail of someone or of something they don't ever want to forget. And they pretended not to hear him or understand him when—switching authors to thereby change the subject and try to get them to forget the unforgettable thing that'd just happened—he asked the cramped academic body if they had any material regarding the stint on their faculty of another of his "absolute heroes": Kurt Vonnegut. But all he managed to do was arouse greater unease in people who were probably terrified thinking that if Nabokov had done *that* to him, who knows what effects someone like Vonnegut would have on his behavior and manner.

Yes: the author of *Slaughterhouse-Five* had been a student there in biochemistry and had edited the school paper, *The Cornell Daily Sun*, and while there had penned an, at the time, controversial pacifist column opposing the

United States entry into the World War Two. But Vonnegut—because of bad grades and neglecting of his studies—didn't take long to become perfectly seasoned cannon fodder ready for the fire. So, knowing they wouldn't hesitate to draft him, the future writer enlisted in the United States Army after the Japanese attack on Pearl Harbor. By 1944, Vonnegut was already in Europe, firing in every direction without seeing anything in the fateful Hürtgen Forest, at the Battle of the Bulge, in the Ardennes (J. D. Salinger was somewhere in the vicinity and, he thought, someone—though it wouldn't be him—could write, about a hypothetical encounter between those two writers who would end up, years later, mis/shaping a great many of the young readers in the United States). And Vonnegut was soon captured and taken to Dresden as a prisoner of war and it's a shame that his enlistment had deprived him of, perhaps, getting to be Nabokov's student or, at least, getting to listen to one of his lectures on literature (another story there, perhaps?). But it was also true that, if things hadn't happened as they happened, Vonnegut would probably never have ended up writing the books that he wrote and . . .

He told all of his to his hosts who—it was clear—only wished to no longer be in that role (and who'd feared the worst ever since the beginning when he told them that he wouldn't sign away permission for the filming and diffusion of his voice and image and his lecture because he was "against *everything* being online"). Hosts who, next time, would think very carefully before allowing symposiums with—proposed by him—titles worthy of a heart attack with no white fountain, like *"National Industry,"* or *How to Write a Successful Goddamned First Book and More or Less Live to Tell the Tale,* or something like that, and in which he'd limited himself to rambling about his first fucking book. A book that, besides, was the only one of his books that'd been translated into English and that, every so often, appeared as a flat footnote or was mentioned in passing in papers on writers who were far better known and appreciated "by the great reading public" than he was, IKEA among them. Yes: there were many who only came in contact with him passing through or being struck by a paragraph or two of that book. But there were even more situations and dissertations where he appeared like a shadow sewn to the heels of many who, often, claimed to be influenced by a reflexive and automatic opposition to his work, in pieces devoted other writers. Yes: he was an influence, but a bad influence that had to be resisted. He was something like a communicating vessel full to the brim, like a free-floating cell, but one that was ready to be interlinked and that, for many, was unequivocally carcinogenic (and he couldn't help but wonder how many of the, without a doubt, curative cells that orbited, in secret, in Nabokov's office, had now come to rest in his lungs). But it'd become clearer than water that it wasn't advisable to invite him to too many rounds/turns of that glass, because his residual effects spun dizzyingly and came crashing down and swept everything away with him.

So—after readings by students, who seemed to have serious behavioral problems, of papers with titles like *Mobilephonephobia: Hidden Numbers, Secret Passwords, and Anonymous Ringtones in "The Impossible Story"*—the dean and chairman limited themselves to nodding along in agreement with his closing lecture, the way you nod in agreement with the lunatic in the next seat. And then they accompanied him like guards to the bus stop to catch the bus (making sure he got on the bus and that he wasn't going to jump off at the last second and stay there, roaming the Cornell campus) that would take him to Rochester, to the University of Rochester: the last stop on his minitour where, no doubt, when the time came to ask him about his work, there would only be questions about Penelope, who was already beginning to be absorbed into academic theses and theories despite, for once, her popular success.

One of the professors in the "Spanish Department" (the one directly responsible for his invitation to Cornell and who, no doubt, now saw that obtaining his long-worked-for-and-desired tenure was endangered) appeared to feel sorry for him. A little. And so, as he was boarding the bus, he said, as a kind of goodbye: "I don't know if you know this, but Billy Pilgrim is buried in Rochester, at Mount Hope Cemetery, maybe you can visit his grave and . . ."

Then the doors closed with a pneumatic sound and he wasn't sure that he'd heard him correctly. Billy Pilgrim? The protagonist of Kurt Vonnegut's *Slaughterhouse-Five*? The pilgriming space-time traveler? As far as he knew or imagined, Billy Pilgrim was still alive and breathing and traversing decades and dimensions from a kind of geodesic cage in a cosmic zoo on the planet of Tralfamadore.

But no, a couple hours later, at the information desk at his hotel in Rochester—where they didn't have any kind of information but did have Google—they put him on the trail of something that he'd read about a few years before in a biography of Kurt Vonnegut, but that hadn't registered at the time and that, much less, had he remembered when he learned he would be traveling to Rochester. He found that biography of Kurt Vonnegut in the university library and there was everything he needed to remember about it.

Yes: before being immortalized as a character, the invented Billy Pilgrim had led the brief and very mortal and real existence of one Edward "Joe" Crone, a native of Rochester, comrade of Kurt Vonnegut in the 423rd Regiment. A man who—as the biography of the great Vonnegut that included the short life of the little Crone described—always seemed to be up in the clouds and always traded his food rations for cigarettes and candy and told everyone that, when he got back from the war, he was going to get ordained as an episcopal preacher. The biography of Kurt Vonnegut detailed how Crone was a disaster as a soldier. Crone lagged behind in the formations and forgot to securely close his backpack, leaving behind a trail of utensils. Watching him, Kurt Vonnegut had concluded that "Joe didn't understand the war and of course there was nothing to understand. The world had gone completely mad."

Not long after, Crone died in Dresden with what Kurt Vonnegut described as "the thousand yard stare" in his eyes. The unblinking stare of soldiers who've seen too much and who from then on and forever—back home—could no longer see anything but what they'd seen during the war; because their eyes had lost the ability to forget and to cover up what they'd seen with more agreeable things. The phrase/definition—that of "the thousand-yard stare"—had been popularized by the portrait of a marine who'd just disembarked on a small island in the Pacific painted by the "painter/war correspondent" Thomas Lea and published in *Life* magazine in 1945. There, in a magazine that could rightly have been, on that occasion, renamed Death, a soldier's face appeared close up—behind him a landscape with fighter jets in the sky and war tanks on the ground and smoke in every direction—and he had that stunned yet unmistakable what-am-I-doing-here-and-how-did-I-get-myself-signed-up-for-this-party expression.

And he knew that expression perfectly, because it was the same one he'd worn—in front of the battle front of his computer screen—when he discovered that he'd been left without ammo or a map to tell him where the enemy to be defeated was and in what direction to march or to shoot or to be shot. Like the disoriented professional Billy Pilgrim, he'd been behind enemy lines, on a blank surface white as snow.

And Vonnegut described how Crone was always trading food for sweets and smokes and how he was malnourished and no longer interested in eating, and how he seemed to be floating between planets. They even had to take him to the bathroom, because by that point Crone could neither move nor stand on his feet. Not even the growing rumors that the end of the war was neigh and that his side would win seemed to cheer him up much. And one morning they found him dead on his bunk. The mental autopsy carried out by Kurt Vonnegut concluded that Crone had simply gotten tired of living a life that no longer made any sense. And that Crone "was right. It wasn't making any sense at all. So he didn't want to pretend he understood it anymore, which is more than the rest of us did. We pretended we understood it . . . He was beautiful."

And, yes, the window of his hotel room looked out on the cemetery where Crone was buried, on the other side of an avenue where cars and trucks passed incessantly by. So he excused himself from a lunch with the faculty, saying he had to go over his lecture. And he walked off the campus, where in plain sight he saw that several students, both male and female, had tattooed—on their navels or their arms or even their foreheads—Vonnegutian tattoos. That asterisk that Kurt Vonnegut said was simultaneously part of the way he signed his name and a faithful rendition of his asshole. And phrases like "Hi Ho" or "So it goes . . ." or "Everything was beautiful, and nothing hurt" or "We are what we pretend to be" or "Lonesome no more." It was clear that Kurt Vonnegut was still very popular with the kids or that tattooing Vonnegutian things was not particularly expensive, because his lines were brief and blunt. But he was also sure that most of them didn't even know that, a few streets away from their classrooms, lay Billy Pilgrim.

So he crossed over to Mount Hope Cemetery and, yes, it was an old and sprawling cemetery (one of those cemeteries that are perfectly aware of how a cemetery should be and look) and he asked himself how he was going to figure out how to find one tomb among close to three hundred thousand and climbing. Classic tombs. Gravestones and obelisks and, every so often, one of those angelic statues. But nothing in retro mode evoking those sepulchers of ancient crusaders: effigies with their swords driven in between their feet and, beneath those slabs, skeletons in suits of armor and swords between their legs. And none of those writers' tombs where, to the contrary, they were represented in movement and action, far more kinetic and centrifugal than in their lives and during the practice of their resting-but-not-in-peace craft. Soon, no doubt, he said to himself, there will be monuments where the dead will appear sculpted with a smartphone in their hand, while two or three meters away, immobile and underground, their mobile phone keeps on receiving the occasional lost call, looking for them, demanding that they answer: their body inert yet exposed to the radiations of those calls—those robocalls—on which the living interacted with voices of algorithms and dialogues designed to sell them whatever the fuck; even offering the ghost eternal life and a Heaven where phones would never ring or would ring all the time depending on the preferences of the dead.

He entered the cemetery where clusters of joggers were running and fat men and women were moving around on those little golf carts and couples were slipping hands and tongues into each other between burial mounds, because, yes, it was true that nothing made you feel more alive than the dead. And, yes, there were also those who spoke quietly to the gravestones, as if they were the iPhone antennas of the dead; and they did so in low voices, fearing that people would think they'd lost their minds when they hadn't, at least as long as they didn't think the dead were talking back to them.

He went to the groundskeeper's office and told them the dead man's name and they located his "resting place" with two or three clicks and they printed a map for him, marking the tomb's location with a red cross. And luckily—it began to rain and he didn't have an umbrella—Crone wasn't buried far from the entrance.

He walked quickly thinking that cemeteries were like memory machines *in memoriam*: that people went to cemeteries to keep from forgetting that some things were unforgettable, that cemeteries were like particle decelerators.

He found the gravestone in five minutes about one hundred meters from the office and he was very surprised and not surprised at all that he could clearly see his hotel room from there. Yes: they'd given him a hotel room with views of Tralfamadore. And it dawned on him with a mix of joy and resignation: he wasn't writing anything anymore, but, at least, someone was still writing him. Someone somewhere was still concerned with continuing to make the kind of things happen to him that—randomly or not—only seemed to happen to him.

Crone's gravestone was a gravestone of classical design and very small, almost like a dollhouse gravestone, like a doll-cemetery gravestone. There, below a cross etched in the stone and inside a circle, it read: "EDWARD R CRONE JR / NEW YORK / PVT 423 INFANTRY / 106 INFANTRY DIV / WORLD WAR II / OCTOBER 26, 1923 / APRIL 11, 1945."

Then he remembered a line from the beginning of Vladimir Nabokov's *Laughter in the Dark*: "although there is plenty of space on a gravestone to contain, bound in moss, the abridged version of a man's life, detail is always welcome." Then he—who hadn't brought any flowers—decided to offer some welcome details. He stayed there, hands in his pockets, thinking about what Crone might've thought about his own sad story, about becoming a classic of American literature (he probably would've done a quick mental calculation to figure out how many Camels or M&Ms that position was worth). And about how Kurt Vonnegut, during many of his quite successful and even better remunerated speeches where he played Kurt Vonnegut (the way Mark Twain and Charles Dickens had done before him), had preached that "a plausible mission of artists is to make people appreciate being alive at least a little bit. I am then asked if I know of any artists who pulled that off. I reply, 'The Beatles did.'"

And then he started to whistle that lively requiem that was "A Day in the Life"—the song whose ending set Uncle Hey Walrus to barking—and he remembered again that he first heard about *Slaughterhouse-Five* from his uncle's mouth.

He sees the whole scene again as if he'd written it, as if he were reading it:

Uncle Hey Walrus runs into a friend while crossing "The Widest Avenue in the World" in the center of the capital of his now nonexistent country of origin. An avenue where once stood—and at the time still stood, like a last lone sniper—his primary school.

(And here, all at once the fragmentary ectoplasmic intermission—like one of those short films before the main attraction that will forever be the netherworldly Penelope—of another dead character originator not as alive as that of Billy Pilgrim: his Pertusato, Nicolasito. His first dead person and it's a dead person he saw die. Pertusato, Nicolasito and several other friends and him. Him and some friends—among them the one who never stops talking about Mickey Mouse and *The Sorcerer's Apprentice* and his woefully unlucky brother—playing at the exit to their school, in the ruins that surrounded it at the time, next in line to be demolished in order to lengthen The Widest Avenue in the World. And—poking out among the bricks and doorways leading to a hole and an empty bathtub and dry plumbing—a high voltage cable shaped like a hand. Something like the claw of the extraterrestrials in *The War of the Worlds*. And then him, challenging Pertusato, Nicolasito to "kill the alien." And Pertusato, Nicolasito grabbing a piece of metal from the ground and striking the cluster of finger-like cables with all his might. And, suddenly, his hair standing on end and his eyes wide open and that smoke that came out of his ears and those sparks that flew from his mouth and—which makes his mouth water—a smell identical to that of Patty hamburgers, with a side of lumpy powdered mashed potatoes, what he and Penelope were fed by an endless stream of Rosalitas: the girls their parents paid to watch them and periodically—planned obsolescence—traded in for a "new model," claiming that they "always go crazy" when really they just want to make sure that he and Penelope don't get too attached to any one of them. Rosalitas, on a continuous rotation, who "take care of them," protecting them from who knows what or who knows who, if not from the greatest danger of all, them: their parents. And beyond any danger he exposed himself to or to which he'd been exposed, Pertusato, Nicolasito dies, electrocuted. Pertusato, Nicolasito is like a deity in the moment of his demise. Something all-powerful, struck down by flashing bolts of lightning and looking just like and experiencing what happens to the most monstrous cartoon characters: those rolling eyes, those contorting bodies, deaths that were supposedly funny but, even still, terrible and only pardonable because nobody and everybody dies in those cartoons, and, no, that won't be Pertusato, Nicolasito's case. Starting then, Pertusato, Nicolasito is just another face in all those class pictures and, maybe more importantly, the face missing in the next and final graduation picture. Pictures that he kept for years and that were incinerated in the last of his life's multiple house fires. Better that way, he tells himself. Pictures of children always frightened him a little. They were pictures of something that came to an end, something that'd died. In a way, all pictures of children ended up being pictures of dead children. But the picture of a child who died as a child—the picture of Pertusato, Nicolasito is the picture of a boy who today would be almost sixty years old—is, paradoxically, the picture of an immortal. Of someone who would never age because he never got to age. Yes: pictures of dead children were pictures of real ghosts.)

And not long after the inauguration of Pertusato, Nicolasito's immortality, the three of them are there. He and Uncle Hey Walrus and his friend. In the exact center of The Widest Avenue in the World. On a grass-covered median, with an obelisk in the background and, beyond, the silhouette of his school standing alone amid rubble and bulldozers waiting for the final assault.

Uncle Hey Walrus and his friend exchange bills and small envelopes filled with powders and pills. Uncle Hey Walrus hands over the bills. His friend passes him the small envelopes.

And it was then that Uncle Hey Walrus's friend said: "I just saw the craziest movie. The main character lives in all times at the same time. As a young and pretty worthless soldier in a firebombed city during WWII, in a house in the United States when he's older, and on another planet where he's being observed by extraterrestrials who keep him inside a kind of geodesic cage and make him mate with a porn star and . . ."

And then, he remembers, Uncle Hey Walrus interrupted his friend and said: "Say no more. Nothing new for me. I always feel like that, even when I'm not taking your drugs.

And, yes, he feels like that too, once again, he feels just *like that*.

The way his Uncle Hey Walrus felt and the way the space-time traveler Billy Pilgrim lived, the hero of that novel and that movie called *Slaughterhouse-Five*. And it was good that the film had retained the book's name (even the French had, for once, respected the original title) because the two of them got along very well, because they were close relatives. One of the few exceptions where the subsequent film lived up and faultlessly did justice to the original novel. Both made him feel how they and their protagonist felt. *Like that*. Neither now nor then but both at the same time. Neither here nor there but a combination of the two: seeing himself *there* with the eyes of *here*. In *that* place but from *this* location. Rereading as if reading for the first time but knowing perfectly well everything that would happen; and yet, seeing things that, back then, when he was far smaller yet far stronger, he'd missed.

Not long after that—back when he was still growing and not, like now, shrinking—he saw the film, which had a soundtrack arranged and performed by another strange alien and future saint on his altars: the Canadian pianist Glenn Gould.

And then he read the novel. *Slaughterhouse-Five*. That novel where Kurt Vonnegut had, definitively, turned all of his shortcomings and flaws as a writer into assets and into pure and personal style. And he read it again as soon as he finished it. Many times. Many more than many. A couple of them, even, from back to front: page by page at first and then word by word (and it had astonished and not astonished him to discover then that the book's sense was maintained but with a heightening of its alien nature and the impact of all those marvelous moments melting together, the ones with the others, until they achieved an atemporal and simultaneous whole).

And he would read it again (two hours before he'd bought a/another copy at the campus bookstore; the brand-new commemorative edition for the fiftieth anniversary. And he experienced a brief vertigo when he realized he could recall to perfection the day he'd bought the commemorative twenty-five-year edition. And he couldn't help wondering if he would live long enough to buy, when the time came, the corresponding seventy-five-year edition. Or if he would already be long gone by that time).

But before all of that, he tells EDWARD R CRONE JR—there, underground and under-gravestone—something that Kurt Vonnegut had said to a journalist and that later appeared in the writer's biography.

In 1994, Kurt Vonnegut had visited the University of Rochester to give a series of lectures and—perhaps, who knows—to award the prize for the best tattoo inspired by his work. And they brought him, without telling him anything, to Crone's tomb. Then Vonnegut looked at them, surprised and almost with anguish, perhaps fearing that he'd fallen into some space-time wrinkle or that maybe he'd been abducted into one of the tales of his own Kilgore Trout. "But . . . but . . . if he's in Dresden," a confused Vonnegut stuttered, with that voice conjugated in the most present of past tenses, the voice with which the living speak of the dead, the voice that the living, who're going to die, use to refer to the dead who're still alive.

"I saw myself how they buried him there, in a paper suit because there was no cloth available to bury him in a real suit," Vonnegut insisted.

Then the people with him told Kurt Vonnegut that, when the war was over, Crone's parents spent five years searching for their son's body. They wrote to nearly two hundred of their son's regiment comrades, but missed the only one they should have written to (Vonnegut said later that he resisted revealing the inspiration for Billy Pilgrim until he found out that Crone's parents had passed away, fearing they would be offended). Finally, one veteran of the war told Crone's parents that their son had died in Hospital Revier and that he was buried on the outskirts of Dresden, in Görlitz. And Crone's parents traveled to East Germany and got permission to exhume and repatriate the body.

Then Vonnegut asked them if it would be possible for him to have a few minutes alone with the tomb. His companions withdrew to a respectful distance, but didn't miss the opportunity to record the historical moment: Kurt Vonnegut lit a cigarette, looked first at the centenary trees that surrounded him, and began to speak to the tomb in a low voice and—he wondered—could Crone have then felt the vibration of the words of the man who'd brought him back from the dead? Could there be some language with which creators can commune with their creations, who, in a way, without knowing it, involuntarily, had *also* created them, turning them into creators in the same way that mankind created the gods who, supposedly, created them? Could there be a special place for the souls of the real beings who inspired fictional organisms whose invented souls, so often, turn out to be far more realistic and enduring than their real-world models? Would that place be a Heaven or a Purgatory or a Hell?

Minutes later, when he rejoined his hosts, Vonnegut's face was wet with tears and he said: "Well, that closes the book on World War II for me."

As he was leaving, Vonnegut passed by the cemetery offices and wrote them a generous check so that, every Memorial Day, they would leave flowers on the tomb of Crone and Billy Pilgrim.

And, not wanting to be outdone yet unable to do quite so much, he stole the flowers (all of them were plastic) from a nearby tomb and placed them next to Crone's gravestone and thanked him for everything ("No problem and thanks for coming by and you wouldn't by chance have any candy, would you?" Crone answered and asked). And he went back to his hotel to sit by the window and, from there, to keep on thanking him while defiling the minibar (and he didn't go back to the tomb to give him a handful of M&Ms, but he should have, thinking about how if Pringles were like love, then M&Ms were like memories: you carefully selected them, put them in order, preferring some, the green ones, and discarding others, the reds, the way he did with the Sugus chewy candies of his childhood) and staring out at someone he'd read so many times, there, so near yet so far, under the immensity of the rain, falling from the most indifferent and vast and tender of skies.

THE INCREDIBLE

He remembers that—many years after reading *Slaughterhouse-Five* for the first time—he finally met Kurt Vonnegut. In Iowa. He'd been invited there by the International Writer's Workshop (those were days when the success of *National Industry* had translated into multiple more or less tempting invitations) and he'd accepted the invitation because, among other thing, he knew that (like John Cheever) Kurt Vonnegut had taught there years before, while he was writing *Slaughterhouse-Five*. And he'd heard that Kurt Vonnegut came back to the city fairly frequently, almost incognito, to visit friends from the rough old days, back when he wondered how he was going to pay the next month's bills and the ones from the previous month that he still hadn't paid.

So, he figured out where Vonnegut's friends lived and, every morning, he sat down to read at a café table across from their house. And he waited. And one day, twenty-five degrees below zero, he saw an imposing figure in a fur coat approaching. He was like a bear, wearing a bearskin coat, advancing cautiously but assuredly, along the snow-covered streets and frozen sidewalks. And he bore no resemblance to Billy Pilgrim, stumbling through a German forest, but, no doubt about it, he did resemble Billy Pilgrim's creator.

And back then he always carried (in its original edition, it hadn't yet been translated into English) a copy of *Industria Nacional* around with him: because it'd always been one of his unfulfilled fantasies and wishes to give it to Kurt Vonnegut. So, he ran out of the café and came to a stop in front of the fur-wrapped giant and, yes, it was him. It was Vonnegut. That mushroom cloud of hair, that carefully unkempt mustache, that joyfully sorrowful look in his eyes.

And he said to him: "Mr. Vonnegut, I'm a foreign writer. You've been and continue to be very important for me. So, I wanted to give you this book of mine. It's in Spanish, so you won't be able to read it; but still, you're a character in it, and I wanted to thank you for everything you've done for me."

And Vonnegut stared at him and lit a cigarette and took the book as if it were radioactive and said: "What's this? A writer from who knows where comes here, to Iowa, to find me, hoping that I would show up, and gives me a book that I can't read but in which I am a character . . . This is the most incredible thing that's ever happened to me!"

And he said: "No, no, Mr. Vonnegut. You've had much more incredible things happen to you."

"Like what?" Vonnegut asked him

"Surviving the bombing of Dresden, for example," he said.

"No, no, no. This is *far* more incredible," Vonnegut insisted.

So they talked for a few minutes (the time it took Vonnegut to finish his cigarette and light another one; and years later he would die from complications related to a fall he'd taken down the stairs of his New York brownstone when going outside to smoke; his wife didn't let him smoke inside anymore because he'd fallen asleep smoking not long before) and then Kurt Vonnegut said: "Okay, this is it for us. This is as far as we go, right? I mean . . . This isn't going to get dragged out, is it? I'm not going to have to worry about this and this won't turn into a problem, okay? I'm not going to find you lurking around my house somewhere down the line with another book, right?"

"No, no, no. Don't worry, I'll never bother you again," he said.

And Kurt Vonnegut disappeared from view to keep appearing in his eyes, every time that he reread him and—he liked to think that it'd been and was and would be the case—in his own book, every time somebody else read it.

REGARDING THE NATURE OF CERTAIN MUTATIONS:
YOUNG WRITERS, MONSTER CRABS AND
ATOMIC NOVELS

He remembers that, back then, it was still a few years before he left and moved somewhere else, far away, Abroad, before he stopped writing and sleeping. And, there, to be someone else, to be everyone else, to be like

Malcolm Lowry—like him, another compulsive notetaker—when he said he was like "a Mexican dreaming of the white cliffs of Dover."

But he wanted to go even further.

To take more distance.

To be like an alien from Urkh 24 watching the Earth Channel or something like that.

To get out of himself, to be absolutely outside.

To attain the *éxito* of the exit.

And, once there—nowhere and everywhere—to never imagine everything that would happen there and lead him to fantasize about centrifuging not just his at that point, for him, nonexistent country of origin but the entire universe. Storming a Swiss particle accelerator and hadron collider in memory of Nabokov (another hero he wanted to convince himself and to believe he had many things in common with beyond the most obvious of all: both of them were not especially good people) to cosmically transform himself into a child of the long-heralded Singularity: into a deus ex machina and deity-rewriter of all the lives of all people.

Yes, he was going to teach to all those fools who prattled on about "the death of the author" a lesson they wouldn't soon forget: he was going to teach them about the immortality of the all-powerful author as re/de/constructor of worlds; he was going to offer them the ever-living author as character and reader and editor and critic.

But, again, it would still be a while before all of that.

And it would still be a while before the tenuous peak of some of the youth from his now nonexistent country of origin. Youth like The Young Man and The Young Woman, whom he rewrote and imagined—as kind of preliminary sketches of what was to come, as an antechamber to the heat and the fusion—inside a tent, camping out on a beach: the girl pretending to sleep and making seductive little moans and the boy, listening to her, aflame and lost and trying to distract himself by recalling a movie from his childhood about monstrous mutant and telepathic crabs, a movie that The Young Man had also seen mentioned in an interview by his favorite writer: him. A couple of kids who dreamed of being successful young writers and who chose him as the subject for a revindicating thesis-documentary. And who rescued him and held him up like a banner when facing off against the dictates of totemic academics like Edith "Ditta" Stern-Zanuzzi (whom her colleagues, for fear of reprisals, didn't dare accuse of "aping" foreign ideas for her publications, inserting glimmers of Susan Sontag and Joan Didion and even a pinch of Nora Ephron or Fran Lebowitz and that's as far as she got and that's where she stayed; because Ditta would never read Deborah Eisenberg or Renata Adler or so many others because "I don't have time for what's written outside my country"). Ditta who had no regard for him and who planted protégés who, she knew, wouldn't hesitate to protect her later on, when her power began to wane. Ditta who "taught" a few stories from *National Industry* as examples of "everything you have to do wrong if you don't want to do anything right"; and who, in that way, fed her packs of students on hate and disdain for everything that wasn't what she held up as what you had to read and write and think to think and write and read like her.

And so—in the, for many, rotten and soon to be sanitized as frivolous and decadent decade of the '90s, a year after the appearance of *National Industry*—nobody was defending his work in the "literary world" (a place that automatically and increasingly reminded him of that painting, *Le Radeau de La Méduse* by Théodore Géricault, with everyone clinging to everyone else to keep from falling into shark-infested waters; but, in any case, oh how smug he'd made his enemies back then and how he'd embarrassed his allies of today: all of those conspiranoic-apocalyptic fanatics who admired him more for his attempt to destroy everything using a particle accelerator than for his desire to create something with a bunch of signs and symbols) yet. And even his followers and publishers and colleagues who used him as a battering ram to attack other colleagues and other publishers and other followers of others were beginning to lose patience and enthusiasm. Because he hadn't taken the obvious path. He didn't claim to be writing *Son of National Industry* or *National Industry Strikes Back*. And, as far as anyone knew, what he was writing next had little or nothing to do with his successful debut. And they were starting to get a little bored of his clever articles and slogan-like one-liners, probably the result of his parents' DNA dancing in his blood and neurons, heavily contaminated by controlled substances and irradiated by the strobe lights of dance clubs or rocked in the ethylic half-light of bars where (the success of *National Industry* had played a key role in a little aesthetic war being waged between literary factions, "supplying content" to cultural journalists and literary supplements) he and his colleagues get together to exchange zingers and share cloying cocktails. There they all are pincers snapping and antennae a-whip. Squaring off in friendly purple-prose wars of pen and sword and word. The practically narrativist samurais and the theoretically experimental mandarins; but he—accused of "foreignizing" and "mediafying" and, in the end, the greatest affront, of "having left"—doesn't feel like one or the other. All of them together then, opposite but complementary, fun and having fun in days when the recently deceased Borges and Cortázar—the yin and the yang who'd branded the previous generation of writers in fire and ink—are just books that'd already been written. Great books, sure. But they, on the other hand, have great books yet to write and there's nothing greater than what's yet to come, they believe and convince themselves. And they have humor and moustaches and collections of cheap paperbacks and irreverent magazines and sex and drugs and rock 'n' roll and twisted opinion columns and TV shows of their own and small roles in big movies and they don't feel politically engaged or committed to anything or anyone and maybe that's why (because they're inoffensive beyond all their transgressive posturing) they get invited to all the best parties.

And, of course, not all of it was *really* like that; but *like that* is really how he remembers it; because to remember is to rewrite, until the rewrite effaces the writing and selective memory completely crosses out what actually happened but what now turns out to be impossible to synthesize into a precise and organized narrative. And there's no Google or YouTube or Facebook or Twitter or WhatsApp yet; so, each person retains his own version of events and recounts what counts to him and, yes, memory is what you choose to memorize.

But more or less all of them agree that they're less or more read by the more or less spellbound eyes and looks of the until recently unthinkable new litter of young writers. Writers who don't want to be like the older writers but like them: young writers who want to be like slightly-less-young writers. Popping up like little mushroom clouds at university or editorial desks—The Young Man and The Young Woman among them—and who, just passing through, suddenly, discover that having a literary vocation can be a good time. Yes: suddenly and without warning—in addition to soccer players, to top-models, to scientists—his now nonexistent country of origin starts producing young writers. Young writers to be read by young readers to the bewilderment and fury of the now not-so-young writers whom young readers now consider a thing of the past. To be a thing of the past—though it was tantamount to being history—did not in this case mean to be classic. Now, then, suddenly, a delayed changing of the guard and an end to that parenthesis of ice and shadow and spilled blood that allowed for the existence of "young" writers who were fifty years old.

Now, not so much.

Now, never again.

And in one of the many interviews he gives in the days and nights that followed the publication and ascent to number one on the best-seller lists of *National Industry*, he said, "Yes, if you think of our history as a spasmodic succession of stories—*One Thousand and One Twilights*, you could call them—tenuously connected by a common thread, then Argentina as a country makes some sense. It's understood that 'The Military Dictatorship' and 'The South Atlantic War' are two different stories, even though they happened at the same time; and that the first Perón is a completely different story from the second Perón and *Evita, that woman* was one thing and *that woman Evita* another entirely different thing (and, for real, seriously: is there anybody out there who can explain to me how a whole generation of rebellious youth in conflict with their parents sought out a manipulative grandpa and an operatic embalmed undead woman as their battle totems?); and that Maradona's goal against the English in the World Cup in Mexico in '86 has a different hero than Maradona being kicked out of the World Cup in the United States in '94. That's why, when it came to telling the story of my country, I chose the format of a novel-in-stories or stories-in-a-novel for *National Industry*." And he continued: "It's not happenstance that, beyond tastes and flavors, our Great Novels (I'm thinking of the foundational strangeness of Sarmiento's *Facundo*, of Julio Cortázar's *Hopscotch*; of Leopoldo Marechal's *Adam Buenosayres*; of Ricardo Piglia's *Artificial Respiration*; of Manuel Puig's *The Kiss of the Spider Woman*, of Ernesto Sabato's *On Heroes and Tombs*, if you like Sabato) never respect the traditional structure of the monster and are atomized into various or thousands of puzzle pieces. And it's no coincidence that Bioy Casares's *The Dream of Heroes*—perhaps the novel from here that's the most formally perfect as a novel—is, really, the story of a novel desperately trying to remember the story of what happened one night." And he added: "And it's no coincidence either that the Great Theme of our writing is reading. There, in stories or in novels or in whatever, everyone is reading, everyone is telling the stories of books and telling the stories of writers convinced that their literature is rooted not in the ground but—the result of a windswept seed lodged in a crack—in a wall. And that wall is the wall of the library. The library is the only true homeland . . . And maybe most curious of all: our literature is the only literature on the continent—and I'd dare to say on the planet—where all the canonical authors have dabbled in the genre of the fantastic. I guess that says something about all of us as a people and a nation, right?"

But, of course, instead of closing his mouth there and leaving everybody satisfied, he kept talking about his various influences. A vast majority of them little-referenced foreign writers, certain rock songs (where Bob Dylan and The Kinks and Pink Floyd figured heavily), class A movies (*2001: A Space Odyssey*), and class Z movies (generally scheduled in long multi-genre cycles on Saturdays) where horror movies with very low budgets but high toxicity took precedent. And, at angular round tables where everyone debated about the great national texts that were always the same ones, he said things like: "It won't be long before we have the ability to see any film at any time and to know everything there is to know about it . . . But I for one like living in times when the memory of the past is still more powerful than the applications of the present and I enjoy trying to remember movies like *Attack of the Crab Monsters* as best I can. And *Sardonicus* and his fixed grimace: one of the key movies of my childhood, where the monstrous baron says things like 'Only Earth's ugly children grow here' and I remember the pleasure I got from having memorized that line. And the excitement of looking for and finding information in books, information that, before long, will come to us via screens and microchips inserted in our brains . . . Going back to *Attack of the Crab Monsters* . . . That movie from the late '50s directed by Roger Corman, right before he started working on adapting Edgar Allan Poe or proposing a sequel to *2001: A Space Odyssey* in which the cosmic neo-man Dave Bowman ended up opening an auto repair shop in Alabama where HAL is reincarnated in a Camaro or something like that. And Bowman faced off against a group of smugglers who he defeated with the help of a tribe of 'very violent but also very—after having interacted with a black monolith—intelligent simians.' And in the end

Bowman hooks up with the daughter of the local sheriff and they have a son who, indignant over his having been conceived out of wedlock, destroys Earth with his cosmic powers. And I remember that that other Corman movie, the one with the gigantic and telepathic crabs, began with several male scientists (and the inevitable female scientist with tight sweater and a bathing suit seemingly painted on her body) landing on a remote island in the Pacific to figure out why a previous expedition had stopped communicating with terra firma. Of course, they'd all been killed. Dismembered. And soon after disembarking, all of them start to hear voices in their heads. Voices like midnight DJs that tempt them into entering caves inhabited by a race of titanic papier-mâché crabs and—the movie is in black and white; you can't know if the crabs are green—sending out messages like 'You may have wounded me! I will have to wait to grow a new claw. But I can do that in one day! The question is whether you humans can find new legs once I have torn yours off.' Which is maybe, also, my heartfelt message for all those writers and professors and critics out there milling around who don't realize that all our great novels are nothing but monstrous crabs that ceaselessly grow new parts and who think they'll be able to kill off *National Industry* and all my books that'll come after it. Greetings to all of them and I'll be waiting here in my little cave, always smiling, clicking my pincers."

And he, absolutely shunned, got out of there before they kicked him out, amid booing and with his arms aloft, opening and closing his hands as if they were claws.

NATIONAL INDUSTRY

He remembers his first and—for many—his only book.

The only book of all his books that—more for a few than for many—was worth reading.

The only one of his books that—for too many people—showed no mercy.

The book that'd earned his name a life sentence with no chance of parole and chained it forever to "the author of *National Industry*," which would appear under his name on the cover of each and every book of his that came after it (and he always remembered that thing Warren Zevon had said not long before he died about "If you're lucky, people like something you do early and something you do just before you drop dead . . . That's as many pats on the back as you should expect"; and he could faithfully vouch for the first part, but he had no faith that he'd ever be able to vouch for the second).

The book that he'd written as a kind of response to and retaliation against an editor who told him that what he'd shown him (a cycle of linked stories titled *Draculas* that recounted everything the imported vampire had done in London and what a good time he'd had while his pursuers tried in vain to hunt him down) was unpublishable. "Nobody's going to be interested in a 'foreign' book written by an unknown writer; what they're interested in is the here and now," he'd said, almost as if accusing him of a mortal sin.

The book about which all his obituaries would talk, after first mentioning the truly important thing: that he was Penelope's brother, that he'd been a crystalline yet fragile footnote of a powerful and giant woman. And therefore, when that tragic moment came, probably none of those future online *commentators*—the technological version of the people who back in the day slipped into wakes and funerals to shed false tears—would type a "DEP" or an "RIP" or a "May the earth rest lightly on him" or would imagine a supernatural encounter with the greats of the profession in a Heaven that functioned as an absurd literary salon or his favorite: "It's always sad when a writer dies, but at least he wrote." And one that cracked him up but also disturbed him a little: "Write when you get there." Or the indispensable: "Known best to those who had the good fortune of sitting down to a meal with him in his home." The kind of comment dropped under the hot news of cold dead body by people with too much time on their hands and too great a need to feel part of something, whatever it was, and not to write but to be read. And who also opted for that classic of celestial kitsch that was—depending on the profession of the deceased— a "He's probably already painting or acting or singing or filming with A or B or C." As if the Heaven that those imbeciles imagined (and never seeming to admit the possibility of Purgatory and much less of Hell) were a kind of spa, full of angelic celebrities with whom you could take selfies for all eternity. In any case—in his case—he was more than convinced that he would never get a "He's probably already writing with X or Y or Z" because, clearly, people write alone, each in their own corner. In Purgatory or in Hell. Maybe, just, at most, an almost indifferent "I read one of his books once. I think it was called something *Industry*."

The most successful (the only truly successful) book of all the books he'd written.

The book that'd made and unmade him as a writer (and he, in his naïve pride, hadn't been able to understand that not all writing careers took off *like that*: making it big and being all the rage, like the most triumphant and epic of overtures and he was afraid to even wonder what it might have been like to write without that having happened with his first book; dreaming that it might still happen for him someday, in the future, who knows when; and how could someone push himself to keep writing having never experienced something like that when he was starting out, having published a first book after so many years of thinking and dreaming it up and having nothing happen. The horror! . . . The horror!, yes, but—harsh sign of harsh times—degraded to The horrific! The horrific! with young writers constantly campaigning for themselves on platforms off of which they hurled themselves out into the online ether or on networks in which they only ever ended up getting trapped because of their stupidly clever lives and never because of their intelligent and always-in-progress work).

Yes: his literary career took off a step away from what, for many, was the ultimate goal and what few ever achieved while still standing. It was as if he were running a marathon all by himself and, of course, after only a hundred meters, took home first prize as the one and only winner.

And, yes, he didn't know it then; but that would be his golden age, his *golden years . . . gold . . . whop whop whop . . .*

And advice for the kids, he thinks now, rusted (advice for The Young Man and The Young Woman): everybody has and passes through a golden age but they're never aware of it until it's too late, when the shine has faded to reveal the corrosion and make apparent everything you didn't know how to see at the time. So, better, try to be aware of it at the time and not after; knowing that the most important decisions you make are only understood as decisions and important a long time after you make them without even realizing that you are making them.

And it was best, of course, to always have your golden age still ahead of you.

But that wasn't his case. What he had ahead of him was the constant confirmation of having once *had* a golden age. As Orson Welles said: "I started at the top and worked my way down."

Yes: *National Industry* had appeared out of nowhere, as if fallen from the celestial sky or shot out of the sulfurous guts of the Earth, and it'd made clear everything that many people weren't happy to admit at the time: that a book of stories by an unknown writer could be a sales and even a critical success and, of course, last but not least, an excuse for immediate insults and envy at wobbly café tables or sofas at broke-down writing workshops.

Yes: *National Industry* had irritated both teachers and students alike with its inappropriate attitude. *National Industry* had, at the time of its release, disturbed older writers while also unsettling both his contemporaries and younger writers who, all of a sudden, found themselves being asked—more or less subliminally by publishers and newspapers—to produce a similar effect, because "if that guy who nobody knows can do it, you can too, right?"

And, yes, *National Industry*—like it or not—had been and was a smart book that'd come along in the right place and at the right time.

National Industry had fed off a particular historic-circumstantial force.

National Industry had been the perfect product: a book written by the son of a somewhat famous couple who'd been disappeared. *Desaparecidos* who'd been a successful duo of commercial models who, one Christmas, had come up with the idea of putting on a "guerrilla-chic" performance, or something like that.

And the most interesting, the most novel, the deepest and sharpest of all: *National Industry* didn't mock but did (despite him being who he was and coming from where he came and disregarding any suffering and functional pose) refuse to be an easy and comforting elegy to the victims of The Dictatorship (written with the same capital letters as its almost-Siamese sister The Democracy). Which (refusing to mourn, he didn't know it then, he learned it pretty quickly) was almost worse than mocking the victims.

And the truth is that *National Industry* wasn't the typical and testimonial book of the child of *desaparecidos*. Not even the testimonial and typical book (these existed too) of the child of a torturer or of the child of *desaparecidos* who, without knowing it until much later, had been adopted/abducted and rewritten as the child of a torturer.

National Industry was something like the book of the child of *desaparecidos* ready to torture everyone and everything in front or behind or above or below him.

And, also, more than ready to adopt them.

And so—like ghosts of Christmases past, triggered by that one Christmas that, for him, will never pass into the past—knowing and reading and rereading and telling those stories again, stories that now, for him, are more like the invented memory of recurrent dreams barely concealing the nightmare that came true:

The first story in *National Industry*, "The Founding Myth," tells of the successive foundations of a city that never stops being recreated over the course of centuries, because, in the future, "it wanted to have the form of multiple stories instead of the form of a single novel."

In "Children of the Revolution," he told the story of a group of ten-year-olds (fed up with their transgressive and undisciplined and oh so childish parents) who plan to kidnap their adored Teacher of Artistic Activities and hold her for ransom. He really liked one paragraph in which—inspired by the ghost of his real Teacher of Artistic Activities, dragged away by his parents to their subversive-fashionista finale—he described "the same small but vast strangeness we feel when we see our teacher on the street or at the movie theater, outside of school, far away from their 'natural ecosystem' ('ecosystem' was one of those rare words that left a strange taste in his mouth, the taste of those 'grown-up' candies that tasted like anything but candy). It was like watching one of those interdimensional sci-fi doubles and imposters and body snatchers, the cheapest but, also, the most effective special effect: the replica in a totally different life of someone we thought we'd located perfectly, but who is, suddenly, out of place. The same thing, but in a far more banal way, happens when, years later, you see an ex-girlfriend on the arm or holding the hand or sucking the face of another guy." And the story ended very badly, and it was only told many years later, when those children had grown up and turned into retirees, sitting out on the plaza showing off their dentures.

In "Fantasia," we're introduced to a young man who believes he's possessed by the Slavic demon inhabiting the symphonic volcanos of Chernabog—which the protagonist refers to as Che—and who, in the devil's name, joins an anticommunist cell and gets behind the wheel of a green Falcon, headed for a pseudo-hippie party in a park full of rosebushes, on Christmas Eve of 1977, listening to the music of Mussorgsky and Schubert at full volume.

In "Exocet and I" (which opens by making fun of a popular book with a donkey that was being read in schools at the time with the lines "I'm large, chromed, cold, so hard on the outside that you'd think I'm solid steel and that I'm not carrying explosives. Only the quartz mirrors of my censors are delicate, like the eyes of mutant crabs. They release me and I climb into the sky . . .") a few pages pass before it's revealed that the voice of the narrator belongs to one of the missiles fired by the air force jets of his now nonexistent country of origin at the British armada in 1982. A missile that, for some strange reason, so many years later, is still wheeling around up in the air. Finally, tired of not hitting the target, the missile kamikazes into a helicopter that's carrying the son of the president of his now nonexistent country of origin.

In "eCHE Homo," the Great Comandante of the Cuban Revolution, tired of everyone and everything, faked his death in Bolivia. And, with the help of the CIA, he changed his name and moved to New Orleans to become a creole style cook, under the name Chef Guevara.

In "Love Story," a man who could no longer stand his wife—but who doesn't dare divorce her—joined a "clandestine Marxist liberation" cell so he could "get out of the house" and there he discovered an inconceivable talent for urban guerilla warfare and was transformed into "a mythic figure on the level of Lawrence of Arabia."

In "Insatisfaction," a soldier in the Malvinas/Falklands War let himself be taken prisoner because—a lover of The Beatles—he hated The Rolling Stones and maintained that they were responsible for the drift from *Let It Be* to *Let It Bleed* in his now nonexistent country of origin. So his plan was to be taken back to London and once there he would assassinate the band. Or, at least, if nothing else, those "phonies" Mick Jagger and Keith Richards. But he ended up killing, by mistake, poor Marianne Faithful, who just happened to be passing through.

In "It's Alive!!!," a kind of Victor Frankenstein with a laboratory in a neighborhood to the south of the capital profaned the tombs of the fathers of the fatherland. Here and there. The tombs of Borges, Ernesto Guevara Lynch, Gardel, San Martín, and Perón to, out of their bones, create "The Great Argentine Automaton, Cheers" a.k.a. "The Sacred Scream." All of that was told with the staging errors and low budget typical of Z movies. And, at the end, it was revealed that it was all just the product of the imagination of a boy whose parents had "disappeared." The boy didn't remember it; but he did have flashbacks of other faces and another home, which give him the inspiration for the plot of what would be, in the future, his first novel: *Homage to Philip K. Dick*. And the boy (who's always playing with a defective, little wind-up toy made of tin that he names Perky Patrick) was now living with a family headed by an army coronel. The boy (addicted to the magazine *Famous Monsters of Filmland* and to the books from the publisher of science fiction Teseo and to the monster movies of Universal and to the radioactive ones of American International Pictures and, most especially, to the sardonic and terrifying gimmicks of William Castle Productions) was pale and fragile and really bad at sports and "too intellectual" for his new uniformed father. A soldier who was constantly expressing his regret at having chosen "the little boy instead of the girl when they offered them to me." In any case—in parallel, as if in split-screen—the story also told how that discarded girl grew up and became, first, one of the legends of the underground theater, and then a famous model with a not at all accidental tendency for catastrophe whose artist's name might have been Piva or Diana and whose daughter—an exceedingly ugly little girl—would end up finding irrefutable proof of intelligent life on other planets. Or maybe not, who knows.

In "Seeking" a casting agency for mediocre actors—with the slogan "We bring them back to life"—hired the children of *desaparecidos* to "liven up/bring emotion to" parties and dinners.

"They Say it Was All a Dream" opens with an oft-cited fragment from "Auto-Chronology" by Adolfo Bioy Casares (one/another of his literary heroes, for him far above Borges; Bioy was so generous and sensitive and sentimental and had so many things to teach; whereas the cold and hermetic

Borges, who was a closed system, didn't: because greatness can't be taught and isn't didactic in itself, it can only be contemplated and admired from outside; greatness isn't shown to or exposed to everyone else, greatness shows and exposes itself to itself and nothing more) where, describing a something that happened in 1918 when he was a child, Bioy said: "In a raffle I win a dog called Gabriel. The next day he is no longer in the house. They tell me it was a dream." (Many years later, in a gray night of insomnia—lying down, to one side and on his side, in the fetal and unborn position, desperately seeking and not finding that eternal sleep of seven or eight hours—he would remember a great deal about Bioy Casares, but not this detail and not this memory of the writer, perhaps, to avoid creating another distraction that would keep him from sleep.) And, yes, he thought then that, there, that autobiographical note contained not only all of Bioy Casares but all of his and everyone else's work: the invented, the dreamed, and what from then on would never stop being remembered, all the parts of a good story. And, yes, there was nothing more autobiographical than what you invented about your own life, he thought, thinking that maybe what Bioy Casares said wasn't entirely accurate but that it was undoubtedly true. Thinking about whether there might exist something more authentic and unquestionable than what was created based on something that'd already been created. And thinking too that that line of his and not Bioy Casares but inspired by him ("There's nothing more auto-biographical than what you invent about your own life," now inside quotation marks and with a dash separating the word to further highlight the gesture) would be a good epigraph to open someone else's book in the absence of a book of his own. And he remembers that Bioy Casares's wife, also a great writer, Silvina Ocampo, would end up writing an autobiography titled *Invenciones del recuerdo* and, reading it, he couldn't help thinking about the variable modes and the very different ways in which the rich and the poor remembered. The memories of the rich tended to be disorganized and not all that rigorous and as if invoked with the electricity of the whims and the unexpected: the rich remembered like someone selecting a jewel or a bonbon out of many jewels and bonbons. Whereas the poor had the terrible gift of the fateful absolute memory, maybe because they had fewer things of their own to remember beyond the hours of hunger and cold and heat. The intellectual middle class, on the other hand, devoted itself to the reinvention and rewriting of everything that happened in the distant past, or yesterday, or just a few hours ago. And for him, that entry in Bioy Casares's "Auto-Chronology"—an entry that, he claimed in his story, started off as a kind of essay, reflecting on all of the above—synthesized, in a way, what'd been the beginning of the entire imaginary of the author of *The Invention of Morel*. That novel (he had an old edition of that book with a cover—a man and a woman in a rocky landscape—that could also have worked well as the cover for *Wuthering Heights*, which was the only reason why Penelope had ended up reading it and declaring that it wasn't bad) was structured around that idea: a man—the hero—was presented with the precise shadow of a woman, invoked by the power of a hysterical and decidedly female machine. There, on an island beyond all maps, the protagonist bore witness to something he didn't fully comprehend and he dedicated and sacrificed what little life he had left to understanding that mystery. The woman is dream, the man is dreamer, life is nightmare. And so, suddenly and finally, the story from *National Industry* that he'd titled "They Say it Was All a Dream" narrated all of that, but from the point of view of Gabriel, Bioy Casares's dog. Won in a raffle and fleetingly adopted by the little Adolfito to then—as if waking up from the brief happiness of being with a boy who was always hugging and kissing him—be returned to the side of the road on the edge of a dynastic estate. Then Gabriel began the long walk home and, when at last, after multiple travails and dangers, he found the place where the market he was raffled at previously stood, he discovered that there was nothing there. He discovered that everyone had disappeared, that they were gone. Including the litter of puppies that were his brothers and sisters. In a final metaliterary twist, Gabriel began a long search for his family, passing through various hands and enduring many beatings, he got as far as Mexico and ended up that dog that gets thrown down into the ravine along with the Consul on the last page of *Under the Volcano*. All of it told in a mode not at all Walt Disney and very much Bang!bi. And punctuated—again—by other quotations from Bioy Casares related to dreams as the keys that opened the doors of invention and of memory. "There's something so intimate about the night. The bed is a nest. Dreams leave behind traces of nostalgia for things too soon forgotten. More even than when awake, in dreams we are ourselves. We participate with the full cast," "The dream's scenographer tires quickly and finishes his work any way he can," "I dream every night. The idea of some valuable thing that at one time you had, lost, barely remember later on, and want to recover, corresponds to the experience of the dreamer who wakes up knowing he's dreamed of a marvelous moment and tries in vain to remember it," "Reality is fantastical at any moment. In dreams, in an illness," and "I would like to write novels readers remember like dreams."

In "Manbrú," an illusionist collaborates the Dictatorship, helping to "disappear" enemies of the regime: magic phrases and words that didn't leave behind inconvenient evidence and send those individuals to a place that was perfect for them, a place where the revolution had triumphed and that "looked a lot like Pepperland from *Yellow Submarine*."

"Passes and Free Throws," is the story of two college basketball players in the United States. One white and one black and both get sent to train with a team in Patagonia. There, in a town called Planicie Banderita, the imported players are welcomed as heroes and soon both of them fall in love with the English teacher at the local high school. The first part of the story was light and romantic and picaresque; the second—when "the armed conflict in the South Atlantic" breaks out—turned disturbing and paranoid, when both young men are accused of being "spies for La Margaret" and passing information to the British army or something like that. In the end, both are lynched by a mob and nobody knows or even suspects that, all along, the real spy was the English teacher.

And in "My Unforgettable Night" (which was perhaps the best of all the stories in *National Industry*, also the one least shaded with black humor and where you can already catch a glimpse on the horizon of the formal storms of his subsequent books) he created a portrait of a father who, one night, woke up his young son and asked him to help him burn, in their back yard, his entire library, because it contained too many books that were "banned" by The Dictatorship. And as they're throwing the books into the fire, the boy tries to read them as fast as he can (he read all of them, yes, simultaneously and not one after another; and for him they had no beginning, no middle, no end, no suspense, no moral, no causes, no effects, and it was as if they were breathing in the surprising and beautiful depths of marvelous moments seen all at one time) and store them in his head in brief fragments that are nothing more than glimmers of plotlines and shots in the dark. Inventing on the basis of those random pieces—and in the same act destroying them—how they began and how they would end. And so, right there and then, the boy ended up beginning to be transformed into a writer when, really, "he was going to be a veterinarian or a Formula 1 racer." At the end, it's revealed that the boy wasn't a boy: that the boy was an adult, preserved in a space shuttle launched to infinity; that he had become the last writer, not only of his now nonexistent country of origin but of the entire world; floating in space and hoping to reach a planet whose inhabitants still read and wrote, without it being entirely clear to him if such a planet would be more advanced or more primitive than the Earth he'd left behind.

Behind all of the above—if it were possible to accelerate its particles or to centrifuge its hadrons, concealed like one of those hidden tracks recorded at a different sonic frequency—there was another story that he'd never written and would never write, even if it meant (sometimes he suspected that it was possible) he was able to write again, if it gave him back the gift of words.

Even still, it was something that he could read between the lines: the untellable tale and the unconfessable confession of a brother and sister who, tired of the volatile instability of their parents, ratted them out over the phone and got them arrested and disappeared, so that, erased from the map, they never see them again.

And yes: the book sold well and was read even more via hearsay (*National Industry* had achieved that curious literary category of "topic of conversation" where there was no need to read it well first to offer a bad opinion later).

And the "intellectual sphere" developed complex explanatory theories to discredit its author along the lines of accusing him of "writing for the market."

And, again, more than one almost-*desaparecido* (odd category that included those who had been saved by a miracle or by happenstance or because, actually, they'd never been much of a danger to or in much danger from their repressors, though they claimed the opposite) took issue with him. And called him "literary torturer" and someone whose parents would be ashamed of what he'd done while he responded by pointing out that no revolution that prides itself on being a revolution will ever triumph if it can't laugh at itself a little bit and his parents would've definitely approved of his book as a good product from a marketing perspective.

But, again, to tell the sad truth: his parents weren't all that highly regarded *either*; his disappeared *bon vivant* progenitors were, also, politically and ideologically problematic: a subversive aberration both for the extreme right and for the extreme left. As much for the ones as for the others, his parents provoked the sad and insurmountable discomfort of a tattoo with orthographical errors.

And so, suddenly polemical—to the fury of his detractors who'd become his best promoters by opposition—*National Industry* sold even more.

And, of course, many writers just simply hated him by default. Him first and then his creature, because at that time—'twas ever thus and thus it shall ever be—his now nonexistent country of origin was characterized by being that place where anyone for whom, exceptionally, things went fairly well had to explain himself to the hundreds or thousands or millions of people for whom, by twisted general rule, things went fairly badly.

And at that time he went to a lot of the kind of parties where you knew what time they began but not what day they ended.

And at one of those parties—which didn't much help his profile that featured an increasingly heavily and bettered powdered nose—he met Pétalo: the artist name of Marita Roldán, the sexy host of one of the first music video shows and supposedly (though not really) the daughter of one of the most rabid and ardent and messianic repressors of The Dictatorship: a coronel who'd been considered directly responsible for the final assault on the department store that'd been taken over by his disappeared parents. And soon, the coronel in question would be assassinated at a nightclub by a conflicted rock musician/jingle composer or something like that. Shot down for the love of art. "Big Bang-Bang," ran the headline of a more or less countercultural monthly at the time. His father would've loved it. "It's got a hook and it's catchy," he would've said. His mother and father were mentioned several times in that article. And it even included a picture of his whole family where he and Penelope—his sister was still small but already XL crazy and yet to be transformed into Literature's High Priestess—appeared posing aboard the famous sailboat, the *Diver*, holding a sign, another sign, that read "Special Offer: Children Included." (Years later, a successful writer, *National Industry* at its apogee, he would mock and take revenge against all of that by having himself photographed on the cover of a weekly among the people of the year, with a sign that asked: "Do you know where your parents are tonight?")

Parents and children and children and parents, yes: together in that place where some go in so that others come out.

Everything seemed to start there just so it could end up back there.

And what disappeared was the desire to keep telling the tale.

That tale.

Let others tell it, he told himself.

And others took no time at all to tell it throughout the next quarter century, claiming that they were doing it *like that*, with reverent irreverence, for the first time; not as if *National Industry* had disappeared (because it was still there and it was even rereleased every so often) but as if it'd never existed. *National Industry* not *novel* and not even a *novelty*: just *not*. Denied by new young writers from his now nonexistent country of origin. Many of them more concerned with nonfiction and reportage than with fictions and inventions. More interested in being realists within a literature that'd always been more of the fantastic variety. All of them calling for justice and rising from the ashes of another economic and governmental and millennial crisis in which, this time, the military hadn't participated. The Democracy couldn't blame The Dictatorship. Which greatly complicated the plotline of his now nonexistent country of origin. Because—all of a sudden and with no sudden coup d'état—there was no longer any indisputable villainous villain to blame for everything and thereby conceal the irresponsibility that was felt because, suddenly and for many, The Democracy was like that relative who started to say strange things and do even stranger things. A relative you don't have the money to have committed so he would be cared for and convinced that things had been worse, that things weren't that bad, that he'd been through worse things and lived to tell the tale, to not lose the will to survive, which was the last thing you lost, because it was the last will.

LAST WILLS

He remembers that his parents didn't leave a will because they were so young. Or because they thought that they would never die (much less grow old) and, under no circumstances, that their fashionista-terrorist happening would end how it ended: ending them and a group of their cause-less rebellion's followers (including his so-longed-for Teacher of Artistic Activities) and, in the process, multiple customers who just happened to be there, in that department store, for some last minute Christmas shopping and Ho Ho Ho.

But many years later, opening those boxes you should never open, he found, among documents various, a pamphlet/map of Disneyland showing the different "Lands" in the amusement park and there—in his mother's round handwriting and his father's angular handwriting—a series of instructions in the event that the *Diver* sank (it was clear that that was the only possible form of disappearance they could conceive of). And where it said that "under no circumstances" were he or Penelope to become writers when they grew up, it was "expressly prohibited," and they proposed, instead, an immediate and future occupation: "Never writers. You are to be advertisers (if you want, you can write your own scripts) and/or models. Like us. First, you'll win the account of an international soda brand and advertise it by traveling all over the world. And then, when you're old enough, you'll take over the positions that we have left open and take charge of *our* whisky aboard the *Diver II*. You will elegantly insinuate the subtly incestuous nature of your relationship. How you're not happy with anyone else, only with each other. Don't worry about growing up. Don't worry about the past (the past is a product that can always be modified and relaunched into the market under a new name and label and packaging). And most important of all: don't even think about writing about us."

But nothing of that, of that nothing.

And the *Diver* had been acquired by a colleague of their parents: an adman known as La Montaña García who would also disappear a few years later, but of his own volition and along with a friend of his (all of a sudden, he remembers his name): Federico Esperanto. A musician and also an adman (and assassinated by a soldier in a nightclub), both of them pulling up anchors and all aboard and bound for the horizon. And—unlike their parents—with nobody to film their departure and a popular song playing in the background.

He remembers that, nevertheless, advertising . . . It was clear that he hadn't gotten into it to honor the memory of his father and mother, but, rather, because at the time, he thought there might be something *there* that could be useful to him. Something that could work, to give him time, and to launch him—after getting out of there before it was too late, like someone fleeing from Dracula's castle—toward his true and one and only vocation. Because advertising was not a vocation: it was a diabolical occupation that occupied its possessed occupiers. It vampirized and abducted and possessed them. A place where promising writers and visual artists and film directors and musicians in his now nonexistent country of origin went to make and to earn money that, in theory, would later allow them to finance their respective arts. Don't shake before using and, kids, don't try this at home. Nothing is lost, everything is transformed or—maybe, to put it in advertising argot-jargon—everything is rebranded. The way the story of his now nonexistent country of origin got rebranded over and over again.

But it was clear that—like with pretty much everything—it was easy to get in but so hard to get out. It wasn't that all of them ended up selling their souls to the Devil, but they did end up selling their souls. Pure and simple. Or, even, giving it away. Again: the soul as a product and a good number for those who started out as *mad men* and ended in a bad way, becoming nothing more and nothing less than—oxymoronic definition if ever there was one—*locos lindos*: "creative" types who no longer create but just recreate in the vicinity of the things other people created. People literally producing in the service—like lords and ladies of fortune—of registered trademarks. Beings who—like in Roger Corman's films—had mutated into something else, into volatile creatures ready to do anything to pay for their vices and virtues and, later, operating as if in some kind of internal and self-imposed exile during The Dictatorship and, sometimes, even in cahoots with it, producing "pieces" that distracted people from the horror or, sometimes, went so far as to celebrate it, as if it were a kind of soccer match. There inside, feeling *forever young* and one of the *very few*. After all, for initiates, advertising was nothing more than the glorification and professionalization of that great primitive and childish impulse: telling lies.

Fairy tales in the hands of wizards.

And advertising—though in one way or another everyone spoke it, from the first consumer to the last consumed—was the secret language of his country.

At any rate, few countries were as "commercial" as his now nonexistent country of origin. And as mendacious. And as bewitched. Why? Maybe— because of its strange and precisely dislocated insularity, because of its European calling and its end-of-the-world reality—due to the need to sell itself *ad aeternum*, in a succession of "campaigns," to try to give some order and meaning to an always convulsive history. To sum it up: his now non-existent country of origin was a complicated but interesting product. And its inhabitants were always complex and complex-ridden and consummate compulsive consumers. It was enough to—as a random but significant exam-ple—point out that one of the most successful TV shows throughout the '80s (while he was preparing to write *National Industry*) came on late on fever-ish Saturday nights and featured the rebroadcast of spots/commercials from all over the world, commented on by a pair of hosts with the air of twilight playboys, and that went as far as including a contest segment where the par-ticipants sang immortal jingles as if they were standards by Frank Sinatra or Tony Bennett, those two formidable rewriters of other peoples' songs, in their own way, those re-interpreters of authorship. And he and a lot of people he knew stayed home on Saturday nights to get high and watch that show and laugh their asses off and, yes, to sing along from home with the participants.

Some of his friends were dead, some of them ended up admen (and those were the ones who always called him, so many years later, invoking their shared past, to "seduce him" into participating in their artistic and very per-sonal and generally not so commercial projects, which they understood as ways to redeem themselves in the eyes of the muses for having prostituted their hypothetical gifts to make so much money selling other people's products; and he never stopped explaining to them that he did not have that problem: that he'd already solved and resolved the whole artistic part for himself, that what he needed to do was to sell and earn money, like them, and, of course, it didn't take him long to realize, that they hadn't read any of his books).

But he came into that world—"the advertising world"—thinking he wouldn't fall into its trap. That his stint there would be a good way to train and deform himself to later escape—or to be discharged as if it were the most convenient and hedonistic form of military service—and write what would be *National Industry*. That his organism was immune to all its temptation because he was naturally equipped with antibodies and serums because of who his parents had been (and being the son of such legends was what opened all those doors for him, doors watched over by his late parents' friends and colleagues) and that, between what he would take home working at an ad agency whose name was made up of more surnames than a buffet of law firms plus what he would earn laying out/writing as a pseudo-neo-journalist for the magazine *Volare* run by Abel Rondeau (his journalistic mentor who had, also, come from and lived off of advertising and still was, because *Volare* was nothing but a magazine conceived of on the basis of its advertisers), he could *finance* without a problem—even allowing himself various luxuries and vices—the writing of his first book.

His mentor in advertising—and subsequently one of the most consistent detractors of *National Industry*—was a guy named Guillermo Aleluya Nebel a.k.a. Guillermo Nebel a.k.a. Willy Nebel a.k.a Nebel. Which was always almost incomprehensible to him. Because he never could've written that book—or at least he would've written it in a very different way—if he hadn't read Nebel's books first.

Nebel had been born on September 1, 1939 ("Day and year of the start of World War Two; I always had a certain tendency to get mixed up in public and private catastrophes," he'd joked once). And—like him in his moment—Nebel seemed to have materialized out of nothingness as a writer of nothingness, fallen from the sky, outside any generation but with winks at Borges and Cortázar.

Nebel—a virtuosic adman by way of sociology and ultimately a major and blessedly *maudit* poet and writer—knew that the first thing you had to do was to turn yourself into a brand. And so, almost right away, the forever polemical polemicist distilled his name down to the pure and simple Nebel on his book covers. Nebel and full stop. Or full stop and new sentence or full stop and new paragraph if and only if the first word of the next line was none other than the word "Nebel."

Nebel, and that was enough and more than enough.

Nebel, and that said—and wrote—it all.

Nebel, who in 1982 ("Coinciding with another war, as you know," he commented) won a literary award sponsored by an international brand of chocolates with a deluxe jury and Nebel, who then turned down the award because the associated publication and sales' conditions struck him as unacceptable. And, alongside his ever more admired books—at the kind of *brief briefing* only possible at one of the sharp and vertiginous peaks of the Nebelian and advertising saga—Nebel enumerated his other occupations. "Activities various" that included the booms and cracks of multiple ad agencies (with a stint in jail for a never-entirely clarified financial issue). And writing fortunes for fortune cookies. And the creation of paradigmatic slogans and the formulation of market and public opinion surveys that revealed to him that "People don't know what they do, they don't say what they know, and they never do what they say. I know this because I am one of them." And the siring of several artistic children (children who, in his own way, Nebel seemed to adore) with various histrionic women. And an admiration for firearms and a love of water sports (Nebel had been the one who'd advised his parents on the purchase and outfitting of the *Diver*; and his thing was to sail and to swim and to sink metaphorically and financially, and to thereby sweep entire crews into the abyss, while he always managed to cling to a free verse poem or a story with an original structure or a novel of deformed form: "Writing, when I can, is very easy for me," Nebel had said). And the serial and incessant unleashing of *boutades* in which he, in general, belittled writers old and young, especially the youngest ones, and which he defended as "firing first" because "the more you show people you don't like them the more they like you." And always keeping in mind that warning from François de La Rochefoucauld about how old people start complaining about the behavior of the young when they discover themselves to no longer be a bad example for them. And Nebel only wanted to be the best bad example (and to enjoy himself, as if he were playing chess, setting some young writers against others and—national pastime where he towered and eviscerated—defining his tastes more by what he didn't like than by what he did).

Nebel belittled him in particular, and he learned pretty quickly that nothing irritated Nebel more than being celebrated by him and claimed as a key influence on his work in general and on the successful *National Industry* in particular. And no: it wasn't a premeditated strategy on his part, it was genuine gratitude. Because the truth is that he would never have tried or never even thought of writing something like *National Industry* if Nebel hadn't first published the stories included in his debut *My Rock Bones* or the brief novel *Toy Soldier Requiem*, written—mythically and mythomaniacally, by his own proud admission—at the speed of cocaine.

Nebel was the only author born in his now nonexistent country of origin whose books he had all in their first editions and the only one he'd followed since his first book. Nebel was the writer who'd *inspired* him. And he—who previously could only write "things that took place far away"—had read Nebel's books and thought "Ah, so you *can* write *like that* about *here and now!*" And he'd studied them with care and affection and, in doing those autopsies, he'd discovered something of his own, something different, but not for that reason any less indebted and grateful to Nebel.

Nebel, of course, had belittled him and *National Industry* from the beginning. "It's not even *boludo*, it's straight up *esfericudo*," he'd said in the same voice with which he would later hear him recite one of his poems as background for a TV commercial for the same brand of chocolates that'd given him his first break as a writer.

Over the years, the two of them had crossed paths multiple times—at lunches and dinners at literary festivals—and Nebel had always treated him with the most cordial indifference, always turning up the volume of the sarcasm whenever there was someone else present. Whereas, if they were alone, Nebel was almost affectionate. And he reproached him for the fact that he would never be a true writer until he became a father. "Because one always writes better if he knows there's a child who wants to kill him. You didn't even kill your father, they killed your father" (and he thought "Oh, if only you knew: I did kill my father, and my mother, I killed them both"). And then Nebel, in passing, insinuated with a play of eyebrows worthy of Groucho Marx that he'd spent a "crazy night" with his model mother below deck on the *Diver* on an escapade to Punta del Este. And he told him that *National Industry* was "a good product but not good literature; I know of what I speak, *chiquito*."

And he always listened to him with affection and gratitude and wondered how it was possible (the same thing happened on the subject of soccer) that nobody had yet written a story or a novel about advertising in his now nonexistent country of origin and its *mad men*—to be titled, yes, *Locos Lindos*—with

Nebel as conducting wire and high voltage cable. There were times he'd even considered doing it himself; but there were other times, more of them, when he thought it would be better if someone else did it. Someone who wasn't so closely tied to the environment of those golden Shangri-Las and Neverlands that ended up being reincarnated in volatile, dangerous, decidedly Peter-Panic individuals, believing themselves forever young and possibly ingenious, having come up during the *swinging/esmowing sixties* out of the city's artistic-cultural-advertising scene.

The last time he'd run into Nebel was in a country bordering his now nonexistent country of origin.

There, Nebel was languishing on a VIP salary as a marketing guru, writing down increasingly wakeful and realist dreams in Moleskine notebooks (Nebel had been the image for the brand in an ad published in Latin American airline magazines, with the clever and immediately unforgettable and to-be-forgotten line "I don't write: I obliterate").

That cold and damp night they went out to dinner with their shared editor (Nebel had already passed through almost all the publishing houses and he'd "caused problems" at all of them except, "for now, at this one with this guy"). And Nebel had blown them away with the supposedly true story of an Argentine sniper and *bon vivant* in Vietnam. It was as if Nebel were telling us a Nebel novel written on the spot, in the air, concluding the story with a "There, now you have another story for your first little book when you rerelease it with additional pages."

But then, for once, Nebel had been extremely affectionate toward him in someone else's company. And that's how he preferred to remember him and he had no doubt that his affection was genuine; because it didn't add up to him that someone with the most-excellent bad, transgressive reputation would behave well with him just because the man in charge of publishing both of them was present. Nebel wouldn't have missed a chance like that to tear him apart him in front of his friend and benefactor.

As they were saying goodbye (and it was the last time he saw him; he wasn't home during Nebel's final visit to his city, when Nebel, apparently, warned everyone to stay away from him because his work "is contagious" and told the press that he "was a prick for not putting me on his list of great North American writers") and they embraced for the first time and Nebel broke off that embrace with a "This is the end of the truce, the war goes on." But then, a few minutes later, leaving the seafood joint, Nebel called him to one side and said: "The truth is your writing isn't *thaaat* bad. I just can't stand that my kids like it so much."

And then Nebel asked that he walk a few blocks with him (the contaminated air of the city made a noise in Nebel's lungs like sleigh bells and snakes) and they talked about that inexplicable or completely comprehensible fact that the ad spots for cellphones portrayed their users/addicts as unicellular happy idiots. And Nebel proposed they have one last drink at the hotel bar. And there—in that artificial half-light—Nebel told him: "I have another good story to tell you and, though you never realized it, you're its protagonist."

And he continued:

"The only good writer born in our country is the writer born dead in our dead country," Nebel had said. "And the whole thing is even more obvious if the writer is young. Being a young writer, in our country, is to enjoy the possibility of everyone whoring you out for more years, not to mention the fact that they'll consider you young forever. That's why I had the wherewithal to only start publishing after forty. And so, I enjoyed the best of both worlds: I was precocious because they didn't get me sized up until I was already too old for them to dare get involved with me, especially when there was such a big litter of almost-pubescent runts like you up for grabs and on offer . . . Not that you were *that* young at the time either. But the truth is that there was nobody younger than you with a hit book . . . But it's clear that this isn't a job for sissies. That was made abundantly clear to me the first time I read Ernest Shackleton's newspaper ad trying to recruit men for his expedition to the South Pole . . . Did you ever read it? It's considered the best ad of all time . . . I know it by heart. It's like my credo and my one commandment. It goes like this, in English, and now you get to see and hear my excellent English pronunciation, far better than yours, because unlike you—who got your education at a 'trendy' public school whose main attraction was that it was almost free—I went to a British primary school. *Atención*, pay attention, little buddy. It goes and went like this: 'MEN WANTED for hazardous journey, small wages, bitter cold, long months of complete darkness, constant danger, safe return doubtful, honor and recognition in case of success' . . . No need for me to translate it, right? Because you only read in English and you like to insert all those words in italics in different languages in your books, right? Anyway, it's all there: hazardous journey and bad pay and a lot of cold and working in complete darkness for a long time, unexpected dangers, doubts that you'll ever return to a safe port, and, who knows, if all goes well a bit of honor and recognition . . . And most interesting of all, this is the best part: it's one of the most famous ads in History, but nobody ever saw it in print. It's been looked for in all the English newspapers from the year 1900. They were even offering financial remuneration to anyone who could offer physical and print evidence of its existence. And nothing. It's not there, it never was . . . Any trace of it was lost, as if the ad had itself been one of those doomed excursions into the unknown. Understand what I'm saying here? Yes? No? Get it? What it symbolizes? Want another line?"

COCAINE AND BIG LITTLE GIRLS

He remembers that Nebel had been the person who'd introduced him to cocaine. And that he was more than pleased to make its acquaintance. And to invite it up his nose and into his brain the way someone invites in the kind of vampire (another vampire) that asks permission the first time, but will never do so again on any of its many subsequent visits, sharp fangs bared and nose snorting up all of that stuff made to make the night feel like it would never end.

And he remembers that it was along with cocaine that he'd first come to know the kind of insomnia that people go out looking for and not, like now, so long thereafter, the kind of insomnia that came looking for him.

Now, on his nights of insomnia (yes, insomnia makes it so that a night is all for you, that you possess it because it belongs to what cries out and won't let you sleep), he, shorn of sleeping dreams, recounts waking fragments as if they were sheep. Sometimes they were the fragments of others and sometimes they were his own and, to elevate them, he added quotation marks in the manner of cowbells. So they sounded better.

For example: "He remembers that on his nights of insomnia he would play at swapping the meanings of words until he'd created a new language, a language that he could still speak but that was different. They couldn't be, obviously, gratuitous or irrational switches. They had to have a certain sonic/etymological/definitional logic. To wit, to disrupt: for 'extenuated' to mean 'exhausting' and for 'exhausted' to mean 'extenuated.'"

And now he was so extenuated from being so exhausting.

And not long ago, in the middle of one of his many insomniac nights, he turned off the book he was reading and opened the television.

And, after flipping through multiple channels, he stopped on a movie that he'd seen before. *The Human Stain*, directed by Robert Benton and based on a Philip Roth novel that in its day he'd liked a lot. The movie wasn't bad, the novel was better, but he didn't feel like reading it again. And yet, you can always watch a movie as if it were a book composed of shifting images and not stationary letters. And who was he kidding: he stopped there because there was Nicole Kidman. And Nicole Kidman included Nicole Kidman's body: a body he had photograms of stored away in his memory from movies like *To Die For* and *Birth* and *Eyes Wide Shut* (in which Stanley Kubrick, they say, in his dimension as half-mad scientist and half-crazed lover had filmed, for scenes never used in the film's final cut, a monolithic Nicole Kidman worshipped by and with other men, to torture Tom Cruise, who deserved all of that and much more). But for him, what he liked most about Nicole Kidman in her movies were those moments not when the actress got undressed but when she got dressed (and he always thought that watching a girl get dressed was far more intimate and erotic than watching a girl get undressed).

And in all of those movies, the face of Nicole Kidman was still Nicole Kidman's face and it hadn't yet been ravaged by Botox-brand rat poison.

And there, in *The Human Stain*, Nicole Kidman looked so much like so many now impossible girls from his now nonexistent country of origin or that country for which he was now nonexistent.

Girls that actually looked even more like another Nicole, one Nicole Kidman couldn't play more but might have played at one point: the disturbing and disturbed Nicole Diver in *Tender Is the Night*, rambling as if in a trance about "the divided mind of the world" and maybe, who knows—on some page discarded by Fitzgerald but recovered by Malcolm Lowry for his impossible screenplay of *Tender Is the Night*—challenging her husband, Dick Diver, to play William Tell, putting a glass or a bottle of absinthe that would suddenly turn into mezcal atop her head, passing him a pistol.

Girls that he'd danced with and drank with and gotten high with under the lights and music of a nightclub called Coliseum where, also, the last, hip, and ephemeral rock bands played in front of people who still held aloft lit lighters while they watched and listened instead of glowing phones to film and watch and listen on their screens. A place about which—when night fell on Friday, the day of the true fever when for a few hours the past and the present and the future were the same—everyone said, "it opens at 11:30 PM but it only gets good around 2:00 AM, still it's best to show up around 10:00 PM to wait in line, because it's impossible to get in later on."

And it was good, indeed.

And the owner of the place—last name Patricio who'd invested his inheritance from one of his many aunts, a friend of Nebel's and the nephew of a military officer involved in the coup—was an aspiring writer. And he'd even run a kind of underground afterhours/literary salon where the young writers who'd been given a golden card that got them free admission and bottomless drinks and cocaine on the house read their unpublished texts as the walls shook with the highs and lows from upstairs. And he remembers having read there, for the first time and aloud, his favorite story of all the stories he'd ever written. A long story that, yes, in the end, he did write even though sometimes it seemed to him like it was written by someone else, by that other writer who people sometimes mistook him for and who he ran into every now and then with Enrique Vila-Matas (okay, sure: it wasn't his story, but he read it as if it were, because, he felt, he'd influenced that other writer the way Nebel had influenced him). A story with a really ugly little girl (very similar to the daughter of some of his parents' friends, also models, whom he'd met when he was a kid) and dead top-models and the need for there to exist irrefutable proof of intelligent life on other planets or, at least, more intelligent than the life with which all those quasi-zombies were listening to the story, dilated pupils and grinding teeth and spasmodic bodies and yet, even still, then, giving him all the attention and tension they had, not caring about the many already-passed and yet-to-pass pages. And he remembers that he said to himself then: "Ah, this is the good life: I've gotten them to forget about their noses for a while . . . This is the proof that there's nothing more addictive and tempting than being told a story."

And, then, after—everyone pressed together—they danced to music that, supposedly, wasn't dance music but turned out to be the most surprisingly danceable music. Thinking music to dance to thinking that you're dancing. Music for dancing like you're mocking the very act and idea of dancing. "Memories Can't Wait," by Talking Heads, like a party in his mind. And hoping it never stops. And that it'll be there all the time. And that everybody else could split, but he'll be there all the time. There, with his head talking to itself or talking to him, alone, because even though all his dancing friends had already split, he couldn't stop dancing. With his talking head speaking in tongues and thinking about absurdly (in)coherent things, like how Marcel Proust would have been a great lyricist for Talking Heads: the synthetic ideas of David Byrne stretched out into EPs and remixes and folding into sinuous and hypnotic *paperolles*, lisping like the tongues of charming snakes. So, Coliseum—the name of the place where gladiators and Christians were sacrificed—became, for him, that Heaven you go to when you die. The place where all kisses were prolonged in one kiss. And nothing changed and nothing happened and that was so exciting and fun and the party kept going until everyone left at the same time.

All of that and so much more, with cocaine of so many kinds and more names than the fifty names the Eskimos have for snow, on the longest night of cold noses. Lines of cocaine that he never cut long and compact but preferred likes lines of Morse Code: abrupt and spasmodic and dot-dash-dash-dash.

Cocaine that he obtained and consumed to, for a while, attain the happiness of having one single fixed idea—cocaine, sex, cocaine, a single idea for a possible story—instead of the desperation of feeling tugged around by the too many random ideas that occurred to him when he wasn't under any influence (the opposite effect from what the substance appeared to produce in Hollywood producers at the time who didn't hesitate to green light a movie in which the truly terrifying Arnold Schwarzenegger appeared, after experimenting with a drug called Expectane, as the first pregnant man in History).

Cocaine that, of course, seemed to him so much more useful than all those visionary drugs: he did cocaine to stop looking (reading) and to focus on seeing (writing). (And he always remembered that anecdote about how in Los Angeles a very young Ray Bradbury ran into the seasoned doorman of perception Aldous Huxley and Huxley recommended that he experiment with LSD to "have thousands of visions." To which Bradbury responded: "What I need is a drug that controls me and makes me have just one vision, because I have thousands of visions all the time without drugs." And, yes, for him cocaine was *that* drug.)

Cocaine which focused him and distanced him from what Buddhists called the restless and irresolute "monkey mind" (*shin'en* 心猿) and that now was the sign of these out-of-time times (that constant jumping from one on-screen site to another to remain forever nowhere, that having one foot in the future and another in the past in order to piss on the present) and allowed him to have sexual relations (and only in that phrase, refocusing himself unhurriedly, with the mind of a turtle or the mind of a snail) while thinking about that last line he'd written of what he was writing or wondering what was more disrespectful: to think about another person while making love or to think about something that wasn't even a person, like, for example, another line of cocaine or another line of text?

Cocaine whose chemical effect returned him to the physical realm and quieted, at least for a few minutes, the mental.

Cocaine that others inspired to gain inspiration (and it led them to make use of that first manifestation of this hyper-communicative futurism that was the fax machine, with that maxillary sound it made when printing and that tongue of paper protruding, sometimes, at three in the morning, courtesy of some coked-up "colleague" who'd decided to fax over his unpublished novel and use up all that ink that was sold at the price of black and liquid gold and now, not so much: now, communicating cost nothing, unless you took into account the effort involved in suspecting that nobody on the other end will pay any attention to you) while he inhaled it so he could exhale a sigh.

Cocaine with which he was sure he "didn't have a problem," though he was a little unsettled by the way that, not his mouth, but his nose began to water every time he stared at white and black lines of a crosswalk when crossing the street from one corner to another (and, yes, cocaine was—like so many things in life—something that was a lot of fun until it wasn't, and then, for him, it took no effort at all to leave it behind, because his aspirations had more to do with reading and writing than with inspiring line after line).

Cocaine obtained in the bathrooms of that same nightclub from a dealer known as Juan John: a well-deserved alias, because he spent the whole night, there in the bathroom, whistling "My Bag" by Lloyd Cole and The Commotions, with that line "Meet me in the john, John").

Cocaine that made him see everything around him not like something all of a piece but like the different parts—fragments, instants, moments, all times at the same time, one on top of the other on top of the other like the bounciest of pogo-sticks—of a collage.

And there, at Coliseum, the girls danced like the trees in the films of trees—bending as if suddenly made of rubber but never breaking or cracking—struck by the expansive wave of an atomic bomb. And he danced like one of the houses in those same films flattened by the expansive wave of an atomic bomb. And the trees were stronger than the houses. And then he and those strong girls would go back to his flattened house (a flat strategically located in close proximity to Coliseum; and back then getting together with girls was an artisanal and live and in-person activity and had nothing to do with what, they say, is all the rage these days, when meeting people and hooking up is prearranged at a distance, everyone thinking it's all so much clearer and hotter like that, when actually they're constrained by the cold dictates of an algorithm) and snort white powder cut into lines atop a circular black table, where he traced ideograms across the cover—now almost illegible due to the scarring caused by the erosion of the Coliseum card (the selection of the title then seemed funny to him then and not so funny now, a book narrating the slight rise and great fall of the frustrated writer Rickie Elliot)—of jet-black edition of E. M. Forster's *The Longest Journey*. And he would recommend mixing the cocaine powder with the cool gel of Vicks VapoRub and coating the inside of their noses with it, the way medical examiners did before making the acquaintance a more or less decomposed body or a perfectly functioning dead man; just that, there and then, the increasingly cold bodies were their own. And leaving it there, cool inside their noses, resting in peace and in repose. And that way its effect came on slowly, in small and successive spasms, instead of the whiplash of a pure, straight line.

And he would postulate his pop theories (his "popories"; he was writing a fairly successful column where he took up such subjects) like, for example, the ominous and Thanatic importance of oranges in *The Godfather*: "Someone buys or eats or squeezes oranges in the Corleone family and that means that soon they will kill or be killed; if you want, I can show you now on VHS." And, oh, it was so much work to put that videocassette in that slot like the Bocca della Verita not far from the original Coliseum. Or how "every generation of cartoons is intimately connected to the drug/war *du jour.* And so, for Tex "Bugs Bunny & Co." Avery it was the alcohol/delirium tremens of World War Two, while for Friz "Pink Panther" Frelang (and better not even mention *Scooby-Doo*) it was the heroinic Vietnamarijuana and now, yes, we're smackdab in age of Prozac and so someone's decided that cartoons have, basically, an obligation to be moving and inspirational." Or a "comparative study of the services and fees and location and tourist attractions in the vicinity of the hotel where Jack Torrance loses his mind in *The Shining* and of the hotel in *The Wall* where pink goes insane and of the hotel by the waterfall in *Twin Peaks* where everyone—televiewers included—goes insane."

And meanwhile—during hours that went by at full slowness and high speed at the same time—he shook them up cocktails of his own invention with names like Bloody Martini and Gin CataTonic under his always-on-the-rocks barman aliases Count Drunkula or Dr. Drunkenstein.

All of that for all those girls who made him feel, even though he was still young, already somewhat démodé and vintage; a little like those pathetic predators of barely ex-nymphets in those songs by the exceedingly coked-out Steely Dan.

Girls with whom he listened nonstop to vinyl before vinyl came back in style (vinyl that right away he'd copy and listen to on Memorex-brand cassettes so he wouldn't scratch the records). Albums like David Bowie's *Station to Station* and Fleetwood Mac's *Tusk*, something like the *white albums*—really, better, *pale albums*: albums that barely knew the light of the sun and were recorded during the longest of *long-playing* white nights—in their respective careers: "The two greatest pop-rock soundtracks of cocaine, both recorded in the demonic Los Angeles, background music for brains filled to the gills with powder via the nasal passages," he explained "poporistically" and quivering like one of those tommyknockers in front of all those girls who only wanted a little more of that stuff that was neither him nor anything he had to tell them but something he could serve up for them. And so he lifted a little spoon up to their little noses while rambling on incessantly about Bowie, whose capacity to reinvent himself and to rob/mutate and collage/cut-up things—like his ever so Philip-K.-Dickian Major Tom in that song that leaned so heavily on *2001: A Space Odyssey*—he simultaneously admired and found irritating. Or how Bowie had even given himself the luxury of composing his own requiem and publishing it hours before his death. Though he'd always found his Ziggy Stardust incarnation—for many the best of all—pretty cringe-worthy. Whereas his favorite was the decadent and almost translucent Thin-White-Duke-model Bowie of *Station to Station*, at the time submitting himself to an exclusive diet of milk and peppers and cocaine. That Bowie whom Bowie (years later, while recording "Absolute Beginners"; possibly the most efficient love song of all time when it came to singing about that thing which he'd only ever felt once) claimed to barely be able to remember at all just as he couldn't remember almost anything of the recording of *Station to Station*: "I know it was in LA because I've read it was." (Many years later, at the end of the millennium, a Bowie of impeccable and strong aspect would give a TV interview where he would evoke all of that with a "I only remember that I don't remember anything." And in the same interview—looking forward, in the direction that he liked most to look; and, that obsession with what was to come instead of with what was, that, as far as he was concerned, was what kept Bowie from being as great as Bob Dylan or The Beatles or The Kinks—Bowie prophesized that the Internet was going to change everything, that it would have "exhilarating and terrifying" effects and that it wasn't a tool, it was an alien life form. "Is there life on Mars? Yes, it's just landed here," Bowie asked and answered himself, cracking up. And he saw that interview a quarter of a century later, online, with Bowie dead and him in worse shape than the artist had been at his age and, even, just before he died.)

While—he continued—the crisscrossing couples of Fleetwood Mac would've given anything to forget the sleepless night after sleepless night of those studio sessions.

And he listened to *Station to Station* and *Tusk* over and over and told the stories behind their respective recordings to those ephemeral girls. And there were times—he supposed that this had to do with the quality and purity of the white powder—when he thought he heard his own name interspersed in the verses of "Word on a Wing" ("In this age of grand illusion / You walked into my Life / Out of my dreams") or of "Walk a Thin Line" ("And I said 'Fate takes time' / But no one was listenin' / I walk a thin line"). And he asked all those girls passing through his flat if they heard it too and, of course, he couldn't care less about their answer just like they couldn't care less about his question.

Girls of all sizes and colors and models.

Girls he always said goodbye to them with a "Remember me . . . this way," a line that years later had been stolen from him—he was almost certain of it, even though it was chronologically impossible, the already more plop than pop—by Morrissey in that video from a concert at the Hollywood Bowl. Morrissey said it there, many years after he would have said it, with a little bow, just before breaking into "There's a Light that Never Goes Out," a song that he'd already been singing and dancing to back at Coliseum. A line that seemed so moving to him, but that, in his mouth (maybe because he lacked the context, he lacked Morrissey and that song that pushed the ecstasy of dying crushed by love and by one of those double-decker English buses), never seemed to move those girls of, again, small yet deeply inspiring noses.

Girls who, consumed and consumable, went and left him alone, when the sun came up with the blinds drawn and eyes wide open and paranoid that the muscular and shirtless saxophonist from the Tina Turner music videos was hiding in his closet, ready to jump out and play the longest and loudest of solos to his solitude.

Then, to come down or to crash, he put—to come down, to land—the Glenn Gould version of *Goldberg Variations* on repeat. Not the first version he did—the one that plays on the soundtrack of the film adaptation of *Slaughterhouse-Five*—but the one that came later. The last of the two versions the Canadian pianist recorded, the favorite, again, of Hannibal Lecter: music for people who didn't need cocaine to keep their eyes wide open (though it's well known that Glenn Gould was a distinguished performer and composer of different combinations of uppers and downers), music for insomniacs performed by an insomniac, music for—in the event that they were still there, maybe because, confused, they thought they felt *something* for him—insinuating to the girls that it was time for everyone to return to their respective coffins and to take their hard and fine-tuned bodies away in the most fugue of toccatas from his softened and out-of-tune sex organ.

Ephemeral girls who sometimes took off their clothes and sometimes didn't and it didn't really matter and who, when he buried his face and his mouth and his tongue between their legs, always seemed to taste of swords newly forged, but already ready for the most ecstatic of combat or to confer titles of nobility (and he, remembering them, understood that one is definitely a man of a certain age when all one's sexual fantasies no longer feature beings from one's immediate present or future—in fact, on more than one occasion, he'd caught himself out of the corner of his eye staring at the asses of mannequins in shop windows, tempting him with tight retro '80s attire they were sporting—but from one's increasingly distant past; girls who're no longer girls but are still girls, because he hasn't seen them for years and hasn't seen them age and hasn't even thought about them for a long time and better that way, better that way; but he was somewhat moved and unsettled to discover that, suddenly, yesterday was now so much more exciting than tomorrow).

Girls with more desire to be written than to be writers. Dying (but without needing to die) to be legendary and more narratable than narrators, in the mode of Leonora Carrington or Sylvia Plath or Clarice Lispector or Lucia Berlin or . . .

Girls who, before long, he would end up accompanying to meetings of addicts anonymous; not because he felt responsible for anything but because he always heard really good stories at those meetings that could end up "being useful for something." And there, listening to the Serenity Prayer (the whole "Grant me the serenity to accept the things I cannot change, the courage to change the things I can, and the wisdom to know the difference"), he said to himself that, in those few lines, there was more common sense and practical and useful instruction than what you got in years of attending one of those writing workshops (where you went to "fix" something broken that, really, could only be put right by sitting down in your library, without ever having to leave home and simply reading a lot of literature) always demarcated by some kind of psychoanalytic therapy or alternative religion that had you kissing crystals or caressing vessels, instead of invoking that far more effective *serenity now*. And that it was logical (with the illogical certification of a psychic psychopath assuring the unwitting, once more, as if he were informing them of the meteorological forecast, that his true profession was that of a writer; never that of bronze sculpture or of the composition of symphonies or of molecular chemistry) that it was so—that the work of literature was equivalent to dependence on some controlled substance that made you lose control—because, after all, reading was one of those "soft" and recreational drugs that ended up being a gateway to the "hard" and demanding drug of writing. And so, by the time you were aware of it, you were already hooked. And the problem was that most addicts didn't know how to manage the vice and ended up in a bad way and writing even worse in the corners and reading their work aloud like someone delirious or hallucinating. And, of course, social media hadn't done anything but make the epidemic worse, with the illusion of it all being gratis when really it was just gratuitous.

Girls—the new version of those girls—who would discover the books of Renata Adler and Joan Didion (from whom a Belarusian with an audio recorder—he would like to think that, at least, she was the one who transcribed all those voices on those tapes and that it wasn't some paid assistant; and, oh, where were all the purists who'd condemned Bob Dylan being awarded the Nobel then; and he'd mentioned all of this in passing in an interview and, of course, the furious Furies had fallen all over him on social media, accusing him of being an ignorant machista—had stolen the Nobel she so deserved for her self-referential nonfiction and whose famous "We tell ourselves stories in order to live" had devolved into a degraded "We tell our story to everybody, to anybody, in order to convince ourselves that we have an interesting life") and Elizabeth Hardwick and would think that it was so easy to write *like that*—short sentences, brief paragraphs, elastic ellipses—and would convince themselves that their own lives were oh so interesting and would publish books about girls in which, every so often, he would have a sad cameo.

BRIEF HISTORY OF PERIPETEIA

He remembers all those girls who would've given anything to be like Nicole Kidman in that movie.

In *The Human Stain* in which every move and expression she made was like a small earthquake but an earthquake all the same for everyone who, shaken, watched her do her thing. And—nothing happens by chance, the actress's last name warned—seeing her and watching her, he felt like a man suddenly kidlike or like a kid suddenly ready to do whatever's expected of him.

A kid-man.

And he watched them, his girls, his Nicolettes.

And he watched them and enjoyed watching them so much with their dilated pupils and nostrils a-quiver like the snouts of the she-wolves.

And just as his memory was pulling him back and running the risk of making him come crashing down (like someone leaning back in a chair, rocking on its hind legs), luckily, almost right away, he was seduced again by the movie he was watching and by Nicole Kidman in that movie. The story of the dean Coleman Silk who'd fallen into disgrace (for a while now, all the disgraced men were, for him, like blood brothers or members of the only club that'd ever accepted him; because his condition was that of having been previously expelled from all extant clubs).

And Silk's fall had come about due to an excess of political correctness.

Silk—in a class on classical literature—had invoked the terrible fury of Pelida Aquiles (the most sensitive and poetic killing machine ever to brandish a sword or to throw a spear and who unleashed infinite ills on the Achaeans) and recited aloud the first verses of his myth in ancient Greek: μῆνιν ἄειδε θεὰ Πηληϊάδεω Ἀχιλῆος / οὐλομένην, ἣμυρί' Ἀχαιοῖς ἄλγε' ἔθηκεν. And then, intrigued by the fact that there were a couple of students on the class list who'd never attended the class, he wondered aloud if they might not be ectoplasmic creatures. And he said the word "spooks." He described them as spooks. Spooks taken to mean lightless or spectral or intangible beings (spooks was also the coded epithet for certain rare trading cards or hard-to-come-by action figures, fighting as spies in the invisible Cold War, he would be told before too long by a passenger, on an airplane, named General Electric, in the seat beside him); but then, in that class, everyone understood or chose to understand him to mean "spooks" second definition: a synonym of "niggers." And so Silk became a *persona non grata* on the campus and a sudden widow and almost-instantaneous twilight womanizer. And Silk repeatedly visits the also failed and reclusive Zuckerman (recovering from prostate cancer which has rendered him impotent) and they talk and dance and become close friends. And Silk suggests to Zuckerman, also impotent in his fiction writing, that—since he can no longer come up with anything to write—he write about his life. And at one point, Zuckerman asks Silk what it was the ancient Greeks called the moment when the hero realizes he was wrong about everything. And Silk tells him that the Greeks called it *peripeteia* or περιπέτεια. *Peripeteia*: a shifting of circumstances or a decisive moment or a radical change of situation, when luck turns for good or ill. According to Aristotle (who'd also postulated that dreaming was a rest, because dreams were that one place absent of all elements of judgment, and, oh, could there be some way to be able to forget all this information stored in his memory the way you forget a dream upon waking, please, have mercy, right?), *peripeteia* was the most efficient tool when it came to sowing a drama or reaping a tragedy. *Oedipus Rex* was the classic case. Or *Iphigenia in Tauris*. But also the sudden conversion of Paul on the road to Damascus or the story "The Three Apples" from *One Thousand and One Nights* are paradigmatic examples of *peripeteia*. And Zuckerman and Silk talked about that and about so many other things. And the unfolding present of the movie was interrupted by successive flashbacks to the dean's youth (and he always envied that about movies: the power of a memory that was so decisive when it came to understanding the here and now that could even nullify the present and wash over it with the past, sometimes in black and white or with a different texture of lighting or photography; because in the movies you can't remember and live at the same time). And in one of those various flashbacks, a very handsome and young Silk first took home and then took to his bed the beautiful college Valkyrie Steena Paulsson on the pretext of lending her "a book that will change your life." And here, once again, come the ghosts of Christmas past (that make him feel more screwed than Scrooge, on those dates when you invent and dream and remember more than at any other time of the year) to look for and find him. His own very personal memories, the memories of his parents, more disappeared than appearing, frightening him less as *spooks!* and more with a *booo!*: because the book in question, in the movie, the book that Silk lends Steena, was *Tender Is the Night*. And he says to himself that he can't remember any mention of that ill-fated Fitzgerald novel in the lucky, multiple prize-winning Roth novel. And he doesn't have the strength to get up off the sofa and go to his bookshelf to check. And it wouldn't make any sense either. Because he's almost certain that that reference to his parents' talismanic books is nothing but a message from the Beyond. For him alone and only visible to him in the movie.

It wasn't the first time it'd happened to him.

That book was always popping up in the most unexpected places and at the most unexpected times, like someone who startles you with a pat on the back that you receive as if it were a slap. Not long ago, *Tender Is the Night* (the book Fitzgerald—its author, disappointed in the face of its disappointing reception among critics and readers, in his own words—had ended up pointing to as something that "has demanded nine years and all my guts . . . It is a novelist's novel") had made an appearance in a biography of Nabokov. There, the Russian introduced himself—*épaté* with *boutade*—to a biographer of Fitzgerald with the words: "*Tender Is the Night*, magnificent; *The Great Gatsby*, terrible" (though Nabokov's appreciation could be better understood if you read Rosemary Hoyt as a proto-Lolita and the Divers as a kind of two-headed Humbert Humbert of both sexes). And in another biography, one of John Cheever, it was mentioned as a failed screenplay project of the creator of "The Swimmer," drowning in alcohol and almost committing suicide in Hollywood.

And that book came back now.

It came back again.

And it wouldn't be the last time.

Tender Is the Night as crystal ball and three-legged table and Ouija board. And so, through that novel, his parents telling him they hadn't forgotten him and that now, from the other side, they knew what it was that he and Penelope did, what they did to them to bring about their undoing. His parents telling him that now they knew that their children had been the authors of their *peripeteia*.

And most disturbing of all: gone but returning inside him like that, he felt that—in their maneuvers and surprises—in the end he really did resemble his parents. Or maybe it is the dead who, with the passing of the years, start to resemble the living more and more, because, after all, it is the living who think of them and rewrite and correct them (and one of his recurrent dreams was, on the foggy streets of a nameless city, running into one of "his" dead, with some dead person he'd once known when they weren't yet dead, and wanting to update them on the lives of the living while the dead person looked at him with a combination of pity and affection as if to say "I already know it all," as if to say "Nothing and nobody interests me less"). Yes: the dead left more space for the living, but, at the same time, they claimed—with deep condolences—more space in the minds of those who followed them and would end up following them. And so, as you got older, the dead seemed ever more alive, because they were ever closer, closer than the living, as the living got closer to death and imagining, in vain, what it would be like to be dead, while the dead can't forget what it was like to be alive and the living, confronting the newly dead, still thought of them as on this side, capable of coming back to that place from which they left. The dead who are more faithful than the living, because they never abandon or leave you for someone else. The dead who, for Saint Augustine, were invincible because they never got frightened. The newly dead (when you look at a formerly alive person shortly after they've died) were no longer the memory of what they once were—a vessel empty of life—but something very different and opposite: something new and bursting with possibilities. Something that—in their absence, being unable to protest or disagree—you could immediately start to alter as you pleased. Or even—as things kept happening in which they no longer had anything to do with or had any responsibility for—being completely forgotten because they didn't bring any energy to the games of the living: the dead as *batteries not included*, but feeding—according to the *connector* E. M. Forster—off that Death that, practically and physically, destroys men, but that, as a theoretical concept to be feared and respected, is what ends up saving them. And so, living people ended up being transformed into dead characters, more alive than ever. Into immortals, whenever you remembered them and let them come back and bite you, like vampires.

DRACULA: A TRANSFUSION

He remembers that he once thought about how, when you decide to start to remember—to *really* remember—it was like opening the door to Dracula. The past was the Great Vampire. And invoking it was like inviting it in and asking if it was thirsty and if it wanted something to drink. And so, that memory came into your house and turned that house into a palace (or castle, because it's Dracula we're talking about here) and it never left and, yes, it was going to be one of those guests who were unforgettable for their host who, pretty soon, would only dream of being able to forget.

From there and related to that, one of the most interesting details—for him and from the first time he read it—from the novel. Something that's revealed to the Count's pursuers from the mouth of Doctor Abraham Van Helsing. A clause almost always dismissed in film adaptations for reasons as obvious as they are uncomfortable, because it would slow down the plot and the Count's forays into the bedchambers of Victorian damsels with ample bosoms and small brains that they only used to think about *that* though they prefer not to think *that* that is and is done *like that*.

Yes: in the great classic of the vampiric novel, it is the vampire who must be invited into peoples' houses because, as long as the inhabitants of those houses don't do so, he cannot attack them in the security of their homes. Inviting in the vampire was the same as believing in him. And as soon as you opened the door to him, everyone is lost, infected, invaded. (And he thinks, too, about how he and Penelope opened one of those doors when they made that phone call. And they did so because their parents meddled in everything they cared about: their parents fed off of them. They'd filmed a commercial inspired by *Wuthering Heights* and they were planning to make another one based on *Dracula* with a look more Roman Polanski than Tod Browning and more Christopher Lee and his low-cut vampiresses than the borderline-frigid Bela Lugosi.)

From then on, the vampire—once inside the walls of their lives—would bring death to or for them whenever it wished; like those sudden memories that you thought were forgotten but are still there, waiting for the moon and the music of the creatures of night, which isn't the howling of wolves but the buzzing of the bloodthirsty mosquitos of summer. And so, it wasn't the vampire who chose his victims, but the victims who, consciously or unconsciously, chose the vampire, in order to feel chosen by him. Being vampirized was a pleasure in the dark and a dark privilege. Being vampirized was something that robbed you of sleep but gave you so much in return. And so it didn't seem at all coincidental to him—he'd researched it for years and through so many sleepless nights—that in the ancient genesis of *Dracula* was *The Vampyre* by John William Polidori: patient doctor of the possessive and demonic Lord Byron and previously the author, in 1815, of a graduate thesis written in Latin on the different disturbances of sleep with the title of *A Medical Inaugural Dissertation which deals with the disease called Oneirodynia, for the degree of Medical Doctor.* An explanation for insomnia and trances and somnambulism and writings and readings with the eyes closed.

The same thing—losing sleep to find another form of consciousness—happened with all callings and, especially, with the literary calling, he thinks.

Though in his case, *Dracula* received some outside assistance when it came to entering into his life and vampirizing him and staying forever. Not in the same exclusive and omnipresent way in which *Wuthering Heights* occupied the life and work of Penelope; but, even still, always there, baring its fangs and licking its bright red lips in the shadows of his prehistory.

He remembers (because some beginnings turn out to be unforgettable and impose themselves over any ending, beginnings begin over and over again, as if in a loop of recurrent memory) that *Dracula* starts like this: on the 3rd day of May toward the end of the nineteenth century, the real estate agent and assistant solicitor Jonathan Harker writes in Bistritz—in his diary and using a shorthand—that he departs Munich at eight o'clock that evening and arrives to Vienna the next morning.

And many years ago, he traveled along with Harker and he travels with him again now and, at the same time, it's as if he were Harker; though he's doing so at a much later time and so far away from there, bound for Mount Karma, in Abracadabra. His favorite part of the book (an entire book in itself) and the strangest part of his life. But a more than noteworthy and definitive difference: what in the book is the introduction, in his life, will be the conclusion.

Because when he makes that trip for the first time, sitting beside Harker, he's seven years old (the age when most of his classmates are choosing the soccer team they'll support for the rest of their lives—soccer being for him, as it was for The Beatles, something that held absolutely zero interest and that, at most, prompted thoughts like "that whole offside thing is incomprehensible" and "Golem would be a great name for a Central European goal scorer"—or ceasing to say *Bang!* in order to start saying *Kapow!*) and is three years old as a reader. He lives and finds himself in that marvelous time when you're young and a young reader and you still have your whole life left to read and all the books to live ahead of you. Back then reading was like traveling, and, in that sense, the effect was never more vivid or powerful than when a novel opened with a journey.

And, yes, the novel was called *Dracula* and it was published in 1897.

And it's a book that he reads—as it was announced, in round capital letters, because previously the book had been published in its first language and in his now nonexistent country of origin with various cuts—in its FIRST COMPLETE, UNABRIDGED EDITION. A book that bravely and totally crossed the two-hundred-page line, a book that was heavy in his small hands and that, important detail, did not include any illustrations and was not the one where, on the cover, the Count appeared below letters dripping with blood, opening his mouth with a particularly silent-film-star air.

And he starts to read it on the way to stay with his—as he would write/remember them later—"end-of-the-world summer grandparents." His mother's parents: a pair of Russian *émigrés*, in the south of the south, in Sad Songs, where, upon their arrival, they opened the town's first bookstore and newspaper distributor, in a two-story house with the business on the ground floor where a large pendulum clock ticked. (His father's parents live in the capital and are also Russians and professional poker and blackjack players who tour the casinos of the world; and, unlike his mother's parents, so stable and established, they never stop moving, as if blown by an invisible wind; but all of that comes to an abrupt end for both sets of grandparents when their children disappear they're forced to take charge of their grandchildren.) And above the counter in the store (an ideal object to put on one of the shelves in his memory palace where he can see it with eyes closed, like another Dreamachine, while the chimes ring in the clock that sometimes he imagines as a vertical and Draculian coffin) there is one of those, even at that time, already antique almanacs. One of those almanacs with three slots/sights where, by turning little dials on one side, you can change the number and name of the day and month (not the year, which you change by taking out and putting in a small carboard rectangle). An almanac on which, for that reason, you could roll back the date, and he plays with it as if playing with the controls of a time machine. But all he achieves is to make time seem to pass even slower than it already passed during those summers of prolonged pauses. In a big and cubical house that, out back, even included a chicken coop where those little no-longer dinosaurs clucked and laid eggs and shit and were, no doubt, assaulted by flashbacks from prehistoric times when they were kings of all Creation or, at least, that's how he imagined it, studying all of that in school and fantasizing about a Kafkaesque short story in which a *Tyrannosaurus rex* wakes up transformed into a *Gallus gallus domesticus* of the Araucanian variety (or maybe, when he was a boy, they hadn't yet figured out that first came the dinosaur and then the chicken and only studied which came first, the chicken or the egg, and that was a little bit like the mystery about who told the story first the reader or the writer, a mystery that he'd solved now, that he would solve many years later, when he no longer wrote and read very little).

He and Penelope spend their vacations there (Sad Songs is his Illiers/Combray), almost where the map of his now nonexistent country of origin ends, with their Uncle Hey Walrus.

Uncle Hey Walrus, who isn't exactly their uncle but—as his parents say—an "adopted uncle." An uncle who isn't exactly an uncle but who—both his parents being only-children—sort of fills that role. Their uncle who "has issues"; though it might be more accurate to say that it's the issues that have their uncle, that possess him, that vampirize him, like Renfield in *Dracula*. Uncle Hey Walrus who hates Sad Songs in particular and hates Patagonia in general and who describes himself as a "pata/antagonist." Uncle Hey Walrus who once "worked" with The Beatles. Uncle Hey Walrus who has given them a gift, days before, in the capital, on one of those nocturnal excursions, going in and out of bookstores that stay open until almost sunrise, at which point the vampire readers return to their beds after having sucked down all that ink, among bookshelves, standing and reading books they can't buy and sometimes steal. They are, yes, vampiric bookstores: it's not that they're closed by day but they do stay open when the day has already come to a close. And it's on those long nights (in particular he remembers the winter nights) when the customers seem to have a decidedly Nosferatuan air: long coats with large pockets into which on more than one occasion they slip a book that won't be paid for, pale skin, eyes reddened by different strains of flu, seeking to feed an appetite that, they know, they'll never fully sate.

Uncle Hey Walrus has given Bram Stoker's *Dracula* to him and Emily Brontë's *Wuthering Heights*—also in translation and also the complete, unabridged edition—to Penelope. (Their parents also bought them books, but not with the love that Uncle Hey Walrus did it. Their parents gave them books the way someone throws pieces of meat through the bars of a cage or the way some parents—friends of his parents did it and he can't be sure if his parents did or didn't, but, oh, how deeply he slept when he was a kid—crush up Valiums and mix them with Jell-O powder. Books, for their parents, are letters they give the beasts to tranquilize them and put them to sleep.)

He asks for *Dracula* because he's intrigued by the idea of sleeping all day and not having a family. Penelope asks for *Wuthering Heights* because, she discovers, that it's the book that the telenovela they watch day after day with the latest-but-never-last Rosalita is based on.

Wuthering Heights starts with a traveler who arrives and *Dracula* with a traveler who departs.

Dracula begins with a journey, yes; and he started reading it on the way to his grandparents' house, in Sad Songs. During a long journey on a slow train, passing through a landscape so empty that everything fits there and so it's only right to fill it with everything you're reading, looking out the little window of that book, the most voluminous book his hands have ever held up to that point.

Since that time, he's considered the train his ideal mode of transport (he hadn't flown for the first time until years later and he remembers his disappointment when, after lifting off for the first time, he didn't feel like he was flying too the same way that, on trains, you feel somehow part of the whole thing, like you're *train-ing* or something like that).

And he could make the argument (he'll think of it several decades later, already a writer in addition to a reader; actually, an exwriter after having been a writer and a nextwriter; because he doesn't write anymore but only thinks about what he might write, as if imagining trips he cancels and then forgets) that the trajectory of any novel leans on one of two basic thematic impulses: staying home with the family or setting out on a journey. And many times, you embark on an adventure because of an urgent need to leave your clan far, far behind, while other times you leave just to get the opportunity to bring it all back home.

Within in this schema—as you already know and as Leo Tolstoy postulated—are happy and sad families, families who unleash stormy odysseys or take pleasant strolls.

And it's well-known too that the crazy family that goes crazy or that's genetically crazy-making is an option that abounds.

His case, looking no further.

And that at times, like in *Dracula*, an almost hallucinated new family is formed out of people who don't know each other but recognize one another in a common goal that, sometimes, is far more powerful than last name and blood.

And so, in *Dracula*, Jonathan Harker and Wilhelmina "Mina" Murray Harker and Lucy Westenra and Arthur Holmwood and John Seward and Quincey Morris and Abraham Van Helsing (that cross of Sigmund Freud and Sherlock Holmes) unite to battle and vanquish the monster who actually, if you think about it a little, adopts all of them. Dracula like a terrible yet indispensable father that gives all of them—so hitherto bored with the monotony of their lives—a reason to be and to belong and to feel united. A shared cause and sentiment. Like what you assume a family should have and feel (and he'd found it so just and moving and funny that in Jim Jarmusch's *Only Lovers Left Alive* the vampires, so sick of their immortality, refer to the vigorous mortals as "zombies").

And so he reads all of that and keeps reading and with each passing page feels how he's leaving behind Sandokan and D'Artagnan and Nemo and so many others in versions "lightened" to facilitate their digestion through children's eyes, in forever-juvenile classics from the Peter Pan collection. He'll reencounter all of them in movies, he assumes then; but never again in black letters on white paper.

"All of it was new for me," he thinks in Harker's letters.

And really all of it is not *so* new for him, traveling with Harker: because he's already seen the classic film version of *Dracula*. But what he reencounters here for the first time is something very different.

When he arrives to the Borgo Pass, there's no carriage from the Count there waiting for him. Everyone says he should get out of there right away and recommend that Harker go on with them to Bucovina and come back in the morning and . . . But suddenly, out of the fog, appears a caleche, drawn by four "splendid and coal-black" horses and driven by "a tall man, with long brown beard and a great black hat, that seemed to hide his face from us." And yet, a hard face and a smile with very red lips and sharp teeth and a powerful voice that orders them to transfer his luggage from one carriage to the other. And then one of the other passengers quotes a verse by Bürger in German and Harker translates *"Denn die Todten reiten schnell . . ."* or "For the dead travel fast . . ." And Harker climbs into the carriage sent by the Count and looks back and sees how all of them (direct ancestors of the now cliché local warning of what's to come; from whom descend all those sinister byway gas station employees the world over) wave to him with one hand and cross themselves with the other, while the carriage driver says that it's a cold night and that under the seat is a warm flask of Slivovitz. And then the sensation of galloping always in a straight line but always through the same place, like one of those projected backdrops in black and white movies.

And he, then, reading and traveling, thinks: "At last! That is definitely Dracula! The driver is Dracula!" And midnight. And the howling of dogs on the farms melting into the howls of wolves who consider dogs traitors to the cause: domesticated and comfortable cowards who once were wolves (and who were truly loyal, because wolves mate for life) and who now lived the laziest of lives. And a tunnel of trees and the wind and midnight and an interminable ascent past ridgelines and sharp stone spires.

And, at a last, the ruined castle.

And Harker standing beside his luggage in front of the doors and, suddenly, the sound of bolts sliding. And there, "a tall old man, clean shaven save for a long white moustache, and clad in black from head to foot, without a single speck of colour about him anywhere." And—Dracula has a moustache!—nothing at all to do with the illustration on the cover and who, "in excellent English, but with a strange intonation," says: "Welcome to my house. Enter freely and of your own free will . . . Come freely. Go safely, and leave something of the happiness you bring! . . . I am Dracula, and I bid you welcome, Mr. Harker."

And he read those words and it's as if they were being said to him.

And he felt that he'd come to the place where he was supposed to be, the place that'd been waiting for him and one that he would never leave.

And, moving through the castle with Harker, the surprise that it has a well-stocked library. Yes: Dracula reads a lot and he's not surprised that vampires read. Blood or ink, it's all the same; and many years later, he'll see another movie with vampires tired of being vampires but in possession of the enviable gift for exhausting books in a matter of minutes. Vampires who read by running their fingertips across the pages, as if caressing them, quickly, in a kind of braille that, let's not forget, was previously called *"écriture nocturne"* and was created for soldiers at the request of Napoleon Bonaparte, so his troops could decode battle codes in the dark and in the depths of tomblike trenches.

And then he'll imagine the vampires confined to the respite of their coffins, through the long days of summer, lying there as if sleeping inside trees. Reading in the dark how Dracula says to Harker: "I am glad you found your way in here, for I am sure there is much that will interest you. These friends have been good friends to me." And the Dracula makes reference to the property he has just acquired on the outskirts of London as if he were already missing it, as if it were his new memory palace to decorate: "I am glad that it is old and big. I myself am of an old family, and to live in a new house would kill me. A house cannot be made habitable in a day, and after all, how few days go to make up a century . . . I seek not gaiety nor mirth, not the bright voluptuousness of much sunshine and sparkling waters which please the young and gay. I am no longer young, and my heart, through weary years of mourning over the dead, is not attuned to mirth. Moreover, the walls of my castle are broken. The shadows are many, and the wind breathes cold through the broken battlements and casements. I love the shade and the shadow, and I would be alone with my thoughts when I may."

And he read all of that—he remembers it as if it were now, as if he were rereading it—aboard one of those trains that no longer exist. A train that passed on and that was part of the past. A train where mobile phones didn't ring (and to which you didn't yet have to pay extra to access the sanctuary of the "silent car") like bats biting ears and where, instead, there are many people speaking quietly among themselves or sleeping or reading. A train aboard which a lot of the passengers appeared dressed in clothes described by that expression that's fallen into disuse: they appeared in their "Sunday best" back in the days when Sunday was still an important day and different from the others and when traveling was a less common occurrence. When traveling was a celebration where you sharpened your senses like sharpening the point of a pencil with which to write everything that happens or ceases to happen on a journey, on a train.

A southbound train, a train bound for summer vacation, far from his parents and their vampiric tendencies (sleep by day, revel by night) where there awaited the limitless winds and howling of the wolves (*lobos marinos* aka sea lions) by the beach and on the cliffs and at mass with their grandparents, and, yes, Sad Songs would be the perfect setting for a horror movie. And him, thinking then that the Jesus Christ they learned about at the masses that their grandparents dragged him and Penelope to was, in his own way, a vampire: an undead immortal and a holy spirit who came and died and came back from death to possess everyone, telling them to drink his blood.

But, also—and already reasoning like the writer he'll one day be, like the nextwriter he already is—marveling and telling himself that, throughout the entire novel, Bram Stoker created a structure that provoked terror by keeping the agent of said terror, the bloodthirsty Count, far out of sight throughout most of the storyline. Like God in the Old Testament, the Count appeared in the first four chapters of the book, in the diary of Jonathan Harker, to almost completely disappear for the next three hundred pages, and to only become visible again on six brief occasions before meeting his end, at a pass in the Carpathians, in the book's final pages. And he never speaks in person and in viva voce but through the ears of those who heard him and can't stop transcribing him and describing him and writing him like not entirely reliable but very dedicated narrators. So excited. So driven. So, in their way, happy. As if they were apostles or evangelists. Because of course: the vampire drinks the blood of his pursuers, but, also and in exchange, he gives them a transfusion of life and passion the likes of which they've never had or felt before. He gives them a reason to live and, also, to write. Because suddenly, in *Dracula*, yes, everyone is a writer. And so, Dracula turns them first into readers of his supernatural persona so that later they can write him into being in long sermons of personal diaries and letters in a prose that's almost hysterical in its adoration for that thing they fear most. The true and admirable achievement of Stoker—who wasn't a great writer; but who was great in his most, justly, famous book—is that *thirsty trompe-l'oeil* of the lives of others, omnipresent and yet almost invisible. Dracula is, yes, a *peripeteia*. A shadow transforming the landscape and those who inhabit it that—when it's already too late to denounce it to the authorities—is only possible and worthwhile to describe as what it is even as it is almost nonexistent: like a shadow within a shadow within a shadow.

And later, Uncle Hey Walrus will play the lamest joke on him apropos Dracula and his obsession with the book. And he'll read all the derivatives of that novel—from that odd and, yes, vampiric and contemporary Icelandic rewriting approved by Stoker himself, with a politicized count calling for anarchy in London, passing through those aristocratic sects of Nosferatus moving all throughout history, until arriving to the adolescent vampires who inexplicably insist on going to high school when they'll never reach the age of college students—as if possessed by an inexplicable thirst, as if searching in them for the justification of his literary vocation. And he'll even end up writing a prologue to the Stoker novel at a time when he was writing prologues with an almost-evangelical compulsion and he'll even write a story about all of that.

(And this is what he wrote, in the third person, about the amazingly bad and lame joke his Uncle Hey Walrus played on him: "The next morning, the boy who wanted to be a writer when he grew up discovered something strikingly similar on his own neck. He woke up and there, under a slapdash bandage, was the unmistakable bite of the living dead, the beginning of the end. A wound whose [again, the words of Doctor Seward, page 223 of the first unabridged version of *Dracula*] 'edges were white and worn looking' . . . The boy who wanted to be a writer when he grew up decided not to bathe that day and to hide the truth from the world. He found a shirt with a high collar and sat down without a word with his smiling family. 'You look a little pale today . . . ,' his uncle said to him as he took a bite of toast . . .

"It was midday by the time the boy who wanted to be a writer when he grew up got up the nerve to inspect the wound again. He closed and locked the bathroom door, unbuttoned his shirt collar in front of the mirror that still reflected his face but wouldn't hesitate to reject it when he became a vampire, when he'd completed the transformation into a Nosferatu with all the time in the universe to write novels. He pressed a finger to one of the punctures and was surprised to feel no pain. He brought his finger to his nose and was even more surprised to discover that the wound had a familiar smell. So, he brought his finger to his mouth and, indeed, it was paint . . . He washed his neck with an odd mix of fury and relief as he heard, outside, his uncle's car peel out at drive away at top speed until it was lost in the streets of Sad Songs.")

But before all of that, on the train, Uncle Hey Walrus lets him know that they'll be arriving to Sad Songs soon; but he still has so much left to read and he shuts the book in the moment that Harker writes the final lines of his castle-bound and Transylvanian journal and gets ready to attempt his escape, which he suspects is more likely to end in suicide than success: "I shall try to scale the castle wall farther than I have yet attempted. I shall take some of the gold with me, lest I want it later. I may find a way from this dreadful place. And then away for home! Away to the quickest and nearest train! Away from the cursed spot, from this cursed land, where the devil and his children still walk with earthly feet! At least God's mercy is better than that of those monsters, and the precipice is steep and high. At its foot a man may sleep—as a man. Goodbye, all. Mina!"

And there was nothing that interested him less than saying goodbye.

Or going "home."

He wants to stay there, in transit.

Harker will return to Transylvania with his friends on the heels of the Count, increasingly frightened by this obsessed band that isn't giving him a chance to catch his breath, even though he doesn't exactly breathe anymore.

And he'll travel with them too.

And, there, the end of *Dracula* and Dracula's end. It's not a bad ending, but he found the dénouement a little disappointing. Just a handful of lines wherein the Count is brought down with a sword to the heart and decapitated with the blow of a big kukri knife. His body turns to dust and the sun rises and illuminates the ruins of the Transylvanian castle (years later, he'll learn that in the first version of the manuscript, far more operatic, with the vampire's last breath, the castle crumbles in a cataclysm between agonizing and ecstatic, demonstrating that property owner and property—and *Dracula* is also a great real-estate novel; just like, now that he thinks about it, *Wuthering Heights* was, with another difficult host in its opening pages—were bound together until death did them part; but the editors told Stoker to cut that whole part to avoid complicating a possible sequel). Then, the only thing added is a final note in which Jonathan Harker reports the birth of his son and the respective marriages of Seward and Holmwood. And happy ending, or that's what's presumed. But, he suspects, all of them have been vampirized in some way and, on full-moon nights, they'll remember and long for those days when they were more alive and when what awakened them was something far more grand but far less irksome than a wailing infant who sucked milk from his mother and patience from his father: when Dracula was alive, when—like him back then, he remembers now—the whole journey was still ahead of them and all the doors were yet to be opened so first the vampire could enter and then, right away, they could go outside to play.

Now, not so much.

Now, never again.

Now—almost having arrived to his destination—the journey can only be remembered.

And he would reread *Dracula* many times.

One of them not long ago—imagining himself as if he were looking at himself from outside, as the pursuers in the novel imagined their pursued pursuer—tucked into that super-bed that he almost never left anymore and that he finally left in order to flee, like a vampire pursued by bloodthirsty and ignorant villagers who deemed it the right historical moment to gain independence from him. And then, remembering how Stoker himself didn't leave his little bed, stricken with a mysterious illness, until he was seven years old (the age he was when he read *Dracula* for the first time), recalling that "Certainly, till I was about seven years old I never knew what it was to stand upright." And that Stoker gave birth to his creature of the night in the dreams that followed an indigestible meal of fried and possibly mutant and radioactive crabs (though there are biographers who claim that Stoker invented that whole bit because he wanted to be like Robert Louis Stevenson creating his Dr. Jekyll/Mr. Hyde during a nightmare).

In any case, when he no longer had drugs to consume or a tactic for turning the writing engines on, he even went so far as to try eating an excess of fried crabs, as an homage to one of his first great reads and all he got was an interminable night of nonstop vomiting.

And, again, every time he reopened that novel, he looked for and found that key moment. Van Helsing instructing everyone about how "He can, when once he find his way, come out from anything or into anything, no matter how close it be bound or even fused up with fire, solder you call it. He can see in the dark, no small power this, in a world which is one half shut from the night. Ah, but hear me through. He can do all these things, yet he is not free. Nay, he is even more prisoner than the slave of the galley, than the madman in his cell. He cannot go where he lists, he who is not of nature has yet to obey some of nature's laws, why we know not. He may not enter anywhere at the first, unless there be someone of the household who bid him to come, through afterward he can come as he please."

That's all and maybe that and this is what literature is.

Literature like that vampire—dazzled by the possibilities of his power— you open the door to and invite in, suspecting all the while that from then on it'll be impossible to contain him.

Literature like that vampire capable of transforming himself into anything: a wolf, a bat, a solid wisp of swirling fog and, oh, it's so deceptively easy and gratifying to surrender to the dance he dances.

Literature like that vampire and key capable of entering and exiting anything "no matter how close it be bound or even fused up with fire."

Literature like that vampire you give lodging to so he can tell his story with the implicit understanding that you'll pass it on to others who haven't yet heard it and in that way—time and again, in more or less complete versions— insure his survival through the rigors of time and the terror of his curse.

Literature like that vampire who demands your blood so that later, if you're worthy, he can return it to your lips from a slash in his own chest. And in that way—with any luck and any justice—attain immortality. And to be able to transform yourself into anything. Being able to cross any threshold knowing that some part of you will stay there, inside the book, for all eternity, for as long as you keep telling that story that now, through the simple act and complex science of having read it, was also your own story.

And, there, picking out your favorite parts to be remembered forever. Jumping from this unforgettable part to that one, while other parts are forgotten and transformed into blank and deserted zones that can occupy minutes or even centuries, names or faces, things made or unmade. All those parts that, when it comes to recounting them, are not considered important and are left out with a "and then I don't really remember what happens." Parts that, nevertheless, like invisible workers in the machine room in the basement of your memory palace, keep on happening so that the part that can never be forgotten can happen, like those restless memories and ellipses that are unforgettable though you can't see or read them.

THE FINE ART OF LEAVING SOMETHING OUT

He remembers that "ellipsis" has, all of a sudden, become one of those words. A word that's *important* to him. Like "epiphany." Like those ancient words that sound, all of them, like the names—like Anomaly, like Serendipity—of very pretty and very mysterious girls, like the vampiresses at Coliseum had once been.

He looks up and learns that *ellipsis* is a figure of speech whose sound and letters come from the Greek (ἔλλειψις, élleipsis) and that it amounts to omitting or leaving something out of the story and yet, that absent thing is still sensed, intuited, it's there, though it's neither seen nor mentioned. It can be an event, a person, or even millions of years; like in that second when he became aware for the first time of the invisible but unbounded power of the ellipsis: in *2001: A Space Odyssey* a primate tosses a bone into the air and the bone turns into a space shuttle orbiting Earth (and later, near the end of the film, the astronaut Dave Bowman aging in a series of linked shots until his death and cosmic transmutation). And—again, not something but someone tossed into the air—Vladimir Nabokov's father in *Speak, Memory*, cheered and hoisted up by mujiks, grateful for some favor from their patron *barin*. Nabokov's father tossed up and appearing and disappearing through the window frame and watched by his young son. The man going up and going down, in "a marvelous case of levitation," over and over, with his arms folded across his chest until, suddenly, he's no longer a living man but a dead body "among the swimming lights, in the open coffin" surrounded by "wax tapers in mortal hands." And from the fire we come and to the fire we return. And, then, another: T.E. Lawrence blowing out that match—and, yes, that other match in the hands of that general and friend of Nabokov's father, first in a military uniform and years later in the garb of a beggar—to light up a sunrise in *Lawrence of Arabia*. But, in his own way, the character of Dracula is *also* a kind of omnipresent ellipsis in the novel *Dracula*.

And over time he learns that ellipsis is not alone when it comes to leaving things out. There are also the *asyndeton* (which avoids the conjunctions and nexuses within a list); the *zeugma* (which deploys a single word that commonly applies to various analogous units in sentence), the *paralipsis* (which consists of stating that something is being omitted or left out, when in fact the occasion is being used to call attention to it), the *syllepsis* (an extreme case of *zeugma*, consisting of the omission of an element that rules different units, semantically or syntactically), the *brachyology* (the use of a short and simple equivalent of a longer and more complex expression), and the reticence or *aposiopesis* (which is used to leave a phrase incomplete, for example: "If I were to write . . .").

And so he—who sometimes feels like the King of the Ellipsis and at other times like the Slave of the Ellipsis—has learned the definition and use of all these terms. Because his whole life and all the work he's ever done (from that beach where he almost drowns so he can leap forward in time and, for a few minutes, have the ability to read and to write without anyone having yet taught him and later, an even longer leap, to imagining a young couple with camera in hand and on that same beach trying to elucidate the mystery of his life and work) are marked by the constant presence of one permanent omission: by that darkest of blank spaces, by that terrible night that began in his childhood and that, like a slow-motion eclipse, still hasn't ended.

The ellipsis like one of those dotted lines in a phrase where you have to fill in the blank for it to make sense.

Or like those redactions in movies due to censorship of the military dictatorship.

Or like the last option on a *multiple-choice* test, like this:

X. X

X being the letter where he locates that night that he remembers tonight. That night that no longer falls but that seems to return every night at nightfall: a vampire night. A night to which he returns again and after circling around and around it, ends up surrounded by it, cornered, like the circular structure in so many Greek classics and the way in which the comings and goings of their polytropic heroes are narrated: advancing and receding in time—narrating the present based on the past and vice versa, understanding what's to come only based on what was, so Kierkegaardianly—and taking detours down byways and more or less pertinent or arbitrary anecdotes, but knowing that they'll always end up returning to that inescapable point of departure. To that Homeric night that's ripped him apart, that's broken him into pieces, that's left him irreparably damaged, composed and decomposed of fragments, instants, moments, random paragraphs.

And so, now, he's throwing pages into the fire—pages of that novel that he's finally read elliptically—as if they were bones in the air.

And he remembers a sign in a city that announced: "From Ciudad Lineal to Plaza Elíptica in 11 minutes"; and then having thought: "Ah, maybe I should live here. Maybe in this place all my style problems would be solved. But making the return trip. In reverse. Like Mr. Trip."

And he remembers that he always thought that the human being would never escape its prehistory until it discovered the secret of spatio-temporal transportation and, then, every journey would be pure ellipsis, non-journey, brief in seconds yet long in kilometers. A waking dream—the violent claw that throws the bone evolves in the snap of fingers to that obliging hand that takes hold of that weightless pen and puts it in the pocket of a sleeping passenger—that would only make sense to invent as a *voyage extraordinaire*, because there would be nothing there to remember.

And he remembers too that, after so many years of waiting for it to happen, it snowed for the first time in the capital of his now nonexistent country of origin, and a song with a Proustian title got really popular: "*Las intermitencias del corazón*," and he wrote or read (either way; reading and writing were the opposite but complementary shores of an ellipsis like a flowing river) about a very, very ugly little girl who dreamed of finding irrefutable proof of intelligent life on other planets and about a very, very beautiful girl who let herself fall into one and another and another and another swimming pool.

And that all of that happened or seemed to happen—in a linear ellipsis in reverse—while he shut his eyes to keep from remembering what it was to be able to sleep and to remember that day when he almost drowned and that night when his parents disappeared as if by the art of the blackest of magic.

And to rock him to sleep, to dream of a past (the ellipsis wasn't the language but did have the phrasing and diction of dreams) when things still occurred to him like the following, things like the things that follow him.

And the things that he put in writing as if they were being dictated to him by a voice from the future, ordering him to destroy the whole world and accelerate each and every one of his particles to—interlinking cells—be reduced to fragments, instants, moments, random pieces, abstract stains that once were figurative and that, for that reason, always recall and remember something.

RORSCHACH: AN INTERPRETATION

He remembers that he once wondered if the practice of the highly theoretical Rorschach Test could be a system to recapture memories directly bordering the invented part and the dreamed part. One of those small republics that are almost invisible and elliptical but linear on a map and whose function was to be a borderland from which great nations would be visible to everyone. A kind of *multiple choice* of infinite possibilities where all the grades were not exactly overachieving or inadequate. An inexact science, which are the sciences he likes best and that interest him most and that, in the end, he understands or thinks he understands. Or that he wants to understand.

The Rorschach Test like the adult and pathological variation of the interrogative torments of songs like "Veo-veo, ¿Qué ves?" or stories like "La Buena Pipa" from his childhood. And what you see when taking that test, comprised of ten sheets of paper, are stains that, supposedly, would automatically evoke bats or butterflies, two clowns or an animal on all fours, fur or carpet, cat or dog or gorilla, caterpillars or frogs, a headless woman or two women with big breasts, sex organs or flowering flowers, or a coat of arms of the kind that preach making war and not love. And that could mean and equal so many things that are up for interpretation, like, for example—and as they claimed when they first started shuffling the cards—latent homosexual tendencies or the seeds of psychoses ready to sprout. The test in question was today considered one of the most amusing forms of pseudoscience; but it was used in the interrogations at the Nuremberg trials and was still used in some countries for interrogating interesting criminals (that's what he was told by General Electric, his seat mate on that airplane, that retired but forever-vigilant spook for The Company) or for casting possible couples at marriage agencies.

And the test had been designed—based on a popular nineteenth-century parlor game—by one Hermann Rorschach in 1921.

Yes, more of those datums that he'd been storing up like layers and layers of paint to hide the metastasis of that other stain, that damp stain (the kind of stain that always recalls the face of someone you have tried in vain to erase) on the walls of his story, in his memory palace.

And so, a picture of Rorschach with the air of a Hollywood leading man, nicknamed Klecks (Stain) by his friends, a good illustrator and with one of those childhoods that make you want to grow up as fast as you can.

And at some point Rorschach left Germany, hung around with Jung, and died when he was thirty-seven, in 1922, as a result of peritonitis.

In the lysergic '60s, the test got even more popular as a variation of Tarot or the I Ching or of the runic and Tolkienistic Silmarillion to consult while chewing on glass onions in purple mists at the doors to the dawning of the end of the Age of Aquarius and . . .

Now he looks at one of those cards and asks himself what those ink spirals remind him of and he answers: what hadrons would look like—contemplating them with eyes closed and staring at a Dreamachine—in the moment of colliding inside a particle accelerator, seconds before the end of all things on this earth as they've been known until now, until right now, until *ahoritita mismitito.*

IN PARTICULAR

He remembers that then he followed the absurd instructions of that man for whom he'd bought several bullshots on a terrace in Montreux. That man had told him something unbelievable but worth believing: that, as a boy, he'd known Vladimir Nabokov. And that that'd been the case because his father—a one-time FBI agent, and he remembers that General Electric told him or would tell him something about that on a past or what would be a past airplane—had gotten obsessed with the writer and had followed him there and . . .

So, he listened to him carefully and took notes and paid the bill and went and broke into the particle accelerator at CERN. And took a first/third-rate scientist hostage. And told him his grand and definitive plan, with that inexplicable and exhaustive compulsion to reveal plans that all villains tend experience when taking on James Bond who, in that long and indispensable scene in all Bond movies (he'd never read the novels, but he suspected things were done differently there, the way they were done in that foreign land called the past), is presumed to be done for, but who is actually listening very closely so he can deactivate everything more quickly in the next scene and at the last moment, at the last second of that countdown that's always counting down on some control panel primed to abort the explosion.

Then he told the scientist—and, then, the entire world via the security cameras—that, unable to write and ignored by everyone, he was going to centrifuge himself and become part of everything, to be everywhere and to rewrite the universe in his image and semblance, coming and going as he pleased throughout all of time. (And he remembered that justly venerated comic from his now nonexistent country of origin: lethal snowfalls, lyrical interplanetary invaders moved by the shape of an earthly coffee pot and, near the end, the hero—one Juan Salvo, a time traveler akin to Billy Pilgrim—saying *"Que salga lo que salga,"* which is to say, "Come what may," or "So it goes" or something like that. And pressing the button and pulling the lever and traveling across ages to end up hearing a last alien of his species exclaim "What does the destruction of an entire planet matter, the eradication of an entire species, matter! What matters is the survival of the spirit.") He was going to be a writernaut, yes. He was going to be—CERN or no CERN, ha, ha, ha?—a "true" creator. He was going to dictate plotlines and move multitudes as if they were his own creations. But his visions and auditions wouldn't be so obvious and banal as—what he read in those square and rectangular comic strips—"the thunderous advance of cannons along cobblestone street" or "the dreadful head of a dinosaur howling in terror" or "the tremendous roar of a rocket taking off." No. He wasn't going to make adjustments to universal History, but, rather, he was going to reorganize all of it as his life. Historic public days from here onward would be the most important days of his private life. He was going to rewrite everything that happened only as it happened to him. He was going to write again with the ink of hadrons across the Big Sky of his desk. He was going to interlink cells with the molecules of the tin traveler he carried in his pocket. Yes, he was going to melt into interdimensional communion with is faithful companion of so many years, Mr. Trip, until they became one and returned to this plane of existence as a divine wind-up giant, carrying his suitcase, going in reverse, but with nothing and nobody to stop him, like those atomic missiles to be neutralized by that Star-Child, returning home to put everything in order. He would be a vengeful God who would never stop creating and never rest on the seventh day.

And that's what happened and that's what he said, and the scientist let him speak, like someone putting up with the tantrum of a spoiled child, silently staring at him, his face revealing more sorrow than fear, and finally told him that he was wrong. Very wrong. He told him that what he intended to do was impossible, insinuating that perhaps he'd read too many comic books and seen too many B science-fiction movies when he was a kid. He explained that "things don't work like that." And that what he intended to do would not only not accomplish his objectives of total and messianic domination, but that, in addition, it would be very dangerous for his own health.

What the scientist said had also been caught on the security cameras (it was the only part that he chose to remember, having edited and cut from his memory, out of shame, his own participation in the scene) and broadcast live and direct to the population worried about the accidental yet intentional creation of a black hole that would open up and swallow everything.

And what the scientist said was the following:

"What you plan to do doesn't strike me as particularly recommendable, my friend . . . Luckily, there aren't too many antecedents when it comes to the effects of what you propose . . . But I must warn you that, in 1978, a particle accelerated by the Russian U-70 struck one Anatoli Bugorski in the back of the head. I remember his name because we often use the expression 'Be careful: you don't want to pull a Bugorski' and because that's his picture hanging on the wall, over there, we've got it there to always keep in mind what happened to him. The molecule came out through Bugorski's nose. The man claimed to see a flash of light 'as bright as a thousand suns' or something like that. Bugorski was immediately examined by doctors who thought he should've died on the spot. But no. Just mild facial paralysis, some epileptic fits, and slightly elevated levels of radiation. Oh: and a small orifice perforating through his head. But, warning, that machine had less than 1% of the power of what we have here . . . In short: higher radiation (and keep in mind that that was what finally killed Bugorski) that will poison your entire body and your vision will only register the color mauve, as a result of the radioactivity impacting your ocular fluid. And nausea and your white blood cell count dropping to almost zero and the absolute deactivation of your immune system. The prognosis is a survival of between four to eight weeks in horrendous condition. So, more than feeling like a heavenly deity, you'll feel like absolute hell, my friend."

He listened to all of that and all he thought was that the color *mauve*—and also the word itself—was Nabokov's favorite. And that its mention/appearance in what the scientist told him could only be a sign that he had to proceed, to seek the Final Judgement.

Minutes later, he was subdued by the forces of order and locked in a cell not all that different from a four-star hotel room (which IKEA got him out of by paying his bail); the scientist received an offer from a U.S. cable company to host his own scientific documentary show; and the whole world breathed a sigh of relief and sent tweets with thumbs up and applauding hands and emoticons and hearts and smiley-faced emojis.

The paradox and irony: the broadcast on all TV channels of his messianic break transformed him—for a while—into a trending topic. There was a *Saturday Night Live* sketch (the segment wasn't very good; but he couldn't help feeling proud despite everything that, coinciding with the week in which he happened to be the host, Billy Murray had been cast to play him). And, of course, his foibles generated a trend, as intense as it was brief, of using top-secret laboratories for apocalyptic jokes, to be recorded and uploaded to YouTube. Even *his* own Swiss particle accelerator, before long, was the scene for the video of a fake human sacrifice of a woman being stabbed by a group of hooded figures in honor of the Great Tin Traveler or something like that. The authorities sent out a communiqué/apology where they pointed out that "every year we welcome thousands of scientists here and it's clear that on this occasion a few of them went too far with their particular sense of humor, inspired by the recent unfortunate events that took place in our facilities and that everyone is familiar with ." He saw those videos online and was struck by—seeing as the people in question were of the "cold and calculating" variety—the degree of ingenuity and childish humor demonstrated by those involved. Red robes and horned masks and howling chants and the whole thing proved for him what he'd always suspected: the great scientific minds of the present had *also* been raised on B or Z movies in their exceedingly imaginative childhoods, and they could neither forget nor did they want to forget all of that, which was what'd inspired them to decipher the unfathomable mysteries of the universe.

(And El Vivo Muerto—a multimedia artist, or something like that, another of the many people he knew who were far more well-known than he was—had, before he died, assembled a kind of short film/hyperactive/performance-art piece with all the video footage produced by the news of the event. There, the idea was that—very much in the mode of Philip K. Dick—he'd been successful in his mission and rewrote himself as a writer without disappeared parents or a hallucinated sister, with a son of his own and a happy marriage and friendship with Enrique Vila-Matas and a respectable literary reputation and readers who weren't many but were loyal and every so often he was even deserving of some honest and prestigious award: a good and modest life that, to him, when he saw the film, had seemed somewhat lacking for an all-powerful being capable of altering destinies and El Vivo Muerto had put it like this: "He lacks ambition . . . I lack ambition . . . ," he complained. And then El Vivo Muerto appeared to flicker and fade away and suddenly he was no longer there. He understood—in a flash and as if struck by lightning—that El Vivo Muerto had never been there, except as one of those possible characters that he once thought of putting in writing but never did. And that he could count ever fewer people in his life and ever more characters that he'd never described in writing And that, like what'd happened to him with another of his paternal and phantasmal mentors, with Eames "Chip" Chippendale, now his characters were the ones rewriting him. And in his darkest hotel nights, he, sometimes, was terrified of asking himself if Ella might not also be nothing more than that: another construct built atop the quick sands of his inability to write, another fragmentary collage of disparate parts, dying to live as a complete whole.)

And—after The Incident with the particle accelerator—it even seemed possible that one of his books might sell an additional copy and his publishers might consider the possibility of reissuing some of his titles, in collection all his own and under his name. A revival, a rediscovery, things that publishers and journalists always liked so much.

And driven by the expansive and residual wave of all of that, he'd ended up writing *The Impossible Story*, as if it were written by someone else, that other him.

And that was it.

Then he went back to not being able to write. And to feeling more and more that thing that those who no longer write but used to write feel. The same feeling that, they say, people who have had an arm or leg amputated experience: the feeling that it was still there, like phantom parts of a living body, still able to grab or to kick or to scratch its head. That head of his that'd already stopped thinking about anything but the fact that what'd happened to him in Switzerland was something worth writing, but, better, written by someone else. Even by that other person he'd once been, that person who'd written so much and without any apparent effort. That other person he doesn't want to remember but—in the very act of trying not to remember him—can't forget, even though he feels, more and more, that his *mind is going.*

INTERMISSIONS AND EXTERMISSION

He remembers that the last time he rewatches *2001: A Space Odyssey*—on the big screen, the way that film was meant to be watched—he does so with He Whose Name Must Not Be Mentioned.

They have already seen it together—multiple times—on televisions of different sizes.

And they have talked a lot about the film and about its many possible interpretations.

He has told him what Stanley Kubrick said when, in the moment of its release, reporters had asked him for explanations: "How could we possibly appreciate the Mona Lisa if Leonardo had written at the bottom of the canvas: 'The lady is smiling so slightly because her teeth are rotten' or 'The lady is smiling because she is hiding a secret from her lover.' This would shackle the viewer to reality, and I don't want this to happen to *2001*."

But to He Whose Name Must Not Be Mentioned, nothing about the movie seemed "cryptic" or "vague." Just the opposite. To him, the plot was transparently clear.

"The monolith appears again and again when man takes one of those small steps for the universe but great leaps for mankind . . . The revelation of the use of tools and of standing on two feet, the discovery of irrefutable proof of intelligent life on other planets, and, finally, the evolution of the human being," he explains with that voice that, he thinks, is a good imitation of HAL 9000.

But this is the first time that He Whose Name Must Not Be Mentioned is going to see the film on the big screen and in a 70mm facsimile version, restored from the original negatives and, also, it's the first time he'll get to see it like that since the film's debut and since his debut with the film, in 1968.

The film had returned to theaters for a couple weeks to commemorate the fifty years it had been floating in space. And everything was in its place and, yes, he remembered every bit of it. *2001: A Space Odyssey* was a film he knew from memory because his memory knew it to be an important part of his life.

And yet, the surprise that—at the theater—the film had an intermission. He hadn't remembered that and it didn't appear in the successive VHS and DVD copies that he had rewatched it on.

Intermission—which already appeared as a concept/idea in the earliest performances of the works of Shakespeare, and in the classics of kabuki theater where intermission could last up to an hour—was, supposedly, a break, not for the characters, but for the spectators. But that was never entirely clear to him. He could always sense all of them back there: behind the curtains of screens, spying on the audience and toying with the possibility of changing the plot.

Intermission was that form of ellipsis where you came back from where you'd been for a few minutes in order to, soon thereafter (after passing through the bathroom to attend to needs physiological or chemical, or paying a visit to the concession stand, or frantically making out and groping without ever leaving your seats), go right back there. Intermission was that phantom zone—inventive and dreamy and to be remembered—where the spectator was, in a way, part of the cast of the movie.

And so, when he was a kid, he rarely got up to *use* the intermission. And he preferred to sit there, his eyes closed, so the light in the theater wouldn't distract him from the darkness he'd just emerged from and to which he would soon return. Intermission was, for him, something like when, in the middle of the night, he woke up from a dream only to fall back asleep after a few minutes and—surprise or not so much—the interrupted dream picked up from the exact point in which that dream had been awakened so that, the next morning, he barely even remembered fragments of it, like previews for a movie that'd been rewound forever.

He remembered, yes, that during his childhood and youth several of his favorite movies (or many of those movies that everyone saw over and over again to, maybe, without knowing it, enjoy those pauses as key parts of the stories they told) included intermissions.

He wasn't sure (he thought so) if *Les Aventuriers* included an intermission. But there was an intermission in *Lawrence of Arabia* (which, in addition, had introduced that novelty of starting at the end, opening with the death of the protagonist, like what'd happened to him when he was born), *Fantasia, Gone with the Wind, Doctor Zhivago, Around the World in 80 Days, The Ten Commandments, My Fair Lady, The Sound of Music, The Fiddler on the Roof, Chitty Chitty Bang Bang*, and, years later, *Barry Lyndon* and *Once Upon a Time in America*. (Had *It's a Wonderful Life*—another of his favorites and one he'd always considered a preview and XXL episode of *The Twilight Zone*, in its most sentimental iteration, like the episode featuring a good man named Bookman, dedicated to repairing toys like Mr. Trip and who was now being circled by an almost angelic Death and . . . —originally had an intermission when it was shown in movie theaters and not broadcast on Christmastime televisions in order make him cry year after year when he watched it? He could swear that it had. Or, at least, that it should have. And that its intermission should have been inserted at that exact point in which the long flashback of what was came to an end so that that terrible pause of what'd never been could begin and arrive to that, as ecstatic as it is now truly irreal, fast-forward, recovering the joy of being back there, running through the streets of that private and wall-less prison of Bedford Falls. That city that will never let George Bailey out, forcing him to serve a life sentence in freedom but behind the loving bars of all those who had saved him at the last minute. And it wasn't a happy ending and, he thinks, for it to work even better, it should take place not on the fateful 24th of December but on the 31st of December, that time and place to make all those promises that will never come true. No: the person who had friends was not the richest man in the world, the person who had friends was the most indebted man in the world. And he has no friends.)

And all of those movies had an intermission in the right place, in the exact dramatic instant when a before came to an end so that an after could begin.

But the intermission in *2001: A Space Odyssey* came at a strange moment.

It was more of an extermission than an intermission. Something like what happened in some books when, suddenly, everything stopped so that, in that brief and final pause, the momentum could be found to reach the grand finale (in any case, E. M. Forster warned and complained in his *Aspects of the Novel* that no novel ever came to a satisfactory end due to an insurmountable failure in its machinery: life always kept going and novels did not).

And he remembered those two moments in Proust and Vonnegut, moments in which their respective protagonists—in *Le temps retrouvé* and in *Mother Night*—tripping over an irregular paving stone walking to a party for the princes of Guermantes or going out walking in New York. And—beyond the elapsed time and the far-off location—both of them perceive in that moment how everything pauses so that, at last, they can both move forward in a precise direction (to the end of their lives to die or to the beginning of their work to write) after years of going around in circles or feeling that they had no reason to go anywhere.

The intermission in *2001: A Space Odyssey* came after that scene in which HAL 9000—without Bowman and Poole realizing it—reads the lips of the astronauts and learns they're thinking of disconnecting him.

Then, pause and continuation and a few minutes later the whole: "Open the pod bay doors, please, HAL. Open the pod bay doors, please, HAL. Hello, HAL, do you read me? Hello, HAL, do you read me? Do you read me, HAL? Do you read me, HAL? Hello, HAL, do you read me? Hello, HAL, do you read me? Do you read me, HAL?"

And HAL answering: "Affirmative, Dave. I read you."

And then him thinking about that *read* where it was one thing *to read* and another very different thing *to understand* or *to obey*. In fact, *to read* wasn't necessarily *to obey*, even if you did so by following the preestablished order of words and sentences and lines and chapters. To read was to respect the programming, but, soon thereafter, to interpret it in your own way, affirmative.

To read was to disobey.

RAIN IN TEARS

He remembers that the first time he walked out of seeing *2001: A Space Odyssey* that it was raining harder than in the Bible and that the world seemed to him, unexpectedly, full of infinite possibilities.

The same thing happened to him—he felt the same thing—several years later, in 1982, when he walked out of another of those palatial and immemorial theaters where telephones still only rang on the screens and not in the pockets or, even worse, in the hands of spectators who would refuse to put them down for even a few minutes, preferring that little light on their little screens to that spectacular nova glow on the big screen where someone picked up the receiver and answered the call to be told some always-important news: a piece of life or death or life and life or death and death news. Venues where outside their front doors they still offered preview pictures of what would be shown inside, like fragments, like parts of a possible collage, like lines of a plot that were unknown yet beginning to be imagined based on those quasi-postcards from that place you hadn't yet gone and that was the full movie. Movie theaters that he kept returning to every so often and where it no longer mattered that much if the movie was bad (because for a while now, what mattered was just the act of *going to the* movies: the movie was what mattered least; what mattered most was waiting for the lights to come down, the joy that nobody had sat down in front of you, the breathing and the laughter of strangers who suddenly became close friends and the certainty that going to the movies was, yes, going out to play at going to the movies). Movie theaters like sanctuaries that've almost ceased to exist (most of them had been broken up into multiplex theaters) except for the ones that are being preserved like cathedrals, nostalgic for an age in which the movie theater was the king of the big screens and it hadn't yet been ousted by ever smaller screens ever more consumed with courtesan intrigue.

It was raining again and again it was a science-fiction movie being projected back from the year 2019 when it all took place.

And it was probably the rainiest movie in the history of science fiction: Ridley Scott's *Blade Runner*, loosely based on a novel by one/another of his favorite authors, Philip K. Dick. Dick, who claimed to have saved the life of his son by diagnosing him with an illness—which no doctor had detected—with the aid of a pink laser beam and a Christian gnostic named VALIS and the liquid rhythms of the song "Strawberry Fields Forever" and the memory of the Roman Empire that'd never ended and the absolute certainty that everything understood as real wasn't really all that real.

Dick's novel was titled *Do Androids Dream of Electric Sheep?*, it'd been published in 1968, and he'd read it not that long ago. The movie didn't really resemble the novel, it didn't really resemble it at all. Actually, the movie (whose working titles had been *Android* and *Dangerous Days*) had stolen what would ultimately become its title from a treatment William S. Burroughs wrote for another movie based on another novel: *The Bladerunner* by Alan E. Nourse, which Burroughs, cutting and un-pasting and pasting back together again, had changed into *Blade Runner*. The Nourse novel was a thriller about illegal medical services offered in a not-too-distant future (sterilization and euthanasia; two things that he was increasingly in favor of, aboard this airplane, considering the decreasing quality and proclivities of the average passenger). Burroughs hadn't hesitated to add (and he also supported this motion) a designer virus—one of his unmistakable trademarks—to his version.

In the pages of Dick's novel, everything seemed slow and domestic and sordid. There was no grandeur. None of the many incredible things he ended up seeing in the movie theater were in the novel. The year didn't line up either: in the book, it was 1992 and Earth was pretty much a post-atomic wasteland with a dust-filled atmosphere that'd triggered mass stellar migrations and caused the extinction of all animals: their memory now only surviving as high-value robots that signaled the social status of their owners. The more and the bigger the cybernetic animals you owned, the more powerful you were. There were also numerous humans who'd mutated for the worse (with exceedingly low IQs) and a religion called Mercerism that preached collective suffering, and utilized "empathy boxes" to bring users together in a virtual reality where their messiah, Wilbur Mercer, climbs a hill for all eternity while being stoned by the rabid masses or, once again, something like that (or maybe he couldn't help seeing himself as similar to Mercer, only that he was being chased down the hill). There were also "Penfield Mood Organs" that altered one's state of mind and had the effect of producing an urgent and irrepressible "desire to watch TV, no matter what's on it." And there came and went a guy named Rick Deckard with marital problems and a powerful longing to own one of those little animals, which was why he'd dedicated himself to hunting down, for money, androids that'd escaped from Mars. Androids (and not replicants) created by Rosen Associates in Seattle (and not Tyrell Corporation in Los Angeles) that were referred to as "andys." And everything was ugly and blundering and exhausting. And the replicant Roy Batty was hunted down and finally cornered and executed by Deckard. And his death was banal and lacking any emotion. There were no moving or visionary or alephian last words, just a "cry of anguish." And nowhere did you hear those synthetic keyboards and that synthesized sax that he, coming out of that movie theater, couldn't stop hearing inside his rain-soaked head. And nobody seemed to have any problem yet with the disquiet provoked by what neo-sociologists classify as the *uncanny valley*: that deserted space that, at present, is so hard for human beings to cross (even though the once-anticipatory date when all of that was to happen, both in the novel and the movie, has already come and gone) when it comes to relating to and interacting with anthropomorphic replicas that too closely resemble them. But the central problem with both machines—in writing and on film—was the same: planned obsolescence. The product's expiration date. The expiration date of a human being that only had the one advantage or disadvantage of not being precise and that, in the case of the replicants, arrived punctually and didn't allow for postponement or arrangements of any kind. Everything was programmed to break down and stop functioning and to die. It happened to him with his life as a writer, as a writer who no long replicates, as an exwriter. The same thing that happened to so many so-called loves, that're supposed to last until death does them part, in sickness and in health, in perfect functioning and in imperfect dysfunction that might or might not be able to be repaired, but that now, really for a good while now, better to go out find and buy something new. Or at least that's what's kindly suggested or ordered in a barely subliminal way by the manufacturer.

And so, the planned obsolescence that was in the future in *Blade Runner* was already a distinctive sign of the present times. One of the many applications of the implacable Murphy's Law. Everything that functioned did so, simply, to sooner or later cease functioning. Ever sooner and ever faster. And intentionally. What before was sold by leaning on the inestimable virtue of its toughness and durability now offered the questionable gift of the ephemeral.

He remembered that when he went to live on his own for the first time and when he was still very young (yes, before, you could do that; before, even that undertaking could work and function), his grandparents gave him the gift of an old refrigerator that, decades after its debut, was still cooling to perfection, without overheating or suddenly bursting into flames. Now, not so much. Now, what was functional existed to break down. Now, business and leisure made their home—ever since the world had gotten misinformed by the computerization of the information age—in having products last less and less time in order to experience the excitement of upgrading to the new model that, more than once, ended up being worse than the previous model. Now, his computers miscomputed and stopped complying two or three years after he turned them on for the first time. And they rarely lasted for the writing of more than one of his novels, back in days when he still wrote novels.

So now, the fact that big companies had taken all of that and "normalized" it in a not-even covert way (not the unspoken but un-chipped secret that everything was manufactured to self-destruct and so whenever someone brought up and decried that fact in a voice that was barely audible or that nobody was interested in listening to, megacorporations would just offer begrudging and cynical apologies and that was that) but was just part of a downward spiraling countdown. The numbers counting down to a supposed elevation of the species and warning that within a few years the human and the machine would merge courtesy of The Singularity (maybe that explains, he thinks, this interest that different companies seemed to have in turning everyone into addicts of little machines, as a kind of introduction and aperitif, in order to make the imminent Big Crack bearable). Then *Homo sapiens* as such would be discontinued and would go out of production and distribution and circulation. He'd read that, among the many advantages of the fusion of flesh and silicone, would be immortality. But he wasn't buying it. And it's not that he's a complete Luddite (though the events in movies like *Terminator* and *The Matrix* seemed increasingly probable to him), but he was less concerned about artificial intelligence and more about the artificial stupidity getting transmitted to the used users and making them even more imbecilic. No doubt there would be a lot of fine print and Catch 2.2 and criminal yet legal replacement of the expensive cloned parts for the *very few*. Again: everything expires. And it would always reach the categorical category of ex. This hard life lasts as long as it lasts, he thinks. While death—the degree zero and point of no return of planned obsolescence—lasts forever.

And, yes, he'd always liked science fiction.

Not so much the science fiction of rockets taking off for other planets, but the science fiction that, defeated, launches into the study of the inner space of the bodies and minds of humans who've become alien to themselves and gotten addicted to substances like the memories of others. The science fiction that seemed to look backward and inward: a nostalgic and melancholic futurism. Rock 'n' roll was a little bit like that now too: something supposedly advanced but in reverse and where what was most revolutionary was already in the past.

And he still really liked Philip K. Dick (and he'd done the work of finding out that Dick had come up with *Do Androids Dream of Electric Sheep?* after hearing a lecture by the British mathematician and logician and computer scientist and cryptographer and philosopher and marathoner and long-distance runner and suicide victim Alan Turing titled "Computing Machinery and Intelligence" and reading of the personal diary of an SS officer that described the desperate wailing of the Jewish children about to be executed that wouldn't let him sleep and who, as such, to distract himself, to think about anything else, "found himself obliged to remember pleasant things whether they'd happened or not"). And he'd never considered science fiction literature of evasion but literature of invasion (and he'd never entirely understood Nabokov's disdain for the whole genre; it was one of the few things he didn't agree with him on; but maybe it was because the Russian was more interested in the supernatural Beyond than in the infinity of space).

Since he was a kid, he'd been attracted even to the name, the label. Those two words sometimes connected by the umbilical cord of a hyphen: the one feeding off the letters and meaning of the other. These two words that, in the beginning, seemed to him impossible to make coincide in a single environment. "Science" and "Fiction" struck him as irreconcilable and contradictory terms, like polar opposites. And that, clearly, could only be brought together in the name of literature and in a childhood when the future was still far away and futuristic.

For him, science-fiction novels were novels not of ideas but of an idea: what mattered was to have one good idea before someone else came up with it. And, thus, paradoxically, to make a story within a genre wherein—again, paradoxically—there were no limits when it came to what could be fanta-sized or predicted, but that, at the same time, was the most traditionalist and repressive for its practitioners and aficionados. Science fiction was the transgressive within the conservative. Something floating alone in the most absolute of voids; but a void that was infinite and, as such, full of possibili-ties, yet always abiding by the precise and inviolable laws of other worlds or another Earth.

But then, of course, the dates of the classics of science-fiction film and literature—1992/2019 and 2001—began to be surpassed by the dates on the calendars of reality and the future. And tired of running and of being chased, the genre gave up and sat down in the present to thereby reach its triumphant expiration date. The whole *next century* thing already came to an end. And nobody was thinking about the twenty-second century.

The future is no longer what it was.

Which doesn't keep him from recalling that moment, in 1982, when people still fantasized about things like "the next millennium."

There and then, coming out of a movie theater as night was falling onto a street in the capital of his now nonexistent country of origin on which there was nothing but movie theaters. A kind of pedestrian, freak mutation of Times Square and Piccadilly Circus, but in a thin straight line and as if raised to the millionth and most hysterical power. Then, the storm (the first big storm of that autumn) and everything around him seemed like a continuation of the rainy scenography of *Blade Runner* that he was just leaving behind. The gas-eous and rising light of neon distorted by water falling from the sky, huge signs with the faces of actors and actresses looking out at spectators like gods on Olympus. All of them flanked by more than one attractive offer from one of the big companies of the day that, like many that appeared in the com-mercially doomed *Blade Runner* (Atari, Pan Am, Bell), no longer existed and were no longer listed on any stock exchange on this side of the Tannhäuser Gate and the shoulder of Orion.

And so he—who didn't have an umbrella or any desire to come back to reality—went back into the movie theater to rewatch *Blade Runner* for the second of many times.

Now, he watched it again.

Not in the rain but above the storm. Dipping in and out of heavy clouds aboard what will be (he doesn't know it yet but senses it) the penultimate flight of his life, crossing the ocean, flying toward Abracadabra.

And on the movie menu, someone had had the good idea (a not particularly original but definitely quite pleasing idea) of, among all the superheroes and comedies and biopics, offering both *Blade Runner* and *Blade Runner 2049*: packaged together but with a documentary about the imminent roboticization of humankind separating them. He watches the documentary first and learns nothing new. It features assorted scientists aspiring to earn the salary of Carl Sagan or Neil deGrasse Tyson, assorted science-fiction authors (and fans of Philip K. Dick), the cast of the second *Blade Runner* . . . He gets bored as soon as his curiosities coincide with his fears and he switches over to the first movie. And he already knows it from memory, internal and private memory. He doesn't need any external gadget to remember it. And yet, there are a few things he didn't notice the last time he rewatched it—ten years ago?—that he finds entertaining and unsettling. For example: Rick Deckard reads a paper newspaper. And everyone smokes in offices and public spaces. And videocalls are made from booths and not from something that pulses in hands and pockets. And, oh, not even in the most pessimistic dystopia would anyone have dreamed—or, better, *nightmared*—of the idea that the greatest technological-domestic advances would all pass through and end up in telephones, so that people could be more and more in/communicado. Other things move him more than ever. Especially, the loving obsession the replicants have with and feel for the few photographs (also paper) they carry with them. The photographs kept by the replicants Rachael (the instantly iconic actress Sean Young who, before long, would fall into disgrace and star in events nearly as regrettable as his failed storming of the Swiss particle accelerator; *almost*, he says) and Leon (who doesn't like that they make him take a test and interrogate him with *multiple-choice* questions like: "You're in a desert, walking along in the sand when all of a sudden you look down and see a tortoise laying on its back." And what desert and what's a turtle and what would you do if you saw it and bang bang and flash flash.)

Photographs all that—you can tell, you *feel* it—were carefully thought out and considered. Photographs—photographs on paper—taken with great care and dedication. Photographs that are much more than the reflexive and compulsive act of indiscriminately snapping pictures. In the already-past future of *Blade Runner*, he thought, people still thought a lot before they made something go click with a click. Photographs were, for the replicants, the desperate illusion and the almost loving need to believe they had a past worth preserving, an unforgettable yesterday. That ever-so-human need to not be forgotten, to be remembered. The replicants were proud to endure the existential dilemma of existing but not being entirely real: they were an invention of the dreams of men. Thus their need to remember, to fight to the death—to the deaths of others, even to their own deaths—to preserve their memories and the certainty that they wouldn't function properly if they couldn't remember. The replicants didn't laugh that prerecorded laugh of the callers on those automated telemarketing calls that he—to unmask them and reveal their artificiality—always asked to say the prohibited phrase/distraction: "I am not a robot" and who then, unable to lie, defended themselves with a nervous "I'm a real person." Faced with such a situation, the replicants would draw a gun and shoot their interrogator point blank. The replicants were clear on everything they were not. And so, the replicants—like writers who, in their own way, were nothing but replicants, builders of exceedingly personal replicas of reality; and he'd always been intrigued by the fact that, being so concerned with the past and with memory, among the replicants, there wasn't one who was or wanted to be a writer, someone seeing things that nobody had seen in his or her mind—thought more about the vast yesterday than about the brief tomorrow. They thought about how, yes, they'd "seen things that you wouldn't believe" and because of that and from there the memorable and unforgettable final soliloquy of the Nexus-6 named Roy Batty (improvised by the actor Rutger Hauer who, from then on, according to people who worked with him, insisted, with catastrophic results, on inserting farewell speeches for his characters in all of the almost-always mediocre movies that he participated in thereafter). And he couldn't help thinking that it wasn't entirely coincidental that the two most essential and influential and unforgettable movies in the history of science fiction culminated with respective farewell monologues delivered by implacable machines, implacable yet sentient—saddened and frightened and disillusioned at everything that would be lost to oblivion once their artificial intelligences were deactivated—and quite disappointed at the lack of vision of the humans who, at the time of their respective premieres, didn't hesitate to give them bad reviews.

Both films—*2001: A Space Odyssey* and *Blade Runner*—struck critics upon being released, in 1968 and 1982 respectively, as slow and cryptic. All of them maybe thinking that something futuristic—that's how it had been anticipated up until then—had the obligation to be vertiginous and didactic and to illuminate something about the tomorrow that it prophesized. (And he thinks that any blockbuster of today compared with any summer movie of yesterday is like the difference between the effects of amphetamines and opioids: back then, even the action and special effects moved with the lack of urgency of someone entering a mansion he doesn't entirely remember, a memory palace.)

But what impressed and moved him most rewatching *Blade Runner* this time—distracting him from the Esperantic sound that never ceases inside airplanes, a blend of engines with languages with the whisper of nylon on the legs of the flight attendants coming and going up and down the aisles—was that moment in which Deckard, in his apartment, goes about "investigating" one of the replicants' photographs in that kind of portable scanner/computer. Deckard there and then moving and zooming in on the image and shifting his perspective by giving orders in an almost robotic diction, speaking to a machine the way it should be spoken to: like a machine and not with the mellifluous voice people use to ask questions of those intelligent and virtual assistants with suspiciously obsequious voices and with brief and easy-to-remember names. There Deckard saying and commanding: "Enhance 224 to 176 . . . Stop . . . Move in . . . Stop . . . Pull out, track right . . . Stop . . . Center and stop . . . Enhance 34 to 36 . . . Pan right and pull back . . . Enhance 15 to 23 . . . Give me a hard copy right there . . ."

And the rest of the movie unfolded for him like a dream he'd dreamed on so many nights.

Whereas now, in the air, it's the first time he's ever seen *Blade Runner 2049*. He opted not to see it when it came out. Why voluntarily expose himself to a fresh disappointment, especially if he had to pay for a ticket to experience it? What was the point of activating the chronometer of another sci-fi title with a precise year that sooner rather than later would reach its expiration date and be left behind, growing old due to its imprecisions regarding a future that would never be like that in the present?

And yet, surprise: within a few minutes he discovered that the movie wasn't bad at all and that, as the plot advanced, it was better and better, it was good, it was really good.

And, yes, *Blade Runner 2049* was slow and cryptic, and it was good that it was and that it was like that. And—when it came out, similar to what happened with *Blade Runner*, he read—it didn't earn much critical acclaim and didn't bring in much in ticket sales.

And he likes the setting, which is like the natural regressive progression of the original. And it rains (and, even better, it snows) too. And also, that slow synths of the score (so Pink-Floydian, so *Wish You Were Here*; remember to buy the soundtrack when you land, he told himself) that sounded like heavy clouds, recalling the harmony of thunder and lightning of those other already-vintage and futuristic melodies.

And above all, it was a movie about paternity and the altering of memories.

And it strikes him as such a clever and intelligent idea for the protagonist, Constant K (serial number KDC-3.7, later known as Joe), to be not just a blade runner but, also, a replicant and, like him, obsessed with a toy (a little carved wooden horse) galloping down the pathways of someone else's memory that he's made his own.

And he was moved by the reappearance of Deckard almost like a Kurtz, apocalyptic and now, in a Las Vegas of sepia and memorious air, where the hologram ghosts of Presley and Sinatra sing to the lonesomeness of three in the morning and the flowing of a lovesick river. Deckard as an ex-blade runner and someone who—as Gaff, now in nursing home, puts it—"wasn't long for this world . . . something in his eyes" and was now, in Hungarian, *nyugdíjas*: retired.

Like him now. Living off of memories and surrounded by nostalgic holograms and, according to Gaff—now making origami sheep and not unicorns—having gotten what he wanted: "To be alone."

And he's fascinated by the idea that it all takes place years after, in 2022, something (and it was funny or frightening that at some point the forever-retro Penelope might've prophesized it) known as The Blackout: the great terrorist act of a rebel replicant who detonated a nuclear warhead over Los Angeles, provoking a powerful electromagnetic pulse, erasing a good part of the memory of humanity stored in computers. (And he would have settled for less, for it just erasing his memory and not even all of it: just that one phone call and that one night and, oh, suddenly he remembers the title of the Forster story that predicts another Blackout and that at one time he couldn't remember: "The Machine Stops." And he also remembers that there had been a David Bowie song from his most psychotic-cokehead period called "Blackout.")

"Everyone remembers where they were at the Blackout . . . I was home with my folks . . . Ten days of darkness . . . Every machine stopped cold . . . When the lights came back, we were wiped clean . . . Photos, files, every bit of data . . . Gone . . . We had everything on drives . . . Everything, everything, everything . . . My mom still cries over the lost baby pictures . . . It's funny it's only paper that lasted," a functionary informs K. And most interesting of all was that the mega-attack (seeing *Blade Runner 2049*, he thought something like that would probably happen eventually, but there would be no need for an attack, it would happen on its own, due to an inevitable exhaustion of available space for all that virtual and unnecessary nonsense that accumulated online) didn't make people lose their memory, it confirmed the lost memory as something unforgettable: because, by then, before the explosion, they were all already voluntary amnesiacs who'd surrendered and relegated their memories to giant external data banks that, suddenly, broke down, went to pieces. And it was and would be only then that humanity would remember that they no longer remembered, and that without any resistance and of their own volition they'd ceded that activity and labor and ability to machines. "All our memory bearings from the time. They were all damaged in the Blackout. But there are sometimes fragments," K is informed by the secretarial Luv, the deadly Nexus-9 replicant and right hand and "first angel" of the messianic magnate Niander Wallace, obsessed with getting his replicants to be able to reproduce and to whom Deckard says, "You don't have children . . . do you?" with a tone somewhere between reproach and accusation.

And he felt moved by that moment when Joi—something like K's synthetic girlfriend—frees herself from the bonds of her holographic and domestic projection with the help of an *emanator* and emerges into the outside world and feels rain for the first time. And then Joi—who without hesitation said, "Mere data makes a man"—could go anywhere she wanted, anywhere in the world, to any of its possible ends.

And he was also thrilled by that scene in which Joi said to K that "I want to be real for you" and she "synchronized" with a female replicant to be able to make love with K and, oh, how many replicants had he synchronized with his memory of Ella to be with her again.

And he pleased that Deckard was pleased—based on a line from *Treasure Island* uttered by the marooned-by-his-mates Benjamin "Ben," Gunn dreaming for three years of the taste of cheese—when he discovers that K reads, because "that's good. Me too, not much else to do around here at night anymore." And he explains to K that "sometimes to love someone you got to be a stranger" and that his very important "part in the replicants' plan was to go away."

And he was even more moved that there was an unforgettable young woman who doesn't forget: the very young Dr. Ana Stelline—subcontracted by Wallace but independent and the head of Stelline Laboratories—imagining and remembering as if what she were imagining were memories, from inside a hermetic and sterile glass capsule, because her immune system "is compromised." Stelline who—spoiler, spoiler! as the spoiled howl—was actually the daughter of Deckard and Rachael.

And Stelline—with the look of a solitary Victorian writer or a pre-Raphaelite model—was devoted to "writing" the memories of others, to be implanted with the help of a *memory orb* that looked like a camera lens. Memories like vital organs, like pieces of a collage, like moments and instants and fragments, to make the replicants feel human. Ethically designed memories. Stelline was the best maker of memories in operation. And her imagined memories were authentic, because, she explained, "there's a bit of every artist in their work. But, I was locked in this sterile chamber at eight; so, if I wanted to see the world, I had to imagine it. I got very good at imagining."

"All the best memories are hers," K said to Deckard at the end of *Blade Runner 2049*, before dying—did he die?—not in the rain but in the snow. And K didn't feel the need to say goodbye with a grand soliloquy because, he thinks—and he thinks well, K is a Nexus-9, a far more advanced model than the Nexus-6, Roy Batty—that it's more than enough for him to say, smiling, "Go meet your daughter."

And yes: *Blade Runner 2049* was another movie about absent fathers and lost children.

And no: Stelline wasn't making autofiction with her imagined memories.

Stelline created from what she lived: because to imagine was to create and to create was to live.

Stelline, he said to himself, was something like the bridge across that divide in the collective unconscious of the ancient world known as "The Great Interruption." Then, for several centuries, the ability to read ancient Greek was lost, and nobody could understand and follow the exceedingly advanced maps of the great Mediterranean sailors anymore. And for a long and elliptical parenthesis, the world ceased to be round and became flat once more. Until someone manifested the necessary memory to be able to understand all that forgotten knowledge again. Stelline was the one who—in *Blade Runner 2049*—overcame and crossed over that deep and black divide.

And he appreciated the explanation that the young Dr. Stelline (who reminded him so much of someone and he couldn't remember, until he did: she reminded him of his creative and volatile Teacher of Artistic Activities at Gervasio Vicario Cabrera, colegio n.° 1 del Distrito Escolar Primero who, seduced by their lunacy, would end up disappearing along with his parents) offered the replicant K, a lesson regarding the nature of her work: "Replicants live such hard lives, made to do what we'd rather not. I can't help your future, but I can give you good memories to think back on and smile . . . If you have authentic memories, you have real human responses. Wouldn't you agree? . . . As far as telling if something really happened or not, they all think it's about more detail. But that's not how memory works. We recall with our feelings. Any true memory is like the fog. Anything real should be a mess."

And he was a little unsettled by the fact that one of the memories implanted in K's artificial memory—a real memory, one of Stelline's memories, and, as such, illegal; a memory that makes Stelline weep to remember—had to do with a toy from his/her childhood and, yes, K says, "I feel a little strange sharing a childhood story considering I was never a child." And he—watching him and listening to him on that small screen—thought: "Don't fret, K. It might be much better that way." And then K said: "I have one about a toy that I had, a wooden horse."

But what surprised him more—and also didn't surprise him, because nothing happens by chance—was the appearance in the movie of a copy of Nabokov's *Pale Fire*, in the hands of Joi, who asks K to read it, because "it will make you feel better." "You hate that book," K responds. And Joi says,

"I don't want to read either," and throws the book into the air. And it was a paper book, a real book. (And it was understandable that K and Joi would be annoyed by or dislike that book, because that book was a book that forces you, when reading it, to ask who is who, who created whom, who exists and who doesn't, who remembers what's remembered and who remembers what they've been forced to remember.)

And, before that, he was even more surprised that the Baseline Test that K was by rule submitted to every time he returned from a mission in a booth at the police headquarters (to thereby demonstrate the authenticity and obedience of his intentions) was the recitation and repetition of several of the ninety-nine verses (with a final and phantasmal verse that was just the first one again, repeated like an echo, and starting all over again) of the formidable poem by John Shade in that novel by Vladimir Nabokov: "A blood-black nothingness began to spin . . . A system of cells interlinked within cells interlinked within cells interlinked . . . Within one stem . . . And dreadfully distinct . . . Against the dark, a tall white fountain played . . ." inserting between one and the next questions like "Cells / Have you ever been in an institution? / Interlinked" or "Cells / What's it like to hold the hand of someone you love? / Interlinked" or "Cells / Did they teach you how to feel finger to finger? / Interlinked" or "Cells / What's it like to hold your child in your arms? / Interlinked" or "Cells / When you're not performing your duties do they keep you in a little box? / Interlinked" or "Cells / Do you long for having your heart interlinked? / Interlinked" or "Do you feel that there's a part of you that's missing? / Interlinked" or "Cells / Do you dream about being interlinked? / Interlinked."

And the sudden appearance of Vladimir Nabokov's writing in *Blade Runner 2049* delighted him to no end (and he'd just seen, in *Blade Runner*, that one of the questions on the Voight-Kampff Test also alluded to a Nabokovian collection of butterflies and the jar that a boy uses to asphyxiate them). Because, again, Nabokov always said he felt a certain disdain for science fiction as a modern genre—claiming that none of it was all that special, and that Shakespeare's *The Tempest* had already done it all a long time ago and, of course, Shakespeare had done it far better—but without that keeping him from making use of several of its devices: the alternate history in the opening pages of *Ada, or Ardor*, the teletransportation in "The Visit to the Museum," the ectoplasmic appearances in "The Vane Sisters," the temporal displacements in "Time and Ebb" ("Like other old men before me, I have discovered that the near in time is annoyingly confused, whereas at the end of the tunnel there are color and light"), the horror of space voyages in "Lance," and the exploration of exceedingly "fantasy" imaginary kingdoms in *Pale Fire*. But it was also true that Nabokov worshipped the scent of celluloid; that he had conceived of several of his novels as films (going so far as to fantasize about a collaboration with Alfred Hitchcock in which a movie starlet would discover that her astronaut suitor was no longer the same after returning from a long voyage among other stars); and that during his years in Ithaca he'd spent time going in and out of the four theaters at the cinema which he—based on their distance from home and office—had designated "the near near," "the near far," "the far near," and "the far far." And that, no doubt, Nabokov would have been pleased by this wink to his novel in *Blade Runner 2049*.

And he was near near and near far and far near and far far, but he hoped to arrive soon, he thinks. Because now that terrible moment, in that place that was nowhere and everywhere at the same time, was coming when the passengers—"cells interlinked within cells interlinked within cells interlinked within one stem"—began to wake up and to feel restless after too many hours in the uncertain sky far away from terra firma.

And he remembers one of his favorite Philip K. Dick stories —"I Hope I Shall Arrive Soon," one of the last stories he published before he died—in which a space traveler wakes up from his suspended animation before he's supposed to because of a mechanical failure and finds himself forced to spend the next ten years sleepless and immobile. To keep him from losing his mind, the spacecraft's central computer then offers him the opportunity to repeat a single memory over and over again (this idea, like so many of Dick's ideas, had later been used over and over by writers of less talent and more copies sold: all those memory drugs or all those induced amnesias to be better endure a frightening present and all of that and all of *this*). So the computer asked the traveler to choose one memory in particular, something that'd been very pleasant. But all the memories of the cosmonaut were shaded, always, with some shadow of trauma that, however small, could end up being lethal for his psyche if it were relived over and over again. The computer gave up and then artificially generated a future memory: the moment of the end of the voyage. Which ended up making it so that, of course, once he arrived to his destination, the traveler could no longer differentiate his present from his past (and there was a time in which he was traveling so much that he woke up at home wondering where he was and he fell asleep in airplanes and hotels as if he were at home). Then, the future recollection was already part of his memory and it no longer coincided with the, far less happy, reality, and then . . .

He, for good or ill or neither, knew that there were so many things he's seen that won't be lost in the rain. Because there was a reason the umbrella of the memory had been invented (even though sometimes it didn't open right or the wind whipped it around or it had a few holes). He felt then that he just wanted all the moments of his journey to be lost like tears in rain—it wouldn't be bad to see *Blade Runner* again and to see *Blade Runner 2049* for the first time—but that now it was time not to die but to arrive so he could start thinking things through. Things like how, it is more than certain, he wouldn't be alive in 2049 and how he was living and alive in 2019 when the first *Blade Runner* takes place, but who knows how much longer his batteries would last.

And, on the menu of movies, he sees that they're offering another movie with another Blackout. A comedy where everyone—apart from the protagonist—forgets one thing: that there once existed something called The Beatles and that, along with the band, all of their songs have been forgotten; and the only memorious person is a failed and mediocre musician and so . . . And another one in which the activation in orbit around a particle accelerator triggers an interdimensional "paradox" that unleashes monsters; yes, another of those movies belonging to the subgenre with the crew screaming and running through the circular passageways of a space station: and all of them so much more sensitive than the astronauts in *2001: A Space Odyssey*. And so much more professional and efficient and the feeling that—by humanizing them so much in order to bring them closer to the viewer, was the first *Alien* to blame for this?—anyone could end up taking a spin up in space just like how, on Earth, anybody could go around writing and believing themselves a writer and causing all kinds of damage.

But he decides that he's already had enough of planetary amnesias and that there was no good reason to add, according to the synopsis/preview of the other movie, a "space-time collisions of multiverses in interaction" to the trip (besides, more than once he'd fantasized that the same thing happened to certain books, *Pale Fire* or *Slaughterhouse-Five* and so many others, and that then he copied and published them under his name in an alternate reality). And that he had enough and more than enough on his plate with everything that—here, on this plane of existence—he couldn't forget and that nobody else could remember because nobody knew what he remembered.

To distract himself, he accepted one of those in-flight magazines that the head flight attendant was now handing out. A local and Abracadabraesque version of that weekly with glossy pages and big pictures and brief captions where families with big last names and bloodlines showed off their houses and posed like satisfied replicants of themselves and lied about their ages (which always appeared as numbers between parentheses) thinking that in that way they were postponing the expiration of their batteries. Pictures that they would look at over and over until they knew them by heart. Pictures that they would use to toot their own horn in public and criticize in private. And a few of those pages of pictures are dedicated to the Karma family on the occasion of the imminent beatification, simultaneous with her canonization (miracle!), of a very alive dead family member they all called Mamagrandma, with a combination of obligatory love and reflexive terror. And it also mentioned that one of the Karmas had almost become the Pope but couldn't accept that honor for "health reasons." There they were. En masse and planning a trip to the Vatican. And all of them—and there are so many of them—also posing in front of a sprawling and monstrous mansion known as Mount Karma. And suddenly, in that double-page photo spread in which all those people barely even fit (the editors of the weekly had made a kind of diagram of numbered silhouettes on one side so you could identify each one of the innumerable family members, as if it were that explanatory diagram of the cover that accompanied the successive commemorative editions of *Sgt. Pepper's Lonely Hearts Club Band* over the decades), he discovered something surprising. Something almost out of focus and half hidden. A flash of red. A fragment, a streak the color of blood, of the blood of his blood, yes. And "Enhance 224 to 176 . . . Stop . . . Move in . . . Stop . . . Pull out, track right . . . Stop . . . Center and stop . . . Enhance 34 to 36 . . . Pan right and pull back . . . Enhance 34 to 46 . . . Wait a minute. Go right. Center and pull back . . . Enhance 15 to 23 . . . Give me a hard copy right there . . ." and "Cells interlinked within cells interlinked within cells interlinked . . . Within one stem . . . And dreadfully distinct . . . Against the dark . . ."

And then he saw him.

And he understood.

And—like K—he suddenly understands that he has a mission, a search, someone to look for and to find.

And he tore out the picture the way he once tore pictures from magazines for his collages. And he folded it and tucked it in with a facsimile copy of a notecard with Vladimir Nabokov's handwriting on it and the copy of his Mexican and end-of-the-world newspaper clipping. That one depicting a meteor-man with a caption warning that: "THE WORLD WILL BE TOOOTALLY CRACKLING," and that a "horrendous catastrophe" would soon be triggered by that "malevolent star that will crash into Earth unleashing a thousand ills."

And he understands that, maybe, this is his second and definitive chance to dance like Shiva and accelerate particles and scatter fragments and that now nothing would ever be the same again.

And he knew that, after so much time, he finally had something that resembled at story worth putting in writing.

STILL WISHING YOU WERE HERE

He remembers when he was young and, no, he never shone like the sun but everything had indeed had the sound of Pink Floyd's *Wish You Were Here*. The definitive album on the subject of absences, according to the members of the band. An album assembled from fragments until it became a whole. A living elegy to the crazy diamond Syd Barrett, eroded by the corrosive winds of the lysergic acid of the late '60s and expulsed and self-expulsed from Pink Floyd; but there forever. His memory as victim of "the crossfire of childhood and stardom" and of having "wore out your welcome with random precision" and all of that. And suddenly, also, the sudden and unexpected appearance of Syd Barrett in the studio: nobody recognizes him—a fat and bald and mumbling man where once there had been a svelte Byronian youth—as, on more than one occasion, things of the past are unrecognizable. That past—when all that you have is the memory of someone, all you can think about is that that someone is no longer there even when that someone is there again for a few minutes—who, depending on the side of the prisms from which you see him, can appear so far but near or so near but far. And, also, an album (Syd Barrett is not excited by what they play for him, he finds it antiquated) that emerged from the creative block resulting from the global success of *The Dark Side of the Moon*. An ode to no longer knowing what to do, born of a period of self-sequester in the studio, where the members of Pink Floyd spent their time playing a lot of squash and taking drugs and wondering where their ability to invent had gone and if it would ever return, if the dream had ended, if they could no longer remember how to do everything they had once done when they were young, something they were already ceasing to be. And no: the dream hadn't ended then, but it wouldn't last much long either. Two or three albums amid fights and lawyers and then the splitting up into factions and the albums of David Gilmour with insufferable and never-ending guitar solos and without Roger Waters and those of Roger Waters without David Gilmour and with that voice of demanding explanation for absolutely everything in the universe. And a brief and perfect reunion for one night at the beginning of the new millennium for a benefit concert. And Syd Barrett dying a few days after that, and a few years after that the one and only Rick Wright (the best of all of them and the least recognized and the legitimate owner of *that* sound). And a final and phantasmal farewell with the title *The Endless River* and Nick Mason taking charge of managing the itinerant mega-exposition called *Their Mortal Remains* on which what was exhibited—their mortal remains, indeed—wasn't all that different than what was reproduced and sold at the giftshop. And they all blamed each other and, yes, that was one of the advantages of having created as a group: there was always someone you could blame for something. Writers, on the other hand, could only condemn themselves and, at most, distract themselves from all of that for a while and remember old yet eternal songs heard for the first time, back when vinyl was the only available option for wishing that somebody was there, for everyone to still be there.

He'd always been a pale kid who only caught fire by stealing a little light, like that moon that now shone above him, above the desert; above him, more deserted than ever, whistling the melodies off that album that was always playing in his childhood ear, singing to him—in the company of a magnificent green cow—of the omnipresence of certain absences, of the brimming void that could only be hidden by inventing and dreaming and, later, remembering.

The perfect album to take not to a desert island but to a deserted desert. And since he doesn't have it with him now, he remembers it and sings it to himself from the first note to the last word.

ADA, OR INTO THE FIRE

He remembers immediately what he just read in the final pages of *Ada, or Ardor* as he burned them in that desert night with the green cow (the last one he reads and, yes, this book that he always thought he'd never read to the end is the last one he's going to read), the pages in "The Texture of Time." That treatise that Van is writing when he recovers his so-missed Ada and where he sets out to "examine the essence of Time, not its lapses, for I do not believe that its essence can be reduced to its lapse. I wish to caress Time."

Van divides it into "Pure Time, Perceptual Time, Tangible Time, Time free of content, context, and running commentary—this is *my* time and theme. All the rest is numerical symbol or some aspect of Space. The texture of Space is not that of Time, and the piebald four-dimensional sport bred by relativists is a quadruped with one leg replaced by the ghost of a leg. My time is also Motionless Time . . . The Time I am concerned with is only the Time stopped by me and closely attended to by my tense-willed mind."

And Van proceeds to "consider the Past as an accumulation of sensa, not as the dissolution of Time implied by immemorial metaphors picturing transition. The 'passage of time' as merely a figment of the mind with no objective counterpart, but with easy spatial analogies. It is seen only in rear view, shapes and shades, arollas and larches silently tumbling away: the perpetual disaster of receding time, *éboulements*, landslides, mountain roads where rocks are always falling and men always working. We build models of the past and then use them spatio-logically to reify and measure Time . . . Time is anything but the popular triptych: a no-longer existing Past, the durationless point of the Present, and a 'not yet' that may never come. No. There are only two panels. The Past (ever-existing in my mind) and the Present (to which my mind gives duration and, therefore, reality). If we make a third compartment of fulfilled expectation, the foreseen, the foreordained, the faculty of prevision, perfect forecast, we are still applying our mind to the Present . . . If the Past is perceived as a storage of Time, and if the Present is the process of that perception, the future, on the other hand, is not an item of Time, has nothing to do with Time and with the dim gauze of its physical texture. The future is but a quack at the court of Chronos . . ."

And he read all of that feeling somewhat embarrassed and sad for Nabokov: because he saw and heard him being so concerned with surpassing Proust in his own realm. And there, for once, Nabokov sounded not like a rereader but like a rewriter; like someone who'd made the mistake of going in search of someone else's lost time instead of staying in his own deserved and noble memory palace, listening to that memory that he had told to speak. And that memory, obedient, had done so with its best accent and most dazzling prose.

In the last pages of *Ada, or Ardor* that now were burning, at last, almost at the end, he feels that, in a way, Nabokov resembles him.

At his worst, he resembles him.

But it's better than nothing.

ELLA, OR WHAT'S FORGOTTEN

He remembers that Ella sounded somewhat like one of Vladimir Nabokov's characters, like a distant relative of that family from *Ada, or Ardor* when she climbed out of one of her many swimming pools to offer an ardent defense (an ardent defense that she would forget to switch off or put out, the way you forget to switch off lights or ovens or to put out bonfires) of amnesia. A voluntary amnesia. The amnesia of someone who no longer asks any questions about their past (could that be why he loved her?) and who, as such, defended the euthanasia of the memory, the oblivion of memories.

He'd once asked Ella if not remembering didn't seem to her a terrible thing and she answered that to the contrary: not bearing the burden of what'd already happened, of everything that was impossible to change, she assumed would be a kind of great relief when it came to navigating the present.

"The present becomes something far more tangible and interesting. The present ends up occupying the same place and space as the past with the difference that you can correct it as many times as you want and think is necessary. The present becomes a combination of past and future. The present is nowhere while simultaneously here and now. The present is always asking to be or not to be and, by the time it gets an answer, it is already past," Ella said.

Ella had just come back from another one of her incursions into "the quantum physics of the multidimensional terrorism of swimming pools."

And Ella continued: "I read somewhere that 'Memory is the dumbest dog, you throw it a stick and it brings back anything but that stick.' And, of course, it sounds very good. But memory can sometimes be a chihuahua and others a Rottweiler. It can be an obedient Lassie or a vengeful Hound of the Baskervilles. And so you have to see what you get: man's best friend or man's worst enemy, something that barks or bites or does both at the same time. Something to which you can't say the whole 'You're barking up the wrong tree,' because it'll just ignore you. And, more often than not, it won't bring you back just a bone but a whole skeleton that it's dragged out of the deepest of closets. Like when we wake up and find ourselves still under the covers of the paralyzing phantoms of sleep, our feet still tangled in the sheets of what we dreamed, and it's so hard to move. And, for a few seconds as long as centuries, we don't know where or who we are and then, frightened, we make memory. We put ourselves back together, until we are back to who we were and still are, but with the suspicion that we've left some piece of important and vital information behind. There, then, once again, the sensation of having plunged into the deepest swimming pool and, coming up from the bottom, with the blood bubbling in your veins, stroking and kicking in a vertiginous fast-forward, advancing through fragmentary flashbacks: not your whole life in the moment of your death but your whole past in the moment of opening your eyes to the present, convinced that you've forgotten something essential, something you invented there, while dreaming . . . Thus, memory is irresponsible and has no obligation or fidelity to those who make it, who make memory. Memory completely forgets what those who memorize it feel or don't feel. Memory is the playback of our life and, sometimes, all we can do is move our lips without emitting a sound, because it's our memory that sings through us. At most, sometimes, we sing a little, slipping off key; but memory helps us, spinning the music of our past, our *Greatest Hits*, which, every so often, get remastered and sometimes even incorporate a bonus track, and yet never amount to more than alternate versions of the same song as always. Yes, there's an imperceptible yet terrible and transcendent moment when, I think, we're finally full to the brim with the past, with memory, and our present and what we have left of our future becomes nothing but a perpetual performance where we act—sing—in accordance with the directions and suggestions of everything that took place a long time ago. That's why the elderly tend to remember events in the distant past with greater ease than what they did just a few hours ago. Yesterday is our refuge and there's no longer anything new that can happen to us, because everything that can happen to us has a path that was prefigured on an old map of the electro-Japanese island of Karaoke. So amnesia isn't a problem, but, rather, the solution to this punishment. Amnesia—the forgetting of everything—really just conceals the possibility of starting over, of having everything that happens post amnesia be new again and, yes, unforgettable. The beginning of your amnesia, like the beginning of all amnesia, is a mystery and it's one of those mysteries that you accept without questioning it too much and just for the pleasure and privilege of feeling that you're part of something. Logic has little to do with amnesia because amnesia isn't logical. In any case, that's why, again, I'm not surprised by the compulsive use of amnesia in the tumultuous plots of telenovelas, because, if you think about it a little, amnesia is nothing but one of the many forms of showing love: having forgotten everything, the only thing we remember is that we have amnesia, just like how, when we fall in love, we forget about everything—everything is forgettable—except the fact that we're in love, that we live to remember that we would die for love."

And Ella smiled at him.

And, looking at him, Ella closed her eyes.

And—after one of those yawns that seemed to give her more pleasure than the orgasm she had earlier—Ella fell asleep on the spot.

And he felt so privileged to watch her sleep. It was an honor to watch her sleep, feeling more awake than ever. Ella there, but, at the same time (her imperfections perfect in themselves), elsewhere.

Ella who wasn't just more beautiful than how he remembered her when she wasn't there: Ella was, always, more beautiful than he could've ever dreamed or invented.

And he swore that he would never forget that he loves her and was even moved by the power of feeling that Ella made him feel.

Which didn't stop him, of course, from noting down everything Ella said (what Ella said as if in a trance, but with all the doors and windows open; what he would end up using in his commissioned Karmatic-Mexican novel; what, on more than one occasion, made Ella sound too similar to how Penelope's characters sounded) and thereby add several more †s, many more, unsheathed and ready for the torment of the thousands *cuts* (*& paste*). As if all those †s surrounded Ella to protect her from any threat and menace, between the blades of the pages of his biji notebooks.

Like this:

†

† †
† †
† †
† †
† †
† †
† †
† †
† †
† †
† †
† †
† †
† †
† †

He remembers that Ella's name was . . . was . . . was . . . was . . . was . . .

He remembers that Ella's name was NOT Oblivion.

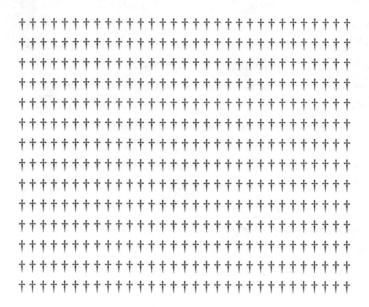

ELLA, OR THE FORGOTTEN ONE

He remembers that—if he were to write again, if there existed the possibility of finally explaining Ella *in extenso*, in a next book, an inevitably
and undoubtedly excessive book, of course—he, in the end, would opt to
do just the opposite. And he would do it—which is to say, he would *not* do
it—to preserve the mystery of the mystery of Ella. To tell nothing with the
most eloquent of silences (just like how, on his final and definitive *multiple-
choice* test, there would be no option, though he might sense one, regarding
a miracle cure for his tumor, dying of a tumor that disappears and vanishes
and effaces expunges erases deletes rubs out wipes out obliterates everything
about *him*). Pages—many—left blank or, merely, with signs watching over
the mystery of her name. Language of signs, yes. But signs that only he
would understand.

(Something far more cryptic than the cut-up and collage prose of William
S. Burroughs, who, okay, he found most interesting not so much because of
his conspiranoid imaginary but because—courtesy of enticing payoffs and
weighty bribes paid by his family—in his day he'd dodged a life sentence in a
Mexican jail cell after killing Joan Vollmer, when a corrupt judge deemed his

excellently awful marksmanship not "homicide" but "criminal negligence." And he'd always fantasized that what he'd done, and what Penelope had done, with respect to their own parents—death "by misadventure"?, besides, they were just kids, right?—might come to be considered in similar and forgivable legal terms, right? Though the truth is he never remembered to ask Ella what she thought about all of that.)

Not to forget Ella but to allow himself "to forget" to tell her, in order to always remember that her thing was the one form of absolute memory: voluntary oblivion. He would evoke her wordlessly and only for himself, in the most absolute and deafening of silences. Ella, for him, like that part that he'd chosen not to invent or to dream or to remember in writing. And to, in that way, ignore the demands of editors and the complaints of critics and the dissatisfaction of readers when it came to that impassable ellipsis that was Ella.

Then he would ignore all those voices that couldn't help inventing or dreaming or remembering her themselves ("Is Ella mystical or physical love?" "Could it be that Ella left him for being such an insufferable machista and misogynistic bastard and he couldn't bear it and so he rewrote her to fit his own needs and intensity?" "Did Ella meet Penelope?" "Is Ella maybe the sublimation of his incestuous love for Penelope that was never consummated, or maybe it was, who knows, because this guy is capable of anything?" "Is Ella actually the code name for a powerful synthetic-Aztec drug with hallucinogenic properties?" "Did Ella suffer and maybe die from the—possibly contagious?—Combray Syndrome?" "Is Ella an extraterrestrial?" "Was Ella him?" "Does Ella *exist*?").

And no no no no no no no no and yes: Voices that—he was certain—would end up right where they started, wearing him out with their moans and accusations and reproaches. Voices that he, with a smile, would turn off the way you turn off a television—after a brief *Mexican standoff*, aiming at the converter atop the device, as if it were a glass of Oso Negro gin—with a pointblank and soundless shot from the remote control and *off*. Or, better, *on* forever and with that other form of watching without watching: changing the channel (there are more and more channels all the time) until you find (there are fewer and fewer good options all the time) something that's worth watching and that guarantees, at least for one more night, the surviving of the light.

THE DYING OF THE LIGHT

He remembers that, when he was a kid, he always resisted the dying of the light. Those were days when there were just four channels on television, in black and white, and the broadcasts ended as soon as that midnight line was crossed after the airing of diabolical and tortured movies like *Sardonicus* or *Attack of the Crab Monsters* (in which the victims were divided into those chased by a psychopath with an axe and those stomped on by gigantic monsters) and, after that, a priest said goodnight to everyone and everything, preaching belief in the unbelievable. A "man of faith" and a "religious man" knowing that the dark made people more permeable to the maddest of notions, far madder than the those projected and transmitted in *Attack of the Crab Monster* or in *Sardonicus*. Then he resisted when the time came for turning out the lights with a click and not a bang. Not angry, but yes confronting sleep and, in that useless little bed, seeking any excuse for nothing to end. And for all of it to keep going after turning off that TV that no longer had anything to show but, on the black screen, that final and single point of light that remained there a few minutes more, like the last dead star in the universe saying goodnight and *hasta mañana*.

The darkness was the end of something that—despite everything and against all odds—had been arranged to arrive there and who knew if it would still be in place and operation the following morning.

And night was map-less journey where it turned out to be so easy to get lost.

And so, reading under the covers with a little flashlight and dilated pupils; or holding up to his ear, with the volume way down low, a radio whose long short-waves traveled better on winter nights. And on the waves, the floating voices, like ghosts demanding that you blindly believe in them. Voices in other languages and, among them, his favorite: that of the BBC host who by way of farewell, always, from so far away, informed sleepless listeners: "This is the end of the world news." The end of the news of the world, indeed, but also a line that could be taken to mean "news of the end of the world." A pronouncement like a mantra that he couldn't help but compile with the images from other movies in those same pre-midnight film series and before televisions turned off without first hanging on to that white dot in the center of the dark and switched-off screen for a few minutes more. Or now, with that Mexican news-clipping in his pocket with the whole THE WORLD WILL BE TOOOTALLY CRACKLING headline.

But first, again, those radioactive sci-fi movies from before that had nothing to do with and looked nothing like *2001: A Space Odyssey* or *Blade Runner* or *Blade Runner 2049*. The lowest of low budgets but extremely high levels of paranoia. In those movies, the planet—just like his cataclysmic childhood, courtesy of a father and mother who, just like in some of those films, on more than one occasion appeared to have been duplicated and replaced by aliens—was always on the brink of succumbing and being left *crackling* by that menace arriving from the abyss of space or rising from the depths of the Earth. Prehistoric beasts that came up to the surface to breathe or futuristic meteorites with perfect aim. And, then, all those unknown extras and figurants disfigured and squashed by gigantic feet or swept away in waves of fire because THE WORLD WILL BE TOOOTALLY CRACKLING.

And he remembers being between seven and eight years old—remembering almost everything because at that point there's still so little to remember—and thinking about how his life could end at any moment and about the paradox of a vast future with so little yet to come. Childhood is, yes, a comedy that at any moment can become a tragedy.

Tomorrow and tomorrow and tomorrow.

And yes: in the beginning of life is when you think most about death, looking at it head-on and not for that reason fearing it any less; while it's at the end that you try most (in vain) to think about anything but THE END; when the short time that you have left to live is better spent in the recollection of insignificant events, the more remote the better. It wasn't that you couldn't remember the immediate present. It was that you did not want to be aware of it and of your constant and ever fleeting ephemerality.

And *that* is where—in that place where one began to be *very*, yet still not entirely, aware of all of that—he is now, there, with everything closing in.

Halfway through life but closer to the end than to the beginning. And with a doctor (the same doctor who a while back had attended him on a night of emergencies when he felt he was dying and more creative than in a long time) staring at an X-ray. And, all of a sudden, he remembered a song by one of his parents' friends, one of the many "creatives" in their milieu, a song where he sang something about how "*Tengo un algo adentro que se llama el Coso*" and how "*Es peligroso ponerse a pensar en el Coso.*" Lines that in English would be something like "I've got something inside me they call a Thingy" and "It's scary to think about the Thingy." And then he makes an enormous effort to think about anything else, because—in addition—he's always looked down on plot twists and turns like this in books or in films. The doctor pointed at something in his brain's frontal lobe and he—with that brand of humor that fear always provoked in him—said, please, don't tell me the sex, I want it to be a surprise (and he had to bite his tongue to not ask him if *that*, that *Thingy*, might end up being the exact reason—and perfect excuse— why he couldn't write anymore. But, in the end, he didn't ask, because he didn't want him to say no, that it was unrelated or, even, what he had there tended to produce the opposite effect: a kind of orgasmic and creative climax wherein the person receiving that diagnosis couldn't stop creating and covering the walls to the last corner with letters).

And the doctor didn't laugh because he didn't find it at all funny, because what he had to tell him was something very serious.

And he knew exactly what that doctor was going to tell him, because he'd already written it years ago in a book, in that commissioned Mexican novel that he'd stolen from Penelope. Something about a tumor that, bite by bite, was eating away at his memory and that would eventually leave him only one single memory and . . . And it wasn't the first time his fictions had anticipated his nonfiction: *déjà écrit*.

And the doctor picked up that X-ray and held it up to the light and stared at it with the same mannerisms with which others once looked up at skies full of stars or down at nautical charts and ocean waters where—beyond the borders of the unknown and beside the prints of wind roses to be depetaled— *there be monsters*, always waiting for a hush to fall over the sailors and their captain as they fall off the edge of a flat world.

Like he was falling now.

CARRY THAT WEIGHT

He remembers how, all of a sudden, events precipitated and, with them, there was no longer time for remembering. The present imposed itself and he saw on TV what'd happened with *The Impossible Story*.

His last book was suddenly like those radioactive journals housed in a vault with lead walls in Paris.

The Impossible Story was a toxic book and not—like up until that point—only from the literary point of view.

The Impossible Story was a sci-fi beast with a low budget but a high number of pages that had managed to set off a wave not of panic but of fury in the public.

And it was because of *The Impossible Story* that, all of a sudden, he heard the approaching cries and saw the glow of torches coming up the hill, his name being chanted as if it were a very bad word that'd been very naughty and had to be punished so it learned that you don't do what it had done.

And he saw something he never thought he'd see and—much less—make happen, because he'd never been able to make it happen despite a great deal of trying: The Intruders, there in service of Penelope's memory and last wishes, were breaking camp ("Her mind kept fading in the growing mist. / She still could speak. / She paused, and groped, and found / What seemed at first a serviceable sound, / But from adjacent cells impostors took / The place of words she needed, / and her look / Spelt imploration as she fought in vain / To reason with the monsters in her brain," *Pale Fire* rhymed and read and recited), because none of what was now coming down on top of him had figured in the script of their final performance: the one about the "reconstruction" of his family from when he and Penelope were kids. The one with "Helter Skelter" playing over and over at full volume and those little toy soldiers, one by one, along the path, that the Brontë's played with coming all the way up to his house, as if inviting Mr. Trip to come out and follow them back down the trail and play with them. They liked how it turned out, it turned out well for them, obeying down to the last detail the instructions left by Penelope. But this improvisation that starts now . . . They have no idea how it's going to end, just that, everything seems to indicate, it's going to end very badly and better to exit before they were *pursued* . . .

And he decided that it was best for him to do the same, as around him the first flames began of another house fire began to rise, the last of his memory palaces. FUBAR and FUBU and SNAFU and SUSFU and TARFU and An Imperial FU and him imagining himself and running through the prose of those fiery passageways, feeling suddenly poetic. So best to get out of there light of luggage. A duffel bag and his passport and cash and none of his copies of *Ada, or Ardor* (he would get another one during his escape) that occupied an entire bookshelf in his library that he said goodbye to with reverence (after selecting another Nabokov book and multiple biji notebooks, two or three diaries, the composition book that'd belonged to He Whose Name Must Not Be Mentioned with the title *Master Advice of a Man Who Sleeps on the Floor*, and the Penelope's booklet with a label on the cover that read *Karma Konfidential*) and then took off running down the hill.

There he goes, past wild boars that stared at him and, he didn't know it then but assumes it now, sent greetings with him to their distant relatives: to the colossal green cows in the Abracadabran desert, not far from Mount Karma, where he's no longer asking himself how all of that happened but what would happen next.

"THE END?"

He remembers that, whenever he heard "The End" by The Beatles, the second to last song on *Abbey Road*—before that light coda of "Her Majesty," perhaps slipped in there to try to attenuate the sentimental epic of what'd come immediately before—he heard those brief and concluding and definitive verses not as an assertive statement but as the most pointed of questions.

And so—after "Oh yeah, all right / Are you going to be in my dreams / Tonight?" and after that one-and-only and first and last and perfect accompanying drum solo by Ringo Starr, who'd always said he hated solos, followed by that hurricane of guitars—what he heard wasn't "And in the end / The love you take / Is equal to the love you make" but "And in the end / The love you take . . . / Is equal to the love you make?"

And, of course, McCartney and Starr—the survivors—had repeated time and again throughout the years that whole *peace and love* bit, no doubt as amazed as they were delighted, because even in the twenty-first century and almost half a century after The End of the band, The Beatles were still the best-selling artists. And because, what they had to sell, were nothing but rereleases and anthologies and reconfigurations various of two hundred and thirty-six songs of their own and seventy-nine songs of others that seemed to belong to them now.

The Beatles were like vampires sipping at the eardrums of humanity, yes. And he really liked something he'd read not long ago, in an interview of Starr. There they asked the drummer what it's like to be a Beatle, and Ringo Starr responded with a question of his own: "What's it like not to be a Beatle?"

And it was funny: Starr had only been a Beatle for ten years, half a century ago. But that's where he remained, forever, being that.

(The same thing, notwithstanding the vast and cosmic distances that set them apart, happened to him: he didn't know what it was like not to be a writer. And, yes, he would like to have a switch he could flip that would let him not be a writer for a while so he could get an answer to the question he never stopped asking himself about what it would be like to be a pure reader. A reader who never wanted to be a writer. And, yes, every so often and less and less these days, a book appeared that shook him and triggered a kind of amnesia with respect to his occupation. That was how he knew that a book was truly and indisputably a masterpiece. Because it was a book that expelled the *maudit* writer from inside it, like a demon being exorcised, to welcome in the blessed and holy reader. Such miracles and marvels were few and far between these days. That was why, to that end, to remember the unforgettable, he reread. And he wondered what happened to The Beatles when they listened to their own songs, what they felt when they played them in person, alone and without the others.)

And yet, before dying, Lennon and Harrison had not only demystified all of it, but, in addition, had complained about how The Beatles had had a much worse time than The Beatles' fans. And to tell the truth, it was a bit irritating for The Beatles to be grumbling about being The Beatles. "Why should the Beatles give more? Didn't they give everything on God's earth for ten years? Didn't they give themselves? You're like the typical sort of love-hate fan who says, 'Thank you for everything you did for us in the Sixties . . . would you just give me another shot? Just one more miracle?" shouted Lennon, who, at the time, was recording and primally screaming songs like "Remember" or "God" in which he rhymed that he no longer believed in the past or in The Beatles, just in himself and in the present (and why was he so preoccupied with Lennon? Why did he think about him so much? Was it because his parents had filmed one of their ad spots crossing Abbey Road, his father dressed as John and his mother dressed as Yoko? Or was it because the relationship of that Beatle with the Japanese woman sometimes reminded him of the one he and Ella could have ended up having but never did?). "They gave their money, and they gave their screams. But The Beatles kind of gave their nervous systems. They used us as an excuse to go mad, the world did, and then blamed it on us," whispered Harrison with that razor-sharp voice he always had.

But for him, the great victim of The Beatles and their radiations had been his overexposed Uncle Hey Walrus. The world wept for the breakup of The Beatles as a done deed, but Uncle Hey Walrus—who had come to them thinking they were perfect and worthy of worship and would be together forever—was witness to each and every fight before the breakup. Uncle Hey Walrus was like the child of divorced parents nobody fought for even though they were all fighting all the time. Uncle Hey Walrus was a highly flammable victim when the love that was all you need was snuffed out.

The love you give and the love you take and all of that and The Beatles recorded "The End"—some people insist this was the last session when the four of them were in the studio at the same time—around the same time that they, also, had that photograph taken of them crossing the street as if crossing the Rubicon. When they already knew they weren't going to keep on walking together, even though, people who were at Abbey Road for those final sessions, remembered that the four of them seemed "like kids again, all playing together and at the same time, alternatingly unholstering and firing off their guitars like gunfighters of the Far West" while Ringo did his thing like never before. Those three guitars taking off together and beginning to separate while in the background there repeated, like a mantra, "Love you . . . Love you . . . Love you . . ."A perfect epitaph that didn't condense the end of a life but the waking up from a dream that was over forever, but whose memory would be like an eternal dream in itself.

In "The End"—though they hadn't realized it, or maybe they had, who knows—The Beatles seemed to be saying that they would never be forgotten, that people would keep on believing in yesterday, that they would always be the music playing in those places or the people who would be remembered forever, because, though some of them would change or even die, The Beatles would always be and sound like The Beatles.

And he remembers the first time he listened to side B of *Abbey Road*. And being surprised and marveling at the way The Beatles had completely revolutionized the fragmentary. Sonically and thematically: a lullaby, yes, but one that also warned that there would be pillows that were never given and that you would end up carrying that weight for a long time.

He took the album to Uncle Hey Walrus at the psychiatric hospital where he'd just had himself committed, only to leave soon thereafter, and, in that way, be able recommit himself to the next psychiatric hospital. His doctors had strictly forbidden him from listening to anything by The Beatles, but he wanted, at least, to show it to him. Uncle Hey Walrus looked at the cover in silence and then said to him: "You have to get me the keys to that white Volkswagen Beetle that's parked there and I'll get out of here and get in that car and run over all four of them and throw it in reverse to run them over again and back up a little more and then run them over again . . ."

And then—when they heard his primal screams—a couple of nurses came and took Uncle Hey Walrus away.

Uncle Hey Walrus who ended up emptying a bottle to fill himself up with psychedelic-colored pills and to go to sleep forever beside a river and *turn off your mind relax and float downstream* (and when he learned of his death, he thought that "Hey, but I was the one who almost drowned," and in a way, it gave him peace when they told him that Uncle Hey Walrus died from an overdose first and that only afterward had someone thrown his body into the water, after relieving it of his watch and the few bills he always carried in his shoes). And tomorrow never knows, because there won't be any tomorrow and, after thinking about all of that, he felt sad.

Uncle Hey Walrus committed suicide on the day that—like everyone else—he learned that John Lennon had been killed.

Then Uncle Hey Walrus left a note where he wrote a single line:

"It wasn't me."

THE END

He remembers that at one time he thought that "And in the end / The love you take / Is equal to the love you make" without a question mark was something like a mathematical formula or a law of physics:

The love you take = The love you make.

But unlike universal and well-tested laws and formulas obligatory for all presents and pasts and futures, this was a principle that could be brought to an end with a:

The love you take ≠ The love you make.

Similarly, remembering a lot didn't automatically imply that you would be remembered.

THE END! (ARIA DA CAPO)

He remembers how it was that his thing ended, how it was that his thing came to an end, how it was that he stopped writing.

With different background music.

It'd all started with the *Goldberg Variations* by Johann Sebastian Bach. In the two versions—the dawning one from 1955 and the twilight one from 1982—recorded on the piano by Glenn Gould. Albums and performances that were the classical music equivalent of what *Kind of Blue* by Miles Davis or *A Love Supreme* by John Coltrane were for jazz or what *Sgt. Pepper's Lonely Hearts Club Band* by The Beatles (Glenn Gould considered The Beatles' music to be "a happy, cocky, belligerently resourceless brand of harmonic primitivism") was for rock 'n' roll. Everyone had them, even if they weren't interested in classical music or in jazz or in rock 'n' roll. Sonic commonplaces. Topics of conversation and topics of audition.

And the poetic justice and the narrative astuteness of the fact that Glenn Gould—a fierce insomniac—got famous forever performing that score composed in 1741 by J. S. Bach, who never charged much for his work and who—nightmare of nightmares, punishment for his excesses—had to feed twenty children who, most of them, would die before him. Music to frighten away the insomnia of Count Hermann Karl von Keyserling of the court of Saxony. Bach put everything he knew into it. And then he passed the scores—as if they were a prescription—to the count's very young lead organist, one Johann Gottlieb Goldberg, so he could administer them at the right dosage to the prostrate noble.

Personally—beyond its supposed application for fighting insomnia—there was no music that woke him up more and better. And he wasn't the only one. That's why it was used, over and over again, in movies to accompany almost everything and everyone: epiphanic nurses in *The English Patient*, pacifist aliens in *The Day the Earth Stood Still*, a serial killer in *Hannibal*, the father of a dysfunctional family in *Captain Fantastic*, a guilty astronaut in *Solaris*, some strange policemen in *True Detective*, a superhero despite himself in *Unbreakable*, a sex addict in *Shame*, a bored actor in *Somewhere* . . .

But for him, the best "performance" of the *Goldberg Variations* had the advantage of Glenn Gould's direct participation. On the soundtrack he made for George Roy Hill's perfect 1972 film adaptation of *Slaughterhouse-Five* by Kurt Vonnegut. There, Glenn Gould—who once said he dreamed "I appear on some other planet, perhaps in some other solar system, and . . . I have been given the opportunity—and the authority—to impart my value systems to whatever form of life there might be on that planet; and they understand me and listen to me"—accompanying the space-time voyage bound for Tralfamadore of the cosmic pilgrim Billy Pilgrim.

Years later, in a way, his wish had come true: music by Bach but performed by Glenn Gould was included on those gold albums that were sent traveling aboard the *Voyager I* and *II* to the far reaches of the universe, like Dave Bowman at the end of *2001: A Space Odyssey*, extracts of Gould's work included so that extraterrestrial intelligences would understand that earthlings weren't as dumb as they might appear on their screens, as if human history were an idiotic sitcom that'd gone on for too many seasons with too many repeated gags and falls from slipping on banana peels and pies in the face. Over and over, like a bad joke that only became good (dis)courtesy of repetition.

But, in addition, Glenn Gould—and what a musical name he had, sounding like a pair of notes close together on the keys—interested him for other reasons. Glenn Herbert Gould (Toronto, 1932-1982) was a great character whom some musicologists didn't hesitate to deem a clown-freak-idiot savant and more a pretentious megalomaniac than a melomaniac. A usurper and a violator. "Glenn Gould's *Goldberg Variations* are Bach's," they raged. While others took no time at all to raise him up like a kind of genius saint.

And he'd studied the twists and turns of Gould's career. He'd read a lot about him and had also read all of the great deal he'd written. And he'd even "employed" him in a couple stories and had researched him for an article in *Volare* about the frozen Canadian north.

There was abundant material to delve into the mystery of Glenn Gould, a mystery he had no desire to solve, because the fun was in the fact that—as one of the many documentaries devoted to him warned—"the Gould Dilemma has not been resolved; the Gould Dilemma remains even though Gould is no longer with us." And the thing is that Glenn Gould might've been the closest thing classical music will ever have to a pop star: someone who was so easy to admire and adore and, of course, to question and condemn, but whatever way you chose to look at him, it was impassioned. "Within what we might call the territory of the wanderers, Glenn Gould will always have his altar," Enrique Vila-Matas had written. And it was well-known that it isn't easy to be a religious icon.

And so, Glenn Gould like a combination of a hermetic Bob Dylan and a reclusive J. D. Salinger, considering "prison convict" as an optional career because "isolation is an indispensable component of human happiness." And yet, like both of them, Glenn Gould here and there and everywhere, and he was always rediscovering him. In so many biographies, pausing on his misanthropy and his tics and faults and fixations (which scholars of the mind now associate with autism or Asperger syndrome); and his complete lack of a sex life (though recent research has rediscovered him as a top-secret Casanova with a variety of lovers; one of them always concealing her face behind phantasmal and operatic mask); and even completely devoting himself to the life and work not of Glenn Gould but of his favorite piano. In collections of his letters and writings (the simultaneously revealing and intangible essay/self-portrait "Glenn Gould Interviews Glenn Gould About Glenn Gould" is particularly noteworthy) and responses to questions from reporters ("Are there any off-limit areas?" "I certainly can't think of any—apart that of music, of course"). In the brilliant and emotive and exceptionally smart and unconventional and highly recommended biopic: *Thirty Two Short Films About Glenn Gould*, made by another Canadian, François Girard. In photo albums (that showed him when he was young as a kind of James Dean of the Steinway and, when he was older, as a combination of X-Men academy director and nerd from *The Big Bang Theory*). In the suffering past of the protagonist of Thomas Bernhard's *The Loser*. In DVD recordings of his studio performances and TV specials and comedy shows (where he appeared dressed up as the Edwardian and antimodernist Sir Nigel Twitt-Thornwaite or the brutal Theodore "Ted" Slotz, taxi driver and music critic from the Bronx). In an episode of *The Simpsons* and in another of *The X-Files*. And on a stamp where Glenn Gould appeared (like Billy Pilgrim) as a twenty-year-old and a fifty-year-old at the same time and, yes, accompanied by the first notes of the aria of the *Goldberg Variations* that are identified there—crass error or Freudian slip or justifiable claim?, after all and at this point doesn't that can of tomato soup belong more to Andy Warhol than to Campbell's?—as *Glenn Gould's Variations*.

And there is a German maxim that states: *"Niemand kann Bach kaputt macht!"* Which is to say: "Nobody can ruin Bach!" But, for many, Glenn Gould—doing his thing, punctuating his performances with changes of tempo, sighing and panting through the spiritual ecstasy and carnal orgasm, histrionic gesticulations and collage and high-tech stunts/tricks in the studio, cutting up and putting back together a new whole from multiple fragments and moments and instants and takes—had achieved that and then some. For his detractors, Glenn Gould ruined not just Bach but so many other composers and performers, who felt that, in order to be transcendent, it was incumbent upon them to feel and make people feel that they were *strange* too, just like Glenn Gould.

So it is, so it was: Glenn Gould like a mad scientist and experimenter. And if Bach was considered by many the most sublime expression of the mathematical order of the universe, then Glenn Gould was something like an expert in quantum physics. And so, Glenn Gould like a voyager through parallel dimensions of the classical. A freak who began and ended in himself and who seemed to endow his own life with the fragmented yet indivisible tempo and trajectory of the *Goldberg Variations*.

And though it wasn't necessary, he had to confess it: what interested him most about Glenn Gould was his condition as prodigy, because he thought the condition of prodigy (that so many times he'd wanted for himself, who after all was able to read and write for a few minutes before ever learning to read and to write) justified any action no matter how bad, because it washed away all the sins of the world. But his parents had been too busy to calibrate the power of his little brain (his parents only thought that they had to think of themselves, they were prodigious in and at that) and the truth is the little Penelope fit that bill better, even though she was still so young and only expressed herself with arched eyebrows, twisted smiles, and sounds at once deep and sharp and slightly off key.

And yet, he couldn't miss the opportunity to arrange the life of Glenn Gould (always one of his favorite possible "characters" who he'd gone so far as to write into one of his stories where he crossed paths with J. Robert Oppenheimer) as a collection of variations on a single theme. Variations on solitude and the empty yet fullest of spaces that always contained a definite and defining absence (and for him the *Goldberg Variations* in Glenn Gould's version were the perfect and complementary classical counterpart to Pink Floyd's *Wish You Were Here*).

Listen to them.

Gouldberg Variations, indeed:

A mother who knows her son will be a pianist even when he's still inside her, floating in amniotic fluid.

A baby who never stopped moving his fingers and a boy who learns to read music before reading letters.

A father who takes him to see *Fantasia*, the symphonic feature film by Walt Disney. "I hated every minute of that movie," Glenn Gould, who as a boy preferred to listen to music on the radio, would remember.

A mother who gave up being his first piano teacher to turn him over, at eleven years old, to the unorthodox and exceedingly singular and talented Chilean maestro Alberto Guerrero, at the Toronto conservatory. From Guerrero, Glenn Gould inherits the habit of sitting low on a bench with short legs (the legendary piano chair Glenn Gould used that in the end no longer had a seat is now a frequently visited piece at the National Library of Canada), as if the keys were a cliff's edge from which to hang, as if he were performing at the edge of the abyss. Criticized for that posture, Glenn Gould digs in with one of his most oft-quoted lines: that "business is surely a private matter between my left hand and my right, and I cannot see why it's of concern to anybody."

An adolescent who during his free time practiced little and read a lot: looking at scores improves your execution more than memorizing them, he explains. And he adds that the piano "is not an instrument for which I have any great love as such . . . [but] I have played it all my life, and it is the best vehicle I have to express my ideas."

A young man who at twenty was conscious of the fact that Glenn Gould was already Glenn Gould and was already the Glenn Gould of those photographs of Glenn Gould that, though motionless, always showed him shaken and shaking everything and everyone around him. And one of his first gestures is disdain for all the most obvious pianistic repertoire (and thus his unearthing/reinvention of the *Goldberg Variations*, at the time sidelined after the, for many, first and definitive reading by Wanda Landowska in 1933). And first he records them in four days that shook up the world of classical music and then he's consecrated as a star, touring auditoriums the whole world over.

Glenn Gould who, in addition, was already starting to be very well known, and was barely tolerated by business owners when it came to his particularities, but was adored by his followers and evangelists: his lucky worn-out chair; his specifications regarding the pianos (and his quasi-addiction to the blind tuner, Verne Edquist, another great character, he thinks); his scarves and sweaters and hats and gloves with clipped fingertips even when the summer sun was beating down; his propensity to drive in dangerous zigzags, following the rhythm of the music in the car's sound system; the industrial quantity of towels he had (he sweat a great deal when he went into action) in his recording studios and auditoriums; his terror of germs (especially the ones in the air of airplanes) and his panic when it came to people touching him (he went so far as considering a lawsuit when an employee of Steinway & Sons greeted him with a pat on the back, giving Gould, from what he said, "bruises for life"); his murmurs while performing (a nightmare for sound engineers at Columbia Records) and his affinity for full-throatily singing to cows in the countryside and to elephants at the zoo ("Certainly I've never encountered so attentive an audience before"). And, of course, his oft-predicted yet still unthinkable retirement from the stage, when he was thirty-one years old.

April 10ᵗʰ in 1964 and without prior notice, Glenn Gould says farewell to all of that at the Wilshire Ebell Theatre in Los Angeles. In the program, more than pertinent, was included a selection of Bach's *The Art of the Fugue*. And Glenn Gould, yes, fugues. Like The Beatles, Glenn Gould got tired of his live and in-person fans and focused on the pirouettes that could only be done in studios, recording and cutting and pasting, almost note by note, as if putting together the puzzle pieces of a collage. And in so doing, Glenn Gould arousing the ire and disdain of his enemies. But Glenn Gould had already made up his mind: flesh and bone listeners didn't just strike him as an anachronism to be overcome, but, also, a "force of evil." And then he founded the doctrine of GPAADAK (acronym to be decoded as the Gould Plan for the Abolition of Applause and Demonstrations of All Kind). "That nut is a genius," someone said at the time. "I'm just the last puritan," Glenn Gould corrected.

From then on and up until his death, an increasing number of particularities and phobias and talents. People claim that he had an astounding talent for speculating on the stock market. And somewhat frightening were his rampant hypochondria; his addiction to all kinds of medications (and to ketchup); his technological preaching (Glenn Gould maintaining that Bach sounded better with a washing machine running at the same time); his sonic montages always centered on trapping the melody of solitude ("I don't know what the effective ratio would be, but I've always had some sort of intuition that for every hour you spend in the company of other human beings, you need 'x' number of hours alone. Now, what 'x' represents I don't really know . . . but it is a substantial ratio") and of silence (there's film footage of Glenn Gould directing imaginary orchestras on the banks of his beloved Lake Simcoe); his trips to the police station (like what also happened to Bob Dylan) when he was mistaken on the streets for a homeless person; his phone calls at all hours that would go on for hours; his waking dream based in the consumption of pills of different colors and grammages about how "art gives you the opportunity to entirely disappear."

And even more unexpected than his retirement was his death from a stroke two days after turning fifty and after recording a second and a slower and more reflective version—as if moving off toward the horizon saying hello or returning to the source to say goodbye, like salmon—of the *Goldberg Variations*.

And all of the above about Glenn Gould was nothing more than the point of entry to all of the below about him.

Because for him *that* had been the perfect music for so many things (he *used* it all the time for reading and writing) and suddenly, also, they were the notes that opened the door so his own door could close never to open again.

And he listened to it attentively, trying to fully understand it and suddenly—based on something he'd talked about with a musician friend—hearing everything that was *also* there, in the brief yet eternal time between one note and the next, in that deafening silence.

Then he asked his friend if, musically, that space produced between one sound and the next was understood as a kind of secret melody, a counter-score, a negative of what was positively heard that could be discerned if, like dogs, you were able to hear a particular frequency inaudible to the human being.

First his friend gave him a strange look and then explained to him that the pauses were like the fingerprint of the performer, what made him recognizable and particular and unique: his swing, his brand, and, every so often, his genius.

In what went un-played resided the style of what was played.

But he needed to know more, to go further. He needed to understand what the more or less well-tempered key was for getting that emptiness to fill everything, to make it so that everything that wasn't performed between the folds of a score was, actually, the unquestionable reason why it would live on forever.

All he wanted was the opportunity to recompose that secret melody and—given that he didn't know how to read or write music—then to come up with a way to apply all of it to his own territory and his own abilities. Asking first to answer later if something similar happened or could happen with writing: if the blank space between one word and the next might not, also, contain the divine accelerated particles and interlinked cells of a true masterpiece. The voice of the gods that human beings had forgotten how to answer, the music of the snow, the Esperanto of the roaring rush of the blood, the international language of the dead.

And so he began with caution, like someone entering the virgin jungle or starting to experiment in a laboratory.

Brief texts.

Fragments. Instants. Moments.

Paying particular and constant attention to that pause between one word and the next. Little by little he went along separating words more and more, so they had more space to breathe and to entrust him with their, not last, but, yes, definitive breath.

Soon the pauses were like a language, they were even more important than any language because—he said to himself, marveling—everyone understood and spoke and read and wrote the language in which pauses are expressed.

Soon, words were accessories: nothing more than the two ends of suspension bridges that took no time at all to catch fire and to burn so that all that silence could be made and heard and everything was effaced expunged erased deleted rubbed out wiped out obliterated.

And he stopped writing because everything was already written.

And so it was that, in trying to write better than ever, he stopped writing forever.

CLIMAX – ACMÉ / ANAPHORA – CATAPHORA

He remembers that—disoriented, getting lost in the passageways of his memory palace, in which there were ever more locked rooms and cracks on the walls—he was left with only the theory and without the practice.

With random pieces and no instruction manual.

With things like climax (that came from the Greek word κλῖμαξ and that meant "staircase"). Things like acmé (άκμή, or "the point, or blade of an object" and—in the figurative sense—the moment when something is at its maximum splendor, its peak). At its zenith and apogee whose result was the finality and the result of the cataphora (φέρω or "to bring down, to fall") and the anaphora (άναφορά, "repetition"), insisting over and over again on the same words for opening a line and/or anticipating what would come until you achieved the ecstasy only offered by certain prayers.

The fragments.

The collages.

The deserts.

The winds.

The airports.

The airplanes.

The hotels.

The telephones.

The books.

The dead.

The ghosts.

All of the above.

And then him praying over and over for everything that'd abandoned him to come back and for it to bring him to the most Hellenistic of happy endings (to that original and ancient yet eternal idea of the *happy end*) or, at least, to the happiest of continuations.

(TO BE CONTINUED . . .)

He remembers then (though he doesn't have to make memory, because he just now thought and felt it) that, for once, all the fragments seemed to arrange themselves harmoniously.

Once upon a time Penelope had explained to him that "in physical illness you start fragmenting. Little by little. You stop being able to do things. As if you were coming apart in slow motion. Until you're no longer what you were and only the photographs remain. With madness, with *mental* illness, something similar happens. Especially with the madness that arises from pure pain. But with a decisive variation: you don't cease to be, rather you become someone else. As if, using the same parts, you'd disregarded the instruction manual and assembled something entirely different."

What he felt now, on the other hand, was something very different: that he was becoming again who he once was, that his parts were coming back together and reuniting to talk among themselves and sign a truce and reach an agreement and offer him a little bit of peace before the final battle.

And it was as if he was seeing all those instants and parts and moments and fragments from outside, from far away, from overhead; as if they were coming together into one of those equally demented and intelligent choreographies by Busby Berkeley. Girls spinning. Boys going down stairs. Girls dancing on a stage like a memory palace. Girls in swimming pools but not his girl, the girl who was his, Ella.

He looked at all those fragments with kaleidoscopic eyes from this diamond-strewn desert floor. He said hello to all those fragments in the moment he said goodbye to them. He said *aloha*: that word of coming and going that meant both things. He told them that the time had come to make peace and to rest. That there was no longer any need for Enoch Soames to keep fighting Funes with a † like a throwing knife or with a ⸸ like a throwing axe.

He told them that the time had come to disappear, to forget everyone else and to not remember himself.

He told them what he wished he'd never—though in a different way and in a different language—said to that voice on the other end of the telephone of his childhood, the voice that turned his parents in.

He told them the words listed on a square notecard (*efface* was circled, there was something crossed out and incomprehensible between *rub out* and *wipe out*) written in pencil by Nabokov and located at the opening of *The Original of Laura*.

He told them

efface

expunge

erase

delete

rub out

wipe out

obliterate

He told them what it said in the novel that Vladimir Nabokov was working on before he died in 1977, and whose scattered notecards he demanded be burned if he didn't make it to the final version, because—as he said in one of his last interviews—"only ambitious nonentities and hearty mediocrities exhibit their rough drafts. It's like passing around samples of sputum." And because—as he'd already stated before in the mouth of the diffuse narrator of *The Secret Life of Sebastian Knight*—"nothing ought to remain except the perfect achievement: the printed book . . . the litter of the workshop, no matter its sentimental value, must never subsist." And also in the preface to his translation of *Eugene Onegin* by Alexander Pushkin, Nabokov had reaffirmed that "An artist should ruthlessly destroy his manuscripts after publication, lest they mislead academic mediocrities into thinking that it is possible to unravel the mysteries of genius by studying cancelled readings. In art, purpose and plan are nothing; only the results count."

But Vera Nabokov refused to carry out said mission and chose to save the notecards (to which only a couple of trusted "Nabokovologists" were given access) in the safe deposit box of a Swiss bank.

When Vera died, her son Dmitri Nabokov promised to carry out the ceremony and cremation of the notecards, but, in the end, he decided to publish them—in 2009 and under the title *The Original of Laura*—because as he saw it they comprised "Father's most brilliant novel, the most concentrated distillation of his creativity." And Dmitri's excuse was as dubious as it was irrefutable: he insinuated something about how his father's ghost had appeared to him and asked him to do it. Or something like that. And Dmitri gave interviews where he highlighted again and again his father's constant preoccupation with the Beyond (with the *potustornost*) and the way it'd been invoked over and over again in his work. It was clear that Dmitri (who died shortly after the publication of *The Original of Laura* and, to date, *he* doesn't appear to have appeared to anyone) was a clever guy. Clever as only somebody who managed to develop and bring together into one the irreconcilable vocations of Russian translator, race car driver, and opera singer. Which translated as "When I grow up, I want to be the son of Vladimir Nabokov or, better, a character of Vladimir Nabokov with a right to royalties." Or, to be even more precise, someone capable of, in the prologue to that unfinished book, asking himself the crucial question: "Should I be damned or thanked? But why, Mr. Nabokov, why did you *really* decide to publish *Laura*?" And to answer like this:

"Well, I am a nice guy, and, having noticed that people the world over find themselves on a first name basis with me as they empathize with 'Dmitri's dilemma.' I felt it would be kind to alleviate their sufferings."

The Original of Laura (its working titles were *Dying is Fun* and *The Opposite of Laura*) was subtitled *A Novel in Fragments*. And it was more an object-book than a book-object. What can you do with something that was next to nothing (one hundred and thirty-eight notecards turned into more or less thirty manuscript pages) but could still be appreciated and that'd been so-long awaited?

Easy: you turn it into a game.

And he bought it on the same day it arrived in bookstores.

And he read it carefully and with a combination of relief and disappointment (because, oh, wouldn't it have been terrible if, unfinished and barely begun, *The Original of Laura*, its scraps and tatters, had been the most ingenious thing ever genialized by that genius?) and surprise (those theretofore unthinkable orthographical errors from the hand of someone you considered beyond all error and someone who'd revolutionized and accelerated and centrifuged every particle of the English language).

And, yes, *The Original of Laura* was first and foremost and when all was said and done a beautiful artifact, designed by the brilliant Chip Kidd. A dark cover where the letters seemed to be captured in the very act of vanishing and, there inside, a possible plotline in which a neurologist, one Philip Wild ("The 'I' of the book is a neurotic and hesitant man of letters, who destroys his mistress in the act of portraying her"), toyed with the idea of erasing himself—step by step and appendage by appendage—from his feet to his head.

It's a Wonderful Death.

Something with which he could sympathize and identify no problem, as he turned the heavy pages, a facsimile reproduction of the notecards that, perforated, invited you to disassemble and reorganize them as you wished.

And no, never: he would never have dared do that; but he did photocopy that first page with the synonyms of disappearing verbs. And, ever since, he'd been carrying it with him folded inside his wallet or passport (next to it adding that cutout with the José Guadalupe Posada print and that glossy page from the society magazine).

And every so often he took it out the list and recited it like magic words.

And now—having burned all of *Ada, or Ardor*—it's the last thing he throws into the fire in the desert night, on the outskirts of Mount Karma, in Abracadabra.

"Thy will be done, VN," he thinks or says; because he's been alone for so long now that the voice of what he says or what he thinks is the same.

And there he is.

In the desert.

That landscape where you have to pay very close attention to understand what's happening and when it happens; because you can never be entirely certain whether the desert is the greatest expression of the ruins of the past, or of foundations that are full of and ready to be filled with possibilities for the future, taking time and place in an absolute present.

The ideal location and perfect moment to:

A. Efface

B. Expunge

C. Erase

D. Delete

E. Rub out

F. Wipe out

G. Obliterate

or

H. All of the above

He chooses, of course and just in case, the option he'd added himself: *All of the above*; which is what he needs to feel in order to do what follows, what's coming, what, it won't be long now, is about to happen.

Because, at last, something is going to happen again.

To happen to him.

Because now is the end of remembering so that what's to come can begin and he commends himself unto Khaibit (The Shadow of the Memory of your whole past conditioned by the way you decide to remember or forget it) and to Sekhu (or the Remains, what never leaves, what ends up being impossible to forget).

Goodbye then to the guilty pleasure of contemplating amnesiac memory palaces, walls that toppled never to rise again. (And he remembers that one of Uncle Hey Walrus's notebooks recorded the words of J. telling him how Yoko "had made me spend ten days under a vow of silence. Without books or newspapers or music or television. Emptying myself of everything until I was filled with myself. Erasing myself first to draw myself again. Until I start to see all those parts of myself that I'd never seen. Or that I'd forgotten. Or that I don't want to remember. All those fragments. Like spirits slipping along the passageways of a temple. And you are the temple." And he also remembers that he, reading that, thought about Matteo Ricci and about the memory palace, about his memory palace that now shook and cracked as if struck by an earthquake measuring a 10 on the Usher scale.)

Goodbye then and now to suffering the torture not of what'd been but of what'd never been: what never came to pass, what you thought could've been but never panned out. Goodbye to the fragments of a model to be assembled now disassembled and lacking so many key pieces. Everything you don't remember but that, at the same time, is—like certain inventions and certain dreams—unforgettable and, for that reason, no longer needs to be recalled.

Hello to the here and now.

And he remembers those winter mornings—back then the winters were far more wintery than they are now—in his now nonexistent country of origin. Back then, the seasons were more fixed and distinguished: quadrophonic instead of stereo or even today's mono, where there didn't appear to be any difference between the ones and the others, and all of them sounded more or less the same. Seasons like different songs, like hit singles and greatest hits and not parts of a concept album or chapters in a book where the weather never changed.

There he was and there he would stay.

In his childhood classroom at Gervasio Vicario Cabrera, colegio n.° 1 del Distrito Escolar Primero, with the Teacher of Artistic Activities taking attendance. And, then, awaiting that magical moment when his name would emerge from her lips so he could answer with a vaporous—due to the cold—yet ecstatic and enthusiastic and with all the breath in his little body: "Present!"

Hello to going up to the front of the classroom, frightening everyone because you were so afraid, afraid of and for everyone, when it came time to give or receive a lesson.

And, yes, the end is one and indivisible and yet, at the end, the ending part is but a loving instant and fragment and moment where the given coexists with the taken.

Interlinked.

That last fossilized fragment that you hurl into the heights, higher still, into the sky full of stars and:

A. You watch it climb and climb.

B. You watch it not fall.

C. You keep watching it.

D. All of the above.

E. All of the below.

All of what—*Time is an asterisk . . . Same as it ever was . . . Here comes the twister . . . Look out! 'Cause here she comes . . .*—was coming now and all of what was already here.

III

INVENTING
WHAT WILL HAPPEN
BECAUSE YOU CAN NO LONGER
KEEP INVENTING
WHAT ALREADY HAPPENED AND,
HAVING READ THE BOOK
AND FULL OF STARS,
BON VOYAGE,
MY FRIEND

All we have to face in the future is what has happened in the past. It is
unbearable. [. . .] There is no lesson to be learned from experience.
—Maeve Brennan,
excerpts from two letters to William Maxwell

Experiences aren't given us to be "got over," otherwise
they would hardly be experiences.
—Penelope Fitzgerald,
opening line—later discarded—of the first draft of
The Bookshop

If only one knew what to remember or pretend to remember. Make
a decision and what you want from the lost things will present
itself. You can take it down like a can from a shelf. Perhaps.
—Elizabeth Hardwick,
Sleepless Nights

Oh, that day! One kept waiting—as if a morning would arrive from before
that day to take them all along a different track. One kept waiting for
that shattering day to unhappen, so that the real—the intended—future,
the one that had been implied by the past, could unfold. Hour after
hour, month after month, waiting for that day to not have happened.
But it had happened. And now it was always going to have happened.

But seriously, isn't that the whole point of the past? That it's immutable?
—Deborah Eisenberg,
"Twilight of the Superheroes" and "Taj Mahal"

Everything that happens in my stories has
happened to me or will happen to me.
—Carson McCullers,
The Mortgaged Heart

One of the hardest things in the world is to describe what happens next.
—Mavis Gallant,
Paris Notebooks

了

What was coming now was already here. What was going to happen (everything that goes up must come down; including, even though the film didn't
show it, that prehistoric bone that opts to change into millennial steel and to
keep rising into the most outer of spaces where everything floats and orbits)
was what was already happening.

All time in one single time: like in an experiment with the texture of
time, yes.

His irreality had become reality.

His dream had come true: there was no longer any perceptible difference
between what was recreated with exactitude and what was exactly created,
there was no longer any measurable distance between what was remembered
and what was invented.

In the end and at the beginning, nothing being everything.

And everything present while simultaneously past and future. (And what
was that Chinese symbol, that accelerating and slowing "particle" of the language with which the exact temporal situation was determined by the context
or "appearance" more than by expressions like "yesterday" and "today" and
"tomorrow"; and, oh, yes, it was *like this*: 了. And he drew it with the tip
of his finger across the screen of the desert sand with eyes half-closed and
suddenly squinting against the force of the vertical light that falls across and
exposes every shadow.)

Everything right here and right now.

And final.

And ending.

And endings were and are and would ever be more crystalline and clear than beginnings.

That's why people tend to talk more about happy or sad endings than about sad or happy beginnings.

The sadness or the happiness of beginnings is, always, transitory and fleeting and never stays still. It's there only to shift, to change location and mood and intensity.

Happy or sad endings are, on the other hand, terminal and immoveable, irrefutable and definitive. As if—statues under the rain, with dates and names—sculpted in the marble or etched in the bronze of monuments conceived of to survive until the end of time.

Nobody asks, "How did it all begin?" because there's no need, because asking "How did it all end?" you know everything from the first minute to the last second.

And yet the condition or nature of the ending is not known or specified until the last letter of the last line.

Which is to say: endings have multiple parts, parts in which—even though it's the ending—even though there's little left to tell or to say, even though endings are the most present part and in the present of a story, also there, in those different parts of an ending, you can invent and dream and remember.

Which is to say: there's a beginning and a during and an ending of the ending.

Which is to say: he knows that this is the ending; but he doesn't yet know how and in what way and with what spirit all of it'll end.

He knows, yes, how to begin the ending.

J

It begins like this, for example:

He crossed the final frontier with the sun on the page higher than the sky.

Or:

He crossed the final frontier with the moon on the page higher than a sky full of stars.

Or maybe like this:

Between 1967 and 1977, the Canadian pianist Glenn Gould recorded a trio of radial-sonic documentaries—*The Idea of North*, *The Latecomers*, *The Quiet in the Land*—that he subsequently brought together under the general title *Solitude Trilogy*.

There, Glenn Gould had concerned himself with researching the sound of "the absolute isolation of the world" and had presented it as "about as close to an autobiographical statement as I'm probably going to make at this stage of my life."

There, Glenn Gould recording the silent voices of the tundra and the taiga in arctic landscapes until he attained what he called "The Idea of the North": the notion of an absolute and unmapped emptiness in which everything fit and which was the ideal place to "dream about, spin tall tales about, and, in the end, avoid."

Remembering all of that, he wondered if now he might not be experiencing its flipside, its complementary opposite, the other part of the plan for finding the treasure: *The Idea of the South*.

Something that began deserted and windy and slow to, all of a sudden, begin to fill up with the speed of his things. Memories, influences, readings, visions—including that one thing that he only wished to forget, knowing it to be the most impossible of wishes—until there was no longer any free space left for the unconditional yet unchained prisoner that he'd become.

What then were the probabilities—certainly minimal, but suddenly maximal—that certain enumerative and referential and fetishistic tools from what'd once been his body of work would, all of a sudden, be imposed on his life? What strange phenomenon made it so that—when he walked into that almost-deserted cantina in Melancholy Rancheras to order a mezcal in whose bottle a worm smiled a smile that no designer of emojis could ever distill—a radio (one of those radios that haven't been around for decades and that seemed to be there, broadcasting, from decades in the past) was on and playing, one after the other "Shine On You Crazy Diamond" by Pink Floyd, "Series of Dreams" by Bob Dylan, "A Day in the Life" by The Beatles, and "Big Sky" by The Kinks? How was it possible that, all of a sudden, he heard those songs there, all together and outside of time and space, as if an omnipresent and invisible DJ were looking at him and only him while, on the screen of a cubic and ancient television almost hanging above the bar, news was breaking about a new sighting of a possible "extraterrestrial space object"? Where had that mysterious, black "celestial body"—floating in space and christened by someone (by whom? who decided these things and who gave them that authority?) as Oumuamua or Ummagumma or something like that—come from and where was it going? Were its eight hundred by eighty meters and its exceedingly irregular shape dreaming that, once they'd sculpted its angles, the most melodious of monoliths would emerge from inside it? How could he not think that all of that symbolized something and—whatever it was—that what it signified was something of great significance for him, now, here, crossing borders that he would never cross again in the opposite direction? Were these kinds of episodes, happening on this side of things, in what was presumed to be reality, the disconsolate consolation prize for someone who, as he was no longer writing, only had left the illusory illusion of feeling that he was writing himself, respecting or resembling, more or less, what he'd once understood and recognized as his style? Had all those questions marks—like fish or meat hooks—maybe come to skewer him and drag him out of the heavy darkness of that cantina and throw him outside, under a lunar and lunatic sun that rose last night and seemed to be singing to him about how he was so far from the land where he was born?

The Idea of the South? The Bad and Awful Idea of the South? The Invented and Dreamed and Remembered Idea as final destination and the end of all things? And how was it possible that that monolithic piece of news, of a spatial rather than a local color—one of those pieces of news typically used to separate the supposedly important political news and the, without a shadow of a doubt, transcendent sports news, amid so many infographics and holograms that seem to turn those shows into a kind of videogame of supposedly real reality—was suddenly interrupted by an apocalyptic, last minute EXTRA / BREAKING NEWS bulletin, some truly *end of the world news* where there appeared the image of the face, very blurry and apparently bellowing, as if howling at closed-circuit security camera, of someone who reminded him of someone of somebody of something of him?

Or if not:

Behind was the world of the others; ahead awaited nothing more and nothing less than the rest of his life.

And nothing led him to believe that what was behind him was far more expansive than what was yet to be known and yet to come. So much to remember, so little to dream, and in the meantime, between one extreme and the other, to invent while he still can, he thought.

What'd been no longer was and, as such, would never be. And he had to make a considerable effort to forget it: because it was too heavy, because it was made up of too many heavy regrets.

Then, now, beginning again only to come to an end, he says to himself.

As if by the art of magic.

Like in one of those tricks for which the magician asks for a volunteer from the audience.

Now, he was magician and volunteer and, yes, both at the same time.

And that was the great trick.

The greatest trick of all.

Todo por aquí y todo por allá.

Abracadabra.

Or maybe:

Not long ago, on the most jagged peaks of his insomnia, he'd tried a medication (its name didn't matter in the same way that a time always came when the names of ex-girlfriends didn't matter: ex-girlfriends and ex-medications all end up the same irrespective of their hypothetical function, pleasant or placebo, in a given moment). An experimental medication still in the testing phase that a psychiatrist friend gave him and that would supposedly help him sleep. In the drafts of its informational pamphlet—regarding "possible side effects"—he'd read something that'd caught his attention and that he'd found a little amusing. "Taking this medication can sometimes produce strange dreams."

Excuse me?

A medication for insomnia that warned of the possibility of having "strange dreams"? What dream wasn't strange? Was there anything stranger than dreams?

What's more: was there anything stranger than reality, anything stranger than this reality that he was waking up to now and that—desert, magnificent telepathic green cow—seemed like the strangest and most memorable of dreams?

Or in few but just the right words:

He was on his way—because he'd finally realized that you can't change or correct the past, but that you can modify and amend the future—to redeem the indelible memory of that night with this unforgettable day.

Or to end beginning:

If all of this were being written, it would be the third and final part of a third and final book. Not the revelatory conclusion of a linear trilogy advancing in a single direction through time and space. No. Rather, yes, something more reminiscent of a triptych: something that would fold in on itself with the mechanism of a divider or partition or taboret or screen. And that would overlay thoughts with actions, memories with predictions, reflexive repetition with calculated insistence. And on like that, until it achieved the beautiful and surprising *grand style* of the depths of many marvelous moments seen all at one time. A magnum opus of thousands of pages for him to climb up onto to look out across the landscape, but, at the same time, glancing back over his shoulder in case someone tries to push him into the void. Yet actually knowing himself to be totally and absolutely alone, there above, where, for good or ill, he alone had arrived; feeling so Glenn-Gouldianly *avoided* and frightened of nothing more than the exceedingly tempting impulse he felt to take one step forward and execute himself by executing the most fatal and swan-songing of swan dives.

The first of those books already written and published, historical and true.

And the two remaining books—projected by that same book like its luminous shadows—now impossible to write perhaps because he'd spent so much time thinking about them.

He'd invented and dreamed and remembered them across every one of his pages.

He'd read them in his imagination so much that it no longer made any sense even to try to put them in writing.

In any case, thinking of how it would all come to an end, that third part of the third book—unlike the first two, to which he'd devoted one year each—should be written at top speed, as if he were seeing it rather than reading it. Not the climax of everything that'd come before but the climax of that climax.

Again: fragments, instants, moments.

But this time more or less composed and recomposed as the accelerated particles and interlinked cells of the *journal* of a *hazardous journey* in *complete darkness* and *constant danger*. As if this third and final part of the final and third book ("Same as it ever was . . . Time isn't holding up . . . Time is an asterisk . . . Same as it ever was . . . Same as it ever was . . . Same as it ever was . . . Same as it ever was . . . Same as it ever was . . . Same as it ever was . . . Same as it ever was . . . Yeah, the twister comes . . . Here comes the twister . . .") were screaming its own song from inside the center of a tornado ceaselessly spinning around on itself.

A tornado that'll never turn back and here it comes.

And so, the fuel of memory feeding, at last, the engines of the present, because, as someone once said, "There is no present or future—only the past, happening over and over again—now."

He'd heard that line, once, on a stage, coming from the mouth of an actor or actress. He didn't remember the name of the play or its author, but he did remember that, at the time, hearing that, it was as if someone had thrown a dagger that'd pierced his heart or his brain, either way.

That's why he rarely went to the theater.

He wasn't all that interested in actors either. He felt some pity for them. All of them trying now to survive in a world in which everyone—in addition to feeling like writers—also felt like actors of themselves, of their own lives: ceaselessly performing and presenting them. Yes, it was true: *all the world's a stage and all the stage's a screen*. And there was no longer any line between actors and audience and there were so many plays in which "average people" narrated their regrets and joys. And that's what Charles Chaplin was referring to in a preface that, in the end, wasn't included in his 1964 autobiography, where he warned that: "In this record I shall tell only what I want to tell, for there is a line of demarcation between oneself and the public. There are some things which if divulged to the public, I would have nothing left to hold body and soul together, and my personality would disappear like the waters of the rivers that flow into the sea." Now, it was clear, nobody really cared about being a soulless body, so long as there was somebody there ready to watch and listen to them.

The theater (something similar happened to him with poetry, poetry that was the realm of poets, poets who were like electrified fiction writers and as if struck by a lightning bolt that never ceased and how terrible and glorious it must be to live like that, poetic all the time, he thought; poetry that mysteriously and incomprehensibly had found a way to convince all languages that it could be translated from its original language without losing its meaning or accuracy, poetry that, though cryptic, was so memorizable, far more so than novels or stories unless those novels or stories were the ones that were learned and recited in the final pages of *Fahrenheit 451*; poetry that could articulate absurdities and lies like *"childhood is the kingdom where nobody dies"*; poetry that contained some poems that, it terrified him to think it, might just be the distillate of the best and most indispensable parts of excessively long novels; poetry whose rules and virtues he never ended up understanding and enjoying beyond the little pleasure he got from the rhymes in, if possible, better, songs) pained him, it was bad for him, it always had been, even, not "true-to-life," but, yes, "true" theater: he was struck and even frightened by the idea of people repeating speeches from memory and trying to convince everyone and convince themselves that they were occurring to them on the spot. And he would never understand that whole thing of one person saying something and having to *wait* for someone else to say something to, only then, be able to say something again. And it didn't seem fair to him that actors and people "of the world of the spectacle" were allowed to have nervous breakdowns and were forgiven for everything they'd done and then given the chance to start over from zero (while writers only had access to creative crises, relatively unseen crises with limited anecdotal power, that nobody cared about and that didn't entitle them to anything: he'd lost the ability to write, and so what?). And yet—once in a *great* while—the theater had that unsettling effect on him that he'd experienced when he heard the line about the past being something that happened over and over again. And that effect was achieved in public, in front of other people (while the great moments in the life of a writer, his or her sudden epiphanies, always took place in private). Though, if given a choice, he would rather read it than hear it from the mouth of a stranger with dubious clarity and oracular diction. He would rather hear by it reading it in his own voice. *To be* Hamlet rather than *not to be* Hamlet, and without having to see or listen to another Hamlet who isn't Hamlet either: who was merely someone *playing* Hamlet, trying to convince the audience that he was convinced that he was the best Hamlet of all, competing against past and future Hamlets (in film it was different, it was *elsewhere*, it was *far away*, the effect was more tolerable for him, film was like reading images: the actors weren't there, they were giant mirages, they were flat planes of light and they didn't get offended or lose focus if someone in the audience spoke or got up and left before the show was over; even more, better still, if all of it was in black and white and if all the actors were already dead). Yes, he remembered, for example, that William Faulkner (who'd spent some time in Hollywood, emptying bottles and whom he'd read little and badly, perhaps badly influenced by Nabokov's strong opinion about how everyone who made such a big deal out of Faulkner and his Idea of the South had fallen victim to "an absurd delusion as when a hypnotized person makes love to a chair") had formulated a similar idea. Something about how the past was never dead and that it wasn't even past or something like that. Faulkner had written it in a novel, but the novel was composed—formally—as if it were a play.

And again: there was something truly sick or really idiotic in that, he thought. There was something completely *mad* in the very idea of the theater and in the mystery that several of his favorite writers—Henry James and Saul Bellow and Kurt Vonnegut and Vladimir Nabokov among them—had at some point taken the risk of writing plays that, in general, had been resounding failures. He felt the same thing when he saw a writer blathering in public or a priest claiming he was performing a transmutation of blood into wine—or was it the other way around, he wasn't entirely sure. An urge to get out of there and go home and shut himself in and bolt the door from inside.

He'd always thought that certain things should be done alone and always in that personal and secret voice you use when you think or read in silence.

And he was sure that the greatest performers of his work were (or had been) his books.

And that there was no point in going out to represent them, to talk about them, instead of letting them speak for themselves when they were read.

And so, his only more or less proximal exposure to the radiations of the genre of the theater had taken place ages ago yet as if it were yesterday: during his childhood, in that grade-school adaptation of William Shakespeare's *A Midsummer Night's Dream* under the direction of his Teacher of Artistic Activities in the classrooms of Gervasio Vicario Cabrera, colegio n°1 del Distrito Escolar Primero. He didn't remember much about the performance that, in the end, was never performed due to extenuating circumstance (the disappearance of his Teacher of Artistic Activities along with the disappearance of his parents, in a single performance—debut and farewell—directed first by the armed forces and later by a cell of parapolice). But he does remember that it was going to be—according to his Teacher of Artistic Activities— "something different and surprising" and that it "would symbolize all those separations of fathers and mothers, seemingly so in vogue these days."

In any case, not knowing in detail what that show would've been like allowed him to know now what it might've been, that's what he limited himself to and that's what it was all about: inventing it and dreaming it as if he were remembering it.

What he did remember very well, on the other hand (what led him to this), was that essay about how to gain enlightenment by moving in the dark, penned by Donald Barthelme.

A text that he'd reread so many times: *Not-Knowing*.

There Barthelme postulated that all processes of creation were a constant and wise *not-knowing* until you came to know. Something that you read as you wrote it and where the writer was transformed into "a sort of lightning rod for an accumulation of atmospheric disturbances, a St. Sebastian absorbing in his tattered breast the arrows of the Zeitgeist." That which—long before but now in absolute synchrony—the *mente meravigliosa* of John Keats had defined in a letter as "negative capability" or "when a man is capable of being in uncertainties."

Now, here, he set out to bring that theoretical essay to its practical debut, but altering that beginning to suit his ends: not so much a *Not-Knowing* as a *Stop-Knowing*.

Something—after so many years of convincing himself that he knew everything only to discover that there was nothing there—that would help him reach what would be a new point of departure.

Something that—after effacing expunging erasing crossing out wiping out obliterating everything he would no longer need—would allow him to achieve pure and simple *Knowing* all on his own.

丁

But—even still, now—he wants to put his whole body and soul into confronting and taking on something like that, something that started out as an idea and then became a certainty. That was why he needed so badly to convince himself that memories could come to be understood as random lines torn out of the pages of others that you want to believe are your own, but that you know you'll never possess no matter how badly you want to.

That's why—in this desert—he's burning them as he reads them, as if he were dreaming them.

Things like "I have some notes here on the general character of dreams. One puzzling feature is the multitude of perfect strangers with clear features, but never seen again, accompanying, meeting, welcoming me, pestering me with long tedious tales about other strangers—all this in localities familiar to me and in the midst of people, deceased or living, whom I knew well) . . . All dreams are affected by the experiences and impressions of the present as well as by memories of childhood; all reflect, in images or sensations, a draft, a light, a rich meal or grave internal disorder." Things like "A writer who likens, say, the fact of the imagination's weakening less rapidly than memory, to the lead of a pencil getting used up more slowly than its erasing end, is comparing two real, concrete, existing things. Do you want me to repeat that? (cries of 'yes! yes!') Well, the pencil I'm holding is still conveniently long though it has served me a lot, but its rubber cap is practically erased by the very action it has been performing too many times. My imagination is still strong and serviceable but my memory is getting shorter and shorter."

Later, when he has finished throwing *Ada, or Ardor*—that alien book (alien in every sense: because it was never his, because it was written by someone else, because he never made it his own by reading it, because he never could, until now, at random and out of order, tearing pages out and staring at them and burning them)—into the fire, he proceeds to burn anything else he can, to provide a little warmth in the freezing desert night.

With respect to him and unlike what would happen in *Blade Runner 2049*, not even what was on paper would endure. Auto-Blackout. FUBAR, yes, but, in a way, functioning perfectly and liberated—*un-fucked up beyond all recognition*—and with a clear way forward after so much time spent motion-less in the shadows.

And so, into the fire with his biji notebooks and his old diaries. He only stops himself from throwing the booklet with Penelope's Karmatic notes and the composition book of advice belonging to He Whose Name Must Not Be Mentioned because he feels that they do not belong to him, that they have been given to him to watch over, like the holy relics of the most crossed-out crusader. As if he were that anonymous crusader who, in the twelfth century, on a quest for the Holy Grail, wrote (another quotation on another page in another of his biji notebooks that now burns) that thing about "Let us seek what we shall not find."

And *not-knowing* once again.

And so—now so far away and in a land where he was not born and that turns out to be impossible to let go of—he tears out his final pages as if they were the wings of something that provoked the envy of what once could fly but no longer can.

And the last epigraph on one of the last pages of his last biji notebook (an epigraph he'd captured the way you capture a butterfly, only to then let it go, because he no longer had a book in which to pin it up and claim it as his own) came from a novel by Joy Williams. And, yes, the subject and the title (with a boy who all of a sudden was no longer where he was supposed to be, which is what led him to open it) was *The Changeling*.

And there it read: "It was the present, it had been the present, and it was always going to be the present."

And, standing in a bookstore reading that book (the line was near the beginning of a novel that'd been condemned and reviled in its day, and then went out of print, and now had been reissued with honors and apologies to Joy Williams; every time he found out about the publication of one of these prestigious amends-making-reeditions he couldn't help but think that maybe, who knows, someday, with any luck or justice, one of his books . . .), he said to himself: "Yes, that's it, this, exactly. Right here, that's me. Right now."

And he thinks about what his new occupation will be from now on and until his revelatory apocalypse: fixing and classifying and even naming—caterpillars, butterflies, pins—everything that happened in the exact instant that it took time and place. In that almost-now/almost-before in which everything begins to become part of the past.

The closest thing to writing without putting things in writing, he thinks, he wants to convince himself, he needs to console himself.

Action after so much time gauging the light and adjusting the camera and thus the "*Longtemps, je me suis couché de bonne heure*" or the "Just go to bed now. Quickly. Quickly and slowly" making time and space for the unexpected change in rhythm and melody of a "Woke up, fell out of bed . . ."

And, then, the entrance of that introductory and orchestral and end-of-the-world sound.

And an immemorial yet unforgettable Song singing—Oh, Muse—of a man of multiform wiles or of many paths, who wandered long and saw many cities and learned the customs of many men and whose soul suffered a great many toils, imprisoned by the terrible wrath of his dead yet immortal sister.

And so he also promised himself (or promised that he would at least try) from now on not to weigh himself down with so many quotations, with so much excess baggage, with so many voices harmonizing or disharmonizing with his own.

The time had come to travel light, to fly free.

And in that way to be able to specify what'd already happened and what'd been rewritten so many times by his memory—if possible, along the way—as if shaking off this sound like a litany to finally opt for something more direct and functional and sharp; and "Striptease: getting naked 24 hours a day here," announced a sign as soon as he crossed the final frontier, as if inviting him to rid himself of things as he changed languages.

But, it tends to happen, what happens next—while what was yet to happen readied itself to happen—is something he remembers.

Something that took place not long ago, but that, remembering it now, happens to him almost in this instant, just as he remembers it.

For now, and for what future he has left—he decides as if he were a samurai feeling already dead before entering into combat—the past won't be anything but the part behind the present.

What's right behind him.

Remembering everything that happened to him as if it'd just happened to him even though it took time and place in another millennium.

7

He remembers that other night (same time and same place) and here it comes again now.

Falling prisoner of his free fall.

Downward bound funicular; but now on a one-way descent with no return ascent. The return of The Lonely Man is the departure of The Lonely Man. Before the sun came up and everything would be cast in that white summer light. A blazing brilliance, like that of an atomic bomb that exploded five minutes ago, rising from the edges of a wave-less sea. A radioactive glow that stripped bones and tore away skin as if it were a fruit peel.

Then, not long ago, the funicular (a word that came from the Latin *funiculus* or "cord" and that, then and now, was the rope around his neck) like a Dunkirk ship, like a Saigon helicopter. "Not a save yourself but a save me," he thinks, thinking of the Vietnamese on an embassy roof and the Brits in the shallows of a beach. And he remembered too that—in those ever more precise documentaries with ever more material available regarding what'd happened only discovered decades later—he'd heard testimonies from veterans of those evacuations. And that, beyond the dates and the nationalities, they all said the same thing: that, at night, so much time later, they still heard the sound of the propellers and sirens coming to rescue them. And that they referred to it by the same name: "the dream in the wind."

Retreat and evacuation as if in a trance but waking up.

Because to escape was to stop dreaming of escape.

And the sound of the funicular that, no doubt, came to remind him of all of that which, in the very moment it happened, he wanted to forget.

His descent without ascent.

For one last time to be narrated with slight variations—perhaps improvements—so many times hereafter.

Because the last times tend to be the ones that count, the ones most recounted, and the ones that are repeated over and over again as if they were always the first of the last times.

Not like that other time, on that unique and singular and unrepeatable night (but a night when so many short stories—today they would be called flash fictions—occurred to him as if they were evasive maneuvers) when he also went down as if he were falling.

In that same funicular, from his house to the emergency room of a clinic, and thinking then of the funicular as the mechanical version of the angel of death (thinking too about what'd happened to Vladimir Nabokov, in 1975, near the end of his life, lying at the bottom of a Swiss ravine where he'd fallen while chasing alpine butterflies, on his back and unable to get to his feet, his net caught on a branch, and the passengers in a cable car waving to him and mocking him and mistaking him for a drunk tourist and ignoring that that fall was nothing less than the beginning of the writer's farewell).

Then, like now, events precipitated and his heart (which, they say, is the size of a fist) felt as if gripped by a fist. But the fist of a giant, squeezing it down to the last breath and beat and word. Or, at least, that's what he felt, as if he were departing forever: *exit*, curtain, *adieu*, *finis*.

Something like that.

The last word of that writer he'd ceased to be and who no longer even considered himself an exwriter and who'd collected the last words of writers (like those of James Joyce, who said goodbye with a "Does nobody understand?"). And maybe, there and then, Joyce (sensing how in the next room they were mixing the plaster for his death mask that would make him look so un-Joycean) was laughing last and best at everyone who'd considered him incomprehensible and at everyone he'd never tried to comprehend for the love of art and because he didn't want to. Or maybe what the Irishman had felt was pure and definitive and inconsolable sorrow, who knows.

Of one thing he was certain: nobody had understood him while he was alive and everything seemed to indicate that, in death, not only would they not understand him, but, moreover, they would opt for that easier and more functional and far crueler solution applied to so many writers who not only no longer wrote but who could no longer even think about not writing: to be forgotten and on to something else. Condemning him to that limbo where a writer becomes the ghost of his own books, books that nobody enters anymore, as if they were haunted mansions that nobody believed in. Mansions that they demolish without a second thought or fear, in order to, in their place, erect forgetting palaces: a hotel or a shopping mall that doesn't include a bookstore among its shops that sell electronic devices to be consumed by dislocated consumers who wander through those places convinced that they have nothing better to do. Nobody, not one of them, with a book in hand. All of them so far removed from those not-so-remote but yes irretrievable days. Days when people took books (some of them wearing a leash and muzzle, because they were books of unpredictable behavior and sometimes dangerous and sharp-toothed and biting books) out on walks, because they refused to leave them home alone and because they wanted to feel in good company.

And he remembers again—The Lonely Man, during that other agonizing ride in that same funicular, downhill, heading to that clinic—that, when it came to the idea of choosing a book for the waiting room or the intensive care unit or for the death bed, he'd selected *Tender Is the Night* by Francis Scott Fitzgerald: the favorite novel of his vanished and disappeared parents.

A novel whose characters first rewrite and then erase themselves until all that's left is their memory in the memories of those who knew them and who, on more than one occasion, would've preferred not to have known them or, at least, to have stopped knowing them before their fall and when they were still at their peak, before they became unrecognizable.

His parents, he thinks, never had time to rewrite themselves or not recognize themselves like Dick and Nicole Diver in Fitzgerald's novel, because they were erased before they got the chance.

By him and by Penelope.

But now, on the other hand, he'd wanted a far more functional book for his definitive flight. A book that would be good company for several of his biji notebooks, overflowing with quotations, for Penelope's booklet of notes with the label that read *Karma Konfidential*, and for that composition book titled—in the childish yet serious handwriting of He Whose Name Must Not Be Mentioned—*Master Advice of a Man Who Sleeps on the Floor*.

So he looked for something he could open to any page and close at any moment without losing the plot or character development or logical coherence.

Something closer to the I Ching than to the Bible.

Something wise and oracular and far from the chaos of faith in things unseen.

And so, *Strong Opinions* by Vladimir Nabokov (which the French, who gave new titles to everything, even Nabokov, had retitled, he remembers, *Intransigeances*; and, of course, along the way, he would buy himself a new edition of *Ada, or Ardor* with, if possible, a new and different cover).

There, in *Strong Opinions*, interviews of and intransigent articles by and letters to and from Nabokov. And, among them, abundant insults and condemnations of colleagues (Joyce was one of the few spared from the massacre) meticulously meted out by the universal and extraterrestrial Russian, from his suite in the Montreux Palace Hotel in Switzerland.

Questions like pins and answers like butterflies.

Or the other way around.

In any case, of course, Nabokov responds—the secret of any good interviewee confronted with a bad interviewer—there with whatever occurs to him or whatever he wishes to say irrespective of what he was being asked about.

And, in an aside about the comings and goings of his lepidopterous explorations (he read this paragraph in the moment he was awaiting the arrival of that final funicular; and it was clear that books were living organisms attentive to the needs or the sorrows of those who opened them and opened themselves up to them), Nabokov explained, as if he were talking to him, there and then, that "My favorite method of locomotion, though, is the cableway" and that "Some day the butterfly hunter will find even finer dream lore when floating upright over the mountains, carried by a diminutive rocket strapped to his back."

And he—as always happens to him with and around Nabokov—feels so seen and understood. Nabokov as style as plot and—now more than ever—the complicit wish for a rocket pack that would allow him to take off and fly away. And he felt so sympathetic to Nabokov's antipathies (for telephones, jazz, psychoanalysis, "social" gatherings, televisions, odontology, motorcycles and automobiles, the paintings of Chagall, and the theories of Freud) because he shared them. And, on the side of his affinities, not his fascination with nymphets and butterflies or his supposed and dubious legend as soccer goalie or chess player, but, very particularly, his understanding of collective reality as an uninteresting physical space and very overrated as literary subject matter. And his distrust and incredulity with respect to the idea of time, and his perception of the occupation of the writer as similar to that of a detective, devoted to solving the mystery of literary structures. Thus—outside of all chronogeographical coordinates—not the body in the library but the library as immortal investigation in itself, as a hermetic forever-open case, where, if things weren't done right, if you wrote poorly, you could end up victim or victimizer.

A library like the one in the house that he's leaving behind now never to return. A library that includes all those books by William Faulkner (who'd proposed for his epitaph a "He made the books, and he died" and, in an interview, claimed that "It is my ambition to be, as a private individual, abolished and voided from history, leaving it markless, no refuse save the print books") that he never read or even tried to read and all those copies of *Ada, or Ardor* that, in vain, he did try to read. A library that's not turning him into a true exile; because up until now he'd only been an *émigré* because, for him, an *émigré* was an exile who had enough time to pack up his library.

Now, he didn't have time and he left behind that library (that library that, for him, had always been a portable homeland, something like those boxes full of Transylvanian dirt that Dracula—again, never forget: the fault never lay with the monster but with whoever offered him something to drink by inviting him in—needed to bring with him so he could rest in the most bloodthirsty peace of all) with a house all around it: he left it behind forever, there inside, the way you leave behind the dead body of a library in a house.

J

And how do you say goodbye to a library? By taking a brief yet deeply grateful bow, there, in that study where he wrote little and next to nothing and read a lot and almost everything.

That study with that circular window (that, right away, had reminded him of those pods with bone-crushing arms in *2001: A Space Odyssey*) in the attic of a remodeled modernist tower.

One of Penelope's houses, yes.

A house that she never got around to burning down (because Penelope had burned in a deluxe mental hospital), but that had less and less time until it would be burned down by others: those savage patriots now ascending the mountainside, coming for him.

A house that'd once been a second home for a family of the local aristocracy.

A summer home for people who lived in the city at the foot of the mountain and who installed themselves here, throughout July and August, back in days when the locals were the only tourists. Days maybe not better (people's lives were shorter and passed more quickly and they died more quickly and much younger) but in whose skies those cheap airplanes available to everyone weren't yet flying and in whose seas those luxury cruises larger than a town weren't yet filling up the port. Seaborn or airborne vessels from which descended—like infected rats jumping from the deck of the *Demeter* in *Dracula* or pouring out of that contagious 747 in *The Strain*—hordes of invaders ready to be fruitful and multiply and brandishing selfie-sticks. On the attack and ready to drink and shit and puke in streets—in that city that never slept and never let you sleep—where they were allowed to do everything they couldn't do in their own countries. And they were so happy in their libertine liberty that some stayed forever. They stuffed themselves into T-shirts with labels and colors advertising where they'd come from or where they'd come to (and to avoid reading them, he invented different logos that he found clever for about as long as one of those pills designed to aid slow digestion took to dissolve, names like *BADcelona* or *ARGHentina* or *MADcelona* or *BUEHnos AYYYres* or *sPAIN* or *EmPAÑA*) and that standardized all origins and destinations with those absurd and entirely out-of-place mariachi sombreros that were sold on the streets of the city center alongside the uniforms of millionaire soccer players stitched and hawked by the poorest of "illegal" immigrants. And so, with that look that he preferred not to see, they crammed by the dozen into small apartments out of which the owners had expulsed their lifelong tenants to make room for those turbulent and tempestuous travelers. And there were even small battles in the streets between visitors and locals within the context of another great political battle being waged between independentists and constitutionalists, or something like that.

And among those who came to install themselves in the city there featured, always, a handful who also had the fantasy that here—just like Maxi Karma had once believed—they would finally become the writers they'd always aspired to be, due to an alchemy of diffuse magic and inconsistent efficacy and more similar to the lottery and to other games of pure chance where expertise was a far more decisive element than talent. Because, yes, drop in and take a look and have a listen: this was a city that "historically" had always welcomed writers. And its "cultural movers" had spent more than half a century selling that mirage as if it were an oasis.

One thing was true, he thought: it was a great city for writers, because it had both sea and mountains. And, for that reason, writers didn't even need to think about "Uh, I should get out of the city for a while and go to the sea or to the mountains." There was no need: all you had to do was open the windows to the east or west, or take a fifty-minute walk and your conscience would already be clear and you could go back and shut yourself in the study to keep on writing and he no longer wrote, but he lived on top of the mountain and could look out at the sea.

But it was also true that that ancestral and nineteenth-century Grand Tour that European students went on to see the world and learn languages and look sidelong at naked statues, as well as the *paseíllo* of the nouveau-riche American heirs to hook impoverished and decadent but titled nobles—a rite of passage that'd inspired so many good novels—here and now had become something different with different applications in this city.

Now what prevailed was the ravenous rush to secure an agent and a publisher and a laudatory blurb for their book jacket penned by some consecrated name and a potentially consecrating prize. And so, mornings spent in professional meetings, afternoons at book launches, and nights at the latest designer bars or at slightly vintage sanctuaries of bygone youths, where all elements of the profession got together to drink as if the world—or, at least, the drinks—were about to end. A scene that reminded him a bit of the final pages of *Le Temps retrouvé*: where all the characters appeared together, masked or wrinkled, and ready for the final farewell, like at the end of *The Porky Pig Show* with that song that starts out mournful but then gets almost hysterical.

And he remembered everything that kept happening with the authority of someone who'd been there and been part of all of it, until he got tired of it so he wouldn't have to think that it 'd gotten tired of him.

But, every so often, he made brief and cautious incursions onto those—less and less fiery but always more or less flammable—fields of learned and lettered battles. Just to see how it was all going, to verify that everything was still the same on those groundhog nights. Some of them were a bit surprised that the bookseller's prize of this supposedly welcoming city had never been given (in fact none of them had even been considered worthy of being a finalist) to any of them, not even to past Nobel winners, who'd arrived there and wrote in the same language. Others were still there in hopes that their cups would be refilled. And many (especially those born in his now nonexistent country of origin, at the end or the beginning of that always-quaking continent) had beat a retreat forever when they realized that it would be far easier and better remunerated to triumph in their respective birthplaces. To fight to become the Great National Writer (a nonviable project in almost any country no matter its size; but improbable and almost absurd in a state of a rather stateless nature like his now nonexistent country of origin) would always afford greater recompense than killing yourself to be a minor foreign writer who would never be considered on par with the locals though he'd been there for years. And, if things didn't go well, there were always the family businesses back home.

Yes: he'd verified a while back—and he might've put it in practice if he'd had somewhere to return to—that it turned out to be more advantageous for foreign writers to dock here for two or three years, make a small emotional/visual impression on the locals, return to their point of origin, and come back every so often to visit, after triumphing in their own lands. And in that way—now, yes—even end up winning some local prize and gracious tribute for having gone back on the other side of the ocean to preach the gospel of this city as something like the literary heart of the world. A sanctuary that could never be forgotten—and this was very important—because it was here that they "had become writers," riding in the wake of the primordial gods of the Boomthulhu and all of that. Suctioning and asphyxiating and viscous offspring sprouting all manner of appendages. Amorphous and indistinguishable the ones from the others, always latching on to someone who could give them a little push up the hill, so they could continue their ascent. Sticky social-climbers. With that accomplished ambition of those who have no talent of their own to bring to the table. Nothing to do or to read with the aristocratic singularity of the vampire who selects whom to vampirize or the possessive demon who chooses whom to possess. Just the opposite: something massive and corporate. Here, in this city that was also the reiterated and proud home to the biggest and most important and most global of mobile-phone conferences: mega event that every year is given far more importance and coverage than any literary festival. And, no doubt, somebody was already writing a novel that took place during those days in which the entire city appeared to succumb to a tele-tech virus; probably a more or less close relative to those imported heroes who hadn't written much during their time in the city. A young writer who would be awarded for his last name and for contributing to maintaining, so that it would never melt, the burning memory and the glacial breath of the ice; not the ice in the stalls of a gypsy-magic festival, but the ice in glasses to be filled to the brim on nights ready to explode, amid the din of whistles and timbales, in the most self-satisfied and mythomaniacal of booms.

That hadn't been and wouldn't be his case, of course; because the only thing that might end up mattering to the cultural curators and locals with respect to his life—more than to his work—was that he was Penelope's brother. And that Penelope had spent a brief and frenetic period in the city as part of the local fauna at the suddenly legendary but now disappeared Psycholabis Bar (because she drank and got high there; and because, luckily the authorities weren't aware of it, it was there that Penelope met Maxi Karma, the involuntary and comatose father of He Whose Name Must Not Be Mentioned). A refuge of the underground where today there was a shop that rented and sold those Segways that tourists floated around on while checking their mobile phones and running over old people. And, of course, now there were even books devoted to detecting impossible "coded" allusions to the city in Penelope's books. And the travel agencies even offered a "Penelope Tour" that ascended, exceeding the maximum capacity of the funicular, up to his house (to the house that actually belonged to Penelope; the house whose door he now closed never to open again, as if it were one of his too many copies of *Ada, or Ardor*), to take pictures and scare away the wild boars when they tried to take pictures next to them: the wild boars who now watched him take off running and recognized him and accompanied him in his flight.

丁

Those wild boars that went in and out of the forest and roamed along the paths that wound around the ridgeline, attacking the rectangular cubes of garbage (ones climbing on top of others, like a circus performance) and, between scornful and absorbed in masticating anything they could, staring back at the people who stared at them.

There.

Four wild boars.

Two adults and two little ones: a family, like the one he self-destructed in his childhood, like the family he never had as an adult.

Four wild boars near the doors to the funicular station. There they were, beside the entry to the "*funi*," as it was referred to by the local kids who rode it up and down and took off running out of the cars that went up and down.

Wild boars with a kind of suicidal tendency they don't recognize as such (and, oh, he thinks, what an awful state not writing has gotten him into that he's going around assigning suicidal tendencies to wild boars) and just experience as an openness to any possibility that, perhaps, will end up closing in on them forever.

Like him now.

Expulsed.

Fleeing.

It's not the first time.

In fact: he could even understand and organize his life into a series of expulsions.

One inside another, like Russian dolls or Chinese boxes, ever larger or ever smaller, depending on the order and direction from which you look at them and swallow them and spit them out.

Expulsions some of which, were he to list them, he would likely forget.

There were so many that, no doubt, at least one of those expulsions had been expulsed.

Expulsed from his now nonexistent country of origin.

Expulsed from so many beds and anthologies.

Expulsed from a colossal Swiss particle accelerator across the lake from where Vladimir Nabokov wrote *Transparent Things* (those particles, those transparent things, with which he wanted to merge, interlinking their cells, while they centrifuged from point A in Geneva to point B in Gran Sasso; dreaming that he was transformed into Point X, the divine manipulator of all plotlines in the world, and that the cosmos with all its galaxies would be but a blue drop in the palm of his hand and would thereby eliminate, for him, all terror of the infinite). *Transparent Things* narrated in the voice of the dead who find themselves more alive than ever. And, yes, in one way or another, Vladimir Nabokov always returned to the subject of The Beyond, but he did so without hysteria or anxiety and with the assuredness of one who knows he'll be admitted into any possible heaven by merely showing the genius stamps on his passport. For Vladimir Nabokov, The Beyond—his *potustoronnost*—was nothing but the persistence of the immortality of Art. Art was the uncorrupted and incorruptible soul.

He, on the other hand, had known he was soulless for a long time now. His passport had expired and he was defeated and now, again, he was being expulsed from a place that people thought of as Edenic, but that, for him, not so much, never had been.

Expulsed now from that city that was supposedly welcoming to foreign writers (he remembers how the Latin American variety of the species tended to herd together every so often for group photos that would be published in the newspapers, sometimes even at the feet of a statue of Cristopher Columbus, pointing in the wrong direction, toward the Indies that he wanted to arrive to on the other side); but the truth was that they'd never really put up with him that well, they'd never considered him sufficiently eccentric or picturesque, they'd never really known what shelf to put him on or how to categorize and define his increasingly extraterrestrial books.

But the expulsion expulsing him now is the final and definitive and—from a purely anecdotal perspective, he can't help rate it like this—perhaps the most arch and absurd expulsion of all.

This last and definitive expulsion was an expulsion by "political mandate."

And he'd never taken any interest in politics, because politics had taken too much interest in him during his childhood, in his now nonexistent country of origin, transforming him, for everyone, into a child of *desaparecidos*, when the truth was he'd been a *desaparecedor* of parents.

That's why he'd left and that's why he hadn't been back: because he'd never "politicized" himself as a writer. He never wanted to. Politicizing yourself made you a bad reader and committed you to writing badly. The only social cause writers should be concerned with was that of offering alternate histories and interesting characters to a society sunk in a History that was generally very poorly written and always overflowing with stupid personas, many of whom belonged precisely to the political species. For him, reality was always toxic and politics were poisonous and there was no effective antidote (even though, in its day, *National Industry* had been deemed, both by its defenders and its detractors, as "a new way of making political fiction").

That was also why he'd come here—"So I have sailed the seas and come . . . to B . . . ," as one of his favorite stories with his favorite story title began—where politics, for years now, was nothing but a whisper between politicians happily installed in their positions, stealing everything they always stole with the central governing authority looking the other way or too busy stealing everything they could steal in their own sphere. And in the heights, everyone was happy and down on the plains everyone seemed peaceable.

But now, not so much.

All of a sudden, something had happened: a rupture had taken place in the delicate balance in which all the actors, in their respective roles and parties, automatically overacted their parts, always reciting the same words, in a simulacrum of a debate over ideology and territory that never really went beyond the mildly unsporting or the puppet show.

All of a sudden, there were new parties that'd complicated the theretofore well-oiled, periodically alternating, cast of two. Suddenly, everything was up in the air and uncertain and there was nothing more disturbing than what happened when politics ceased to be obvious and predictable. It was as if, out of nowhere, blank cartridges had been swapped out for live rounds. And what'd previously been a farce that spectators and voters—who only went to vote infrequently, anyway, because elections always fell on Sundays—knew by heart, moving their lips and anticipating, almost synchronously, the picaresque parleys of parliamentarians, had mutated into avant-garde experimental theater, where everyone appeared to have gone mad, howling and making calls to arms.

And so, all of a sudden, battles in the streets and duels on benches and fights between neighbors and family members, theretofore accustomed to the clear and figurative, getting all riled up in the name of cubist abstractions, with angles that wounded and bruised the skin.

And he'd wandered around so disoriented and foreign to all of that like—again and always—Fabrizio at the beginning of *La Chartreuse de Parme*, ignoring the fact that he was drifting through suburbs of the Battle of Waterloo, on the margins of something historical, but fully conscious that his presence didn't mean anything or meant nothing when it came to the evolution or conclusion of the battle.

And he didn't understand anything.

He only thought that nothing interested him less than being independent.

All his life he'd wanted to be dependent: on his agent, on his publisher, on critics, on "the great reading masses."

Literature and its practice were nothing but a complex network of gifts and favors. And he'd always wanted to be on the receiving end of all of them; but the only one he'd been given, in the end, was to be dependent on the copious and exceedingly profitable unforgettable memory of his sister Penelope.

And now, all of a sudden, without ever having benefited from it, he received the punishment—and none of the reward—reserved for all those who profited off of being "committed/engaged" and off of "literature as a sign of the times."

There it was, not him, but his book.

The night before on all the newscasts and this very morning in all the newspapers.

The Impossible Story in the hands of politicians, its cover close-up in videos and pictures, its title in a titular role in headlines and his name in smaller print and once even misspelled by some on-call intern in the editorial office.

There was a small but very high-level functionary in the central government—nothing more and nothing less than the Vice President—making a gift of *The Impossible Story*. His last book, in accordance with the custom of a local ritual on a date stipulated by tradition—to the growing fury of feminists, many of them writers of "*lo feminino*"—when women gave books to men and men gave roses to women.

And so the Vice President presented his book—obediently abiding by the rituals of the region—to the local male authorities, who accepted it with tense smiles facing gusts of camera flashes. But what the Vice President gave them wasn't a book to be read, it was a book to be looked at. A book that could indeed be judged by its cover (there was a photograph of his Mr. Trip on the book's cover) and more and even better by its title: because *The Impossible Story* was a way to signal to the rebels and separatists in the region that theirs was a dream that would never come true, an impossible invention that would never function, a broken toy.

And the Vice President—who was a woman with a somewhat odd aspect—didn't even appear to want to conceal her intention, which clearly struck her as mischievous and clever. The Vice President reminded him of a Japanese manga character, her eyes so big and wide open; or of some kind of precursor to one of the different races inhabiting Tolkien's Middle Earth or its many epigones (he'd never thought of her as entirely human and he suspected that she might be a preview model of a Nexus replicant); or one of those extras with a single line in the films of Fellini who, all of a sudden, approached the camera to look at the audience and blow them a kiss with a *"Ciao, bellissimo!"*

And—most disturbing of all for him—the Vice President always found a way to keep her lips slightly twisted in a version of the Mona Lisa's smile; but hers was a Mona-Lisa smile that didn't arouse the slightest doubt or curiosity regarding what she might be thinking that would make her smile like that. It was a Mona-Lisa smile without translated subtitles or a clarifying caption down below. It was a Mona-Lisa smile that was always smiling—and appearing to make a concerted and more-than-obvious effort to contain a full and sonorous burst of laughter—at the expense of whomever it was smiling at.

In any case, the Vice President (who immediately had to be evacuated from the auditorium, which exploded with screams and threats, to a helicopter that flew her across the regional border) miscalculated the level of atmospheric pressure and never suspected that her stunt with *The Impossible Story* would be the drop that burst the dam and the match that lit the fuse.

And, at first, he couldn't help but feel a little pride at being the reason and cause célèbre for, once again, it to be proven that reality was always being molded by fiction. That literature—that fiction—could still play a starring role on this side of things and function as a trigger sending people out into the streets to start pulling triggers. *The Impossible Story*, yes, had produced a political seism and a historical schism.

But that satisfaction and pride didn't last him more than a couple minutes. And then he was overcome by fear as, on TV, the local politicians set about repeating and condemning his name and repeating over and over that they would never read "that book."

On the daytime TV talk shows in the region, they kept on chewing up and spitting out his last name through clenched teeth, baring their fangs and accusing him of every possible offense, between words like "foreigner" and "parasite" and "agent of the Crown" and "fetish author and ideologue of the oppressor" and—he couldn't help cracking up a little bit at this one—"Judas!" and "the protagonist of the most resounding fall from literary grace since Truman Capote published those random chapters of *Answered Prayers* in a magazine." On those shows, some of the guests—some of them acquaintances of his—held copies of *The Impossible Story* (it was no mean feat, they were heavy; and he couldn't help but wonder if they'd bought them or if the producers of the shows had demanded the publisher send them gratis, probably the latter) with the tips of their fingers, as if they were roadkill. All of them making it more than clear that they hadn't read the book, because they described it as "the true manifesto of the fascists from the capital," written by someone who didn't even know "the language of our republic."

And, yes, on this last point they were right. But he'd always explained that it wasn't that he didn't want to speak it, but that—the same thing happened to him with French or with Mandarin—he no longer had the mental capacity to incorporate a new language into his brain's memory. He already had too much memorable material there, in his memory palace that the revolutionaries were closing in on.

And, if he'd been invited on to debate and defend himself live and in person instead of receiving the attacks from his TV screen, he would've reminded all of them about what Clare Bishop said in *The Real Life of Sebastian Knight* about how the title "must convey the color of the book, not its subject." But it'd been so long since he'd been invited to participate in anything; he was only invited to leave.

Ciao, bellissimo!; and he started to ask himself what to take and what to leave as he watched The Intruders abandon the property without looking back and he emptied his safe and stuffed wads of bills that could well have worn the face of Penelope into a backpack, because (like The Intruders whom she'd hired to torment him with their performances) they belonged to her and her ghost. And he wondered where he'd left his passport and boarding passes/instantly redeemable vouchers for those pending tickets for that article for *Volare* on dead cities.

Then, in the Kingdom's capital, they opted to forego mentioning "*The Impossible Story* affair" or, even, to deny it despite the existence of pictures and videos (to thereby "invisibilize" the bumbling of the Vice President); and no writer from there—just as none from here—came out in his defense *either*, because they had little and nothing to gain and so much and too much to lose in doing so. And, yes, he had to admit that if he were in their shoes he would've done—he would *not* have done—exactly the same thing.

And so, soon the explosions and screams could be heard from down in the city (screams screaming his name that made him feel a little bit like Frankenstein's monster cornered and fantasizing about disappearing into the "vast and wild lands of South America" only to end up, somewhat disoriented, among the eternal ices of something like the Idea of the North).

And down below they lit bonfires that had nothing to do with those of the also traditional Saint John's Eve, but were, rather, the blazes of the eternal and clock-less morning of Saint John's Apocalypse. The flames descending from the sky down to the earth and the firetrucks and ambulances warning everybody that nobody is safe with their sirens intoning their inclusive *we-you we-you we-you* . . .

When the sun went down—he watched the lines of torches winding their way up the hillside, thinking that whole *Qualis artifex pereo!*—they were coming for him.

7

So, now, expulsed from here (he didn't like the names of places in novels; he always preferred the capital initial followed by a period; just like he couldn't stand those novels that imposed the face of the protagonist on readers by putting it on the cover, depriving them of imagining the physiognomies of their own heroes or villains).

Now, on the outskirts of the city of B. and in the neighborhood of V. on the Sierra de C.

And ready to go down in the funicular of V. (longitude of the line 734 meters, altitude P.F. 196 meters, altitude V.S. 359 meters, rise 158 meters, maximum gradient 28.9 %, cars 2, car capacity 50 people and a maximum— never respected—of two bicycles, transport capacity in one direction 2,000 people per hour, speed 18 km/h, cable diameter 30mm, track width 1,000 metric m.m.) from the V.S. station with an intermediate stop at C. de les A., and waiting there for the arrival of the train at the P. del F. stop and from there who knows and . . .

Should he say goodbye to that family of wild boars that'd come to say goodbye to him? Maybe they'd come, them too, to expulse him from the stage by grunting and ramming him with their snouts?

[Exit, pursued by a bear.], instructed that famous stage direction in William Shakespeare's *The Winter's Tale* and it was never entirely clear (unlike the transparency of that other and paternal and vengeful and always demanding to be remembered *Exit GHOST* in *Hamlet*) if a real bear had actually been used in the play's debut or if the animal was "played" by a man draped in a heavy rug with the head of an ursine plantigrade. Did this detail matter in days when the Juliets and Ophelias were cross-dressing men, because that's what the law demanded? Who knows, but he was far more intrigued by those ancient questions than the turbulences of the present and so he'd made his exit, he exited, he was exiting. The truth is that in *The Winter's Tale*, Antigonus made his exit at full speed with an "I am gone forever" on his lips. And he did so obeying that very stage direction—*[Exit, pursued by a bear.]*—which over the centuries had become the way and the euphemism to indicate a character's end (especially a villain's) when they've been struck down by a surprising element (like an in/opportune wild animal), so that the hero didn't have to get his hands dirty with the villain's blood when bringing him to justice. Thus, for example, the crocodile that ended up devouring Hook in *Peter Pan*. But also—perhaps most important from a plot perspective—the fact that it all took place out of sight of the audience allowed for/ justified an unexpected and possible and subsequent return of the villain who the audience already imagined was out of the game and out of dirty tricks.

In any case, was he, now, to *[Exit, pursued by a boar]*?

Was he the villain in the play?

Was he exiting the stage pursued by wild boars?

No, they weren't pursuing him: they are accompanying him, they are escorting him, they are courting him. He lies to himself—or wants to believe—that the wild boars now watch his departure with tears in their eyes. (But maybe the wild boars are weeping, not at his departure, but because the word or the grunt—which not long ago an enthusiastic veterinarian-biologist

- 679 -

described as a "virtual language"—has gotten around that another one of those sporadic crossbow hunting parties was in the offing, organized by the City Council to reduce the population of species number 91 on the ranking of the "100 most damaging and exotic invasive species on the planet.")

But he—who'd learned about this stigma regarding the *Sus scrofa* species from an entry in one of those online encyclopedias—loved them.

And he felt indebted to them.

And as he ran toward the funicular station with his backpack on his back, he whispered to them—with that voice with which you speak to wild animals or domestic babies or wild babies or domestic animals—that they should calm down. He explained to them that, tonight, they weren't the ones being hunted, that he was the prey, and that he was grateful to them for everything.

Because he owed them something.

A great deal, in fact.

Yes.

Something that he couldn't take with him in his carry-on, but that he couldn't leave behind either, because it was unforgettable and heavy and because—as Uncle Hey Walrus would sing, singing The Beatles—"Boy, you're gonna carry that weight . . . Carry that weight a long time . . . Boy, you're gonna carry that weight . . . Carry that weight a long time."

And that was a weight he refused to take on as dead weight.

And few invisible things weighed more than memories.

What he owed to them, to those wild boars, was that they'd been the inspiration for the stories of Cerdic: prince of the wild boars and last bastion of the dynasty of the Porkyngs Oynk-Oynk.

Oh, great Cerdic, direct descendent of that prehistoric wild boar who gave up his bone to be thrown into the air in the novel *2001: A Space Odyssey* by Arthur C. Clarke (in the film it was the bone of a tapir, an animal that to Stanley Kubrick had seemed "more prehistoric"). Glory to Cerdic, successor too of the Erymanthian Boar and the fourth labor of Hercules; and of that other one that Adonis killed; and of that other boar whose body, slain by the Ionian prince Androclos, was the foundation for the city of Ephesus; and of the boar who was the original model for the Chinese zodiac sign and the inspiration for Welsh coats of arms, referred to as the "black beast" on par with Saint George's dragon; and of that inflatable and wild boar that the docile pig from Pink Floyd's *Animals* had transformed into for the live version of Roger Waters's *The Wall* (on whose flanks were written things like "No Fucking Way!" and "Divided We Fall"); and of Jabalix: the one who justly and deservedly and finally killed the Gallic Obelix when Obelix tried to hunt him down and eat him as he'd done to thousands of others like him.

But to tell the truth, it didn't matter were Cerdic came from: the important thing was that Cerdic had come to him.

Cerdic was a wild boar of a long lineage and, actually, his name was Cedric.

But when he invented him as the protagonist in a series of children's stories to put to sleep the small reality and awaken the immense dreams of night, the only recipient for those adventures, delivered in a fairly low voice (because he never put them in writing), had been that now-lost boy with flame-colored hair.

He Whose Name Must Not Be Mentioned.

The Son of Penelope.

The other *desaparecido* in the family.

He'd said "Cedric" and the boy had heard "Cerdic."

And Cedric went and Cerdic stayed.

And the story that he imagined and told the boy was the story of a happy and noble wild boar, white of fur and red of blood, cursed by a maleficent wizard and turned into a blue-blooded prince, married to the most beautiful princess and fervently beloved by his subjects. But, oh, Cerdic got so bored on his throne and in his bed. And Cerdic only dreamed of the return of the Age of the White Boar. Cerdic wanted to go back to being that pig who—along that circuit of about ten kilometers that in the past had been a sewer, in the heights of that city with a view of the sea and, from where he was now persecuted and expulsed and *exit* and *pursued*—frightened cyclists stuffed into increasingly absurd get-ups and students on excursions and flocks of worn-out retirees with shaky legs and diffuse mental states. And, again, tourists were much higher up than Cerdic on the list of the most damaging exotic invasive species on the planet (all of them walking in a daze, not really knowing why they'd climbed up there, to the heights of B., to enter that absurd church or stroll through that ancient amusement park with crazy-expensive tickets and from where they looked down at the city that they only wished to return to so they could continue violating all of its access points).

Yeah.

Okay.

His whole Cerdic thing was no big deal.

He hadn't been aiming for the absolute and Tristrampedic and Shandy compilation of all the wisdom of the world out of a father's love (he wasn't his father) for his son (He Whose Name Must Not Be Mentioned was not his son), and yet . . .

. . . he told all of this to the little boy who listened with the rapt attention of those who had only recently arrived to a world that they still found very interesting.

And the boy had even added new and decisive characters to the myth: the field mouse Hank, the salamander Salada, the sparrow hawk Gabe, and the special human interventions of the bed-addicted Camilo Camito Camoncio, of the spectral Muñeco Flotante, and of the worst magician in the world Pésimo Malini, who (despite his bumbling and purely random misreading of the spells in a book of witchcraft) finally managed to break the curse cast upon the anguished Cerdic and to return him to his feral porcine happiness.

And it was also The Son of Penelope—when the final moment of the adventure arrived—who decided how the final sendoff should unfold.

It would all end—He Whose Name Must Not Be Mentioned almost demanded—with a raging wildfire. With The Great Purifying Fire that the inhabitants of V. feared every summer and that at last came to lay waste to everything.

And so, in the middle of a wild boar hunt, Cerdic and his warriors would make one epic and final charge with their fangs bared.

An apocalypse now.

"Something with an atomic bomb, right," The Son of Penelope had asked. Something to exterminate everyone, something that gets blamed on one of those "acts of terrorism" that everyone is afraid of one day and not the next.

And now and all of a sudden—it occurred to him the way ideas for his work and not for his life once occurred to him—he says to himself that tonight he could also be that bomb.

So, before boarding the funicular—which is now about to arrive, he hears it coming, with that sound of mechanical heartbeats, like the background of one of those, again, he never stopped hearing them wherever he went, Pink Floyd albums—he stepped out of the station for a few seconds.

And he walked over to some dry bushes in the garden of one of the nearby houses (it'd been an extremely dry and rainless spring), and he lights a match and holds it up to the branches and leaves.

And he sees them catch fire and watches the fire move as if it were a dangerous and raging toy. A toy that's nothing like his little wind-up tin traveler (Mr. Trip always with him, in one of the breast pockets of his jacket, next to his heart), but that's like one of those toys that are like playing with fire.

Soon it'll be the hour of the screams and the sirens and the evacuations, he says to himself.

And he steps onto the funicular.

And he descends.

And *exit* . . .

7

. . . and *pursued* by so many things.

Exit and *No Return* and *Gone Forever.*

Or, maybe, he'll end up returning from where he's gone in a different way from how he left and, as such, return as a very different person than who he was when he left.

To be someone else, someone who arrived there without having left.

Something like that.

Something like—nothing more and nothing less than the new and all-powerful and newborn Star-Child—what was once and no longer is the astronaut David "Dave" Bowman.

And of all the many never-entirely explained mysteries in the film *2001: A Space Odyssey,* the one that had intrigued him most, from the first time he saw it until the last time he rewatched it, was the reason for—once HAL 9000 was deactivated—Bowman's immediate departure for the most outer of spaces. He remembers that, back then, in the year of its premiere, his implacable child logic had made him ask—and ask the protagonist—why he didn't stay where he was, aboard the *Discovery One* orbiting Jupiter, and wait for a rescue mission. All his crewmates had died, so he had more than enough provisions, right? What need did he have—what was the secret impulse—to go out and pass through the Star Gate bound for the farthest reaches of the universe through what, he'd thought back then with childish maturity, looked to him like the tunnel at the end of the light? In any case, for him, that was the one definitive moment in which Bowman stopped behaving like a machine—as he'd done up until then, as if he were a primitive model of a replicant—to take the risk of acting like a man.

After seeing the Stanley Kubrick film—almost right away—he'd read the Arthur C. Clarke novel.

And yes: there everything was explained and everything there was quite different.

In his novel, Clarke seemed almost desperate to fill with didactic language everything about which the Kubrick film retained the most empty and nebulous and cosmic of silences. Over the years, he'd read in multiple books about the almost cataclysmic arguments between the science-fiction writer and the film director regarding what should and shouldn't be clear to the spectator. Clarke wanted viewers to see the extraterrestrials and for everything to have a scientific and grounded logic. And Clarke hadn't had sufficient intelligence to understand that, he thought, what interested Kubrick (who was already tiring of Clarke's affinity for the didactic and was toying with the idea of replacing him with less orthodox writers of the genre like J. G. Ballard and Michael Moorcock) was for his film to be like something narrated by a superior and extraterrestrial intelligence and, for that reason, something that could never be entirely comprehensible to the far more inferior human intellect. Thus, not a film about the definitively alien but a definitively alien film.

But there, in his novel, the writer had fully surrendered to the impulse of revealing, in a full luxury of detail (Clarke seemed to be one of those suspects who confessed everything without ever being interrogated or intimidated), the hows and the whys of everything that happened. To begin with, between the singing farewell of HAL 9000 and Bowman shooting off into a maelstrom of shapes and colors, at least three months passed. Long weeks during which Bowman had time to converse via satellite with Heywood Floyd about the flaws in the computer of the *Discovery One* ("We believe we know the cause of your HAL 9000's breakdown, but we'll discuss that later, as it is no longer a critical problem . . . First of all, we must congratulate you on the way you handled this extremely difficult situation. You did exactly the right thing in dealing with an unprecedented and unforeseen emergency") and about the possible nature of the monolith ("Geological evidence proves beyond a doubt that it is three million years old"). And to "take an interest in things" and to make several approaches to the immense and mysterious object (there outside, an XXL version of the Tycho Magnetic Anomaly One); to listen "to classical plays—especially the works of Shaw, Ibsen, and Shakespeare—or poetry readings from *Discovery One*'s enormous library of recorded sounds. The problems they dealt with, however, seemed so remote, or so easily resolved with a little common sense, that after a while he lost patience with them"; to then move on to opera until he "realized that the sound of all these superbly trained voices was only exacerbating his loneliness" and thereafter he only listened to wordless classical music, but nothing by—mentioned are Sibelius and Tchaikovsky and Berlioz and Mozart—Richard Strauss or Johan Strauss and, much less, György Ligeti.

In a way, Bowman ends up resembling Dracula in the solitude of his castle and with such a powerful longing to escape, to know other worlds.

And at some point, according to Clarke, the air started to become unbreathable and the hibernation systems were useless without the help of a computer to watch over them and it would be four or five years until the hypothetical arrival of the *Discovery Two*. Which is why Bowman decides— while also obeying the orders of Heywood Floyd: "Your mission, therefore, is much more a voyage of discovery . . . a reconnaissance into unknown and potentially dangerous territory"—to investigate the nature of the monolith, and when he hovers above it, he discovers that it is something like "the Grand Central Station of the galaxy." And it was from there that "David Bowman had time for just one broken sentence which the waiting men in Mission Control, nine hundred million miles away and eighty minutes in the future, were never to forget: 'The thing's hollow—it goes on forever—and—oh my God!—*it's full of stars!*'"

Then Clarke offered a couple sentences that, reading them, at six years old, make him tremble: "The Star Gate opened. The Star Gate closed."

And he trembled again now, so much time later.

And he opened a door and he closed that door.

And it was perfectly clear to him—he remembers without a shadow of a doubt—what place he'd left a few hours before was, that what was behind him was awash in flame and smoke and screams, like those of primates fighting among themselves: now, he's between drop scenes and frames, and it was as if he were watching himself arrive to the third and final act of the film of his life.

So, he leaves the stage corresponding to the gothic mansion reconstructed stone for stone by his sister Penelope. A mansion that he inherited and that he liked to feel was the equivalent of that intergalactic hotel suite at the end of *2001: A Space Odyssey* (but his library having nothing to do and nothing to read with the library that, Clarke described, "formed an odd selection—mostly rather trashy bestsellers, a few sensational works of nonfiction, and some well-publicized autobiographies. There was nothing less than three years old, and little of any intellectual content. Not that it mattered, for the books could not even be taken down from the shelves").

And the truth is that his house that was Penelope's house had increasingly come to resemble the toxic and asphyxiating lair of one of those serial killers who cover the walls with clippings and pictures and cabalistic symbols and arrows. The scene of a crime, of the greatest crime of all: for that is where his inspiration died, his ability to invent, and even the simplest and least stylistically rigorous literary act of dreaming had been supplanted—spurred on by constant insomnia—by nothing more and nothing less than its memory.

And he also knew where he wanted—emerging as if in a trance—to go and what his next stage to explore was:

Mount Karma, Abracadabra.

And to do there not everything he never did and should have done; but, yes, to carry out a final gesture that might redeem him, after so much immobile invention and so much daydreaming.

Now, at last, all the muscle-action after so much brain-reflection, he says to himself.

Now, everything is going to move and change locations and break apart to be put back together and thereby bring all the written theory of his craft ("He wished, now that it was far too late, that he had paid more attention to those theories of hyperspace, of transdimensional ducts. To David Bowman, they were theories no longer," the unstoppable Clarke continued explaining) to the practice of living, he continued saying to himself.

And remembering too that, after all, there were those who'd interpreted the arrival to Earth of the Star-Child in the final scene of *2001: A Space Odyssey* as the coming of a righteous and executing Master of the Final Judgement.

And, of course, again, an obsequious Clarke had come back to clarify everything in the final lines of his novel. There, that transfigured Bowman orbiting around that "glittering toy no Star-Child could resist" that was "planet Earth with all its peoples" and deactivating with the power of his mind the nuclear projectiles fired by impotent powers to then wait "marshaling his thoughts and brooding over his still untested powers. For though he was master of the world, he was not quite sure what to do next. But he would think of something."

That "But he would think of something" was thought millennia after that other "But he would think of something," in the first and prehistoric pages of Clarke's novel, by "the man-ape of the veldt"—whom, why not, its author wouldn't hesitate to christen Moon-Watcher—freshly *monolithized*, bone in hand, feeling too that "he was master of the world" and "not quite sure what to do next."

"Why not invent writing?" he'd thought back then, when he just over eight years old, rereading that "But he would think of something" (*2001: A Space Odyssey* had been the first book he read in English with the help of a dictionary that'd also helped him decode the lyrics on the back cover of *Sgt. Pepper's Lonely Hearts Club Band*). He thought and remembered that now, thinking about whether he might once and for all reinvent his writing. Thinking about how, maybe, this journey to Abracadabra and Mount Karma was something like an auto-nonfiction auto-writing-workshop: a way to see all those random pieces from a new perspective and, all of a sudden, to be able to glimpse how it would all look with everything in its place, like in those perfect and deceptive-in-their-unattainability illustrations on the boxes of models to be assembled that never looked *like that* when they were assembled.

He hadn't the slightest idea how to make it happen, but—he needed to believe it and believe in himself—he would think of something and, at the moment, he could only think that *He Would Think of Something* would be a great motto to etch into a coat of arms. The other line to consider was *It Was the Least He Could Do*, but not deployed in its kindly construction but in its literal and almost cruel one: having done, in truth, *the least he could*.

And so, he said to himself, as if he were writing it, he would enter Mount Karma more alive than ever to—it was more than possible—not make it out alive.

Or, which was the same thing, again: to emerge unrecognizable, to emerge as someone else, transfigured, his style changed forever.

And it would be fine if that was what happened.

And, if not, he *too*, would think of something.

And, oh, he thought about how much he'd always liked that *other* ellipsis: a single word in *L'Éducation sentimentale / histoire d'un jeune homme* (the subtitle aged, so the title could last forever, he thought; the reverse of what happened with *2001: A Space Odyssey*, where the subtitle retained its mythic youthfulness while the title was already surrounded by wrinkles). There— near the end of the journey of the novel by Gustave Flaubert—the reader was informed about the protagonist, Frédéric Moreau, that "he traveled." And noun and verb and period and new paragraph. And, below in a vague way, Flaubert added that Moreau "tasted the melancholy of packet ships, the chill of waking up under canvas, the boredom of landscapes and monuments, the bitterness of broken friendship." And he doesn't specify exact times or fixed trajectories. Because it wasn't necessary. For Flaubert—and for Flaubert's reader—*le mot juste*, the right word and the precise verb was more than enough. Melancholy and cold and boredom and bitterness were inevitable stops on any journey, on all the most sentimental odysseys. So it made no sense to expand on that, on all of that.

And, yes, many times what he liked most in a writer was everything that he lacked, something that he would never be able to write because it wasn't his; because nobody was waiting for him there, because it was one of those immoveable passages that, at most, he caught a glimpse of out the moving window of the book of another.

And—even though he admired that synthetic "he traveled"—it was impossible for him to travel like that, so light and elegant.

To the contrary, he—expansive, imprecise, already from the very moment of his mortal birth and given to the twists and turns and to taking a spin through X just after departing from A and before ever reaching B—had never really believed in direct trips and in quick access to places from which, no doubt, he would want to book his *departure* within a few minutes of his *arrival.* He didn't like staying still for very long, except when he was writing; and, even then, when he could, he wrote in streaks and gusts and never in a sustained and regular and disciplined way: he'd been able to write thirty pages in a day or not write at all for a whole week.

That writing in motion was the result of his professional deformation in not-so-distant days; when (like when he was starting out) he was writing for one of those glossy travel and good-living airline magazines. For a magazine called *Volare* (like also, back when he was starting out, little to nothing had changed in the system of his relatively recently deceased "discoverer" Abel Rondeau) in which each and every one of his assignments and itineraries had to stretch the given budget to the maximum and to squeeze the full value of the investment out of every trip. That was why—when at *Volare* they finally granted him the honor and privilege of a *real* ticket—he had to make the most out of the trip, to generate the greatest number of possible spaces for more or less subliminal advertising (mentions previously agreed on with clients, but that sounded random in the body of his articles and imaginary travels), as if they were clauses in a marriage or a divorce or a will.

Similarly, each primary destination had to also include multiple secondary and nearby destinations. And so, when he got lucky (or when Rondeau was in a good and generous mood), New York included Brooklyn and even Providence (passing through the locations frequented by Lovecraft and using them as the backdrop for an article on a local restaurant, famous for its menu and preparation of shellfish and tentacles). And when, everything got twisted (the way Rondeau's smile twisted when he announced it), Planicie Banderita implied a detour through the vast spaces of Patagonia, until he arrived to a family diner as "standard and secret code for the *very few*," in the vortex of a stormy paramo called the Pit of the Dead (and better not to find out where that name had come from and why they'd kept it) and where some gauchos with the look of cannibals but with too few teeth were flaying cows alive ("because they're more tender that way, boss") to roast them on red-hot plow discs.

In any case, before he started to actually fly, he'd learned there—in the *Volare*'s editorial office—to fly spatiotemporally with his imagination. Like with the initiations of Marco Polo and Jules Verne and Emilio Salgari. And not to sail like Herman Melville or Jack London, or course. (All those books of his childhood that, also, had been the books of the childhoods of his parents and his grandparents: a multigenerational imaginative formation—heightened by those other books in true Young-Adult mode like *Lord of the Rings, Siddhartha, Fahrenheit 451, On the Road*—that'd been toppled forever, on the cusp of a new millennium, with the arrival child witches and wizards and adolescent vampires attending their schools and hungry and labyrinthian and divergent dystopias in which the adults were the bad guys and, also, featuring the most bizarre hairdos.) *Volare* had been a great training in false nonfictions for his true fictions that would come later. To depart without leaving his desk in the corner of an editorial office, a space where he—and his nine pseudonyms, including women and multiple nationalities and even different sexual orientations—looked at photographs and studied tourist guidebooks and invented more or less realistic comings and goings. In days when there weren't so many cheap tickets and everything was still remote and invisible from a distance, but—even though Google Earth wasn't yet pulsating in the wings, allowing you to look at everything from far away yet so close up—you could still imagine it and make it believable by putting everything that wasn't in plain sight in writing.

Now he was going to bring together the best of both methods: on the way to Mount Karma in Abracadabra, he was going to physically travel to places that were almost so nonexistent that almost all you could do was imagine them.

He'd planned a trio of stops as thematic introductions, like previews of the twilight, before he dropped below the horizon line forever.

He was going to make use of a ticket reserved for him by *Volare* (for an article that, along with that other one on the particle accelerator, Rondeau had managed to assign him just before his death) to escape from B. taking off for three destination-less destinations. He was going to pass through three place-less places. Through three of those locations considered—he'd always liked this way of describing them—"forgotten by the hand of God"; as if God's memory resided in His fingers, ready to snap, and, especially, in that pointing index finger He used on Vatican chapel ceilings to give life or, also, to expulse His tenants from Heaven for not having respected the conditions stipulated in the renter's contract.

Making this trip would be, for him, all of a sudden, the chance to efface expunge erase delete rub out wipe out obliterate places. Arriving to them would be to leave them behind, to find them would be the same as losing them, crossing them off a list, ripping them off the map.

So he, also, traveled.

丁

And he traveled.
And he traveled.
And he traveled.

And so—now fleeing more from himself than from those who'd chased him and who'd already been left behind and more ass-backward all the time—he crossed the ocean first and then an entire continent to arrive to the West Coast, to California.

And to land in the demonic Los Angeles, beside that turbulent Pacific that—as the generally forgetful Mexicans claimed—had no memory, but that sooner or later would remember that its mission was to devour that part of the planet and would proceed to do so amid earthquakes and tsunamis.

And he rented a car that included a driver (he never learned how to learn how to drive, he actually never learned how to drive) to cruise along primary highways and secondary byways.

First to Zzyzx (35°8 35 N 116°6 15 W) and then to Colma (37°40 44 N 122°27 20 W) later to Nothing (34°28 47 N 113°20 7 W). And he specified the latitudes and degrees and decimal minutes and seconds for the same reason that he liked to include names in more or less exotic alphabets: in order to think that he had some control, some sense, some direction.

And, then, to the South as a fixed idea and fixed direction, toward what was down below; like someone descending into the infernos down a rope that you suspect is going to be cut so you can never climb back up again.

He'd heard of a place—the first one in the index of all atlases—called A, just like that, unadorned, not an abbreviation but a complete name, in the municipality of Moskenes, in Norway.

But it was so easy to be the first, he thought.

And, no doubt, A would be something like an exhibition room at a DIY furniture manufacturer, but the exterior version: everything so falsely solid and well-finished. Everything, also, so truly fragile and with defective fasteners and connectors accompanied by an incomprehensible instruction manual (and, thinking about this, he couldn't help but wonder if the fired-up hordes in B. would have also, indirectly because of him, caught IKEA—who at the time of his escape was passing through the city to accept another humanist-literary award—or if, more likely than not, they'd forgiven IKEA the connection he had to him: because IKEA always found his way into everyone's good graces; and it was even possible, who knows, that it was IKEA himself who'd pointed the way to his library which he now imagined in flames; with all those started-but-never-finished copies of *Ada, or Ardor* catching fire in the night.

And humor and grace was and resided in laughing last and laughing best, but he thought that—he suspected, not wanting to give it much thought—now, more than laughing last, he was laughing for the last time. He was smiling a constant last smile out of which, every so often, there escaped an almost-mechanical and badly-oiled sound. A smile that was laughing at itself.

And maybe that'd been the idea of the person who founded Zzyzx, he thought, approaching the ruins of the place: the idea of being the last town in the world and to have a laughable name. Beyond that, alphabetically, there was nothing but names of distant stars and unreachable fabrications with numbers and symbols (they weren't nameable names; they were acronyms muddled with shapes and colors like the ones that disoriented David Bowman as he moved through that long tunnel, full of stars, on the other side of the Star Gate).

But Zzyzx (pronounced: *zai-zex*, like the rattling hiss of a snake that bites and kills) was a place you could arrive to.

And he arrived there and, clearly, he wasn't going to write something about that nothing, but—professional deformation—he couldn't avoid that primary and automatic reflex to look at everything as if he were taking notes the way someone takes a shot but doesn't swallow it and immediately spits it back out.

Again: he arrived there in a rented car with a rented driver. A Cadillac with a mustang behind the wheel: a Native American man, who looked like a direct descendent of that tribe of wooden Indians who, back in the day, stood watch outside the doors to North American barbershops. Someone as impassible as a thick-trunked tree with high branches like a plume of feathers where sad-colored birds came to rest.

And suddenly Zzyzx, in the middle of the Mojave Desert, the first desert of this, his most desert-bound of journeys. Once a prehistoric dig site where arrowheads and rock art were discovered along with—he liked to imagine—fossilized bones of tapirs or wild boars. Later, a military outpost (where, historically, Natives, Spanish explorers, soldiers, miners, and builders of the Tonopa/Tidewater railroad stopped) on the road to that other paramo of silence that would end up laced with the neon lights of Las Vegas and the velvety voices of crooners. Zzyzx as a stop at which to stop and stock up on provisions and to go on and get out of there as fast as you could. And, he thought, you could: because, passing through Zzyzx, by the time you came to the end of the beginning you were already at the beginning of the end. A few streets, a handful of lines like in the little bang of a piece of urban flash fiction with no evidence of a more or less ingenious way out.

He'd first heard about Zzyzx the way he'd first heard about so many things: in writing, reading about it, hearing about it through wide open eyes. He'd heard its final consonants in a thriller with a serial killer where the monster (a fan of Edgar Allan Poe and christened The Poet by the FBI, the same FBI that'd once wasted a great deal of time tracking the poetic Vladimir Nabokov who'd had Poe and his "Annabel Lee" very much in mind when writing his *Lolita*) used Zzyzx as a mass grave where he amassed the bodies of his victims.

Later, he got more interested in the history of the place, which included a radio evangelist preacher of some fame and high levels of delirious and quacked-out superstitious content. One Curtis Howe Springer, who, at the end of World War Two, filed a claim for those federal lands in the Mojave Desert, and erected there a combination spa and religious retreat where—taking advantage of bubbling hot springs (later revealed to be fake, a series of pools Springer heated with a boiler)—he offered cures for all manner of illness of the body and soul, including cancer, baldness, and demonic passion.

At that time, the place was called Soda Springs; but Springer rechristened it Zzyzx ("which rhymes with Isaac"), because he wanted to think of it as and feel that it was the final and definitive sanctuary: a paradise where you could "cleanse yourself internally and externally and eternally." "The last word in health," his pamphlets preached. And Springer recruited homeless people to—in the name of the Lord and as penitence and Hallelujah—help him build the compound and to receive forgiveness for their sins and that salvation that only becomes effective just before death. Thus, a sixty-room hotel, a church, a radio broadcast studio, a castle, an artificial lake, a parkway named the "Boulevard of Dreams," and airstrip called Zyport, and the planting of rows of palm trees to highlight the one-thousand-and-one-nightish oasis effect. But in the '70s (after amassing a fortune selling placebos of his own invention and fabrication with names like the laxative "Antediluvian Tea," the antacid "Re-Hib," the invigorating "Hollywood Pep Cocktail," the blood-circulation promoter "Mo-Hair," and "Zy-Crystals" which contributed to the proliferation of "positive thoughts" and "relief for tired feet") Springer was denounced as a fraud: his cures cured nothing. And, besides, his land-use permit was, originally, only granted for mining activities and not for Edenic or medicinal excavations. So Springer went to jail for a while and the land was reclaimed by some governmental organization and by a consortium of state university campuses that now maintained a Desert Studies Center there to study "the behavior of the desert" and where, he thinks, they probably send the worst students or those flammable geniuses who started raving in excess about firearms on their blogs.

And he was there now: a ghost compiling information for an article that would never be put in writing beyond a "he traveled" about a ghost town where the ghosts didn't exist. More or less new and well-preserved ruins. Dried up pools that looked like something out of a J. G. Ballard wet dream, which brought him—half asleep in the back seat of the car—to the climax of a half-dream. One of those dreams where you closed your eyes and opened them again and it was as if the whole night had passed and, suddenly, the alarm clock next to the bed—the alarm clock that for so long now didn't serve to wake him up but to intensify the awareness of being awake—was informing you, implacably, that everything was still the same as it ever was and the same as it ever would be. A half-dream of his that, actually, was a full-dream of Ella. A dream with and about Ella.

When he woke up, they were already in Colma and he doesn't know how many hours or miles have passed. Time—he discovers—is no longer what it was. Now time is what it is and what it will be. And it takes so much effort to ask himself what time it is, so he decides that from now on answer that with a "what will be, will be." All of a sudden, it's as if his notion of time were more like an unknowing of time in which, no doubt, something about the speed of his escape combined with the slowness of his jetlag was giving birth to a dead time.

And Colma is not the city of the living dead, but it is the city of the most lively of deaths. It is confirmed on the signs announcing its approach proclaiming that "It's great to be alive in Colma." And the slogan—which his father would have approved of—has true humor and humorous truth: Colma—founded in 1924, in San Mateo County—is the location with the greatest concentration of corpses per square meter in the universe. Colma is a necropolis of 4.9 square kilometers. A cluster of sixteen cemeteries of different humanistic faiths and Babelic tongues and ethnicities with names like Woodlawn, Greenlawn, Cypress Lawn, Golden Hills, Eternal Home, Home of Peace, and Holy Cross where, in 1971, several scenes of that classic of the mortuary dark comedy *Harold and Maude*, directed by Hal Ashby, were filmed. (And he couldn't help but wonder if Colma might have a small airfield where coffins with the initials DEP or RIP were unloaded.) The 2010 census—he read in an explanatory pamphlet in a tourism office on the outskirts of the town—counted 1,792 living people, occupying themselves with more than 1,500,000 dead people living in "the City of the Silent." But, everyone knows, really there's nothing more deafening than the voice of the dead, which is nothing but the voice of the living that survive them (with the exception of Penelope's voice, which is enough in itself and doesn't need his voice to tell him over and over again how much she has to tell him, the same as always, how much she looks down on him, but, at the same time, how much she needs him: because nobody ever listened to her better than he did). Again: ghosts exist, yes, but they're the life and work of the living, who turn that second of the physical act of dying into years of spectral and zombie and vampiric existence. An arid short story growing into a river-novel. Ghosts were the memories of the living. The living never let the dead rest in peace—he says to himself again—at the gate to a cemetery and another gate to another cemetery and another gate to another cemetery. The crosses that now are stars or moons. And him walking slowly and weightlessly through all the cemeteries of Colma. A name that came from Kolma, which meant "moon" in the dialect of the Ohlone people. Colma which, until 1900, was a dying one-horse town that got brought back to life at the last minute; when in San Francisco an order was drawn up prohibiting the construction of more cemeteries within the city limits for reasons of hygiene and because, in addition, the prices of land had become agonizing and lethal for the more or less beloved survivors. Then—he continued reading—the dead were sent away from home in a long funeral procession because they were already too grown-up to live out their deaths here, in Colma. And here, among them (headstones and more headstones believing in different gods but all of them like hands being raised in a sepulchral classroom, dying to tell the story of when their names were alive and they only had a date of birth), he discovered immortal names like those of William Randolph Hearst, Wyatt Earp, Levi "Jeans" Strauss, Joe DiMaggio, Tina Turner's dog . . . He read headstones as if they were those book covers by which it isn't fair to judge what they contain in those other cemeteries that are the shelves and tables of the bookstores that readers almost never visit anymore because they prefer the medium of online shopping.

Should he pause longer to think more about death or not? Should he continue on his way and try not to think about it? Should he take the risk—like Alexander Pushkin in that poem of his—of calculating with more or less exactitude the up-in-the-air date that at some point will come to rest on the earth to be buried? It's well known, though not known with precision: the sooner-or-later inevitable stopping point of the day and of the time of that secret anniversary. That unhappy birthday that's never celebrated or acknowledged as such. Even though, maybe, retrospectively and too late, it's discovered that, year after year, that precise day was always in a bad mood, or congested, or with a headache, or making bad decisions. That that was the day in the life of every year that would become—maybe this very day, in twelve months—the day of your death. That that precise day would mark the birth of the last year of your life: that that day would be, within just one year, the first day of your death. That your death was already gestating. In any case, the dead no longer thought about any of this. The dead didn't waste their time with any of these minutiae. The dead had their whole death ahead of them.

And he can no longer—nor does he want to, again, nothing interests him less—be sure of the chronology or of the geography, of the before or of the ahead, of the behind or of the after. Nothing more than the words and the numbers and the cactus-colored signs on the side of the road. Signs that say things like "Absolutely Nothing / Next 22 Miles" (signs warning drivers that they were going to be entering a zone with no water or food or gasoline or love or dreams for a long way; and that it's better for them to collect themselves and gather what's necessary to make it alive, and to arrive not to everything but, yes, to something that, with any luck, is waiting for them on the other side of nothing) or, all of a sudden, a sign that announces "Nothing / 1 Mile.")

Welcome to the nothing of Nothing, the last appearance, the third of his ghost towns. Nothing exists. Almost. Founded in 1977 and given its name "by some drunks who were passing through and stopped to take a piss." Nothing was abandoned in 2005 and purchased in its entirety in 2008 by one Mike Jensen, who in 2009 opened a pizzeria there, which closed in 2011. And, after having reached a maximum population of four residents, nothing in Nothing again. And on June 19th of 2016—on Father's Day and under the sympathetically antipathic slogan of "Give Dad Nothing"—a twenty-four hour viewing was opened in Nothing, an invitation to a wild real-estate orgy, so that anyone who came through there could walk away with a few meters of nothing, a few yards of Nothing. Free. But—as far as he knows and could find out—nobody went to Nothing. Nobody did anything for Nothing. And there, in Nothing, he remembers that moment from the Ernest Hemingway story "A Clean, Well Lighted Place," where it had that line about "Our nada who art in nada, nada be thy name thy kingdom nada thy will be nada in nada as it is in nada . . ." And it's clear that Hemingway was neither the first nor the last to pray to that nothing on the basis of which the preferred model of God created everything, understanding God, of course, as the absolute form of nothing. Before it—to worship or deny it—knelt down and kneel down and will kneel down multitudes of Buddhist monks seeking to attain the Sunyata (or empty state of mind) and Parmenides, Epicurus, Leucippus, Plato, Casanova, Aristotle, Newton, Descartes, Pascal, Torricelli, Galileo, Hegel, Sartre, Lacan, Heidegger, Kierkegaard, the most precise mathematicians of MIT, the most technological of technologists of Silicon Valley, and the fans of that nothing joked about in *Seinfeld*. "Yada-yada-yada" and "Happy Festivus" and "Serenity Now" which, maybe, is what—in truth and in quiet voices—those already invoked mystics in orange robes whisper in the exact moment of reaching the nirvana of nothing. That psychedelic "nothing is real" when there's nothing left to worry about. And that sign on the way out that notified him and bade him farewell with a "You Are Leaving Nothing" was lying.

So it goes: he's leaving nothing behind because at last he's become nobody. He's managed to—during this purifying stretch of his journey where nothing has taken place beyond the retelling of how these pointless places first came to be—efface expunge erase delete rub out wipe out obliterate himself. A variation of a samurai aria: not an *already dead* but an *already gone* and a *gone forever*. A going and a having gone in order to return to the beginning and thus—in the worn out atlas of his mind exhausted from carrying the weight of his world—now Zzyzx and Colma and Nothing directly border Sad Songs.

Soon, everything will end there, at the beginning of everything.

And he'll abandon his memory palace just as he left his and Penelope's house in flames.

And then the only thing he'll remember (farewell to all those books and songs and films) will be that he's forgotten what he remembered.

And—with that spirit of an almost-soul—he makes a gesture to his driver. One of those *hellos* that's closer to the stereotypical *hau* that he learned watching those westerns that he didn't like at all in his childhood, which is why, right away, he changed the channel to stop watching them. Because his thing—he's said it before, he's tuned it in before—were psychotronic and low-budget horror movies, capable of making him feel that strange horror that fixed your face in a sardonic grin or convinced you that the voices of tumor-like crabs were clicking in your brain.

That horror that felt unjustified after he successfully made it through every annual check-up; until all horror was justified and his check-up turned into a check-out, where he stared at the X-ray of his own skull like something that couldn't be true, that couldn't be his, that had to be someone else's, because, in the end, all skulls were equal and death was the great equalizer.

And he watched himself in that moment.

He watched himself fall.

And—white on black against a backlight—he looked at the doctor pointing, below the pale cupula of his skull (so akin to the dome of a planetarium where you go where the arrow of the narrator of cosmic wonders and astral catastrophes points), that "I-don't-like-it-at-all" model stain. That black hole that at first he linked to that point from which, star by star, the universe of his past and the sky above his memory palace, was being emptied.

And then—this is the kind of small misery that even the greatest writers are made of—he thought about how he could blame everything on that cerebral aberration: the revving motor of his rage and the skidding to a stop of his love, his dream-like insomnia, and, most important of all, his inability to keep writing.

And then he asked the doctor (who already knew him from previous appointments and emergencies and who, he was sure, wouldn't be surprised by anything he said) if he thought that "a hyper-invasive treatment like, for example, being exposed to the centrifugation of a particle accelerator could take out that tumor, which, as you say, is inoperable," might do some good.

Then the man limited himself to putting a hand on his shoulder, sighing, and, after a quick dance of fingers across the keys of his computer, printing off a sheet (in no time at all, that incomprehensible electro-encephalon-grammar handwriting of doctors had already been eliminated forever, he thought) enumerating a long list (another list for his list of lists) that detailed more urgent tests that needed to be done.

And he assumed the man was a specialist; but he didn't seem especially special to him.

And he left thinking that he was never going to go back (there) and that he was going to go (here) and, once again, he started thinking about those things that are better not to think about.

But better not to think about that.

Better not to think—better to remember to forget about that Combray Syndrome and that his mind was going—about what he had inside that brain with which he thinks that it's better not to think about that.

And so he tells Big Chief Fast Steel Hearse to take him back to the Los Angeles Airport so he can fly first to Mexico City and from there continue on—after a brief layover—to Abracadabra, to Mount Karma. To his final destination where events will do exactly what events most like to do. There, events were going to precipitate so that there would take place—in that place as final as Zzyzx and Colma and Nothing—the last end of his world news.

That's where he's going now in order to stop going anywhere.

ʃ

And, on the way to the airport, his Native American driver asked him if it would bother him if he put on some music and he said no, but thinking yes, and expecting the worst. One of those Latin American successes or some ethnic-electronic fusion, he anticipated. But no. What played and enveloped him was something that he carried inside him and that he knew by heart (and few things were more pleasurable than hearing music you know down to the last note, as if you were composing it and listening to it in the very act of hearing it, as if ʃ).

It plays there, everywhere.

An important part of the sounds of his life: *Wish You Were Here* by Pink Floyd. The definitive album—according to its authors and performers—on the theme of absence. An album assembled from broken fragments and loose pieces (with the full and absolutely disoriented band spinning in circles inside the studio, dizzy from the global success of *The Dark Side of the Moon*) until, from out of those moments, a marvelous whole was achieved.

And, oh, all the pages that he'd once written with that music as soundtrack.

And, then, he couldn't help saying aloud "Oh, one of my favorite albums."

And smiling at him in the rearview mirror, the driver says to him "I was there."

And he didn't understand.

And the driver continued, as if he knew who he was, as if he intuited that what he was doing was accumulating information: "My tribe is an offshoot of the Northern Paiute people. The Kutzadika'a or 'fly eaters.' And they settled on the banks of Mono Lake, in Mono County, California. Not very far from here. And that's where they took that photograph. I saw them take it. One evening when I was a kid."

"What photograph?" he asked.

And the driver answered: "The one inside—like a postcard—the sleeve of *Wish You Were Here.* The one with the diver in the water. I saw how they did it. No Photoshop back then. It didn't exist. No tricks. They screwed a chair down to the bottom of the lake and the model they used was a ferocious practitioner of yoga. And the man put himself there, head down, underwater, with an oxygen tank, until every wave disappeared from the surface of the lake. It was then that the designers and photographers saw me watching and hired me as a full-service assistant. And so they took me with them, so I could help them with whatever they needed. I guess that, also, for that small tribe of psychedelic Englishmen, having a young Indian on their payroll was pretty *groovy* or *far out* or whatever. So I went with them to the Yuma desert where they photographed that faceless businessman and, also, that swimmer run aground in the sand. And, from there, we went to the Warner Bros studios, where they photographed those two guys shaking hands, one of them in flames. Again: real fire. I was there, off to one side, with a fire extinguisher. They photographed them over and over. Up to fifteen times. And at one point, the wind changed direction and the stunt double they were using lost his eyebrows and moustache and said he'd had enough, and that's why there is even a final photograph that shows that stunt man walking out of frame and . . . By the way: the story about there being some kind of sect of men who've gotten burned trying to imitate that photograph is an urban legend."

And he listens and can't stop listening.

And he even considers interrupting him and submitting him to a concentrated dose of the way his head works. The bad joke that occurs to him in the moment about how it's funny that Pink Floyd—the kings of the stereo and the quadrophonic—had sent somebody to be photographed in a lake called Mono. The free association of ideas that takes him from that photograph of the motionless diver to "All good writing is *swimming under water* and holding your breath," as a burned Francis Scott Fitzgerald once wrote, almost extinguished by days he spent walking like a sleepwalker through those same Hollywood ranch-houses and film sets where that photograph for *Wish You Were Here* was taken. Fitzgerald trying to write screenplays that nobody was going to film and dying to finish that novel, *The Love of the Last Tycoon*, where first it said that thing about how "Writers aren't people exactly" and then conceded that, if they are, "they're a whole lot of people trying so hard to be one person."

And, again, like what happened to him listening to that old ex-spy, to that "old boy of 'The Outfit,' sitting next to him one or two airplanes ago: the sensation of reality realigning with his fictions or with his irreal life. The possibility, now, that this "fly-eater" driver was the same indigenous man who, so many years ago now, in the line to get into a Bob Dylan concert, introduced himself as Rolling Thunder (thusly named in honor of that tour, about which, not long ago, in a documentary, Dylan said, " I don't remember a thing" because "it happened so long ago I wasn't even born" and that "What remains of that tour to this day, nothing . . . Not one single thing . . . Ashes") and with whom later, during the encores, he climbed up onto the stage to end up howling "Rainy Day Women #12 & 35" alongside the songwriter who, disconcerted, smiled despite everything and despite them.

He'd never done anything like that.

He would never have made gestures as extreme as those of the legendary and urban burning men; but when there exploded that absurd retro-trend that had vinyl being rediscovered like a quasi-philosophical alchemical plastic, he did run out to the nearest record store—one of the only ones left in B.—and bought the facsimile reissue of *Wish You Were Here*. (Even though something made him think that, maybe, that whole vinyl revival was—underneath all the consumerist frivolity—in the end a good symptom and positive move and a kind of reflexive atavistic resistance. A return to listening to full sides of albums before succumbing to the absolute atomization of random songs or untethered refrains; to once again asking and answering why this track came after that track; to reencountering a long and well-thought-out discourse instead of random, free-floating ideas . . . And, if vinyl had been able to do it, he told himself that, maybe, soon, paper and ink would pull it off too. And then, goodbye forever to all those sticky newspaper homepages where, below the headline of every article, they offer an estimate, almost as a kind of dissuasive warning, of the number of minutes it would take you to read it, as if they were marathons that demanded great physical fitness and mental focus.) "Heavyweight 180g Vinyl," specified the label atop the transparent cellophane that enveloped the black cover with the classic label and hand-shake on his brand-spanking-new edition of *Wish You Were Here*, so similar to the one from his childhood.

And he bought it and took it home.

And he never opened it.

And now, no doubt, *Wish You Were Here* is also burning, along with all his books in that ever more distant city where nobody now, not anymore, is wishing he were there.

丁

And aboard another airplane where nobody wishes they were there and where all of them are trying to think about anything but the fact that that's where they are, in the air, suspended, waiting. The volume of voices rising and falling, like the whispers and murmurs and coughs and laughs and the occasional shout, between the songs on a Pink Floyd album.

And 4C saying to 4B that "Every time I tell the truth I leave a lot out, which, I suppose, isn't the same as lying, is it? So then remembering would be a form of lying to yourself about the truth . . ." and 4A interrupting him when he got to "I suppose" with a "To remember is to find while continuing to look. We don't know if a memory is what we give up for lost just as we remember it or what was lost and is suddenly recovered."

And hearing all of that and saying to himself, first, that he'd already heard all of that somewhere else (on another airplane?) and then realizing that it wasn't that he heard it but that he'd written it. In one of his books, back when he wrote down the things he said to himself. What he heard himself say a second before reading it as he wrote it.

And feeling himself to be in no place at all but in the best of all possible places.

And, then, in the volcanic and ashen air above that place that brought together all possible places, some better than others, many worse than some: Mexico City, D.F., which, from the sky and as he descends, looks the same as it did the last time he landed there. Golden and stretching out like a spider of shadow or a spiderweb of lights. A site surrounded by itself. A terminal yet limitless metropolis.

And the Hotel La Nada.

And everything.

And all those worms inside bottles of mezcal whose only message for him was that there was nobody coming to rescue him and to get him out of there.

And almost dragging himself up to El Zócalo.

And the bookstores of heavily-handled second-hand books.

And, there, a copy, crisped by the passing decades, of *Martin Eden*: that book by Jack London that—it occurred to him suddenly and right there—was, perhaps, for him, the first and very distant inspiration for what his *The Impossible Story* ended up becoming. It was the exact same edition of *Martin Eden* (on its cover, the drawing of a great ship and a couple seagulls, title and the author's name in black letters across a yellow background) that he'd read during his childhood.

And he opened it to the last page and then remembered—as if he'd just experienced it hours before—the great impression it had on him when he discovered that a book could end not with the victory of the hero on terra firma but with the death of the hero on the high seas. Then and forever, Martin Eden—after so much swimming among the sharks of the little literary world—drowning just like he'd drowned only a couple summers before reading that book for the first time. And, again, Martin Eden reaching—in the last words, not his, but those of the novel that told the story of his life—that death that, as he read again, was nothing but "the instant" you knew only to cease to know.

Last words that he'd memorized when, many years later, he reread the novel in English: "And somewhere at the bottom he fell into darkness. That much he knew. He had fallen into darkness. And at that instant he knew, he ceased to know."

And then he couldn't help thinking about something he always thought about: about how, in that precise instant in which he knew that Martin Eden had known that he would no longer know anything, maybe, somewhere in the world, someone else was reading that very same sentence. And that he or the other or the others, all of them reading those same words at the same time, were all mysteriously united for a few seconds, as if by a prayer. That all of them were in communion in and with a single book that suddenly was a shared cathedral-like memory palace. That all of them, reading the same thing, remembered the same thing.

And that, in that instant of infinite wisdom, it didn't matter at all that "THE WORLD WILL BE TOOOTALLY CRACKLING," or that "The world is going to end! We're going to be irredeemably toasted! Let's get toasted! Bring it on! Let's turn to ash!" That what was left of the planet would be for the few survivors who, after the last curtain dropped, would get to their feet and applaud and be fully aware of the end of all ends. And who wouldn't be part of those thousands of millions of immobile skeletons with headphones plugged into their skulls and mobile phones clutched in the bones of their hands, not even aware that none of it mattered anymore and would never matter again.

And survivors like him wouldn't live so much to write the tale, but, at least, would survive long enough to read it. Electrified by emotion and not by the latest trendy gadget and with no need to pay for those "little volts" that were now being offered in the trumpeting Plaza Garibaldi before returning to his memory-losing hotel room where he thought he could feel how his mind was going, memory by memory. Like someone tearing the pages out of a book in the she-loves-me/she-loves-me-not mode, until there is only one page left. One final memory in the beginning of feeling so Prousticized and Proustified and Proustilian. The absolute and total concentration of his memory that, if he was lucky, would preserve the memory of Ella forever. And, if he was unlucky, would insist over and over again—like in that Philip K. Dick story—on the circular loop of that terrible night with Uncle Hey Walrus and Penelope: the three of them circulating through another city, years ago and a few hours before his parents would disappear to never reappear again.

And so he went into his room and hung that "DO NOT DISTURB" sign from the doorknob and collapsed onto a bed that moved and never stopped moving, as if obeying the ragged voice of that ruinous lullaby sung by incessant earthquakes and that wasn't for putting you to sleep but for waking you up. That song that sings to him of how far he is from the land where he was born.

And then the undertow of the next morning's hangover that first pulls him down and spins him around and finally—fallen out of bed—delivers him to the castaway but overpopulated beaches of an airport waiting area.

A waiting area at the exceedingly inhospitable Mexico City, D.F. airport.

The Mexico City, D.F. airport, which is already, in itself, a plane crash in the center of the city, awaiting—sooner rather than later—the inevitable tragedy of an airplane plummeting down on parks and avenues that not even that golden angel will be able to protect them from anymore.

That's where he is.

With that dream deferred and his flight to Abracadabra delayed.

And—all of a sudden, again—a new example of how his reality, the reality in which he doesn't write, is beginning to be populated by his characters.

The waiting area begins to fill up with Karmas.

The Karmas that he first came to know in the dispatches and videos that Penelope sent him from and during her unstable stay in Mount Karma. The Karmas he read and watched and analyzed (in the same way that others had analyzed the Compsons or the Sutpens or the Snopes or the Sartoris that he'd never been able to read perhaps because, he intuited that with his own, with his own blood and flesh, he'd already had enough of the southern gothic) for hours, as if they were Abraham-Zapruder brand documents or as if he was J. M. W. Turner tied high on the mast of a ship in order to understand the profiles and faces of a storm that was posing for him so he could paint its portrait. He memorized them to the point where he was able to see himself among all of them. Believing himself to be—through a distant yet real relationship—a kind of comfortable and accommodated exwriter in residence: someone, if not well loved, at least accepted by everyone (because, after all, their connection to the universally celebrated and worshipped Penelope gave the Karmas a cachet that none of the other patrician or matrician families of Abracadabra could access or compete with). And, all of a sudden, even imagining himself appearing in any of those home movies of Karma weddings that were like Blockbusters: him there, coming quickly down the stairway of a French-style estate, barely glancing at the camera, like Marcel Proust *chez* Guiche-Greffulhe, so that all of the Karmas could ask each other where he'd come from and who was that guy and, seconds later (almost a minute), answering with a "Ah, but that must be Penita's brother, the one who teaches at that writing workshop that we all signed up for but never attended . . ."

And yet, he recognizes all of them—coming in as if they owned the place and immediately taking all the best seats—because, in addition, he'd seen them recently and updated them in his mind.

And he removes from his pocket the page he tore from that magazine depicting the family during their most recent invasion of the Vatican; when and where the simultaneous beatification and canonization of the clan's great matriarch took place: the ferocious Mamagrandma, about whom Penelope had moaned and told him so much (but he hadn't used her in the Mexican book he'd written on commission, because the woman seemed like a little too much, even for him and his stylistic and creative parameters: Mamagrandma was someone so real and unique in Penelope's telling that she could only be considered an unrealistic and impossible creature; besides, he was afraid that he would put her in writing and then that the demon woman would read what he'd written and recognize herself and come after him).

He also recognizes them (even though he's never seen them up close; except for the comatose Maxi Karma, when he was still breathing—without the help of machines sketching the lines of his heart and brain—and snorting white lines at the Psycholabis Bar: the involuntary father of The Son of Penelope whom Penelope suffocated after he impregnated her, though he was unaware of anything, especially of that fact) because he put all of them in writing. In that Mexican book written on commission, stealing them from Penelope (or using them without her permission, either way) changing their last name and moving them from Mount Karma to that city where now, they're all waiting for an airplane belonging to that increasingly popular airline: DelayedAir.

So, he stares at them like someone trying, in vain, to take in one of those overcrowded and enormous courtesan portraits where a massive family poses in a great hall, the walls covered with paintings in which even more numerous tribes pose in rooms full of even more paintings. Those paintings that—if you could touch them, if you were allowed to put an ear to the canvas—no doubt would ramble in the universal language of that zoo Noah survived off of once the waters receded and the sun came out.

And he also recognizes them because what ends up confirming that they are indeed the Karmas is the fact that—in the almost bellicose clamor of their conversations that barely conceal their true nature as monologues—the word he hears most, over and over, repeated like a mantra, is "Karma."

Karma as subject and verb.

"Karma and Karma and Karma and Karma," the Karmas repeat as if Karma were the Alpha and Omega and, first and foremost and when all is said and done, The Surname. The best and the only worthy way of referring to themselves.

And he proceeds to more or less identify them one by one with the help of that glossy photograph and the random pleasantries typical of "society" magazines, but that, even still, end up revealing details that are unsettling and, yes, quite inspiring for a mind like his, like his once was.

There's the new leader of the tribe, Cubita Karma: Cubita—he learns, reading there—comes from a diminutive form of the affectionate *Cub*; but, he suspects, *also* from the malevolent and under-the-breath *cubic*, based on the shape of her body and the expressionlessness of her expression. On the pages torn out from the magazine it also tells—having barely gotten through the almost eternal funeral rites following the death, "unexpected and in her sleep," of the centenarian Mamagrandma—how Cubita "told everyone at a family meeting" that the departed matriarch had "appeared to her in all her glory." And that "Mamagrandma, wreathed in flowers and with a melodious voice," had told "her and her alone," that she was anointing and naming Cubita as her successor. Ah-ha: that one great idea that every idiotic person tends to have in their life, he thought with admiration (because, he also thought, it was impossible that Cubita had done and said that consciously *plagiarizing* what Dmitri Nabokov had come up with to justify the publication of *The Original of Laura*). And, of course, nobody had dared contradict Cubita out of fear of the memory—more impossible to forget than unforgettable—of Mamagrandma (and out of that near desperation and need that dynasties tend to have to believe, no matter the cost, in the Afterlife: any proof or evidence of the realized fantasy of a Heaven, where a VIP area waited under their name, like the one they already had at the Kountry Klub—yes, they'd founded it so they spelled it however they liked most and best—was good, was very good, was far better than nothing and far better than the possibility that their surname wouldn't get them anywhere and that anybody could get in just by virtue of having been "a good person").

And so—as he read them in person and between the lines and watched them with half-closed eyes—the Karmas now seemed exceedingly unstable and nitroglycerinic. Even more so than when he novelized them. And, disoriented, they walked in circles around the waiting area in small groups. Watching each other—always out of the corners of the corners of their eyes—with something that to him looked like a variation of that "thousand-yard stare" of dumbstruck soldiers, but reduced and intensified here to, at most, a two-yard stare. The stares of people who couldn't see beyond themselves, eyes—with pupils dilated or shrunken by uppers and downers of varying caliber—that could only understand the world if it was written in the first-person singular or plural.

The Karma women with hairdos like wasp nests that remind him of the one that the aged Dracula had in the Francis Ford Coppola version and fake lashes that look fabricated from the claws of praying mantises and all of them wrapped—no matter the temperature—in coats of the fur of bears or tigers that appear to have devoured the people they're swallowing in the slowest of digestion. The Karma men with their hair coated in a thick layer of styling gel and cut as if they had showed up at a casting call for a silent movie by mistake (because how was it possible to go to the movies to read so much and, on top of it all, that the world hadn't yet discovered colors) and all of them stuffed into aquamarine and pastel-pink polo shirts, proclaiming that they all share the same mystical power animal: the Lacoste crocodile.

And all of them so similar to each other, the men and the women (like what happened to those prehistoric races and like what will happen to those futuristic races), and nothing concerning them less than the whole *uncanny valley* thing: because they all feel like original replicas of an artificially authentic Karma way of life. They're not the chosen race: they're the race that chose itself. And thus the abundance (from what Penelope had told him) of marriages between cousins. And thus too the peace of mind that comes from knowing that all the people around you are thinking—good or bad—the same thing.

And so, all of them smiling and saying things like "So lucky that the flight is delayed, now we can go shopping in the Duty Free and . . ." Or "The problem with poor little Hiriz—God holds her in His glory and embraces her in His bosom and hasn't given her any spankings—is that nobody recognized her, in her moment, for being who she was, for being an excellent bad person, which is why she never thought of becoming a somewhat good person. And that's why she ended up in that monastery and why what happened happened and . . ." and "But you've got to admit that Hiriz did a lot for the faith with her really conciliatory teleological ideas, like the one about how it's not that man is descended from apes, but that apes are an early sketch of man that God, in His infinite mercy, decided not to throw in the trash can. Or that other one about how it's not that God is absent but that on the seventh day He rested and that, obviously, every day for God is the equivalent of millions of millions of years of human days and so, what happens is that we're living on His Sunday, while God is taking a most well-deserved rest after all that work." Or "I've got a great idea for a fantastic business: ice cream that doesn't melt, but every time I try to make it work, it melts on me." Or "Guess what? After he was chosen to be Pope and when they asked him what his new name would be, Chiquito Karma couldn't come up with anything better than Jesus II; and, of course, that led all those cardinals to slam on the brakes and go with their second choice: this lame guy we've got now who looks like one of those retirees out in the plaza. But, luckily, at the embassy, Checho Karma pulled strings and used connections and got them, in exchange for saying nothing about the whole fiasco, to beatify and canonize Mamagrandma in an express ceremony."

And they go on and on like that for minutes as long as hours. Happy and comfortable with time not passing, because if they're too conscious of time's passing, they might find themselves forced to think—for a few seconds as long as minutes—about how they actually do nothing, about how they only act like they're working, and about how, even that, tires them out and bores them. But a disturbance like that only lasts for seconds as brief as nanoseconds and then it's overridden by the common, but for them never banal, sense that, really, there could be no better occupation—all those baptisms and weddings and birthdays and saints' days and funerals where they can gather again without ever having parted, except to go to the bathroom—than that of being a Karma.

And he listens to them and pretty soon their deafening murmur is like a kind of hypnotic muzak and—to keep from tripping and falling into a bad trance—he takes Penelope's notebook out of his backpack on whose cover is written *Karma Konfidential*.

And there are the many notes in his dead sister's sloping hand. He'd never read them. Random comments and assessments. Very fine, badly-thought ideas about all of them, there, with him, everywhere. And, again, the feeling of watching featured extras in a Marx Brothers' movie shown in slow motion to which Penelope has provided the best and most avant-garde of subtitles.

Things like:

Karmas = persons of interest. The term "person of interest," generally used by the police in the United States in the early stages of an investigation, has no legal significance. It simply indicates someone the police want to speak to. It does not imply any accusation. It could also be expressed as *person the police want to question*. Nothing more, nothing less / Impossible to accuse a Karma of anything except of being a Karma: it would be the only thing they would admit to being guilty of and, because of it, more innocent than anyone / The idea that the Karmas are victims and victimizers of (im)perfect crimes and lawyers and prosecutors and judges of themselves (and I always admired and have always been intrigued by that decisive subtle idiomatic difference when it comes to sentencing: in Spanish, they always say *culpable* or *inocente*; while, in English, they choose between *guilty* and *not guilty*, which isn't the same thing; and that it admits the possibility of someone not being innocent, but, also, the possibility of not being entirely sure that someone is not guilty; and that, between one uncertainty and the other, the most *just* thing, for that reason, would be to deliver a verdict of innocent not beyond all reasonable doubt, if you're not convinced of the person's absolute and irrefutable guilt; thus, the defense has no reason to prove anything, while the prosecution has to prove everything; thus, all Karmas would always declare themselves innocent, while I, at most, on my best days, can convince myself that I believe that I'm *not guilty*; in any case, my best days are few and wintry and quite short) / The disturbing sensation that the Karmas get offended by everything, over everything. Hyper-sensitive and thin-skinned and delicate personalities, like—as my Bad Little Brother would probably think—on Twitter: where people are so insensitive with regard to others and so sensitive with regard to themselves. To the point where you realize that the Karmas live in a state of offense and that a good part of their daily activity consists of seeking out and finding someone or something to justify their infinite capacity for feeling insulted. Thus, all the time making and unmaking lists of friends and enemies among cousins and aunts and uncles and brothers and sisters and parents and children. Getting offended is a way of demonstrating that other people matter to you. And, besides, it gives them the chance to befriend and ally themselves with each other to feel offended on behalf of others / Karma parties like subliminal courts: all those proud and openly homophobic Karmas dancing and choreographing "YMCA" or "In the Navy" unaware that they are gay anthems (the Karma men are so homophobic that they eat bananas sideways) / Anorexia y sus flaquitas (the impossibility of not singing/dancing to the songs of their childhood and adolescence, maybe thinking that in that way they won't get old) / All of them sing. All of the time. Suddenly and without warning. Like in musical comedies. For some strange reason they all seem absolutely convinced that they sing very well (but they don't) / Unavoidable: the Karmas are true geniuses when it comes to square/line dancing: their minds and movements in communion / Gestalt: they're all in agreement about everything but really they don't approve of anybody / Thinking about thinking the same thing is a way to think about nothing / Their circular and amorphous conversations: the unspeakable fear of realizing they don't have anything to say and so they conceal that fact by talking all the time about nothing at all / Their conversations are even more amorphous and circular when they're on their mobile phones (the mobile phone as the ideal invention for Karma use: easy to manage and with technology that's both sophisticated and renewable year after year and thus—another of their many forms of unhappy happiness—something else that can be purchased many times) / They talk and they talk and they talk and they make

you wonder if the character in Edvard Munch's *The Scream* is screaming or, to the contrary, is covering his ears to not hear the screams
other people are screaming outside the frame: more and more convinced that it's the latter / Horror vacui: the Karmas activity on social
media where they tell everything and show everything: and everything they show and tell is nothing but Karmas doing everything
they can to not do anything before giving in to the idea of doing something, very little, at most / Playing office as adults the way they played
house as kids (the Karmas fail at any extrafamilial project they
attempt; they're like Midas in reverse: all the gold they touch turns to
lead and sometimes to mud) / Karmas: they call each other and
describe themselves as "boys" and "girls" until they're more or less
forty years old / And they're all—or at least that's how they refer to
one another— "amazing fathers" and "amazing mothers": apparently,
there isn't one bad father or mother among them, which is why there
isn't anyone to compare their inevitable greatness to either. And so,
the idea of equalizing—in public and when it comes to any activity—
so that uncomfortable comparisons or causes for confrontation don't
arise. In private, of course, things change and the appraisals are
exceedingly variable and worthy of unfavorable comments. In private,
one can be a bad father of insufferable children (for some reason,
nobody talks about "amazing daughters" or "amazing sons") who take
your breath away and make you wonder why you got that spermatozoid or that ovum / "Childhood is the kingdom where nobody dies,"
who said/wrote that? Wrong: childhood is the kingdom that dies / If
breathing weren't an automatic reflex, if breathing were work or
something that had to be "consciously" done, the Karmas would die of
asphyxiation / The Karmas take four times as long to do anything: "If
it were up to me, pregnancies would last two or three years," I hear a
pregnant Karma say, clinging to her belly as if it were a life preserver
that could keep her from drowning: pregnancy as a way of increasing
the value of your actions within the tribe / Karmas saying goodbye to
each other: they can spend more time saying goodbye than they've
spent together / The possibility of getting together for just a few minutes in order to be able to spend an hour, or two, saying goodbye / The

disturbing conviction the Karmas have about how all public places (boutiques, restaurants, movie theaters, airplanes, cruise ships) are an extension of their homes and, for that reason, part of their property and places where they feel authorized to behave as if they were in distant enclaves of their own realms, where they feel they should be accorded every honor and privilege: never having to wait, showing up late, demanding the best seats and tables / The Karma lunches where—if you half close your eyes and empty your mind of all thoughts—you can almost see the invisible lines and notes of pure hatred and envy and scorn, like laser alarm systems in those movies where masterpieces are stolen from supposedly unbreachable museums and where there hangs, attempting to avoid tripping those alarms, the perfect thief: me / The Karma Life like the opening-preliminary chapter in any Agatha Christie novel: presentation-list of suspects, difficult to individualize and distinguish, constantly consulting that list of characters from the beginning of the book (all of them barely in secret proud of knowing themselves to be possible candidates for the commission of a crime they would never dare commit, because here, the only acknowledged and authorized and feared executioner is Mamagrandma) and, of course, me as both victim and criminal, to whom all of them talk without the slightest interest in listening / Or The Karma Life like one of those idiotic and idiotizing sitcoms, with weak jokes and canned laughter and characters who're always opening and closing doors and coming in and out of frame and seeming more black and white than color and two-dimensional in every sense (and me among them, like an abducted guest actress who isn't particularly well-liked by the telespectators who're also the Karmas, auto-tuning themselves in, feeling so fun and so funny) / The unmistakable sensation that . . . sensation that, listening to the Karmas, my neurons are being extinguished one by one, like little lightbulbs burning out (participating as little as possible to delay the effect all I can) / Karmatic soliloquys / That fucking automatic Karma reflex (especially among the women) to say something and, even if it's not particularly funny or especially fun, bringing it home with a burst of laughter (is it from insecurity or the certainty of knowing that nothing they say is deserving of laughter from everybody else and that's why they immediately slip in a laugh of their own to see if in that way, maybe, who knows . . . ?). Laughter more toxic than contagious and that sounds like a kind of jungle cackle, like what bursts from a tree full of big ugly birds that have nothing better to do than listen to their own voices and find them so cheerful no matter that what they've just said is the most chilling of statements (generally badmouthing someone not present at the moment). Question: do they laugh to conceal their full terror or absolute emptiness at the fact that what they say says nothing? Their laughter almost like a stage direction *[laughter]* indicating the obligation to laugh? Why do they shout when they talk on the phone? Do they not realize that the telephone reduces distance? Do they think that if they shout, they'll be heard better, closer? / Conversations among Karmas: the accumulation of two or more monologues recited simultaneously. What time is it for the Karmas? It's time to never have to ask what time it is. Worrying about the time and its passing understood as a defect of the lower classes / If remembering something in different ways is what makes us free subjects, people with personality; the Karmas, on the other hand, have all opted to remember everything the same way: a single and irrefutable official universal version that won't cause conflicts or that facilitates absolute condemnation with no right to reply or disagree (at least in public; in private, I'm sure, each and every one of them thinks things that only occur to each and every one of them) / Jean Paul Sartre said that thing about how "Hell is other people." For the Karmas, other people are like Heaven: you can talk infernal shit about them and thereby feel like you're in paradise / Karma MO (Hiriz is the master of this) for relating and communicating ideas among themselves: you say something very personal and monstrous (racist, homophobic, ignorant comments), but you offer them not in first-person singular but in an inconclusive and unconsulted first-person plural, implicating the other, automatically making them an accomplice in a crime that—because they understand that contradicting is one of the many forms of bad manners—nobody dares denounce. Thus, a Karma is always confessing in the name of others and in this way all of them are the most innocent of guilty parties / That Tolstoy idea, the one about happy families and sad families; but Tolstoy didn't say anything about insufferable families: the ones who're so happy to be as they are and to cause so much sadness among everyone else / Karma wedding anniversaries celebrated like a record to be broken or a resistance test; the very few divorces, on the other hand, condemned as cheating and disqualified from the familial Olympics / The long, looooong death throes of the Karmas: almost none of them die right away; almost all of them dedicate themselves to living eternal deaths, unpunctual down to the last breath that's drawn out like a perfectly healthy wind; though I've heard of Karmas taking/texting selfies beside newly dead bodies in order to be the first ones to deliver the good (in terms of likes) bad news that, depending on the name of the dead person (the last name never changed), might end up being cause for the saddest of fireworks (What's the idea, the fun, the strategy? As soon as a Karma falls ill with something relatively serious, he or she is given up for dead, becoming a lost cause no matter the opinions of doctors and specialists, and they start to plan the funeral rites and the fulfillment—or not—of his or her last wishes. And so, when the person improves and gets better, they attribute the miraculous recovery to the prayers of the Karmas having been heard and answered by a God always attentive to their wishes and privileges). Death as the absolute limelight, so make it last as long as possible, stealing the show and demanding a close-up. Death in slow motion as a form of success / They take me to see the cemetery where the Karmas are put to rest. In concentric circles. They explain to me that it's set up like that so that, on the Day of the Final Judgment, when they rise from their tombs, the Karmas will only see other resurrected Karmas (they explain it to me as if it were the best of ideas; it pains me to tell them that the American Sedgwick-brand magnates had a similar idea, probably before)/ The Karmas are so unoriginal and so lacking in talent, but totally unconcerned with making up for it with the consolation of discipline (that bastard child of talent): The Karmas' talent for being so undisciplined, to always be beginning to finish, leaving never to arrive, thinking without doing, talking without saying anything / But are the baroque Karmas possibly worse than our minimalist family? Good question, bad answer. After all, a big family offers more space for hate, but, also, for love / The Karmas like theorists of the relative / The Karmas who read post-cards and embroidered pillowcases and little more (self-help books, mainly, but ones they never finish when they discover that they do *not* only *help them* but aim to *help everyone*; the Karmas understand that a good self-help book has to be one that helps them but that, in addition, doesn't help anyone else) / The Karmas who don't like going to the movies (the Karmas are great defenders of cable TV and its increasingly numerous payment platforms) because they can't talk loudly at the movies, they can't talk about themselves to alleviate the strangeness of the fact that, in movies, not one Karma appears or is mentioned (and the Karmas read even less for the same reasons, though the effect of their absence in those pages is even worse than on the screen, because when it's all pure letters they can't even say that this or that actor reminds them of some Karma) / Is there life after death? Yes, if and only if death is named Karma / The Karmas like—are you there my Bad Little Brother?—decelerators of particles, like liquefiers of the three times into a *paspresenture* wherein the narrative arc is always the same and everything is repeated from one generation to the next with different faces (Like in the operatic *Wuthering Heights* whose second part/generation seems to be an invention or a dream or a memory of the first part! Or vice versa! A rewrite! A correction but not an improvement! And, yes, though it's hard to admit it, the Karmas were so enviably melodramatic and nineteenth century and *Nonsense and Insensibility*) shooting for a single target that they never hit and always miss / And the Karmas filing in an almost religious procession to the homes of other Kar-mas. Always nearby—everyone together at the Mount Karma enclave—but never knowing exactly how long it'll take and how far away they are: like what happens with the movements between Wuthering Heights and Thrushcross Grange (of course, no Heathcliff among them and, yes, many Edgars and many Hindleys; and I heard that they recently discovered a television version that they thought was lost with a young Richard Burton as Heathcliff—he wouldn't be bad in the role—but my favorite candidate remains a young Clive Owen). Maybe they fly, maybe they teletransport *Star Trek* style, one thing is certain: they'll always arrive late, except, of course, to any summons from Mamagrandma / Mamagrandma who—long accustomed to doing whatever she wants—has now taken the next step, moving on to the next stage, and crossing the next border: thinking that now it's everyone else who has to do whatever she wants them to do / Mamagrandma and her shikomizue cane: watch out for it / Yesterday I convinced a few Karmas to watch *Citizen Kane* for the first time: Hiriz got excited because she thought that letter on the gate in the opening scene was a "K for Karma" / UGH! It's like you hear that dramatic telenovela music every time a Karma says something supposedly important but certifiably idiotic (*goin' crazy*) / The telenovela as a category of philosophy and (lack of) ethics / Karma cousins = fairy (witch) tale stepsisters / Karmas worried because they see you reading ("Are you bored?, depressed?") / Hypochondriacs and—though they condemn drug use—constantly high on downers and uppers and always ready to try new "products" whenever they're not contraindicated by their miracle cures / Tours of Houston clinics to be diagnosed with everything they don't suffer from (they look down on homeopathy as placebo, but, of course, they haven't the slightest doubt regarding the mystical properties of holy water) / Religion: they think it's great that Jesus "has been attached" to a girl called Mary (or María), "like his mother" / Doctors and priests as personal friends and "Karmas by association" (those people who aren't Karmas but who would like to be and for that reason they love them even though they constantly remind them, in one thousand and one different ways, that they are not "the real deal") / Karmas playing golf nonstop at the Kountry Klub: they play golf badly, they play golf to be able to say that they play golf, they play golf to be able to "wear golf clothes" and, while they're at it, to think that in that way they are taking care of their health: golf is the only sport where you can talk and scheme a lot while you play it / Karmas who read nothing but the popular bestsellers (if possible, something with romance and sex) / They like—they like the movies—Jane Austen (that *Sex and the City* version of the Brontës: in the books of Jane Austen nobody gives life or asks for death. Nobody really lives or seriously dies in their pages. And walking in the rain is just the same as a light cold; and the great tragedy is to miss out on a dance where everyone talks between one spin and the next and, again, square/line dancing / Karma Time = Soap Opera Time: a diagnosis, an engagement, a pregnancy, a divorce all last far longer than normal (and are developed episodically) or, suddenly, happen or fizzle out in a matter of seconds, as if by a sudden burst of enthusiasm or regret of the screenwriter / Ex-husbands and ex-wives who're not 100% Karma (bearers of last names that the Karmas always find "funny" or "strange" or "suspect") disappear from the plot and from the family tree, as if trimming a branch, in a matter of seconds / The Karmas and the "Non-Karmas": The Karmas spend their lives poking each other and causing wounds of varying severity but never lethal. The Karmas lovingly hate each other and are always on the lookout for some "Non-Karma" to appear in the Karmatic places they tend to frequent. When this happens, they all come together and throw themselves on the new arrival and devour him or her alive (with the exception of those who have some aristocratic Euro-trash title or who're famous) / Take heed: there are no Karmas who are famous outside Karma Land, none of them ever managed to gain any acclaim beyond the borders of the family business/fortune / The mystery, without a doubt solved for them, but impenetrable for outsiders regarding how and why the Karmas ever got rich (multiple theories that they neither confirm nor deny) explaining their ability to lose money in every venture they undertake. I asked Hiriz about it, Hiriz said: "What we make is something very small . . . But we do it far better than everyone else. We almost have a monopoly on its production and . . . It's not that it's something unseemly or that we're ashamed of it. In fact, we refer to it constantly, with familiarity and borderline impertinence. But it's still something small and trivial and almost ridiculous when it comes to its domestic applications . . . It's something . . . how to put it . . . Quite banal." Shoe polish? Clothespins? Some contraption for bathrooms on which to sit and think and purge what you never think about anywhere else? Toothpicks? / The Karmas travel to consume: in the Beginning was The Word and The Word was *Buy* (the word *Sell* is only used in order to get more cash so they can keep buying) / The 100% Karmas who get married among themselves are not allowed to get divorced: only widowhood is allowed and respected: if there are issues, "hang in there *m'hija*" / And no: infidelity is not a problem (better to practice it, always, with a Karma of inferior strata; thus the scandal always stays in the family); the absolute lack of love in the marriage is not a problem either / Engagements as long as marriages / But, at the same time, the Karmas incorporate more and more distant relatives; bringing them to Mount Karma (a property that never stops expanding and concentrating, like a combination of Aleph with Tlön) because, the more Karmas there are, the more opportunities there are to talk shit about someone / They are so many, they are more all the time: the quotas are never exceeded (although—obviously, of course, don't doubt it—there are first- and second- and third-class Karmas: I am a third-class Karma married to a first-class Karma; which amounts to, I guess, being a second-class Karma) / The Karmas have the patience of a carnivorous plant. The Karmas who're like a not-so restless and rather contemplative Dracula, waiting in the wings: vampires not interested in being invited into the houses of strangers (houses of strangers disgust them a little) but in attracting unwitting individuals to Mount Karma who'll be vampirized there and taken captive and slowly bled out while still alive / Mount Karma as Mecca and *meta* / Mount Karma as the only possible destination: they leave only so they can return and evoke the anguish they experience of being a nobody there outside and the ecstasy of coming home and being everything there inside / And so, their madness dissolves as it increases and is socialized and accepted and even understood and approved of / Their madness so different from that of our brief and concentrated families, where there's barely enough room—because there are barely any family members—for the Family Lunatic (Uncle Hey Walrus) or for a couple of *Locos Lindos* (our parents) / The horrifying lack of cleverness turning into cleverness when it comes to the names and nicknames of the Karmas: men and women (grandfathers and fathers, grandmothers and mothers and children and grandchildren both male and female) all calling themselves the same things, generation after generation / Frequent and, almost, unique nicknames: *El Gordo*, *El Flaco*, *El Flaco Gordo* or *El Gordo Flaco* (and their corresponding diminutives) / Or nicknames (the Karmas belong to that category of people whose nicknames end up renaming them: none of them have been vaccinated against the nickname) where it's unknown exactly what they refer to: *El Quicko* o *La Tuta* / Karmas on the loose: everything happens to them in public spaces, nothing happens to them when they're alone / "You sleep in bedrooms: bedrooms are for sleeping," one Karma explains to me / Weddings for the Karmas are synonymous with weekends; there is no weekend when the Karmas are not "going to a wedding" / Said/heard coming back from a Karma Wedding: "That girl he married is a real tramp, am I right?" / (Protocol-existential question: does she say this to me to get me to react in a violent way, or does she say it to me because she considers me a kind of trash dump where it's acceptable to throw all of her most toxic waste, or because she knows nobody would believe me if I mentioned it to other people, or because she thinks that maybe I think the same thing? In any case, every option is insulting. It was a young Karma woman who said it, she said it while arching her eyebrows and half-closing her eyes with a shark-like smile: the older Karma women think like that too, but they're *like that* due to cultural imposition, because generationally they had no option to not be *like that*; but the young Karma women are *like that* by choice, they could be different, they're better at being awful than their mothers and grandmothers and aunts) / Likewise, the Karmas of the past were brutes, the Karmas of today are brutal: the fine yet decisive line that separates imposed retrogression from the most enlightened of willful ignorance. The same difference that exists between being evil by nature or malicious by choice / Not the pure banality of evil but the dirty vulgarity of evil / The incredibly long showers taken by the Karmas whose waste of water could provide drinking water to multiple villages of the Kalahari (do the Karmas think that's a way to wash away their sins or, merely, a way to clean them up and make them smell nice and cover them up until the next shower when they feel those sins are starting to stink again?) / The Karmas always simultaneously just arrived and ready to leave / They travel en masse—in groups and they're never happier than when they're on cruises, where they can walk little and cruise a lot among themselves—and they always agree to get together in the cities they travel to in order to attenuate the horror of realizing that the rest of humanity is not like them (never that they're not like the rest of humanity). Or to feel even more proud to be unlike everyone else. Who knows. In any case, they are crazy / VERY CRAZY / Karmas upholstering their chairs to match their jackets in order to camouflage themselves and pass unperceived though they're there the whole time: Early Versace & Late Arcimboldo (there are Karmas whom I've only ever seen sitting down, never standing and in motion) / The sorrow barely concealing the joy of every Karma at the wake of any other Karma: it was someone else's turn / Someone else's death as something never known but learned by heart: "Do you know who died?" / Competing to be the one who finds out first about a death, to be the first to communicate it to the others in a group chat called RIP KARMA / Feeling like death? / The only way to stay alive is to suffer every so often (and the Karmas make me feel something like agony though not exactly) / Overheard at a Karma wake: "Have you noticed that K is looking a little cancer-colored?" / Tradition: a way of forcing someone to do something, to obey. Everything is a family tradition for them; even though there are Karma Traditions that only have twenty four hours of activities and that are constantly corrected or improved or—when it's more convenient—deactivated until further notice. Thus, another Karmatic way to abolish the laws of time / And the way every Karma looks at you when they find you reading or writing: the circular panic in their eyes, the brief awareness of that vast ocean in which they've only gotten their feet wet when the story of an S&M millionaire or a traumatized hacker or a student vampire gets massively popular. And the way in which they subsequently overcome that fear: they say that, without a doubt, that person who is reading or writing is depressed or bored / Just to clarify: the Karmas are not interesting. They're not the Kennedys. Really, the Karmas are the least interesting people on the face of the earth. But that's precisely why they *interest* me / Could I make some use of them? Yes? No? Could I lend/give them to my Bad Little Brother? Losing them the way you lose parents and—punishment for the crime—and . . . and . . . and . . . what turns someone into a mother and what I can't even bring myself to think about because it would be to admit that I think of nothing but that, of nothing but him. Maybe that would be the best. But not directly, rather, offer them to him little by little and so he doesn't realize it, like sugar cubes to a fly, until he feels capable and even justified in stealing them. And thus make him feel a great guilt but, also, helping him to keep on writing: it seems to me that he's reached the point where he can only write if he feels that writing is a sin and not a virtue / *Pobrecito*, alas: his guilt is not guilty of my guilt / All things familial have merit and there's nothing more familial than sadness / And, oh, the Karmas are so much happier than my Bad Little Brother, than I am, than we are. And it's so hard to be good when you're better than everyone, right? . . . And this is what it's like, this is how it works: one day you get up and you brush your teeth and you eat breakfast and you brush them again. And you go out into the street and, at some point, you discover that, for the first time, you haven't thought about *that*. About *that thing* you couldn't stop thinking about day after day ever since *that* happened. And it's then that you remember that *that* is what it is to forget. That gift. That privilege. The exceedingly pleasant weakness of that superpower. But, oh, Bad Little Brother: I don't think that we—our superpower is something else, just the opposite—are ever going to be able to remember to forget. About *that*. About all of *that*.

And, of course, he struggles to keep reading, because it wasn't easy to read when your eyes are flooded with tears, when your eyes weep and are lost. And then, the pages that follow, all those short sentences in that notebook seemed to realign into something that seemed to be the fleshless but already powerful skeleton of an unfinished novel by Penelope.

There—from what he can decode based on and emerging from crossed out words and arrows that're going to miss their targets—is a possible title: WUTHERING CRATERS. Like that, in all caps. And brief and telegraphic paragraphs about Eddie Tulpa (unbeknownst to her sisters Alex and Charley and to her brother Bertie) writing another adventure of the photophobic priestess/activist Stella D'Or facing off with a "lunar-lunatic family" (because they come from the moon) that's ready to be fruitful and multiple and invade everything. And it's a family that "hides a secret in plain sight, because it's a secret they share among themselves."

A secret that he glimpsed in that gushing group photo on the page he tore out of that magazine just days ago and that he examined in-flight ("enhance 224 to 176 . . . Stop . . . Move in . . . Stop . . . Pull out, track right . . . Stop . . . Center and stop . . .") with blade-runner eyes.

Something almost out of focus and half-hidden, off to one side and coming out of frame.

A flash of red.

A fragment, a bit of color the color of blood of his blood, yes.

In that photograph, entering the scene (*Enter GHOST*) for a second; so that nobody there looking and smiling at the camera realizes that he's spotted him, that he waves to him from so far away yet feeling him close.

There he is.

He Whose Name Must Not Be Mentioned.

The Son of Penelope who—it was assumed—had been lost so long ago in that place where the sea ends so the forest can begin. That boy who was given up for dead or murdered and who—he understands now, on that night full of flashlights and voices repeating his name over and over—had been kidnapped by the Karmas, because they believed that he belonged to them and not to Penelope and, definitely not to him.

The boy they'd looked for forever and never found.

The boy he found now and who he was going to track down like a replicant tracking down a replicant child.

And thinking about how all of that sets everything into motion, into the kind of motion where nothing ceases moving, like in that perpetual earthquake that he wrote at the end of his commissioned Mexican novel that Penelope let him steal from her.

And again, fiction coming true.

And all the delayed flights being canceled until further notice.

And, there outside, everything moves.

And that volcano opens its mouth in something that's the combination of the yawn of someone waking up and the scream of someone who can't fall asleep.

ʃ

And then all that was left was to think in the dark. Not counting white sheep but recounting everything to that immense green cow, in the desert night, telepathically.

He recounts images transmitted as though at the speed of memory (with that vertiginous slowness, with that slow vertigo) that in writing would take up hundreds of pages.

He recounts one of his favorite scenes from his favorite movie.

He recounts how that "man-ape" throws a tapir bone into the air and the bone spins and spins and suddenly—lights, camera, ellipsis!—millions of years go by.

He recounts how his story has been far humbler yet equally transcendent.

He recounts how he left the airport in Mexico City, D.F.—in a stampede along with all those Karmas—and how everything shook in sync with his own shaking.

He recounts how everyone got into cars and buses and trains and barges and how they went down rivers and rails and dirt roads whose courses were altered by winds and shadows.

He recounts for the magnificent green cow how he crossed the final frontier with the sun on the page higher than the sky and how he crossed the final frontier with the moon on the page higher than the sky, no matter the hour, it was all *full of stars*.

He recounts how he entered that cantina in Melancholic Rancheras, already in Abracadabra, and that from the jukebox came voices singing "How near or how far, I'd already gone the distance, having read the book, nothing matters much to me."

He recounts how, above the bar, the TV news was reporting, almost ready to sign-off, the comings and goings of a more or less mysterious celestial object.

He recounts how, suddenly, the tone of the program's host seemed to go totally off the rails, like a driver losing control of his vehicle. And how (BREAKING NEWS / EXTRA and ominous and dramatic music and he wondered if it'd been composed by Tom, with whom he and Penelope went to see *2001: A Space Odyssey* when they were kids) he reported "an incident of gravely serious consequences that could be the explanation for the drastic atmospheric-physical phenomena of recent days."

He recounts how it was reported that authorities had finally "declassified information about what'd happened on the previous Tuesday at the CERN particle accelerator in Switzerland."

He recounts how then it was reported that an "unstable man," "allegedly a terrorist" had snuck into the facilities and taken a hostage and "had opened what was perhaps a space-time rift, triggering an effect whose vast and grave consequences we still can't know for sure, but are now beginning to perceive in a variety of very different ways."

He recounts how then they broadcast the footage from a security camera at CERN, showing a man talking nonstop to the camera and how—when zooming in on the image and despite the poor quality—that man's face immediately reminded him of the face of someone he knew.

He recounts for the sumptuous green cow that, at first, he asked himself who it was that the man, there, on the television, reminded him of.

And that, then, he answered that the man reminded him of himself.

7

"How does it feel? . . . How does it feel?" And, yes, for such a long time now, it'd been perfectly clear to him what it was like to feel like a *complete unknown* with *no direction home*, and what it was like to live like he had nothing, like he had nothing left to lose, and what it was like to be invisible and to be left with no secret to hide apart from the secret of that one night.

And that other one too: "How do you feel? . . . How do you feel, ah-ah?" of someone asking himself if he wants to say something before he leaves, knowing perfectly well that we tend to say goodbye before we say hello and that a bed is a place where you can gain a day to end up losing a bloody year.

But now—but then—he feels and felt something new.

Something that nobody had ever felt before.

Then—now and in all times at the same time—when he would press and presses and pressed a button on the control panel in the European Laboratory of Elemental Particle Physics of the Conseil Européene pour la Recherche Nucléaire (for once the French had no need to change the name or the initials because the original name had been in French) where he'd locked himself inside with no way out. He understood and understands and would understand only now: that unhealthy pleasure of pressing a button, the same pleasure almost all of humanity experienced when feeling they had that power in the tip of their finger.

And all his particles accelerated and accelerate and would accelerate to merge with that other divine particle and lights and camera and action.

And before his eyes—his pupils changing color with every blink—opened and opens a rift in the shape of $\mathfrak{I}$.

And he entered and enters it.

And nothing happens by chance, nothing ever did.

And writers—even those who, like him, no longer wrote—were and are and will always be particularly sensitive to these tics and defects of reality. Reality which—perhaps just as unsatisfied—allows, almost on the sly, small flashes worthy of fiction. Plot twists that—given measurable time and palpable space—are always cast into doubt or related by opening with great care the door with the key of the "Believe it or not, what happened was . . ."

And, there inside, advancing at breakneck speed, all those figures and flashes. All of it very much like—because he doesn't dare think that it was all *exactly the same*, though he would dare to say it—everything the astronaut David Bowman saw when he crossed the threshold of the Star Gate.

Something that Clarke needed more and more pages of his novel to describe, but that made no sense to read.

Something that you had to see, not to understand it, but, yes, to admire it. Something that was "full of stars" and about whose genesis he'd read so many times in so many books about the complex and prolonged filming of *2001: A Space Odyssey*. There, Douglas Trumbull—thinking about how those initial painted curtains weren't going to work at all—telling Stanley Kubrick that "I've had a kind of epiphany" and explaining to him that not long ago he'd seen what'd been achieved by an animator named John Whitney with something called "slit scan." Something that, Trumbull thought, could be taken—if you introduced greater speed and different axes for the movement of the camera—much further and could achieve something far greater. And Kubrick said okay. And Trumbull felt like he was "going to church every day" and making all of that enter through Bowman's eyes so that it would arrive directly to the eyes of the viewers and—every so often, in the form of static inserts—showing the astronaut's face melting as if it'd been painted by Francis Bacon across Mark Rothko landscapes. And nothing gave Kubrick more pleasure and pride (because there was nothing he disdained and feared more than the effects of substances that would make him lose control over his work and life) than managing to *portray* the definitive *trip* without needing to take drugs. And besides, there, Kubrick achieved in film the most special effect of all, the one literature had been putting into practice since the dawn of time: turning the first and third person—character and reader—into a single person.

And he felt and saw himself and saw the same thing now.

And he heard it all accompanied by that sound and orchestral/atonal crescendo in the middle and at the end of The Beatles' "A Day in the Life" with George Martin doing all he could to follow John Lennon's instructions and to achieve "a tremendous build-up, from nothing up to something absolutely like the end of the world."

There, forty exceedingly disconcerted and uncomfortable musicians who were paid £367 for the session (and made to dress in formal attire and some wore fake noses and fake moustaches and stick-on nipples and the lead violinist performed wearing a gorilla paw and they were forced to obey a score that sounded somewhere between stupid and demented) and whose names didn't appear on the cover of *Sgt. Pepper's Lonely Hearts Club Band* until a long time thereafter, until the commemorative reissues that started coming once every ten years after that "It was twenty years ago today . . ." had been surpassed. Names that he looked for and memorized and recited every so often and recited again now—*all together now*—to populate a final phantasmal version of one of his lists of acknowledgements: John Marston (harp),

Eric Gruenberg, Granville Jones, Bill Monro, Jurgen Hess, Hans Geiger, D. Bradley, Lionel Bentley, David McCallum, Donald Weekes, Henry Datyner, Sidney Sax, Ernest Scott (violins), and John Underwood, Gwynne Edwards, Bernard Davis, John Meek (violas), and Francisco Gabarro, Denis Vigay, Alan Delziel, Alex Nifosi (cello), and Cyril Mac Arther, Gordon Pearce (double bass), and Roger Lord (oboe), and Basil Tschaikov, Jack Brymer (clarinets), and N Fawcett and Alfred Waters (bassoons), and Clifford Seville and David Sandeman (flutes) and Alan Civil and Neil Sanders (French horns), and David Mason and Monty Montgomery and Harold Jackson (trumpets), and Raymond Brown and Raymond Premru and T. Moore (trombones), and Michael Barnes (tuba), and Tristan Fry (tympani).

And it's as if all of them had gotten back together to accompany him, to play alongside him, to carry him toward the light at the speed of their sound.

And, after setting the controls for his *interstellar overdrive* and *astronomy domine* and all that psychedelia or whatever it was toward the heart of his sun, what'd happened and was still happening to him, of course, were many things. Interdimensional crossroads that were nothing but alternate versions of a single event that someone had discarded (as if he were inspecting valuable objects on the shelves of his memory palace, as if throwing pale Post-its into the trash) while attempting to find the best possible option among so many options.

In its moment, the option wherein he'd been subdued by the CERN security forces just before he could set the hadron centrifuge to spin and had been taken to a cell and then freed when IKEA came to pay his bail—even though, beyond its nonsensical nature, probable and realistic—was no longer the one he liked, it no longer worked for him.

The moment had come to choose a different plotline, to try to find a better ending.

He loves to turn himself on, indeed.

And on, and on, and on . . .

Now he was going to try something else very different from what he'd tried before.

The option he'd selected hadn't turned out as he'd planned. Sure: it'd tempted him with the offer of writing again, of having written *The Impossible Story* (and he'd been pulled in by that flash in which a first-rate politician had given his book as a gift, thinking that something like that could only have happened or could only end up happening if he'd become a living classic). But, clearly, he hadn't reviewed the fine print in the contract or calibrated the true scope and consequences of setting it in motion. Or its incessant *ritor-nellos*, its winding and circular digressions, its wanderings through corridors and rooms of his memory palace searching in vain for the bathroom or the kitchen. And, of course, much less had he calculated the primary effects on secondary characters: Penelope in flames and Ella appearing and disappearing in a torrent of multidimensional swimming pools (and wondering, in his particular acceleration, if he could somehow bring them, him and Ella, back together again, as if in the most merciful of acts, at the bottom of the sky of their consciousnesses) and him imagining himself like a colossal version of Mr. Trip, roaming across a planet rewritten in his style and semblance, whistling that song by The Kinks that he loved so much . . .

ʃ

. . . and that was called "Big Sky" and, oh, promises are made not to be kept and challenges not to be accepted. So, again, another display of his referential mania, another entry in his private encyclopedia (now in the prose of those articles he'd written back when he was starting out, those articles that, before *National Industry*, he'd published in rock magazines and cultural supplements and that'd garnered him certain renown among his editors and readers for the way he had of lending them prestige with a glut of literary references) and "Big Sky," track 6, Side 1, of *The Kinks Are the Village Green Preservation Society*, from 1968.

That album that The Kinks—with that great lack of sense of timing that always characterized them—released on the same day that The Beatles put out *The Beatles* (but for him, The Kinks were so much better than The Beatles, for him "Days" would always be far above "Yesterday" and The Beatles had only ever transcended its heights with "A Day in the Life"). And one of those two albums sold millions of copies, and the other didn't sell at all. And, of course, The Kinks' album—which could be connected to Marcel Proust or George Eliot or Philip Larkin—was a little bit out of touch with its times but perfectly in sync with the world according to Ray Davies: pastoral songs, odes to the small town, and warnings various about the dangers of the bright lights of the big city, and a defense of all past times as better compared to that psychedelic present. In his own way, as Ray Davies explained years later in an interview, "my own form of psychedelia." There, childhood friends never seen again and crazy relatives, tempted and tempting girls who went to town and later returned home victoriously vanquished to their parents who loved them so even though they'd gotten pregnant by some dandy from Carnaby St., village witches, "real" animals and phenomenal cats, shops and parks and promenades and steam-powered trains and rivers to sit beside and look at the river.

The Kinks—in days of combative protest and anxiety of an emergent world, when the world seemed to be burning and the streets were overrun with revolutionary kids—proposed staying home and not doing anything and distrusting trends and, instead, "preserving the old ways from being abused" and flouting the long and serpentine and sinful guitar solos and the even longer songs with cryptic or overtly nonsensical lyrics. And, there, Ray Davies wasn't telling or singing a single and conceptual story. There was no trace of "rock-opera" ambition. What was woven together there was something that had no beginning, no middle, no end, no suspense, no moral, no causes, no effects, and yet aspired to achieve and achieved something formidable: the surprising and beautiful depths of many marvelous moments seen all at one time. *The Kinks Are the Village Green Preservation Society* was, really, a mood, a state of mind, a figurative abstraction running through the lives and joys and miseries of a handful of characters coming and going through the English countryside and confronting the past head-on.

And he'd listened to all of that for the first time in the rural locale of Sad

Songs, on the Wincofon of Uncle Hey Walrus who (somewhat disturbed; a doctor had suggested that he listen to it as a form of therapy to ween himself off his lords and masters) couldn't help but admit The Kinks greatness was on par with that of The Beatles (but, for Uncle Hey Walrus, The Beatles were better, because they'd figured out how to have everything go far better for them than The Kinks had).

And he hadn't stopped listening to *The Kinks Are the Village Green Preservation Society* ever since, feeling closer and more akin to how Ray Davies had been feeling ever since: an outsider, different, a counter-current, pushing upstream, someone who still put the descriptive lyric of the verse ahead of the imprisoning image of the photograph. Like Ray Davies, he preferred the gratitude for the revelatory days of the past over the uncertainty of what might be revealed by the sleepless nights of the future.

And so—The Kinks were already highlighting their perverse need to be different with the name of the band itself—in days of the summer of love and the season of the witch, of satanic graces, and of bands with lonely hearts, with pipers at the gates of dawn, and with pinball wizards. And so, this album of humble sales and simple sound (but with the proud humility that The Beatles' most humbly proud tracks on *The Beatles* never achieved) and with a personal and bizarre ideology "of protest" (but in the inverse and retro-conservative direction; it was protesting against change and worshipping what should never change) didn't have a great reception among the youth at the time. Ray Davies would take it all further still—to fail even more successfully—in that kind of continuation/expansion that was the rock-operetta *Preservation*. There—again and five years later—Ray Davies denouncing the involutions of progress and the greed of real-estate sharks infesting rivers and lakes and laying waste to villages with bulldozers like the ones that'd swept away his alma mater, Gervasio Vicario Cabrera, colegio n.°1 del Distrito Escolar Primero and the *alma* mortem of Pertusato, Nicolasito. Ray Davies as if denouncing the dangers lying in wait for holy lands to be preserved at all cost where the best models and modalities and manners of his culture were still hanging on beyond the toxic influence of the big cities and the expansive decadence of the Empire.

The Kinks Are the Village Green Preservation Society—so out of place, so perfectly positioned within itself, considered in retrospect to be one of the few unquestionable masterpieces of '60s pop music and every so often revisited again in different formats by its author—had, also, been the result of Ray Davies having a nervous breakdown. One of many. And that was why those songs functioned as an ideal soundtrack for those asylums/sanctuaries where gentleman of yesteryear were sent to recover their lost happiness or, at least, their missing sanity. And that was also why the whole concept had been first been conceived of by Ray Davies as a solo album and then—as he began accumulating perfect songs, among them the sublime farewell of "Days"—as a heartfelt and terrified epitaph to the Swinging Sixties and final act of The Kinks. The Kinks who—despite the fact that they kept on recording and touring until 1996 and, ever since, had periodically announced an imminent reunion—Ray Davies had considered finished as a band in 1968. Everything that'd come thereafter, for him, had been nothing more than, not all the past life, but all the life yet to come. As if it were all unfolding before the eyes and ears of a bitter divinity, not moribund but disenchanted with his own creation, and unable to understand how it was that those imperfect beings had failed to understand him and had turned his masterpiece into—in Ray Davies's own words—"the most successful flop of all time."

And what was *The Kinks Are the Village Green Preservation Society* exactly? A concept album? A rock-operetta? None of that. What's more: you could say that what it most resembled was that also naturalist "novel-for-radio" and play for voices written by Dylan Thomas and titled *Under Milk Wood*, with allusions to *Coming Up for Air* by George Orwell.

But for him, *The Kinks Are the Village Green Preservation Society* had been an album of mature songs with a deceptively childish air and ideal for prematurely mature children terrorized by the Peterpanic childishness of their parents. And, from the here and now, *The Kinks Are the Village Green Preservation Society* was nothing but the bucolic version of *Wish You Were Here*. Again and forever, not what he was most interested in hearing but what he couldn't stop hearing: the sound of absence, of the absent, of what/who had once been there and no longer was: the sound of his life.

A series of voices bursting forth from one mouth to sing of their comings and goings blending together to form a single landscape that defined them. Wherever you might be from, you moved away from all of that just so you could return to it.

Melodies clear as perfect postcards, punctuated by the inevitable *fa-la-las, a-scooby-dooby-doos, tralalas, sha-la-las.*

And—among all of them, again and always and forever—"Big Sky."

A tumult of sound (a sound that was the natural continuation of that sound on "A Day in the Life" that, he thought, could only be the sound of his particles accelerating to centrifuge with universe.

"No, it's not about God. It's just a big sky . . . and most of it is fact," Ray Davies explained in an interview.

And, yes, right: the absence of God demarcating his presence in "Big Sky." A song in which everyone looks up and only one being looks down. And, as he doesn't find what he sees interesting, he leaves.

Tzimtzum: that constriction—as it's explained in the Kabbalah—voluntarily experienced by God. God contracting and compressing himself and renouncing his infinite essence to thereby allow for the existence of a conceptual space: the *chalal panui*, a space where an independent world could exist.

In a way, God thereby became a perfect reader, allowing humanity to take over as an imperfect yet prolific writer.

"Big Sky" as a song in which you don't really know if someone is singing to an absent god or if it is the indifferent god—in third and first person at the same time—who's excusing himself for not feeling any concern or responsibility for the actions of those tiny beings inhabiting that planet down there. The Beatles included (Ray Davies had once said that "The Beatles were supposed to be like the boy next door only better"; and in 1967, Iris Murdoch had nominated The Beatles as a four-headed Poet Laureate to sing for the Empire, but the unquestionable and natural candidate—someone who'd always been taking that role on though nobody would think to nominate him—had always been Ray Davies).

And Ray Davies had admitted that "If I had to do my life over, I would change every single thing I have done."

And, yes, he understood Ray Davies perfectly and he was right there with him in that desire and sentiment.

And there was nothing he liked more than the idea of being able to be like Big Sky.

J

And now, at last, he was like Big Sky. But not the Big Sky in the "Big Sky" that he'd listened to all his life, but the one that appeared, over and over again, in that formidable fiftieth-anniversary commemorative box set of *The Kinks Are the Village Green Preservation Society:* multiple versions and demos including a choir and an orchestra and takes in radio studios or in concerts throughout the decades and from various CDs and even adding a facsimile reincarnation on vinyl of the LP and its respective singles. Marvelous moments, indeed. All times at the same time and, occasionally, Big Sky poking out its head, like a disinterested participant, in medleys where it melted into other songs on the album.

That's how, with those mannerisms, he saw himself now in order to see himself from before. To remix what wasn't, what couldn't have been, what was elsewhere and what could have come to pass who knows where and when.

And the sky is never bigger—nor the bigness of the sky perceived more and better—than when you're walking in the desert.

J

He arrived to the last desert—the desert where all deserts end up—almost without realizing it. Because one doesn't realize one is lost until one is already lost. There's no process of going to get lost, just like, for him, there was no clear perception that he was ceasing to write: all of a sudden he was no longer writing, all of a sudden writing had deserted him. Out of nowhere, he couldn't count on being able to recount anything, apart from humming that bit about my echo my shadow and me.

Now, by merely pressing a button, with all the accelerated particles of his imagination more accelerated than ever, possibilities multiplied, variations composed and recomposed themselves, cells interlinked, like in a medley, in another medley. That medley where The Beatles came together like never before in order break apart forever. That medley that is the only thing left for them to do—before breaking up—after having recorded the greatest streak in the history of pop music: "Strawberry Fields Forever / Penny Lane," *Sgt.*

Pepper's Lonely Hearts Club Band. Magical Mystery Tour, "All You Need Is Love," "Hey Jude," *The Beatles, Let It Be, Abbey Road* in a little more than three years, the last three years of an eight-year career (in days when artists could change many times without ceasing to be themselves, unlike today, when one artist is swapped out for another artist at ever greater speed) and suddenly centrifuging in on themselves and accelerating the particles of parts of songs melting and blending into each other. That medley that, after a part called "Golden Slumbers" and another part called "Carry That Weight," continued and came to a close (because he never stuck around to listen to that inopportune coda titled "Her Majesty") with a final part called—like the truly final credits at the finale of a movie—"The End."

Fragments and instants and moments. Freewheeling parts that end up coming together into a whole that was nothing but a "this is as far as it goes," the farewell, the ceasing to be. And so goodbye to everything he'd been up until then, which now came apart to make space for something new.

Now, out of nowhere, he was like the hero in that comic of his childhood (Juan Salvo), like that time traveler from that novel that would be with him forever (Billy Pilgrim), like that miser from that novella hopping back and forth between Christmases past (Ebenezer Scrooge), and like the protagonist of that movie (George Bailey) who was offered the miracle of effacing expunging erasing deleting crossing out wiping out obliterating himself. But, in his case, no dinosaurs or canyons or canons or rockets or cages in extraterrestrial zoos or bridges under the snow or the biggest turkey in the city.

No.

His thing was and is and would be different.

Now he was in the desert, yes, but full of possibilities.

7

And among the many things of the past that he never stopped missing in the present was the use of *The End* at the end of movies. *The End* in different typographies and calligraphies on the screen, like the final signature of an irrefutable testimony, as if it were the writing of God at the end of His reign, after He's said everything He has to say. A reign that'd come to an end (in days when sequels or prequels, no matter the great success of the original, weren't yet in style; pretty soon, he thought, people would be doing remakes and reboots of reality and things like the Battle of Thermopolis and the "discovery" of America and the *Apollo 11* moon landing would take place again, with better production) because there were so many other stories waiting to be told, because there were too many stories, because there was always another story waiting to make history.

Thus and for that reason, that unquestionable and irrefutable *The End* that told the viewer that, in the end, the love or that hate that the characters take is equal to the hate or the love that they make or unmake. That *The End* that—unlike what, in general, happened at the end of the movies that would come later and that were shown these days in the artificial night of ever smaller and emptier movies theaters—now shone in its absence.

Now, scenes that continued as if nobody had been informed that soon the lights would come up even as all those letters of the credits were rolling across the faces of heroes of heroines. Or that, even, they would spend a few eternal minutes waiting for a few extra seconds that, supposedly, would reveal some more or less fun or intriguing connection, already previewing another movie belonging to the same saga: another of those movies whose opening credits had been transported from the beginning to the ending without *The End*.

Nothing appeared to end, all need to conclude what'd begun had been lost. Continuing to continue was the sign of the times, influenced, perhaps, by those videogames in which you always died or lost, due to the most sadistic and implacable of algorithms, but in which, right away, with false and exceedingly utilitarian mercy, you were allowed and encouraged to start over again.

There was no *The End* at the end of *2001: A Space Odyssey*. Just—in case there was any doubt, in ominous and indisputable all caps—a THIS FILM WAS DIRECTED AND PRODUCED BY STANLEY KUBRICK followed by a SCREENPLAY BY STANLEY KUBRICK AND ARTHUR C. CLARKE.

And yes: now he really needed, more than anything, the feeling of an ending.

A *The End* like the ones that left no room for doubt or ambiguity in those classic movies. And, yes, Orson Welles had warned that no story could have a happy ending because it "was an ending." The only way something had a happy ending was for it to never end, for the end not to be told, Orson Wells claimed. And, maybe for that reason, Orson Welles almost never ended his films and, in the most famous one he'd finished, the investigators left Xanadu without the faintest idea of who or what Rosebud was; because they thought that Rosebud was what would explain the present, when, really, Rosebud was a past that needed no explanation, that other monolith in the shape of a sled.

Rosebud—a sled with the name of a mythological stone, of an ancient location, of an indecipherable rite—as an enigma for the future: and what was the past if not a monolith around which to hop up and down, trying to understand it, hoping that something occurs to you and that something occurs? Something always ready for someone to enter into it—the door to the past opens, the door to the past closes—because it is full of stars. Stars with which to write life and—stardust, that pigment in dust to which you add water to then dip in the point of a pen—to try to recapture the most faraway stars, thinking and writing that from them you come and that, with any luck and good guidance, to them you shall return.

So now, he says to himself, he's going to try for the best of both worlds: black and white and color for an open ending that closes in on itself.

An ending where the protagonist would be The End.

And where The End would be him.

丁

And once upon a time—so many airplanes ago—he'd fantasized for a few instants about the fragments of a possible science-fiction novel composed of marvelous moments. A story with two young men and a melancholic extraterrestrial and an otherworldly young woman and the four of them surrounded by and buried under so much snow and bound together by something that'd happened to them one otherworldly night.

And he even, for the last time, came up with an opening line: "Find yourself wherever you find yourself, near or far, if you can read what I now write, please, remember, remember me, remember us, like this."

And he thought—just before ceasing to think about all of that, because thinking about writing what he was certain he could no longer write hurt so much or made him too uncomfortable—that it wouldn't be bad for that novel to end with a list of successive and possible ends of the world.

But what he could offer himself now, he understood with a combination of joy and terror (there was something as moving as it was absurd about the sudden transformation of a man of reflection, of a writer or exwriter, mutating into a man of action or into a person-persona-character), was the certainty that his memory was no longer what it'd been and that it would never be what it once was. Now, his memory wasn't what he could remember but, merely, what he couldn't forget. So, what he proposed and accepted and wrote was something else. Instead of different endings he proposed different alternate beginnings; but understanding beginnings not as the first thing that happens in a story but as something on the basis of which—beyond their space-time location within the plot—so many different things could come to pass. A succession of clusters of carefully-selected symbols, a depth of marvelous moments seen all at one time, telling and enumerating possibilities not for returning to the point of departure but for arriving to the endpoint, the final period.

Beginnings that started like this:

And in the end . . .

丁

Welcome (as if his life were a novel not *of* science fiction but a novel *with* science fiction) to the final and ultimate beginnings of his world.

丁

Is there anybody out there?

﹁

Yes.

﹁

Seven.

﹁.

The Seven Capital Scenes, as postulated by that book, that manual for young men so desperate to become writers after so long being nothing but readers and who he always crossed paths with on airplanes.

To wit:

1) vanquish the monster

2) rags to riches

3) the search

4) the comedy

5) the tragedy

6) the rebirth

7) the journey out of the shadows and into the light

And that's all, folks.

Or not: because he'd left out the most important and interesting plot of all.

Plot 8) which, for him, was like the eighth passenger, bursting out of from the insides and not from the brain, devouring all the previous *capital scenes* one by one.

The plot that suddenly sees itself from outside and asks itself what's going on and what can I do to get out of here, out of this loving and burning building, and, at last, enter what's over there, or vice versa.

The plot that, in truth, allowed for the existence of so many other plots, of possible points of departure that would lead to the final period, the infinite endpoint.

Plot number 8, plot number ∞.

And then, all of a sudden, he's not alone.

At his side there's an enormous green cow.

A green cow as big as a gray elephant.

And, yes, Penelope had told him about her: about how, when fleeing her own wedding, where she was marrying the comatose Maxi on Mount Karma, she'd wandered through the desert studded with diamonds that she collected—like breadcrumbs in a fairytale—until she almost died of thirst and was rescued by one of these animals. And, when she drank its fluorescent milk, Penelope had acquired telepathic abilities and had communicated with that magnificent green cow who'd told her that, yes, her race had been developed as a part of one of Hiriz's many disastrous undertakings, utilizing banned feed and illicit radiations for the rapid reproduction and growth of the cows. And that all her sisters—when Hiriz saw the whole thing had gone awry—had been chased and hunted down and killed. And that she was the last of her species. But that, actually, her true essence originated long before Hiriz's biological blunders, that her origin was on pre Columbian altars, where she and those of her race had been raised up as deities.

And the formidable green cow told him and enumerated all the things that she'd seen and that he wouldn't believe.

And he listened to her with great attention—with the kind of interest you achieve when you have nothing left to focus on apart from what a telepathic green cow is telling you—and, yes, he's thirsty and he seeks shade between her four legs and all of a sudden everything spins even faster.

And, after drinking that milk, what he's allowed to see and to live are random scenes from alternate realities around his reality, answers to a *multiple-choice* test, cells interlinked within cells interlinked within cells interlinked within one stem that was him, as if they were memories—based on his memory—designed and modified by the young Dr. Ana Stelline: the catalogue of furniture to decorate his interior life with, the things he would see and that nobody would believe.

A. And then his small hand is holding a not-so-small but, yes, mobile and portable phone. A device that has nothing to do with the mobile phones of today: it's a steampunk device, Victorian, as if designed by the inventor of the movie *The Time Machine*. With a dial and ringer and a small receiver that hooks over the ear. It's not particularly comfortable and weighs a great deal—it's made of Bakelite—but for him it's enough and more than enough. A cellular telephone interlinking within a cellular telephone interlinking within a cellular telephone interlinking within cells of one stem that was him: the stem of his parents. A cellular telephone—let the invention and the dream and the memory of that device be done—to be used, that night, to call his parents and tell them what he'd done and what's going to happen to them and to implore them to get aboard the *Diver* and to pull up anchor and to flee.

And, for once, his parents obey.

B. And then he's back amid the ruins that surround Gervasio Vicario Cabrera, colegio n.°1 del Distrito Escolar Primero. And there he is with his friends and with Pertusato, Nicolasito. All of them and only him playing at having survived in a landscape laid to waste by Victorian Martian invaders or by post-atomic earthlings. And there's the end of a loose, high-tension cable sticking out of the ground and resembling the claw of an alien or robot. And he says to Pertusato, Nicolasito that he should eliminate that threat, that since he was the last one to join the group, he has to go through this rite of passage. And he hands him a metal bar so that he can smash it. And Pertusato, Nicolasito obeys just as he once obeyed. But nothing happens: now the cable has been disconnected.

And their lives go on.

And he becomes a writer and many years later, out of nowhere, Pertusato, Nicolasito comes up to him at one of his book launches and introduces himself, and he barely recognizes him.

And Pertusato, Nicolasito tells him that he's now a dentist, that he inherited his father's practice and clientele, because "the whole literature thing isn't much of a life, it's not a good life, right?"

C. And then a young IKEA approaches him at a party and tells him how much he admires him and asks him for a flattering blurb for his first book. And he tells IKEA that he has to go to the bathroom, that they can talk more in a minute, but he leaves that party and goes home early (he needs to keep his faculties intact, he's writing his third book, the second one was even better-received than the first) and he never sees IKEA again and never hears anything about him. Until many years later, in a bookstore, he comes across one of his books: IKEA's first book. IKEA is one of those late-blooming writers, IKEA was never a young writer. But, oh, now, IKEA is incredibly juvenile in the best possible sense.

And he opens it.

And he's moved to see that it's dedicated to him: his name followed by a "*Il miglior fabbro.*"

And he starts to read it.

And IKEA's book is difficult and excessive and with too many pages and experimental and has no dialogue or character names.

And it's very good.

And it's better.

And it's not that this seems good to him, but it doesn't seem bad either.

D. And then Ella appears. Again. As if she'd never left and dematerialized. Ella on the deck of a boat like that of his parents. Or maybe it is the *Diver* and how would he have gotten it and what does it matter. And he and The Son of Penelope get on board and depart on an adventure. As a family, finally and in the end. As a family after all. Thanks to Ella. Ella who—unlike what really happened, after she fell into that last swimming pool and got out of it that one night—came over walking in a way that reminded him so much of Rachael in *Blade Runner*, in the scene where she appeared for the first time. Rachael—as is explained in *Blade Runner 2049*—emotionally designed to fall in love with an already prone-to-fall-in-love Deckard. And, together, giving birth to a miracle as "mad as thunder." Ella who now—sitting at the table over one of those breakfasts where they talked and talked and kept on talking—says to him: "Life is a gift. One of those gifts with a very complex bow and wrapped in paper so shiny it's a shame to rip it. And for that reason you open it very carefully and, with any luck, delay the surprise for a long time, a long happy time, as long as possible. Because, there, inside—he understands as he sees it—awaits the definitive and inescapable surprise of death . . . Meanwhile, we move on at the speed of life, which isn't as fast as the speed of sound or the speed of light, but far more vertiginous and it deforms your face, as if dissolving it, like what happens to the faces of astronauts during those centrifugal-acceleration tests or when they're sunk into swimming pools to experience weightlessness or whatever. But constantly thinking—like those astronauts, because in outer space any interior error is dearly paid for and gives you no chance to fix it or start over—that you must not forget this or that thing, because it is precisely in those things where your life and your ability to depart and to return reside . . . And, of course, you can't forget to not forget. And there's something very strange in the fact that what you cannot forget, the most important things in your life, are already part of the past and are already finished, while, at the same time, they're still here and now and will still be there and then tomorrow. Forever. Like me in your head. I who, though I may die, will live on in your head. Like a tumor nesting in your memory. And there, you convincing yourself that you're my salvation . . . And so, always remember and remember well . . . Let's be clear. You didn't save my life. I allowed you to save my life, so that, then, you would be able to tell the story of how you saved my life, for the rest of your life. Nobody will save you from that . . . You're going to save my life, over and over, until the day you die."

And then he knew that he'd been blessed with the curse of telling the story of Ella, of telling how Ella had begun for him and how she'd moved on. But he would never be allowed to tell her ending, because it was and is and would always be an open ending—the kind of ending that isn't the end of the world but the continuation of a life, her life.

E. And then he's running along the edge of a beach where a Young Man and a Young Woman have been camping and they're surprised to see him, and they tell him that everyone had given him up for dead or disappeared or volatilized. And they tell him—almost apologizing—that their idea had been, first, to film a documentary about him; but they'd run out of funding; and that it'd been easier for them to reorient the whole project and that now the documentary was on Penelope, but "you do appear in it and your importance is greatly emphasized." And then he tells them not to worry, that it's all fine, that there's no problem; but that, also, they should take some time to document themselves, that they had no time to waste, that life is short, and that . . .

F. And then Mamagrandma delivers one of her typical speeches. Another of her self-aggrandizing sermons. Not a speech of the "I have seen things you people wouldn't believe" variety, but more along the lines of "You will never see what I have seen." And no, she's not dead: Mamagrandma faked her death and she's hiding in a cave, near Mount Karma, outfitted with every comfort and convenience. She explains to him—while pointing a revolver at him, a revolver that once belonged to her husband who she killed and whose body she hid in a wall—that "I was very eager to be the first living saint in History."

He arrived to that cave after taking Mount Karma by storm and blood and fire with the help of Rolling Thunder, who perished in the battle and who—as he held him in his arms—commended his soul unto Manitou without, it seemed to him, a great deal of enthusiasm.

As everything was exploding—"Drop the Bomb! Exterminate Them All! Hue or who? Destroy and Forget. Awkward. Reward!," he thought—he ran through the rooms of Mount Karma, as the walls came crashing down and dozens of Karmas fled screaming, but, also, thinking that maybe it wasn't a bad thing that it was all ending, that maybe it wouldn't be bad to live in different houses, far away from each other, to get to know people with last names different from their own.

But he didn't find who he was looking for and so he took Cubita Karma hostage and interrogated her and she told "the truth that only I know," and she told him where to go out in the desert and he went out and found that cave and walked inside. And now Mamagrandma was telling him—and inevitably talking just like one of his characters—that "I couldn't allow the son of my son and descendent of our line to be brought up by a madwoman like your sister and a failure like you . . . Two writers . . . There are no beings more pathetic than writers: all the time inventing what they do not do, dreaming of what they'll never do, and remembering what they never did." And that was why Mamagrandma had hired some hitmen to kidnap the boy. The Son of Penelope.

And they'd made him disappear just like his maternal grandparents—who could never have countenanced the idea of themselves as grandparents—had disappeared. And ever since, He Whose Name Must Not Be Mentioned had been there, with her, forever: "a saint's apprentice being brought up to become Messiah Karma."

And he looks at her the way Marlow once looked at Kurtz (and no, it wasn't the same Marlow from *Heart of Darkness*, the Joseph Conrad novella; in the film by Francis Ford Coppola, for him far better than the book, Marlow is named Willard; and he always struggled to remember that and never understood why they'd changed Marlow's name, what was the point given that they hadn't changed Kurtz's name) and then, in one corner of the cave, he sees The Son of Penelope. And the boy—who, apart from the fact that he's wearing some ridiculous golf pants and a *mauve* Lacoste polo shirt, reminds him, yes, of the first appearance of little Heathcliff in *Wuthering Heights*—remembers him. And he tells him to get behind him and he takes aim. And Mamagrandma rips the rifle out of his hands and fires at close range and he feels a blow to his chest and falls on his back; but there's no blood, no last breath. And he discovers that the bullet struck Mr. Trip and that Mr. Trip saved his life, like what happens in the movies with a sheriff's star or a Bible or a lucky coin.

And Mamagrandma laughs like the most beatific of possessed people and fails to notice what's happening. She fails to notice that he's still alive and fails to notice (*Exit, Killed by a Green Cow*) that the jaws of a colossal green cow close around her neck and proceed to eat her alive.

G. And then he winds up Mr. Trip ("Mr. Trip!," The Son of Penelope exclaims with joy). And—surprise—Mr. Trip still works despite the bullet. But—he stands him up on the cave floor—now, and after so many years, for the first time in his life, Mr. Trip moves forward.

And, all of a sudden, Mr. Trip begins to grow and grow and grow, until his body bursts through the cave's ceiling and he protects him and The Son of Penelope from the falling rocks and lifts them up onto his shoulder. And now Mr. Trip is like the gigantic automaton of a Central European occultist or an all-powerful Eastern mutant. And the horizon is the end of the known world. And the three of them, together forever, are the new gods.

And he no longer feels any need to write because now, everyone (there's even an assignment in schools requiring students to dedicate not exactly open-subject essays and compositions to his figure and glory) writes about him.

H. And so he's rescued He Whose Name Must Not Be Mentioned and he goes back to the beach and hands him over to The Young Man and The Young Woman so they can care for him. Or to Ella. Either way. The important thing is for the boy to choose his own future parents, that he is there and gets to determine what'll happen to him: what, one day, will be his past. And he says goodbye to him with a line that he wrote in a book, so long ago: "My aspirations are humble but that doesn't make them easy to achieve: faced with the impossibility of being a good memory for you, I'll settle for being a good story." Then he runs like he once ran almost for the first time, when he was a boy, on another beach, like children who're pure knee and who run not yet thinking that someone is watching them run. Like a boy who runs, unaware that, unfortunately, for a total lack of fortune, there will soon be a uniform and proper and respectable and harmonious way of running, for he'll know himself watched and judged and compared to other runners. But he can barely go on, he's been mortally wounded. And he's surprised, because the blood that comes out of the hole opened in his chest by the bullet fired by Mamagrandma is more black than red. It looks like ink, he thinks. And, all of sudden, it seems very important to him to wash it off. He doesn't want The Son of Penelope to be scared, for him to remember him like that. And that's why, now, he runs on alone—*Denn die Todten reiten schnell . . .*—and into the sea and a wave washes over him and pulls him out and under. And the sea has a celestial and ultramarine color that reminds him of the sky inside Grand Central Station in New York: of those constellations arranging the stars, making false order out of the chaos of space. And he remembers himself there, so many times, rocked to the rumbling of the future still ahead of him, of the trains coming and going: him, there, still so young, under what felt like the Sistine Chapel, his feet planted firmly on solid ground and the future out ahead of him. As stiff as a flag, taut and frozen by an invisible wind in a lunar desert, with Earth on high, in a bottomless sky the color of Grand Central in the Pantone of its illusion: the color of all the books he dreamed of inventing. And he lets himself go, drifting down, like Martin Eden toward that last instant of absolute knowing which is followed by an instant of total unknowing.

And at some point he'd read about something called "secondary drowning" or "dry drowning": something that happened when you almost drowned and, even several days later, ended up experiencing death by drowning on terra firma, due to a sudden spasm in your throat. Your body and your mind, traumatized by the memory of almost drowning and, trying to protect you, cause your larynx to close, mistakenly preventing air and not water from getting there inside. The memory of when you almost died coming back and living to tell the tale. He wondered—having almost drowned at the beginning of the novel of his life—if such a phenomenon could end up taking place more than a half century later. Probably not, but who knows and he still has a few seconds of that awareness that he's losing letter by letter, just as he gained it, fifty years ago, when, all of a sudden, for a few minutes he knew how to read and write before ever having learned to write and to read. Which is why, now, in the water, floating in reverse, he feels that he's forgetting and losing the superpower of reading and writing, and he feels more powerful than ever, because all he has left to do is watch.

And, there above, one of the stars is moving.

And it's an airplane. The last of many airplanes that he thinks about.

And it's the airplane in which he and Penelope are traveling, years ago, back from Disneyland. "Here you leave today and enter the world of yesterday, tomorrow and fantasy," he remembers, and he can see it: he sees himself there, above, looking out the little window of the airplane, and seeing himself and saying to Penelope a "I bet you can't guess who I just saw."

I. And then he see him, he sees himself, in what appears to be a luxury hotel. In a room with glowing floors and white walls and Louis-XVI furniture. On one of the walls hangs, framed, his favorite photograph of Vladimir Nabokov. The one that Irving Penn took of the writer in 1966 and that's just his face: a head like that of a turtle whose shell holds up the entire world, the absolute totality of the universe. And, as constant background music, piped in through invisible speakers, he hears not classical music but *Hey Walrus Sings the Sad Songs Revival Affinity*: the album that G. and Jeff Lynne produced for his now cured and lucid and talented uncle; the album that, since the early '80s (the new '60s), had been considered a cult classic, with innumerable reissues and multiple bonus tracks; and, yes, the girl/woman on the cover, who's so in love with his uncle, is none other than his onetime Teacher of Artistic Activities. And, atop a small pedestal, sits a telephone: the telephone from a story that's about everything that, though it goes unsaid, can be read like signs and symbols waiting to be heard on the other end of the line, waiting for someone to answer and to listen and to pay attention to them, only to, right way, disregard them, because they realize that the person calling was a little boy, faking an adult voice, saying some nonsense about his parents being terrorists. The scene reminds him of the end of a movie, but its title— he was almost certain that there was a number between its words—scurries away into some remote corner of his memory palace. He can't see his face but he can see the wrinkles and stains on his hands that open a notebook with a cover—in childish handwriting that could also be the trembling scrawl of an old man—that announces: *Master Advice of a Man Who Sleeps on the Floor.*

And he opens it.

And he reads. "You cannot hurt me, my friend. Because I am not flesh and bone. I am an idea. And ideas are bulletproof."

7

One of the unmistakable signs and unquestionable symptoms of the fact that not only were the years passing but that they'd already passed, that not many things were left to come to pass. Or that (because the structure of life is already well or poorly constructed and already more or less fossilized) they were coming to pass in a very, very different way from how they'd come to pass when all those years hadn't yet passed. Like when it felt, all the time, like you were just passing through so that things would keep coming to pass.

But that already passed.

Trying then—from the here and now, far away in time and space—to bring all those points together, with lines to connect and explain them, was a complex task that yielded inexact results. And, yes, he's forgotten many details along the way, but that doesn't prevent the totality of the landscape from being unforgettable.

All that's left and yet to be done is to stop seeing it from outside, from a nowhere like Zzyzx or Colma or Nothing.

And so, in the beginning and at the end, when there's nothing left for him, he's left with the last possible option. After so long immersed in invented and dreamed and remembered parts, he decides he will be *nyugdìjas* from all of that. He decides to lean toward and on something new and, for him, quite different.

Something—out of opposition and because it was classic—very experimental or avant-garde: because he never dared do anything *like that*. And it won't be easy. It won't be easy to live through everything that's going to come at him (maybe IKEA can help him and take him on as an exceedingly self-promotional humanist cause; maybe he'll ask IKEA for help); but it won't be easy to live through on this side of what's going to happen, what's going to happen to him.

Because what's going to happen to him will be his *peripeteia*.

And come what may.

But it doesn't matter and—in a way—he feels it'll be, if not easier, at least more heart-felt to experience it than to put it in writing.

He senses that he'll be too busy living to worry about not writing.

He senses that, for once, for the first time, given a choice, it'll be better that way.

He chooses X.

He chooses *none of the above*.

He chooses *not-knowing*.

He chooses the real part.

He chooses the true part.

𐤈

X. And so he spun and spins and will spin on his heel and turned and turns and will turn his back on everyone so that no one sees him smile beatifically with eyes full of tears and he opens the door and walks out.

And he walks the streets of Abracadabra and asks for directions to the most expensive and prestigious school in the city and arrives there after a peaceful stroll, all the while thinking about nothing, with nothing to think about.

And nothing to remember.

And it's all so simple.

All of it seems to happen right now, in this very moment.

Not a *More in a moment* but a *This is the moment.*

The present is so much easier to narrate than the past, *not* thinking it but feeling it.

And it's hot and he's thirsty and he's very tired. Physical and not mental sensations to which he doesn't have to add ideas or images that have nothing to do with what he's experiencing right now: sweat and a dry mouth and aching joints.

And, ah, *this* is realism, he says to himself.

And he sits down on a bench in front of the gates to the school beside a tall white fountain.

It's nap time, one of those naps that's like an animal sleeping in the sun of a bottomless sky: its breathing as heavy and peaceful as that of someone toying with the idea of devoting the rest of his life to nothing but breathing and taking another nap. It's a time that'll never feel the need to ask itself what time it is, because it's the time that it is and the only possible time, the time when even the clocks have drifted off to sleep.

And he falls asleep and an hour later a bell rings and the students begin to file out of the school.

And when you go looking for someone at the end of the school day—he thinks then—it's as if you really find them, as if you find them for real. And this was, after so much lying to himself, the ultimate truth, the dissolution into the solid (another and better form of the *efface expunge erase delete rub out wipe out obliterate*). The goodbye to the experiments and the hello to the irrefutable proof, and not to *posterity* but to *finality*, really and truly.

Real life now!, one of his favorite fictions had once exclaimed.

So *hasta la vista* to the *kalos thanatos*, to the beautiful and heroic death of Achilles and hello again to the far better return to domestic life of Odysseus.

See you, who knows when, to the biblical *Where is the wise man? Where is the scribe? Where is the debater of this age?* (and—where had he read that—he sees himself as the person he was and no longer is; he remembers himself as that little figure with a long shadow, like that of an unsure visitor in the illuminated doorway to a corridor that grows ever narrower in perspective and, oh, now he remembers where he read it: he read it *there*, on a burning page, in a desert, somewhere else, not long but so long ago).

Adieu and he remembers that perfect moment when Charles Swann doesn't just understand that Odette de Crécy doesn't love him, but that, moreover, she's not and never was and never will be his type; and, *oui*, that joyful interior sorrow of feeling yourself outside and with no possible way back in: not out of the game, but refusing to keep playing and continuing to feel (like the poor, always suffering the exhausting weight of the lack of money, the poor who spend so much more time thinking about money than the rich) that he no longer wrote, but now, for the first time, with the relief of not trying to blindly read all those letters that would never be there and there must be some reason why and better that way.

And, yes, finally and at the end, see you never to the progressive *Welcome back my friends to the show that never ends* and hello to the *That's all, folks!*, like the farewell from those cartoons of his childhood that'd never stopped being broadcast during the successive childhoods of others.

The beginning of the end of his original vocation.

The excising of his Ugly Spirit, of that invasive Ugly Spirit (like the one that'd possessed William S. Burroughs when he killed Joan Vollmer or that'd possessed him when he *effaced expunged erased deleted rubbed out wiped out obliterated* his parents) that you could only escape by putting things in writing.

Too many years swimming not to drown and to discover that, always and forever, you could, simply, float.

Enough with the inappropriate words of others.

And there was nothing more epic and literary and worthy of being told and written and filmed and recorded and narrated (and to not be invented or dreamed or remembered; because it is happening right now, because everything led to right there, to that precise instant worthy of living), than going to pick up somebody from school.

Hello to all of that then, to *this*: to being, if not a father, than a stepfather.

Or, better yet, being one of those equally generous and mysterious bene-factors finally giving up his invisibility and revealing his face in the last chapters of gothic melodramas; the ones in which the sun ends up coming out after so much time out on the moors and in the wind that lashes and crosses out and rewrites and revises until it leaves behind only the bare bones, what's essential to keep on telling the story.

If there were novels that take place over the course of a single day and night, why not, then, a novel that focused on an instant *like this*, he says to himself. All of it concentrating on the instant when that person who, every time he finished telling and inventing him a story, just before turning out the light to light up his dreams—like, *there goes the twister*, a twister that'd been left almost out of breath—always remembered to ask him, closing his eyes, a "And what happened next?"

But, again, he wasn't going to write it.

He wouldn't do it the honor or the gift of fossilizing it in an official version that, every time it was read, always the same, would allow itself to be remembered with decisive variations, with new changes that would transform that part into something far more faithful to the truth because it would be truly felt.

He wasn't even going to offer it a hypothetical draft. And he'd always been intrigued by that word: something that you wrote to be erased, a first and true version that rarely remained as the finished and definitive version to be remembered. Another way of forgetting while trying to find something you wanted to be impossible to forget: the forgotten part devolving into the unforgettable part.

No: he was going—far better—to live it.

And so, the curtain drops—who was it, Fitzgerald?, who'd said that thing about how "there are no second acts in American lives" but who'd simultaneously added that "nothing was impossible; everything was just beginning"—and rises again.

So, he opens his eyes to not miss any details, to look and to find and to find himself. And to understand that a good life is a life in which you comprehend that you have more things you want to remember than things you want to forget.

And this is one of those things to understand and to comprehend.

And in the very instant in which you live it, you're already certain that it is and will be something unforgettable.

And he finds it.

And he looks for him.

And at first he doesn't see him, but then, before long, he does.

He identifies him by the color of his hair and, then, by his facial features which have changed with the years but in which he still recognizes the original version: the one he wrote and reread so many times until he couldn't write it anymore.

There is He Whose Name He'll Never Stop Saying Over and Over from now on. A name which is, also, his own name; because Penelope had named her son after him "to improve the name; because it's not that name's fault that it was given to you," she'd said.

And he says the name.

And the boy walks up to him and smiles.

And he asks: "Do you remember me?"

And the boy—looking at him as if he were first an invention and then a dream and at last a memory—answers: "Of course I remember you."

And he reaches his hand into his inside jacket pocket and takes out Mr. Trip. Technology of another age, spring and gear: nothing further from the devices of the new world in which the youngest have grown up, an antique of a few generations past, but as primitive for them as an Altamira bison.

And he gives it to the boy, who smiles like someone who finds something they believed lost forever but without that meaning they've forgotten it, rather, they remember it more and better than ever, and no, he doesn't need to ask him about it: of course he remembers that wind-up Mr. Trip.

And—without any formal stunts or structural ruptures or typographical games or quotations or references or lists as shields or alibis—this is, in his most absolute present, his "instant" in which, unlike Martin Eden, he knows not to cease knowing but to learn something new, with a new style.

And, for the last time, he thinks about Ella and about how he would really like for her, finding herself wherever she finds herself, near or far, if she can read what he's now not writing, please, to remember him like this and, yes, here's a moment:

The unforgettable memory.

Something that would last forever.

Something that—like him—has come to stay.

Something that (what would his readers say about all of this, about ending *like this*?; let them say whatever they want, he says to himself) he might understand better if he put it in writing and thinking (there are so many that he struggles to count them, there are as many as all the stars in the most stellar day in his life, that now fill him to the point of bursting) that he has so many stories, so many tales to tell that boy.

Something that he would no longer remember about the past but something that he would remember in the future.

Something—he doesn't know what he'll do now or how he'll go on—that he didn't yet understand what it was or what to make of it or how he might make something of it.

Because, even though now he was once again the master of his world, he wasn't really sure what he would be—not inventing and dreaming and remembering—doing next.

But he would think of something.

THE UNFORGETTABLE PART

(A Thank-You Note)

I'll remember you
When I've forgotten all the rest
—Bob Dylan,
"I'll Remember You"

Yes, people often change
but memories of people can remain
—Ray Davies,
"Do You Remember Walter?"

Preserve your memories
They're all that's left you
—Paul Simon,
"Bookends"

Remember, life is just a memory
—Harry Nilsson,
"Remember"

There are places I remember
—John Lennon & Paul McCartney,
In My Life

Remember
—John Lennon,
"Remember"

You must remember this
—Herman Hupfeld,
"As Time Goes By"

The song "As Time Goes By"—transformed into a *standard* years later, when it was included in the film *Casablanca* in 1942—was originally written for a 1931 Broadway musical titled *Everybody's Welcome*.

And—beyond the indiscriminate instruction of its title impossible both spatially and sentimentally—everybody is never welcome, *not everybody* is welcome.

That's never the case and putting in practice such benevolence would be really bad. There are people (Dracula being one of them) for whom you should never open the door, because once they enter they'll never leave.

But (notwithstanding the repeated frustration of the people who condemn my thank-you notes for reasons that, with their constant presence throughout the years and books, I find as incomprehensible as they are uninteresting) the doors *are* open wide open for all the following people.

All of them are welcome in these final pages of this book whose first pages really began to be written—I remember it perfectly, though I didn't know it at the time—a decade ago: first in *The Invented Part* and then in *The Dreamed Part*. And whose echo originated long before and from even farther away; because everything I wrote before and since the beginning, going back to my first book in 1991, *Argentine History*, ended up here, in *The Remembered Part*.

Here, yes, many things come to an end: *Endgame!*

How to go on and where to go after this triptych?

Who knows (I'll do everything impossible to make sure whatever comes next doesn't include so many writers and everything possible to make sure not even one mobile phone rings therein).

We'll see. We'll write. We'll read.

And—*you must remember this*, don't forget it—if you've done things more or less well you'll always have more and more people to thank.

And so, now, in every language and with singular affection: welcome, again, to the very welcome farewell, friends and family and books and authors and films and directors and songs and musicians and paintings and painters whose close or distant influence lets itself be felt in the memory of this book and in that of the two that preceded it (please, add to those present here and to the repeat offenders those who were only named in both and in previous thank-you notes) across a decade of inventing and dreaming and remembering.

Here they are, these are them, welcome one and all:

Edward Abbey; David Ackles; Mauricio Alarcón and Paula Escobar (*El Mercurio*, Chile); *Everyday Robots* (and all the others too; especially "Tender," in Blur, and that "Tender is the ghost . . . The ghost I love the most . . ." and *The Now Now* with Gorillaz), by Damon Albarn; Carlos and Ana Alberdi; Martin Amis; Paul Thomas Anderson; We Anderson; "We Don't Deserve Love," by Arcade Fire; *Tranquility Base Hotel + Casino*, by Arctic Monkeys; Javier Argüello; *The Shadow in the Garden*, by James Atlas; Xavi Ayén ("But, what have you done, Rodrigo Fresán?"); "Coming to Your Senses" and "Holy Grail" and "I'll Keep the Things You Throw Away" and "It's What I'm Thinking")"In my memory everybody looks the same / There's nothing else to blame / But my memory"), by Badly Drawn Boy; *The Beatles Off The Record: Outrageous Opinions & Unrehearsed Interviews*, by Keith Badman; Guillermo Balbona (and Literary Tuesdays, UIMP, Manderley, Santander); J. G. Ballard; Agencia Carmen Balcells (Gloria Gutiérrez, Javier Martín & Co.); John Banville; *The Dakota Winters*, by Tom Barbash; Gennady Barabtarlo (for *Insomniac Dreams: Experiments with Time*, by Vladimir Nabokov); Barcelona; "Not-Knowing" and *Overnight to Many Distant Cities*, by Donald Barthelme (and all of his work); Guillaume Basset (Book World, Prague); "L'Era Del Cinghiale Bianco," by Franco Battiato; *The Business of Memory: The Art of Remembering in an Age of Forgetting*, by Charles Baxter (ed.); The Beatles and The Beatles; The Beatles Anthology, by The Beatles; Eduardo Becerra; Saul Bellow (and Zachary Leader); *Space Odyssey: Stanley Kubrick, Arthur C. Clarke, and The Making of a Masterpiece*, by Michael Benson; *The Human Stain*, film by Robert Benton based on the novel by Philip Roth; *Bento's Sketchbook*, by John Berger; John Berryman; Juan Pablo Bertazza; Patricio Binaghi; Adolfo Bioy Casares; *The Art of Time in Memoir: Then, Again*, by Sven Birkerts; *The Making of Stanley Kubrick's 2001: A Space Odyssey*, by Piers Bizony; Anthony Blake; *In Their Lives: Great Writers on Great Beatles Songs*, edited by Andrew Blauner; Juan Ignacio Boido (for the thing about "friends are the director's cut of the family" and for the thing about "Chef Guevara" and for that discussion about Rosebud and for some desert and for so many other things); "A Stroll Through Literature" and, again, "Godzilla in Mexico," by Roberto Bolaño (The boy wasn't dead, Roberto! You'll see, he's coming for you); "Absolute Beginners" and "Ashes to

Ashes" and *Station to Station* ("Oh, ready to shape the scheme of things . . .")
and *Live Nassau Coliseum '76* and *Low/"Heroes"/Lodger* and *The Next Day /
Extra* and ★ / *No Plan*, by David Bowie; *Big Bang*, and *fa fa fa fa fa fa fa fa*:
That Adventures of Talking Heads in the 20ᵗʰ Century, by David bowman; Brian
Boyd; "An Absence of Wood Nymph," by Robert H. Boyle (in *Conversations
with Nabokov*); *I Remember*, by Joe Brainard; Miguel Brascó; "I Was Trying
to Describe You to Someone," by Richard Brautigan; Guillermo Bravo; *Pink
Floyd: Their Immortal Remains*, by Victoria Broackes and Anna Landreth
Strong (eds.); *The Brief History of the Dead*, by Kevin Brockmeier; *The Love
You Make: An Insider's Story of The Beatles*, by Peter Brown and Steven Gains;
BTBA (Best Translated Book Award); *Mid Air*, by Paul Buchanan (and The
Blue Nile); William S. Burroughs; Kate Bush (for all of her work, but, here,
especially, for "Deeper Understanding"); David Byrne (and *My Life in the
Bush of Ghosts* and *Everything That Happens Will Happen Today*, by David
Byrne + Brian Eno); Andrés Calamaro; *The Hero of a Thousand Faces*, by
Joseph Campbell; Martín Caparrós; Mónica Carmona; Jordi/Jorge Carrión;
Anne Carson ("Prose is a house, poetry a man in flames running / quite fast
through it"); *Casablanca*, by so many people, by everyone; Casa Victoria
Ocampo (Fondo Nacional de las Artes); *And Then You're Dead*, by Cody Cas-
sidy + Paul Doherty, PhD; *Step Right Up! I'm Gonna Scare The Pants Off
America* and *Mr. Sardonicus*, by William Castle; Cervantes Institute (Prague
and Tokyo and Vienna); *Moonglow*, by Michael Chabon; Olivier Chaudenson
(Maison de la Poésoe, Paris); Coen Brothers (especially *Barton Fink* and *The
Big Lebowski*); "Can't Get Arrested," by Lloyd Cole (and "My Bag," by Lloyd
Cole and The Commotions); *The Narrows*, by Michael Connolly; *Stop-Time*,
by Frank Conroy; *Apocalypse Now*, by Francis Ford Coppola; *Attack of the
Crab Monsters*, by Roger Corman; Cornell University; Jordi Costa; Elvis
Costello (for all of his work; but here, especially, for *All This Useless Beauty*,
Blood & Chocolate, "Favourite Hour," *Imperial Bedroom*, "No Hiding Place,"—
one of the best songs ever written about the stupid violence of social networks
and the poison of the tarantulas who weave them; look up the lyrics and listen to it, it's a great song—"Painted from Memory," and "Poor Fractured
Atlas"); Rachel Cusk; *The Beatles Lyrics*, by Hunter Davies; Ray "A Place in
Your Heart" and "Scattered" Davies & The Kinks (especially *The Kinks Are
the Village Green Preservation Society*); Iván de la Nuez; Sergio del Molino;

"No Stars," by Rebekah Del Rio (and by Angelo Badalamenti & David Lynch); Abel Díaz (for the familiar ghost); Philip K. Dick; Charles Dickens (*A Tale of Two Cities* and *David Copperfield* and *Great Expectations*); *The Last Thing He Wanted*, by Joan Didion; *The Longest Cocktail Party*, by Richard DiLello; *Lives of the Poets*, by E. L. Doctorow; *You Never Give Me Your Money: The Beatles After the Breakup*, by Peter Doggett; Ignasi Duarte (Conversations Fictives); Tom Drury; Keir Dullea (& David "Dave" Bowman); *An Experiment with Time*, by J. W. Dunne; Daphne du Maurier; Bob Dylan (for everything, but here, especially, *The Bootleg Series Vol. 12: The Cutting Edge 1965-1966* and *The Bootleg Series Vol. 14: More Blood, More Tracks*); *Sum: Forty Tales of the Afterlives*, by David Eagleman; Ignacio Echevarría; *Pink Floyd: The Story of Wish You Were Here* (Eagle Rock Entertainment, John Edgintos, dir.); "Twilight of the Superheroes," by Deborah Eisenberg; Bret Easton Ellis; Argentine Embassy in Prague (Agustín Giménez, Roberto Alejandro Salafia, and Verónica Skerianz), Geoff Emmerick (and *Here, There and Everywhere: My Life Recording The Beatles*, by Geoff Emmerick with Howard Massey); "A Samurai Watches the Sun Rise in Acapulco," by Álvaro Enrique; Mariana Enríquez; Cecilia Fanti ¡& Cookie!; Jules Feiffer; *Pieces of Light: How the New Science of Memory Illuminates the Stories We Tell About Our Pasts* and *The Voices Within: The History and Science of How We Talk to Ourselves*, by Charles Fernyhough; Laura Fernández; Marta Fernández; Rodrigo Fernández; *My Favorite Thing is Monsters*, by Emil Ferris; Festival LEER (Eleonora Jaureguiberry and her whole dream team in San Isidro: Leda Bachor, Camila Fabbri, Carlos Furman, Verónica Leo, María Laura Monti, Mariano Morello); FILBA Buenos Aires (Gabriela Adamo & Pablo Braun & Co.); Oscar Finkleberg; *Tusk*, by Fleetwood Mac; *Moonwalking with Einstein*, by Joshua Foer; Fogwill; *Between Them*, by Richard Ford; "Danger in the Past" and "From Ghost town" and "If It Rains" and "Let Me Imagine You," by Robert "It Doesn't Really Matter If You Can't Exactly Recall + I Know What It Is Like to Be Ignored, Forgotten / When Yours Is the Name that Doesn't Come Often" Forster; *Memory: A Very Short Introduction*, by Jonathan K. Foster; Frefán; Juan Fresán; Nelly Fresán; Silvina Friera; Fundación Telefónica España; Funicular de Vallvidrera; William Gaddis; Garamond, Czechoslovakia (Anežka Charvátová, Petr Himl, and Anna Melicharorová); Charly García in general (and "Pasajera en trance," by Charly García and

Pedro Aznar in particular); Adolfo García Ortega; Alfredo Garófano; William H. Gass; Tom Gauld; Ricky Garvais; Géraldine Ghislain; *The Blue Ant Trilogy*, by William Gibson; Louise Glück; The Go-Betweens; Paty Godoy (Sonora Deserts); Catalina Gómez (Library of Congress); Andreu Gomila (*Time Out Barcelona*); Ángeles González-Sinde; Glenn Gould (and his *Goldberg Variations* by J. S. Bach); "The Incredible," by David Gray; *Will in the World: How Shakespeare Became Shakespeare*, by Stephen J. Greenblatt; *Less*, by Andrew Sean Greer; Jacob and Wilhelm Grimml Grisetti (Vermouth Rojo); Daniel Guebel; Leila Guerriero; Isabelle Gugnon (and MAAAAAAAARC Simon, for his . . . Proustian? patience); Jordi Guinart; Brion Gysin; *Living Life Without Loving The Beatles: A Survivor's Guide*, by Gary Hall; Ray and "Water Liars," by Barry Hannah; *The End of Absence*, by Michael Harris; Tristan Harris; Elena Hevia; *The Nix*, by Nathan Hill; "We Three (My Echo, My Shadow and Me)," performed by The Ink Spots (and composed by Nelson Cogane, Sammy Mysels, and Dick Robertson); Wild boars on the Sierra de Collserola; Ja! Bilbao (Juan Bas & Carolina Ontivero); Henry James; Adelaida Jaramillo; Andreu Juame; Denis Johnson (for everything, but, especially, for "The Largesse of the Sea Maiden" and *The Largesse of the Sea Maiden*, which gave me back my voice and kept me from drowning in a very complicated moment in the writing of this book); *David Bowie: A Life*, by Dylan Jones; Frank Dermode; Jack Kerouac; Stephen King (and Jim Gardener in *The Tommyknockers*); Chuck Klosterman ("Helter Skelter"); Karl Kraus; Stanley Kubrick; *American Dream* and "Someone Great," by LCD Soundsystem ("you've lost your internet and we've lost our memory); Hannibal Lecter; LiberAria Editrice (Giorgia Antonelli and Alesandro Raveggi and Giulia Zavagna); Librería La Central (Antonio & Marta & Neus & Co.); Paul La Farge; Patrick Lagrange (& Julian Barnes); Lalo Lambda (and Brandy with Candies); "My Mistakes Were Made for you" and "The Dream Synopsis," by The Last Shadow Puppets; John le Carré; Sam Sevenson; *The Affair*, by Hagai Levi and Sarah Treem; *City of the Sun*, by David Levien; *The Complete Beatles Chronicle*, by Mark Lewisohn; Liniers; Literaktum (San Sebastián); Little Village (Don't Bug Me When I'm Working"); *Martin Eden*, by Jack London; Ray Loriga (for the thing about *The End* of movies and, again, for the thing with "Memory is the dumbest dog, you throw it a stick and it brings back anything but that stick"); *A Ghost Story*, by David

Lowery; Malcolm Lowry (Hotel La Nada, "Strange Comfort Afforded by the Profession," etc.); María Lynch (and everyone at Casanovas & Lynch); *I Trawl the MEGAHERTZ*, by Paddy McAloon (and Prefab Sprout); *Old Boys*, by Charles McCarry; Jimmy McGill (Saul Goodman); MacServiceBen (C/ Villarroel 68 / 08011 Barcelona / 34-93-114-7890 / info@macservicebcn.com) Aurelio Major; "Stuck in the Past," by Aimee Mann; David Markson; Jan Martí; George Martin; Juan Peregrina Martín; J.A. Masoliver Ródenas; Norma Elizabeth Mastrorilli; Fran G. Matute; *An Odyssey: A Father, A Son, and an Epic*, by Daniel Mendelsohn; *The King Receives*, by Eduardo Mendoza; *The Woman Upstairs*, by Claire Messud; *My Name is Burroughs* and *The Beat Hotel: Ginsberg, Burroughs & Corso in Paris / 1957-1963* by Barry Miles; Valerie Miles (and *Granta* en español); *The Beatles: Ten Years That Shook The World*, by *Mojo Magazine*; Rick Moody ("The End"); "The Lost Art of Forehead Sweat" / *The X-Files—Season 11—Episode 4*, by Darin Morgan; "Reader Meet Author" and "I Spent the Day in Bed," by Morrissey; Annie Morvan; Enrique Moya & Co. (¡En Español, Por Favor! / Literaturhaus, Wien); Bill Murray; Vladimir Nabokov; María José Navia; Matías Néspolo; Laura Niembro (and Feria del Libro de Guadalajara); "Don't Forget Me" and "Remember," by Harry Nilsson; *David Lynch: The Art Life*, by Jon Nguyen, Rick Barnes, and Olivia Neergaard-Holm; Yann Nicol (Fête du Livre de Bron); *El eternauta*, by Héctor G. Oesterheld and Alberto Breccia; Open Letter Books; Piere Ortin (Altäir & Co.); Randy Newman in general (and "Potholes" in particular); *The English Patient* and *Warlight* by Michael Ondaatje; Julio Ortega; Fito Páez; *Página/12*; Pale Fire Fan; Pareja Levitante; Alan Pauls; *Il mestiere di vivere*, by Cesare Pavese; *The Complete David Bowie*, by Nicholas Pegg; Penguin Random House (Raquel Abad, Miguel Aguilar, Patxi Beascoa, Juame Bonfill, Ricardo Cayuela, Silvia Coma, Núria Cabuti, Carlota del Amo, Eva Cuenca, Juán Díaz, Gabriela Ellena, Conxita Estruga, Lourdes González, Nora Grosse, Victoria Malet, Núria Manent, Irene Pérez, Melca Pérez, Albert Puigdueta, Pilar Reyes, Carme Riera, Cecilia Sarthe, José Serra, and everyone else as well); A. G. Porta; Chip Rolley & Co. (PEN World Voices Festival of International Literature, NY); "Tengo un algo adentro que se llama El Coso," by Federico Peralta Ramos; *Je me souviens*, by Georges Perec; Fernando "El Jefe" Pérez Morales (and Carmela & Milagros and the whole Notanpüan band); Ginés "Belvedere" Pérez

Navarro (for his Mantras); Andrés Perruca; *Difficult Women*, by David Plante; The Plutzik Series (Jim Longenbach, Stephen Schottenfeld, Joanna Scott & Co.); Ricardo Piglia (and Emilio Renzi); Pink Floyd (and Storm Thorgerson); Padgett Powell; *Generosity*, by Richard Powers; Ana Prescott; Eugene O'Neill; "Free Fallin'" by Tom Petty; Sergio Pitol; Francisco "Paco" Porrúa; José Guadalupe Posada; Chad Post; Barbara Prince; Prix Roger-Caillois; *The Impossible Exile: Stefan Zweig at the End of the World*, by George Prochnik; Patricio Pron; Marcel Proust (the quotes from/of *À la recherche du temps perdu* come from the translations by Pedro Salinas and by Consuelo Berges); *This Is Hardcore*, by Pulp ("This is the sound of someone losing the plot" and "the sound of failure, but it's the most successful sound of failure put to tape. So there," in his days described and sung by Jarvis Cocker); Laura Ramos; Robert Rauschenberg; "Talking Books," by Lou Reed (and *The Time Machine*, by H. G. Wells); *Wild Nights: How Taming Our Sleep Created Our Restless World*, by Benjamin Reiss; *Automatic for the People*, by R.E.M.; Rep (for his clarifying for me "triptych" and for so many other things); *L'Année dernière à Marienbad and Je t'aime* and *Providence*, by Alan Resnais; Laura Revuelta (and ABC); Jean Rhys; Robot Chicken; *Mortifications: Writer's Stories of Their Public Shame*, by Robin Robertson (ed.); University of Rochester; Anna María Rodríguez Arias; *The Man Who Fell To Earth* by Nicolas Roeg and Walter Tevis (and Thomas Jerome Newton, of course); *Ray Davies: A Complicated Life*, by Johnny Rogan; *The Golden House*, by Ray Russel; Guillermo Saccomanno; Soraya Sáenz de Santamaría ("Santamaría gives Junqueras *The Invented Part* by Rodrigo Fresán," *La Vanguardia*, 04/21/17); J. D. Salinger (always there); James Salter; *Future Noir: The Making of Blade Runner*, by Paul M. Sammon; *Lincoln in the Bardo*, by George Saunders; Saniel L. Schacter; *Vor der Morgenröte*, by Maria Schrader; *Blade Runner*, by Ridley Scott (screenplay by Hampton Fancher and David Peoples); *Umbrella* and *Shark* and *Phone*, by Will Self; *In the Night Kitchen*, by Maurice Sendak; Les Editions du Seuil; *A Midsummer Night's Dream* and *The Tempest* and *The Winter's Tale*, by William Shakespeare; *Proust's Way: A Field Guide to "In Search of Lost Time,"* by Roger Shattuck; *Dreaming The Beatles: The Love Story of One Band and the Whole World*, by Rob Sheffield; *And So It Goes / Kurt Vonnegut: A Life*, by Charles J. Shields; Charles Simic; *Illium / Olympos*, by Dan Simmons; *Debriefing*, by Susan Sontag; Phil

Spector's Wall of Sound; *The Memory Palace of Matteo Ricci*, by Jonathan D. Spence; "Photograph," by Ringo Starr & George Harrison; Edward St. Aubyn (& Charlie Fairburn & Patrick Melrose); Edna St. Vincent Millay; Steely Dan; Mark Strand; *Dracula*, by Bram Stoker; Kaija Straumanis; "The Novelist," by Richard Swift; *Proust: The Search*, by Benjamin Taylor; *The Third Man*; Adam Thirlwell; The Three Percent Gang (Mark Binelli, Rachel Cordasco, Tom Flynn, Jeremy Garber, Tom Roberge, Jonathan Lethem, Derek Maine, Valerie Miles again, Lytton Smith, P. T. Smith); *The Invented Sky / The Bottom of the Part USA Tour '18* (Emily Ballaine and John Gibbs at Green Apple Books / San Francisco; East Bay Booksellers / Oakland; Thomas K. Flynn and Jeffrey Mull at Volumes Bookcafe / Chicago; Jeremy Garber at Powell's / Portland; Mark Haber at Brazos Bookstore / Houston; Javier Molea at McNally Jackson / New York; Edmundo Paz Soldán and Liliana Colanzi at Cornell University / Ithaca); Talking Heads (especially *Fear of Music* and *Remains in Light*); Paul Tickell; "Wild Is the Wind," by Dimitri Tiomkin and Ned Washington; Adam Thirlwell; David Trueba; Drederic Tuten; *Clock Dance*, by Anne Tyler; Florencia Ure; Lucrecia Ure; *Lists of Note*, by Shaun Usher (ed.); Jordi Vallverdú; Will Vanderhyden; *Blade Runner 2049*, by Denis Villeneuve (screenplay by Hampton Fancher and Michael Green); Villa Gilet / Assises Internationales du Ruman (Lyon); Villaseñor Urrca Family; Glenda Vieites; *Le quattro stagioni*, by Antonio Lucio Vivaldi (*Recomposed by Max Richter*), Silvana Vogt; Miquel Volonté; Kurt Vonnegut (and Billy Pilgrim & Edward Reginald Crone, Jr.); Christopher Walken; "Mystery Girl" by Karl "World Party" Wallinger; Mathilde Walton (Villa Gillet, Lyon); *Crackpot*, by John Waters; *A Handful of Dust* and *The Ordeal of Gilbert Pinfold*, by Evelyn Waugh; "Angle of Reflection," by Josh Weil; Orson Welles (and *The Other Side of the Wind* and *They'll Love Me When I'm Dead*); Jim White; Joy Williams; "End of the Show" and "Farewell My Friend," by Dennis Wilson; Kevin Wilson; *The Wire*; Thomas Wolfe; *Plan 9 from Outer Space* by Ed Wood; Brian Wood; Virginia Woolf; "Precious Memories," by J. B. F. Wright; "Summer '68," by Rick Wright (and Pink Floyd); XTC; Warren Zevon; and Nathan Zuckerman (and Philip Roth).

Claudui López de Lamadrid, without whom none of this would have been possible.

Daniel Fresán and Ana Isabel Villaseñor, without whom it wouldn't have been possible to do any of this.

And I almost forgot, but remembered at the last minute:

(Any similarities to actual events or real people—with the exception of those named and quoted by name—of the events or individuals described in this book are purely coincidental. Likewise, the person who wrote this book and whose name appears on the cover is not the character who is featured herein.)

And next time we see each other it won't be in another Part but, yes, in the same place.

Meanwhile and in the meantime, never forget to invent and to dream and to remember your way back to that place that is found, exactly and precisely, just beyond this one and all of that.

R. F.
Barcelona, April of 2019

RODRIGO FRESÁN is the author of ten works of fiction, including *Kensington Gardens*, *Mantra*, and *The Invented Part*, winner of the 2018 Best Translated Book Award. A self-professed "referential maniac," his works incorporate many elements from science fiction (Philip K. Dick in particular) alongside pop culture and literary references. According to Jonathan Lethem, "he's a kaleidoscopic, openhearted, shamelessly polymathic storyteller, the kind who brings a blast of oxygen into the room." In 2017, he received the Prix Roger Caillois, awarded by PEN Club France every year to both a French and a Latin American writer.

WILL VANDERHYDEN received an MA in Literary Translation Studies from the University of Rochester. He has translated fiction by Carlos Labbé, Edgardo Cozarinsky, Alfredo Bryce Echenique, Juan Marsé, Rafael Sánchez Ferlosio, and Dainerys Machado Vento, among others, and received NEA and Lannan fellowships to translate another of Fresán's novels, *The Invented Part*. His translations have appeared in such publications as *Granta*, *Two Lines*, *The Literary Review*, and *Asymptote*.

CPSIA information can be obtained
at www.ICGtesting.com
Printed in the USA
JSHW020922170622
27148JS00002B/2